THE TARNISHED COLLAR

FUTURE NOVELS

What Do Readers Say about The Tarnished Collar?

The Tarnished Collar is a compelling story that connects the intimate lives of its characters and shows glimpses into their shattered worlds. The author's use of language and descriptive images presents delicate subject matter with sensitivity and grace. Lang's extraordinary literary ability creates powerful images and brings insightful messages that will inspire readers to be moved in a profound way. A must read, hard to put down book that relates to ever-present human conditions and the need for much deserved critical attention.

Yvonne Marie Moroni, Oconomowoc, WI

Spellbound, I hated when I had to put the book down. I sat in every room and could feel and see all the surroundings. I knew each character. What a page turner!!! A mesmerizing story.

Patricia Deyhle, Carmel, IN

The Tarnished Collar is a thoughtful page turner rich in descriptive detail. The intersecting plots kept me reading, guessing, and wondering how the story would come together in the end. And it did.

Charles Schroeder, Rome, WI

The intrigue of the book is, I didn't want to put it down…and anticipated picking it up again and again, a real page turner. My highlight was getting to know each character personally, a real study in human nature. A book I could reread and enjoy all over again.

Herb Schmiedel, Summit, WI

Quiet, reluctant heroes pushed to act against the forces of evil in a 1950s small mid-western town. A story of common characters caught in a web of lust, love, abuse, murder, and revenge that could be ripped from the headlines of today's news. *The Tarnished Collar* highlights the greatest of dignity found in all of us….and the horrendous depths to which human foibles can take some. Robert Lang sheds light on the common hero's ability to rise up against the disregard of human dignity and injustice.

John Czarnecki, Wauwatosa, WI

A spell-binding novel set in the mid-50s, a page turner. I could not put the book down. Some of the aspects in the novel were the same as experiences I found in the years in the seminary in the early 1950s. I knew a few good priests like Father Sullivan. How did you ever write such an intriguing first novel? *Unbelievable.*

Jim Phillips, Milwaukee, WI

The Tarnished Collar is a morality play, written like a thriller novel. For a work of fiction, the book is as believable as it is disturbing. The characters in *The Tarnished Collar* are people that I can love, admire or…despise. I've known folks like these in my life. I feel empathy for them. I feel sorrow for them. For some of them I feel nothing but dread, disdain, and disgust. The book begs the reader to ask the question; what is more reprehensible - the sin of commission or the sin of omission?

Tom Lubbers, Wilmington, NC

Crime and punishment in America's heartland – both beyond the law. Welcome to the jury.

William Stouffer, Wabash, IN

Wow! Quite a read. *The Tarnished Collar* certainly had me hooked. I found the writing engrossing, the reenactment of the 1950s compelling. The author captures the culture with accuracy and believability. The story takes me back to another world. The abuse that has taken place in our Church is beyond despicable. Bob Lang's passion and insight presents a horrifying disorder. His descriptive writing-style draws the reader into each engrossing scene.

Edgar Wolgamot, Peoria, IL

THE
TARNISHED
COLLAR

ROBERT ALLEN LANG

This book is a work of fiction. The characters and situations described in *The Tarnished Collar* may resemble certain people and events alleged to have taken place. All of the characters, including Pope John Benedict, and all of the encounters described in *The Tarnished Collar*, are completely fictional and figments of my imagination. Wabash, Indiana, including some buildings, streets, and locations, might be actual places caught in the setting of the story. The characters, however, are not imagined from anyone who ever lived or now lives in this small traditional Midwestern town.

ISBN: 978-0-9909758-0-9

Cover Design and Staircase Drawing by **Susan Winget**
Cover Typeset by **Karen Erickson**
Three Drawings by **Geri Bourget**

**Please address all comments,
questions, suggestions or reviews to:**

**ROBERT ALLEN LANG
LANG BOOKS
514 Wells Street
Delafield, Wisconsin 53018
robertallenlang.com
262-646-3388**

The Tarnished Collar is dedicated
to all abused children who harbor memories of the past.
May they find hope in the future.

ACKNOWLEDGMENTS

… man can never accomplish success alone

WRITING a book is a solitary endeavor. Early in the morning, late at night, you are alone. The only companion is your pen and paper, and your imagination.

A writer once said, "The story tells itself." For the most part, I believe that to be true. **The Tarnished Collar**, being my first novel, I was unencumbered by any preconceived notions of how to write. Pen in hand, the characters told the story about the pursuit of justice.

I could not have written **The Tarnished Collar** without support. My wife, Susanne, is a good Catholic. From the very beginning, I thought the subject might be too disconcerting and controversial for her. Wrong. She was an avid supporter and harsh critic. Her editing was invaluable. An avid reader herself, Susanne reminded me all along, "Bob, this is a good story."

To Suzanne Schroeder, my trusted and devoted assistant, I thank you for being there every step of the way. Your technical computer skills and continual encouragement have proven invaluable. You became an accomplished assistant editor.

To Susan Winget, I am appreciative of your artistry. The cover design and staircase sketch suggest the hidden story. Carolyn Madison, Dana Cole and Jonathan Gullery of *Self-Publishing*, your patient support, editing, and direction will always be appreciated. Mike Smith, a friend of many years, deserves the credit for suggesting the idea that I write about this challenging subject back on a cold winter's day, January 11, 2011. I extend my appreciation to Karen Erickson for her creative design, calligraphy, and advice. To Geri Bourget, thank you for your descriptive sketches of some main characters in the novel.

A heartfelt thank you, Mark Salmon. By chance, we met during the writing of **The Tarnished Collar**. Your experiences of abuse during the 1960s were a firsthand telling of reality. Although I did not use Mark's horrific experiences in my novel, his sincerity, openness, and trust validated that my story was on track. Of anyone, Mark knows best what this book is all about. Mrs. Salmon, Mark's mother, told him, "I'm sure Bob Lang was abused. His story is so real, so true, he could not have just made it up himself." Thank you, Mrs. Salmon for the kind words about the realism of my story. **The Tarnished Collar** may seem real, but fortunately, I was never experienced sexual abuse.

I extend special thanks to my six advanced readers: Jim Phillips, Tom Lubbers, Charles Schroeder, Herb Schmiedel, John Czarnecki, and Yvonne Moroni. All avid readers themselves, they honored my request to pull no punches, "hit me between the eyes" with valuable constructive criticism, and evaluation. Each liking the story for different reasons, the advanced readers were concerned about the length of **The Tarnished Collar**. However, considering the interconnected plots, twelve main characters, and a cast of significant supporting characters; I decided the length is necessary for the reader to fully understand the story, the characters, and the mystery within each chapter.

Thank you, Ellen Pederson, for your interest and support as first reader. Dan Potter, thank you for your continuing encouragement.

All that is good, along with lives filled with hardship, is found in the heart of small towns across America. To my good friends, Bill and Ellen Stouffer, thank you for your insight into the history of your beloved Wabash, Indiana. Bill was an encyclopedia about the history of Wabash. His heart is on the pulse of the community. I extend my appreciation to you, Bill, for sharing the photographs of Wabash, from The Ruth Stouffer Photography Collection.

To all the wonderful people in Wabash, thank you for being a part of and supporting me in the use of the historic name. I am fortunate to use the name, *Wabash*. Although I chose the location of your fair city as the stage for my story, in no way does this novel draw from any of the lives of your citizens, past or present.

And to you, Father Cyril, a priest at Holy Hill in Wisconsin, thank you for keeping me grounded, and for being a constant reminder that we are blessed today with many good priests. You are my shining example. In memory of all the priests and sisters that were an integral part of my life in grade and high school in Danville, Illinois, I will always be appreciative of your positive influence.

Pat Wolgamot, Tuck Meyer, John Fredrickson, and Dan Brink. I am very appreciative of your sound legal advice. Ted Wolgamot, thank you for your insightful foreword. You, of all the readers, based on your experience as a priest for twenty years, know the realities of injustice from within the Catholic Church.

To my dad, Richard Lang, thank you for showing me that a strong will, tenacity, and perseverance will always prevail. Your pursuit of ideas and dreams were part of your life. Somehow they became a part of mine.

To Pope Francis, thank you for your concerns. Your commitment to review and question the church's past and present is encouraging. Your leadership into the future is integral to the future direction of the Catholic Church. We all pray for and with you.

The Tarnished Collar can remind us all about injustice in the world. We will see that hope and justice can prevail. May all of our combined efforts waken the soul of the Catholic Church and citizens everywhere. Indeed, *The Tarnished Collar* is a story about justice that needs to be told. To all of you readers, please accept my sincere appreciation for reading *The Tarnished Collar*

Most of all, to Susanne and my beloved family ... everything I do is for you.

Thank you all so very much.
Life is a Journey,

Robert Allen Lang
Robert Allen Lang

FOREWORD

In May of 1967, I was ordained a Catholic priest. One month later, I arrived at my first assignment: a large parish in a relatively small town in the Midwest.

I can still remember how excited and thrilled I was to finally be able to do the priestly ministry I had dreamed of for so long. But, soon after I began my work in this parish, a very sad and tragic piece of information popped the bubble of my enthusiasm.

In a discussion I was having with one of the other priests in the parish, he told me something very dark and disturbing. It seems that I had been sent to this parish for the purpose of replacing a priest that was involved in an issue I had never heard of before, an issue I never dreamed possible in the Church that I knew and loved.

According to what I was told, the father of a high school student had approached the pastor of this same parish and, in a rage, informed him that if they didn't get rid of this particular priest, he was going to the sheriff. The priest, he claimed, was sexually abusing his son, and others.

This was shocking enough. But the attitude of the pastor and of the bishop was even more troubling to me. This priest/abuser was simply sent to another parish!

This bothered me to the point that I approached the pastor and asked him about this whole matter. First, I asked if what I had heard about all this was true. He assured me that it was. I then asked if it was also true that they had sent this priest on to another parish. He told me that the diocese had.

I can remember being angry at that response. So, I asked: "How does that help the situation? He'll just do the same thing there."

I will never forget the pastor's response: "Well, at least we got him out of our hair. I don't care what happens to him someplace else. Let them deal with him."

That priest went on to abuse scores of young boys. He was removed from active ministry in the early '90s – some 25 years later. What has happened to those boys as a result can only be imagined. Adding to the tragedy is the knowledge that it could have been stopped. But it wasn't.

This issue of the scandalous and criminal betrayal of trust certainly ranks as one of the most heinous crimes of the entire history of the Catholic Church. What is even sadder and more troubling is that it continues to profoundly affect the lives of far too many people in the most damaging of ways.

In my present role as a psychologist and addiction specialist, I have had to deal with the aftermath of terrible traumas suffered by people who made a seemingly harmless mistake: they trusted. They trusted a priest, and then trusted a diocese, and then trusted a bishop.

Fortunately, in the diocese of which I am a member, we have a bishop and a diocesan staff who have been dedicated to doing everything they can to provide a safe environment for all the children under their care, and to support a thorough review of all candidates for the priesthood and the deaconate.

Bob Lang's novel is an effort on the part of a man who dearly loved the Church of his childhood to the extent of doing all he could to cry out for justice. With great passion and with enormous love and with consummate skill, Bob tells a story that begs and pleads for an end to all the cover-ups, and an end to the kind of attitude that I had to deal with on the part of that pastor way back in 1967.

Bob's belief is very strong: this can only end when the people at the very top of the hierarchical structure, beginning with the pope himself, make it crystal clear that cover-ups will no longer be tolerated, and that those in the highest positions of authority must all agree to live out a single message: "Never again."

You will find Bob's story line compelling and riveting. But, in the end, it is his fervent plea for justice that will stir the hearts of many to want to join with him in his passionate demand for full integrity on the part of a Church that preaches the gospel of Jesus Christ.

Read this book and weep. Then, join the fight.

Ted Wolgamot, Psy.D.

INTRODUCTION

THE *Tarnished Collar* is above all a story about the *pursuit of justice*. From a small town parish in Indiana to the inner circles of the Vatican, the lives of the abused, their parents, priests, and the hierarchy are intertwined into a web of secrecy, denial, pain and suffering. A good priest begins his quest to right the wronged and cleanse the Catholic Church from the demons within.

I am not an historian, scholar, advocate, or expert on the subject of the story that follows. I may oversimplify for the purpose of not sensationalizing. I do not pretend to be an investigative journalist. All the characters, plots, descriptions and narrative are from my imagination. I have not interviewed anyone for this book. I know a friend who was abused in grade school. I know another familiar with some abuses in the seminary. Neither are portrayed or personalized in this book. I was never abused.

Another close friend's brother left the priesthood after twenty-five years. The former priest knows firsthand above coverup within the hierarchy of the Catholic Church in the United States. He told me directly, "I could expose lies told in deposition, under oath, absolute perjury, all in real time of situations that took place in the 1980s." These lies are still covered up.

For over three generations, I have experienced much of what life has to offer. I have met people from all walks of life. I have enjoyed happiness, success, and love. I have learned from the challenges and disappointments in life. I have seen, read, and watched the struggles between good and evil. As an ordinary person, I am inclined to cheer for the underdog, support the common man and defy the abuse of power. *The Tarnished Collar* is drawn from these experiences and an understanding of my insight and concern for others.

Until January 11, 2011, I was simply a Catholic who was aware of the scandal of abuse in the Catholic Church. I found the accusations of priests to be, not only horrific, but also seemingly unbelievable. How could a priest treat children in such an abusive and horrific way? Then on that day in January, my life was affected when I began to write this story. With the best of intentions, I wrote a story with narrative that could draw attention and expose abuse of power and search for justice.

I am blessed with having experienced eight years of Catholic grade school and four years of Catholic high school. I loved the good priests and sisters that were such a wonderful and influential part of those rewarding twelve years. My memories of that time long ago, I will cherish forever. I never knew or was aware of any abuse, pedophilia, sin or secrecy within the Catholic Church during the decades of the 1950s and 1960s.

My memories are of my first communion, Baltimore Catechism and St. Joseph's Daily Missal, which I still have. I cherish the memory of our good pastor, Father Siesel, a devout and holy man, and a true father figure. For him, I served Mass, poured the sacred wine, held his chasuble and rang the bells during the Holy Mass. I responded to his prayers in Latin. The priests of my youth were models for all that is good about the Catholic Church.

The nuns—strict, but kind—taught us the Our Father and Hail Mary. We memorized the Commandments, were taught respect and manners and practiced for Holy Week. The Palmer Method of handwriting, spell-downs, religion class, and diagramming sentences were part of daily life within the circa 1906 brick schoolhouse. Wooden desks and inkwells were standard. Fountain pens were a must. We would obediently follow sister in single file, as we marched to church for First Friday Confession. The sounds of their black shoes on wood floors, the rattling of their long rosary beads that hung waist to floor at the side of their all-encompassing full-length black habits, stir my soul with lasting memories. Indeed, I am fortunate for all I was taught and all that I learned from these good priests and sisters.

The Tarnished Collar takes place in 1958 in Wabash Indiana. This fictional book raises the question: could the horrific scandal that plagues the Catholic Church today have been avoided? If the hierarchy of the church would have addressed the situation over fifty years ago, then our Catholic Church could be in a far better place today.

Hopefully, my purpose and approach in writing this book will make you more aware of the injustice within the Catholic Church, Protestant Church, schools, scouts, or anywhere children are found. At the same time, I have no intention to challenge faith, negate the charitable works, or defame all the good that the Catholic Church does for all that accept the faith. May this book be a foundation for awareness of injustice that permeate all walks of life. *Those who inflict injustice are not to be free*, as in this story they are to be held accountable.

May this story bring you awareness and inspiration that, indeed, it is not too late.

Robert Allen Lang

Robert Allen Lang

CONTENTS

PART I

ABUSE AND CONFESSION

CHAPTER 1

FORGOTTEN

Gordon Yoder—July 22, 1934, 9:44p.m.

THE darkness of the room was broken by the faint glow of a single light bulb. A bent metal shade covered with tarnished gray paint hung from the low ceiling, hovering over half of the faint light. Tired and exhausted, a man rested on a simple wooden bench, leaning back against the metal lockers. Propping his tired feet on a canvas bag of dirty towels, he relaxed. The sultry heat of the day had pushed the thermometer to a humid ninety-four degrees. A cool shower offered the only relief.

As the man reached around and opened his locker, the tinny sound of the metal door and creaky hinges shattered the silence in the room. The tired worker pulled out his street clothes and tossed them across the bench. After he undressed from his green uniform, he stood alone and naked. He enjoyed the natural feeling in the large dark room, at least most of the time. His body carried a pungent smell of grimy sweat as he sauntered toward the shower. The solitary time provided enjoyment. Being stripped of all clothing gave him an unencumbered feeling of anticipated relief—his time for simple comfort. The shower would be his only one of the day.

The exhausted man turned the cold water on full throttle. For minutes, he just stood there staring at the beating stream. He turned and rotated, allowing every inch of his body to be drenched. Time lapsed. Slowly, he added a hint of warm water. In total relief, he stood alone. Exhausted and in his own personal world, his body discovered full pleasurable relaxation from the staggering heat of the day.

Returning to his locker, he stopped at the sound of faint voices coming from the floors above. At first he thought he detected laughter and then cries of "Stop! No!" and then quiet. He paid little heed, as he thought it could be some boys horsing around after-hours. Once he was completely dressed in his street clothes—a gray button-down shirt and pants—he propped his ankle-high brown leather work boots on the bench. Slowly, he tied the worn dark laces. When he was finished, the sound of two stamping feet echoed in the locker room. Boots secure, the tired man headed up the stairs.

The faint light bulb remained on, sending just enough light to the top of the stairs. One at a time, the man shuffled each boot up the steps toward the back hall. He stopped at the last step, once again hearing cries for help. Dropping his knapsack, he raced toward the screaming: "No! Please no!" Within seconds, the cries turned to a muffled plea for help as if someone had put a hand over the boy's mouth to quiet him. Then a man screamed, "Goddamn little bastard bit me!"

As the worker approached the last room on the right, the door burst open. Out rushed two men, one tall with a thin face and dark hair. The other was of medium height with a full mustache. They both wore white shirts, their jackets clutched in their hands. They turned toward the startled man in the hall. The taller man stopped dead in his tracks at the sight of the oncoming stranger. His face froze. The worker in the gray shirt caught a full glimpse of the tall intruder's face.

"Turn back," the tall man commanded his companion. "Side door!" Immediately, they both reversed, ran down the hall and around the corner to the door, and then disappeared into the darkness.

Within an instant, the startled worker began to follow, but he was brushed aside by a frantic terrorized boy rushing out of the room with his clothes in hand. The workman turned and watched the boy flee down the hall and dash up the stairs toward the dormitory. Rattled, his heart pounding in his chest, the man stopped his pursuit and walked into the abandoned room.

A floor lamp stood at the far end of an old leather couch that had been shoved against the back wall. He noticed two empty wine bottles on the table in front of the couch and a blanket spread over the couch pillows. On the floor, for whatever reason, lay an initialed gold tie clasp, which he picked up to examine. He stared at the two unusual initials. Knowing he had to leave immediately, the man stuffed the clasp into his pocket and turned toward the door. Turning around to face the couch, he saw what looked like a body underneath the blanket on the couch. He slowly walked over to it. Hesitantly, he lifted a corner of the blanket and found a small boy.

The contorted look on the boy's face was shocking. The man pulled the blanket away to discover the boy's naked body. The boy's face was bruised, and his eyes were shut. He could see blood between the boy and the middle couch pillow. Placing his head close to the boy's nose, the man heard nothing. The boy was not breathing.

Carefully, the man laid his open hand across the boy's chest. No movement. The man in the gray shirt knew the boy was dead. He leaned closer, his nose only a few inches from the boy's lifeless face. To the left of the boy's head and against the back of the couch, the man noticed a bloodied pillow, the blood forming almost a circle. Among the blood, he saw what he thought to be skin and then flesh underneath. *Strange. No bone.*

In a state of shock and not wanting to be discovered, he pulled the blanket over the boy's head, stood, turned, and left the room. Heading back in the direction from which he had come, he heard voices. Lights came on. Someone rushed down the stairs. "Call Mr. Showers! Call Mr. Showers!" The footsteps on the terrazzo floors grew louder. He heard several voices. Changing direction, the man in grey headed back down the hall to the side door through which the perpetrators had fled. Out the door and into the night, he disappeared. Never seen, never discovered, the man could only remember the dead boy, the frozen face of the tall perpetrator, and the tie clasp in his pocket.

Returning to work the next day, all he heard was the buzz and talk about Gordon Yoder being found dead the night before.

Three days later, Gordon Yoder was quietly and discreetly laid to rest in Friends Cemetery just down the road from the Wabash Reform School and above the banks of the Wabash River. The boy had no parents or next of kin, so the small one-foot gravestone was engraved, *Gordon Yoder, April 2, 1922–July 22, 1934.* The perpetrators were never found and the murder still remains within the darkness.

5

CHAPTER 2

TOGETHER

The Seminarian—August 23, 1906

DAYS had passed since the seminarian waited for his friend at Hannah Park. One more week and he would be returning to St. Albert's Seminary to begin his fourth year of studies. By late Thursday afternoon, he worked up the courage to walk into the bookshop. He found her placing books on a top shelf.

"Need any help, ma'am?"

Startled and embarrassed, she stepped down from the stool and immediately apologized for failing to meet him three days before at the park. She was delighted to see him again. Reserved, handsome, and polite were all the qualities of a good person. *Of course he should be a priest. No way could it work out*, she thought. They visited for a few minutes.

He wanted to invite her to meet at the park. Glancing out the window, he saw the threatening skies that might again spoil their rendezvous.

"I didn't know if I'd ever see you again after the other day. I'm so sorry, but … " She paused. "I'm so sorry, but there was a family problem."

"No explanation due. I know family is more important than spending time with a wannabe priest."

"Stop it. I was longing to see you, but I had, you know, family. It was Pa."

"Relax, relax. I understand." Compassionately, he looked at her beautiful brown eyes.

"But I'd still like to see you. I'm sure you're leaving soon?" she said, hoping he still had some time.

He reached over and picked up a book from the table, buying time. "Oh, *The Scarlet Letter* by Hawthorne. It's a beautiful but heart-wrenching novel. Takes place more than fifty years ago. Romantic." He looked directly at her. "Sounds a little opposite my theology books."

"Yes, but you are going to be a priest. Confessions. Hawthorne writes about real life."

"Of course. We were, weren't we, talking about my departure this weekend?" he asked, still clutching the book. "Yes. I have to be back on Saturday. Those priests run a tight ship. No second chances with the Jesuits. I was thinking we could try and meet at Hannah Park, if that would be okay?" He looked at her hopefully.

"Sure, but it seems to be raining every day this week."

"Let's chance it."

She turned and walked over to the window. He followed. The foreboding clouds were coming in from the west. *Should I ask?* She wondered.

She turned back to him. "Okay, I'd love to spend some time visiting, talking. Would you … ?" She took a breath.

"Okay, cut the suspense. Say it. Would I what?" He asked, handing her the book.

"Then I will. Being a priest, you might think this quite, well, you know what I mean. Quite forward."

"You've lost me. Forward? What do you mean? Yes, I will buy this book."

"No, no, not the book. I mean would you … would you … ? All right then, my aunts—you met them once—my aunts Margaret and Patricia, their house down at the end of Hill Street on Comstock. They're both away visiting their other sister in Indianapolis. Took the train yesterday. I'm staying there, keeping an eye on the house. Could you … I mean … would you want to come over there? You know, it might be raining. We'll be safe. Maybe tomorrow after work? Oh, I'm sorry. I'm too forward. Sorry. Should not have asked," she said, not giving him a chance to reply.

He raised his eyebrows. Her words were as shocking as the thunder and lightning he was hearing outside. As if he could not control his own words, he said, "Sure. Why not? We can visit. Catch up."

Equally as astounded, her pulse racing, she replied, "That's the best.

Oh, I'm sorry. I mean that would be nice. Maybe around six o'clock or six thirty. Okay?"

Having composed himself, he said, "Quarter after six it will be. At Aunt Margaret's house."

Both surprised by each other, finding the right words became a struggle.

"Well then, the rain is easing."

"Thank goodness. I better get home. Tomorrow, six fifteen, I'll be there."

Searching for a composed smile, she responded properly, "I look forward to your visit."

"Me too. See you tomorrow." He picked up her hand, patted it, turned, and left the store. From the sidewalk, he looked back and tipped his hat.

Did he say yes? Dear Jesus, what have I done? No one heard her sigh of relief.

The rain subsided as he walked back down Canal Street. *Totally proper. A visit between two good friends.* After just a few blocks, he arrived home, and the rain started again. He opened the door just off the street and headed upstairs to his home above the tavern. Something told him he shouldn't mention his planned visit tomorrow to his mother and dad. He didn't know exactly why, but he decided to trust his instincts.

Sitting at his desk late into the night, the seminarian dutifully read the Bible. His mind wandered. Setting the Bible down, he stood and walked over to the comfort of an old cushioned chair and settled down with *The Scarlet Letter*. He knew unfamiliar thoughts were creeping into his mind.

He struggled in resisting temptation, so he prayed to Jesus and Mary about his vocation. *Our Father, who art in heaven, hallowed by Thy name.* Unknowingly, he thought, *Oh, my God, I am heartily sorry for having offended Thee.* Unprovoked, the righteous man's subconscious was attempting to distract his thoughts with temptation. For a brief moment, his desiring mind was taking him to a place he did not know. He visualized himself with her.

The rain subsided during the night. At daybreak, he peered out his bedroom window overlooking the back alley and the carriage barn. He saw Frank, his dad's horse, in the side fenced corral, peering out the barn window in the direction of the Wabash River Valley as if he had something on his mind.

After taking a brief midmorning walk uptown with his brother, Jack, he spent most of the afternoon in his back bedroom, reading and praying but mostly anticipating his visit. By afternoon's end, he was over halfway through the provocative novel. *Where will she end up?*

Around 5:50 p.m., he told his mother he was going to meet a friend after supper. A light rain picked up again. Quickly stepping down the stairs, he peeked into the tavern door, gave a wave to his dad, and then bounded out onto the sidewalk, heading north on Wabash. Previously, he had counted four blocks up the hill on Wabash Street and then left three blocks to her aunt's house on the west end of Hill Street. His steps were slow but deliberate. The rain had reduced to a slight mist. His heart raced with unfamiliar anticipation, although it was somewhat disguised by the ascent up Wabash.

Planning her time perfectly, precisely at 5:00 p.m., she flipped the sign in the window to the closed side. Book and bag in hand, she locked the door and made her way across Canal to Wabash. She held her dress up in front, as the walk was still wet. Focused on her prepared agenda, she had made a batch of lemon cookies the night before. Along with sweet tea, they could enjoy visiting while sitting on the back porch. The shade of the early evening would be a perfect setting compared to the glare of the setting sun on the front porch. *The back porch feels more at home anyway.* Besides, the view of the carriage house and the backyard and garden were so tranquil. *Quiet and private.*

Feeling comfortable in her casual ankle-length checked skirt and full-sleeve white blouse with a high-buttoned white collar, she looked in the full-length mirror in the front foyer. As she turned around, her skirt swirled. Comfortable brown wicker furniture, two chairs, and an armed bench provided a welcoming atmosphere to the back porch. The small round table between the two chairs was perfect for beige napkins, a plate of cookies, and a pitcher of tea. She placed chipped ice in a pewter bowl. All was ready, including the presence of her aunt's cat, Thimble, who was passing the early evening on the comfort of the wicker bench.

The cadence of his steps sounded steadily as his leather shoes echoed on the wood walk. Steadily, the seminarian ascended the slight grade of Hill Street. Just ahead, he could see the corner of Comstock. There, he turned left and saw the large house at the end of the street. As he walked up to the front steps, he could see the Wabash River. *Beautiful.* The Victorian brick, pitched gables, and white trim of the house offered a welcoming invitation to anyone who walked by.

Confidently, the young seminarian made his way up the brick walk and onto the meandering front porch. Through the double black doors, each with vertical glass panes on the top half, he glanced in at the high ceilings in the front foyer. He lifted the brass knocker and knocked twice.

She appeared in the foyer and opened the door. "So good to see you," she said in a somewhat planned welcome.

He was amazed with the grandeur of the house. The ceilings had to be pushing fourteen feet. The front parlor to the right was formally furnished with a large black horsehair couch and side chairs. The drapes hung to the floor. The dark red-and-blue Oriental rug was almost as much the focus of the room as the marble fireplace mantle on the outer wall.

"This is their dining room."

He stepped just to the archway, peeking into something he had never seen before. The long mahogany table and high captain and side chairs were grand but almost uncomfortable looking with the presence of formality.

"Let's step into the kitchen."

He followed her. When walking by the stairs, he glanced up and stopped. She continued toward the kitchen. As he looked upward, his thoughts opened the bedroom door at the top of the stairs. *No. Go away, Satan. Do not tempt me.*

From the kitchen, she called, "Where are you?" Turning, she stepped back into the foyer from behind the stairs.

The seminarian's mind had already entered the upstairs bedroom and disappeared into the darkness.

CHAPTER 3

SHERIFF THUROW'S VISIT

Father Warren—October 14, 1957

THE all-brick rectory stood beside the majestic stone edifice of St. Thomas Moore Catholic Church. Separated by a passage sidewalk flanked by three-foot-wide perennial flowerbeds on each side, the two buildings provided easy access to one another. The school next door and the church were hubs of activity within the parish community.

Late in the afternoon, Sheriff Thurow knocked on the front door of the rectory. Sister Agatha opened it within two knocks. "Good evening, sir. You're here to see Father Warren, I assume. He's expecting you." She turned toward the direction of Father Warren's study. "Please wait right here."

"Thank you, Sister," the sheriff said in response to her matter-of-fact greeting.

Sister Agatha walked in her usual brisk step back to Father Warren's study. "Excuse me, Father. There is a gentleman here to see you. He's in the front foyer."

"Thank you, Sister. Please tell him I'll be right there." The priest set his pen on the letter at his desk, straightened his collar, and fastened the top two buttons of his cassock. As he walked down the rectory's main hall, he could see a gentleman dressed in a suit and tie, hat in hand, waiting. At first glance, he recognized the tall man's chiseled face.

"Good afternoon, Father."

"Why, Sheriff Thurow, good to see you," Father Warren said with a slight nod. "It's been a while."

"Oh yes, Father. We haven't talked lately, but I'm at seven o'clock Mass every Sunday."

"Oh, I know, my friend. I see you there frequently," the priest responded with a pleasant smile. "You're not in uniform today."

"Day off, Father."

"Oh, of course. I know you deserve it. What brings you here?"

"Father, I need to talk with you. Could you spare a few moments?" Sheriff Thurow asked.

Father Warren detected the sheriff's serious frown. "Here." He gestured with an open hand to the front parlor. "Let's sit over here. Have a seat. Please tell me." He motioned again to a place at the end of the 1920s dark brown spring and down sofa.

"I could take a nap on these cushions," the sheriff said, testing them with his left hand when no one was looking.

"Yes, I've done that a couple times," Father Warren replied with a chuckle. "Well, what is it, Sheriff?" he asked with comforting openness. "I'm a far better listener compared to my sometimes lengthy Sunday sermons."

The sheriff leaned forward on the sofa, his hat still clutched in his hands. "Father, I'd like your advice. Have a couple questions. This is confidential and unofficial."

"Sure, I understand. Just like confession. Go ahead."

"Well, Father, I'm not here for confession, although I'm a little overdue. It's about the reform school. I've had reports, anonymous phone calls, and two unsigned letters about somebody abusing boys. Sexually, I'm afraid to say."

"Sheriff, I hate to hear that," the priest replied.

The sheriff, wrapped in his own concern, did not detect the furrowed frown across Father Warren's brow. The priest abandoned his relaxed position and sat up more erectly in his comfortable reading chair.

"Yes, Father … I don't have details or even circumstances. So I came to you for advice." *Now, Father Warren could take that statement a couple of ways*, Sheriff Thurow thought.

Just two words—*abusing boys*—aroused Father Warren's internal concern. An immediate reaction hidden within Father Warren brought forth memories from the past. "Do you by any chance have a name?" he asked rather quickly. His thick white hair and pleasant face gave him a look of distinction.

The sheriff paused before answering but was interrupted by a soft knock at the parlor door.

"Yes, yes, Sister. What is it?" Father Warren responded in a most unusual curt tone at the unwelcomed interruption.

"Excuse me, Father. So sorry to bother you," she said defensively. "It's just that Mr. Mason and his friend from the Knights of Columbus are here for your meeting."

"Yes, Sister. Thank you. Tell them I'll be there in a few minutes. Please offer them some tea," he said in his more typical pleasant tone.

"Yes, Father." She left, closing the double doors tightly behind her, ensuring the father's privacy.

"You were saying, Sheriff?"

"Well, Father, I was given the name twice by two different people."

"Yes? Yes, who?" Father Warren asked.

There was a pause. "It's a ... it's a Bernard ... a Bernard Bednar. Do you know him?"

"A Bernard Bednar? *Hmmm.* Let me see. No, no, I don't ... " he said with a puzzled look. The elder priest thought, placing his right hand to his chin and rubbing. Then he paused and said, "Wait a minute. Yes, I think I do know him. Yes, Bernard lives with his elderly parents over on, ah, I can't remember the street. It's just a couple blocks south of Pike."

Immediately Father Warren was conflicted. "Bernard was a student in the grade school long, long before I became pastor. There are no records, but I recall his father once told me Bernard was involved in a confrontation that happened when he was in seventh grade. It was very tragic, but a public scandal was avoided. Because he was a minor, Bernard's situation was addressed within the parish. Our bishop was not involved. Again, all this is conjecture. It is only what I've heard from what has been passed down. I'm sure they were rumors."

The look on Father Warren's face and his hesitancy in response to the sheriff's inquiry raised a question in Sheriff Thurow's mind, but he did not mention it.

"Now, please understand, Sheriff, it was Bernard who might have been abused back in grade school. I would hope that Bernard would not abuse someone else."

The sheriff listened intently. "Yes, I understand. I just wanted to know if you knew anything about him."

"Thank you, Sheriff. I hope this can help somewhat," was all the priest could say.

"Maybe just one more thing," Sheriff Thurow added. "Today is simply an unofficial inquiry, our visit and all. But could we talk later if I need to? Would that be okay?"

"Of course, of course … I am here whenever you need anything. Contact me anytime."

"Father, could I ask one more question about Bernard now?"

Father Warren nodded in reply, glancing at the clock on the mantel.

"You mentioned confrontation. Could it have been that Bernard was abused? In all my years of dealing with abuse, there is one common thread. Often the abusers were abused as children."

"I just wouldn't know," the father said. "Yes, Sheriff, yes, I do know that abusers were often abused themselves, but unfortunately I do not know the Bednar family well enough, and as I said, we do not have records or files that go back that far."

"If you do think of anything, you have my number. Like I said, I just stopped to hopefully receive some insight. I need to check around, inquire a little more. Maybe someone will recall more about this Bernard Bednar fellow."

"That will be fine. Just call ahead if you can," Father Warren politely suggested.

He led Sheriff Thurow to the door. The sheriff extended his hand to the good priest.

Father Warren responded as he shook the sheriff's hand, "Bless you. Bless everyone involved. I will be praying for all of this to end."

Sheriff Thurow pulled the collar of his long wool coat up, pulled down the brim of his hat, and made his way into the darkness that now encompassed the St. Thomas Moore rectory. As he walked toward his car, he could feel the gathering of the chilly winds of autumn. While driving home that evening, he could not help but wonder what Father Warren had meant when he said, *"Yes, I do know. I know all too well."*

Father Warren spent time in the side chapel of St. Thomas Moore, just off the front right side of the church, close to the rectory. Ten rows of pews faced a simple wooden altar. St. Michael's statue stood to the left, set back in a simple alcove. Several votive prayer candles burned in their small jars on the metal stand. Twenty-five-cent donations were the norm. The warmth and comfortable feel of the chapel encouraged prayer. Father Warren seemed to be spending more time there lately. St. Thomas Moore, unlike most parish churches, was fortunate to have a dedicated side chapel. St. Michael, the patron saint of law and justice, was an inspiration to Father Warren.

An hour or so passed. His deep focus was not only on the future but also on the past. The priest stood, genuflected, and then returned to his study and read—a late-night ritual. Before retiring, he continued reading *Scandal from Within—The Church's Role in Child Abuse in Ireland*. It was a book he had been reading as a result of a suspicion within his own parish. The father reflected on his visit with Sheriff Thurow. He hoped the sheriff had not detected any alarm written on his face. Father Warren's own concerns about sin and possible deception within his parish rested heavily on his mind.

I must first contact Sheriff Thurow. I'll wait until next week, Father Warren thought. His deep concerns about a scandal were a totally unacceptable reality. This confirmed his suspicions. If something was to become of any serious alleged abuse within the reform school, the publicity and exposure might spark insinuations and accusations in his own parish.

This cannot be allowed to happen. One parishioner had already come forth just last month. A few weeks after school started, Father Warren contemplated what he should do. First of all, he had to know the reality and truthfulness regarding his perception of the "seeds of sinfulness" among his very own staff. Father Warren, aware of potential problems, knew he must address them. With only suspicions, he would need to proceed cautiously. He was not ready to broach the subject until he was more sure.

The next evening, Father Jaeger came to dinner. "Good evening, Father,"

Father Jaeger said as he sat at his usual place at the table for the evening meal.

Father Warren preferred that he and his two assistant pastors always ate supper together at 6:00 p.m. sharp. "Have you seen Father Sullivan?" he asked his assistant.

"Yes, Father. He said he would be here in two to three minutes," Father Jaeger replied.

"Sister Agatha has prepared pot roast this evening," Father Warren said, trying to initiate light conversation.

"Oh, here he comes. I detect his hurried steps."

"Father Sullivan, right on time by fifteen seconds," Father Warren said with a relaxed smile.

Father Sullivan hurriedly took his seat without explanation for his last-minute arrival.

"Let's bow our heads and say grace." All three priests bowed their heads in reverence. "Bless us, O Lord, for these our gifts for which we are about to receive. From Thy bounty, through Christ, our Lord … Amen," Father Warren said and then began to carve the roast. "Michael, Jerome, I would like to ask you to assist me."

"Sure, Father, of course. What is it?" Father Sullivan was first to ask. "Bet you want me to take all the 5:30 Masses for the rest of the month." He lightly elbowed Father Jaeger.

"Seriously, there is possibly a growing problem at the reform school. Sheriff Thurow stopped by to see me just yesterday. It seems that a long-time attendant may be … " The good pastor paused. "The sheriff thinks"—he raised his finger—"but is not for sure that a long-time attendant may be taking liberties with some of the boys. Seems it has to do with a Bernard Bednar. He went to our school many years ago. Being that you each have said Mass at the school, maybe we can help."

"I have seen a fellow. I have heard of the name Bernard. Let's see, it was my turn last month. Yes, I remember. There was this guy helping set up chairs in the hall for Mass. Didn't talk to him though," Father Sullivan recalled. "Oh, I hope that cannot be."

Father Jaeger continued to eat his meat and didn't say a word. Father Sullivan made mental note of Father Jaeger's expressionless face.

"We may be needed to help. All is very confidential, of course. Very quiet," Father Warren continued.

"Who knows about this?" Father Sullivan asked with deep concern.

"I do not know who else has been informed. Sheriff Thurow has suspicions it could be this attendant at the reform school. A few anonymous phone calls and two letters have alerted him."

"That's good. These things have to be kept quiet," Father Jaeger chimed in.

What does he mean by that? Father Sullivan thought.

"Well, as I was saying, I'd like for one of you to meet Sheriff Thurow and discuss this in more detail. He wants to keep this very low-key before he actually has to begin an official investigation. See what you can learn. The sheriff wants our help."

"Father, what can we do?" Father Sullivan asked, looking puzzled.

"There's one thing."

"What's that?" Father Jaeger asked without hesitation.

"I was wondering if maybe you knew of or had met Bernard or his parents. Maybe at Sunday Mass?"

No response. Father Sullivan shook his head. Father Jaeger looked puzzled, which Father Warren noticed immediately.

"Jerome?" he asked Father Jaeger.

"Not right offhand, Father. Never heard the name."

Father Warren went on, "I believe Bernard lives with his parents over on the south side of Wabash, a few blocks off Pike Street. The area is called Monkey Town. A strange name, I thought. Anyway, I recall meeting his dad once. I can barely remember anything else from more than twenty-five years ago," Father Warren said. "That goes with being the senior pastor. I assume Bernard may be in his late forties now."

"No, Father, that doesn't ring a bell with me," Father Sullivan said. "Are the suspicions well-founded?"

"That's the sheriff's call."

"You know, come to think of it, I've noticed maybe a couple times a person of that age—a quiet, loner type guy—every so often. I've seen him in the hallways," Father Jaeger said. "I even saw him one time with two boys walking down the hall. Yes, yes, a boy on each side of him and his hands on their shoulders. Let me see," Father Jaeger said, scratching his chin. "They were headed toward the back stairs."

"What are you insinuating?" Father Sullivan looked at Jaeger deliberately.

"Ah, nothing. Nothing," Father Jaeger responded.

"I've been saying Mass there for a couple years," Father Sullivan said. After a thoughtful silence, he went on, "I have no reason to suggest or accuse this Bernard." Father Sullivan glared at Father Jaeger.

"Okay, okay, we're not getting anywhere," Father Warren said. "I'll ask Sheriff Thurow to stop by the rectory again next Thursday afternoon to meet with all three of us. We can discuss this more thoroughly in his presence."

"Sure, Father," Father Sullivan agreed. "How about three o'clock?"

"Yes, Father. I can also," Father Jaeger added.

"Three o'clock it will be. I'll call the sheriff to see if that works for him."

Together they proceeded with supper. Conversation centered on the Boy Scout troop and their request for some new camping equipment. Although Father Jaeger was the liaison with the troop, Father Sullivan seemed to have most of the ideas for fund-raising.

"Excuse me, Father. Good meal. I have some things to do this evening. You can count on me Thursday," Father Jaeger said as he stood up to depart.

"Thank you, Jerome. Good evening."

"Goodnight, Michael," Father Jaeger said to Father Sullivan. "See you at the confirmation meeting tomorrow morning." He wiped his lips with a white napkin and hurried away.

Sitting at the table, Father Warren and Father Sullivan enjoyed their after-dinner coffee. They didn't talk, each wondering what the other was thinking.

Setting his cup down, the senior pastor leaned forward and looked at Father Sullivan. "Michael, between you and me, do you think Father Jaeger seemed a little ... hmmm ... maybe a little uncomfortable talking about ... well, you know ... troubles at the reform school?"

Father Sullivan took his last sip of coffee and then looked directly at Father Warren. "Yes, Father, I did." He paused, leaned in, and looked toward the kitchen to make sure Sister Agatha wasn't close by. "Yes, Father, quite uncomfortable. One more thing." Father Sullivan hesitated and then went on, "This isn't the first time Father Jaeger has raised my suspicions. He just seems secretive. Sorry to say that behind his back, but it is the truth."

Father Warren sat back in his chair and sighed. He had been blessed during his twenty-plus-year stewardship as pastor at St. Thomas Moore. The parish was the religious foundation of Wabash, Indiana. He had a supportive congregation, the school was excellent, and the Franciscan Sisters were a strong support in all activities throughout the parish. A concern about a possible abuse situation at the reform school, if true, would be such a negative for the community. In addition, during the past year, Father Warren had been having some doubts and suspicions about Father Jaeger. He hoped to discover that his suspicions were unfounded.

CHAPTER 4

LAST AN ETERNITY

The Seminarian—August 24, 1906, early evening

STILL standing in the foyer with his friend, the seminarian shook his head. "Oh, yes. Yes, we were going to the kitchen. I was just looking at this beautiful staircase." He rubbed his hand over the smooth mahogany banister as he followed her into the kitchen. "This is quite the place," he said, taking it all in.

"Aunt Margaret and Aunt Patricia have lived here all their lives. Their father was a successful banker, and I might add, he owned hundreds of acres of farmland out west of Pike Street. My aunts never married."

"Oh, you mean living like nuns, or should I say a priest?"

They both smiled at his attempt at humor. After looking around the kitchen, especially at the modern gas stove, they retired to the comfort of the back porch.

He said, "That carriage house is nicer than our home. In fact, that little privy over there is quite large. All brick."

"Oh, that's never used. The house has all inside bathrooms. Three to be exact."

They spent the next hour in delightful conversation about Wabash, their families, childhood memories, the bookstore, and the seminary. As darkness began to engulf the backyard and porch, she stood, struck a match, and lit the lone kerosene lamp.

"I'll be right back." She walked back into the kitchen and returned with a fresh bowl of ice. "Some more tea?"

"Yes, it's delicious."

She filled his glass and sat down. She moved Thimble away and sat on the bench directly across from him as he remained in his chair. As darkness fell, their presence was accompanied by the low warm glow of the lamp. Enjoying the cool iced tea, she stood, reached over, and softened the glow of the lamp.

He repositioned himself in his chair. Searching for words, he said, "This is so pleasant. I've never felt, I don't know, like I've never felt so comfortable. I mean so comfortable with someone."

She folded her hands on her lap, sitting erect on the bench. "Me too." She paused. "I never want to forget this moment." Silence became their companion, along with the advancing presence of late summer's lightning bugs. "Looks like stars moving around."

Iced tea in hand, he sat comfortably in his chair. Looking across at her, he summoned the words. "You are beautiful. Just beautiful." He said the words like never before.

"Thank you. You are so kind." She lowered her head and then heard Thimble scamper across the wooden porch. "Would you like some more tea?" There was a long pause. "Would you like to sit here with me?" She patted the cushion.

Thomas took a long, slow drink of tea and looked over at her. "I'd like both. Yes, I'd like both very much." Together they sat. Time passed slowly.

The lightest of breezes floated through the leaves of the solitary sycamore tree centered in the backyard. The stillness of the late evening surrounded the porch. Conversation drifted. Serenity and peacefulness touched them both as they now sat closer on the wicker bench. Discreetly, she closed the space between them even more while reaching her hand over the top of his. He raised his arm, resting it on back of the bench, as she was now very close. They felt each other's presence.

Slowly and softly, she tilted her head to his shoulder, and he dropped his arm around her shoulder. She felt the gentle strength of his hand clasp her arm. Her hands folded together, and he reached his left hand to hers and rested it on her lap. Totally at ease, they listened to the soft sound of the evening breeze. Together they shared the tranquility of the stillness of the night. Looking down at her head, he raised his hand and touched her cheek. Gently, his fingers glided across her skin and then around her neck.

"Are you okay? Comfortable?" he whispered.

"Oh yes, more than any time in my life." She closed her eyes as if to capture the memory of the moment. *Oh, if only forever.*

"Look over there," he said. Together they watched the lightning bugs twinkle in the yard.

Silence overpowered their need for words. They listened to the song of the mockingbird hidden away somewhere beyond the carriage house. She raised her head as her right hand turned his chin. She gazed into the seminarian's eyes, reached up, and kissed his cheek. Without hesitation, she stood up, looked down, and pulled him upward. They embraced slowly, gently. The seminarian stood in front of her, his right arm still around her shoulder.

"Come with me." She took his hand, and he followed her through the kitchen.

As they stopped in the foyer, the moon's glow drifted through the front door window just enough to catch the side of his face. They stood still, her hand still clutching his, and he squeezed tightly as if saying *yes.* Neither heard Thimble scamper through the parlor and dart up the stairs. She followed by taking the first step. He reached his hand around her waist. Now side by side, they ascended the stairs. Not breaking her stride, she turned and led him down the hall to her room. Stepping inside, he followed. She reached into the drawer of a table that stood next to the closet door. She drew a match and lit the kerosene lamp. The flickering flame danced across the floral wallpaper. *Alone, peaceful, quiet.*

On the far wall, he saw the high carved headboard that dominated the room. The wallpaper was almost completely hidden in the darkness. He took in the comfort of the surroundings. He touched the stained glass of the Tiffany lamp standing alone on the marble-top table just inside the door.

"I prefer the moon's glow and the dancing flame," she said.

He pulled his hand away from the lamp. He could feel his nervousness as he reached down and felt the softness of the wool coverlet atop the bed. He watched as she moved the floral pillow and then pulled the coverlet to the foot of the bed. She walked around to the darker side of the bed, pulled the other side down, and squared the ends. Feeling still a little awkward, he stepped toward the foot of the bed. She first thought he was moving in the direction of the door. He rested his hand on the footboard as if to brace himself for what was about to happen. His eyes remained focused on her standing alone on the other side.

He whispered, "I shouldn't be here. No, I shouldn't. I am feeling the strength of temptation pulling me in your direction." Lust was their only companion.

"Everything will be all right," she whispered softly, trying to ease his mind.

He watched as she lifted her hands. Her gentle fingers unfastened the line of buttons from her high collar to her waist. He was overcome by feelings with which he was not familiar. For a reason he did not know, he sat on the bench at the foot of the bed. A rush of desire and confidence in the moment entered his soul. He stood, tucking his thumbs under his suspenders and lowering them so he could remove his trousers. His back to her, he took his time. The seminarian's shirttail hung far below his waist. Not looking, hoping to hear her voice, he untied his tie and began to unbutton his high collar.

In a low whisper, he heard her beckon, "Come over here. Come over here with me."

He turned. Her face half hidden in darkness, he could see the shadow of the flame dancing and flickering behind her body. She wore no clothes, just her hands crisscrossed across her breasts. The high bed hid just below her waist. She stood alone, enticing him to come nearer. He removed his shirt and slowly walked around the bed to her side. He stood before her. Gently, he clasped his hands around her wrists and pulled her to him. Her supple breasts were totally exposed. He looked down and then into her eyes.

Their bodies were close. He placed his hands on her exposed shoulders and pulled her nearer. Their lips touched. The immediate pressure of her breasts against his chest provided an ecstasy he had never known. Pulling her tightly against him, he lowered his face to her shoulder and breasts and then up to her neck. Slowly, he caressed her neck. Then ever so gently he lowered his head and kissed, kissed them both. Rushed by arousal, he kissed more and then more.

"Gentle. Gentle, my dear." She squeezed him tightly as she lowered her hands on his body. She totally succumbed to his embrace. His skin felt the warmth of hers. She whispered, "This is my first time."

He pulled her down onto the bed. Their entire sides touched. His arm around her shoulders, he continued to kiss the back of her neck faster, more intensely, sending feelings throughout her entire body.

"This, too, is my first time," he whispered breathlessly.

She reached around and wrapped her body around his, pulling them both to the coolness of the sheets. As one, their bodies clung to each other in the total freedom of touch, wrapping themselves around each other. She rolled to her back; they never lost the touch of their embrace. She closed her eyes. He felt the warmth of her body and whispered in her ear. Their movement together became ecstatic. The strength of his embrace heightened her arousal, as it did his. Their movement was caring, and their tantalizing hearts beat ever so faster. Back and then forth.

"More! Oh, yes! More!" she begged. "This night must last forever."

He granted her every wish. "Oh, yes! *Ahhh*." His words and sounds transcended the room.

Her pleas vanquished. The world was forgotten. The two of them were lost to only each other. Together they created a bond that would last a lifetime. Moments became minutes and then an hour. They slumbered together. The flicker of the dancing flames subsided. Still locked in their embrace, their eyes closed, their hearts touched, and their dreams pulled them together, alone in the darkness.

CHAPTER 5

FIRST ENCOUNTER

Father Jaeger—October 21, 1957

DARKNESS was falling on the late October afternoon. The study was wrapped in an aura of fading tranquility. The deep tapestry sofa was positioned in front of the floor-to-ceiling wall-to-wall bookcase. With just enough room to walk in front of the books, Father Jaeger's private study was a place of solitude, a place of privacy. Total and complete privacy, however, was not an option.

The lone Tiffany lamp rested on a small table, providing just enough light to allow one to maneuver about the room. Opposite the sofa, a walnut desk stood backed against the wall, allowing the priest to sit at the desk and converse with anyone sitting on the sofa. A dark-framed horizontal mirror hung above the credenza behind his desk. Family pictures were noticeably absent. He often retired from his desk and sat on the sofa, depending on his visitor. A dark antique oriental rug covered the two-inch-wide dark oak floorboards. The doorway to the right of the desk led to the back hall of the rectory. A second door off the far end of the couch opened into the hallway of the rectory. Immediately off the front hallway, stairs led to his living quarters, offering a more secluded place for complete privacy.

Pastor Warren's bedroom was on the first floor at the other end of the hall. A staircase there led to Father Sullivan's bedroom on the second floor. The long hallway separated the two assistants' quarters.

Father Jaeger enjoyed the solitary privacy of his study, stairs, and second-floor sleeping quarters. Privacy was important to him.

He heard a knock at the door. "Come in. Oh hello, Peter. You're right on time."

Peter stood, school bag and hat in hand. "Yes, Father. You said six o'clock."

"Yes, that I did. Come on in. Thanks for stopping by. Did you have a good day at school?"

"Yes, Father. You know, the usual."

"Here, have a seat," Father Jaeger said, extending his hand.

Peter sat on the desk chair nearest to the light by the sofa.

"There's a reason I wanted to see you, Peter. I am wondering if you would like to begin learning to be a high server. I think you would do very well. I thought we could visit, talk about it, and get to know each other better." Casually, Father Jaeger reached behind his neck and unhooked his white collar. He placed it neatly atop the ivory lace doily on the table beside the couch, across from his desk.

Peter nervously watched as the priest sat down at the far end of the couch. The boy noticed a worn, frayed missal behind the aged Tiffany lamp, which provided just enough light to create minimal shadows in the darkening room.

Father Jaeger patted Peter on his knee, smiled, and said, "Why don't you sit on the couch, closer to the lamp?"

Peter accepted the invitation, though he felt a little tense.

"Does the light help?" the father asked.

Peter nodded with a nervous smile. He could not explain the reason for his uncomfortable feeling. At eleven years old, he was not aware of the realities of life outside of his home, the Boy Scout troop, the YMCA, and St. Thomas Moore's parish school.

Looking at the priest, Peter focused on the slight mole above the father's lip, to the left of his nose. His full head of black hair was parted on the left and perfectly combed. *Probably uses Brylcreem*, Peter thought. A slight amount of pudginess padded the priest's face.

Father Jaeger unlaced his shoes and neatly sat them side by side next to the table at his end of the sofa. "It's been a long day, Peter. How about you?"

Father Jaeger is a very orderly person. Peter nodded and smiled. *But his shoes are off.* "Yes, Father. It has been," he said.

"Let's see, what time is confirmation practice this evening?" Father Jaeger asked.

"Seven o'clock, Father. Remember, our sponsors will be here."

"Oh yes, of course. Let's see, that leaves us some time. Did you tell your parents you were coming here before practice to meet with me?"

"Yes, Father. Mom even packed a peanut butter sandwich. Did you know my mother works in the lunchroom, and she's on the parish council?" Peter said, bragging, trying to make conversation.

Father Jaeger paid no attention, having other things on his mind. "Do you want to eat the sandwich now?"

"No thank you, Father. I ate it after school over at Johnny's house."

"Oh, Johnny's house. Would that be Johnny Olsen? Did you tell him about coming to the rectory?"

"Oh no, Father. Johnny had to go with his mother to his sister's house. She's having a baby soon. Johnny's sister, I mean."

"I see. So they are not aware that you are here?"

"Well, I guess not since I didn't tell them," Peter said bravely with an unintended note of sarcasm.

"Say, would you like a soda?" Father Jaeger offered.

"Sure, that would be great, Father," Peter responded, trying to buy time for a reason he did not know.

"Okay. I'll be right back." The priest stood and turned toward the door.

"Father … " Peter paused. "Your shoes."

"Oh, yes. Thanks, Peter."

Within a few minutes, the priest returned with a 7-Up in his hand.

"Thanks, Father. How'd you know that's my favorite?" Peter asked.

Father Jaeger thought for a few seconds. "Because I know a lot of things about boys like you."

What does that mean? Peter thought, unaware of many realities of growing up in the 1950s.

"Peter, I asked you to stop by so we could talk about you becoming a high server. You have done so well your first year. Your Latin is perfect. You are attentive. You're a leader, Peter. I'm sure you already know the responsibilities of high server during Mass."

"I'd like that. I've always wanted to be an altar boy since second grade when I made my first communion, except—"

Father Jaeger cut Peter off. "Except what?"

"Well, I'd miss ringing the bells."

"Oh yes, of course."

They both smiled at Peter's attempt at humor.

"When I was your age, I served Mass almost every day," Father Jaeger said proudly, seeing if he could get a rise out of Peter.

"Really, Father?"

"Look there on the table. That's my daily missal—my *Saint Joseph's Daily Missal*. Pick it up. That was mine when I was about your age."

Peter reached for the sacred book. "Sure looks old." He rubbed the worn black cover, opened it, and paged through it.

"Page 642—turn to it, Peter. You recognize those words? *In nomine Patris.* Amen. Oh, those words … beautiful. We use them every day. Here, let me show you something else." Father Jaeger scooted over, now sitting next to Peter, with his left arm still on the back of the couch and now closer to Peter's head. He was excited. His pulse elevated. His body tingled. He was not thinking about serving Mass or his *Saint Joseph's Daily Missal.* Father Jaeger was totally focused on Peter.

Innocently, Peter said, "I appreciate you inviting me here, Father. Your study is beautiful."

Father Jaeger pulled his knee up onto the cushion and leaned over to reach for the missal. Peter now felt the priest's knee at his side. *Must be okay*, Peter thought. *He's a priest for gosh sake.*

Within a second, they were holding the missal together. Father Jaeger's hand touched Peter's hand as they held the book. *Smooth*, the excited priest thought. The father was feeling not only anxious but also quite confident in his approach to Peter. Having been this far on so many other occasions with others of Peter's age, he forgot about confirmation practice. When alone and in the presence of youth, Father Jaeger focused on only one thing. All else was blocked out.

Father Warren, the senior pastor, was absent from the rectory for the evening. Peter didn't know. Father Jaeger felt empowered by the indulgence of the moment, a rush from deep inside—anticipation.

Peter felt awkward. "What time is it, Father? Maybe I better check and see if Uncle Bob is here to meet me for practice."

"It's only 6:35. I want to know your feelings." *A slight slip of inappropriate words.* "I mean, what do you think about becoming a high server? I think you are ready. I know I'm ready," the priest said inadvertently.

Peter's innocence prohibited him from picking up on the priest's suggestion. He noticed some beads of perspiration across Father Jaeger's forehead. *It's November. Doesn't seem hot to me,* Peter thought. "Excuse me, Father. Could I have another soda, please? Maybe you might need one too," he said, referring to the perspiration on the priest's brow.

"No, not yet. You still have a few swigs left in your bottle." Peter detected some slight aggravation in the priest's voice. "I'll get one in a minute. I want to show you something ... I want—"

"Jerome! Jerome! Are you in there?"

Both Father Jaeger and Peter recognized the cheerful voice of Father Sullivan coming down the hall. He knocked on the half-open door and bounded into Father Jaeger's study. "Oh, I mean Father. You have company. Sorry, Father. Why, Peter, hi."

Father Jaeger was annoyed by the unwelcomed intrusion. Peter was relieved to see Father Sullivan.

"Good evening, Father Sullivan," Peter said with a sheepish grin.

"Thought you were with the Doyle's this evening," Father Jaeger said to his fellow priest.

"Back early. The meeting with Mr. Doyle was cut short. His wife called. Can you believe their dog is loose in the neighborhood? So Mr. Doyle had to leave." Father Jaeger slowly stood up, hitched up his belt, and bent his knees.

Father Sullivan said, "Oh, I'll let you be. I'll just grab a sandwich before confirmation practice. See you in thirty." He turned and was gone.

The chemistry in the room had changed from inviting to departing. Attempting awkward nonchalance, Father Jaeger asked Peter if he'd like to borrow his missal for a few days or so.

"Wow! That would be great, Father." A wide smile appeared on Peter's innocent face for the first time that evening, though he was happier to leave the study than to take the missal. "I'll bring it back of course," Peter assured him. "Better go look for my uncle. Thanks again, Father." Feeling relieved, he stood up and turned to exit the room.

"One more thing, Peter. Can you return the missal within the next week or two? Just let me know ahead of time so I can be ready for you."

"Oh sure, Father. Be glad to. You can tell me more then."

I will, Father Jaeger thought. *I surely will.* The illumination from the Tiffany lamp didn't catch the slight smile on Father Jaeger's face. Standing beyond the light, anticipating Peter's departure, he said, "You have beautiful skin, Peter," trying to pay a compliment that would entice the boy to stay.

"Beautiful skin?" Peter asked, thinking how weird it was for him to say that. "Well, I gotta go find Uncle Bob." As he passed quickly in front of the priest, he added, "Thanks again for the 7-Up."

Father Jaeger tied his shoes, hooked his collar, and headed upstairs. His only relief was that Father Sullivan had left.

As Peter exited the rectory, he thought, *Why tell me I have beautiful skin?*

As Father Jaeger climbed the stairs and Peter left the rectory, Father Sullivan finished fixing his dinner. After cutting his sandwich, he poured some milk and sat alone at the kitchen table. A thought occurred to him. *Now what was that all about? Father and Peter? Strange to say the least.*

CHAPTER 6

RAISING SUSPICIONS

Sheriff Thurow—October 15, 1957, late afternoon

SHERIFF Thurow thought about his meeting again with Father Warren. *Hope I get some answers.* Pulling up to the rectory, he admired the two-story building. After parking in front, he looked to the end of the block, stopped for a moment, and stared at the historic courthouse, admiring its stately grandeur. Most of all, he was in awe of the bigger-than-life statue of Abraham Lincoln.

Sheriff Thurow was anxious to meet with Father Warren and his assistants. He anticipated a more thorough conversation about the alleged abuse than in his first meeting with Father Warren.

"Good afternoon, Sister."

Bowing her head, Sister Agatha said, "And to you too, Sheriff Thurow. Come right in. All three fathers are in the parlor. Please follow me." Turning around, she asked if she could bring some coffee or tea.

"Thank you, Sister. Coffee would be perfect. Straight black for me."

Father Warren stood as he saw the sheriff enter the parlor. "Good afternoon, Sheriff Thurow," he welcomed, extending his hand.

"And to you, Fathers," he said as Fathers Sullivan and Jaeger stood and shook hands with the out-of-uniform sheriff.

The two assistants sat at opposite ends of the couch. Father Warren and the sheriff sat in the wingback chairs positioned at either end. All were grouped around a high coffee table in front of the old heavy tapestry sofa.

Sister Agatha had prepared a fire, which crackled and popped from the dry hickory logs. Late in the afternoon, the parlor was dim and offered an environment for a good book by the fire as opposed to a difficult conversation about reprehensible acts against innocent children.

"Thank you, Sister," Father Warren said as she set the coffee tray on the table.

Father Sullivan and the sheriff lifted their cups as Father Warren served. Father Jaeger declined, just sitting back, wedged into the farthest corner of the couch.

"Please close both doors, Sister."

She complied with a nod and closed the doors as she backed into the foyer. Total privacy.

"Allow me to get right to the point, Father," the sheriff said. "I am opening an official investigation into an alleged abuse that might have taken place at the reform school. I am sad to report that we believe this abuse may have been taking place for several years."

"How is that possible, Sheriff?" Father Sullivan asked, leaning forward, hands on his knees.

"Cover-up. That simple. There's abuse ... children without the guidance of parents. The abuser scares them and threatens to harm anyone who talks. We even think there could be some older boys, fifteen- and sixteen-year-olds taking advantage of the younger ones. As a matter of fact, there have been rumors about what happened back in 1934 when one of the boys died. He was about twelve or thirteen. His name ... *hmmm*, I can't even remember. Anyway, he was buried over there. You know, in Friends Cemetery, just east of the school back toward town. The rumor is that he was sodomized. Supposedly something went wrong and he died. I was on the force but not involved. Guess the sheriff at the time looked into it, but nothing came of it. The boy had no parents. No kin. Always kind of a looming mystery. Wish I could think of that kid's name. Officially, the coroner ruled it death caused by influenza."

Father Warren somehow recalled *Gordon*—a name not easily forgotten. "Yes, Gordon. Gordon Yoder. I heard it a long time ago," he said as he brushed his hand through his pure white hair.

"Back to today. We all know the tough prey on the weak," Father Sullivan said.

"You are exactly right," the sheriff confirmed. "For now, we have only one person we suspect, and that is Bernard Bednar. Of course, this is confidential."

"He is taking sin too far. If this is happening, the abusers should be removed and tried, and if guilty, they should go to prison," Father Sullivan said with inflamed passion.

"We understand, of course." Father Warren calmed the young priest by using his hand to gesture to Father Sullivan. Father Jaeger did not comment.

"Father, do you have any suggestions that could help us before this becomes public?" Sheriff Thurow asked, looking directly at Father Warren and then at Fathers Sullivan and Jaeger. The priests looked at each other.

"Not really," said Father Jaeger. "I'd keep this quiet. Not tell anyone and maybe move this Bernard guy to another place in the building. If the abuse is happening in the area where he works, it would stop."

"Isn't that just masking the problem?" asked Father Warren. "Moving from one place to another?"

"Maybe for now, Father, but maybe it will eliminate the problem. Just my thought, just my thought," Father Jaeger replied.

"Sheriff, what if Father Jaeger or Father Sullivan paid a visit as a priest of the parish? Simply went to his home to talk and visit with Bernard, talk with his parents. As you say, he may be a suspect, but there is no proof. Sometimes people will open up to a priest. Sometimes not. It's worth a try."

"That's a good idea," the sheriff replied.

"Well, what about that, Father Jaeger, Father Sullivan?" Father Warren asked.

"Could be a start. I'd recommend that would be a perfect assignment for Father Sullivan. He's so good with people," Father Jaeger suggested, trying to put the burden on his fellow assistant.

"I'd be glad to," Father Sullivan said, taking advantage of the perfect opening provided by his associate.

Father Warren was at first silent on the matter, knowing that only Father Sullivan would be able to handle the subject with Bernard. "Well, Michael, you'll need to tone down some of that Irish passion," he said with a smile.

"Of course, of course, Father. I am anxious to help any way I can. And yes, I will leave my Irish passion here."

"I trust the three of you for that decision," Sheriff Thurow concurred.

Father Jaeger was relieved that he would not be involved regarding his knowledge of abuse.

"Could we all agree that Father Sullivan's mission would be a low-key visit to try to see if Bernard would want to talk or if anything is on his mind?"

"I'll contact the family and ask if I could just stop by and pay a visit as a priest from the parish," Father Sullivan said.

"They might be quite reluctant. His parents, I assume from what I've heard about them, will probably be there," Father Warren informed them. "I've heard they are a strange family. Just the three of them. I once heard they only leave the house once a week on Fridays. You will most likely be visiting all three of them."

"Well, that should do it. Do you think you could try and then get back to me?" the sheriff asked.

"You can count on me, Sheriff," Father Sullivan assured him.

They all stood. Sheriff Thurow took the last drink of his coffee, turned, and walked to the door. "This is such a beautiful room. Never seen so many books. Mighty comfortable chairs too." As he opened the door, he almost bumped into Sister Agatha.

"Oh, excuse me, Sister. I didn't mean to startle you." The sheriff stepped back, allowing the sister to walk through. Turning to wave, he said, "Thanks again, Fathers."

"Just returning for the tray," Sister Agatha said shyly.

"Always good timing, Sister," Father Warren said with a smile. After Sister Agatha closed the door, he said, "Well, what do you think, Michael? Jerome?"

"Such a disappointing surprise to me," said Father Sullivan. "They don't know for sure about Bernard. I do intend to find out the truth. Just because the family is odd doesn't mean Bernard would harm any of the boys. The whole situation sounds so strange to me."

"I'm sure it's only one isolated incident and this will all go quietly away," Father Jaeger said, downplaying the suspicion. "Sometimes these accusations have no merit."

"I wish it were so, but I'm not so sure," replied Father Warren.

As the two younger priests left the front parlor, Father Warren asked, "Did you see that Sister Agatha was right there when the sheriff opened the door?"

"Do you think she could have been listening?" Father Sullivan asked.

Father Warren did not respond, with the exception of raising his eyebrows up and down a couple of times. "We all hear confessions. You never know who is trying to listen," Father Warren reminded him.

CHAPTER 7

LATE WALK HOME

Monkey Town—October 17, 1957

THE full moon shined bright in the late harvest season. The fires of autumn bellowed smoke from the tidy rows of houses on the south side of town. The smell of burning leaves was characteristic of peaceful neighborhoods where folks raked piles of fallen maple leaves to the street's edge. Neighbors visited on front porches. Ladies borrowed eggs or sugar from next door. Children played and frolicked all over the neighborhood, which was named Monkey Town for reasons not known.

The name provided identity. Locals were proud to say they lived in Monkey Town. The northern edge of the quiet, sleepy neighborhood was bordered by Pike Street, just across from the Stouffer homestead. South of Pike, Monkey Town included McKibben, Columbus, Chester, and Webster Streets. A few people on the northern side of downtown frowned at or looked down on the names when they heard them.

Three blocks south of Pike Street, soft lights could be detected from within the Boy Scout meeting hall next to the old St. Ignasius parish churchyard at the corner of King and Webster. After the fire of 1896, the church was never rebuilt. A new parish, St. Thomas Moore, had replaced the old small-frame nineteenth-century church of St. Ignasius. St. Thomas Moore was located downtown, atop the hill just across from the county courthouse at Hill and Wabash Streets.

Boy Scout Troop 33 was gathered inside the small hall, which rested on a crumbling brick foundation behind the former church. The hall had been saved from the fire. The bi-monthly Scout meeting was in session.

The single-room hall was filled with the anticipation of the thirty-two dedicated, fun-loving Boy Scouts. They were preparing for their fall camping trip, which was set for that weekend. At 8:30 sharp, the lights dimmed, and the Scouts were dismissed. They spread in all directions in the neighborhood. Most headed straight home, per their parents' demands. Carefree eleven- to thirteen-year-old boys freely walked the streets. Even after dark, unencumbered by fear of strangers, dangerous dogs, or any unknowns in the darkness of the night, the boys felt safe.

One block from the meeting hall, an unpainted neglected gray clapboard house stood isolated from the rest of the neighborhood. Chestnut Street was a dead end, along with the house and the three inhabitants who resided within it. Elmer and Gladys Bednar lived there along with their only son, Bernard. All three were strange—creepy, to be exact. The weathered house, unkempt yard, broken fence, and leaning single-car garage all contributed to the aura of mystery and eeriness. The aged gray window shades were always drawn. The three inhabitants were rarely seen. Bernard left his house only to walk to and from work. Some days, he left in the early morning. Other days, he left the house in the early afternoon. He always walked alone.

Friendless, Bernard had maintained a job as an attendant at the Wabash Reform School for more than twenty-five years. Located on Pike Road a mile farther west of Monkey Town and adjacent to the southern bend in the Wabash River, the school was an early 1900s brick institution. Separate from the goings-on in town, the school was like an isolated island within itself, though it was funded by the county.

Quite often, strange stories leaked from the doors and windows about various goings-on inside. Rumors were usually produced by a few of the stranger folks who worked there. One incident had gone beyond the stage of rumor, that being the quiet and strange death of Gordon Yoder back in the summer of 1934. Rumor had it that Gordon had suddenly died just three nights after a small group of well-wishers and a few staff members celebrated the retirement of Herman Lawrey, who had worked at the school for the previous thirty-two years. Having no next of kin, Gordon had been quietly buried in the Friends Cemetery on July 25, 1934. A small, nondescript gravestone next to the giant maple below the hill marked his last day. School records noted that Gordon Yoder died from the flu on Sunday, July 22, 1934, at age twelve.

A few blocks away from the Bednars' home, Eddie Baker, Dan Grimm, and Dennis McCormack left the Scout meeting hall. They headed up King Street and then straight for Pike, never wandering or even looking down Chestnut Street toward the mysterious old decrepit house. The wind was picking up on this hazy full-mooned mid-October evening. A few remaining leaves of fall scampered and skidded across the street. The boys instinctively walked at a quicker pace. Eddie noticed a shadow of a figure walking in their direction. Dan and Dennis continued to chatter about the upcoming camping trip.

"Stop," Eddie commanded quietly. "Stop, I said." He reached for the back of Dan's heavy flannel shirt, pulling him backward. Dan fell back a step. "Look ahead! Who's that?" Eddie pointed straight down the sidewalk. The three stood still. "Is that him?"

"Him, like in who?" Dennis asked with a note of fearless sarcasm, pulling the brim of his red wool hunting hat lower over his eyes.

"That guy. You know. The one down on Chestnut." Eddie pointed back over his left shoulder to the street behind them.

Before they could reply, the figure suddenly stopped, turned right, walked a few paces back, and headed down Columbus in the same direction as the dead-end Chestnut Street. The night darkened as a billowing cloud passed in front of the full moon. Eddie turned around as if to retreat back toward the meeting hall.

"Come on, Eddie. This way," Dennis said.

Dan and Dennis proceeded forward. Eddie scampered after them, close to their heels. Approaching Columbus, the boys did not notice a man watching them from the shadows of a large barren maple tree.

Suddenly headlights flashed as a car turned off Pike and onto King. The boys stopped in their tracks. The headlights glared forward just a block away. The car came closer, muffled past, slowed, and turned right on Chestnut. It disappeared down the dead-end street. Ahead one block, the unknown figure was definitely gone.

"Let's go back. I don't like this. Feels freaky. That car had to be his old man. That's the clunker. I've seen it before. Did you see inside?"

Eddie asked. "You know, they say the creep spends all his time over in that woods, chopping with an ax as large as a wagon tongue."

"Ah, you been seein' too many Frankenstein movies. Come on, Eddie. Gotta get home or Ma will wonder where I am," Dennis said.

Dennis and Dan proceeded toward Pike Street. Eddie continued to follow closely. As they approached Columbus, Dan and Dennis stopped and looked down the street. Nothing.

"See, Eddie. Nothing."

Dim lights outlined some homes on both sides. Quiet, stillness … except for the wind, which was now just a lonely howl. Suddenly, out of nowhere the rattle of a car or pickup truck pulled up from behind them and next to the curb. With the headlights shining, the boys couldn't detect the driver of the vehicle.

"Holy shit!" Dennis cried out.

"Who's driving that truck?" Dan said, clinging to Dennis's buckle coat.

"Hey, guys. Need a ride? Hop in," the man directed without waiting for an answer.

Dennis peeked around the headlights. "It's Mr. Krueger, our smiling scoutmaster," he said, alerting Dan and Eddie.

"Oh hi, Mr. Krueger," Dan said, still startled. "You scared the crap out of us."

"Oh sorry, boys."

"Thanks, but we all live close by. We'll walk," Dan replied with hidden purpose.

"Ah, there's room. The three of you can all squeeze into the front seat with me."

"Nah, we're all stopping at Dan's house for a few minutes. He's gonna show us his new backpack and the army canteen his dad gave him. Carried it all through the war."

"Okay then, another time. See you all Friday. Lots to do at Portland Arch." Mr. Krueger hung his elbow out the window and headed slowly toward Pike.

All three boys smelled the dark exhaust from his old Ford pickup. "Puke! You bet he wanted us to all three squeeze into the front seat," Dan said in disgust.

"You bet. That's not all he'd be squeezing," Dennis fired back.

"That's right there, Danny Boy. He'd have hold of you sitting closest to him." Dan pushed Dennis forward.

"His truck doesn't bother me," Dennis said. "Krueger makes me puke. I love the Scouts, but that guy gives me the creeps. I sure wish Mr. Batkus was scoutmaster. How'd Krueger become scoutmaster anyway?"

Dan, who always had an answer for everything, said, "Dad told me that decision comes from the priests. Father Warren, I guess. He appointed Krueger. Although Dad said once that the real guy in charge of the Scouts is Father Jaeger. I hate it when he comes to our Scout meetings now and then. Remember last spring when Father Jaeger said Mass at our spring campout?"

"Yeah, I remember," Dennis chimed in. "Wasn't that the time Mark Ross came to school with his parents after the outing and had to go see Father Warren?"

"Yeah, Mark said something happened that weekend … but he was mum to everyone," Dan replied.

Fat little Dennis was a conspiracy freak. Always thought something was wrong behind the scenes. Sometimes Eddie had a tendency to believe him.

"I don't like Father Jaeger," Dan said. "Hey, how about this one? You know one time after Mass, I was bringing in the wine from the side altar and then took off my cassock. Jaeger comes right up behind me, puts his hands on my shoulders, and says something like … I can't remember exactly but like 'You got a good build, Dan. Bet you're gonna be a football player … or a swimmer.' It felt creepy. Then he said, 'Do you like to swim at the Y?'"

"Creepy. Creepy SOB. I don't care if he is a priest."

"You're kidding," Eddie replied. Eddie was the oldest of the trio; he just turned thirteen.

"That does sound creepy," Dennis added. "Ah, come on, guys. Let's get to Dan's house. Maybe his mom will have her apple pie. Right, Dan?" Dennis said hopefully.

"Let's just get to someone's house," Eddie said from behind Dennis and Dan.

"Yeah, maybe. She bakes all the time, especially if she knows you're coming, Weesbo."

"Up yours, big guy," Dennis said, hoping she had made pie.

They dropped the subject of Krueger and Father Jaeger. As they crossed Columbus, the boys heard a bark. Then a dog squealed like he had been hit, kicked, or just startled by someone unexpected. The mutt's echoes could be heard half a block away. Their heads turned left. The streak of a hound dashing across Columbus and then disappearing into the night once again startled the boys.

"What caused that?" asked Eddie, his imagination in full gear.

"Ah, nothing. Just a scared dog," Dan said, the most daring of the three.

"Yeah, but what scared him was on the street that creepy guy went down. Bet it was him. That's creep number three for this evening. Don't like it, guys. There's something gonna happen," Dennis conspired.

"Ah, quiet, Dennis," Dan ordered. "Too much darkness, clouds, and creepy guys for you two meatheads?"

"Hey, Dan, there's your dad on the front porch. Let's go see that canteen of yours." Pointing toward Pike Street, Eddie asked, "Say, Mr. Grimm, isn't that the Stouffer milk farm over there?"

"Sure is. I used to work there for twenty-five cents an hour when I was a kid."

"Yeah, I been there a couple times. Played in the barn with Billy. He's our age. Goes to public school. He loves milking. He showed me how. Made me squeeze those teats. Yuck!" Dennis said, shaking his right hand. "Billy said when he grows up he wants to be a milkman or a race car driver. Figure that."

"Ah, who cares," Eddie said. "Let's go get some pie."

Their minds switched back to camping gear as they quickly stepped up to the porch and walked into Dan's house. Dennis still had pie on his mind. Nobody noticed the red lights. A truck was parked on the opposite side of the street about a half block from Pike.

Eddie and Dennis sat and had some pie with Dan and his dad. Like on a number of occasions before, Dan's pop was open about sharing war stories with Dan and his friends. *Okay for them to know the harsh realities of life*, Dan's dad thought. Keeping in mind their age, he carefully edited many of the truths he didn't want them to know, and the ones he wanted to forget.

Sitting around the kitchen table, the three boys listened intently to Dan's pop as he told them about being surrounded in a farmhouse in France just one week after D-day.

"You mean you carried this canteen for two years during the war?"

"Every single day," he replied.

Dennis, ever so analytical, thought Dan's dad looked like an ex-infantryman. He was still slender and dressed in a T-shirt, and the hair on his muscular forearms was bristled. His face was angular, and his head was topped by thick black hair. The slight gray at the temples gave him an authoritative look. Dan often bragged about his dad, the tough army sergeant of WWII.

Eddie and Dennis each wanted to hold the canteen, as if it might have some mystical power.

"It's just a canteen, boys. The real story can be seen in the hundreds of photos." Dan's dad stopped himself.

Surprised, Dan looked at his pop with a question across his face. "You have photos?" he asked.

His pop hesitated. "Well, yes. They're all packed away in the basement."

"Can we see them?" all three boys asked almost simultaneously.

"Not tonight. Save that for another day. You were too young to see the grim realities of war. Maybe you guys are ready now."

"Yeah, Mr. Grimm, we would love to see them. Wow!"

"Another time, boys."

"Hey, we better go," Dennis said to Eddie. "Thanks, Mr. Grimm. Night, Dan."

"See you guys in school tomorrow."

As Eddie and Dennis stepped from the porch and continued toward Pike Street, Dan noticed what he thought to be that old pickup parked just a half block away. *Nah*, he thought. He stepped back into the house and locked the door behind him. As he walked upstairs, he thought, *I'm sure Eddie and Dennis will be okay.*

Within a minute or two, the motor started. The truck slowly turned right on Pike Street. Eddie's house was just a block or so from Dan's, a block before McKibben Street, and just a few houses out of Monkey Town. Nothing else happened that night. Dan, Eddie, and Dennis were reminded again how they disliked their creepy scoutmaster, Mr. Krueger. The thought of the man in the shadows gave Dennis a lot to dream about, but it was Dan who really knew who the stranger was lurking that evening in the darkness.

CHAPTER 8

QUIET TOWN
ON THE WABASH RIVER

Wabash, Indiana—Circa 1957

WABASH, Indiana, was a quiet town of 11,462 proud Hoosiers, located on the banks of the meandering Wabash River. Huntington, a much more Catholic-dominant town, was twenty miles to the east. Although Huntington had far more Catholics than Wabash, neither of the town's churches could match the magnificence of St. Thomas Moore.

Wabash was adorned with stunning turn-of-the-century buildings in the downtown, including the majestic county courthouse, the Carnegie Library, and the twin spires of St. Thomas Moore Catholic Church. Neat rows of gothic brick and clapboard houses lined the streets of the quiet neighborhoods. Wabash had always been the center of commerce, sports, and civic pride within Wabash County. The town had become a cultural center after WWI and during the mid-twentieth century.

The downtown was a lively center of business and commerce. Handsomely painted signs proudly adorned retail establishments like King's Hardware, Beckman Bros. Department Store, and Gackenheimer's Drug Store. These three stores offered goods and services to the entire community and farmers from the surrounding countryside.

Each summer during the National Plowing Contest, Wabash was a center of activity; Vice President Nixon himself visited the event in 1955. Wabash had much to be proud of. Friday nights and Saturdays came alive as Middle America came downtown to shop or just to run into friends they hadn't seen for a while. The Rock City Bar and Grill, the Union Cigar Store, and the Sweet Shop were social gathering places. John Dillinger especially liked the fried chicken at the Rock City, while Hoagie Carmichael spent many an evening entertaining locals on the second floor. Wabash was proud of its civic organizations like the Lions Club, chamber of commerce, and Moose Lodge. The town even had its own River Bend Country Club.

Stately old brick houses lined Maple and Oak Streets. The south side, with Pike Street being the main artery leading out of town, con-sisted of more modest clapboard two-stories and bungalows. Toward the end of Pike Street, Monkey Town offered an array of hard working, middle class residents. Every so often sprinkled with a few more savory characters, the likes of which were reserved for the west side of Wabash. Brick homes could be seen here and there. They were older. Across from Pike, a gothic 1850s brick farmhouse graced the farm of William Parker Stouffer. The farm was divided by the Wabash River. The Carroll Street Bridge provided egress from the south side of town to the north.

St. Ignasius Church once stood proudly on the corner of King and Webster, just three blocks from Pike. It succumbed to fire in 1896. Mass and parish activities had been held in the community center until the new church, St. Thomas Moore, was built in the early 1900s. Second only to the Taylor Bros. Community Center, St. Thomas Moore was the social hub of Wabash. The largest parish, St. Thomas Moore's design had been taken directly from its ancestral namesake in Chesterton, England. Wabash, however, was still dominated by the quiet influence of the Quakers, dating back to its origin. Quaker farmers had settled around Wabash in the 1830s, even before the advance of the Wabash Railway in the early 1850s. Wabash was first officially settled in 1835.

The Taylor, Zilbar, and Anthony families were the original organizers of St. Thomas Moore. Their families left St. Ignasius Catholic Church after the fire. They worked under the kindly patronage of Bishop Sheldon in the diocese of South Wayne in 1897 as they built the new parish. With the consent of Bishop John Henry Larson, the first bishop of South Wayne, Father Theodore Hendricks laid the foundation of St. Thomas Moore in October of 1901.

Commerce and agriculture provided numerous families in Wabash with wealth. The founding families were very philanthropic and gave vast amounts to build the new church. Constructed from Indiana limestone, the grand church's engraved cornerstone read, *Saint Thomas Moore, dedicated to all Catholics who share their faith for the honor and glory of God. Founded August 1, 1901.* Once completed, St. Thomas Moore was known for having one of the two tallest steeples in northern Indiana.

The grandiose, awe-inspiring edifice of St. Thomas Moore was the pride and joy of Wabash's Catholic community. Parishioners came from all around Wabash County, and more than fifteen percent of the town were faithful parishioners. The parish was led by its first pastor, the Reverend John Howard. A smaller parish, St. Bernard's, was equally respected, attended, and supported. Unusual for a small-town church at the turn of the century was St. Thomas Moore's side chapel, which was dedicated to St. Michael, the patron saint of law and justice.

The four founding families, whose wealth had been built on banking, finance, farming, and law, remained at the core of the spiritual, civic, and financial structure of the parish for more than three generations. The Zilbar's, prominent in banking, law, and investments, had been instrumental in naming the parish St. Thomas Moore. Of equal importance, good, hard-working, and dedicated middle- and lower-middle-class families were the epicenter of all church functions. The parish council took pride in assisting the good priests and nuns in all aspects of church and school activities.

The Brennan, Smith, and Meyer families were also third generation parishioners. Active in fund-raising, PTA, and the annual Summer Festival, they were fixtures in all parish activities. John James and Daniel Jackson were both WWII veterans and members of the American Legion. John Meyer and his young wife, Betty, were coordinators of the Summer Festival, the grand fundraiser held every August, one week before the start of school. John was a steadfast pillar of the parish.

Ralph Smith, along with his wife, Grace, were the go-to people for Father Warren whenever he needed advice or a most important project handled within the council and central body of the parish. The Jacksons, Smiths, and Meyers were all good parish people.

Father Warren—December 1, 1957

"Say, Ralph ∴. any chance you could see me after Mass?" Father Warren asked as he saw Ralph and Grace Smith walking up the sidewalk on their way to the 8:30 Sunday Mass. Having two assistant pastors provided the large parish with five Sunday Masses beginning at the 5:30 Mass and ending with the 11:30 Mass. Father Warren always preferred to say the 5:30 and 8:30 Masses, while Father Jaeger and Father Sullivan said the 7:00, 10:15, and 11:30 Masses. In addition to Sunday Masses, they also held Mass every weekday and Saturday at 6:00 a.m. and 8:30 a.m.

"Sure, Father. Should we come to the sacristy?" Ralph replied.

"You could, or just knock on the rectory door. That would probably be much easier. How about fifteen to twenty minutes after Mass? Will that hold you up?" Father Warren asked considerately.

"No, not at all, Father. The kids will be able to walk home after Mass."

"That'll be just fine," Grace added. "That will give me some extra time to light a candle after Mass. I do have a special intention," she said, smiling at Ralph. "See you then, Father."

Later, after Mass, the priest heard a knock at the front door. Sister Agatha was off that morning. "Hello, Ralph, Grace."

"Father." Ralph stepped back and followed Father Warren and Grace into the front parlor. Ralph was dressed in his wide-lapelled Sunday suit and blue tie. Grace was wearing a silk dress, short jacket, and brimmed hat. The Smiths were like the rest of the congregation—respectful of Sunday morning dress.

"First of all, Ralph and Grace, I want to thank you both for all you do behind the scenes for our parish. You are a fixture on the council. I'm glad you keep serving."

"Father, I really enjoy it. This parish is so important to our family. The school—all our kids love their classes, the good sisters, everything. There is nothing more important than a good Catholic education."

"Yes, and now you both are doing so much in getting ready for our Thanksgiving pageant."

"Yes, Father. Lots of work, lots of fun. We both enjoy it."

"Now, why I asked you here. You remember, Ralph, when you and I talked about your Boy Scout experience as a youth? I believe you said you were an Eagle Scout."

"Yes, I was. That was before the war, one of the best experiences of my life."

Grace added, "You know, Father, every so often Ralph talks about those good old days."

"Yes, Scouts helped me prepare to be a better soldier … and hopefully, a better person."

"You know, Father, Ralph was at Normandy. Landed in the first wave," Grace said.

"Now, Grace," Ralph said bashfully.

"I didn't know that," Father Warren replied.

"Yes, and by the grace of God, I'm still here today. I never stopped praying until we destroyed those German bunkers," Ralph said with a very serious look on his face.

"You can understand then why our troop is an important part of the parish's life." Father Warren looked directly at him. "Ralph, I need your help. Freddie Klaman is moving away, and that leaves a vacancy as assistant scoutmaster. I'd like you to volunteer."

Ralph looked a little surprised. He looked at Grace. "Well, Father, I'd say I'll think about it … but if Grace agrees, I'll say yes right now. You know, Russell is already a second-class scout, and Gary will join next year. I'd have more time with them. Yes, that would be great."

Father Warren felt immediate relief. He had dual purpose in asking Ralph. He was cautious about disclosing too much about his second reason during their first meeting.

"Then let's call that final, Ralph. I'll tell Father Jaeger. He oversees the troop from a parish point of view." Trying to brief Ralph about Father Jaeger's total involvement, he continued, "He's also chaplain for Sunday Mass on four of the weekend camping trips. Father Sullivan covers the rest." Father Warren stood up and extended his hand. "Thank you, Ralph. I'll feel much better about you being involved."

"You can count on me," Ralph assured his pastor.

As they were leaving, Father Warren said, "One more thing. Scoutmaster Phillip Krueger is quite busy in many activities around town and out at the reform school. He's an administrator. Kind of keep an eye on him for me. You know, does he give enough time? How does he get along with the boys? Know what I mean?" he asked with a serious look on his face, hoping Ralph could read a little between the lines.

"Again, Father, anything."

As Ralph and Grace left the rectory and walked toward their car, Father Warren thought, *I need a good man like that. He'll let me know if Father Jaeger and Phil Krueger are handling everything the way they should be.*

CHAPTER 9

UPSTAIRS ROOM

Peter Goodnar—December 4, 1957, late afternoon

TWO weeks flew by quickly. An appointment was set for after school. Peter Goodnar thought he really hadn't spent enough time reading Father Jaeger's missal. *Hope he doesn't quiz me.* Peter stepped through the side door from the church onto the sidewalk separating the two buildings. Opening the door, Peter stepped into the back hall of the rectory and proceeded a few steps to Father Jaeger's office door. *No answer.*

Having left his bedroom door slightly open, Father Jaeger anxiously listened for Peter. He waited after hearing the first knock. After opening the door, he stepped to the top of the stairs. "Oh hi, Peter," he said in a soft voice. "Up here."

Peter looked up the stairs. "Oh hi, Father," he said, expecting to have found Father Jaeger waiting in the study.

"Come on up. I'm not quite ready. Do you have the missal?"

"Sure, Father," Peter said as he agreeably proceeded upward, taking each step more slowly as he approached the top of the stairs.

"Come on in. Take your coat off," the priest said with a false casualness, disguising the eagerness within him.

After slipping off his coat and changing the missal from hand to hand, Peter gave his coat to Father Jaeger, along with his side-muffed hat. As he straightened his sweater and looked up, Peter was suddenly shocked. "Father, where's your collar? I've never seen a priest in, well, just in a T-shirt. Seems a little ... well, Father—"

Father Jaeger cut Peter off. "Now, Peter, priests are human just like you. That's a part of God's plan. Shoes, hats, food, sleep—we still do everything you do."

Looking around the tidy but sparse room, Peter noticed an unusually high stack of magazines neatly arranged on the floor next to a comfortable-looking easy chair. The one on top was open, with numerous pages bent under the back page. Peter was startled by a quick glimpse of the exposed picture on the opened page. *Looks like two ...*

"Oh sure, Father," Peter responded, quickly looking up before he had a clear focus on the image. "Whatever you say," he naively agreed. "Are we going to discuss the missal?"

"Sorry, there's only that straight chair and this easy chair. Don't have a sofa up here like down in the study," Father Jaeger said with a forced smile.

"Father, is this—me being up here—all right?" Peter asked with a very perplexed expression.

"What do you mean, Peter?"

"Well, for me to be up here, up here in your room, kinda … kinda alone with you?"

"Peter, of course. Others come up … Sometimes I have counseling and even one-on-one prayer sessions in here."

Prayer sessions? Peter thought, questioning in his own mind what he had heard. "What about Father Warren … Father Sullivan? Do they come up here for prayer sessions?"

Keeping a straight face at such an unexpected naïve question, Father Jaeger replied, "Oh no, Father Warren's never been up here … and Father Sullivan? Nah, he has his own room for prayer and a bedroom at the other end of the hall. I just have these two rooms. This little sitting room, and then of course my bedroom," he said, pointing to the open door. "Here, I'll show you. Come look." Father Jaeger immediately proceeded into the bedroom, assuming Peter would follow. "Come here, Peter. Bring the missal."

Reluctantly, Peter followed the priest's suggestion. Swirling questions raced through his mind. *Is this okay?* he wondered. A beautiful wooden crucifix hung above the priest's bed. Peter was drawn to it immediately.

Standing behind Peter as the boy stared at the crucifix, Father Jaeger closed the door and quietly flipped the lock. Peter heard the latch. He turned. As the father lifted his own shirt over his head, Peter stepped back, startled by the shirtless priest.

"Father, maybe I should go." He instinctively felt something was wrong.

Ignoring Peter's question, the priest said while looking up at the crucifix, "I just want to show you my scar, just like the wound on the side of Jesus." He pointed to the three-inch scar right above his waist. "Oh, I wasn't lanced, Peter. That's from an appendix operation. To me the scar is a symbol that I am to be like Jesus."

"Father, please. I better go. Please. I'm kind of really warm."

"Sure, you can leave, but let's pray first."

"Pray? Heck, I'm hot. I just wanna go. Here, you can have your missal," Peter said with a trace of aggression in his voice.

"Now, Peter, relax. Just take your sweater off if you're too hot."

"My sweater? I only have a T-shirt on underneath."

"Well, that's good. Just like me."

With that, Father Jaeger reached around Peter, tucked his hands under Peter's sweater, and slowly pulled it and the T-shirt off together. He turned and laid them on the straight wooden side chair next to the small dresser. Peter froze.

"Let's pray," the father said as he knelt at the side of the bed. Reaching around Peter with his right arm and hand, the priest gently pulled the boy next to him.

Peter's mind was ablaze as Father Jaeger pulled him down to a kneeling position beside him, defenseless to resist.

"Our Father who art in heaven … " Father Jaeger began. "Come on. You too."

Peter chimed in, "Hallowed be thy name … "

They said the next verse of the prayer together. "And lead us not into temptation, but deliver us from evil."

"Stop, Father. Is this a sin?"

"Why of course not. We are friends. As Jesus said, 'Love thy neighbor as you love yourself.' This is beautiful. Jesus wants us together," the priest said, drawing himself ever so close.

After they finished their prayer, the father stood up, unbuckled his belt, and slipped off his trousers and shorts. Peter was startled as he looked at the excited priest. Father Jaeger sat on the side of the bed and pulled Peter up next to him. Momentarily they sat side by side, their feet dangling above the floor beneath the high black metal bed. Gently, the priest placed his left arm around Peter's shoulders. In a continuous motion, Peter felt the father's right hand fold and cup around his waist, unbuckling his belt; then the priest stood Peter up and pulled off his pants and shorts. Peter was now hotter than ever. Together, they glided onto the bed, both looking up at the ceiling.

Father Jaeger said, "Hail Mary, full of grace."

Peter stared at the crucifix, trying to hold his trembling body still. He followed along with the priest, feeling he had no choice. "Father, please no. I'm scared."

Detecting some defenseless resistance, Father Jaeger slowly turned onto his side, pulling Peter with him. Feeling the smooth beautiful skin on the young man's back, Father Jaeger embraced Peter … all in anticipation of the moment. On his side, with his eyes closed, Peter no longer focused on the crucifix overhead. The suffering Jesus was now out of sight.

While Father Jaeger was lost in his own warped world of sinful passion and at a moment when the man could not halt his dastardly deed, all Peter could do was lay there, pray for forgiveness, and count the seconds until he could leave and run away from this unexpected nightmare. His only feeling was of the tears welling in his eyes and trailing across his cheeks. Then he felt the uncomfortable pain. Plugging his ears to block out the moans of the man behind him, Peter prayed for escape and wished only for this to be a bad dream.

Peter Goodnar would never forget what happened that day, each disgusting detail. He could not recall how he got away to the safety of his parents' home. That dark, dank day in December 1957 was embedded in Peter's mind—a horrid, deranged memory that would affect his life forever.

CHAPTER 10

LONG WAIT TO REPENTANCE

Linda Singleton—December 7, 1957

4:40 P.M., *Saturday afternoon. Perfect timing,* Linda Singleton thought as she approached St. Thomas Moore for her long-overdue confession. Clutching the collar of her below-the-knee-length wool coat, Linda walked toward the front entrance of the church. She glanced upward at the tall steeple. *How glorious.* The silence of the early evening was broken only by the crunch of snow beneath her feet. The streets were quiet. No wind, just cold.

Pulling the heavy oak door open, Linda stepped inside, immediately feeling the warmth and protection from the declining temperature. Tightening her scarf, she peeked into the church through the small window of the vestibule door. Lines of ten to twelve repentant stood along both side aisles leading to the confessionals in each of the back corners of the church.

Having checked the confession schedule before coming, Linda knew Father Warren was in the confessional on the left side and Father Sullivan was hearing confessions in the opposite corner. She genuflected and stepped into the pews about five rows in front of the priest's solemn closet. She checked the confessional door. Father Warren's nameplate was in place.

Praying and preparing her thoughts, Linda kept her eyes closed and her head bowed. The line was now only six deep. Making the sign of the cross, she stood and took her place in line. After so many years of the anxiety and stress, the time to confess was near. Linda closed her eyes and thought, *Let me say the right thing*. Very near. Another ten, maybe fifteen, minutes passed. When she was next in line to enter the confessional, her heart raced.

Complete darkness had engulfed the outside of the church. Only every third hanging light in the church was lit. As Linda faced the main altar, which seemed so far away in the front of the church, the glow of moonlight illuminated the stained glass windows high above and to the side. Her eyes were transfixed by the crucifix hanging above the gold tabernacle. Remorse, guilt, and sorrow intensified within her being like a sharp pain to her soul.

Three years had passed since this guilt entered her life. Being with him was wrong, very wrong, and the burden of sin she carried daily was heavy. But being without him was even worse. She knew it could not be. Confession was her only option. An eternity seemed to pass as she waited for the next person to leave the confessional. Fortunately, three more parishioners remained in line in front of Father Sullivan's confessional. They were all strangers, just as she had hoped. After confession, Linda would have plenty of time to leave the church before the other confessional emptied.

Even though he would be silenced by the seal of confession, Linda worried that Father Warren would know who she was. She knew that although priests were men of the cloth, they were still men. They were human and shared weaknesses along with all of their good. Linda really respected Father Warren and wanted no chance that he could link her to the grave sin she was about to confess.

As Linda walked toward the confessional, she looked back to the altar and happened to notice Father Jaeger in front of the church. He genuflected before the altar and disappeared into the sacristy. She knew him. Linda waited outside the confessional. She could faintly hear the small black frame between the priest and penitent close. The other side slid open. Linda would be next to enter the confessional.

The door opened, and out stepped Roberta Geboy, Linda's neighbor just three houses down. As Linda entered, they exchanged a nod and a smile. *Thank you, God, for having Charlotte before me. Please have her leave church before I finish*. It was now Linda's turn. She entered the confessional, knelt, and waited. In moments, the small door would slide open. Linda prayed and waited.

Father Jaeger—December 7, 1957

Father Jaeger flipped the light switch in the sacristy. He knew Alan Palmer would be waiting for him. He had asked Alan to stop around 6:30 p.m. He had told Alan he would give him a ride to the K of C Hall's eighth grade night out. Saturday evenings were always open to high school students—music, dancing, and just a place for kids to gather. It was co-ed, and there was even a pool table and two ping-pong tables in the back. The first Saturday of every month, eighth graders were welcome.

Members of the Knights of Columbus and sometimes a priest went along to chaperone. Father Jaeger knew Alan was a little bashful, even timid.

"Good evening, Father."

"Oh hello, Alan. Sorry I'm a little late."

"That's okay, Father. I was over in the Mother's Chapel waiting for you. I saw you walk by the altar, so I came over. Here I am," Alan said a little nervously. "Nice of you to give me a ride. I've only been to K of C's once before, so I'm just a little nervous. I'm glad you'll be there, Father."

"I had a late lunch, and then my altar boy meeting went a little longer this afternoon. Before we leave, I have to go to my room. My wallet and heavy coat are there. I've been in church all afternoon, but I know it's really supposed to get cold this evening."

"Father, I walked over. I just live two blocks from here. I about froze. Dad said the temperature was about eighteen degrees and going down to single digits tonight."

"Guess I better get an extra scarf and gloves, Alan. It's just through that door. You can wait there while I go upstairs."

"Okay, Father." Alan followed the priest. "Wow, this sure is a nice office, Father. Kinda dark though. I've never seen so many books."

"You just make yourself comfortable while I go upstairs. Would you like a 7-Up while you wait?"

"No thanks, Father. I kinda want to get down to the K of C's."

"Okay then. I'll be right back. Try that ol' sofa, Alan."

Alan made himself comfortable.

Father Jaeger could feel some anticipation. Stepping onto the first step, he stopped and waited as he had planned. "Say, Alan," he called back. "Why don't you come on up? I'll show you my room." No response from Alan. "Come on up." He climbed a few more steps, stopped, and waited. "Alan?"

Five seconds, maybe ten, and no reply. Then Alan suddenly appeared at the bottom of the stairs. He looked up at Father Jaeger. "Sure," he said with unquestioning innocence.

The priest turned, didn't say another word, and climbed the stairs. Father Jaeger's pulse climbed even faster. At the top of the stairs, he stepped across the hall, opened his unlocked door, and entered his room. Alan followed a few steps behind Father Jaeger. Once inside, the priest stopped and waited for Alan to enter. He did. Father Jaeger reached his arm around Alan and shut the door. In a continuous motion, he discreetly turned the lock, ensuring total privacy.

Linda Singleton—December 7, 1957

The small confessional door slid open. It was dark, but Linda knew good Father Warren was there. "Bless me, Father." Linda immediately paused, now knowing Father Warren was listening.

"Go ahead, my child. I'm here for you." The whisper from beyond the black screen was low and soothing.

"Yes, Father. Sorry. I'm a little nervous," she whispered, knowingly disguising her voice. "Father … " She paused. "Bless me, Father. My last confession was about five years ago." She paused again.

"It's good you are here then. Go on," Father Warren patiently encouraged the reluctant repentant.

"Father, I try to lead a good Catholic life, but I am unable to because of my sin, a very serious sin, Father. You see, I am a divorced Catholic. I have been for twelve years, so I cannot partake in communion, and this hurts me so very much." Relieved to have said that, Linda paused. The priest waited. "Father, my son was born one year before the divorce. My husband left town against the orders of the judge. He has never returned. Never," she said. "I'm raising my son the best I can alone. Father, there is more. About five years ago, that's when I quit going to confession, I took up with another man for about three years," she said, beginning to be more open.

"Well, that is understandable. However, the church does not recognize divorce, as you know."

"Yes, Father. It is heartbreaking to me. I'm here to confess. Father, please understand, though, there is more. I loved this man—not my husband—very, very much. We both knew the secret of our love could never come out and that we could not be together as we both so desperately wanted." Linda's heart was beating so hard. Her emotions started to take hold. It was becoming difficult to talk. She felt she could not explain the way it had been.

"I do understand. You knew it couldn't be because you were divorced."

"No, Father, that is not the reason." The detail of confessing was now more complex than she had expected. Linda could not see the puzzled look and furrowed brow on the other side of the covered door, but she felt her confessor's confusion.

"Please remember, our Savior died for our sins. He is all knowing and aware of your sins. You are repenting. You are asking for forgiveness. Repent your sin," Father Warren said calmly.

"Yes, Father, I will," she said with some reassurance.

The long pause that came next seemed like an eternity for Linda. Father Warren waited, giving her time.

"Yes, I can say this, Father. My love is for a priest. He is the man in my life." Her words were like whispering into a megaphone.

Father Warren could hear her sigh of relief. Even having listened to about all sins in the confessional for more than fifty years, this was a first for him.

"There have been secret love affairs, which are wrong if you are not married, but love with a priest is equally or even more sinful," Father Warren said as his first reaction.

"One more thing, Father. Please, I cannot disclose who this man is. Please, Father, I just—"

Father Warren cut her off. "The intent, the act, is the sin. You do not have to disclose the name to gain God's forgiveness. What you do have to do now that you have confessed is to not see this man anymore. To stop the sin."

"Oh, Father, I have. We stopped being with each other more than two years ago."

"Do you intend to see him again, or should I say *be* with him again?" Father Warren asked with a tone of caution.

"No, Father. I mean, I do see him. We are not ever with each other, not for the last two years, although it seems like an eternity to me. Father, I still do love him."

In the extreme seriousness of the moment, the pastor knew his next few words would be difficult for her to accept and equally challenging to execute. "You must first control your mind. Your confessed sin deserves our Lord's forgiveness, but you must commit yourself to pursue the difference between love and lust. Choose the former. Discard the latter. This will be between you and your Redeemer. I hope you can understand, my child."

"Yes, Father … I do," Linda replied.

All that could be said in the solitary privacy of the confessional had been exchanged between the priest and the repentant sinner.

"Our Lord loves all sinners. He forgives those who repent with a firm commitment never to sin again. You know the darkness of your sin. Now you're on a path to heaven."

"Yes, Father. I know. So well, I know."

"I would like for you to pray and be thankful for His forgiveness. Go forward and sin no more. For your penance, I would like for you to attend Mass one extra day a week for the next year. Be thankful for His forgiveness and pray for the strength to take you on the right path to God, for the one you loved and for yourself. You are forgiven."

The sliding door of the confessional closed, signifying the reality of the lifting of guilt and suffering. Linda made her way to the far front of the church and to the confines of St. Michael's side chapel. There she lit a candle, knelt, and prayed. So overwhelmed with the spiritual cleansing of her soul, Linda totally forgot about Father Warren possibly leaving the confessional and recognizing her.

The repenting lady was lost in the recollection of the priest's powerful words. *Pursue the difference between love and lust.* Bowing her head in her hands, she thought, *What if they are the same?*

CHAPTER 11

UNEXPECTED TRIP HOME

Father Sullivan—December 12, 1957, early morning

RING, ring. "Hello, Father Sullivan here."

"Michael, this is your dad."

"Hey. Hi, Dad. Good to hear your voice."

"Michael, I better get right to the point. I know you are very busy, but I think it would be a good idea if you could come home for a few days. Your mother ... " He paused. "Your mother needs you. Actually, Michael, she is not doing well."

"What's wrong? Dad, what's wrong? Tell me."

"Well, son, for the last few months your mother hasn't been feeling well. Kept saying she had pains. Pains around her shoulder and under her left arm."

"What happened? Did she fall? Did she break something?"

"No, it wasn't that kind of pain. It wasn't like a bone thing. She kept saying more like stiffness, like a muscle. Doctors took X-rays and tested, but they couldn't find a thing."

"Gosh, Dad, this sounds terrible. Of course I'll come home."

"They've checked her heart. That's fine," he said with deepening concern. "They just don't know."

"Is she in the hospital?"

"No, she's home now. After all those tests, she's just so tired."

"What doctor is she seeing?"

"What doctor? Why, Doctor Templeton of course. He's been our doctor since before you were born. He's the best. Of course, we both trust him so much."

"He's the only one?" Father Sullivan asked.

"Well, there's Dr. Stadler. He does X-rays. But that's not the problem. We want just Dr. Templeton."

"Okay, okay, Dad. Listen. Father Warren will totally understand. He'll want me to be with Mom. Father Jaeger can pitch in a little extra. This won't be a problem. You know how kind and understanding Father Warren is. He'll pray for Mom. Probably say a Mass. He'll have the entire congregation and convent praying for her. Dad, she's going to be fine. Tomorrow's Friday. I'll leave after I say Mass."

"Son, that would be great. Your mother will be so happy. You'll give her such a lift."

"Can I talk to her now?"

"Not really. She's been in her room now for about a week, just resting in bed. Doc is due to stop by and see her tomorrow. She's sleeping now. She's just always so sad and quiet. I know she's in a lot of pain, but she never complains. Actually, Michael, I noticed yesterday that, well, I noticed her arm is kind of blue in places. I just don't know."

Like a giant hammer, a realization suddenly struck Father Sullivan. *Blue arm,* he thought. *Blue arm.* He didn't want to alarm his father. He knew both of his parents really needed him. "Dad, I better go. I'm going to see Father Warren now. What about Nancy? Does she know?" Michael asked about his younger sister, toward whom he was very loving and caring, as well as toward his niece and two nephews.

"Yes, she does, but her hands are full with those little ones. Anyway, Evansville is such a long trip. I just told her to wait, that you'll come home first."

"I understand. Right choice, Dad. Of course, I won't ask about Richard. Won't even ask. Okay, Dad. Gotta go. See you tomorrow. Tell Mom I'll be there. I love her so much."

Like Father Sullivan, his dad also knew his oldest son, Richard, would have some reason not to come. Either he was too busy or he'd come next week when his schedule would work better. "Thanks, Michael. See you tomorrow."

"Bye, Dad. I'll be praying for you both." He hesitated. "Oh, Dad, one more thing."

"Yes, what's that?"

"I love you too."

As he hung up the phone, Father Sullivan had a sinking feeling in his stomach. He knew something was very wrong. He recalled that a parishioner, Mrs. Wallace, had a similar problem. The blue arm was telling. He just knew. *I had better pray very hard*, he thought.

Father Sullivan immediately confided in Father Warren, who was most understanding about the assistant pastor's need to go home to his ailing mother. "You leave first thing tomorrow," he said to Father Sullivan. He looked straight into the younger priest's eyes. "Son, remember … God, family, and your church. You go to your mother now. I'll be praying for her, you, and your entire family."

"Thank you so much, Father. You're such a true friend."

Father Warren put his arms around Father Sullivan and gave him three hardy pats on the back. "You go to your mother."

Father Sullivan thought all evening about his mother. The next morning, he said the 6:00 Mass, packed his bag, and was ready to leave by 8:30 a.m. *Just one more thing*, he thought. He might have enough time to make a phone call to one other person before leaving. He knew she would be concerned and would want to know. He had to tell her. It had been a long, long time since they last talked.

Father Sullivan dialed the phone. He hoped she hadn't left for work yet. Ring, ring, ring … no answer. Michael was aware that there was still something between them, even though they were now far more distant. When they were alone before, he had talked to her often about family. She knew how much he loved his parents.

The drive to Huntington was about seventeen miles. Huntington was blessed with two Catholic churches. St. Mary's had been founded in 1858. St. Monica's had been established earlier in 1834. Father Sullivan had attended all eight years of grammar school at the old St. Mary's school. He was looking forward to next year when his family parish would celebrate its centennial.

Father Sullivan's thoughts focused on his folks as he drove along the flat Indiana countryside. His thoughts went back and forth between the pleasant memories of his grade school years and his present concern for his mother.

He thought about his love for Linda Singleton and their mutual decision to break off their intimacy. It had been the right thing for both of them. However, he still had feelings, but they were controlled by his own will, his vows, and the moral code of the priesthood. Having confessed his sin while on a retreat more than three years ago, Father Sullivan was now at peace, although thoughts sometimes prevailed.

But he could never totally discard his thoughts. She was an ever-vibrant, loving, caring, and attractive person. Her wavy chestnut hair, high cheekbones, brown eyes, soothing voice, and attractive figure presented an alluring attraction to anyone she encountered. She was never totally out of Father Sullivan's mind. Late at night when he put his head to his pillow and closed his eyes, he often fell asleep with thoughts of her permeating his dreams. He knew she could not be in his life, but that did not stop him from thinking, loving, and lusting for her embrace. Father Sullivan knew he was not without sin. He also knew that Jesus, first of all, had been a man.

The two-lane highway held a dusting of snow but not enough to be dangerous. Father Sullivan could see the city limits sign: *Huntington, 17500*. As he drove through town, familiar memories surrounded him. Huntington's neighborhood streets were tree lined. The downtown was a time warp from the 1840s.

Passing the Eagles Theatre, he noticed *Giant* with the names of Rock Hudson, Elizabeth Taylor, and James Dean lettered on the marquee. Everyone in the entire area knew James Dean was from nearby Fairmount.

Susie's Drug Store and King Hipskind Hardware Store stood on the left side of North Street. As he drove into his old childhood neighborhood, memories of friends, baseball, and his old secondhand bike flashed through his mind. Most of all, he could hear his mother's voice calling from the back door, *"Michael, time for supper!"*

There is Dad's four-holer Buick. Father Sullivan slowed and turned into the driveway right behind Dad's car. No sooner had he pulled in, stopped, and grabbed his bag from the trunk than Dad was there waiting on the porch.

A white clapboard front porch wrapped around the driveway side of the house, which had been built in 1923. It stood on Poplar Street, just a few blocks from St. Mary's. As he walked up to the porch, he noticed the single window in the gable of his second-floor attic bedroom. *Home. Memories.*

Entering the house, Father Sullivan threw down his bag. Dad gave him a big hug. Everything looked so familiar.

"Let's go up. She's anxious to see you," his dad said with an enthusiastic smile.

Slowly, Father Sullivan ascended the stairs, looking up through the railings toward his mother's room. He set his suitcase down at the top of the stairs. Walking into her room, he first stopped in the open doorway.

"Hi, Ma. It's Michael. I'm here for you," he said as he continued over to the side of her bed. He then leaned down and gently kissed her forehead.

"Oh, Michael. Michael, it's so good to see you. I've been waiting." She reached upward with both arms. They hugged. "Now hug like you mean it, Michael."

"Didn't want to squeeze too hard, Ma."

"Now just look at you. You handsome priest … that collar. Your black wavy hair. Your beautiful smile. You look so good. The Lord is fortunate to have you, but many a lady wanted your hand," she spoke in an elevated whisper. Michael could tell she was in pain.

"Mom, don't you get going. I love being a priest. You know that. All I ever wanted since the sixth grade. You and Dad helped me secure my vocation."

"We love having a priest in the family," she assured him.

"Ma, I'm able to be here until Sunday evening, so whatever you need, I'm here for you."

Michael sat on the side of her bed, her hand clasped in his. They talked for over an hour about seventh grade report cards, his first puppy, little league ball, his first girlfriend. Mr. Sullivan sat in a chair on the opposite side of the bed. He was a quiet man, taking it all in. As conversation moved on, Michael could tell how tired and sleepy his mother was getting.

"Honey, maybe you should rest for a while. Michael can go and check on his room," his dad said. "Remember, we have him all weekend. There will be all kinds of time."

"I know, Jerry. You know best. It's just so good to see him. Feels like 1924 all over again. You were twelve," she replied groggily. They both could see her eyes closing.

Father Sullivan and his dad walked back to his room at the far end of the hall. The room was decorated with a Notre Dame pennant, a model airplane atop the bookcase, and—his favorite—a Dizzy Dean signed baseball. Michael had been a good athlete. Walking over to his desk, he reached for a framed picture.

"Senior prom, Ellen Pederson." He smiled. "Does she still live in town? We agreed to go to the prom even though she knew I wanted to become a priest. We had a great time."

"Oh, yes. She and Jim still live in her mother's house over on Grant. Three kids, all boys. The oldest is now in high school. You remember Jim. He worked down at the electric company for thirty years."

"I had a place in my heart for Ellen for quite a few years. We really had some great times for a while there. Good Catholic. Came from a large family. Twelve, fourteen kids, if I remember correctly. I'm sure she's a wonderful wife and mother."

"Michael, I'm going downstairs to prepare a little bite to eat. Your mother will be hungry pretty soon after her nap. I've become quite a cook. I specialize in soups. She loves soup the most. Just easier for her. You rest up. I'll be in the kitchen."

Father Sullivan walked around his bedroom above the front porch. Mom had kept the room just about the same since he left. Although Richard had shared the room with him when they were young, his older brother rarely came home anymore. The room was still to Father Sullivan's liking. The focal point was his grandmother's high carved headboard bed from the 1880s. There was nothing better than that down mattress and the sounds of rain beating on the slanted roof.

Father Sullivan could feel the bond between his parents becoming even closer. Dad had settled in as a caregiver, much different from the hard-driving insurance business he had pushed for more than forty-five years. How long they would continue to live in the house together would mainly be determined by the prognosis of his mother's illness.

With Michael's mother being too weak to make it downstairs, he and his father set up a card table in her room. They used placemats, their good china, and two candles and enjoyed the best pea soup with ham the three had ever tasted. Mrs. Sullivan even summoned the strength to sit in the chair between them. The evening was pleasant and heartwarming.

The three spent the better part of the evening reminiscing about Father Sullivan's childhood, his sister, and her family. Father Sullivan especially enjoyed hearing about his folks in their early years before they had children. He learned that it had been his mother who had actually popped the question to his father, saying, "Jerry, if we are ever going to be married, it's time for you to gather some courage, talk to my father, find a ring, and learn how to bend your knee for something other than genuflecting in church."

Father Sullivan chuckled. His father contributed more of a sheepish smile and admittedly said, "That's exactly how it happened."

Father Sullivan detected sleepiness in his mother's eyes. He reached over and gave her a hug of appreciation, thankfulness, and love. He and his father helped her back into bed. Then he leaned over her, gently kissed her forehead, and said, "I do love you so much." She smiled beautifully.

Mother retired for the evening. As Father Sullivan and his father sat down at the kitchen table, his father said, "Michael, I received a call late this afternoon. Dr. Fox took more tests this week. He'll have the results Monday. He doesn't know for sure, but he said he is anticipating it will be cancer."

Father Sullivan closed his eyes and rubbed his brow, but he was not overly shocked, as he had been thinking that all along.

He and his dad spent hours talking about life, family, church, the priesthood, and of course, Michael's mother. They shared everything about Michael's vocation, from his beginning years as an altar boy right up to ordination and this very evening. They talked about his dedication to the church and life. Like never before, his dad explained just what having a priest in the family meant to them and to Michael's sister.

Father Sullivan shared with his father the joy of being a priest, as well as the trials, tribulations, happiness, and satisfaction of giving to his fellow man. He shared many stories and experiences like never before. Michael's heart was overfilled with nostalgia, new understanding, and elevated love for his parents.

His father listened intently to every word, and Father Sullivan felt a new level of understanding with his dad. He did not know, however, if he should mention the thing that had begun to weigh heavily on his mind ever since his brief chat with Father Warren about Father Jaeger. *Will Dad understand?*

"Dad, could I ask a question? It's rather delicate."

"Of course, anything," his father said, expecting Michael to bring up something about the family.

Beginning cautiously, Father Sullivan said, "It's about our church. About some priests."

"Be specific, Michael."

"Dad, it's about our assistant pastor, Jerome Jaeger."

"Oh yes, you introduced me to him. Seemed like a nice young priest. Is he sick? Hurt? Leaving?"

"Let me finish, Dad," Father Sullivan said, now wanting to get to the point. "We have reason to believe he might be sexually abusing boys. Still, what we know is only circumstantial." His father looked startled. "If it is true, of course, we need more confirmation. I was wondering if there have been any problems in your parish."

Father Sullivan's father paused and then stood up to get a cup of coffee. "Want some?" he asked, raising the percolator in his son's direction.

"Sure, just a small cup."

Mr. Sullivan sat back down. He looked down at his cup of coffee and said, "Our parish, I know of nothing like that." He hesitated and took a sip of coffee. "Michael, there's something hidden deep in our family. Let me tell you." He paused and then added, "I'm sure, considering the circumstances that have developed in our family lately, your mother will approve of me telling you this."

"Telling me what?" Father Sullivan asked. "What could it be? I was telling you about possible sexual abuse in my parish."

"Let's sit in the front room. I'd be more comfortable."

Father Sullivan followed his father into the front room. Dropping into his favorite easy chair, Mr. Sullivan kicked off his shoes and rested them on the cushioned foot stool.

"Michael, as I said, there is no problem at St. Mary's that I am aware of." Then he proceeded with his story. "Back in '22, when you were too young to understand, your brother Richard came to me saying Father

Simmons had been touching him. Then he said the father made him take his clothes off. They got into bed together. I recall him insisting that it had been happening since October, just after Richard's birthday. He was telling me this in April of 1923."

Mr. Sullivan's directness startled Father Sullivan. Set him back. "I wasn't expecting ... What'd you do, Dad?" he asked in disbelief that it had happened even in his own family.

"Immediately I told your mother. Like me, she couldn't believe it."

"Did you believe him?"

"No, not really. I knew a priest couldn't do such a thing."

"What if Richard was telling the truth?"

"Well, Michael, we found out. Your mother and I, against my better judgment, went directly to meet with Father Simmons without Richard. We didn't take him along. Looking back, that was a mistake. Anyway, we did meet with Father Simmons. He was nice and receptive as could be. Of course, he denied all of it, explaining that as young boys enter puberty, their imaginations run rampant. He was thorough, helpful, and—most of all—convincing. Yes, we believed Father Simmons. Like I said, he was a priest. All perfect.

"Seems like from then on Richard lived in a downward spiral. As you yourself grew older, don't you recall the trouble, the endless arguments he had with your mother and myself, his consumption of alcohol, flunking out of school? Most of all, his sad, unfortunate marriage and divorce. Richard—sad, sad, sad. After that, he convinced us about Father Simmons. Remember back in '37 when the father suddenly left? He was reassigned to another parish someplace in southern Indiana. I was told the reality by our new pastor, Father Burke. Now there's a good priest."

"Dad, I just never knew. My own brother," Father Sullivan said. "How did you find out?"

His father took another sip of coffee. "After Father Simmons's reassignment, I found out a few years later that he was reassigned again. Remember my good friend Mark, Mark Meyer? What a great guy. You know he thought about becoming a priest? He knew the pastor who informed him about Father Simmons's problem. He was caught abusing one of the boys. Mark would never lie. Then I knew Richard had been telling the truth all the while, and I hadn't believed him. I will feel guilty forever. Can never make it up. Looking back, Richard was never the same after Father Simmons. I'm glad I told you, Michael. This secret was life-affecting to Richard, your mother, and myself. Now you know. Here we believed that horrid priest. How unfair we were to Richard."

"And Nancy?" Father Sullivan asked.

"Oh no. No purpose. No need to tell her." Reaching up, Mr. Sullivan pulled the chain on the table lamp to his left. As his father laid his head back on the chair, Father Sullivan noticed the sorrowful look on his face.

Walking over beside the chair, Father Sullivan picked up his dad's left hand with both of his and then patted it. Mr. Sullivan didn't raise his head.

"It's been quite a day, Dad. Quite a day."

Father Sullivan walked to the kitchen to turn out the lights. The faint moonlight shining through the front window gave just enough light for the priest to find the stairs. Looking back, he could hear that his dad was asleep. Checking his mother's room, he peeked inside. *Peaceful.* Lying in bed that memorable night, Michael thought back to his youth. *Indeed, it's been quite a day.*

Later that evening, Father Sullivan looked out the gabled window in his room. He noticed the moon shining. He closed his eyes and fell asleep thinking of his wonderful parents, his brother and sister, and the lasting memories of his childhood.

That weekend with his parents would live forever in Father Sullivan's heart. So much of life had taken on new meaning. He was overwhelmed with love for his parents. They had disclosed so much about their lives. He loved them even more. That most memorable weekend was the last time Father Sullivan would see his loving mother. Just one week later, she passed away. He was unable to make it home in time.

Driving home to St. Thomas Moore after his mother's funeral, Father Sullivan reflected on their special weekend together, just the three of them. He was so thankful for that time and was glad he had told them so much about being a priest. He had literally tried to share everything with them. *Well, almost everything.*

Chapter 12

Mysterious Family

Bernard Bednar—January 8, 1958, early morning

BERNARD knew all the boys in the Wabash Reform School. Although he did not talk much to any of them, he knew who they were. Everybody knew Bernard by his looks, manner, and actions. Bernard was a different character no one could forget.

From his house at the end of Chestnut Street, Bernard Bednar always walked to work at the reform school, two blocks to Pike and then west one mile from town. Walking against the traffic each way, Bernard never changed his pattern. He would only stop to wander through the cemetery. He always pressed forward, living in the present, with no eye to the future and only memories of the past.

The flat, rich fields outside town offered some of the best farmland in the county. Large houses of the more wealthy farmers dotted the countryside. The area was known as King's Row. Bernard found solitude walking along the vast, sprawling fields. The Wabash Reform School was just west of Friends Cemetery. Even on bitter cold days, the hottest days of summer, and days of heavy rains and snows, Bernard never wavered from his routine. He beat the same isolated path to and from home to the school, six days a week ... forever.

The back entrance of the reform school was on the north side, backing up to the Wabash River. From there, the cemetery was in full view. During lunch, after eating alone in the cafeteria, Bernard liked to walk through the cemetery. The older the gravestone, the better. He would think about the past. After walking to the crest of the hill, Bernard would return down the other side. Seven rows to be exact … turn left, count eleven headstones, stop. There, next to the large maple, the stone was weathered and tarnished with spots of black, but it was still readable. *Edgar Malcolm Cambridge, born April 6, 1869, died October 9, 1882.* Bernard often wondered about the young boy's life oh so many years ago.

For years, Bernard had walked the cemetery every third day without exception. From within the reform school, his habit did not go unnoticed. Everyone who knew Bernard thought his routine was strange, as strange as Bernard himself.

After stopping at the first grave, without fail Bernard would continue on and check a second tombstone, this one nestled at the bottom of the hill. The small stone was etched with the name *Gordon Yoder.* Long forgotten and with no family, Gordon was fortunate to even have a headstone. Carrying a heavy secret inside, Bernard always made sure Gordon's plot was cared for. Each visit, he remembered. *Someday I'll see the man in the white shirt, the tie, and the initials.*

The back entrance of the school was on the north side, adjacent to the cemetery. The loading dock was opposite the entrance. A long cyclone fence housed trash bins. The attendants filled them every day. Located fifty yards beyond the building, the burners could easily handle the daily rubbish. They were constructed like giant ovens that could burn even the most undesirable discards and waste.

Just inside the back door of the reform school, a long hall led to the second main corridor of the school. The stairwell, concrete encased in steel frames, led to the lower level boiler rooms, coal bin, and attendants' room. The staff locker room at the base of the stairs included two showers and walls lined with green metal lockers. Like everyone, Bernard had his own private metal locker. The vents at the top of the locker door were at the same height as the top shelf. Bernard kept his few personal items on the shelf. A brown canvas bag with leather handles stood folded on the floor of his locker, seldom used.

Bernard opened the back door to the school, removed his hat, and proceeded to the lower level. His locker was located in the corner. The lockers on either side of his were unoccupied, which was fine with Bernard. He sat on the long wooden bench carved with initials and dates of those who had served at the school over the last fifty-nine years.

"Morning, Bernard. What don't you have to say today?" David Klark asked, just as he did at precisely 6:52 a.m. each day.

Bernard responded, as always, "Nothing much."

"That's good to hear," David responded with friendly sarcasm. "I'm always glad to hear what's going on with you, Bernard. Oh, you ask about me? Same ol', same ol'. Won two bucks last night playing poker. Thanks for asking, Bernard." David stood and patted Bernard on the shoulder. "Good talking to you, ol' boy."

Bernard never looked up. "*Uumpgh.*"

"Enjoy another great day. Remember only 278 left till my last day here in this ol' brick barn," David informed Bernard. "Hope you come to my retirement party. I'll teach you how to play poker after all these years." He patted Bernard again and walked away.

Bernard changed into his green work shirt and work pants. He tied the heavy laces of his work boots at the top eye after twice encircling his ankles with the extra-long laces; only God knew why. *Secure.* Bernard never wore socks with his work shoes. His oversized brown belt was always pulled high above his waist and tight. He bothered no one. David accepted Bernard just as he did the wooden bench in front of his locker. Bernard's strangeness did not bother David or the rest of the crew.

After his shoes, Bernard buttoned his work shirt over his worn undershirt. Always routine, clothes put on in the same tedious order—pants, shoes, shirt. Nobody paid attention. Despite all this, however, Bernard was accepted for the quiet, hardworking, keep-it-to-himself kind of guy he was.

At 7:01 a.m. the work routine began. Bernard's first task of the day was to walk up to the main floor, go to the kitchen, and fill the pushcart rack with trays of nondescript but edible food. He looked forward to his routine. Always beginning in the service area next to the kitchen, he would uncharacteristically speak and greet a member of the staff. He always kept to himself with the exception of a few boys like Eddie Small and one other person.

"Morning, Bernard!"

"Morning, Miss Gladys Louise." He always responded to Gladys Louise. In his mind, she was special. They had known each other since their days in grade school at St. Thomas Moore. Like Bernard, Gladys was quiet and mainly kept to herself. Her pleasant demeanor and her respect for others had been recognized by the nuns and a few classmates, especially Bernard. Now Bernard was able to see Gladys Louise on a daily basis, though they did little more than greet one another. Bernard often thought about her.

From there, he proceeded to the bottom of the back stairs. Twelve trays, six trips, one tray in each hand. Up one flight to the landing, up a second flight, through the steel door, and to the second floor secured dormitory.

"*Uumpgh*," Bernard routinely grumbled in greeting. Twelve trays, six rooms, one bunk bed per room, one table. The small group of twelve boys always ate in their rooms for well-earned disciplinary reasons. The occupants always had a choice. Eat at the tables or sit on the beds with the trays on their laps. Half sat on their beds. The top bunkers usually used the table.

Bernard, the main attendant for unit 7, kept the boys fed, clothed, and supervised in the shower room, which had no partitions, two toilets, one urinal, two showerheads, and two sinks. Everything was open. The only authority he had in life was his command over the twelve boys in his unit, and he served with pride. The boys ranged in age from ten to thirteen. Few other attendants ever came into Bernard's unit. It was his domain. The fellow attendant on the other side of the twelve-hour shift was given the same responsibilities and authority as Bernard. Orville Smith respected the boys, took good care of them, did his job, and then went home to his wife and four children. Bernard and Orville were a strange team, separated by the clock. Each minded his own shift without concern or curiosity about the opposite time period. Bernard had always wanted to be an altar boy. Orville's last dream was to be a teacher. They both cared about the boys.

The boys in unit 7 knew Bernard's ways, demands, and even the way he dressed. Breakfast, lunch, and dinner each lasted thirty-five minutes. Bernard delivered the twelve trays to the floor with perfect timing. Periodically, he checked each of the six rooms. The boys adhered to Bernard's insistence that meals be eaten efficiently and each plate be completely cleaned.

"Breakfast trays here. *Uumpgh.* Say your prayers. *Uumpgh.* You don't waste the good food, boys," he told them.

They dared not cross Bernard when it came to tidiness, cleanliness, and cleaning their food trays. Of medium height, Bernard had a broad build with large hands, and he was very strong, especially in the hands and forearms. He had noticeably thick fingers. Despite the perception of meekness he presented, not one of the boys would dare defy Bernard.

"Okay, everybody up. Open doors. Breakfast trays here," Bernard said.

Bernard's usual routing was to randomly take two trays to each room. Some days he'd begin with room 2; other days it might be room 5, ending with room 1 … maybe room 3. The boys understood the routine but not the purpose, if there was one.

Bernard brought the trays to his first room of choice. Before eating, each boy knew he had to kneel on the floor and pray. To the boys and Bernard, both acts had meaning. This Wednesday would be no different. Today, Bernard served room 3 first.

Strange as strange could be, the boys liked Bernard. He helped them with special needs and favors. They could depend on him to protect the weaker boys if they were preyed upon by the older ones.

Joey Carter never knew his mom and dad. He had lived in the orphanage for ten years. Mike Glover's family had left him on the front steps of the courthouse in nearby Huntington when he was about two or three. His real age and birth date were unknown. Mike couldn't remember his parents, let alone what city or state he had lived in.

Mike's early memories in life were limited to the yelling, fighting, and screaming among his parents, brothers, and sisters. Cousins had always been around, left for days at a time by drunken, jobless, or dysfunctional aunts or uncles. Mike had been abused by two of his uncles, although that information had been kept within the family.

"Here comes Bernard." Mike stood up along with Joey, welcoming Bernard.

"Here's your food, boys. *Uumpgh.*"

"Hey, smells good to me," Mike said, patting Bernard on the back.

"Yep. Good for you boys. Eat it all. Say your prayers." Bernard set the trays on the table and watched as the boys prayed. Then they eagerly began to eat. As Bernard moved toward the door, he didn't say a word but reached over and patted Joey and Mike's shoulders.

Having delivered the trays, Bernard moved on to complete his rounds. Mike always felt more secure knowing Bernard was around—a security he would later have to call upon.

CHAPTER 13

WEEKLY MASS

Linda Singleton—January 14, 1958

LIKE her devotion to St. Thomas Moore parish, Linda was equally dedicated to her position in the probate office at the county courthouse, which she had acquired after graduating in the top ten of her class at Wabash High. During the Depression and the war, few women went to college. An excellent student with high grades and recommendations, Linda had secured her position in the probate office within one month of graduation.

By 1958, Linda knew the structure, operations, and procedures within probate like no other. Unfortunately, her advancement was not in proportion to her experience and knowledge. Linda was liked and respected by most employees throughout all the departments of the courthouse, including the register of deeds, the park department, and most of the entire staff of the sheriff's office.

Weekly Mass, although a penance from her confession, had become a blessing for Linda. The peace and quiet she found at the Tuesday morning Mass offered her time to reflect, make amends with her Lord, and continually pray for inner piece regarding her love for Father Sullivan. She knew acceptance was her only option. But as hard as she tried, as much as she prayed, her penance was made more difficult whenever Father Sullivan said the 6:00 Mass.

Keeping her distance, Linda sat toward the back of the church. Father Sullivan turned and faced the few parishioners scattered in the pews. For Linda, the memories became nearly unbearable when it was time to receive Holy Communion.

"*Misereatur Vestri omnipotens deus.*" After completing the verse, Father Sullivan descended the steps and walked to the communion rail.

Linda stood and walked up the center aisle, genuflected, turned right, and knelt at the rail. She could feel his presence advance closer and closer as he distributed the sacred host to those who knelt before him. The slight whisper of his prayer became more formidable. She could feel the altar boys' white stiffly starched surpluses as they brushed her folded hands. Then she knew he was there. Closing her eyes and tilting her head backward, Linda could feel the closeness of his hand as he laid the sacred host upon her tongue.

Although she tried, Linda could not always keep her eyes closed. Just at the moment he laid the sacred body on her tongue, direct eye contact would sometimes occur between them. It was trying, caring, and very unnoticeable as the good servers looked on, oblivious to any presence of feelings. In that split second, her eyes opened. They met his. *Dear Lord, help me.* Solemnly, Linda stood and followed the side aisle back to her pew. Her heart languished for the man in her past.

After that Tuesday morning Mass, having left the church via the front door, Linda did not see him again until their next encounter the following Sunday. She, along with her son, Joey, always attended Father Sullivan's Sunday Mass. When she was lost among the crowd in the full church, Sundays offered her fifteen to twenty minutes to listen to his sermons. She thought his words and delivery were most sincere, meaningful, and eloquent.

While at Sunday Mass, Linda had more of an opportunity to sit toward the front of the church. She and Joey usually sat in the fourth or fifth row. As she listened, Linda would drift in and out of her memories of Father Sullivan during their time together. She thought of how difficult and clandestine it was. Now there was no contact between them. They had not, however, completely eliminated all communication. But a call or letter was rare and logistically difficult. Meeting was impossible.

That Sunday, thinking of her only real love, Linda listened as the priest announced at the end of Mass: "And lastly, I would like to remind all of you that we are beginning to plan for our annual spaghetti dinner in February raising money for the less fortunate within the parish. We still need a few volunteers." Father Sullivan raised his hands as if to tell them to settle down and then extended his engaging smile. "No, no, you don't need to raise your hands here, but thank you for your enthusiasm anyway. Please contact Mrs. Sanford in the church basement after Mass. You know, if you do volunteer, remember Mrs. Sanford runs a tight ship in the kitchen."

Soft chuckles could be heard throughout the congregation. Everyone loved to listen to the words of Father Sullivan.

As he approached the end of his sermon, he said, "So as you know, our Lord and Savior Jesus Christ is all-forgiving. All you have to do is commit yourself to Him, overcome the temptations of jealously, disobedience, hatred, and lust to name a few. Commit yourself to pray, live a good life, and love your neighbors. Promise to never sin again." Linda thought back to his words about forgiveness. She blinked and then heard, "Go in peace in the name of the Father and of the Son and of the Holy Ghost … Amen."

All too fast. His sermons and Mass are too short, Linda thought. She could listen so much longer to Father Sullivan's melodious, compassionate, and sincere voice. As hard as she fought, the struggles were still deep within her soul. *If only he knew,* she thought. But her routine of the daily Mass continued to afford her new strength and resolve. *Thank you, Father Warren,* she thought, thinking of her confession. The penance of weekday Mass was her blessing in disguise.

Just being close to him sometimes grabbed ahold of Linda. While reading the weekly bulletin that evening after Sunday Mass, she glanced at the schedules for the week ahead. St. Thomas Moore's policy was to name the celebrant of each Mass and also list who would be hearing confessions on Saturday afternoon.

The idea of going to confession to Father Sullivan had first entered Linda's mind at the beginning of the year. *Could I?* she quietly asked herself. Then of course she replied, *No. That wouldn't be right. Too awkward. Would that be a sin in itself? It would be wrong.* Of most importance, she thought, *It would be asking too much of the man.*

The following week passed slowly. Linda made her decision to go to Father Sullivan's confession early. Her normal Saturday morning was routine. She was nervous with anticipation. Her timing would have to be just right, just as it had been with Father Warren.

The day drifted by slowly. When Linda walked to church, her thoughts of him and what she would say raced around in her head. Confessions began at 4:30 p.m. Linda entered the church at exactly 4:40. Both priests were in their confessionals. Linda immersed herself in the quiet, dark, and solemn atmosphere. Tightening her silk scarf, she genuflected and knelt in the third pew from the back. Different from her confession earlier with Father Warren, Linda knelt on the opposite side of church, where Father Sullivan was hearing confessions. She confirmed again by checking his name card on the center confessional door.

As Linda took her place in line, she felt her heart race. Receiving communion and staring at him during his sermons was one thing. Kneeling across from him, protected only by the thin black cloth covering the small sliding door of the confessional, she imagined how close they would be. She would hear the whisper of his voice like so many times before, several years ago under much different circumstances. So close, his breath, warmth. And now the circumstances had changed drastically. Now they would not see each other.

His presence would be so near. What would she say? How would he respond? Would he even recognize her whisper? Would the surprise be unfair? Yes, he would recognize her but only by what she would say.

Linda could feel her eyes begin to water in anticipation. She felt her pulse. Her heart throbbed. Now second in line, Linda heard the left confessional exterior door open. A slightly stooped elderly gentleman held the door at the same time he pulled his prayer book close. Glasses resting on the end of his nose, he glanced over the top of the rims and smiled warmly at her. Recognizing Mr. Kobel from the bookshop on Market Street, Linda returned the smile. Her heart raced faster. She would be next, close to Father Sullivan.

The blast from the organ above startled her. She jolted in her stance as the melodious voices sang out in unison. *Of course, choir practice.* The noise was like an awakening to her focused train of thought. With the shock of reality, Linda suddenly turned, walked to the center aisle, and blessed herself with holy water as she quickly genuflected. Then she turned and left the church.

Driving home that late afternoon, Linda questioned not her intentions but her response. The depth of her desire, caring, and love for this man could not be measured. All she knew was the reality of its existence. Frustrated, disappointed, and anguished that she had not completed her mission, she now had only daily Mass to look forward to. *Monday can't come soon enough.*

CHAPTER 14

FIRESIDE CHAT

Father Sullivan—January 26, 1958, early evening

"**FATHER**," Father Sullivan said, stepping through the parlor door. Father Warren laid the book on his lap, tipped his head, and looked across the room toward the young priest. "Come on in, son." He loved to call the younger man that every once in a while, not being a paternal father himself.

Father Sullivan had presence. His full-length black cassock was contrasted by the starched stiff white collar showing from behind the cassock collar. The endless row of black buttons from the collar to the ankle shined in the faint glow of the parlor light. Father Warren thought, *What a handsome young man. What a charismatic young priest.* He motioned Father Sullivan to take a seat.

"A little cool in here this evening," Father Sullivan said, making more of a statement than asking a question.

"It makes the crackling fire all the more welcome and appreciated," Father Warren said as Father Sullivan walked over to the chair in front of the fire and stared into the red-hot embers.

"You have such a nice way with words, Father," Father Sullivan said, complimenting the elder priest.

"Maybe, but look at how many years I've had to practice. I can assure you, am, you'll be there someday. And sooner than you expect, I might add," the wise old priest said. "You are a gifted man, Michael. You attract the confidence and respect of our parishioners and anyone you come into contact with. You'll go far in our church, and the good Lord knows we need more priests like you." The moment moved Father Warren to say, "And, Michael, I suggest to you, keep control of all your talents, your principles, and your passion to do good. Never let it escape in a way that could lead you astray."

Feeling the seriousness of Father Warren's words and this solemn moment, Father Sullivan did not respond. He knew what Father Warren was saying.

The *tick tock* of the swinging pendulum on the tall, elegant century-old clock dominated the hush that swept the room. Having taken a seat in the winged armchair opposite Father Warren, Father Sullivan simply said, "Your words mean a lot to me, Father. I won't let you down."

"I know you won't, Father." Father Warren paused. "And don't let yourself down," he advised.

The older priest rose, approached the warmth of the crackling fire, and leaned against the wooden mantel. He bent over, reached into the wood box, grabbed a piece of split cedar, and tossed it onto the fire. Sparks flew like firecrackers in the sky, crackling and flashing at the room.

He stared at the pulsating coals below the burning wood and said, "You know, Michael, a burning fire reminds me of both good and bad. The red-hot coals from below remind me of what could happen if we helpless souls fall, go astray, and never return. The jumping sparks and ascending smoke show me what happens when we sinners stoke the fires within us with prayer to our Lord and helping others. We must love our neighbors. Most of all, we must love our Lord and our God more than ourselves."

Father Warren stood erect, turned around, and looked directly at Father Sullivan. "Our job is to share the message to those poor souls without faith."

"That's moving, Father. I enjoyed every word. I'd seriously think about that story as a part of your sermon for Sunday," Father Sullivan suggested.

"*Hmmm.* That's an idea. Maybe I will. Now," he said to the young priest, throwing one more log on the fire. "What brought you in here this evening, before I got so carried away?"

"I just wanted to say thank you. Thank you for trusting me. I know a couple weeks have passed, you know my mom and dad, the funeral … "

Father Warren interrupted, "Michael, I understand. Life is a choice of priorities."

"Yes, Father. Thank you for understanding. I want you to know I'll be stopping by Bernard's house tomorrow. You remember Bernard Bednar?"

"That's good. That's really good. I'll leave it all up to you, Father. You'll know the right thing to do for the sheriff, our church … and most of all for Bernard and his parents. He must have a very troubled soul, and we have to help him, not hide him."

Father Sullivan frowned as he considered the meaning of the priest's comment. *Not hide him?* "Yes, Father, I understand. I better go now. Have a good evening. Enjoy that book you're reading."

Father Warren retreated back to his chair and picked up the book. As Father Sullivan walked up the stairs to his quarters, he thought, *A wise, wise man. I believe I understood everything he said to me.* He entered his room, closed the door, and flicked the lock behind him. "Tomorrow I will knock on Bernard's door."

Minutes later, as he was turning off his bedside light, he had one other thought about another troubled soul. Then he fell asleep and dreamed, his mind drifting on into the darkness.

CHAPTER 15

THE VISIT

Father Sullivan—January 27, 1958, 3:30p.m.

THE '53 Chevy was Father Sullivan's one pride and joy, a remembrance of the material life. The two-door car—with its six-cylinder engine, stick on the column, and whitewall tires—truly set the priest apart, though that was not his intention. Father Sullivan enjoyed driving his unconventional two-tone green Chevrolet. Most priests drove black cars. As in many ways of the priesthood, Father Sullivan thought he was somewhat unconventional.

Pulling up in front of the Bednar house on Monday afternoon, Father Sullivan turned the motor off and sat for a moment. He pulled up his collar on this damp, chilly, and gray February afternoon. He could not help but wonder what lay within the old weathered clapboard house. He would have preferred to set an appointment, but the Bednars did not have a telephone. Everything surrounding the structure needed attention. Two solitary elm trees stood in front of the house, one on each side of the lot. Although it was winter, he could tell at least one was probably dead, and the other was not far behind. The missing and peeling bark supported his conclusion.

The cracked sidewalk leading to the porch looked older than the house, but he knew that could not be. Or could it? There were three steps up to the porch. All squeaked. One was broken. Pausing before the front door, he noticed the torn screen, seemingly out of place in January. More startling, however, was the rusted padlock barring the main exterior door.

A faded wood shingle was nailed to the door: *Use Side Door.* A painted arrow pointed in that direction.

Walking around the corner of the house, Father Sullivan stepped over a rake and shovel half hidden in the snow. Proceeding to the enclosed side porch, he knocked on the screen door. The porch was cluttered with stacked cans, dead potted cacti, and several bundles of stacks of newspapers, which were partially covered with snow that had blown through a broken windowpane.

The storm door rattled with each knock. After a minute or so, the priest assumed nobody was home, or possibly they were just not answering. As he stepped back onto the gravel walk leading to his car, the door creaked opened about a foot. A hollow-faced elderly man stepped onto the porch. Father Sullivan looked up. The man's head was about two feet above the priest's. His face was wrinkled and gaunt, and his hair was thinning, gray, and disheveled.

"Good morning, sir. My name is Father Sullivan from St. Thomas Moore."

Standing behind the door, his hands hidden behind the bib of his soiled overalls, the elderly man responded, "Yep, I know." He stared. The stubble covering his face hid his nonexistent smile. His gray frayed shirt was most appropriate considering his overall persona.

Father Sullivan nodded determinedly. "My purpose, sir, is with Bernard. Bernard, your son, I presume?"

"Yep, that's him."

"May I please say hello to Bernard? I would like to meet him."

"Why?" the old man asked, continuing to glare.

"Just a private matter, sir, if you don't mind."

"What if I do mind? What if I do mind and don't want you to see him?"

"Well, sir, with no disrespect, I would think that would be Bernard's decision, being that he's now probably in his forties."

"Well then, with respect back at you, young man, I don't care for you to see him at all."

Startled, the priest noticed the shade move aside in the window over the old man's shoulder. He saw the face of an elderly woman who looked almost like the man's twin sister. Her woolen gray scarf was pulled tight against her head.

Noticing the priest staring over his shoulder, the man turned his head and looked directly at the window. The shade quickly dropped. Father Sullivan noticed the old man give an unwelcoming glance down the gravel drive as he opened the screen door and stepped onto the porch steps. He maintained his elevated position, having stepped onto the middle step.

Father Sullivan backed away from the steps, still in line with the old man's stare.

"Bernard, this here priest is here to see ya," the man said to his son as he saw Bernard walking up the drive.

Father Sullivan had not seen or heard Bernard come up the driveway. The man kept walking, saying nothing. Stepping in front of Father Sullivan, Bernard took up position in front of the old man. "What fer? Why's he wanna see me?" he asked, looking at the old man. "*Uumpgh.*"

"How the hell should I know? I see you every day. Maybe he wants you to go to church and become an altar boy," the old man said unkindly.

Father Sullivan began again by saying, "Well, Bernard ... can I call you that?"

"What else you gonna call him?" Mr. Bednar asked, answering for his son.

"Yeah, right. *Uumpgh,*" Bernard added.

"I'd like to speak privately."

Bernard looked up at the old man. They all waited in silence. Saying nothing, the old man stepped back onto the porch. Bernard stood frozen. Father Sullivan shivered from the damp cold. Slowly, the old man reopened the screen door, threw his head back, and gave a nod directed at Bernard and Father Sullivan. He turned and walked into the kitchen.

"*Uumpgh.*"

Hat in hand, the priest followed Bernard. The porch had an offensive smell. *Maybe cats.* Inside the cluttered kitchen, Father Sullivan detected a closed-up scent permeating the room. He immediately noticed the back of a woman who was walking into the front room from the kitchen. Scarf still on and an apron tied around her neck, she kind of hobbled in quick steps, stooping as she walked. Immediately, she sat in a black wooden rocker. A gray cat scurried under the table next to the rocker. Resting his head on his paws, ears erect, he stared directly into the kitchen. The cat's companion, now rocking back and forth, did the same.

"Have a seat," Bernard suggested.

The old man pointed to an empty chair at the small square kitchen table.

Father Sullivan sat down, his back to the porch door. He could feel the glare of four eyes staring at him from the front room. Bernard quietly sat opposite the priest, his back to the wood-burning stove. The black stove was piped into the interior chimney wall.

Mr. Bednar remained standing, resting against the kitchen counter, still in a position to look down at Father Sullivan. Reaching over and removing a stack of newspapers and magazines from the table, the old man threw them to the floor next to the wood box. Bernard reached across the table and stacked three chipped green dinner plates.

"Coffee?" the elderly man asked.

"Sure, that would be nice. Thank you," Father Sullivan said, accepting their abrupt hospitality. *I can use some warmth.*

"Bernard!" the elder commanded.

"*Uumpgh, uumpgh.*" Bernard stood, walked over to the cupboard, pulled out a can of Maxwell House, and carefully measured six scoops into a porcelain blue-gray coffee pot.

"Throw some wood in," Bernard's dad commanded again, still leaning against the counter by the kitchen sink.

Bernard picked up what looked to be three perfectly split hickory logs and tossed them into the stove. "Burns good, that hickory. Like it better than oak. Crackles. Good smell. *Uumpgh.*" As Bernard waited for the coffee to brew, he left the room and walked down the hall.

The rocker continued, back and forth, in the front room. When the door slammed, it startled the sleeping cat. Father Sullivan saw the cat run around the corner of the hallway from the front room and down the hall toward Bernard. Moments of silence passed.

"Coffee'll be ready soon," the old man said, but he initiated no conversation. *Silence.*

The priest glanced out the window to the left of the cupboard. It had two cracked panes and another that had been replaced with cardboard.

Years of use had given the cabinets almost a dirty gray look. Father Sullivan saw a small house in the back, but it was bigger than the outhouse, which was a few steps beyond. *Must be a woodshed.* He saw Bernard walking toward the woodpile.

Bernard reached for the ax buried in the stump. With one tug, he pulled the ax from the dense block of wood. Then he sat a round log on the stump. With ease, he used his muscular arms to fling the ax deep into the wood with enough force that the log split, jumped, and flipped to the ground. After splitting several round cuts of hickory into perfect triangle splits, Bernard walked back into the little house and then returned to the chopping block, carrying a small silver hand ax.

Meanwhile, inside the main house, Bernard's dad stepped to the window. He saw Bernard splitting the hickory. Before returning to his resting place at the kitchen sink, the old man peered through the cracked pane and stared at the small mound of dirt with a wooden cross at the end of the picket fence. He remembered.

Bernard picked up some kindling and diced up some wood into small one-inch splits as easily as if he were dicing carrots. Once finished, Bernard turned and easily flipped the hand ax end over end, burying it in the side of the house. Bending over, he pulled up his right pant leg to the knee. From a brown leather sheath strapped to the right side of his calf, he drew a ten-inch straight knife. Like with the ax, Bernard meticulously split the kindling into even smaller pieces. Once finished, he slipped the knife back into the sheath. Father Sullivan noted Bernard's dexterity with the blade.

After picking up the split wood and placing it in his left open arm, Bernard returned to the house, walked into the kitchen, and stacked the wood in the wood box next to the stove. A few moments later, Father Sullivan heard the rattle and clang of a metal bowl. The cat scurried back and took his place under the table in the front room. Again, Father Sullivan felt the stare of four eyes.

"Coffee's ready."

"*Uumpgh*, coffee ready?" Bernard opened the cupboard, returned to the table, set out four cracked, aged cups, and poured the coffee. The cups were not level as they sat on the table. The old oilcloth tablecloth covering the surface was lumpy. Father Sullivan could tell papers and letters were hidden below it. That's just what some folks did, he remembered. An old aunt of his had the same kind of filing system.

Bernard took a cup to the front room and handed it to his mother. They didn't say a word. *Rock, rock.* With both hands clutching the cup to her face, she rocked back and forth in the rocking chair and continually drank as if this was her only coffee in a week. The old man reached over, took a cup, and leaned back against the sink. Bernard set a cup in front of Father Sullivan. He then sat at the table opposite Father Sullivan, his back to the black stove. His father watched. Indeed, by now the priest thought nothing would seem strange anymore.

"Thank you, Bernard." Father Sullivan knew by instinct that he dare not ask for cream and sugar. "Any chance Bernard and I could visit alone?"

"No," replied the old man, still leaning against the counter. "You talk to him right here in front of me."

Bernard showed no response. Then he said, "No, *uumpgh.* Talk right here."

"Yeah, no secrets—the three of us!" Mr. Bednar exclaimed. "Me, Bernard, and Farnsworth."

Farnsworth? That sounds like an unusual name for Mrs. Bednar. "Farnsworth?" Father Sullivan asked.

"Yeah, my cat. *Uumpgh,*" explained Bernard.

"Me, the cat, and Bernard," the old man replied. "No secrets."

Father Sullivan looked into the front room. *What about Mom?*

"Pay no mind to her," Mr. Bednar said as he waved his hand dismissively in the old lady's direction. Four eyes. *Rock, rock.* "She hasn't talked for years."

Don't even ask, Father Sullivan thought. *They don't even refer to her … just the cat.*

The sofa to the side of the rocking chair became a resting place for Farnsworth. Magazines and newspapers occupied two of the cushions. Reconciled to the reality of the definition of privacy within the Bednar household, Father Sullivan realized he needed to talk to Bernard here at the lumpy kitchen table in front of the dizzying motion of the rocker and the prop holding up the counter.

"Would you excuse me, please?" Father Sullivan stood up. "I'll be right back." He proceeded to the side porch, walked out the door, and went straight to his pride and joy. He opened the door of his Chevy and picked up his missal from the front seat. Then he walked back to the house. Laying the *Saint Joseph's Daily Missal* on the table next to his now lukewarm coffee, Father Sullivan removed a rosary from his pocket and neatly laid it atop the book.

"What's that?" the old man asked.

"My rosary and missal," he said, hopefully without sarcasm.

"What fer?"

"I want it to remind you that I'm a priest." Father Sullivan's confidence reminded him that nothing was too strange in this house.

"Already figured that out. Didn't think you were a nun. That upside down collar and all," the old man said.

Hoping to have gained their attention with the missal and rosary, Father Sullivan took a long first sip of his coffee. *Yuck!* he thought with a smile on his face. A perfect complement to this strange day. He allowed plenty of silence to cleanse the room. "Bernard, you've lived here a long time?"

"Yep."

"How long?"

"All ma life. *Uumpgh.*"

"Where did you go to school?"

"Ah, ah, the holy school. That Catholic one up across from the courthouse."

Father Sullivan let that go, knowing he meant St. Thomas Moore. "Did you enjoy the school?"

"Yep."

"Why?"

"Liked all them nice kids."

"Nice kids?"

"Yep, them boys."

"How about the girls?"

"Nope. *Uumpgh.* Likes some them girls."

"How about the sisters?"

"You mean them nuns? Ones with those long black dresses? Yep. Liked some. The nice ones."

"Did you like the priests?"

"Yep. Liked them priests. Maybe ones like you," he told Father Sullivan.

"All the priests?"

"Yep. All except one."

"Which one?"

"Don't remember. Just the bad one. The mean one," Bernard answered. "He tried to hurt me once. I stopped him. Bad man. Grabbed me once. I pushed him away so hard he fell to the floor. Bad man."

Noticing an oak clock hanging on the wall in the front room, Father Sullivan realized this endeavor might take some time. "Do you work now?"

"Yep, out there."

"Out where, Bernard?"

"Out at the big school. Big brick school."

"The Wabash Reform School?" Father Sullivan inquired.

"Yep, the one with all them boys."

"Do you like it there?"

"Yep. Most time. People's nice to me. Well, most of 'em."

Father Sullivan gained confidence that Bernard was beginning to open up. His mother still had not moved. Her cup sat on the table. She just rocked. Mr. Bednar reached over, picked up a couple logs, and fed the stove behind Bernard. *Get to the point*, Father Sullivan thought. "Bernard … Bernard, have you ever been in trouble at the reform school?"

Silence.

"Ah, trouble? *Uumpgh*. Nope."

"Are you sure, Bernard?" Father Sullivan could tell Bernard sounded hesitant.

"Go ahead. Tell the priest," he heard Mr. Bednar say.

"Well … well … *uumpgh*. This one time … *uumpgh*."

"Tell the priest."

"Yep. I can. Pa?"

"Go ahead, Bernard," Father Sullivan encouraged.

"One day I was passing trays. You know, trays with food. For the boys. Take it to 'em every day. Three times. Three times a day. *Uumpgh*. Took trays to them boys. Like them boys."

Father Sullivan reached for his coffee and took a long cold swig. *Bitter.* Having been startled by the longevity of Bernard's reply, he didn't have time to ask another question as Bernard continued to say, "This one day. Went to my unit with them trays. Saw Eddie cryin'. I like Eddie. He's my friend. We do things for each other. He looks up to me, that Little Eddie Small."

"Like what?" Father Sullivan asked innocently but with purpose.

"Eddie's nice to me. Makes me feel good. I like that. I like nice people. *Uumpgh. Uumpgh.*"

"What happened this one day, Bernard?"

"Well, well, this one day. Yeah, this one day Little Eddie Small's cryin'."

"Crying? Crying where?" the priest asked.

"In his room. Where else?" Bernard's unexpected words of sarcasm took Father Sullivan aback. "No place else for Little Eddie to cry. In his room. Yep. In his room. *Uumpgh.* Little Eddie. I like Eddie. He's nice to me."

Father Sullivan didn't feel comfortable asking Bernard about what he meant by "nice." *Just listen,* he thought.

Bernard took a swig of coffee. "Eddie's cryin'. 'What happened, Little Eddie?'"

Father Sullivan could see that Bernard was kind. *Compassion doesn't know the difference between smart or dumb, young or old,* he thought as he listened to each word Bernard said.

"He was cryin'. Not loud. But cryin'. He hurt. I asked. I asked what happened. He said, 'Big Billy, Big Billy. He scared me. He hurt me. He made me. He made me.' Little Eddie cried hard. Then he told me. Big Billy came into his room. Closed the door. Everyone else was gone. Big Billy, he threw ... he threw Little Eddie on the bed. Then he took off his belt. Eddie said he was so scared. Big Billy took off his pants. He told Eddie, 'You wanna ... you wanna this? You better wanna this.'"

"Okay, Bernard. Are you saying he forced Little Eddie?"

"Yep, yep, he did. *Uumpgh.*"

"Did Eddie say what happened?"

"Yep."

Quit the questions and just listen, Father Sullivan told himself.

"He told Eddie he'd better start prayin'. 'Now, you pray to this.'"

"Okay, Bernard. I get it. No need to tell me any more."

"He made Little Eddie do it all," Bernard offered up without being questioned.

"What did you do, Bernard?"

"I helped Eddie. Little Eddie. I like the little boy. Eddie was a little boy. I liked Eddie. He was my friend … *uumpgh*."

"How old was Eddie? Can you remember?"

"Yep, thirteen. 'Member exactly. Thirteen … *uumpgh*."

"Do you remember what you did then?"

"Yep. Sure do. Can't forget that. Can't forget that Big Billy guy. He hurt my friend. My friend Little Eddie."

Lost in the moment and mesmerized by Bernard's story, Father Sullivan could only hear the *tick tock, tick tock* of the clock. He glanced into the front room. The rocker was empty. Now just two eyes stared from the cushion on the couch. Looking to his right, he also noticed the absence of Mr. Bednar. Turning his head, he saw the tall man sitting, elbows on his knees and big hands clasped together, in the straight chair in front of the window to the front porch.

"Can you tell me what you did?"

Bernard's dad rose from his chair. Placing both hands on the kitchen table, he looked Father Sullivan directly in the eye. "Shoulda killed him. You 'buse little boys. You need ta die. I know. Been there. Took care bad man myself."

Puzzled, Father Sullivan watched as Bernard's dad stepped back and leaned against the kitchen counter once again. *What'd he mean by that?*

"Yes, kill them rapers."

Father Sullivan took in the comment but did not reply. Did Mr. Bednar mean Bernard should have killed?

"You said you were in trouble one time?" Father Sullivan prompted Bernard.

"Yep, yep."

"Were you in trouble because of Eddie or because of Billy?"

"Neither one. Didn't get in trouble at the school. Me, I got in trouble once back in grade school. Not my fault."

"What did you do?"

"Can't tell you now. This time, I did it to him. I did it to Big Billy. Can't tell you 'bout long ago. Not now."

As darkness settled into the kitchen, Father Sullivan could smell kerosene and a match. Mr. Bednar sat back down after lighting the lamp on the kitchen table. The priest had not even noticed darkness. "Go ahead, Bernard."

"Nope. Tired. I like Little Eddie. Tired. Time for supper. Then gotta go to bed. Tired. Coffee's gone."

"Do you still like Little Eddie?"

"Yep, he's my friend. Watch out for him. Big Billy leaves him alone now." Bernard dropped his head. Not one word. Then he said, "Eddie knows he's my friend." With that, Bernard stood up and walked back down the hall. Darkness covered the broken window. Father Sullivan could not see the little house.

"Enough. Gotta cook 'em some supper." Mr. Bednar walked onto the porch.

Father Sullivan followed. "Thank you, sir. Thank Bernard for me. We'll have to visit again."

Mr. Bednar nodded and opened the porch door for Father Sullivan.

"No need to say thanks. Didn't give ya nothin'."

What a strange thing to say. Father Sullivan slowly walked down the gravel drive toward his Chevy. He clasped the collar on his overcoat. Snowflakes began to fall. He looked up at the half-full moon. *Well, guess I learned something today. Have to pray for Little Eddie.* But he wondered what exactly happened to Big Billy.

The visit with the Bednar family had affected Father Sullivan very deeply—not only what Bernard had told him but also what Bernard had not disclosed. He shifted his Chevy and drove back to the rectory.

The next morning, in the solitude of his room, Father Sullivan dialed Sheriff Thurow.

"Good morning. Sheriff Thurow's office."

"Oh, hello. This is Father Sullivan from St. Thomas Moore. May I speak with the sheriff please?" A moment passed.

Father Sullivan heard the sheriff come on the line. "Father, Sheriff Thurow. Are you calling about the Bednars?"

"Yes. I met the entire family yesterday, all three of them." He didn't dare mention the fourth.

"And?" the sheriff asked.

"I'll get to the point. Private line, I assume?"

"Of course, Father."

"Bernard Bednar is involved with boys in a caring capacity. Surprisingly, he was very open with me. You would not believe that household, the surroundings, his parents, and Bernard himself."

"Has he molested anyone? Did he admit to anything?" The sheriff was a direct, straightforward man.

"No. I do not believe Bernard has abused anyone, but he is aware of problems of abuse and is concerned for the boys' safety. I need to meet with him again. It was late. Bernard said all he could, or should I say would, at the time. I have confidence, Sheriff. I'd like to have yours."

"What do you mean?"

"Sheriff, I'd like to meet him again. He's especially concerned about a boy named Eddie. He also mentioned one of the bullies named Billy, who may be an abuser. I am concerned about the school, the boys, and Bernard. If you'll allow me, I'd like to become more involved."

"Father, you are part of my posse." Sheriff Thurow knew Father Sullivan was passionate and concerned. He could tell the priest was determined to get to the bottom of the problem.

"Thank you, Sheriff. I'll be back to you. Good-bye."

"Oh, Father. One last thing. Let's meet in person after your next visit with the Bednars."

"Yes, back to you soon." *Better be back real soon,* Father Sullivan thought.

CHAPTER 16

NEW POSITION

Clarence Wolfe—January 30, 1958

CLARENCE Wolfe, the director of the reform school, sat behind the large desk in his office on the first floor. His office, located adjacent to the foyer, was off-limits without specific invitation from the director himself. Wolfe reported directly to the head of social services in the county courthouse. This was his fourteenth year as headmaster and school director.

He had no parents to deal with. No board of directors functioned within the school. Visitors were few. The county chain of command consisted of an annual visit from the director of social services. Clarence Wolfe ruled the school just like he had served as a sergeant during WWII fifteen years before—with an iron fist. First through Africa and then on to Normandy, all across Europe, and straight into Berlin. A man of no fear, Wolfe always demanded and then received compliance.

The Wabash Reform School had been a most unlikely career change. Randall Zilbar arranged for Clarence Wolfe to meet with Harold Fowler. Payback or hush money was long overdue. Fowler, the Wabash County Executive, was a friend of Zilbar's, during and after the war.

As the Director of the Reform School, Wolfe found time, security, and an environment that allowed him to command the staff, the facility, and the boys within the institution. The thoughts he harbored about an unpleasant memory of the past between the walls of the school, he suppressed in his mind as if it had never happened. He led a life with no external threats. However, in 1951 Wolfe had fallen on difficult financial times.

Old haunts and habits had been aroused, and he had needed relief. Fowler had linked him to someone he said would be able to help. A renewed association Wolfe made with Randall Zilbar that year would affect him for the rest of his life.

Clarence Wolfe had called Phillip Krueger from his office at the end of the hall the day before. Wolfe was going to promote Phillip Krueger to relieve Wolfe of much of the ordinary daily operations. Their meeting was scheduled for 7:00 a.m.

"Phillip, I want you to be in my office tomorrow. Evaluation. See you then," he had informed Krueger. *Click.* His plan was set. Clarence Wolfe communicated by commands. As first sergeant in the war, he had never discarded the power of structural hierarchy.

Phillip Krueger had performed well during his twelve years on staff at the Wabash Reform School. Born, bred, and raised in Wabash, he had been civic-minded since grade school. His participation as a Cub and Boy Scout, 4-H member, Eagle Scout, National Honor Society member, and altar boy completed a resume of the student achiever during the pre- and postwar eras. As an adult, Krueger was actively involved in the Masons. Unmarried, he was totally consumed with civic pride. He especially enjoyed his total involvement with the youth of the Wabash Reform School and the Boy Scouts. Krueger's community involvement never included any organization in which members relied on membership by invitation or recognition by election.

Krueger was always punctual, especially with his meeting that morning with Clarence Wolfe. The sound of Krueger's leather shoes on the shiny terrazzo floors echoed down the hall leading to Mr. Wolfe's office. Miss Gardner heard the approaching footsteps. Her hair was pulled tight in a spinster's bun. A long straight pin with a ruby top was embedded in the collar of her silk blouse.

As Krueger entered the office of the director, she immediately greeted him. "Yes, sir. Mr. Krueger, we are expecting you. Have a seat," she commanded.

"Thank you. Yes, good morning, Miss Gardner," he responded. He wondered if his uneasiness was apparent. Every visit to Mr. Wolfe's office was as intimidating as the man himself.

A door behind Miss Gardner's desk opened suddenly, and there stood

Clarence Wolfe. He was a big man, filling the oak frame of the door. "Come right in, Phillip." He turned and proceeded to his desk, which was almost as imposing as the man himself.

Krueger followed.

"Have a seat. Are you well?"

"Yes, sir. I am. Thank you," Krueger responded nervously.

"In all the years you've been here, I have been impressed with your work, ethics, dependability, and relationships with the boys," Wolfe said with an air as if he was bestowing the compliments out of his good nature.

"Well, thank you, sir. That means a lot to me." Shifting in his chair, Krueger now sat more erect, feeling much more confident having received such unexpected compliments.

"With the retirement of Harold Mayer, I have decided to promote you to director of operations. Your responsibility will be to oversee all units within the school. Each of the ward leaders will report to you. You will be in charge of personnel, discipline, and all educational instructions throughout the school. Senior and professional staff will report to you. The daily operations of maintenance, food service, housekeeping, and the grounds staff will remain with Bud Jackson. You will report directly to me. Bud will continue to do the same."

Phillip Krueger was taken aback by the sheer magnitude of Clarence Wolfe's compliments. He had not received a total of that many in all his twelve years at the school.

"Now, Mr. Krueger, I must mention that you have had a few indiscretions along the way, but I have overlooked those in my evaluation. I feel assured that we won't need to address anything of this nature in the future."

Knowing the conversation needed to be short and direct, Krueger said, "You can depend on me. The school and these boys are the most important part of my life. I look forward to the opportunity and challenge. I promise I won't let you down."

Wolfe looked pleased with his response. "We run a tight ship here. Lately some situations, discipline, and relationships have gotten a little out of hand. We both know what I'm talking about. I will announce your promotion effective Monday. Number one on your agenda will be to structure weekly meetings with the boys' personnel staff. Your first direct assignment will be to meet with Bernard Bednar and find out about what happened with Billy Hackett."

"Yes, sir. I do know a little about that."

"Me too. I have a few questions about unit 7. I want you to keep an eye on those particular boys. For instance, are any of the older boys preying on the younger, weaker ones? You address that first thing. You understand? See you back in my office next Monday, four o'clock sharp. Bring some answers. And one other thing. A couple of those little side issues you handled for me. That won't change."

"Oh yes, sir. Whatever you need," Krueger responded eagerly.

"That's all for today, Phillip."

Krueger expressed his gratitude to Clarence Wolfe and, with a sigh of relief, left the office. "Have a good day, Miss Gardner. See you next week."

She did not look up from her typewriter.

Phillip Krueger boasted to himself as he walked down the wide hall to his own office, which was located just across from the stairs to the boys' dorm. *New opportunities to work with the boys,* he thought. *New opportunities.*

Krueger felt more powerful in his new position. Finally, he had gained control of his fate. Only Clarence Wolfe loomed over him. Here, in this office, in this position, Phillip could be closer to the boys, do more for them. Also, he thought, he could do more for himself.

A meeting with all the floor leaders was first on his agenda. Three floors, three leaders. They ruled over the misfits, the tough delinquents, the unreformed, and especially the third-floor east-wing sociopaths. Or as Clarence Wolfe liked to call them, the hardcore.

Phillip knew his main job was to maintain control, a continued tight grip on all levels of disciplining the boys, just as Wolfe had structured. Discipline was now primary. He had a way with some of the boys. Most still did not like him. The same was true with the Boy Scouts, the boys at the Y, and the boys at the gym in the Honeywell Center. Some boys' basic instincts did not allow them to take to Phillip Krueger. Some saw straight through him. One of those boys was Christopher Leffler. Christopher lived in unit 3. Strong, quiet, and determined, he would always stand up for the defenseless. Nobody messed with Christopher Leffler, not even Big Billy.

CHAPTER 17

SHAME, SIN, AND GUILT

Peter Goodnar—February 7, 1958, mid-morning

FATHER Sullivan walked down the side aisle of the quiet old church. As he passed the confessional, he noticed the "on" light above the left confessional door. Father Warren's placard was in the slot on the door. After walking to the center aisle, Father Sullivan genuflected and proceeded to his confessional on the other side of the church. The line for confessions was much longer on Thursdays preceding the First Friday's all-school Mass at St. Thomas Moore.

Father Sullivan enjoyed hearing confessions of grade-schoolers. "Disobeyed my parents five times"; "Used a swear word three times"; "Had impure thoughts six times"; and "Hit my younger brother once" were all reminders of the innocence of youth. He thought it was certainly a far cry from Saturday confessions of "I committed adultery"; "I stole from work"; and "I hit my wife.' *God loves all, especially the young.*

Walking into the confessional, Father Sullivan closed the door, took comfort in his chair, and slid open the small confessional door.

"Bless me, Father, for I have sinned," he heard from the other side of the black cloth.

A half hour and a number of confessions passed. Father Sullivan heard the door close. The next penitent knelt and waited until the priest slid the small black curtained door open.

"Bless me … " There was a pause. "Father, I … I … "

Father Sullivan detected sniffles from the other side of the covered door. A low muffled cry erupted. He could tell it was the voice of a young boy. "Now, my son, I'm here to help you, not punish you."

"Okay, Father. I'll try."

Father Sullivan could hear a big sniff as the boy took a deep breath.

"May I start over, please, Father?"

"Sure, take your time," he responded, as he always tried to make the penitent feel relaxed and comfortable.

"Bless me, Father, for I have sinned. I disobeyed my mom three times, I said damn two times, and I talked during Sunday Mass two times."

This is a reason to cry? Something doesn't add up, Father Sullivan thought.

"I stared at Mary Ann's ... well ... you know, Father, but I will stop."

"Yes, son, I understand."

"I, ah ... I, ah ... "

Father Sullivan detected reluctance and said, "Is there something you are trying to say and you'd like to tell me? If so, it's all right. Go ahead. Our God is a forgiving God. Your repentance is good."

A gush of sobs tore through the covered opening. Father Sullivan waited.

"It's okay. It's okay. I'm here for you."

Another deep breath. "Yes, Father, I sinned. I committed a bad, bad mortal sin. I ... I ... oh, Father, I'm sorry. I ... I was in bed. Oh, Father, I was in bed with a man, and he ... and he ..." More sobs.

Father Sullivan braced himself. The shock was startling. *Calm, calm control*, he thought. "Take your time. You can tell me exactly what happened."

"Well, Father, this man took off his shirt. I saw him. Then he took off my shirt. I wanted to run away, but I couldn't. I knew he locked the door. I didn't want him to see me. I was scared. So scared. Then he put his arms around me. And he ... he touched ... " Silence.

"Now, this does not mean you sinned." *Stay calm*. "Did you have intent to sin?"

Peter responded, "No, no, Father, I wanted out of the room. But, Father, there's more. Father, then he made me. Oh, Father, I didn't mean to. Will God forgive me? Father? Father?" The boy's confession transformed into a plea for help.

"Of course, He will." Father Sullivan knew the seriousness of what he had just heard. They were far beyond sin and repentance. *I need to find out who this is so I can help.* "Son, we are in confession. You are safe with me. Please listen. I want to help you, but you need to meet with me outside the confessional so we can be more open."

The sobs turned to a whimper ... a sniff ... and then silence. Suddenly, all Father Sullivan could hear was the closing of the exterior confessional door. Helpless, he was bound by the seal of confession. *He's gone.*

Peter walked as slowly as he could, following his mind, which had already fled the church. Up the aisle toward the side door at the front of the church, Peter exited with his back to his classmates, who were still kneeling in the pews. Hopefully, they would not detect his red eyes and cheeks stained by the flow of his tears. Approaching the side door, Peter put his hat on and pulled the bill low over his tell-all eyes. *I can't stay in church. They'll see me.* The thought of school and the shame everyone would see across his face made him hurry. *I can never go back. Where? Where can I go to hide?*

Keeping his head down and staring at his feet, he raced down the sidewalk between the church and school. Suddenly Peter heard some voices and looked up.

"Hey, good morning, Peter," said a somewhat startled but calm Father Jaeger as he came around the corner.

Peter had no time to respond to the priest, as the man and two boys kept walking toward the side entrance of the church from where Peter had just come. "Yeah, hi there, Pete," said the older of the two boys.

When he passed them, Peter recognized Joey Singleton striding step-by-step with the priest. The thought of Father Jaeger's bed entered Peter's thoughts. He knew Father Jaeger and Joey were friends. Very, very close friends if Peter could believe all the talk he had heard. Knowing Father Jaeger, Peter concluded it was probably true. Excruciating nausea clenched his stomach. Gag. If he could, he would have. He immediately harbored the thought of the privacy, solitude, and escape of his own room.

Peering back over his shoulder, Peter noticed Father Jaeger's right arm on Joe's shoulder. Peter knew. He raced straight home. Oh, the horror, the sin. *Now if only I can convince Mom that I am sick and must stay home all day.* Hopefully, she'd never know.

Peter's mother was most understanding that Thursday in March 1958. She knew Peter was coming down with a bad cold. He spent the rest of Thursday, all of Friday, and the weekend home in bed, reeling with guilt. He also added lying to his mom to his ever-growing list of sins.

That weekend, for the first time in more than five years, Peter missed Sunday Mass. Deep inside he knew he had sinned even more. It wasn't missing Mass or lying to his mother, however, that would be the sins to send him straight to hell; it would be the mortal sin of being with that priest.

That early winter of 1958 offered little relief from his tormented mind. Peter looked forward to spring and then summer when he would be away from school. Still months away, summer would bring freedom from Father Jaeger, except for Sunday Mass. Attending Sunday Mass with his folks, younger brother, and sisters, Peter was always overjoyed when Father Warren or Father Sullivan said Mass. Still, summer seemed like an eternity away.

Peter's life continued its downward spiral. Unable to resist and scared when cornered, Peter did not know how to stop the advances of the priest. He fell into sin on two more occasions at the hands of Father Jaeger. His grades and overall school performance deteriorated.

Time marched by slowly. The absence of Father Jaeger for any amount of time—hours, days, a week—provided Peter with some peace of mind. However, he always felt on guard for what loomed in the unknown.

Peter was active in the local YMCA, where swimming was the main sport. Every boy in town learned how to swim at the Y, if not taught earlier by a parent or a friend or a buddy down in the Wabash River by the Huntington Bridge.

Looking across the pool during free swim one day, Peter saw Father Jaeger swimming and frolicking around in the pool with a couple of other boys. The priest didn't seem to notice him. Peter knew one of the boys was Joey Singleton. *He's always around Father Jaeger.* Like most Y's across the country, the policy was for all boys and instructors to swim in the nude at all times for health and sanitary reasons. The thoughts haunted

Peter. Swimming underwater to the far side of the pool, closest to the exit and lockers, Peter slipped away unnoticed by the pandering priest.

Peter was determined to keep away from Father Jaeger. Daily, however, he still thought about Father Sullivan wanting to help. *I need to go back to confession*, Peter thought, finding relief in the suggestion. Peter knew he would have to be even more forthcoming. He decided to try to go to confession. Like the last time, he would make sure Father Sullivan was hearing confessions. He could help Peter.

Two weeks after first confessing about Father Jaeger, on a late Saturday afternoon, Peter walked to church and waited in line for Father Sullivan to hear his confession. "Bless me, Father, for I have sinned again."

Upon hearing those eight words, the good priest knew the troubled boy was back.

CHAPTER 18

THERE'S MORE THAN ONE

Father Sullivan—February 12, 1958

FATHER Sullivan knew of only one way to contact or meet with Bernard Bednar again. *I'll have to go to his house.* Not knowing Bernard's exact work schedule, he decided to knock on the door late Wednesday afternoon two weeks after their initial meeting. He knew Sheriff Thurow was anxious to learn more about Bernard and the goings-on at the reform school.

Pike to King Street, left three blocks to Columbus, right at the dead end, and then down four doors to the west, the Bednar house stood alone on the south side of the street, up against the woods. He drove slowly. As he approached the Bednar house, he could see a figure walking down the drive toward the side porch adjacent to the woods. Bernard was home.

Knock, knock. Waiting and hoping Bernard would come to the door, Father Sullivan expected Mr. Bednar. The priest could see the shade being pushed aside in the kitchen window. He briefly saw Bernard. He knocked again, hoping to draw Bernard to the back door. He waited by counting the small holes and tears in the screen. The inside kitchen door opened slowly. Bernard stepped onto the porch.

"Good afternoon, Bernard. I expected to see your father."

"Not home. They're gone to Peru."

"Oh. May I come in? I'd like to visit some more if you have some time."

Looking directly at Father Sullivan, Bernard said nothing. He turned and walked back into the kitchen, leaving the door open. Father

Sullivan accepted the open-door invitation. He walked past the clutter on the porch and accidently brushed over a brown sack full of tin cans. The rattle of the cans startled a third pair of eyes. The cat jumped from behind the door and shot through it before the priest. The smell was familiar now. The combination of wood burning, old stacked newspapers, the cat box in the corner, and the dilapidated furniture gave off a smell of age, must, and stuffiness.

"Coffee?" Bernard asked.

"Sure, that would be great. Chilly day," Father Sullivan said agreeably. He removed his black overcoat and hat and laid them across a straight chair that was piled high with newspapers. He looked into the parlor. The black rocker was empty.

Bernard set the porcelain cups on Father Sullivan's side of the table. His back was to the kitchen door. The priest felt right at home.

Attempting conversation, Father Sullivan said, "Have you been to work today, Bernard?"

"Yep. You must have seen me walking home."

Father Sullivan then asked, "Bernard, could we continue our talk? I think we were talking about Billy. I believe that's what you called him?"

"No, he's Big Billy. *Uumpgh.*"

"What did you do to Big Billy?" Father Sullivan asked.

"Well, Big Billy's room was down the hall, way at the end."

Father Sullivan listened without questioning.

"I went down there and walked in his room. *Uumpgh.* My friend Artie runs the unit—the unit Big Billy lives in. Tough kids in there. Unit 10. Artie let me in. He kept everybody away."

"And what did you do?"

"I closed Billy's door. Just me and Big Billy was in there."

"How big is Billy?"

"He's really big." Bernard raised his hand above his own head about six inches.

"Did you say anything to Billy?"

"Big Billy asked what I wanted. I said, 'You hurt my friend Little Eddie.' Billy said Little Eddie called him a name and then kicked him. I knew he was lyin'. Big Billy said to get out of his room. Then he said he would tell Mr. Krueger on me."

"Who's Mr. Krueger?" Father Sullivan asked.

"He's boss man. Nobody likes him. *Uumpgh.*" Bernard paused and then said, "He makes some them boys like him. He's a bad man."

"What did you do then?"

"I told him he hurt Little Eddie."

Father Sullivan waited without another question.

"Then I told Big Billy to go ahead and tell the boss man. Big Billy stood right up and yelled at me to get out."

"Did you?"

"Nope."

"What did you do?"

"I took off my shirt. Billie yelled at me and said no. He kept yelling no."

"Did you stop?"

"Nope. Big Billy said, 'Please, no.' So I told him, 'Remember what you did to Little Eddie?' Big Billy said he was sorry. Won't do it again. I told Billy to look at this. Remember Little Eddie? He kept saying, 'No, no, not me.' Then I told Billy to get down. Told him, 'Get on your knees.'"

"Okay, Bernard. That's enough. I don't need to hear the rest."

"Yes, you do. *Uumpgh.* So I pulled my belt off. Put my hand behind Billy's neck. *Uumpgh.*" Father Sullivan saw a smile across Bernard's face. "I squeezed his neck. Then I"—Bernard raised his clenched right fist in front of Father Sullivan—"*pow!* I slammed Billy's face with this. *Uumpgh,*" Bernard said, holding up his clenched fist. "Scared him to death. He cried out real loud."

Father Sullivan felt the vibration from Bernard's right fist slamming into his cupped left hand. The hot coffee rippled in the cup front of him. "You mean you, I thought you … Did you do sex with Big Billy?"

"Nope. Don't do that stuff to boys. Don't hurt them. That's bad."

Father Sullivan watched Bernard's face and detected a slight smile.

"I hit Billy 'cause he hurt my friend. Nothing else. I don't do them bad things to boys."

"What happened then, Bernard?"

"I got blood all over my hand. Big Billy, he fell on the floor."

"So what then?" Father Sullivan asked in amazement.

"Well, poor Billy, he was cryin'. Not loud. I picked up his tooth—two of them. Set them on the table. *Uumpgh.*" Bernard's little smile was gone. "I took a towel and scrubbed my chest. Blood. I put my shirt on. My belt too. Then I picked Big Billy up and put him on his bed."

"Did Billy do anything?"

"Nope. Just lay there. I told him, 'Never hurt Little Eddie again.'"

"Did anybody see this?"

"Nope. They all stayed in their rooms. *Uumpgh.*"

"What'd you do next?"

"Told Artie goodnight. He's got a big family. Went back to my locker. *Uumpgh.* Then walked through the cemetery. Stopped at little Gordon Yoder's grave. Walked home."

Father Sullivan took a long drink of the bitter, thick coffee. "Did you get in trouble after that?"

"Nope. Walked out back and chopped wood. *Uumpgh.*"

"No, no, Bernard. I didn't mean after you walked home. I meant did you get in trouble at school?"

"Billy didn't tell Krueger. He just told Artie. *Uumpgh.* Artie told me about Big Billy falling in the shower room. *Uumpgh.* Artie said he broke his nose and two teeth came out. Artie knew better."

"So did anybody know aside from you and your friend Artie?"

"Yep. Yep, Father. Big Billy knew. He never hurt my friend again. *Uumpgh.*"

"Bernard, do you think anybody else hurts boys at school?"

"Yep. Sure do." Bernard was warming up to Father Sullivan. A kind person, he respected the priest. He thought back to his days in grade school. "I liked them sisters."

Father Sullivan was puzzled. "Sisters? At the reform school?"

"Nope. Ones that taught me when I was little. Liked the priests did."

"Bernard, the last time we visited, I thought you did not like the nuns?"

"Nope. Liked some them sisters."

Father Sullivan was taken aback by the sudden shift in the subject. He just listened.

"Yep. Liked them priests. All 'cept one. Nope, didn't like him. He touched me close one time. Only time. I stopped that."

Father Sullivan decided to not pursue that topic.

"I like you. You're like Father Kasemeyer. He was old. Liked him. He's dead now. Nice man."

The priest enjoyed listening to Bernard. He was saying much more this visit. *Maybe because his dad's not here.*

"Yep, boys been hurt out there. I know for sure. Long time ago. I was young. One boy hurt real bad. They killed him. *Uumpgh.*"

Father Sullivan shook his head, not believing what he heard. "Killed him? You mean murder?"

"Yep."

"When? Where?"

"In the school. Saw the man. Saw the dead boy. Gordon Yoder."

"Who was it?"

Realizing he may have said too much against his own secret, which he had hidden for years, he said, "Done. No more. Boy just died. That's all. Done. Rich man. Bad man. I'll get him. He'll pay."

"What do you mean, Bernard?"

"Rich man hurt the weak. *Uumpgh.* He thinks he too big. He forgot he hurt little Gordon Yoder. He'll have to face me. Bad."

Father Sullivan knew not to push Bernard.

"Somebody else hurts boys now. *Uumpgh.*"

"They do? Can I ask who?"

"Me and Artie knows. *Uumpgh.* We both know. Mr. Krueger likes boys a lot."

"Did you ever see him alone with a boy?"

"Yep. Sure did. Me and Artie both did. Lots of times."

Father Sullivan concluded that Bernard might know a lot more than he was saying. "Bernard, one more thing. Do you think Artie would ever talk to me?"

Bernard didn't answer. He just stood up and retrieved the coffee pot. Then he said, "'Bout all gone. Just a little bit. *Uumpgh. Uumpgh.*"

Father Sullivan did his penance by finishing his coffee. Bernard poured, filling each cup halfway.

Bernard took a drink, set his cup down, and kind of leaned forward as he supported himself with both elbows on the table. He clasped his broad hands together. "Yep, Artie will talk to you. Me and Artie both like them boys. *Uumpgh.*" Leaning forward one more inch, he entered

Father Sullivan's space. "Artie and me, we's know a lot. *Uumpgh*. We will help you, Father." Then Bernard stood up and said, "I'm done now. Got some chores before Ma and Pa get home. Need to chop more wood." A second smile appeared. Bernard didn't say a word. He didn't need to. He had already said a lot.

As Father Sullivan drove home that afternoon, he thought about all Bernard had told him. Then out of nowhere, he thought, *Who's Gordon Yoder?*

Father Sullivan called Sheriff Thurow the next morning right after his 8:30 a.m. weekday Mass.

"Sheriff, we need to meet soon. I learned a lot from Bernard. There are definite problems at the reform school. There may be more than you think.

"Can you be here this afternoon?" the sheriff asked immediately.

"Sure. How about middle afternoon? Say three thirty?"

"Works for me," Sheriff Thurow responded.

"See you then, Sheriff."

Little Eddie Small, the unknown boy in the confessional—I wonder how many more there could be. Father Sullivan made a special visit to St. Michael's chapel that afternoon. He thought, *Maybe I have more to pray for than just the unknown boy and Eddie.* He lit three candles that afternoon. He knew he might need St. Michael's help more than he had originally imagined. Little did he know.

CHAPTER 19

JUST ANOTHER VISIT

Joey Singleton—February 12, 1958

THAT evening after supper, Linda and her son, Joey—now thirteen—were sitting in the living room together. Linda was knitting, and Joey was reading *Mad Magazine*.

"Mom, is something bothering you?"

"No, not really anything. Maybe it's just work. Sometimes the staff at the courthouse can be, well, let's say nosey."

"You know, Mom, I do understand. Same at school." Joey stepped into the kitchen to get his mother another cup of coffee. He could tell she had something on her mind. He listened.

"Joey, there's something I've been wanting to ask you," she said with a serious look on her face.

"Sure, what is it?"

"Well, I hear you talk a lot about Father Jaeger lately, like … 'Going to be with Father Jaeger after school' or 'He gave me a ride home' or 'Saw him down at the Y yesterday.'"

"Yeah, sure. I like him. He's a real nice guy. Not just an ordinary priest."

"Do you think it may be because you never knew your father? You were only four months old when we divorced and he left." Rubbing her forehead, she paused and then said, "Left forever. You just have me."

"No, Mom. It's not about Dad. Father is just nice to me, and I, well, I—no, it doesn't make any difference."

"Go on. If it's important to you, it's important to me. I know you seem to like him very much. Then of course you're with your friends Bryan and Mitch so often. Even seems like it's always the four of you."

"Well, Mom, I really like all of them a lot, including Father Jaeger."

"Joey?" she asked with a question written across her face. "Joey?"

"Yes, Mom?"

"Are you thinking about … Well, you're in the eighth grade, and if I can say, you never talk about a girlfriend. Now, that's okay. You have plenty of time."

"Mom!" he responded, as if saying, *Don't interfere*. "Don't ask about girls."

"Let me just say … " She wanted to ask so much. "Joey, are you … Do you think you are … well. Are you thinking about the priesthood? Do you want to be a priest like Father Jaeger? Like Father Sullivan?" Linda did not permit herself to ask the real question she wanted to ask.

Internally, Joey felt the pressure of this conversation going too far. Shaking his head, not knowing how to respond, he just looked her in the eye. "Mom, I'm just trying to figure things out. Tryin' to just sort it out, so can we just leave it at that?"

Acknowledging her own personal questions and that she herself was trying to figure things out about where she was in life, Linda responded, "Joey, I love you so very much, and yes, I do understand. I really do. Just promise me one thing."

"Yes, sure, Mom. What is it?"

"Promise to always talk with me about any problems or questions that you have, like what you want to do with your life. Anything. Just promise you'll always discuss your concerns and your direction in life with me. You understand, don't you? You know I'll always love you and respect your decisions no matter what. As you know, I'm a little experienced in those departments."

"Yes, Mom, I promise. I'll let you know when I figure it all out. Okay?" Joey said matter-of-factly.

Linda smiled. Joey stood up and started to walk away. Then he turned around and looked at his mom.

"Mom, I really do love you." He bent over and gently kissed her on the forehead. "Gotta go. Father Jaeger's giving us a ride downtown. Goin' to the movies."

Staring at her coffee cup, Linda reached over and pulled her rosary from her purse. She clasped her hand around the wooden beads and squeezed. *Two men in my life, my son and a priest. Close to my heart but oh so far away.*

Late afternoon the next day, Joey stood alone on the corner of Huntington and Canal. Just two blocks from the downtown, the neighborhood was quiet and tranquil. A few homes, a couple of small brick apartments, the gas company, some workshops, and a small leather tannery checker-boarded a three-block area. Joey stood in front of the brick tannery building, which closed at 3:00 p.m., as it had for the past sixty years. He did not mind the ripe smells leaking from the doors, windows, and the vented roof. By 4:00 p.m., the light of afternoon began to fade. Joey stood unnoticed, alone, and waiting. He thought he would try a cigarette again. He felt excitement as he watched for the black car and the arrival of his friend.

A farmer pulling a wagon of pigs slowly passed. Joey turned toward the tannery. *Nobody'll see me here.* He coughed twice—a hard cough—as he tried to inhale the Lucky Strike. Turning to his right toward downtown, he detected the distinctive front end of the black Studebaker approaching the quiet street corner. Slowly, the car pulled to the side of Canal about a half block away. He recognized the figure inside, wearing his usual coat and hat—both just as black as the 1950 Studebaker Commander. Manufactured in South Bend, just north of Wabash, the car was different than the typical Fords and Chevys driven by Father Warren and Father Sullivan. Different was the perfect analogy for both the car and driver.

Joey took a last puff, coughed again, and then tossed the Lucky to the pavement. He twisted his shoe atop the half-smoked cigarette. Not noticing the puddle of slush at the edge of the street, he stepped into the center, completely submerging his right foot. "Damn!" he said without looking down or breaking stride. Joey knew how to remain calm and cool even though he was still privately gagging on the Lucky Strike.

Slowly, he crossed the street and walked directly toward the parked car. The car idled at a low *purr*. The priest's fingers tapped on the side of the metal door as he hung his arm out the open driver's side window.

He kept glancing at the side mirror, which faced in the direction of the downtown. *All's quiet.*

Looking straight ahead, Joey walked closer to the black Studebaker. The darkness inside was only broken by the white banded collar around the driver's neck. The figure reached across the seat to unlock the passenger's door handle. The tilt of the car at the side of the road allowed the door to open wide even before Joey approached the passenger's seat.

"Hello, Joey."

"Hello, Father. Right on time as usual."

"Have to be," Father Jaeger said as he gently shifted the car into first gear.

Pulling onto the pavement, the Studebaker seemed to automatically know the way out of town. Although this rendezvous had taken place several times during the past six months, an initial nervousness always permeated the atmosphere. Conversation was minimal. Both had a mutual intention and understanding. The routine was becoming more familiar.

"Does your mother know you're at the server's meeting?" he asked Joey.

"Sure. She always trusts me," Joey confidently reassured his friend.

Father Jaeger turned left onto Huntington Street, drove under the railroad viaduct, continued through Choke Town, turned right onto Highway 24, and then drove another three miles to Lincolnville Road. The Studebaker paced steadily at thirty-five to forty miles per hour. Joey purposely sat low, slouching a bit until his head rested on the top of the passenger's seat. He could feel his hat tipping low on his forehead.

The tight grip of both hands on the wheel reflected the driver's determination for safety and purpose of direction. Ahead, he could see the sign for Gravel Pit Road. Turning left, Father Jaeger headed directly to the old Parker Farm. During the summer of 1957, Max Parker had passed away at the age of eighty-three, ten years after his wife, Millie. Having no living children, the one-hundred-and-twenty-acre farm had been left to St. Thomas Moore. Father Jaeger was well aware that the Parkers had lost their only daughter, Gladys, at twenty-one years old. She had been found murdered over by the gravel pit back in 1942.

Father Jaeger never brought the tragedy up to Joey. *It's just an old farmhouse.* After Mr. Parker's death, his personal items had been boxed up and donated to the St. Vincent DePaul Society. The furniture was left to be sold at the estate sale, which was scheduled for late May. Father Jaeger was in charge of keeping an eye on the house and grounds. He made sure he checked the house every week, whether he needed to or not. Father Jaeger loathed the thought of the furnishings being sold, disturbing his private hideaway.

Joey could see the familiar mailbox and driveway ahead. Slowing down, Father Jaeger gently steered off the road, turned, and drove up the long lane to the house. The ground was patched with melting snow. The white clapboard house stared them both in the face. Closer and closer. Giant old maples surrounded the home. Tall cedars guarded the north side. Seclusion—completely uninhabited, remote seclusion. Perfect.

At an even pace, Father Jaeger turned and parked behind the house. Nobody would ever see. Nobody knew. Not a word. Both exited and vehicle and automatically walked onto the unlocked back porch. Father Jaeger pulled a flashlight out of his pocket and then opened the door into the kitchen. Joey began to feel his usual emotions of uneasiness, guilt, and even sin. Momentarily, he thought of his mother.

"A little cool in here still. I threw some coal in the stove this morning," the priest told Joey. "Maybe it needs another bucket now." Neighbors were not alarmed by the smoke exiting the uninhabited house, although their houses were few and far between. Everyone knew the parish took good care of the old place.

Before going upstairs, Father Jaeger threw some more coal in the stove. Then he put his arm around Joey. Immediately, they walked to the staircase. The sheets on all the furniture gave Joey an eerie feeling every time they arrived. But not Father Jaeger. He had another focus on his mind.

Everything was as usual, all according to plan. Father Jaeger checked the floor register. Already he could feel the heat on the rise. His own internal furnace was rising much faster. Needless talk had been abandoned. Joey followed Father Jaeger up the stairs and then right to the main bedroom on the west side. Simultaneously, both discarded their coats and hats on the upholstered chair in the corner of the room. Father Jaeger pulled the chain on the floor lamp. Just enough light hidden in the corner. First, as always, he removed his collar and then his shoes, shirt, and trousers. Joey sat on the straight chair next to the dresser, keeping the same pace—shoes, shirt, and corduroys. Apprehension and guilt still loomed in his mind.

Father Jaeger walked to the bed. He pulled down the top sheet. Joey stood at his side. There they stood together, side by side. Naturalness took hold. Both were moved by the spirit of the moment. Father Jaeger always moved first. Joey knew the routine as he pulled the switch on the lamp by the side of the bed. Father Jaeger put his arms around Joey. Together they lay back, entwined in their own secret world.

Afterward, they both just lay there. The barren cracked plaster ceiling was their only audience. Father Jaeger's rush and anticipation was long gone. The ecstasy had passed. Some guilt set in. Such a fleeting moment, all for the temporary feelings of physical pleasure. Now the letdown. Time to go back to reality. Father Jaeger knew they would return another day.

A half an hour or so passed. The priest sat up, got out of bed, and pulled the chain on the bed lamp. He dressed in a deliberate manner. Joey did the same. After he took the small Eveready flashlight from his coat pocket, they carefully descended the stairs. A chill began to filter through the house. Joey walked onto the porch and made straight for the car. He slouched. He was tired. Father Jaeger checked the stove, closed the back door, checked the lock, and walked to the car. He could barely see Joey slouched in the front seat.

The ride home was quiet. Joey's head rested back on the seat. He pulled his wool hat lower over his eyes as if seeking sleep. Thirty-five miles an hour back home to Wabash, and Father Jaeger was quiet as usual. Each time after, guilt played its role. Joey looked forward to being in his own home later that evening, in the solitude of his room and bed.

A half hour later, Joey walked into his house. Linda heard the back door slam closed.

"Hi, Mom," Joey said as he walked briskly through the kitchen.

"Hi, honey. I was worried about you."

"Ah, remember, I think I said I'd be at the altar boy's meeting after school."

"Must have been a long meeting," Linda said, inquiring about his whereabouts.

Joey tried to change the subject. "Mom, we all wanna go to the movies this weekend. *The Defiant One* is playing." He always tried to tell the truth, but sometimes a lie was just unavoidable.

"I'm sure that will be okay."

Joey's understanding of himself was becoming quite clear, all with the help of Father Jaeger. He was seriously beginning to think about becoming a priest, although he was confused about his mentor's ways.

CHAPTER 20

DEFENDING THE INNOCENT

Sheriff Thurow—February 13, 1958

SHERIFF Thurow was anticipating his talk with Father Sullivan. He greeted the priest in the front lobby of the police station.

"Glad we can finally talk this afternoon. Let's step into my office."

"Well, Sheriff, I want you to know I'm here to help the best I can."

"Here, have a seat," the sheriff said, pulling the straight chair in front of his desk out for the good priest. The sheriff, dressed in his uniform, clasped his hands across his chest. Leaning back, he said, "Tell me, tell me, Father."

"I've met with Bernard Bednar twice now. He likes the boys, yes, but not in a perverted way. Different? Yes. Perverted! No. Bernard has been there for twenty-plus years. He's different. Maybe just slow, not retarded. He's the kind who watches. Takes it all in. Actually, in one incident he confronted an older boy who took tremendous advantage of a thirteen-year-old. Bernard took things in his own hands, vigilante style."

"Agreed, but we can't condone that," the sheriff said.

"I agree, but we don't have much on anyone. Although, Bernard referred to Phillip Krueger. You know him?"

"Sure," Sheriff Thurow responded. "Phillip's involved all over town. Boy Scouts, YMCA, Lion's Club. He'd be the kind who would be watching out for anyone who was hurting the boys. Nah. He wouldn't take … nah, not Phillip. He wouldn't take advantage of the boys."

"I know him but not well," Father Sullivan said. "He's our scoutmaster.

Bernard knew of a boy named Eddie Small, who he says was taken advantage of by a guy he called Big Billy."

"Oh yes, I know that name. I received a letter a month or so ago from an Ed Small. Must be his father. I think he said he lives alone in an apartment over in Muncie. Says he has no car. Can't see his son. Eddie wrote letters to his dad. I meant to meet with Ed Small. I'll make sure that happens soon."

"Anyway, after Bernard took care of this Big Billy, Big Billy threatened to report Bernard to, well, report him to … to … I hate to tell you, Sheriff, but to Phillip Krueger," Father Sullivan said. "I have the feeling this Billy is friendly with Krueger. Just a gut instinct. Nothing for sure."

"So, if Bernard is correct and this Billy abused Eddie, could there be any connection with Phillip Krueger, like some kind of favoritism, or even cover-up? Is that what you are saying, Father?"

"No. I think Billy would tell Krueger to try to get Bernard in trouble. Pass the buck. Maybe that's Krueger's style, playing favorites. Sheriff, I don't know much for sure, but I do know there is some no good taking place out there, and it seems it might start from the top. Possibly with Krueger. I don't know anything about Clarence Wolfe or anyone else on his staff."

"That reminds me. Come to think of it, you should read the letter." The sheriff reached over, pulled some papers from his top desk drawer, and shuffled through them. "Here it is," he read it over and then passed it to the priest.

January 17, 1958

Sheriff:
My son has been at the Wabash Reform School for fourteen months. He writes of being terrified of the big boys and men who are doing bad things. He said bad sex things. I live in Muncie. I have no way to get to school. Eddie won't tell me who. He said he's scared and wants to leave. I live by myself. My wife is gone. Can you help me and Eddie? I have no telephone. Can you come see me? Need help.

Edward Small

P.S. I live at 516 Grant Street, Apartment 2

Father Sullivan shook his head.

"I received this letter ... What's the postmark? January 17? I saved it until I learned more about Bernard," the sheriff told Father Sullivan.

"I can assure you that Bernard is not the one who hurt Eddie. He protected Eddie from Big Billy," Father Sullivan said.

"I'm going to have to look deeper into this whole situation." Sheriff paused, rubbed his chin. "I know you are not on the force, Father, but as a priest, you can continue to be a benefit in my investigation."

"That you can count on," Father Sullivan said. "Sheriff, Bernard mentioned an Artie," Father Sullivan continued. "Bernard said Artie oversees unit 10. I think that's the third floor where all the really tough kids are. My instinct tells me Artie's not like Bernard. But it's possible both are concerned and protective of some of the boys and men, if there are men involved.

"Father, it's time to move more quickly. Can you stay with this case? Do you have the time?"

Father Sullivan looked at the sheriff. "I'm very concerned on a couple fronts about youth in our town. Sheriff, I'll make the time. The only way, however, is through Bernard. I have much in my own parish to handle, so I can't go directly to the reform school."

"I understand, Father. Just being my conduit to Bernard will be a big help." The sheriff glanced at some papers on his desk. "Here is what we will do. I'll go to Muncie next week. I have an address. Let me see. What is it? Oh yes, Edward Small, 516 Grant Street, apartment number 2. I can just see a two-room upstairs flat, old house, truck in the yard that doesn't run. The whole nine yards. Oh, these poor kids. Let's talk at the end of next week," the sheriff suggested.

"Will do. See you, Sheriff."

"Father, thank you. Thank you very much."

"Of course, Sheriff. We just have to help these boys." The concern in Father Sullivan's mind ran deep as he thought about those innocent and helpless boys. He knew he could learn more from Bernard.

The sheriff, for his part, was sleepless that night, thinking about how to keep this quiet.

CHAPTER 21

CONFESSION

Linda Singleton—February 15, 1958

ALMOST two months had passed since Linda's confession with Father Warren, much time to think about what she should do to overcome her longing for the man she loved. Linda decided it was time to go back to confession. This time it would be a confession with Father Sullivan, as she felt she had to talk. Be close. Her intentions were good.

As she knelt within the dark confines of the confessional, Linda waited. Her heart raced. Father Sullivan was near, oh so near. The confessional door slid open. She pressed her face closer to the black cloth. Father Sullivan did not know who was in the next confessional.

Linda began in her practiced whisper, "Bless me, Father, for I have sinned." She paused. She could faintly smell his Old Spice cologne.

"Yes," she heard from the other side.

"I have sinned, but I have been forgiven."

"Forgiven?" He didn't immediately understand.

"Yes, Father, I was forgiven months ago." Not wanting to blindside the good man, now that the ice had been broken, she said, "Father, this is Linda. Please hear me. Please listen, Michael. I mean, Father. Please?"

Holding his composure, the conflict between being a man and a man of the cloth presented itself in Father Sullivan's mind. His immediate reaction was a flash of their time together. "Yes, yes, Linda. This is fine. Of course I'm here. I'm here to help those who pursue forgiveness. Does your confessor know who you are?"

"No, Father, he does not. He does not know who you are either. I didn't mention a name." No reply came from the priest, though he was relieved. "Father, I told him that I was with a priest. He was not concerned about who the priest was. I mean who I was with."

"That does not matter. Your repentance and forgiveness is what matters to our Redeemer," he said, still talking in a priestly style. Father Sullivan wanted to say all the right words during this unusual confession. "Then why are you here, Linda, if you have been forgiven?"

"Well, Father, I am truly sorry. I want you to know that I am not only sorry to our Lord." She hesitated. "I want you to know that I am sorry for whatever effect I had on you."

Father Sullivan was not expecting her concern for how he was affected. "Linda, I too have confessed. You need to know that. I went to confession a few years ago, while on retreat."

"I assumed you too confessed, Father." Linda added, "Yes, I know. I'm sorry, oh so sorry, about your mother. I heard."

"Yes, I know. And thank you, Linda, for the nice letter you sent afterward."

"Father, I work hard every day proving my repentance and my will to be a better person. But, Michael, I must confess to you. Oh, I know I shouldn't say it."

"Go ahead, Linda. Just say it. Say whatever. The Lord understands," he said, though now talking more personally.

"Father, I still think about you. Every day. Always. It's so very difficult. It's like a huge cross. A huge cross I must carry. And I do. I do try so hard. But I still miss and long for you. I just have to say that. I need for you to know so I can keep going." *Say the right thing for me, Michael, to help me live with this burden, this hidden secret.*

Father Sullivan was taken aback. Touched. Almost shaken. A man who always had the right words, he just didn't know how to respond. Maybe she was expecting some words that could pull them together.

The silence gave them time. A few moments to think. Having gathered his thoughts—and being conscious of her emotions, feelings, and desires—on the other side of the cloth, he said, "I know, Linda. I know. I know, but—"

"Please, Michael, don't say it. I know we can't. I know you are a priest. I'm not here to ask you or tempt you. I just have to share my feelings. Let them out. I have to admit that I find comfort in knowing and hoping you understand." Linda braved the words. "I better go now. I ask for your forgiveness, Michael."

"You were already forgiven, Linda."

"Thank you."

"Linda, before you go … one more thing."

"Yes, Father?" Her heart leapt, wondering what he'd say.

"Linda, you are always welcome to return. Welcome to return to this confessional," he said in a slow, hushed whisper. "For this is a place not only for forgiveness. The confessional is a place for understanding."

"Thank you. Oh thank you, Michael." She felt the intensity of her emotions subside. She slowly stood up.

"Linda. Linda. I do think of you often. God bless … "

Before he could finish, he heard her say, "Thank you, Michael. I must go now." All he heard was the door closing.

Late that afternoon before supper, Father Sullivan visited the chapel. As a priest, he had confidence in his life. Committed to God, his Lord, and the church, he prayed for support to address the evolving problem within the reform school and his own grade school. Men preying on little boys were reprehensible in thought and deed. He prayed for the courage to address the problem head-on.

Lighting a third candle, Father Sullivan looked to the crucifix and then the statue of St. Michael. "My Dear Lord, I am still a man. I pray for Your guidance to do the right thing, to say the right words for her. And, dear Father, I pray to do the right thing for myself. Amen."

CHAPTER 22

THE TRUTH BE TOLD

Peter Goodnar—February 18, 1958, early evening

INSIDE their quiet white-frame family home, George and Audrey Goodnar were seated together in their living room, worrying about their son. Always a good boy, always a good student with lots of friends, Peter had never really caused problems or concern. Of average size and looks, he was an achiever with a desire to be good, grow up, and go to college. St. Thomas Moore's parish was a huge part of Peter's life as a sixth grader. His days had been formed with altar boy practice, baseball games in the neighborhood, and Boy Scout camping trips.

Now Peter remained in his room most of the time. His grades had fallen, and he had no desire for his normal routine, including his parents, friends, and parish activities. For over a month, his days and nights had been dominated by fear, shame, and the fires of hell. The three encounters inflicted upon him by the selfish, depraved, and sick mind of a priest had engulfed Peter's entire life.

Peter thought about Superman, the Lone Ranger, and Sky King ... and priests. They were all the good guys. Priests helped people, priests prayed and said Mass, and ... Peter's mind stopped. The enormity of another thought struck him. Priests turned bread and wine into the body and blood of Christ—Holy Communion. Peter could think no more. The glass world of his church was cracking. Father Jaeger, he thought, had thrown the huge stone. Little did Peter know that stones had been thrown for centuries.

Alone, by himself, Peter struggled for a friend. He knew he could never confide in his parents. He was too embarrassed and ashamed. Most of all, he did not want to disappoint them. No relatives, teachers, or friends could help. Peter remembered Father Sullivan's words. *You did not sin. You are safe with me. I want to help you.* Peter repeated the priest's words over and over again. *I want to help you.* Peter wanted to believe. He wanted to trust the priest, but he knew he had trusted another priest before.

Peter was aware he needed help. He tossed and turned night after night. He dreaded the images of Father Jaeger. He feared the confining darkness. Throwing his pillow to the other side of the bed, Peter felt the dampness of sweat absorbed into his sheets. Then he would see them—the wolf and fire, the man and hell. He knew the images both so well. Peter was scared. Fear of another encounter with Father Jaeger far exceeded any concern of asking for help.

Finally deciding that something had to be done, Peter planned his strategy carefully. At Saturday confession, he would be less noticeable than standing in line on a weekday during school hours.

Arriving through the side door of church that Saturday, Peter first went to St. Michael's Chapel. There he planned to practice. He observed the number of people in church, and then he noticed Father Warren walk down the far side aisle, approach the confessional, and quietly disappear behind the door of secrecy. A line had already formed on Father Sullivan's side. *Perfect,* Peter thought. His prayers had been answered. Father Jaeger was not hearing confessions today.

Peter walked from the chapel and down the aisle, unintentionally clinging to the wall as he approached his place in line. He did not recognize anybody in church, at least not on this side. Praying as he advanced to next in line, Peter saw Virgil Campbell's parents kneel down on Father Warren's side of the church. Peter turned away in the direction of the wall. He checked the name on the door to confirm Father Sullivan's presence. Peter felt a calmness, a confidence in what he was about to do. He was mature enough to have concluded that he had no other choice. The door opened, and an elderly woman exited. As she held the door for Peter, he said a quiet thank-you and walked into the dark sanctuary.

Alone. Peter waited anxiously for the familiar sound of the small sliding door to open. Hearing the sound briefly set off his internal alarm. *Take a deep breath.*

"Bless me, Father, for I have sinned. My last confession was about two weeks ago." *Another breath.* "Father, you said you would help me ... so I ... so I came back. Please, Father, will you help me? I have nobody else."

Father Sullivan knew immediately. *Thank you, God,* he said to himself. *He's returned.* "Yes, I will help you. You are safe with me."

Without the priest having to ask, the boy said, "Father, this is Peter. Peter Goodnar."

That's not who I expected, Father Sullivan thought immediately. "Yes, Peter. All is okay. I'm here to listen," he knew he could not show emotion, surprise, or any reaction. Just like his visits with Bernard. *Go at Peter's pace. Gain his confidence. Create the environment for Peter to feel free to say anything.*

"Father, what do I do? I am so scared, if he ... if he tries again."

"Peter, I know. I understand. Peter, that will never happen again. Never. Peter, I promise you. I am your friend. I will make sure this man will never come close to you again."

A feeling of relief overwhelmed Peter. Now he felt his own tears, tears of relief. "Oh, thank you, Father." He knew he would always remember those words. That moment. *I will help you. He'll never be with you again.*

"Peter, we need to talk more. You and I can meet together alone. We can talk about how I will help." A moment of quiet calm engulfed the boy's space. Father Sullivan sensed the moment. "Now, Peter, you know I need to ask you the name of this man."

"Yes, Father, I know. That's okay. I feel safe telling you."

Now the good priest knew he had gained Peter's confidence. Trust was in his grasp.

"Father, this is very hard. Hard to say his name. You have to believe me. It all happened. So bad. So awful. I can't forget. I think about it all the time."

"I know, Peter. I understand." *Let him talk. Don't ask for the name.*

"Father, can I ask a question? There's something I don't understand."

"Go ahead, Peter."

"Father, aren't all priests good? Priests are like Jesus."

Preparing himself, Father Sullivan waited for Peter to utter the name. Like a lightning bolt, he knew immediately. He knew before Peter could even say it. *Don't react,* he told himself, as he knew Peter thought this is going to shock him.

"Father, I never knew. I never knew a priest could … Father Jaeger. It's Father Jaeger," Peter blurted out the name, thinking Father Sullivan might not believe him.

"Peter, it hurts me to hear that man did this to you. I hurt for you. I hurt for him. Peter, if what you have said is exactly true, then this man is the sinner, not you. Peter, please hear me. Just tell me one more time, Father Jaeger sexually touched you?"

"Oh yes, Father. Much more than touch. Many times. Awful things."

"I do believe you. I know you are telling the truth. I will help, and I will protect you."

Peter just listened.

"Now, all that you have said stays within this confessional. I will not approach this man yet. I will not disclose it to our good pastor, Father Warren. I will not call your parents. What we must first do is talk, you and I."

Peter continued to listen.

"Peter, can you come to my office in the rectory tomorrow after school?"

"Yes, Father, I can. I sure will," Peter said with relief.

"This is good. You are being brave and doing the right thing," the priest said, trying to reassure Peter.

"I don't want to hurt Father Jaeger. I just want him to go away. Leave me alone forever," Peter pleaded.

"Now, Peter, you have not sinned, but I would like for you to pray. Pray to God for strength, as you will need God's help."

"Yes, Father. I will. I really will. Should I just come to the front door of the rectory?"

"Peter, it may be easier for you if I just meet you in the chapel. Then we can walk over to the rectory. We will just talk about all this. We're going to make things better. You and me."

"Thank you, Father," Peter said as he felt continuing relief.

"Go in peace, my son. The Lord loves you and is with you." With that, Father Sullivan slid the small door of the confessional closed. He paused. Reflected. He thought immediately about Peter's confession. It was a moment he would never forget.

That evening, Father Sullivan prayed. Little did he know of the journey ahead.

PART II

CONFRONTATION
AND EXPOSURE

Chapter 23

True Identity

Phillip Krueger—February 18, 1958

PHILLIP Krueger had confidence in his assistant, as he had schooled him well. "Mr. Sizemore, I want you to bring these three boys to my office tomorrow afternoon at five o'clock. You know, the ones you recommended. The ones who've been causing all the ruckus."

Later that evening, after the scout troop meeting, Krueger drove his truck slowly toward Pike Street. Then he turned onto King Street. Glancing at both sides of the street, he found nobody walking home. He had hoped to see Dan or Dennis. Slowly, he turned right on Columbus. Pausing at the end of the street, he detected a dim light leaking from behind the torn shade of the rundown house at the end of Chestnut. *Wonder if that pervert Bernard is home.*

Eventually Phillip Krueger returned to his own house alone. He had hoped for some company that evening. He wanted to be with somebody new. Just introduce them to his place. After turning the lights off in the front room, he retired to his bedroom. He undressed, sat in the chair, and thought of the box below the bed. Standing up straight and erect, he slowly walked into the bathroom. Looking at himself, not ready to shower, he returned to his bedside, knelt, and slid the box from underneath the bedframe.

Placing the box and then the lid on the bed, he removed some pictures and some magazines. The boys' photos and the pictures in the magazines looked very similar to some of the boys in the scout troop. Others looked like ones down at the Y. Three of them had a strong similarities to the boys in the school. He placed the lid back on the box, turned out the light, and thought about his meeting at school tomorrow. Phillip Krueger's lustful mind knew no boundaries.

As planned the next day, Charlie Sizemore approached Phillip Krueger. "Excuse me, sir. Shall I go get the boys now?"

"Yes, Charlie. It's almost five o'clock. Have you told them they are coming to my office?"

"Yes, told them this morning. I gave them the word, kinda shook 'em up a little."

"Ah, that's good, Charlie. They need a little bout of fear before ... "

"I'll go get them now for you, Mr. Krueger." Charlie Sizemore was a loyal assistant.

Sam Elmore, Jerry Tipton, and Eddie Small did not know each other well. Phillip Krueger knew all three. Privy to their personal records, he knew their backgrounds. He knew all of the boys in the school, at least by their faces. A few he knew much better than others.

Carefully selected, Sam, Jerry, and Eddie had much in common. Sam and Jerry were both orphans. Eddie's parents were both alcoholics, and his mother had deserted the family. School records did not indicate his father's whereabouts. His mother had five years yet to serve in the Indiana State Women's Penitentiary. None of the three boys were leaders on the floor. Although their backgrounds were records of delinquency, petty thefts, fights, and some sexual problems—mainly with girls—all three showed psychological streaks of submissive dysfunctional behavior.

"Oh, Charlie, change of plans. Take them down to the mechanical storage room," Krueger ordered. "Might put a little more scare into them."

"Yes, sir. I'll be there in fifteen minutes. All three, sir?"

"Yes, all three." Phillip Krueger felt in control. He knew the storage room, as he had used the quiet space before. The place was perfect, quiet and secluded as long as it was after the first shift. The janitor left at 3:00 p.m., and the room would not be used until the next day. Shelves lined the walls. Two rows dissected the center of the room. Cleaning supplies, tools, and paint were in ample supply. A table, a couple of chairs, and a long bench the maintenance crew used stood against the back wall. From the entrance, a view of the back wall was blocked.

At precisely 5:05 p.m., Phillip Krueger turned off his light, placed some papers in his briefcase, and put on his knee-length winter coat. Hat in hand, he exited the front door.

"Miss Gardner," he said. "Have a pleasant evening," Krueger then said as he passed Mr. Wolfe's office door and headed toward the front door.

"You too, Mr. Krueger."

I will, he thought. Walking around the side of the building, he went directly to his pickup. After opening the door, he threw his case on the seat and then drove around the side of the school, stopped, and parked by the back entrance.

Krueger skipped up the steps, entered through the metal door, and went down the back stairs. He passed the locker room.

"Oh, Bernard, how are you doing?" he asked as he stepped aside.

Bernard ascended the steps, not saying a word to Krueger. Krueger proceeded down the hall. Bernard continued up the stairs, heading for home. *Strange fellow, that Bernard,* Krueger thought.

Slowing his pace, Phil Krueger approached the storage room. There was no light on at the end of the hall. Charlie Sizemore stood outside the storage room door.

"They're in the back as you asked," Sizemore said, wanting to acknowledge his importance.

"Lock the door, Charlie, and follow me. I want them to know you're here. After we talk, you come back here, leave, and wait at the stairs. Make sure you lock the door from the outside." Krueger knew he could unlock the deadbolt from the inside.

"You know you can trust me, Mr. Krueger."

Krueger turned and walked into the storage room. Sizemore followed, locking the door behind him. The two of them headed to the back of the room. Sizemore followed Krueger as instructed. Their conversation and actions were unknown to the boys, who could only hear muffled words from beyond the packed shelves. Sam and Jerry paced around the small space. Eddie sat on the bench. Then they heard the footsteps.

"They're both coming," Jerry said with alarm on his face.

"Oh shit! Wonder what he wants." Sam said.

All three waited the approaching storm.

CHAPTER 24

THE ABSENT PARENT

Sheriff Thurow—February 19, 1958

DRIVING his unmarked car—a '57 Ford, fins and all—Sheriff Thurow saw the melting snow and thought of the spring to come. Ahead he noted the sign that read Muncie City Limits, Population 41,602. He knew Muncie well, mainly because his family had lived there for years. The sheriff drove to Muncie to visit family every other month or so. His destination was locked in his mind. Driving through town, he headed directly for Second Street, turned right, and then drove three blocks to Grant. He stopped right at a dilapidated two-story house on the left.

There it is, apartment 2, second level. He parked his car directly in front on the curbless street. Looking over the place, he thought the refrigerator on the front porch should be illegal. The small two-story was badly in need of paint. A rusted Ford pickup truck rested in its side yard. The tilt indicated flat tires on the right. The house next door was lined with three garbage cans and a broken tricycle. Two cars were in the side drive of the neighbor's house. Both looked old—a '43 Plymouth and a '41 Chevy. *No wonder Eddie is in reform school*, he thought as he profiled the neighborhood.

The side stairs to apartment 2 looked old but moderately safe—if the treads held. Carefully, he climbed to the less-than-sturdy platform at the side door. The sheriff knocked, but there was no answer. He knocked again and waited. Then two eyes, a scruffy face, and a mouth with two missing teeth appeared from behind one of the unbroken panes as the shade was pulled aside. The door opened, a chain pulled tight.

"What do ya want? Not buying anything."

Sheriff Thurow immediately flipped a leather wallet open, exposing his badge. The door closed, and the sheriff heard the chain drop immediately.

"Have some time? I'd like to have a few words about Eddie. You know, your son?"

"Sure, I know," the man said with apparent apprehension.

The sheriff slowly stepped through the door and entered the kitchen. He scanned the room. "I received your letter. Mr. Small, I presume?"

"Yeah. I mean yes, sir."

"I stopped by today to talk to you about your son."

"Why? Is he in more trouble?" Mr. Small asked with a furrowed brow.

"No, he's not in trouble. I'm here to help your Eddie." Having put Mr. Small at ease, the sheriff asked, "Can you tell me what Eddie is like? Why is he in the reform school?"

With that, Eddie's dad opened up and talked continually for twenty minutes. He told the sheriff how he was concerned about Eddie's safety. He first explained that Eddie did not have a mother; she had run away with a no-good drunk before Eddie was one.

"She was a drunk. No good. Just no good. Didn't have a job," Mr. Small said. "Eddie was in and out of trouble all through grade school. For a couple years, he lived in foster homes. Eventually Eddie ended up in the Wabash Reform School. Just look around this place. Can you imagine my boy living here? It's all my fault. My poor Eddie," he said despondently, sitting down in an old threadbare upholstered chair. "Have a seat there, Sheriff," he said pointing to an equally worn easy chair.

The sheriff noticed the disarray of the apartment, especially the empty wine bottles on the kitchen table, a few on the counter, and one half-empty bottle next to Mr. Small's chair. The room smelled of stale smoke. The ashtray on the table next to the chair was filled with a pile of Chesterfield cigarette butts. No job and no car—the sheriff could see why Ed Small did not get the chance to see Eddie. All Mr. Small wanted from the sheriff was some help for his son.

"Sheriff, you see, I know what they're doing to him. Eddie's not a bad kid. He's always needed someone. I wasn't there. Now they are using him. You know, sexual things. Bigger boys, they use him all the time. I just know it. I remember when I was a kid."

"I understand, Mr. Small. That's why I'm here. I do want to help your Eddie."

"That's good. Thank you. Guess I better tell you, sir."

"Tell me what?" Sheriff Thurow asked, looking puzzled.

"Well, about a couple months ago, I got this letter from Eddie. Actually, I don't know how he got it mailed. They read the letters, you know. I mean those staff people. They really guard that place."

"Yes, I am aware." *Well, I'm learning*, the sheriff thought.

"Anyway, I got this letter. Eddie tells me all these bad things are happening to him. There's this Billy guy and his buddies. Lord knows how many more. Tough kids. They're doing it to my Eddie. Then he goes on and tells me of these two guys who are trying to help him. You know, Sheriff, kind of protect him."

"Did he give their names?"

"Let me see. I can't remember."

Mr. Small stopped, sat up in his chair with his hands on his knees. He pushed himself to stand and then walked over to a cheap-looking veneer chest of drawers. It stood just to the left of the only window visible in the apartment—a double window with some cracked panes, like the front door. Opening the top drawer, Mr. Small pulled out what looked like mailing envelopes. He walked back to his chair, sat down, and sorted through the letters. Sheriff Thurow noticed the cancelled four-cent stamp. The disheveled man pulled the letter out and scanned the sheet. "Yes, yes, here's their names. Bernard and Artie. 'They help me sometimes,'" he read from the letter.

Sheriff Thurow immediately thought about what else might be in the letter.

"But here's what scares me the most, Sheriff."

"What's that?"

"Eddie says there is a man who is worse than the boys. Worse than the big boys."

"Which man?" Sheriff Thurow asked without hesitation.

"Well, yes. He even writes one of their names."

"Here, can I see that letter?" the sheriff asked.

"Sure. Take a look. It's all right here," Ed Small said, pointing with his dirty, cracked index fingernail.

Sheriff Thurow looked at the letter. It was as if John Hancock himself had signed it. The sheriff was jolted back in his chair as he read Eddie's printed letter. There was the correctly spelled and perfectly clear name of *Phillip Krueger*. Sheriff Thurow's suspicions immediately aroused his questions. *Who let this letter pass their scrutiny?*

Mr. Small watched and noticed the sheriff's reaction. "Does that help you, Sheriff? Now do you believe me?" he asked as if maybe he'd done the right thing.

"Well, Mr. Small, I'm very thankful you saved this particular letter."

"Does that mean you can help my Eddie?" Ed Small asked. His hopeful eyes beseeched at the sheriff.

Sheriff Thurow looked directly into the neglected man's storied face. "Mr. Small, you can be assured I'll do everything I can for your Eddie. May I have this letter?"

"If that helps Eddie, you sure can, sir."

"These letters are going to help more than just Eddie," the sheriff assured Mr. Small.

The disheveled man smiled, a smile that spread wide across his face, exposing his yellowed gapped teeth. He was a slight man, rather bent from years of wear. He looked up at the sheriff. "Thank you for helping my Eddie. Thank you for coming over to this ... this ol' ramshackle place. Sorry about that," he said apologetically.

Sheriff Thurow put his hand on the man's shoulder. Looking down at Ed Small, he said, "I will help Eddie. He deserves as much, considering your situation, Mr. Small." The sheriff was deeply touched as he looked into the Mr. Small's eyes. He thought this could provide some hope, which Eddie's father hadn't felt in a long, long time.

Ed Small opened the door and reached out his hand. He returned the sheriff's firm grip with the clasp of both of his hands. Neither man said a word. Sheriff Thurow tightened his lips, nodded, and descended the shaky stairs. When he looked back up, Ed Small's face was framed in the broken windowpane. He noticed the remnants of a small smile. Sheriff Thurow was full of empathy. Ed Small's only concern was his son. Driving back to Wabash, the sheriff thought over his plan to help and knew what he had to do.

CHAPTER 25

SCARED TO DEATH

Phillip Krueger—February 19, 1958

THE storage room felt like a jail cell to the three waiting boys. "You boys know why you're here," Krueger said sternly. "Sit on the bench, all three of you."

He nodded to Sizemore, and the assistant departed back toward the front of the storage room, out of sight.

"Discipline. Wabash Reform School is first built on discipline." Krueger could feel the rushing excitement of his authority and position. "I have had reports. Reports on all three of you. Your lack of respect, talking back to the staff, stealing from your fellow students. Or should I say your actions toward your fellow inmates? Neglecting duties, up after hours—this list goes on. What do you have to say for yourselves?"

"Well, sir, we maybe sometimes, but—"

"But hell. No excuses. Let me ask, do you boys know each other?"

Sitting on the bench, looking up at Krueger, Eddie said, "Well, not very much. I see them around sometimes." The other two nodded in agreement.

"Well, boys, you are here to be punished for your deeds."

"Punished? Wha … wha … what, what do you mean?" Eddie asked with a slight stutter.

"You are all being punished, I said. You know what for. I just explained." The three watched as Krueger took off his belt. "Discipline is a must. Take off your shirts."

"You're not going to lash us!" Eddie yelled.

"I'm out of here," Sam said.

"Mr. Sizemore! Now, boys, there are two of us. Mr. Sizemore is at the door. You'll accept this punishment, or your lives within this institution will be a living hell. Let's get this over with now. It will be over, and then you'll be straight." Krueger could feel their submission.

Slowly, they took off their shirts.

"Now your pants. Your backsides will take the brunt. Turn around and face the wall. All three of you. I said your pants. That means both pants."

"What the hell? Our pants?" Sam blurted out. "I'm not taking off my pants. Not me!"

"Shut up and do as I say," Krueger said with force.

Eddie and Jerry immediately obeyed. Standing in blind confusion, they stood frozen.

"Your pants, Sam. Take 'em off," Krueger ordered Sam.

"To hell with you. No way. You're queer." Sam darted toward the front door. Krueger calmly followed with his belt in hand. Sam leaped toward the door and grabbed the handle. It was locked. "Oh shit!" Turning away from the locked door, he stared into the demented eyes of the man behind him.

Krueger wrapped his belt once around his hand and snapped the floor with it. "I'll tell you just one time. One time or else."

Sam knew he was trapped. Trying to catch his breath, he walked around Krueger to the back of the room.

"You ever cross me again and I'll beat the life out of you."

Returning to the back of the room, Sam saw the terror in Eddie and Jerry's eyes. Slowly, Sam took his pants off and stood with his hands cupped in front of him.

"As I said, stand there. Don't turn around."

Waiting in terror, the boys stood, anticipating the lash of the belt. Nothing, not yet. Silence. Moments passed. Eddie heard what he thought sounded like the buckle of the belt hitting the floor. Then the muffled sound of cloth followed. *The belt's coming soon.* Still no pain. The boys shivered as they stood naked, unprotected from the cool air. Krueger's breathing grew louder—heavy, deep breaths. Groans followed. Still no belt.

Eddie looked at Sam. "Here comes the belt," he whispered.

"Stay there. Don't look around," Krueger said, trying to catch his breath. Sam heard a sigh.

Seconds passed like minutes. Soon the boys could hear the muffled movement of clothing. Without meaning to look, Eddie turned slightly and caught a glimpse of Krueger pulling up his pants with his back to them. Krueger then turned.

"Turn around, I said!" Krueger screamed.

The three boys froze in terror.

A minute later, Krueger's voice called from the entrance door, "Put your clothes back on."

Sam peeked around. Krueger was gone. Eddie moved first. Sam and Jerry followed suit.

"Come up here now," Krueger commanded from the front of the room.

Buttoning up, the three boys slowly walked toward the front door between the storage aisles of maintenance supplies, tools, and the like. Sam moved first. Eddie and Jerry followed. Sizemore and Krueger awaited their arrival.

Now Krueger spoke in a stern voice with venom in his eyes. "You see, boys—discipline. The belt was not necessary. You won't ever cross me again. This was a lesson. You understand what could have been, especially you, Sam. You hear me?"

"Yes. Yes, sir," Sam said, choking on his words as he bent over gagging.

"Yes, sir," Eddie said with tears of fright in his eyes.

"Yes, we do. This will not be necessary again," Jerry said.

"We've all learned our lesson," Eddie said, trying to reassure Krueger while Sizemore looked on. "Thank you. Thank you, sir, for not … "

"Quiet!" Krueger cut Eddie off. "That's good. Real good. One more thing. Not one word to anyone, not a soul, about your visit here. This was for your own good. Is that clear? You hear me?" Krueger said with convincing authority. Three "yes, sirs" were delivered in thankful unison. "Not a word. Mr. Sizemore, take these boys back to their rooms."

"Will do. Right away. Come on, boys."

As Sizemore unlocked the door, the boys started to exit.

"Stop!" Stepping into the hall, Krueger snarled, "Boys, remember, discipline and not a word."

Simultaneously, still shaking, Eddie, Sam, and Jerry followed Sizemore out of the room, down the hall, and toward the stairs. Sam was first. Trying to banish the thought of what had just happened, he focused on the worn heels of Sizemore's shoes leading the way up the stairs.

Krueger followed and exited through the back door. Moments later, driving away in his pickup, Phillip Krueger felt content, relieved, and full of authority. Nobody was around. *I don't think I'll take a ride this evening. Just not necessary*, he thought with a satisfied smile as he drove on.

CHAPTER 26

CHARACTERS IN CONFLICT

Father Jaeger—February 20, 1958

DURING supper hour, Father Jaeger felt uneasy. He sensed that Father Sullivan, although quiet, wanted to say something to him or to Father Warren. At one point, he felt uncomfortable, feeling the penetrating gaze of his fellow priest.

Father Sullivan said little. He fought the urge to put Peter Goodnar's name on the table, right there in front of Father Warren and Father Jaeger. Remembering the promise he had given to Peter, Father Sullivan refrained.

After supper, Father Jaeger excused himself. "I have some things to get done," he said, looking directly at Father Warren. "Good evening."

Things to do, Father Sullivan thought. *Like what? Do you think about Peter? Have you no shame?*

Father Jaeger fought the urge to go to the privacy of his own room. He walked past the stairs that led to his quarters, down the hall, out the side door, and down the sidewalk to the front of the church. As he climbed the front steps and continued through the vestibule, the priest was in darkness except for one ceiling fixture that threw just enough light to shadow the overhanging choir loft. The heels of his shoes on the terrazzo floor were the only sounds. *Echoes.*

Respectfully, Father Jaeger genuflected completely and then made his way to St. Michael's side chapel, where he knelt and bowed his head in his hands. He could feel his own perspiration. He knelt and prayed.

144

Forgive me, Father, he repeated to himself. *I have lost all control. Help me*. Remorse and guilt were his only companions.

Linda Singleton—February 21, 1958

Linda's life was conflicted. She continued to long for Father Sullivan and ponder over the uncertainty about the direction of Joey's life. Going to confession and being close to Father Sullivan in that quiet dark place had temporarily relieved the desire to be close. However, now she was in limbo, realizing there could be no finality unless she walked away totally. *The mind is hard to control,* she thought.

Joey continued to mention Father Jaeger's name. Linda knew the priest was having an impact on Joey's life. Having no father of his own, Linda wondered if Joey was in search of a father figure in the priest even though he had denied it. In her heart, Linda knew there was more. She was beginning to conclude that Joey did want to become a priest. *Still,* she thought, *there is something else about Joey and his friendship with Father Jaeger.*

Father Jaeger—February 22, 1958

Walking into church that Saturday morning, Joey Singleton greeted Father Jaeger. "Good morning, Father," Joey said.

"Oh hi, Joey. Glad you're here. Almost time for Mass," Father Jaeger said with a smile on his face.

Joey enjoyed being around the sacristy. He took pride in caring for the cassocks and surpluses, checking the wine, assisting the priests, and helping out with whatever Father Jaeger needed. He enjoyed his role as a high server. Joey simply enjoyed everything about the Mass and the priest himself.

"I'm here to help. Whatever you need, Father."

"Okay, Joey. After Mass, why don't you first check the supply of wine in the basement? Oh yes, make sure that all the surpluses are cleaned and starched for next week. Then if you have a few minutes, I have something I want to show you. It's up in my room."

"Sure, I'll remember." Everything was now ready for Mass.

Joey, along with Martin Davis, waited for the priest to give the signal.

Martin was the only Negro at St. Thomas Moore. He was quiet, well-mannered, and liked by everyone. But he knew his place among all the other kids.

"Ready, boys."

Joey rang the bell, alerting those waiting in the pews that Mass was now beginning. Father Jaeger followed the two servers into the sanctuary. In unison, they genuflected.

Father Jaeger began, "*In Nomine Patris, et Filii, et Spiritus Sancti. Amen.*"

Joey and Martin responded, "*Ad deum qui laetificat juventictem meam.*"

During Mass, Joey was not totally focused on serving. He had other things on his mind.

Father Jaeger said in closing, "*Ite Missa est.*"

Joey enthusiastically responded, "*Des gratias.*"

After Mass, Joey was prompt, remembering Father Jaeger's request. He and Martin extinguished the candles, put away the wine, and finished their post Mass ritual. Joey was anxious to see Father Jaeger, but Martin was already out the door to his piano lesson.

When he was finally finished, he made his way to Father Jaeger's quarters.

"Come in, come in. Hi, Joey."

"Everything is all taken care of, Father. Before I forget, we do have enough wine. Six cases in the basement."

"Good, good. You and I should take care of a few other things. Did anyone see you come up?"

"No, Father. I always check first."

Father Jaeger made sure the lock on the door was secure. Joey had already proceeded to the bedroom, pulling his shirt off while he walked into the room. Father Jaeger followed. He locked the second door. Joey stood waiting, already by the bed. Father Jaeger pulled the shade, turned, and faced Joey. Saturdays were quiet days around the church and rectory.

An hour later, Joey glanced at the clock. "Oh my gosh, it's ten thirty, Father. Better go. Mom always has a list of chores on Saturdays."

"Sure, I know. You shouldn't be late. Be careful going downstairs. You know, before you step into the hall."

"Don't worry, Father. I've got it handled," Joey replied with confidence. He was advanced beyond his thirteen years in many aspects of life.

"Before you go, there's one thing I want you to do. Make sure you drop the word again to Rusty Nader. Just give him a little nudge. You know, make sure he doesn't decide to say something to his parents or anyone about, well ... you know what I mean, Joey."

"Father, these kids know you and I are just friends. That's all they think. They won't cross me. I make sure they keep their mouths shut. I can handle these guys, Father. Trust me. They like you, Father," Joey said in an attempt to reassure Father Jaeger. "Nothing to worry about."

Father Jaeger looked up at Joey from where he still reclined on the bed. "You are a good friend, Joey. You know I care for you very much."

"Yes, Father. Yes, I do know."

Father Jaeger knew that in his own special way, he loved these boys. Joey, however, was different. Special.

Father Sullivan—February 24, 1958

Father Sullivan accepted the inevitable. The meeting with Peter would require a response, first from Father Warren and then from Father Jaeger.

Father Sullivan was friends with Sister Mary Michael, Peter's sixth grade teacher. A visit with the sister would be a good start. Father Sullivan was confident in the good sister. She knew her students well and could give him insight into Peter and how well he was doing in her class. Immediately after school on Monday, shortly before his meeting with Peter, Father Sullivan walked upstairs to the sixth-grade classroom.

"Don't you ever stop?" he asked the kind sister as he walked into the room, noticing her behind the desk, grading papers.

"Why hello, Father Sullivan. Come right in. It's always good to see you."

"Thank you, Sister," he said, glancing at the chalk-covered blackboards that bordered her classroom. He noticed several diagramed sentences—remnants of the day. He smiled when he read, *I must not talk in class*, written twenty-five times and signed by Fred. Sister Mary Michael stood up behind her desk. Father Sullivan sat in the front student desk. *Tight squeeze.* "Sister, I would like your help."

Sliding into the wooden desk across the aisle from Father Sullivan, she responded, "Sure, Father, of course. What is it? Ask anything."

Sister Mary Michael was the most beloved and respected nun in the school. Loved by all, she displayed an unending passion for her religion, her fellow sisters, and her students. All of the sisters looked up to her. Priests and parents always felt free to come to her for advice and guidance. Somewhere in her middle forties, the sister was wise beyond her years.

Father Sullivan began, "Sister, it's about Peter Goodnar."

"What about him, Father? He's such a fine boy."

"Well, Sister, this is very confidential, just between you and me," he said, looking around the room.

"Assume we are in the confessional, Father. Not a word."

"Peter has come to me with … let's call it a situation. I want to help him so much. I'm going to be there for him. However, I'd like to know a little more about him. What's he like in class? How does he relate to other students? How does he relate to adults?"

"Well, Father, to begin with, Peter is a fine student. He seems to get along with everyone. He always does his work and participates in class. Oh, every so often he might be a little extra talkative or inattentive, but that's normal for eleven-year-olds. Why do you ask, Father? Is he in some kind of trouble?"

"No, Sister, he hasn't done anything wrong. Let me ask you this: how does he get along with the boys?"

"I'd say just fair to that. He's friends with Tom Grites and David Mayoras. They're more popular, leader types. As I said, he gets along with everyone. I like Peter. I like having him in class." Then the sister paused. "You know, Father, come to think of it," she said, shaking her head. "Lately he has seemed somewhat not his usual self. More quiet, subdued. Like something is bothering him. Oh yes, Father, one other thing. Peter's a Boy Scout and an altar boy. He's told me that he loves being an altar boy. I think Peter has a deep faith."

"This really helps, Sister, especially when you said he hasn't been himself lately. That makes sense to me."

As Father Sullivan eased out of the desk and walked toward the door,

Sister Mary Michael said, "Father, if I can do anything, anything for you and Peter in any way, please let me know."

"I might just have to take you up on that, Sister. We'll probably talk later. I appreciate your time. Thank you, Sister." Father Sullivan left the room. Sister Mary Michael went back to her papers. "Oh, one other thing," Father Sullivan said, peeking back into the room. "I think you are really a fine sister and a shining example to all your students."

The nun smiled. "Why, thank you, Father Sullivan." Resting her chin in her hand, Sister Mary Michael gazed out the window and wondered what on Earth that had been all about.

Peter Goodnar—February 24, 1958

Father Sullivan knew Peter would be waiting in the church. As he entered from the back vestibule after his meeting with Sister Mary Michael, he could see Peter kneeling in the front pew with his head down. The church was quiet with the exception of Mr. Pantazon putting a finishing coat of varnish on the door to St. Michael's chapel.

"Peter, Peter," Father Sullivan whispered in a low tone, leaning over with both hands braced on the end of the pew.

Peter looked up, immediately grabbed his school bag, and followed Father Sullivan to the rectory. He abruptly turned his head away as they passed the stairs that lead to where he had originally met with Father Jaeger.

Peter followed Father Sullivan into his study at the far end of the middle hall. "Nice room, Father. I like your view out the window. I can see the convent, park, and even President Lincoln's statue in front of the courthouse."

"Thanks, Peter. Yes, our church is in a nice neighborhood. Why don't you sit down? Make yourself at home."

A lamp and a few books sat on Father's Sullivan's desk. Peter noticed a Bible, *Gone with the Wind*, and *Catcher in the Rye*. "Which books do you read?"

"All of them, Peter. I love to read."

He reads more than the Bible, Peter thought. "Me, too," he replied. "I just finished *Huckleberry Finn*."

"I've read *Huckleberry* twice. I loved it so much. That's been at least thirty-some years ago, when I was about your age." Father Sullivan turned his chair so it was more in direct line with Peter. Both were now comfortable. The priest looked compassionately at Peter. "Peter, we both know why we are here. I'm here to help and protect you. You have my solemn word. You can always trust me," Father Sullivan said, trying to instill confidence in Peter.

"I know. I trust you, Father. I really do," Peter said nervously.

"Now, Peter, I need to know when and what happened that afternoon when you were alone with Father Jaeger. Of great importance, Peter, I want to know what he actually said to you."

"Okay, Father, remember that day you came into the study? The night of confirmation practice?" Peter squirmed in his chair.

Father Sullivan nodded. "Yes, I do. Vividly."

"Well, Father Jaeger sat close to me on the sofa. My dad doesn't even sit that close. I felt awkward and strange, but I didn't think at the time that he'd, well, that he'd do anything. Father, I've heard guys call guys queer, but I didn't know exactly what it meant. Then you came in, and now as I think back, I'm sure glad you did. Father Jaeger gave me his *Saint Joseph's Daily Missal* from when he was my age. Said he wanted me to read it but that I had to bring it back. I just took it and was glad to get out of there."

"Well, you did the right thing, Peter."

"I know, but I realized when I got home that he said to bring the missal back real soon. When I came back like he told me to, that's when it happened." Peter felt very anxious. He could feel his heart beating fast. "Father, it was so terrible. When I returned, he wasn't ready, so he said to come on upstairs. Father, I didn't know. So I went up, although I felt uneasy. He said others came up for prayer sessions. And then he showed me his ... " Tears welled in Peter's eyes. "He showed me his bedroom. I saw him take off his shirt. Then he locked the door, took my clothes off, and then we were on the bed. Father, I can't. I can't say it. I prayed. And then I felt his arms go around me. No, no, that's it. I can't say any more. It was awful. It hurt so much."

Father Sullivan was sickened by Peter's words. "Okay, Peter, that's enough. No more."

Peter pulled a handkerchief from his pocket. "I'm sorry, Father. I'm so sorry."

As the priest tried to calm Peter, he could feel his own anger and disgust raging inside. "Peter, just sit here. I'm going to the kitchen to get us a couple soda pops."

"Oh, that would be great, Father."

Father Sullivan left the room. He wanted to give Peter time on his own to gather himself. Even more he wanted to cool down his rage. A few moments later when Father Sullivan returned, Peter had calmed down. The father handed Peter a cold 7-Up.

"Thank you, Father."

"You okay?"

"I'm okay, Father. It's over. Do I have to talk any more about him?"

"No, that's enough. Not today."

"Father, did I sin? You know, a mortal sin?"

"No, Peter. He's the sinner."

"Yes, Father, but … but I don't understand. He's a priest."

Father Sullivan could read the disappointment in Peter's eyes. "Peter, I don't understand either." He was at a loss for words to explain. Then he said, "Father Jaeger was not acting as a priest or a man of God. He was merely acting as a man, a very bad man."

Father Sullivan went on to tell Peter that he was going to take this issue to Father Warren. Although Peter was first concerned that Father Jaeger might come back at him, Father Sullivan assured Peter he would not let that happen. "Peter, you are safe. Remember, you can always come to me. Anytime."

Peter left the rectory feeling like a huge burden had been lifted from his mind and his heart. In the following weeks, he felt better as long as he could keep that priest out of his mind.

Father Sullivan was sleepless that evening. He spent a long time kneeling at the side of his bed. *How could he? How could he do this to that young boy?* He prayed to overcome the rage he held inside.

The next morning, Father Sullivan anticipated having to face Father Jaeger. He knew Father Warren would be there. *Please, God, help me say the right thing.*

CHAPTER 27

SECRET MEETING

Phillip Krueger—March 6, 1958

THE windshield wipers on his pickup truck swept back and forth, pushing aside the light misty rain. Phillip Krueger drove past the Honeywell Center and then turned left on Market Street. Two blocks ahead, he could see the neon sign and the dark red Dye's Tavern sign. At 9:30 p.m. there were only a few cars parked in front. He pulled up and parked on the opposite side of the street.

At this hour, he knew the regular patrons, mainly from the Strawboard Box Factory, would have long since left after a few beers before supper. Most of the customers were from the south side of Wabash. The downtowners usually hung out at the Green Hat or the Club Royal in the Indiana Hotel. Dye's was off the beaten path. Phillip Krueger liked Dye's. The prominent and civic-minded did not patronize the bar across from the factory. Dye's was a good place to meet on the sly.

Krueger did not recognize the two cars parked in front. A few spaces down he saw Joe Stouffer's '40 Ford pickup. Everyone in town knew Joe Stouffer as the milkman. Dye had a small grocery in the rear of the tavern. Joe delivered fresh whole milk from his farm over on Pike Street every Tuesday and Friday. Occasionally on a special Saturday delivery, his son, Billy, would ride along. Dye always gave Billy a Hershey bar.

The bell above the door jingled as Phillip walked in. The tavern's interior was several different hues of brown with the exception of the worn black paint of the booths lining the far wall. A small room in the back housed a pool table. Its green felt was worn and as old as the sixty-year-old building itself. Simple wood pillars separated the three mirrors behind the back bar. A black tin sign with a tarnished gold beer mug hung at the end of the bar to the side of the archway to the pool room. *Beer, fifteen cents*, was painted in uneven sized letters.

Phillip Krueger nodded to the bartender, who was dressed in a white shirt just two shades from worn gray. His black tie was loose at the top. Recognizing Krueger, he immediately popped off the cap of a Falstaff beer, poured it into a small glass, and sat it on the bar. Phillip dropped a quarter and a nickel in anticipation of his second beer, nodded to two patrons, Jimmy Phillips and Herbie Schmiedel, who stopped by to see Reg each night of the week, except for Thursdays. Bowling was always a prioriity.

A few stools away, Joe Stouffer looked at Krueger and said, "Howdy."

Krueger just nodded. Bottle in one hand, glass in the other, he walked over and slid into the second booth from the end.

Having previously spotted the two cars and Joe Stouffer's truck in front of Dye's, Phillip Krueger did not make note of the fourth man at the end of the bar, sitting alone, hovering over his beer. Krueger checked his watch: 9:36 p.m. *He should be here.* Krueger, his back to the pool room, watched the front door. Soon the bell jingled. A man in black trousers, a black waistcoat, and shirt with its collar open stepped in. Father Jaeger noticed Krueger in the far booth and walked over.

He threw his black hat on the seat and said, "Hello, Phillip. Sorry I'm a few minutes late." The priest slid into the booth, leaving his coat on.

"No problem, Father. I'm sometimes late for Mass. Have a beer?"

"Don't mind if I do. Long day. First Friday confessions."

Phillip Krueger lifted his hand, two fingers. Within a minute, Reg—the bartender—walked down the long walnut bar toward the pool room, bringing two more Falstaffs and one glass. As he set the bottles on the table, Phillip slid another quarter and nickel across. Reg looked down at Father Jaeger as if he recognized him. He pursed his lips but didn't say a word.

Father Jaeger felt the glare. "Think he recognized me?"

Walking back to the bar, Reg said to the patron sitting alone at the other end, "Have another?"

"Yeah. *Uumpgh.*"

Reg turned, opened the cooler below the back bar, popped the lid on a Weidemann's, and slid it back to the strange looking man, who never looked up.

Phillip Krueger continued, "Yeah, you probably hear the bartender's confession every Easter week. I've heard him cuss a lot, Father. Uses SOB all the time."

"Ahh, I hear worse than that!"

"How ya been, Father?"

"Been well. Quite well. Really like St. Thomas Moore, especially my pastor, Father Warren. The other assistant, Father Sullivan, that's another story. Let's say we tolerate each other."

"How 'bout the school? Bet you like teaching those sixth and seventh graders," Krueger asked.

"Yeah, as a matter of fact, I sure do. Religion class once a week."

"Course, I'm sure you favor the boys. Ever have any special one-on-one tutoring?"

"Come on. Don't go there," Father Jaeger shot back. "Well, I know you like those Boy Scouts, camping trips and all."

"Damn right, Father. I admit it. Oh excuse me, *darn*. There's some real sweet guys in our troop. Speaking of camping, I just wanted to remind you, Father, about our spring trip in a few weeks. Remember you are saying Mass. "

"Of course. I didn't forget. I really look forward to those trips with the boys."

"That's good. I thought you … "

Krueger was interrupted when he overheard, "Reform School. *Uumpgh*," from the far end of the bar. He turned his head in the direction of the patron. Krueger saw the profile of the man when he looked up the bar to the two men sitting together about six stools away. Krueger listened. Father Jaeger watched.

"Yeah. Been there 'bout twenty-four years. Yeah. *Uumpgh*."

Krueger looked over at Father Jaeger. "That's the creep. Bernard Bednar, janitor. Damn. Why is he here? Oh sorry, Father. Works at the school. Creepy guy. Don't like him." Krueger lifted his right hand and propped up his elbow as if to hide his face from Bernard. "I stay away from him. When we meet in the hall or wherever, he gives me a glaring look. Wish Wolfe would fire him. Get rid of him."

"What's wrong?" Father Jaeger asked. "Why? Has he seen you, or should I say caught you, with someone?"

"Nah, nothing like that. Just a damn creep. Oh excuse me, Father. There I go again."

"Relax." Father Jaeger waved his hand at Krueger. "That's okay. Make sure you are in confession Saturday though."

Both men laughed.

"I'm not confessing my sins to you," Krueger said.

"You're a sinner like everyone else, including me," the priest admitted as he took another drink of Falstaff.

"Anyway, back to the camping trip. I'm so glad you will be able to attend. You know, get out in nature with the boys. You always have such a good time."

They both kind of smiled at each other. Father Jaeger asked, "Say, is a … is Peter Goodnar gonna be there? Nice kid. Been givin' him some guidance. You know. Troubles at home, his grades."

"Sure, sure. Peter's coming. Paid his three dollar fee at last week's troop meeting. I like the kid too."

"You know, Phillip, these boys at this age just need us. Someone who really cares for them. I've learned that boys of this age don't get love and affection at home, especially from dads. Some dads are so tough. Still have the war in their minds, work in the factories. Others have dads working too much at the office, the bank. You know, the supervisor-boss type."

"Same in the scout troop. I do go by my motto: *be prepared*. Always ready, if you know what I mean, Father."

Krueger heard a bar stool slide back on the aged oak floors. From the corner of his eye, he watched Bernard walk up the bar toward the door, passing the two other drinkers.

"See you next Friday, Bednar," Reg said with a half-mock smile.

"*Uumpgh.*"

"Glad he's gone. Creep. Strong as an ox, I hear. He does the heavy stuff around school. Wouldn't want to mess with him. That I know for sure. Just one more, Father?"

"No thanks. Early Mass and it's First Friday."

"Okay, okay, but let's do this more often, Father. Like talkin' here? Beats the confessional, eh?"

"Ah, Phillip. I'll have a beer or hear your confession. Whatever suits your fancy. I know some of your dirty little secrets. We have things in common."

"That's not fair, Father. You know what you guys call it? Seal of confession."

The priest stood and picked up his black brimmed hat. "See you next time, Phillip."

"Yeah, probably at the camp outing. Could be a good time. And of course, the boys would enjoy a field Mass." Phillip watched the priest leave at the same time Reg walked to the window and pulled the string on the Falstaff neon sign.

"Lights out, fellas. Five more minutes. Drink up."

The two drinkers donned their hats. Each threw two quarters on the bar. "Right, Reg. See you tomorrow."

Phillip Krueger took one last drink, stood, and walked toward the door. "You're last out. Don't be a stranger. By the way, do I know that guy with you? Seems I've seen him somewhere before."

"Ah, he's just a friend. I'll bring him back." Phillip walked over to the bar and leaned across the back of the barstool. "Just don't cuss when he's around. Night, Reg."

"You button up there. Still damp and cold," Reg said as Krueger walked out the door.

As Krueger stepped to the curb, he wondered why Father Jaeger specifically asked about Peter Goodnar. *There has to be a reason*, he thought to himself…as he watched the black Studebaker drive away and disappear into the darkness.

CHAPTER 28

TOGETHER BY CHOICE

Father Jaeger—March 11, 1958

WITH spring approaching that year in 1958, Father Jaeger was about to complete his second full year at St. Thomas Moore. Feeling confident in his position as assistant pastor, Father Jaeger looked forward to continue working with his mentor, Father Warren. He enjoyed his assignment as the chaplain of the Boy Scout troop, in addition to saying Mass every third Sunday at the reform school. He especially enjoyed his friendship with several staff members, especially with Scoutmaster Phillip Krueger.

On some occasions, Father Jaeger stopped by the reform school for visits with Krueger. He especially enjoyed his time spent at the YMCA. The all-male atmosphere and the large pool facility was great for a number of reasons.

When alone, Father Jaeger sometimes suffered with his demons. His deep-seated desires and feelings were hard to control. When his mind was clear, he asked for forgiveness, but he could never confess. He fantasized and rationalized that the physical contact was beautiful. It was love that allowed him to ease the pressure within. In rare moments of regret, shame, and remorse, he prayed and promised never to commit deeds of sin again. The desire always returned, and he focused only on the moment.

Now in his early forties, Father Jaeger deeply desired to remain at St. Thomas Moore. He was tired of transfers. He was tired of answering questions about his last parish. The bishop, however, was convinced that each time Father Jaeger was given a chance to start over, and knowing the consequences of leaving another parish so soon, the priest would repent and promise to discard the hidden shadows governing his life.

Father Jaeger viewed befriending Joey Singleton as a sign that this was meant to be. Although Joey was underage, he was mature and willing, and they were together by choice. Father Jaeger felt they both were willing by choice, free and natural. He knew Joey needed and wanted to be with him. He rationalized the good, knowing that he was also influencing Joey to seek and accept a vocation to become a priest.

However, Joey was also a threat. Overprotective of Father Jaeger, he bullied the other boys if they dared threaten to expose the priest's exploits to another priest, a sister, or the boys' parents. Joey had a way of keeping his eye on certain young boys within the parish who Father Jaeger asked him to watch. The word was out not to cross Joey Singleton. Father Jaeger's worst fear was what would happen if *he* ever crossed Joey, considering all that Joey knew about the priest secretive life. Joey justified knowing about the abuse of others because of his love for Father Jaeger.

Father Sullivan—March 11, 1958

"Good morning, Father Warren," Father Sullivan said as he sat down for breakfast in the rectory dining room Tuesday morning.

"Hello, Michael. How was Mass this morning?"

"Six o'clock? Early," Father Sullivan answered with a big smile. "It was fine, Father. Tucker Logan and Danny Johnson were there, as dependable as always. That Danny is a character. You know, one Saturday I found him sleeping in the choir loft? Good kid though." Wanting to get right to the point with Father Warren before Father Jaeger arrived, he said, "Say, Father, you think you might have some time to talk this morning? Just you and I, confidentially?" he asked the elder priest.

"Good morning, Jerome," Father Warren said as Father Jaeger walked into the room.

Father Sullivan nodded the same.

"Morning to you both, Fathers," Father Jaeger said, sitting down and pouring his first cup of coffee.

"Yes, sure, Michael. How about ten thirty in my study?" Father Warren responded to his question, which had been interrupted by Father Jaeger's entrance.

Father Sullivan nodded, not wanting to draw attention to their meeting. The sight of Father Jaeger negated his appetite for breakfast. Sitting next to him at the breakfast table and seeing his face reaffirmed Father Sullivan's commitment to help Peter. Peter and others of whom he probably did not know.

Throughout breakfast, Father Jaeger sensed the same coolness about Father Sullivan that he had previously. It seemed like avoidance, and that made Jaeger feel uncomfortable.

Father Warren, however, was oblivious to any possible friction. He was more engrossed this morning with his coffee and reading about the Chicago Cubs' exhibition schedule. Later that morning he would learn far more than he cared to know.

Father Jaeger—March 11, 1958

Before the 8:30 Mass, Father Jaeger noticed Neil O'Connell seemed very quiet, much more than usual. Even during the liturgy, he observed that Neil wasn't focused. When he had to turn and nod to Neil to ring the bells during the consecration, he knew something was wrong. Father Jaeger always displayed a friendly concern and interest in the girls and boys at St. Thomas Moore, especially the boys. Altar boys always received special attention.

After Mass, Neil took extra time in the post Mass routine. He spent an especially long time retrieving more wine from the cellar for the next Mass. Neil's friend, James, who was the other high server, and the two low servers, Frank and Dave, left for school. Neil remained in the sacristy while Father Jaeger was still there.

"Neil, thank you again. You know, I always appreciate your service. You are a good altar boy," Father Jaeger mentioned.

"Thank you, Father," Neil said bashfully, even lowering his head.

"Today, however, you acted like there was something on your mind. If so, that's normal. Young, old, children, adults, teenagers—we all face certain challenges and troubles in our lives. That's understandable."

"Gosh, thank you, Father. Then maybe there is. I just don't have anybody to talk to."

"Could I help? I'm a pretty good listener," the priest said to Neil.

Neil thought for a moment. He always felt comfortable with Father Jaeger. Since the father had arrived at St. Thomas Moore, he seemed to have a way about him that most of the kids were attracted. This was certainly true for Neil. "Sure, Father. I'd like that," he answered with a positive smile.

"Okay, how about right now? I have some time before a meeting later this morning."

"That would be great, Father. But what about … ? I've got class," Neil said with concern.

"I'll send a note back with you to Sister Georgene. I know you do well. She'll be okay with it," Father Jaeger reassured the boy. "We're finished here. Hang up your cassock, and we'll sit in my study and just visit." He watched as Neil walked into the closet. He then walked toward the door to the sanctuary. *Candles are out. Church is empty. All's quiet.*

"Ready, Father. I'll take my books with me. Okay?"

"Sure. Follow me," Father Jaeger said.

They left the sacristy and walked into the hallway to the rectory and immediately went into Father Jaeger's study. The priest sat down in the easy chair, while Neil took a seat on the sofa.

"Feel like telling me what's on your mind, Neil?"

"Well, you see it's like this. You remember my older brother, David, who was killed in the car wreck last year?"

"I know, Neil. I remember his tragic death," Father Jaeger said empathetically. "Everyone in our parish was touched with grief for you and your family. I can only imagine how difficult it is. I pray for you often."

"Yes, Father, it has been most difficult. My parents live with it every day. My dad even changed jobs so he wouldn't have to travel. He wanted to be with Mom. But, Father … " Neil paused like he couldn't go on. He put his face in his hands and leaned on his knees. Father Jaeger could hear the sobs reverberating through his hands. "It's just so terrible … so terrible." Neil sat back up.

Father Jaeger asked, "Neil, how has all this affected you? You seem—"

Neil cut the priest off. "It's bad every day, every single day. You see,

David was older. He was my parents' favorite. He did everything the best. Best grades, everyone liked him, most popular kid in the freshmen class. Then he was an all-star in Pony League. But, Father, I loved him so much. He was there for me all the time. He was the best big brother a guy could have." Neil's emotions climbed. "That awful night when the police came to the door. I'll never forget. Mom, Dad, and me. It was terrible."

Father Jaeger just sat, listening and letting Neil talk it all out. "Father, you should know. Why? Why? How can a good God let this happen? It's just not fair. Now Mom and Dad don't have time for me. It's David this, David that. You don't understand. Somebody has to help me." With that, Neil just flopped back. Laying his head back against the sofa, he tried to regain his composure by taking a deep breath.

Father Jaeger stood up and walked over by the window to think. Returning to his chair, he sat down and waited. When he thought Neil had calmed down, he said, "Neil, your problem is very difficult. It's natural for you to have all these feelings."

"But, Father, what do I do? Can you help me?"

"Yes, I can Neil. I can be honest and direct with you. Maybe the most difficult problem in life is for a parent to lose a child. That is contrary to the natural scheme of things. Parents are supposed to leave first. They should go to heaven first, and not their children. They weren't prepared to lose David. They would not have been prepared to lose you. Neither of you. They would feel the same losing either one of you. So what I'm saying is look to your parents." Neil listened, focused on every word. "Neil, have the strength to understand them. Be there for them. Be good. Help when you can. Cause them no worry. Good deeds, love, understanding, and time will help to heal the wounds. Of course, you must pray. Ask our dear Lord and God to give your entire family strength to address this tragedy together. For now, always try to think of your parents. You see, Neil, you are in control. You can do this. You just have to commit yourself to being there for both of them. Be strong for your parents. Then I believe you will see things improve." Father Jaeger waited for Neil to respond. He watched as Neil rubbed his eyes and brow with both hands.

"Maybe, Father. Maybe I've been looking too much at my loss. How I'm hurt." He paused. "Actually, I think you're right, Father. I must think of Mom and Dad first."

"That's the idea. And you pray every day for our Lord to give you the strength. All right, Neil?"

"Yes, Father. I can try, since I know it has to be harder for them."

"I think you'll see results. It may be slow at first, but have faith. I think you're going to help your family make things better. All three of you will come together."

"Father, that does help me. I'm going to work hard at doing exactly that. I've got to be there more for Mom and Dad instead of thinking of what they are doing for me."

"You're a good boy, Neil. Now come on," Father stood, patted Neil on his shoulder. "I had better write you a slip for Sister Georgene. She'll understand. Now remember, you can come to talk anytime. I'll be here for you."

"Thank you, Father. I serve next Saturday morning. Maybe I could see you then?" Neil left with a smile on his face and some weight off his shoulders. *Father Jaeger really is a good priest. He really listened. I can go back and see him again. I know he cares about me.*

Father Jaeger walked up the stairs. Entering his apartment, he thought, *God, I love these boys.*

Father Sullivan—March 11, 1958

Father Sullivan felt some apprehension before his visit with Father Warren. *Knock, knock.* "Michael, come on in."

Father Sullivan entered Father Warren's apartment. Situated on the first floor, his space included a parlor, study, and bedroom. It was more gracious in size than the assistants' apartments but still homey and comfortable. His room even included a small galley kitchen between the parlor and the bedroom, though he rarely used it.

"Your rooms are even nicer than I last remembered," Father Sullivan said, trying to relax his manner before opening up to Father Warren.

"Well, son, this goes with being the old man of the group. Have a seat. Tell me what's on your mind. Can I help?"

"Father, I'll get right to the point. It's Father Jaeger." Father Sullivan immediately noticed the tightening of the good priest's brow. Concern covered his face. Father Warren had been expecting Father Sullivan to come forward.

"Father Jaeger? What about him?" Father Warren responded naturally, not wanting to seem overly concerned.

"Father, one of our boys, a good boy in school, came to me about being in bed with a man."

"Father Jaeger?" Father Warren immediately asked without hesitation. "Was this in confession?"

"Yes. The first time he came, he wouldn't even give me his name or the name of the man. Let's just say, he came to me for help. Before I could learn the name, he left the confessional."

"What did you do?" the elder priest inquired.

"All that I could, which was to pray he'd return to see me. About two weeks passed, and he came back. This time he gave me a name. However, that was not during confession. I insisted we talk alone outside, so never breaking the seal of confession."

"And it was?" Father Warren asked immediately.

"It was Father Jaeger."

Father Warren's look was one of huge disappointment and disgust, but he was not surprised. "You're sure this was not during confession?"

"Yes, Father. We met in my study, and he spilled out the whole story."

"Could he be mistaken or making this all up?"

"No, Father. I am confident that what he says is true. An eleven-year-old boy couldn't make this up."

"Who is he, Michael?" Father Warren asked.

"Peter Goodnar."

"Oh, Peter, I know him. Wonderful altar boy, good parents."

"Yes, Father, and I even talked to Sister Mary Michael. She is very fond of Peter. He's just a good kid. Knowing Peter and listening to his remorse, his shame, and his guilt, I know he is not making this up. Father, we have to do something now. God only knows if there are others Father Jaeger is with. I would think that this didn't just begin now."

Father Sullivan continued, "We know this life of celibacy can be most difficult. I am not perfect. I have sinned in my life," he said with remorse in his voice. "But, Father, this is a little boy. Naïve, a sixth grader. He didn't even know what the word *queer* meant. He couldn't understand because this was a priest. He looks up to the collar." Father Sullivan tugged at his own to make the point. "The priesthood has failed this boy. He's scared. Scared for his life. He'll never forget."

"Okay, Michael, just settle back. Relax. Let me think on this. Yes, we must do something, but what? I ask you, what do you think we should do?"

"Father, there is only one thing we can do. We need to address this directly with Father Jaeger. We must tell him of what Peter has accused him. Father Jaeger needs to explain, and then we need to go to the police. This is not only against God's commandments; this is a crime, a crime against this little boy. This cannot go unaddressed. Let me ask you something. Father Jaeger has been here for two years now. Where was he before?"

Father Warren raised his eyebrows, tilted his head, and sheepishly said, "Well, he was an assistant at a parish in Evansville, Indiana."

"How long was he there? Why did he leave?"

"If I recall correctly, I think the bishop told me he was there for a year or maybe two years."

"A year? Two years? That is such a short time. Do you know how many parishes he has been assigned to? How many other places has he been? More importantly, Father, I ask, has he possibly abused other children at other parishes? I'm sure this didn't start just now. Is there something you are not telling me? We need to know more about his history. I'm sure the bishop has files of his past records."

"Michael, I have to say this is very troubling. Two years ago, I was informed by Bishop Powers—you met him in South Wayne—that he wanted to assign a second assistant here at St. Thomas Moore. The bishop knew that our parish was growing. He said he had a fine young priest he would like to assign to our parish. The bishop did suggest that the priest was very good with children and that he worked well with the parishioners. The bishop thought a change would be good for Father Jaeger. Then he told me that the father had what he called a slight psychological problem. Who was I to question our bishop? Within a month, Father Jaeger arrived here as our new assistant."

"Father, with all due respect, have you suspected anything during the last two years?"

Father Warren was silent. He propped his chin between his thumb and forefinger. He didn't say anything. He raised his eyebrows and then looked directly at Father Sullivan and said, "Yes, Michael. I have had suspicions."

"Did you say anything? To anybody?"

"Michael, who would I say this to? You? It was only a feeling, a slight suspicion. I had noticed on a number of occasions the way Father Jaeger looked at boys. He would put his hand on their shoulders. Of course, he was very careful when I was around. But I have to admit, there was something there I suspected. Michael, you know Father Jaeger can be very likeable. He does make friends easily. He's nice looking, friendly. Kids like him. So I didn't think too far beyond. Maybe I should have. I recall last October, late around Halloween, the Samuels spoke to me about Father Jaeger spending an extraordinary amount of time with their son, Johnny. No accusations. Just concerns."

"Father, from my point of view, this is not only a sin against the commandments of our religion, but a sin against this young boy. If this is true as Peter describes, this is a crime. There is no other way to look at it. This should be reported. I hate to say it, but it should be reported to the police. Of course, we should talk to Father Jaeger first. He deserves a chance to comment on the accusation. Perhaps eventually we'd talk to Father Jaeger and Peter Goodnar at the same time. Peter's parents should be there. We have to hit this head-on," Father Sullivan outlined his plan to the elder priest.

"Oh, Michael. Just hold on. We're getting way ahead of ourselves. This would be scandalous to our parish if this is true. This would be horrific for the diocese. This would be in the papers. Now think. We can't have that. If it is true, hopefully we can talk with Father Jaeger. Maybe he can take some time off, get away for a while, and really try to understand what he has done and then repent and seek forgiveness. We both know our Lord forgives those who confess."

"Father, if this is true, we must go further. Forgiveness and confession doesn't bring *justice*. That said, can you and I meet with Father Jaeger? It's not time to call in Peter, but you and I should address this immediately. This afternoon, Father?"

"Michael, you are a good priest. Your intentions are pure, but I need some time to think and pray and search for the right answer. Let's discuss this tomorrow. Then I'll give you my recommendation on what we should do."

"Yes, Father. I will respect your decision. Let's talk tomorrow for sure."

Father Sullivan spent the rest of the day in turmoil. Frustration, anger, and sadness consumed his being. Thinking and praying was not enough to address this horrific issue. He did not want to go it alone. He wanted the support of Father Warren. Without that, however, he knew he would face the issue alone if necessary.

Peter Goodnar—March 13, 1958

The following weekend was the annual Boy Scout spring camping trip at Portland Arch, about twenty miles south of town on the Wabash River. Phillip Krueger and Ralph Smith had been planning the excursion with the troop for the past month. The spring camping weekend was always a big event for the boys. All the scouts made the trip.

Although reluctant, Peter wanted to attend his first camping trip ever. He wanted everything to be okay. On Thursday after school, he stopped in at the church. He solemnly walked up the center aisle to the pew in front of the Sacred Heart. He knelt and prayed.

Oh God, help me. Help me be strong and to avoid the occasions to be around Father Jaeger. I want to be good. I want to avoid sin. Dear Lord, just keep him away. Give Father Sullivan the strength to help me. Keep my parents from finding out. I do not want to disappoint them or my little brother and sisters. I promise to be good always and to not commit sin. I ask you to help Father Jaeger become a good priest again. Please let my mind be clean. Let me get rid of my terrible thoughts and the nightmares. I want things to go back to the way they used to be before him. Dear Lord, You are all good, and I want to be good like You. Amen. Our Father, who art in heaven …

Peter spent a lot of time by himself that week. He had been looking forward to the scout campout trip as a chance to get away from everything he had experienced this past year. His mind was tortured with the daily thoughts of the inflictions imposed on him by the wicked priest.

CHAPTER 29

THE CURTAIN IS RAISED

Ralph Smith—March 23, 1958

HAVING returned earlier than planned from the Scouts' weekend campout, Ralph sat alone in his car on Sunday morning. He had arrived at church a half hour before the end of Father Warren's 8:30 Mass. Ralph knew he had thirty-five to forty minutes before he could meet with Father Warren. The appalling events of the night before had to be disclosed to the pastor. He waited in his car at the end of the parking lot. With his head back and eyes closed, Ralph relived the past night's nightmare in his mind. The weekend spring camping trip had ended in tragedy.

As he sat alone, Ralph thought back to the events of the past evening. After the confrontation Saturday evening, Ralph Smith, the assistant scoutmaster, had decided to break up the Scout camp early on Sunday morning. Father Jaeger's outdoor Mass was canceled. A bitter argument had ensued during the wee hours of the morning between Phillip Krueger and Ralph Smith. Ralph knew Mass had to be canceled, and the troop returned to town earlier than planned. He had simply taken control. Phillip Krueger had no choice; he knew Ralph was close to Father Warren.

Once the troop had taken the old Scout bus back to town, the boys were dropped off at the Scout meeting hall behind the St. Ignasius churchyard. Most of the boys lived within walking distance. Once they arrived in town, some parents were called to pick up the boys early. Phillip Krueger, against Ralph's better judgment, gave some of the boys rides home. They had jumped in the back of Krueger's pickup with their gear. The fact that it was Sunday morning provided an element of safety.

Once all the boys had left the churchyard, Ralph had driven directly to the rectory. His son, Russell, had walked home. Although Russell didn't know what had happened the night before, he knew something had taken place and that his father was very upset.

Ralph Smith dozed off that Sunday morning as he waited in the car to see Father Warren after Mass. He relived the night of horror in his mind.

"It's 9 p.m. boys … all lights out!" Scoutmaster Phil Krueger announced to the boys. "In bed, five minutes. All's quiet."

The cabin was primitive with no electricity and no plumbing. The outhouse was fifty yards back around the base of the hill. The cabin included three rooms. The center room provided a recreation area. A wood-burning cooking stove on the back wall, eight tables, and benches were enough for the small troop of twenty-five boys to gather for meals, crafts, or a late afternoon meeting. The cabin slept thirty boys. The scout leaders slept in the small room on the other side of the central room.

"Phil, we've got two groups out in the woods for their outside camping merit badges. I'm going to take a walk and check which group Father Jaeger is with," Ralph Smith said to the scoutmaster.

"Let's see. Father Jaeger is with Paul Woodward, Mark Salisbury, and Henry Langley," Phil Krueger informed Ralph.

"Well, who's with the other group?" Ralph asked.

"They're with Bob Wilkus and Gene Stefaniak. They're Eagle Scouts. No worry there. It's a beautiful evening. Just look at that full moon. The father's group is at the far end of the ridge, just above the arch." Phillip Krueger pointed down a path that led deep into the dark woods.

"I'll check them first," Ralph said.

"Oh, that's really not necessary. All's safe with Father Jaeger," Krueger told Ralph.

"Ah, just a good walk, Phil. If I see them, I'll just say hi and won't be a bother."

As he began walking toward the ridge, Ralph could feel the early chill of the evening. Picking up a broken branch for a walking stick, he enjoyed the sights and sounds of the woods settling in for the evening. He heard something move to his left just off the trail, but it was hidden in the darkness beyond the reach of the moon. *Just a deer.*

Ralph knew the path along the base of the ridge, as he had hiked it earlier that afternoon. Darkness was everywhere. The full moon was partially hidden by the clouds over the ridge to his left. He figured the distance to where they were camping was about half a mile. The outside world was nonexistent. *Quiet, stillness.* Just him and the nighttime mysteries of the woods. Ralph could hear the echo of some coyotes barking at their prey far in the distance. The spring air was cool, and an earlier light rain provided a softened trail. He could feel the exposed rocks and broken sticks beneath his feet. Although Ralph was an experienced outdoorsman, the darkness still provided an eerie sensation.

Suddenly branches to his left rustled. He heard an unfamiliar sound. Startled, he stopped. *Couldn't be the boys.* He took a breath and marched on. *They've got to be close.* He thought he heard laughter, some voices. *They're just ahead.* Soon, Ralph saw the flickering light of a campfire. He didn't make his presence known. As he got closer, his steps slowed and then stopped. He stood there, blinking his eyes in disbelief. His mouth dropped open, yet he waited to confirm that what he was seeing in his own mind was actually happening.

Around the fire, he saw the figure of a man and three boys, all unclothed. He watched in dismay and horror. *What am I seeing?* Suddenly the man reached for a boy's hand, turned, and pulled him toward some large oaks into the darkness. The other boys then crouched and hovered around the fire. At the same time, Ralph heard the words from the darkness beyond the fire: "No, no, please don't, Father ... "

He charged the campsite, so intent that he stumbled almost to the ground on an exposed rock in the trail. Catching himself, Ralph continued to charge toward the sounds of the boy in the darkness beyond the campfire.

"Stop! Stop! What the hell is going on?" Arriving at the campfire, panting, his heart racing, Ralph asked Mark and Henry, "Where did they go?"

"Mr. Smith, this is not our idea. Honest." Mark said, terror written across his face. "He made us. He made us do it. We all wanted to run back to camp to get away from him. He's scary!"

"But he warned us. Father Jaeger warned us not to tell anybody or he would ... I can't say, I just can't." Henry clutched his arms around his knees and stared at the dimming fire, shivering, speechless, and naked.

"He took Paul over there." Mark pointed toward a large oak just within the fading campfire light.

"You boys get your clothes on. You'll be okay. Then wait here for me." Ralph shined his flashlight toward the oak. He saw not a soul. "Stop! Stop!" he shouted as he challenged the darkness in the direction of the pleas. "Father Jaeger! Paul! Call to me now!" Not a word. "I know you are there! You know you can hear me! The only way out is to step forward! For God's sake, you don't even have clothes on!" To his far right, he heard some rustling in the brush. "Come on out, now!"

Then ... "Please, Mr. Smith. Help me. Help me."

Ralph snapped his head to his right. He saw Paul run forward with both hands covering below his waist. Beyond the boy, he saw a figure wrapping a blanket around himself.

"Run! Run, Paul!" Ralph heard the screams from the boys by the fire.

Still sitting in the car that Sunday morning, Ralph Smith suddenly woke up and blinked. He sat up from his reclining position. *I wish it was a dream*, he thought, thinking of the night before. But he knew it was not. Straightening the Scout handkerchief around his neck, he got out of his car and walked to the rectory. *How am I going to tell this to Father Warren?*

Ring, ring. Ralph pressed the doorbell on the front door of the rectory. "Good morning, Sister. I didn't expect to see you here this morning."

"Well, I'm just helping a little extra. Only Father Warren and Father Sullivan are here. Father Jaeger is away."

"Oh, I see. Is Father Warren back from Mass yet?"

"No, but he'll be here soon. I have his breakfast almost ready. Please come in, Mr. Smith. You can wait in the front parlor."

"That would be fine," Ralph said, still holding his Scout hat in his hand.

"Have a seat. I'll bring him in as soon as he arrives. That sofa is mighty comfortable," the sister said, trying to coax Ralph into the parlor. *He seems tense*, she thought as she headed back to the kitchen.

Ralph was anxious. He paced the floor and then walked over to the beautiful painting of the Last Supper hanging above an antique chest on the far side of the parlor. *Peaceful. Beautiful.* Ralph picked up an album on top of the dresser and paged through photos taken during construction of St. Thomas Moore in 1901. He noticed the close-up of workers laying the cornerstone and then more photos taken during various stages of construction, all the way to the final completion of the steeple. Ralph loved the old black-and-white photos.

"Oh, good morning, Ralph," Father Warren greeted as he rounded the corner. "Thanks for waiting."

"Father, I'm so sorry to come unannounced, but it's very important. I just got back from the camping trip. We had an awful incident. Can we speak in private?"

Tapping his hand on Ralph's arm, Father Warren said, "Just a minute." He walked to the hall. "Sister Agatha, please just cap my breakfast. I'll have it later." She nodded back to him with a little displeasure, as she knew father needed his breakfast. "Here, let's sit down," he said to Ralph as he took his familiar chair at the end of the sofa.

Hat in hand, elbows on his knees, Ralph anxiously leaned forward from his seat on the couch. "Sister's right. This is comfortable," Ralph said, pushing his left hand across the cushions. "Oh, I'm sorry, Father, to take this time on Sunday, but there is something you have to know."

"Ralph, if it's important to you, then it's important to me."

"Father, this weekend was our spring camping trip out at Portland Arch."

"I know. I've heard the boys talk about it for weeks."

"Yes, the trip was great. The boys always love the campouts. However, last night this most awful thing happened."

"Tell me. Tell me what happened," Father Warren said, sitting back in his chair, anticipating what Ralph had to say.

Father Warren always had a comforting, pleasant manner about him. Ralph went on to tell him everything just as he had remembered it during the last forty-five minutes in the car. At first, the priest didn't say a word. He just looked in awe at Ralph.

"What happened after he came out of the darkness?" Father Warren asked in a horrified tone.

Almost going into a trance like he had when he retraced the event in the car, Ralph relived his confrontation with Father Jaeger. Father Warren actually stayed quite calm. Then he heard a wrap on the parlor door. "Excuse me. I'm sorry to bother you. You have a call."

"Just tell them I'll call back."

"Well, Father, he says it's very important."

"Tell him—"

"Sorry, Father, but it's Father Jaeger. He says he's not well and must talk to you now."

Father Warren lifted his head. Ralph was startled.

"Excuse me, Ralph. I had better take this."

"Yes. Yes, of course, Father. I want to know what he tells you."

Father Warren walked to the phone in the back hall. "Hello, Father Warren here."

"Good morning, Father, this is Father Jaeger." Father Warren detected a strained and tense voice on the other end of the line. "I, ah ... I wanted to tell you I'm not feeling well. I left the Scout camp last evening and drove to Chicago. I'm here at home with my parents."

"That's a little sudden, Father Jaeger. Did something happen? Why did you drive all night if you aren't well?"

"I can't talk now. I'll call you this week. Have a good day, Father Warren," he said hurriedly and then hung up the phone.

Father Warren paused and gathered his thoughts, trying to make a connection between Ralph Smith's bizarre account and Father Jaeger's unusual disclosure. *Something doesn't add up.* He then returned to the parlor.

"Father Jaeger said he was in Chicago, went to his parents. He told me he was not feeling well. Said he would call this week. The call was strange but so obvious with what you're tellin' me." He paused. "Go ahead, Ralph. Where were we?"

"Okay, Father, back to ... " Ralph said. "Let's see, I stopped with, *hmmm.* Oh, yes. Then Jaeger said to me as he walked from the woods, 'Now, Ralph, I can explain all of this. There was no harm intended. Nobody was hurt. The boys are okay.' I turned around, and I saw the three boys huddled around the dying fire, bewilderment and terror paralyzing their faces. I said, trying to control my voice and a desire to punch him, 'Father Jaeger, I am at a loss for words. I have never ever seen such … ' I cannot describe how terrible the fear was in those boys' eyes. I told him to go get his clothes on as I pointed toward the darkened path behind the boys. Disgusting, simply disgusting. 'And you're supposed to be a priest?' I asked, trying to contain my outrage. 'An example and mentor to these young boys?'

"I thought I'd said too much in front of the boys. Jaeger said he could explain to me. I told him to get out of my sight. Then he went off behind the trees and dressed. I even told him to fold his disgusting blanket and take it home. I then turned around, walked over to the boys, reached down, and threw a couple of logs on the fire to keep them warm. The boys leaned back in amazement."

Ralph continued, "In the flash of light, I could see Father Jaeger walking back toward the fire. I called to him to stay right there and not to move. I didn't want the boys to hear what I was going to say, although they probably did hear me. I wanted the boys to stay where they were and to keep warm. I tossed them an army canteen full of water. I then slowly stepped toward the priest. He stood directly in front of me. We were almost eye to eye, even though he's taller than me."

Father Warren sat in disbelief. Ralph went on, "I looked Father Jaeger in his eyes and said, 'Now you listen to me. I'm going to tell you exactly what you are going to do,' I commanded him. Jaeger then reached his hand out as if to rest it on my shoulder. I jumped back. I said in disgust, 'Don't touch me.' Now, he may be a priest, but I did the talking. I thank God he had just those tan pants and a shirt on, nothing black to remind me he was a priest. He is despicable. I told him he was a disgrace to the priesthood and the collar he wears. 'I will not forget or keep quiet about this,' I told him.

"Jaeger said, 'Yes, but I can—' But I said, 'I'm talking.' I was sure this was not the first time. I asked him how many young boys were out there in the dark and how many more had been abused, mentally tortured, or raped. I was pretty harsh with him. Then Father Jaeger said to me, 'How dare you talk to me like that. I'm a priest.' I stepped closer. We were almost nose to nose.

"Then I said, 'Quiet. There is no excuse. Naked with these boys. A blanket in the woods. You head right down that path, get in your car, and drive straight home. Don't stop at the cabin. I do not want you near the other boys.' I was now sure the boys had heard everything I said. Neither of us said another word. I then turned and walked back toward the boys. I stopped. My heart was racing. My mouth was parched. I shook. I gathered my thoughts. My focus immediately turned to the three hovering boys.

"Getting back to the campfire, I sat on the log opposite the three frightened boys. Lifting a poking stick, I stoked the fire, trying to show them calm. All three stared into the burning coals. Their thoughts were their own, but I could tell they were wrapped in fear. Mark asked, 'Why would he do that to us? He's a priest.' I couldn't answer. It was then that I needed to see you, Father Warren. On Monday, I'm going to the police." *Dear Lord, forgive me if I said anything wrong. I was talking to the man, not the priest and collar.*

Ralph went on to say, "I asked the boys, 'How did this happen?' Paul spoke first. 'We finished our stew and biscuits and were sitting around talking.' Then Henry added, 'I said it's sure hot. All of a sudden, father stood up. I think he said, "Me too." Yeah, then he took his shirt off.' I shook my head. 'Then he told us to take ours off.' Paul said, 'We thought it was okay since he took his off. He started telling us how beautiful nature was. How we were a likeness of Jesus.'

"Henry thought he was talking crazy. Father Jaeger then told the boys, 'Look, I'll show you.' That's when he took off his pants, everything—totally naked. He said, 'You're like Jesus. You boys do the same.' Paul explained, 'I just wanted to get away from him and go back to the cabin. But then he said, 'Jesus loves the human body. He made us in his likeness.'" Then he walked over and hugged each of them really close and said, 'Like Jesus, I love you boys. I want to show you first.' He sounded excited and was breathing hard. 'I closed my eyes. I couldn't look.' Paul shook his head then told me this wasn't the first time. 'He's done it to us before. Me for sure. Several times. Like in school, his car. It's awful.' I asked him, 'Why didn't you tell your parents?' 'Heck, no way. Who's gonna believe us? Our parents think the priests and sisters are perfect. We just kept quiet. Now this again. I'm tellin' you this time.

Never again.' "I promised the boys this will never happen again. I promised. I'm going straight to Father Warren. Father Warren will take care of everything. I assured them of that."

Ralph Smith startled himself. "Oh, did I tell too much?" he asked Father Warren. Ralph looked at the priest, who had his elbow propped on the arm of the chair and his head in his hand. He continued, "As we stood around the campfire, I explained to the boys that what had just happened was by a very sick man. I told them that what he did was sinful and morally wrong. Now they needed to be brave. Not that I wanted to brush it aside, but I told them to keep this among themselves until I met with you. I told them I would talk to you, and you would be there to help them. I also told them that they would not be contacted by Father Jaeger ever again."

Father Warren was inwardly shaken. "Ralph, I know that was hard to tell, let alone what you had to endure last night. I am horrified," he said. "Just sickened." He paused and shook his head. "You remember, Ralph, I asked you to help by keeping an eye on Phil Krueger," Father Warren said, not wanting Ralph to be aware that he had previously been suspicious of Father Jaeger. "Go ahead. Continue, Ralph."

"I am so disgusted," Ralph looked at Father Warren. "Father Jaeger gives communion. He touches the Host. How despicable then to indecently touch these boys. It's against everything I've been taught about the Catholic Church."

Father Warren looked at Ralph. "You are right. Father Jaeger is a sick, sick man."

Father Jaeger—March 22, 1958

Father Jaeger had to get away. As he followed the path through the dark woods, he looked back over his right shoulder and saw Ralph sitting with the boys around the fire. He stopped. *What will he tell them?* A huge spark jumped from the fire. A flash. He began to walk fast. He stumbled. *Where's the damn path?* Loose rocks made his pace uneasy. Trying to move faster, Father Jaeger lost the path and stumbled over a fallen tree, scraping his face on the stump. For a moment, he lay face down on the cool earth, a mixture of decayed leaves and green sprouts searching for new life. Alone and scared, his mind raced with thoughts. *This is the worst. What have I done? What am I going to do now?*

Almost in a panic, Father Jaeger pulled himself up, turned, and tried to run. He circled around. *Where am I?* Noticing the fallen tree, he stepped to the side from which he had come. *Yes, yes this way.* He ran with his hands in front of him, groping through the darkness. He slowed down and then rushed again, taking irregular steps with hands outstretched, bracing himself for a fall. Suddenly his feet went out from under him. He fell forward and then down. Bracing his fall with both hands, he immediately felt loose pebbles, rocks, and dirt. *Ah, the path. Please, God, please.*

Ahead he saw the dim solitary light of the cabin. He escalated his pace, and the light grew closer and closer. Stepping into the open area that surrounded the cabin, the desperate priest stopped, exhilarated that he had found his way back. *Krueger. I've got to see him.* Then he remembered Ralph Smith's warning to not stop at the cabin. *To hell with that.* Taking a deep breath, he tucked his shirt in, straightened his belt, and wiped the dirt from his forehead and left cheek. Slowly, he stepped to the porch. Two light knocks. "Krueger, Krueger … it's me."

Slowly, the door opened partially. It was Phil. Through the half-open door, he could see two other fathers of the boys sitting at the center table, a checkerboard between them.

"What the hell?" Phillip Krueger asked.

"*Shhh, shhh.* Quiet. Shut the door. Come out here."

Phil Krueger stepped onto the porch and then turned and shut the door quietly. Without a word, Father Jaeger stepped into the yard.

"Come here."

Krueger followed. "What the hell happened?" he asked as the moon shed light on the open yard. "Who hit you?"

"Nobody. I fell," Father Jaeger said, patting his cheek. "Now listen, I need your help. Why in the hell did you let that Ralph Smith come out snooping around?" he asked in disgust.

"He's an assistant. A volunteer. I couldn't stop him. What was going on? What were you doing? Jerome, were you doing something with the boys? You wouldn't be so dumb as to try and do something with the boys here? I've warned you before."

"Warned me before? Heck, you encouraged me to come on this trip. You set up those boys to camp with me," Father Jaeger said in a threatening manner. "How was I to know? The situation was perfect. I couldn't pass it up. I just got in a trance, forgot everything. The boys, they agreed." Krueger just listened. "We were all standing around the fire. Then Paul and I, well, we just took a walk, and all of a sudden Smith was there. It was, it was … damn! I was in a difficult position. Phil, you've got to help me."

Krueger shook his head, pushing his shoe across the ground. "How stupid. That's all I can say," he said, scolding the priest.

"I said I need help, not a sermon. Listen, you've got to talk to Ralph Smith. Tell him this will look bad for me, bad for the troop. It can't get back to Father Warren. God Almighty, he even said he's going to see Warren and then the police. The police, for God's sake. You've got to talk some sense into this guy."

"Okay, okay. I'll calm him down. I'll do my best to have him keep this between us."

"Yes, yes. Then you tell those boys not to say a word. Shut them up, Phil. You have to do this. If you do, I'm going to straighten everything up. I will. I will get control. Promise. I'll get control of myself. God help me. I'm leaving now. I'll call you tomorrow. Maybe Tuesday. I'll call to see if you've got it all under wraps," Father Jaeger said, speaking very hurriedly. "You can do it. For me. Please, Phil. I beg you. I need your help."

Father Jaeger turned in the direction of his car. "Time to go." He walked a few steps, stopped, and looked back at Krueger, who was still standing in front of the cabin. Father Jaeger approached his space. "One more thing. You handle this, and you promise never, never to mention that I've ever visited the school. Never, other than for Mass. That's it. I've never been there otherwise. You get it, Phil? Not a word." He stepped backward one, two, three steps. "You know, Phil, if I go down, there's no telling what I'll say about all that goes on at your school. You and that Clarence Wolfe. You know what I mean, Phil? Goodnight. I'll call you Monday."

Father Jaeger turned and rushed to his car. Phillip Krueger took it all in. Then, taking a deep breath and shaking his head, he walked up the steps of the cabin. As he stood on the porch, Phillip Krueger looked back around. All he could see were two red taillights disappearing into the darkness.

Father Warren—March 23, 1958

The pastor would never forget that morning with Ralph. It was then that Father Warren's life took a turn. He prayed for the strength to do what was right for the poor young boys. His disbelief was shattered by reality. He knew it was up to him. Father Warren knew he would have to decide how and what to do about this horrid, sick cancer within his parish. As a priest, he had to think about the sinful man and what to do about him. Most of all, he asked himself, *How does God forgive?*

Late that Sunday evening, Father Warren sat alone by the dim table light in the front parlor. The rest of the room was encased in darkness. A few burning embers crackled in the fireplace. He heard the front door open and then footsteps. Father Sullivan walked into the open doorway and stood there.

"Hello, Michael," the elder priest said in a low monotone voice.

Father Sullivan didn't respond at first. Then he said, "I've been on a long walk. I heard, Father, this afternoon at around three thirty. I received a call from Joe Woodward, Paul's dad. He told me what happened to Paul this weekend."

"Who told him?" Father Warren asked.

"First, I guess it was Paul. Then Mr. Woodward called Ralph Smith. What an awful day for those boys, for their parents."

"Yes, Michael, it is." Father Warren paused. "And I think ... oh, pray to God ... I'm worried this could be scandalous for our parish."

"Father," the younger priest said. He had walked over and now stood at the end of the sofa. He looked at Father Warren, who was still sitting in his chair at the opposite end of the sofa. "First, we have Peter Goodnar. Now these three boys. Tell me it can't be. Father ... " Father Sullivan was almost pleading for some relief. "Father, I think there could be more," he said, even while finding it hard to believe his own words.

"What do you mean, Michael?"

"I suspect another," Father Sullivan warned. "Yes, Joey Singleton.

Not for sure, but I have reason to believe that Father Jaeger and Joey are close. Too close. God help me for thinking there could be other boys."

"Michael, I'm seventy-two years old. I've been a priest for almost fifty years. I have devoted my life to sharing Christ's love with the people. Now this. I simply do not understand how a priest could do this to these boys."

Father Sullivan raised his finger to his lips. Looking at Father Warren, he said, "Father, between you and me, we knew about Peter. We had our suspicions about Father Jaeger. And now this. We should have done something immediately."

Father Warren sat back and listened. In a hushed, low tone, he said, "I've been aware of this … this horrid sickness. I knew about it when I was in the seminary. I heard *hush-hush*. Then as a pastor I've been told by other priests from other parishes that the abuse continues. Then there are the bishops." Father Warren spoke with hesitation. "They never— don't repeat this—but they never seem to step forward. They defend, defend, and then nothing happens." Silence. "What's hard, Michael, is … well, I've never been this close to a situation … " Father Warren hesitated. "And right here at our own beloved St. Thomas Moore."

"Father, I know how terribly difficult this is for you. You don't deserve this in our parish, in our church that you love so much," Father Sullivan caringly said. "Dear God, Father, you've given your life."

"Thank you, Michael. Your words mean a lot to me."

"But, Father, there's one most important thing. We have to think of the boys first." Father Sullivan knew he best leave Father Warren alone in his own contemplation and prayer. "Good night, Father."

"Yes, Michael." He shook his head. "I know we must address the cancer now."

Father Sullivan turned and walked away, leaving Father Warren alone amongst the dying embers in the darkness.

CHAPTER 30

CONFRONTATION

Sheriff Thurow—April 14, 1958

SHERIFF Thurow drove out of town, west on Pike Street, directly to the Wabash Reform School. Driving ten to fifteen miles per hour over the speed limit reflected his anxiousness to address Clarence Wolfe. Past Friends Cemetery, he could see the foreboding reform school ahead. The three-story brick edifice, built sometime in the early 1900s, looked daunting and unwelcoming. After walking up the worn limestone steps, the sheriff opened the equally imposing front door.

"Good morning, Sheriff Thurow," Miss Gardner said with a curt, forced smile. "Are you here to see Mr. Wolfe?"

"Yes, ma'am. As a matter of fact, that's exactly why I'm here," he replied.

"He's busy right now."

"Would you please tell him I'm here? I'd like to have a meeting," the sheriff said anxiously.

"Why sure, if you don't mind waiting," Miss Gardner said. She thrived on control.

"Thank you, ma'am. I will wait. Tell him I'm right here by your side. And yes, I am busy today also."

Miss Gardner dutifully walked back to the door with a sign that read *Conference Room*. She opened it, entered, and then slowly closed the door behind her, muffling the latch. Sheriff Thurow waited an uneasy couple of minutes. He watched and listened to every tick of the Seth Thomas wall clock hanging on the far side of the room. Finally, the door opened, and a group of men walked out, followed by Clarence Wolfe and then Miss Gardner with her stenographer book in hand. The sheriff noticed one of the men was Phillip Krueger. Talking in a group, Krueger walked right by the sheriff. He didn't say a word, although he recognized the sheriff, having met him several times before at the annual Lion's Club banquet.

Bud Jackson, head of housekeeping, maintenance, and the grounds staff at the school, stopped. "Hello, Sheriff." Bud always volunteered to work at county functions such as the March of Dimes benefit.

"Bud, good to see you. How's your family?" Sheriff Thurow asked.

"Fine, just fine. Thanks for asking, Sheriff."

"Are you going to be at the benefit this year? Always can use your help."

"Sheriff, you know I'll be there." From the corner of his eye, Bud noticed Mr. Wolfe approaching. "Well, gotta go, Sheriff. See you again this summer." He was pleased to speak with the sheriff but anxious to leave when he saw Clarence Wolfe returning.

"Thanks, Bud. You take care now." Bud Jackson was a good man. One of the few Negroes in Wabash. Bud was known as a kind, hard-working family man, unaffected by some of the prejudice within the small northern town.

Extending his hand, Clarence Wolfe greeted the sheriff. "Sheriff, what brings you here unannounced?" The sarcasm in his voice did not go over the sheriff's head.

"I'd like to have a few words with you if you could spare the time, Mr. Wolfe."

"What about?" Wolfe asked in a commanding tone.

"Maybe it would be best to talk in private?" the sheriff suggested.

"Sure, sure. Of course. Let's go in my office."

Moments later, Clarence Wolfe took his position behind his large oak desk. Sheriff Thurow sat in the straight back chair in front of Wolfe's post.

"Let me get right to the point. I have spoken with a parent of one of the boys here in your school. The boy has written to his father, and I have met with him."

"What's it about?" Wolfe asked suspiciously.

"The boy alleges that he is being abused by boys within the school—"

"Sheriff Thurow," Wolfe said, cutting the sheriff off. "Sometimes there may be a slip and one of the bigger boys can punch, threaten, hit, or just bully another one of the boys. But I can assure you, we run a tight ship. We don't spare the discipline."

"Excuse me, Mr. Wolfe, but I'm not referring to bullying. I said abuse—sexual abuse."

"Impossible! Not here. That can't be. As I said, we run a tight ship,"

"Mr. Wolfe, let's get to the bottom of this. There is more."

Clarence Wolfe's defenses were raised like a drawbridge. He knew exactly to what the sheriff was referring. A *letter*. A *letter from whom?* "What do you mean there is more?"

"This young man alleges that he has been abused, sexually, by one of your staff members."

"Now, Sheriff, you are going too far. That, I can assure you, is impossible. Never happened. I know my entire staff. That can't be. Who is saying this? I want to know the accusers, their names. We simply don't allow that kind of thing around here."

"Mr. Wolfe, I am going to investigate this matter, and I will appreciate your full cooperation," Sheriff Thurow said, taking control of the dialogue. "You will receive a letter from me with the names of a few individuals I'd like to talk with. I will return here next Tuesday, and I'll meet with them. I'd prefer that you not be in attendance during our interviews."

"Sheriff, I understand your position, but to be honest, I do not like your accusatory tone."

"Well that makes us even, as I don't like the fact that I have been called to your school about sexual abuse, to be more specific." Sheriff Thurow leaned forward, placing his elbows on Wolfe's desk.

In a hushed voice, he continued, "Mr. Wolfe, your defensive tone alone, not to mention your tapping fingers on the desk makes me very suspicious. I'll see you next Tuesday. You will receive a letter within two days. Thank you, Mr. Wolfe." With that, the sheriff stood up, nodded to Clarence Wolfe, and left the room.

"Now, you have a nice day, Miss Gardner," he said to the secretary's back as he walked by her desk. She was totally focused on her Corona, just typing away. Sheriff Thurow thought he could feel her piercing eyes on his back as he approached the front door.

The sun shone directly overhead. Sheriff Thurow glanced at his watch—12:07. Driving home, he thought about the meeting. He had sensed red flags of deception during the conversation with Mr. Wolfe. *That man is hiding something, and I intend to find out what.*

Bernard Bednar—Monday, April 14, 1958

Bernard Bednar walked the crest of Friends Cemetery, as he often did on his noontime break. He could see the front entrance of the school. Bernard noticed the sheriff's car exit the campus and head back to Wabash. He thought, *Why's the sheriff out here?* As usual, Bernard's walk took him over the hill to the far side of the cemetery, where he stood for a few moments in front of Gordon Yoder's tombstone. Bernard always remembered that day back in 1934.

Bernard returned to school and walked into the locker room. Still dressed in his uniform, he knew he had three hours remaining on his shift. The room was empty. Just then, Artie walked in. "Hi, Bernard, what's you been doing?"

Bernard responded, "*Uumpgh.* I was out walking. Saw the sheriff's car. He was driving away. What's the sheriff's car doing out here, Artie? Why would the sheriff come to our school?"

"Now, Bernard, he comes out here ever so often. We've both seen him before. You and I know some things are not right. These big boys are doing some bad things to the younger guys. Maybe sheriff knows something. You and I are trying to help. When you rescued Little Eddie by pounding on Billy up on my floor, I was surprised Billy didn't go straight to Krueger. We both know Krueger is no good, but who's going to say anything against him? The boys are all scared of him. Billy too. So, Bernard, you shouldn't be surprised. Maybe that's why the sheriff was here."

"He's not a good man, that Krueger. *Uumpgh.* I know he hurts the boys. I know some of those things he does, those sex things. If I ever catch Big Billy again, *uumpgh*, I'm goin' to take him apart this time and shove his—" Bernard stopped. "Right in his mouth. *Uumpgh.*"

"I'd like to see that, Bernard. You are concerned about the boys just like I am, but I have to be careful. I have a family. Four kids. I need this job. Lord knows it's not just Krueger. It's that Wolfe too. I don't want to mess with him. I think Wolfe knows what's going on. For some reason, I think he's protecting Krueger. Maybe, just maybe, the sheriff is checking some things out here. Whatever it is, I don't want to be involved. I gotsa take care of my family."

"*Uumpgh.* I'll just keep watching."

"See you later, Bernard. I have to get back to my floor."

As Artie walked away, he thought, *I know I can't do anything, but I wouldn't be surprised by what Bernard would do. He cares for those boys, and he has nothing to lose.*

The clouds in the western sky hung low that evening. Bernard was finishing up his first shift duties. Making the rounds on the second floor, he picked up the green canvas laundry bags. Flinging two over his shoulder, he dragged another two behind him. Bernard was strong. The hallways of the school were vacant. The 5:45 p.m. supper hour had passed. The muffled echoes of the bags thumping down the stairs were the only sounds throughout the echoing halls. Reaching the lower level, Bernard pulled the bags past the locker room, past the maintenance storage room, and into the laundry room at the end of the dark, narrow hall.

After stacking the bags in the laundry room, Bernard headed back down the hall toward the locker room. As he approached the bottom of the stairs leading to the first floor hall, he heard a sound from behind him. It was the sound of a boy's voice, then a shriek, and then a muffled scream. He immediately turned toward the origin of the sound. Bernard stopped at the maintenance storage room door. He heard more sounds. Quietly, he turned the knob. The door was locked. Bernard knew someone was inside and up to no good.

Having presence of mind, he turned back around and went to the top of the stairs, where the light was more sufficient. He pulled out his chain of forty-eight keys and found the one to the storage room. Back down the stairs he hustled, inserted the key, and pushed the door open with a violent slam. Bernard heard cries from the back of the room. He could tell from the noise that there was more than one boy.

Without hesitation, Bernard ran down the aisle. He saw a man with no clothes on except for his shoes. Immediately, he threw his arm around the man's neck and pulled him back and away from the little boy. Eddie lunged away, pressed himself against the wall, slid down, and wrapped his arms around his knees, protecting his naked body.

"Let me go, you son of a bitch! Who are you?" the abuser yelled.

Bernard's brutal strength closed off the man's breathing. With his left hand and all his might, Bernard slammed his fist into the man's groin. Then he swung him around, and threw him against the concrete block wall, bent over in agonizing pain.

Bernard turned around. "Eddie, you hurt? *Uumpgh.*"

To Eddie's right, two other boys huddled against the wall, trying to cover themselves. Bernard then reached over and picked up the shirt from the floor. He used it to wipe his left hand clean. Eddie could not respond through his uncontrollable whimpers and crying.

"Go put your clothes on," Bernard directed the boys as he helped Eddie stand.

The man started to stand up again while reaching for his shirt. Bernard cupped his left hand behind the abuser's neck and delivered the full power of his right fist square into his face. Blood splattered, as the man sunk to the floor.

Bernard asked the boys, "Got your clothes on? Can you make it back to your rooms?"

"Oh yes, oh yes, we can go back. We'll be okay."

Trying to control his sobs, Eddie looked at Bernard and said, "I'm so glad you found us. You sav ... saved us." Eddie looked down at the bloody heap on the floor. "I hate you! I hate you!"

With that, Eddie dressed and wiped his tears away with his shirt-sleeve. His shoes still untied, Eddie again kicked with all his might. One, two times Eddie powered his shoe Into the bleeding man. Blood smeared his shoe. "Ahhh, you little bastard. You'll pay for that." As Eddie turned and ran to the door, Bernard reached down and popped the back of the abuser's head. All three boys scurried to the door, down the hall, up the stairs, and back to the safety of their rooms.

Smearing his blood on the wall, he raised himself to a sitting position. Gathering his conscience, he reached for his clothes. Bernard kicked them away. Bending over, Bernard gathered and rolled the shirt, pants, and undergarments together.

"I'm cold. Let me have my clothes."

Bernard looked directly at him and said, "Your shoes will keep you warm. *Uumpgh.*" With that, Bernard tucked the rolled bundle of clothes under his arm. He didn't say another word.

The bleeding man crawled over and reached to a shelf housing a stack of hand towels. Remaining seated, he pulled them to his side. First he used one to wipe the blood from around his face, neck, and shoulders.

Meanwhile, Bernard opened the door into the hall. Looking both ways, all he could see was darkness except for the dim light that reached down the stairs. Closing the door behind him, he locked it. He saw a bench at the end of the hall. "*Uumpgh. Uumpgh.*" Picking it up, he propped one end of the bench against the wall opposite the door. The other end underneath the doorknob. *Almost a perfect fit.* He turned and walked back down the hall and into the locker room. After removing some towels from the top shelf, he took them back to the storage door and wedged them underneath the doorknob and the end of the bench. Bernard pulled the handle. *Secure. Sleep well.*

The clothing secure under his arm, Bernard ascended the stairs and left through the back door. Without breaking stride, he tossed the clothing into the trash bin just outside. Bernard thought, *What a bad, bad man.* He started walking and disappeared over the hill in the direction of Friends Cemetery and into the darkness.

CHAPTER 31

UNEXPECTED DILEMMA

Clarence Wolfe—April 15, 1958

CLARENCE Wolfe drove up the long, straight drive toward the reform school at 6:45 a.m. exactly—the same routine as Monday. Clouds hung overhead. Rain was imminent. Cracks of thunder broke the silence of the countryside. The looming brick structure of the school looked overwhelming in size and appearance.

He thought about his governance, his responsibility of overseeing so many lives. This particular morning, flashes of the shadows hidden behind the walls raced through his mind. He always forced them into his subconscious as best he could. Cover-up and rationalization were part of his psyche. He could never forget or erase that night so long ago.

Wolfe steered his four-holer Buick into his reserved parking space—parking space number 1. Walking toward the front steps, he pulled up the collar on his dark trench coat. The large brim of his hat hung over his eyes. Drops began to fall. Slowly, he approached the front entrance. Pulling open the tall heavy entry door with ease, he made his entrance known. Clarence Wolfe was a strong man. His presence personified his controlling and dominant personality.

"Good morning, Miss Gardner," Wolfe always greeted his secretary with an announcement of his arrival. She was busy at her Corona, rapidly typing dictation from yesterday.

Even before he settled behind his desk, Miss Gardner set a large mug of black coffee next to a waiting stack of papers. Wolfe simply nodded, not even offering a simple thank-you. She obligingly accepted his gesture. *Lots on his mind today.*

Clarence Wolfe was anxious as he awaited the letter from Sheriff Thurow. What he wasn't expecting, however, was an urgent call from Harvey Miller, the chief custodian.

Suddenly, he heard a panicked voice from the other room.

"So is he here yet? I have to see him right now! Please!"

Still standing behind his desk, having just hung up his jacket and taken a first swig of his black coffee, Wolfe looked out into the front office and saw Harvey Miller.

Harvey barged into the room. "Mr. Wolfe, sorry to bother you, but you better come now. Right now before anyone else sees."

"Sees what? Tell me, man. What's the hurry?"

"It's Mr. Krueger, sir. He's … he's … Well, just follow me." Not waiting for Wolfe, Miller was out the door and down the hall.

"For Christ's sake," Wolfe mumbled. "I'll be right back," he informed Miss Gardner.

As Harvey Miller scurried down the hall, he turned to look for Wolfe and then continued his charge to the back hall and down the stairs. Wolfe followed. Past the locker room, Harvey Miller panted as he waited at the storage room door for Clarence Wolfe's arrival.

"What's that bench doing here in the middle of the hallway? Get rid of it," Wolfe said as he approached Harvey. Wolfe was a fanatic for neatness.

"In here. In here, sir. Follow me."

Harvey raced down the storage room aisles to the back of the room. He stepped aside. Wolfe froze. There on the floor was the shocking appearance of a naked Phillip Krueger. Nothing covered him except for his shoes and a couple of green hand towels. Blood was smeared, some caked, on his face. Both of his eyes were swollen, one heavily black and blue. Krueger's nose looked askew.

"Krueger, what the hell?" Wolfe bent down. He took a towel and shook the man's shoulder.

Krueger lay on his side. Knees curled up. He groaned.

"What is this? What the hell happened? What'd you do?"

"I'll call an ambulance, Mr. Wolfe," Harvey Miller volunteered.

"No, no. Do not call yet," Wolfe insisted as he formulated what might have happened.

"But, Mr. Wolfe, he needs—"

"I said, no! Now you go back upstairs. Go to the top, beyond the locker room, and chain the locker room door closed. Tell everyone the lockers are closed for now. Then come back downstairs. Be ready in case I need you."

"Yes, sir," Miller responded immediately, although puzzled by the order.

"Krueger, sit up. Tell me what happened. Is this what I think it is? Who did this? For God's sake, where are your clothes?"

Krueger groaned. "I … I was down here, and this guy attacked me." He groaned again. "He attacked me from behind."

"What guy?" Wolfe asked, wanting an immediate explanation.

"Ber—" Krueger felt his eye. His head jolted as he touched his nose. "It was Bernard, Bernard Bednar." Krueger seemed to go in and out of reality. "Where am I? My nose," he said as he attempted to touch it again but only saw more blood on his hand.

"That son of a bitch! I'll have … I'll have him taken straight to jail!" Wolfe exclaimed.

"No, no! Not jail!" Krueger commanded. The sound of those two words shot like a bolt between his eyes and nose.

Wolfe helped Krueger up and leaned him against the wall. Not wanting to touch or come in contact with the other man's body, Wolfe reached for more towels.

"Miller! Get back in here!" Harvey heard the call. "Go to the locker room. Bring me some large towels and then find some work uniforms. Are the stairs blocked?"

"Yes, sir. Just like you said." Miller was off to the locker room and returned a few moments later with a stack of towels.

"Here. Let's get him up on the bench. He is very groggy. Wonder how long he's been here?" Wolfe asked as he took two clean towels.

Krueger groaned aloud as Wolfe and Miller eased him onto the bench.

"Where are your clothes? You've only got shoes on."

"Don't know. Don't know. Maybe that creep Bernard took them," Krueger replied as he groaned in pain.

"Can you walk to the locker room?" Wolfe asked him.

"I'll try. It's my head, my head. Hard to see … and my nose. Oh God, what do I do?"

"Well, you should be able to walk. You got your damn shoes on," Wolfe said as if to shame Krueger for being in such a compromising predicament.

The block walls swirled, and the ceiling closed in on Krueger as he attempted to stand. He stood naked, knees wobbling, with only his shoes to hide his shame. Krueger saw more blood on his chest, arms, and legs. Nausea was his enemy as he detected all the blood. Miller helped Krueger wipe his blood-spattered body. Wolfe stood back.

"You go with Miller. Harvey, have him shower. You get cleaned up, Phillip. Put on a uniform. Then come to my office. No, no, better not. Staff will see you in this god-awful condition. When he's showered and dressed, Miller, you come up to my office. Leave Krueger here though. Then I'll come back down. Where's your overcoat?" Wolfe asked Krueger.

"In my truck. Threw it in there last night."

"Okay. Miller, you get his coat and bring it back down here. At least he's got that."

"Mr. Wolfe, I'm sorry. I'm sorry for all of this," Krueger said in a plaintive, quivering voice. Wrapped in two large gray towels, he eased into a limp with Miller's help.

Wolfe headed for the door.

"Mr. Wolfe … " Krueger groaned. "Mr. Wolfe, don't go to Bernard yet. I need to explain to you what happened last night."

"Last night? You been in here all night? Like this, for God's sake?"

"Yes, I have. Can't remember the time. It all hurts so badly."

"You've got a lot to explain. A lot. Miller, not one word to anyone about this. Hear me?"

"Yes, sir. Nobody will know. Not a word. Between you and me, sir. I mean between the three of us," Miller said as he looked at the forlorn Krueger.

As Harvey Miller walked Krueger to the locker room, he said, "You look worse than Carmen Basilio after his last fight with Sugar Ray."

Krueger responded in disgust, "That's not funny. You're sick, Miller. I'll have your job."

Harvey Miller smiled to himself behind Krueger's back and muttered, "You'll be lucky to keep yours."

As Wolfe returned to his office, he thought, *I hope this is not what I think it is. God, I hope not.*

"Is everything okay, Mr. Wolfe?" Miss Gardner asked with raised eyebrows, as if she needed to know everything that happened around the school.

"Everything is fine, just fine. Bad leak at the back entrance. Miller will handle it. I'm not to be bothered." Wolfe closed the door with a half slam and returned to his cold coffee. "Goddamn it ... that son of a bitch!" he said aloud but in a controlled tone. *That Krueger can't be trusted.* An hour passed. Wolfe heard a knock at the door. "Yes, what is it?"

Miss Gardner opened the door just a crack. "Mr. Wolfe, I didn't want to bother you, but an officer from the sheriff's office was just here. He delivered this letter. Here. See, it says Clarence Wolfe, personal and confidential," she said, holding it in her hand and reaching out to her disgruntled boss. "I'm sure it's quite important, sir," she said as if to taunt him.

"Hand it here. That'll be all." Ignoring the letter opener, Wolfe tore into the envelope with his thumb. Large jagged tears. All he could see within the letter were four names: *Phillip Krueger, Eddie Small, Bernard Bednar,* and *Artie Morris. Please set up meetings for Tuesday afternoon, April 22, 1958, at 2:30 p.m.*

"Holy shit! Goddamn it! That Eddie Small!" He slumped back in his chair. *Tuesday,* he thought. *That's a week away.* Trying to gather his thoughts, Wolfe contemplated what to do. Within the hour, he concluded a call had to be made. Picking up the phone, he dialed 6-6669.

Ring, ring. "Good morning, Mr. Zilbar's office. Yes, he is. Just a minute please."

Wolfe waited, as Zilbar never picked up a phone immediately.

"Randall, this is Clarence. Got a minute?"

"Sure," Zilbar responded in his usual dispassionate voice.

"Listen, I got a problem out here. It's Krueger. Think he's gone a little too far this time," Wolfe said, anticipating Zilbar's negative response.

"Well, if it's about what I'm thinking about, then keep it quiet. Look, let's not talk on the phone. Whatever it is, you have to handle it. Leave me out."

"Listen, Randall, then I'm giving you a heads-up. The sheriff is involved, and I need your advice. You may be a money guy, but I also know you are a lawyer. I need to meet you today or tomorrow, no later."

"Okay, okay. Meet me at the Indiana Hotel late this afternoon. Keep it brief. I'm busy. I have appointments all afternoon and then a dinner engagement this evening. Make it five thirty. I'll be in the bar."

"Good. That's real good. I know you can control...ah...well, difficult situations. Thanks so much. See you then," Wolfe said thankfully.

Randall Zilbar was the only person Clarence Wolfe feared. He had known Zilbar for thirty-five years. Zilbar was *the man* in town. He was the wealthiest and most respected, or at least most catered to, by business-men. Randall Zilbar was civic-minded and rich enough to be a contribu-tor to worthy causes, especially if he thought they would help him or make him look good. He was a pillar of St. Thomas Moore. His father had been one of the three founding members of the parish when they began construction of the new church in 1901.

Father Warren depended on Randall Zilbar, as he was the wealthiest member of the parish and number one every year on the published list of top contributors to the church. Randall Zilbar spent much of his time in Indianapolis and Chicago.

Clarence Wolfe was anxious about their meeting later that after-noon. Although they were not close, Wolfe—like everyone else—was impressed with Zilbar's money, power, and position. Most accepted his arrogance, shiftiness, and self-centered egotism. Nobody dared cross him. Randall Zilbar always controlled those with less, which basically included everyone with whom he came into contact.

As he drove into town later that afternoon, Wolfe thought of what he should say. Meanwhile, Randall Zilbar arrived at the hotel shortly before Wolfe.

"Good evening, Mr. Zilbar. Welcome to the Indiana Hotel," the bellman said as he opened the stately front door.

Randall Zilbar did not acknowledge the man's presence.

"Have a nice evening, sir," the bellman said as he let the door close at Zilbar's heels. *Rich snob.*

Entering the hotel, Zilbar took off his wide-brimmed hat and looked around, taking in the grandeur of the lobby. To the right of the wood paneled registration desk and just beyond the large Persian rug, Zilbar proceeded through the archway to the Green Hat Bar. He appreciated the fine hardwood booths, which were elegantly finished with black leather seats. Looking at the bartender, Zilbar pointed to the booth in the corner. His usual spot. Armond, the bartender, nodded.

Impatiently, Zilbar waited for Clarence Wolfe. *Good. This will be comfortably private.* Promptly, the bartender—a slight man with a pleasant smile, black vest, and a gift for gab—approached Zilbar.

"Good evening, sir. Will someone be joining you?"

"Yes, soon I hope. I'll have my usual vodka martini. Top-shelf."

"Yes, Mr. Zilbar. Just the best for you."

Ego inflated, he sat back in his seat in the back corner booth and relaxed. Randall Zilbar liked this time of day.

Clarence Wolfe wrenched his hands as he walked into the stately lobby and made his way to the bar.

"Good evening, sir," the bartender greeted him.

Wolfe could see Zilbar in the far corner booth. Armond had just returned from presenting Randall Zilbar with his perfectly blended cocktail. With his black vest, white shirt, and friendly smile, Armond was known well by all the regular patrons. Many secrets in Wabash traveled by way of Armond's bar at the Indiana Hotel. Straightening his back, Wolfe took a deep breath and walked by an empty array of perfectly set white linen tabletops.

"Evening, Mr. Zilbar," Wolfe said as he hung his hat and coat on the hook separating the booths.

"Have a seat." Randall Zilbar raised his finger in the air commanding immediate service. Before Zilbar dropped his finger, Armond approached the booth to take Wolfe's order.

"Whiskey on the rocks," Wolfe said, not waiting for the accommodating bartender to ask. "Thank you for meeting on such short notice. I know you are busy. Hope you have some time here at the end of the day," Wolfe said, hoping to receive approval. He received none.

"You've got about thirty minutes at the most," Zilbar informed Wolfe. "What's going on?"

"I might need some help with Sheriff Thurow. You know the right people in town, so … well, I'm asking you to make something go away."

"Explain more exactly what you need. What's this about?" Zilbar insisted.

"Seems that Phillip Krueger has been caught indiscreetly with three of the boys. Now the sheriff is going to investigate."

"Oh, for Christ's sake! I've told you to be careful, to watch that Krueger. He knows too much. How'd you find out about this?"

Wolfe hesitated and then said, "I was there. I saw the aftermath of his deed, and it wasn't pretty."

"What deed?" Zilbar asked, expecting an explicit answer.

"One of our long-time attendants caught Krueger with one of the boys in a very bad state. Bloodied up Krueger pretty badly."

"How the hell can you allow an attendant to bloody up an administrator? Who's in control out there? Who's this a … who's this attendant?"

"Bednar. Bernard Bednar."

"Then fire him. Get rid of the bastard. First, you have this Krueger banging the boys, and now this Bednar fellow is pounding Krueger. Get control. Hear?"

"Can't fire Bednar, sir. He's been there too long, since back in the twenties. Long before I was. He was there when Horace Showers was the chief administrator. You know where I'm going. He was there when the Yoder boy was murdered, and we … "

"Murdered?" Zilbar responded. "There was no murder out there. I know. I heard it was the flu," he said, playing mind games.

Wolfe looked at Zilbar. *Okay, if you say so.* "Yeah, but that's why we can't fire Bednar. Rumor's always been that he was there that night. Some say Bernard saw it. Saw the murderer leaving the room where the boy was found. I'm told he kind of mentions it every so often," Wolfe said with apparent accuracy.

"You mean like a threat?"

"Yes, so we can't stir him up. Just leave Bednar be. Strange guy."

Zilbar did not add any further comment about Bernard Bednar. Then he replied, "So you want me to cover your ineptitude?"

Wolfe knew any answer would be wrong, so he just nodded and replaced any words with two bountiful sips of Jack Daniels.

"Phillip Krueger?" Zilbar asked, nodding defiantly. "Phillip Krueger. That son of a bitch is weak. Can't be trusted. If he exposes anything, it will be his last act," Zilbar said in a threatening manner.

Clarence Wolfe knew. He took another drink and thought, *Never cross Randall Zilbar.*

Zilbar thought for a minute and then warned again. "If this is true and it ever gets out … it will … it will—" Zilbar stopped midsentence. "Look at me. You make sure you never ever say that I have ever been out to the school. Get it? Get it, Wolfe? How can you have let this happen?"

"Well, sir, let me explain. The sheriff hasn't proven a thing yet. He says he's received complaints. He wants to talk to some staff. We can ward it off."

"You mean you want me to ward it off?" Zilbar asked, disgusted. "Do you realize what Krueger's involved in? The chamber, the Scouts, the Wabash Foundation. For Christ's sake, this must be controlled. Push the button and that weak bastard will talk like a parrot. He knows little but just enough to harm us."

"I received a letter from the sheriff today. Krueger's on the list."

"What list? How do you know?"

"I know some things Krueger's been up to. The sheriff will be talking one-on-one to these four on his list."

"Okay, this meeting's over. We're done."

Clarence Wolfe knew their time was up, though it had only been fifteen minutes. Randall stood up, reached for his coat, thrust his arms into the long black tailored overcoat, and shook it comfortably onto his shoulders.

Zilbar leaned over with both hands on the table. "Let me make this clear. I have never been out to that school alone. Remember! After those meetings, you quietly call me. You hear?"

"Yes, sir, I do. I mean, I will."

"If Krueger has done anything to tarnish my involvement or respected presence in this town, I'll have him. He'll be history. Get it?"

Good-byes didn't seem appropriate. Clarence Wolfe understood. He knew Zilbar had all things only one way—his way. Wolfe sat back. He saw only the back of Randall Zilbar's coat. After Randall left, Armond instinctively walked over to Wolfe's booth.

"Yes, Armond, another," Wolfe said, raising his empty glass and shaking it. "Make that a double." *I've got to shut the guy up. Randall's right. Krueger can't be trusted.*

CHAPTER 32

AND THEN THERE WERE TWO

Sister Mary Michael—April 15, 1958

"OKAY class. That will be all for today. Let's stand and say our afternoon prayer. Peter, why don't you lead us today?" Sister Mary Michael said as she prepared her class for dismissal.

Peter immediately responded, "In the name of the Father, and of the Son, and of the Holy Ghost."

Then, having completed the last prayer of the day, the children automatically packed their books.

"Okay, row one, you're first."

The students walked to the back of the room and gathered their coats from the closet. The other rows followed.

"All right, everyone, let's keep the noise down. The bell hasn't rung yet. Who's on duty to stay after and sweep the room and carry out the trash?" sister asked so that all could hear.

Dennis Rhoades and Joe Kreft raised their hands.

"Okay, boys, you two always do a good job." With that, everyone heard the bell ring. "Walk carefully, everyone. No running. See you all tomorrow," she said as they left the room.

"Goodnight, Sister."

"Goodnight, Donald. Good luck finding more arrowheads. Someday you are going to be an archeologist," Sister Mary Michael said with a smile. "I know you like arrowheads more than your homework."

Donald stopped and smiled, "You bet, Sister, arrowheads, cars, and girls. That's me!"

"Good night, Donald. Now get along. Goodnight to you, Sally. You did a great job today in the spelldown."

Sister Mary Michael remained at her desk. She had a pile of papers to correct. Dennis and Joe had just about completed cleaning the room when she looked up. She noticed Gene Kowolski had remained in his seat. Slowly he walked up to her desk.

"Well, Gene, I didn't notice you were still here. Are you finishing up some work?"

"Sister, I was kinda wondering if I could talk to you in private."

"Why sure, Gene. Sure. Why don't you wait until Dennis and Joe are finished? Just sit at the first desk." She continued with her papers. Gene sat at the desk with his hands folded nervously.

"We're finished, Sister," Joe said. "Can we go now?"

"Sure, boys, that will be fine. Thank you. Don't forget your homework." Sister Mary Michael put her pen down, stood up, and walked around her desk. Gene noticed she was picking up her rosary and holding it in both hands as she sat down across the narrow aisle from him.

"What is it, Gene? What can I help you with?"

Gene knew he would have to show courage to tell the sister what was on his mind. "Sister, this is very … this is very hard. I need to tell someone, and I don't know who to go to," he said hesitantly.

"Now, Gene, you can tell me. I am here to help you, whatever it might be."

"Okay, Sister. You see this problem, this problem I have."

Sister Mary Michael could see his eyes welling with tears.

"This problem started one day before Christmas. It was after Mass. Jerry Arnold and I served Mass. Jerry left, and I was still in the sacristy. Father Jaeger was taking off his vestments. I took off my surplus and went to the back closet to hang it up. I … I started to unbutton my cassock. I felt hands on my shoulders. Sister, I turned … I turned around. It was Father Jaeger. He said I was a wonderful server. Then he said I had beautiful hair. Then he hugged me and started unbuttoning my cassock. As he was halfway down, I felt both his hands go around my waist and then around my front pockets. It happened so fast, Sister. He then unbuckled my belt. Sister, I can't … I can't say any more."

Sister Mary Michael listened in startled horror. She took a breath and held her emotions in check. "Gene, are you sure this is what happened? Are you sure this wasn't a dream?"

Gene responded, "No, Sister. I wish it was a dream. It is terrible. I'm here today because I need help. I don't know what to do. 'Cause it has happened more times since then."

Sister Mary Michael jerked her head. "More? How often?"

"I know exactly, Sister. I know when. I know where. I know how many times. Sister, it's been nine times."

Having been exposed to such crimes, Sister Mary Michael squeezed her rosary beads so hard she thought they might break. She then asked, "Always in that closet?"

"No, just two times there." She could tell how difficult this was for Gene. "There were other places. Once in the confessional, a few times in the father's room."

"You mean you were up at the father's room?" she asked, disgusted.

Gene lowered his head. He felt ashamed. He buried his face in his hands and mumbled. "Sister, I was afraid. I knew he was a priest. I didn't know a priest could be bad."

As Gene kept his face buried in his hands, Sister Mary Michael stood up and walked over to the side windows. She stared out the window, trying to gather herself. Not a word was spoken between the two. She thought. Taking a deep breath, she walked back, her rosary still in her hand.

Sitting back down, she said, "Gene, we have to address this situation now. I will ask you one thing. Please look at me, Gene."

Lifting his head from his hands, his eyes tearing up, Gene looked directly at the good sister.

"Gene, just tell me again. Did all of this really happen? Did it happen this many times? Is this what … " Not believing her own words, she said, "Did Father Jaeger do this to you?"

Gene looked at the sister and said, "Sister, I promise. I promise in … in God's name that this is the truth. Sister, I wouldn't lie."

"Gene, I am going to talk to the father about this. No, not Father Jaeger. I'm going to have to talk to Fathers Warren and Father Sullivan."

"Sister, but I'm scared. What if he does it again?"

Sister Mary Michael looked directly at Gene. "If he even approaches you, scream and run. Just get away. Then you come directly to me. Promise? I'm your friend, Gene."

Gene hesitated, didn't say a word, and then nodded. "Yes, Sister, I promise."

CHAPTER 33

PLANNED MEETING

Father Sullivan—April 18, 1958

FATHER Sullivan was a week behind in reading his mail. A popular and respected priest, he usually received several personal letters each week. Students and parishioners alike were attracted to him. Not only was he was liked, but Father Sullivan was also trusted and respected. Most letters were from adults.

Flipping through the mail on his desk, he recognized the elegant blue script on one envelope. Noticing the absence of the sender's name and return address, Father Sullivan quickly slipped the opener into the envelope, welcoming the letter inside.

April 8, 1958

Dear Father,

I hope this letter finds you well. Please understand that I would like to receive your advice. Would you have some time to meet? I want to talk about Joey. Would it be possible to meet in your office? May I suggest April 22 at 4:30 p.m.? If so, please respond by mail. My address is still 522 Arthur Street.

Thank you for your consideration.
Linda Singleton

Father Sullivan reread the letter. He vividly remembered her confession several weeks prior. His heart remained heavy. Random thoughts of Linda were a temptation deep within his being. As difficult as it was for her, he was keenly aware of his own conflicts suppressed within his mind. Late into evenings, alone by himself, he often thought of Linda.

Trying to fall asleep that night, Father Sullivan was still awake at 1:30 a.m. He got up and went to his desk. With pen in hand, he replied to her letter.

Scripting his own thoughts in response, he carefully and thoughtfully penned the right words without any reflection of his thoughts about her.

Dear Linda,

I received your letter of April 8. I hope you are well. Of course, you are welcome to visit, and we can talk about any concerns you have about Joey. He is a fine boy, and I would be pleased to help the two of you in any way I can. I look forward to our visit on April 22.

Until then,
Father Michael Sullivan

The next morning, after his 6:00 Mass and breakfast with Father Warren, Father Sullivan took a walk downtown. Envelope in hand, he dropped it in the mailbox. The morning was cool and clear, typical of early spring in Indiana. Whenever he walked by the courthouse, he was always struck by the stature of the stately building. He greeted President Lincoln, who stood solitary at the corner of Hill and Wabash. Father Sullivan walked downtown, over around Darnell Lumberyard and the Honeywell Center, and back up to Hill Street. He focused on all the good in his life and was thankful. His thoughts, however, returned to his concerns and stress about the boys and the abusing priest. On his way back to the rectory, Father Sullivan walked around the courthouse and stopped at the corner of Hill and Wabash. As he looked over the city, the priest's mind drifted, and he thought about Linda and their meeting on April 22.

CHAPTER 34

MEETING AT THE SCHOOL

Sheriff Thurow—April 22, 1958

SHERIFF Thurow entered the main office of the reform school. "Good afternoon, Miss Gardner. Mr. Wolfe is expecting me."

"Seems like you were just here, Sheriff Thurow," Miss Gardner said, pressing her lips together.

Not feeling very welcome, the sheriff shot back, "That's right, Miss Gardner. You have a good memory for a person your age. Yes, let me see, it was last week as a matter of fact. Your office almost feels like home. Your hospitality is quite welcoming."

Not knowing how to respond, she paused and then directed the sheriff by pointing to a chair against the wall. "Sit right there. I'm sure Mr. Wolfe is looking forward to your visit."

"Thank you. I appreciate your hospitality," Sheriff Thurow said with a smile.

Miss Gardner raised her nose from her trusty Corona and retreated to Clarence Wolfe's office. A minute passed before she returned. She catered to Clarence Wolfe as if she was first in his will. Her astute awareness of the sheriff's suspicions of Wolfe influenced her attitude and remarks toward the man with the badge.

"He'll see you now, Sheriff. You may go in." She guarded the door until the sheriff entered Wolfe's office.

"Thanks for allowing me the audience," he whispered to Miss Gardner as he stepped around her desk and entered the office.

"Hello, Mr. Wolfe."

"Sheriff Thurow, have a seat."

Trying to lighten the conversation, the sheriff said, "Does she ever smile?"

"No. She's not paid to," Wolfe replied with a straight face. "Okay. I got your letter. How long will this take?" he asked, trying to intimidate the sheriff's authority.

"It will take as long as I need," Sheriff Thurow said, taking command, matching Wolfe's positioning.

"Well, you can cut your time by 25 percent. Krueger's not here. Sick today."

The sheriff did not respond immediately, knowing Krueger was the prime reason for the visit and questioning. Sheriff Thurow remembered his promise to Ed Small. "That's convenient. How sick?"

"Not really sick. He had an accident. Fell down the stairs. Bruised his face up pretty badly."

"That's too bad. Sorry to hear it." The sheriff paused. "Bruised? Can he talk?"

"Yes, I imagine he can talk, but he's not feeling well."

"Not feeling well. *Hmmm* … Mr. Wolfe, let me be direct. I'm not feeling well about this whole situation taking place out here, but I can talk. He will answer. You have him here today. Bring him in while I talk to the other three."

Clarence Wolfe was not accustomed to being bossed around. "Sheriff, you can't tell me what to do. I said Mr. Krueger Is not here."

"Mr. Wolfe, let me inform you. You may run this school, but your school is in my county. I'm responsible for the safety of everyone in Wabash County. So you haul him in here during the next two hours, or I'll have you—along with Krueger—down at the jail before the sun sets. Then you'll both know the definition of police interrogation. I even have a number of questions I'd like to ask *you*. However, that will wait. I'm sure you wouldn't want the newspapers seeing you and your bruised-up friend walking into the county jail. All I have to do is call George Griffin over at the newspapers. They might throw in a few questions also, especially if I give a little advance warning. Now that wouldn't look too good for you and this school, not to mention the civic-minded Phillip Krueger."

"Okay, okay, I'll have Krueger here in a couple hours."

"No more than ninety minutes," he told Wolfe. "Works better for me."

"Miss Gardner, get Krueger on the line for me. You have his home phone number, don't you?"

She immediately began to dial.

"One more thing, Mr. Wolfe," the sheriff said. "I'd like to use a room, a private room. Is there one close by?"

"Yes, over there past the window. Very quiet," Wolfe said, pointing to the conference room on the far side of the large office area beyond Miss Gardner's desk.

"Oh, thank you. I see it's in Miss Gardner's territory," Sheriff Thurow remarked, maintaining his position. He knew he was two up on Wolfe. "Please tell your sergeant at arms that I would like to see Mr. Bednar, then Artie Morris, and lastly Eddie Small. By then, you'll have Krueger back here. Could you please show me the room?"

The sheriff followed Wolfe to the meeting room. Passing Miss Gardner's desk, he stopped and bent down. "Ma'am, when you've finished with your typing, could you please bring me a pitcher of water and four glasses for my visitors? Oh yes, make it six. One for me and one for yourself." With a big grin, he left her and proceeded to catch up with Wolfe. "Oh, one more thing," the sheriff said, turning around to Miss Gardner. "Please have Bernard Bednar come to see me now."

Clarence Wolfe heard the sheriff's request. "I'll handle that. James, come here," the director commanded.

With his door open, James had probably heard every word. James Duncan, the trusty bookkeeper, removed his green visor and came directly to the door of the meeting room.

"James, the sheriff here is going to be meeting with a few members of our staff this afternoon. Just routine. As he needs them, will you go and find Bernard Bednar, then Artie, and also Eddie Small."

"Sure thing, chief. I'm right on it."

"Duncan, it's Mr. Wolfe to you. I don't like that chief stuff."

James didn't respond but enthusiastically left the room, heading down the hall in the direction of the stairs. He handled accounting and many clerical matters within the school. He was a twenty-two-year veteran of the Wabash Reform School, having arrived during the Great Depression in 1936. However, he was tired of numbers. Bound by his job, Duncan wanted to be more involved in assisting Clarence Wolfe in the running of the school. Besides that, he knew most everything going on at the school. Well, almost everything.

As Clarence Wolfe left to pick up Krueger, he stopped at Miss Gardner's desk. "Is Krueger's file up-to-date?"

"Yes, of course," she replied. "Just as you instructed."

When things were not right or just the way he wanted, Wolfe would stop at nothing to set the records according to his rules.

A few minutes passed. "Here he is, Sheriff," James announced as he stood with Bernard in the doorway.

"Come on in, Bernard. Thank you, Mr. Duncan. Please close the door when you leave. I'll call you when I need Artie Morris."

Bernard took a chair at the long table, his back to the door. Sheriff Thurow walked around and sat directly across from Bernard.

"Nice badge, *uumpgh*," Bernard said, pointing at the sheriff's silver star. "You here to ask me about Krueger? *Uumpgh.*"

"What makes you ask that?" Sheriff Thurow asked, taken aback by Bernard's immediate question.

"Well, I did it. I took care of him. He was hurting Eddie." Bernard was blatantly direct.

"When was this?"

"Last Monday, five-thirty." Bernard remembered exactly.

"You mean when he fell down the stairs?" the sheriff asked, fishing for the real answer from Bernard.

"No stairs. He was naked behind Eddie. Had shoes on. I took care of him. *Uumpgh.*"

"Took care of him? What do you mean, Bernard?"

"Easy. I just used this hand around his neck," Bernard said, raising his right arm. "Pulled him right off Little Eddie." As he clenched his left fist, he went on to say, "Then I used this. *Uumpgh.*"

"How did you use your fist?" the sheriff asked again.

"Slam! Right into his stick," Bernard said with a look of disgust. Turning his now open left hand, he continued, "Bad man, that Krueger. Then all the blood on his face. *Uumpgh.*"

"Blood? How'd that happen?" Sheriff Thurow asked again, baiting Bernard.

"Yes, I slammed this right … *uumpgh* … slammed this," he said, holding his right fist up, "in his face. Heard a noise. *Uumpgh.* Think it was the bone in his nose. Maybe his teeth. *Crunch.*"

"What about Eddie?"

"Told him, 'Put your clothes on.' He was cryin'. *Uumpgh.* He gotta out a there fast, along with Sam and Jerry running behind. That's good. He ran from that bad man. I took care of Krueger. He was leanin' up against the wall."

"Was he breathing?" the sheriff asked, just to substantiate Bernard's story.

"Yep, I checked. He'd asked for his clothes. Didn't give to him," Bernard said confidently. "His face was in bad shape. He's a bad man. Bad to the boys."

"Then what happened? You know, after the boys ran?"

"Then I walked home. I was tired. *Uumpgh.*"

The sheriff was busy taking notes, hoping to get down every detail Bernard reported.

"That's all?" Bernard asked. "Am I done? 'Nuff talking, *uumpgh.*"

Sheriff Thurow thought Bernard was for real. His green work shirt looked oversized and was buttoned right up to his neck. Short cropped hair. He had fists the size of mallets.

"One other thing, Bernard." On the surface Bernard seemed slow. His simple direct description gave off an aura of sincerity and truth.

"*Uumpgh. Uumpgh.*"

"Does anyone else hurt the boys? Anyone besides Phillip Krueger?"

Bernard leaned forward and put his elbows on the table. A weird look crossed his face. Lowering his head along with his eyelids, he looked directly at the sheriff. "Yep, yep. There's more that hurt the boys. Bernard knows."

"Who? Who else hurts the boys, Bernard?" Sheriff Thurow asked, hoping to coax more information from the simple man.

Bernard paused. Sheriff Thurow could tell he wanted to say something else, but he seemed hesitant. Bernard looked down at his clasped fists and paused. He looked up and then said, "Somebody hurt a boy long,

long ago. I was young, just started here at the school. They said he died of flu. No way. Somebody killed him. I know."

"What? Killed? Who? How do you know, Bernard?"

Bernard hesitated and then said, "Gordon. I found him. Dead."

"Did you see who killed him?"

Bernard did not reply. The sheriff noted the look on his face; it seemed as if he wanted to say something, but he held back.

"Done. I'm done. No more. *Uumpgh*." Bernard stood up. "Oh. One more thing. When I left Krueger, took his clothes. Threw 'em in trash outdoors. Round back. *Uumpgh*." Bernard poured a glass of water and drank it in one gulp.

The sheriff watched his Adam's apple jump up and down. He knew Bernard was done. Bernard set the glass back down on the oak table and looked directly at the sheriff.

"Done. Got work to do. Boys need their dinner soon."

Sheriff Thurow knew he needed to maintain Bernard's trust. The low-key questioning enabled Bernard to trust him. Bernard knew the sheriff was there to help and that he would handle Krueger. That was all Bernard cared about. Get Krueger. He knew the sheriff could help the boys.

Sheriff Thurow knew Bernard told the truth but knew more. He watched as Bernard stood, walked out past Miss Gardner's desk, and disappeared into the lobby.

Miss Gardner never looked up from her Corona.

CHAPTER 35

WITH HIM AT LAST

Linda Singleton—April 22, 1958

SISTER Agatha responded immediately to the front doorbell. "Good afternoon, young lady. Expecting you. Please step in." Her smile was welcoming. Her caring for the fathers was equally matched by the pleasant manner she extended to all who came into contact with her.

"Hello, Sister, I'm Linda Singleton."

"Yes, I know, Ms. Singleton. Father Sullivan is expecting you. Please come with me."

Linda followed the sister through the foyer. She noticed Father Warren sitting in the parlor. As she walked by, Father Warren did not notice the visitor. Linda's knee-length silk dress was colorfully matched by her shoulder shawl. She carried her best leather purse. She felt the anticipation of seeing Father Sullivan as she followed Sister Agatha down the hall.

Father Sullivan's study door was open. Sitting behind his desk, he made sure he had papers open. His black horn-rimmed glasses sat on the end of his nose. He looked studious and focused while experiencing his own anticipation.

Upon arriving in front of the priest's open door, Sister Agatha stopped. "Father, Miss Singleton is here."

"Oh thank you, Sister."

Sister Agatha reached in and closed the door behind Linda. *What a nice lady.*

Linda stepped forward at the same time Father Sullivan stood, nonchalantly tossing his glasses on top of his papers. Walking around his desk, he extended his hand. He clasped both of his hands around hers. They both knew but didn't say.

"Linda, so glad to see you. You are looking well." *Really well.* He nodded in obvious approval. "Here, please sit," he said, motioning to the chair in front of his desk.

"Thank you, Father," she said as she sat and then fixed her dress neatly below her knees. She longed to call him Michael.

Father Sullivan repositioned the second straight armchair in front of his desk almost squarely to hers. He crossed his right knee over his left, only slightly exposing his long black sock just below the black cuff of his trousers.

"How have you been, Linda? It's been a long time," he said, looking directly at her and smiling his relaxed, pleasant smile. "A hi at school or a hello at the courthouse isn't much of a connection." Neither one mentioned their visit in the confessional, but they knew. "I'm glad you decided to visit today. This is good. It's really private here for whatever you have on your mind. Official business, of course," he said, still with that natural smile.

"Yes, it really has been a long time, Father. Quite a long time."

"Linda, what brings you here?" he asked in a more priestly manner.

"It's Joey, Father. I am concerned about him."

"Concerned? Why? What's up with Joey?"

Linda paused, not knowing exactly how to begin. "Joey's really a good kid. He really is, Father. He's smart, works hard, and doesn't cause me any problems. But … but he doesn't spend a lot of time with other kids in his class. He's in eighth grade, as you know, but at thirteen, he's very mature both physically and just in the way he acts. Sometimes he seems fifteen, maybe sixteen."

"Linda, some boys mature faster than others. I see Joey around school. I know. Yes, I'd agree, he does look and acts older than the other boys." he said, shaking his head.

"It's not just that. My main concern is that he spends most of his time with or talking about Father Jaeger. I know he really doesn't have a father. He has never been around. Never there for him. Joey doesn't even know his own dad."

Father Sullivan was a little puzzled. He sat back, more relaxed, outwardly showing a very unconcerned look. "It's understandable, Linda. Joey's thirteen and trying to find himself." Then he said, "Some boys go through this, just at different ages."

Linda looked at Father Sullivan with wanting eyes, yet she had mixed feelings and was frustrated about Joey and about Father Sullivan. Joey was her main reason for her visit, or so she had convinced herself. "Oh, Michael—I mean Father. Sorry. Father, this is difficult for me to say, but I believe Joey might be homosexual. Just a number of things he says and does. Also, he spends so much time with Father Jaeger and a couple of the other boys."

Father Sullivan leaned forward and then back in his chair. He contemplated. He thought to himself, *Joey's own mother confirmed what Father Warren and I suspect. Father Jaeger. Joey could be one of several involved with the abusive priest.* Linda looked at the priest, amazed how he could always remain so calm, so in control. *He hasn't changed at all.*

"Now, on the other hand, for the past few months, Joey's really been talking about becoming a priest. Now this is good, Father, I know. If that's what he wants, I will totally support him. But, Father, it's the other. If he's that way, I don't understand. I don't know how I would handle it."

Linda took her white handkerchief from her purse and dabbed her eyes. "It's just me and Joey. What if this priest is with him too much? You know what I mean, Father? I just don't know about these things. Father," she said, looking at him with pleading eyes. "Help me. Tell me. Tell me a priest wouldn't … wouldn't … You know what I'm trying to say? Please, Michael, tell me Father Jaeger wouldn't," she said, surrendering to calling him Michael. He noticed but didn't correct her.

Father Sullivan could feel his own pulse. He swallowed. With his elbows on his knees, he bent closer and clasped her hands. "Linda, I have to be honest. Linda, no, I'm sorry. I can't tell you that. I can't tell you Father Jaeger is not like that."

Conclusions, desired answers, and direction were not to be had that late afternoon. Their hands clasped for a long time but too short of a time. The emotions were too heartfelt for Linda.

"Father, please understand. This is much more than I expected. I must go." She took a slight breath. "Michael, this all is just too difficult for me. I need to think. I need to sort out my thoughts." With that said, Linda stood and proceeded to the door.

As she reached for the doorknob, Father Sullivan spoke softly, "Linda, wait. Just wait."

He slowly walked around the chair and approached her. As she reached for the door again, he touched her shoulder. She turned around. Father Sullivan looked her straight in the eye. Her eyes welled with tears. She reached for her handkerchief. Dabbing her eyes, she could feel his arms around her back. His hug was slow, close, and comforting. Closing her eyes, Linda relaxed her head onto his secure shoulder. She savored the moment.

Softly, he whispered, "I want to be here the best I can for you." She could feel his head shake as he took a slow breath. "But we both know that which cannot be."

Comforted by his embrace, Linda instinctively put her arms around his neck. She felt the stiffness of his collar against her wrist—a reminder of his priestly vows. He dropped his hands from around Linda, pulling her hands down from around his collar, and clasping them both within his. Looking Linda in her eye, "Linda, my dear Linda, this...we both know this cannot be." Linda turned. Father let go of her hands. "Here, I'll walk with you to the door," he said. Father Sullivan stood back and reached for the door.

His words seemed dismissive to Linda in her frail state of mind. Without another word, they both walked to the front door of the rectory.

Stepping outside, Linda stood on the steps. Looking back at him, she said with hesitation, as if she wanted to say more, "Thank you, Michael..." She hesitated, "I just want to say..."

For a brief moment, their gazes connected. Then Linda turned and walked away.

CHAPTER 36

A TIME TO TELL

Phillip Krueger—April 22, 1958

CLARENCE Wolfe walked up the steps of Phillip Krueger's front porch. He found Krueger sitting alone at his kitchen table. An unread newspaper and a cup of coffee were his only companions. In his attempt to ease the pain, there was also an aspirin jar and an ice pack. He noticed that somehow Krueger had found a way to have a line of stitches sewn across his cheekbone and above his left eye.

Krueger offered no resistance to Clarence Wolfe's order: "Come with me."

Krueger could feel the weight of the situation as Wolfe drove him up to the school. Sitting in the passenger seat, elbow propped on the door, head in hand, he was a little relieved that the swelling in his right eye had partially dissipated. His left eye was still a swollen black mess, like a freshly packed Italian sausage. His nose had a slight bend but with only a fraction of the pain from the previous week. Krueger's cut lip had been slower to mend.

Wolfe instructed, "Now remember, Bernard hit you and threw you into the wall when you caught *him* naked with the boys in the storage room. Say he had his arms around that Small kid."

"Yes, sir, I get it. And I'll say this was the first time anything like this has ever happened at our school."

"You be confident and convince this sheriff that it's all handled. I was right. I met with Artie White. Bernard told him about what happened.

Artie will say you protected the boys. He fears for his job. Artie will tell the same story I've told you. You know him. He'll toe the line."

"Yes, but what about Eddie Small?" Krueger asked. "He's the one I'm concerned about."

"Phillip, we both know he's a habitual liar. He's always been in trouble for two years now … lies, lies, lies. Just read his file."

"But what if he tells what he really saw?"

"Phillip, we'll show the sheriff. Didn't you hear what I said? Small's file will tell the story. Dates, incidences, the counselor, our nurse, and your comments—even the time you brought him into my office. You remember that. He lied to both of us. It's all right there. Typed perfectly. Miss Gardner double-checked. You must make sure you tell exactly what I told you."

He's got it covered. Phillip's mind was easing.

The two men haltingly went up the steps, and Wolfe opened the tall oak doors. Krueger followed tentatively.

"We're back, Miss Gardner." Approaching Miss Gardner's desk, Wolfe bent over and discreetly asked, "Everything handled?"

"All will be fine," she replied, exposing her confident, coy smile.

Although Wolfe had convinced Krueger and Miss Gardner he was in control, he was having a more difficult time convincing himself. "Is the sheriff in the room?" He pointed to the closed door.

"Artie White's in there now. Bernard was with the sheriff for a very long time," Miss Gardner said with emphasis on the word *very*.

A long time? Wolfe asked himself. *That's not what I want to hear.*

Wolfe did not respond. Krueger, who was standing behind him, gulped and trembled inside. Miss Gardner looked at Krueger, giving him a full inspection. "I heard you fell down the stairs, Mr. Krueger. That's too bad. Hope you'll be okay," she said with a note of fake sincerity.

Miss Gardner and Phillip Krueger each held quiet distain for one another, as they both competed for Clarence Wolfe's approval, which was always sparse at best.

"Phillip, you go back to your office until the sheriff is ready for you. No use presenting a spectacle. I'm sure Duncan already sized you up," he said, looking at the bookkeeper's open door. "I'll call you when the sheriff is ready. Now, you remember everything I told you to say," Wolfe whispered, making sure Miss Gardner's radar did not pick up his words.

Without hesitation, Krueger headed for the safety of his office. Duncan looked from beneath his green visor and watched Krueger scurry pass Miss Gardner's desk. He worked hard to learn and know everything that went on around the school.

"See you soon, Mr. Krueger," Miss Gardner said without looking up from her Corona. "I'm sure you are looking forward to your visit with Sheriff Thurow."

"Bitch," Krueger mumbled as he walked back to his office, not even caring if she heard.

Clarence Wolfe knocked on the conference room door. "Who is it?" a voice came from within.

"Clarence Wolfe," he said, opening the door. "Krueger's in his office. Call when you're ready."

"Tell him he's next," Sheriff Thurow said in a tone that sounded like a warning. "I'm finishing up with Mr. White. Then you can bring Mr. Krueger in. Tell him I'm anxious to meet with him."

Wolfe closed the door and proceeded back to his office. Without breaking stride, he took Eddie's file from Miss Gardner's desk as he would a cold towel while running a marathon.

"All in order, as you asked," Miss Gardner said as he closed his office door.

He slammed the file onto his desk, knowing this process was not going to advance his cause and good name if the county board became aware of these goings-on. On the bright side, Clarence Wolfe was relieved that the sheriff was not aware of Harvey Miller's involvement, at least not for now.

Back in the conference room, Sheriff Thurow was finishing up with Artie. "Okay, Mr. White, let me summarize what you have told me. You know that there has been some abuse of boys by some of the older, bigger guys in the school. You specifically were aware of a staff member, a Bernard Bednar, who defended one Eddie Small against a Billy, a Billy ... What did you say his last name was?"

"Billy, Billy Hackett, sir."

"Now, you said Bernard is one of the staff members who helps the boys, along with yourself."

"Yeah, he took care of Billy Hackett."

"Then you said that wasn't reported."

"No. Billy decided to just stay away from Eddie and not tell Krueger."

"Oh, one last thing, Mr. White. I want to be clear on this. You stated that you are not aware of any abuse of the boys by the staff. You're sure?"

"Well, Sheriff Thurow, it's like this. I have my own floor to take care of, and I haven't seen anything. Not a thing. That's all I know. I like my job here. I have a big family to support. Don't want to be mixed up in anything, so I just do my job and don't bother anyone. Maybe sometimes I … I just keep to myself, Sheriff. Now that Bernard's a good guy. That's all I know happened. Can I go now?"

"Yes, Mr. White. Thank you for your help."

The sheriff sat for a few moments and completed his notes on Artie White. His last line read, *Good guy. Seemed like he knew more than what he told. Fear in his voice not to snitch.*

Sheriff Thurow took a much-needed drink of water. He knew it was close to dinnertime, but he didn't want to stop. He was anxious to hear what Phillip Krueger would have to say. Opening the door, he said, "Excuse me, Miss Gardner. Could you send Phillip Krueger in?"

Miss Gardner pursed her lips and looked up from her typewriter. Then before she could say a word, James Duncan was on his way to Phillip Krueger's office. They soon returned. James had a radar sense of what was happening and was able to respond to a request nearly before it was asked. James Duncan was both intelligent and intuitive.

Phillip Krueger passed Miss Gardner on his way to the conference room. As he walked by her desk, she quietly said to him, "The whole truth and nothing but the truth," just low enough for him to hear. "You know what I mean, Mr. Supreme Commander?" She asked in delight as she observed his psychological and physical discomfort.

"You're next," he replied. Then he leaned over her desk and said, "Then you can tell him everything you do for Mr. Wolfe," he said, smiling from ear to ear. "I mean everything."

"I'm not on the list," Miss Gardner boasted.

"Well, maybe you soon will be after I'm finished," Krueger said, trying to alarm her.

"Come on in, Mr. Krueger. I'm looking forward to hearing what you have to say," the sheriff said from inside the room, not rising from his table as he saw Krueger approaching the open door.

"Yes, Sheriff. I'm here. Here on my day off," Krueger said, trying to show his cooperation while keeping his head down.

"With the looks of your face, you might need a few more days off."

"Well, I'm glad to be here if this will help the boys and the school."

"That's thoughtful of you, Mr. Krueger. I'm sure a man of your position can shed some light on what's going on around here. I need for you to clarify a few things. Have a seat," he said, pointing to a chair across the table. "Would you like some cold water?"

"Don't mind if I do," he said as he poured a glass, subconsciously delaying the anticipated inquisition for as long as possible.

"Let's begin. We'll keep this informal. So you just tell me how you were battered. Where was it? The storage room?" the sheriff asked, starting the questioning. "Don't spare the details."

"Sure, Sheriff. 'Bout a week ago, I had stayed late, catching up on some paperwork. It was around six thirty, and I was in the back hall. Hearing some screams from the lower level—sounded like it came from around the lockers—I immediately ran downstairs. I thought it was from the lockers, but the noise was coming from beyond, farther down the hall in the storage room. Then I heard, 'No, no,' from one of the boys. The storage room was closed, but I could hear the muffled sounds. Fortunately, I had my master key, as Bernard had locked the door from the inside."

"Excuse me. You said Bernard locked the door?" the sheriff said as if he was surprised.

"I then opened the door, and I heard the pleas. I ran down the aisle. Bernard was all over Eddie. None of the three boys had any clothes on. Poor little Eddie," Krueger said, trying to show some sympathy.

"What was he doing?" Sheriff Thurow asked.

"This is difficult, Sheriff, you know. The big strong Bernard was holding Eddie from behind, right there over the bench. I pulled Bernard off. It was difficult because he was really ready when I pulled him away.

It was not very pleasant timing. Well, it was just in time to save Eddie from, from, you know."

"Yes, I know what that means," the sheriff replied.

"It was awful. After I pulled Bernard away from Eddie, he went into a rage. It was sickening to look at. Then I reached to help Eddie. Maybe four, five seconds went by. And then this big sweaty man pulled me up from behind, swung me around, and slammed his fist straight into my face. Not once but twice. I could feel and smell his messy hand. Looking down at the boys hovered against the wall, I saw the terror in their eyes. That's it. I can't talk about it any more. Too hard to go back."

"Now, let me clarify," Sheriff Thurow stated. "Bernard and Eddie didn't have any clothes on?"

"Right, Sheriff. Bernard was naked, and so were the other two boys."

"Did *you*?"

"Did I what?" Krueger asked the sheriff.

"Did you have any clothes on?" Sheriff Thurow asked, startling Krueger with a question from left field.

"What? Me? Why, of course I had clothes on," Krueger said, squinting at the surprise question. "I had no reason to take my clothes off. Eddie was naked, except for I think his socks. Bernard had only his shoes on. I was there saving the boys from this monster, Bernard. It was Bernard, not me, who was attacking the boys."

The sheriff knew he had trapped Krueger. His immediate reply had been defensive, as if the sheriff had accused him of the attack. "I didn't say you were attacking the boys, Mr. Krueger," Sheriff Thurow said. "I just wanted to make sure I understood your story."

Trapping himself again, Krueger replied, "Why? Did someone say it was me? That I had no clothes on? It was Bernard who attacked the boys, not me."

"Oh sure. Sure, of course. I see. Absolutely. You say Bernard did it," the sheriff said. "You misunderstood me, Mr. Krueger. I didn't say you were the attacker, although it does seem strange that you are so defensive. Let me ask, will Eddie verify your explanation?"

Krueger responded, "Who knows. Eddie Small is probably the biggest liar in the school. Just ask Mr. Wolfe."

Now there's a reliable source, the sheriff thought. He listened. He just let Krueger talk. Everything Krueger said was now defensive, as if he thought the sheriff was on to him. Already having an uneasy suspicion of Clarence Wolfe, the sheriff's sixth sense kicked in. He continued taking notes.

"Why, of course. I'm sure Eddie Small will verify everything just as it happened," the sheriff went on to say. "I assume you've explained the entire incident to Mr. Wolfe." Sheriff Thurow said and then asked his most important question. "Unless Clarence Wolfe explained the story to you?"

Krueger jolted. He could feel the sheriff's questioning now centering on him. "Are you saying ... " Krueger paused. He involuntarily rubbed his forehead. The sheriff waited. "I mean, are you asking if I'm telling ... telling the ... Well, don't you believe me, Sheriff?"

"Relax, Mr. Krueger, I know you're in pain. No, I didn't say you aren't telling the truth."

"I'm not, Sheriff. I'm not. I mean I ... " Krueger squirmed in his seat. Putting his hand to his forehead, he said, "Sheriff, I am. I am."

"Am what, Mr. Krueger? Lying? Are you lying or telling the truth?"

Krueger took a deep breath. He felt caught and confused in his own lies. "Bernard. It was Bernard. He hit me. I didn't hit him. You believe me, Sheriff?"

Sheriff Thurow leaned back confidently. His two index fingers touched his lips as if forming a pyramid. "Yes, Mr. Krueger. It all seems very clear."

Despite Krueger's pain and suspicious reactions to the sheriff, he knew he might have been too defensive against the truth. Krueger could feel flush in his face and sweat on his forehead. He said nothing.

"Have there been any other indications of abuse around school? I'm sure if anyone would know, it would be you or Mr. Wolfe."

"That's correct. That would be us," Krueger said, trying to regain his confidence and explain his account of the offensive day. "Oh no, Sheriff Thurow. There hasn't been any other. This was one isolated incident. I can assure you that we've handled Bernard with strict disciplinary measures."

"Oh yes, what's that? If Bernard abused a thirteen-year-old, were you going to report him to me? Law enforcement should be involved. Sexual abuse of a child is a felony."

The word *felony* rang in Krueger's ears. "Sheriff, let me explain. Mr. Wolfe and I knew this was the first time, and Bernard understood what he did was wrong. We kept this away from you, Sheriff, because we could handle Bernard by placing him on probation. Mr. Wolfe and I feel this will not happen again. Bernard has learned his lesson and wants to keep his job. If it would happen again, you can be assured that we would call you and all the proper authorities. We will not allow our boys to be treated like this."

"Well, that's good to hear, Mr. Krueger. I'm glad you feel so confident in yourself and Mr. Wolfe. Our conversation has been most enlightening," Sheriff Thurow said as he pushed back from the table. "That should be all for right now. If I do have some follow-up questions, I might be giving you a call."

Relieved to be finished with the sheriff's interrogation, Krueger stood. "Thank you, Sheriff. I think I'll get back home for some rest," he said, anticipating a safe departure.

"By the looks of your face, you may need a lot more than rest."

Krueger did not respond to the sheriff's remark. Then he added, "One more thing before I leave. If you speak with Eddie Small, remember he's an habitual liar. Can't believe a word he says. He sure can make up stories. It's all documented in his file."

"Thanks for the heads-up, Mr. Krueger," Sheriff Thurow said, delighted with Krueger's last remark. "You sure did pay a price for helping those boys. I'm sure they are grateful to you."

Krueger turned to walk out the door. As he reached for the handle, the sheriff asked, "Oh, one more thing before you leave. Can you show me your identification? Driver's license, social security number? Just for the record, of course." He already knew Krueger did not have his identification.

Krueger reached for his wallet. Then he patted all his pockets in search of his ID. As he checked his front pockets, the sheriff said, "Back pockets, shirt, and trousers but no wallet."

Krueger said, "I must have left my wallet at home."

"Oh, so you left your wallet at home. That's confusing," Sheriff Thurow said, reaffirming Krueger's reply.

"What do you mean confusing? I just forgot it. Mr. Wolfe did say we had to hurry out here to meet with you."

"Okay then. Bring it the next time we meet ... if there is a next time."

"Sure, Sheriff. I will, but there shouldn't be a need for a next time."

"Now you have a nice day, and for heaven's sake, take care of that face."

Phillip Krueger turned without a reply and walked out of the conference room.

"My, my, Mr. Krueger, your face has turned white as snow. How'd the meeting go?" Miss Gardner asked with insincere concern.

Krueger didn't hear a word she said as he headed straight to his office.

Sheriff Thurow stood up, stretched, and walked over to Miss Gardner's desk. Without asking, she said, "Down the hall. Last door on your left."

"Thank you, Miss Gardner. Nothing gets by you."

"That's my job," she immediately confirmed.

"Can you call Eddie Small for me?" From his periphery, the sheriff could see James Duncan already on his way to find the boy. Sheriff Thurow walked down the hall in the same direction as Mr. Krueger's office. "Miss Gardner, could we please have a refill on our pitcher of water?"

"Sure thing. Would you also like a cup of coffee?"

"Why, that would be fine. Thank you."

"I'll bring both," she said, now trying to accommodate the sheriff. She seemed to want to distance herself from her co-worker Krueger, who she noticed wasn't doing well. That was just fine with her.

Eddie Small, according to his file, was thirteen years old. His parents, both alcoholics, had separated after his mother ran off with another man. Eddie had lived with his father until he was eleven years old. He entered reform school in 1956. Belligerent, nonconforming, uncooperative, and with no interest in studies, Eddie's first thirteen years had all been on the south side of life. However, his main rap sheet included a dated litany of *propensity to lie, cheat, and fabricate stories to both staff and fellow students.*

"Come on in, Eddie. I am Sheriff Thurow. Don't mind the badge. You're not in any trouble. I'm here just to check out a few things about the school."

"No problem, man. That's cool. I'll help as much as I can." Eddie's initial appearance and persona gave the sheriff the impression of an average-looking adolescent of average size who was able to communicate comfortably.

"Eddie, I'd like to ask you about an incident that took place last week."

"Yes, sir. I'll do the best I can. It was horrid. I haven't been able to sleep. I've never been so scared in my life."

The sheriff was surprised at Eddie's openness. "I think it involved Bernard … Bernard Bednar."

"Yes, sir, it did. That Bernard, he's a tough guy. I've never seen anyone so strong. He hit Mr. Krueger with his fist so hard. I thought all hell broke loose, but I guess it was just his nose."

The sheriff thought, *This sounds right, although the opposite of Krueger's story.* "Who swung first?" he asked, being more specific

"Oh, Bernard did. He really decked him."

"What about you, Eddie? What did you do?"

"Well, sir, I was so scared. I was shaking. I was cold. This wasn't the first time, so I knew what was coming. I could tell he was all roused up. No clothes on. I couldn't stand to look at him."

"At Bernard?" Sheriff Thurow asked.

"No, not Bernard. I couldn't stand to look at that Krueger. He made us take all our clothes off just so he could see me. Rouses him up when the other guys are with me. He did that once before. Says he likes comparing us. Me, I want a girl, not a big ugly … you know what I mean?" Eddie asked. "It's a nightmare. So hard to say—big ugly stick. I couldn't stand to look at him. To look at it. He just … when he's roused and starts breathing heavy, gets all sweaty, I know what's coming. This wasn't the first time." Eddie started to choke. All of a sudden his demeanor changed. Tears welled in his eyes.

"Here, have a glass of water, Eddie. Take your time. I know it's hard to talk about it."

Eddie gulped the water, paused, and said, "Could I please have some more? Talking about this dries my mouth."

The sheriff calmly poured a second glass. "Go ahead, Eddie. Go ahead just like you were there."

"Thanks. That's better. I can tell it all, anything to get this monster out of my life. Last three months, it's been six, seven times. Then he always wants more. Wants me to do more to him. Likes it when the other boys are there. This time wasn't the worst because he was stopped."

"What do you mean, he was stopped?" the sheriff inquired.

"Bernard. Bernard pulled him away and then decked him."

"Why didn't you report him?"

Eddie was startled by the sheriff's question. "Report him? Who to? Do you know what would happen to me? That would be suicide." Eddie jolted his head back. Stunned, he looked at the sheriff. "No way! No way could I do that. Bernard saved me. The only person who could do anything would be Mr. Wolfe. That's never gonna happen. Those two pricks are close. Real close," Eddie said, raising his crossed index and middle fingers. "They're both on the same side."

The sheriff acted confused so that he could verify. "Wait, Eddie. Report Krueger? You mean report Bernard?" Now the sheriff was leading Eddie because he knew the direction Eddie would take if he was telling the truth. "Let me get this clear, Eddie. Are you saying Mr. Krueger did these awful things to you?" the sheriff asked, now looking directly into Eddie's eyes.

"Yes, sir. Of course. He's been doing it for a long time. I heard it even before I came here. He does it to other boys," Eddie continued. "Krueger was behind me. Roused up. I closed my eyes and was waiting for the pain when all of a sudden I heard a noise, a groan. His hands were on my shoulders. He was touching me with his … Then all of a sudden, I felt him let go when Bernard pulled him back away from me. All I could see was Superman in his blue cape coming to save me."

Eddie was worked up in the moment and very emotional. The words and description just poured out from him. The sheriff remained calm and just let Eddie go. The sheriff thought, *The truth doesn't lie.*

Eddie kept talking. "When I turned around, there was Bernard. His arm was around Krueger's neck, pulling him back, back away from me. Then I saw it happen."

"What happened, Eddie? What'd you see?"

"Well, I'll never forget as long as I live. His big ugly ... ugly ... and *pow*! Bernard brought his fist like a left hook from behind—*pow*—right into his dick. It was like an explosion. Krueger screamed and howled. I remember his face. His eyes pushed open. His mouth was as big as a watermelon ... and then all of a sudden I heard the loudest '*Ahhh!*'—a terrible scream. The pain must have been awful. Krueger was bent over in pain, but Bernard was holding him up at the waist.

"I can remember Krueger bringing his knees up, clutching his balls where Bernard hammered him. Bernard is so strong. He brought his right fist and slammed it into Mr. Krueger. Then he actually threw Krueger with his right arm into the wall. I heard a noise. Then that horrible man, that Krueger, was on the floor against the wall with his hands over his face. There was blood, sweat, and mess all over him. Yuck! Krueger was crying in pain. I just wanted to get out of there."

By now, Eddie was sitting on the edge of his seat, just like he was reliving it all over again. The look on his face spelled horror, hate, and anguish. "*Wheeewww!*" Eddie leaned back in his chair. Then he bent over and put his head in his arms on the table and sobbed. He couldn't catch his breath. Sheriff Thurow reached over and lightly patted Eddie on the back of his head.

"It's over, Eddie. It's all over. You're safe. I promise you he'll never touch you again. You've told me enough." Eddie kept sobbing, but his pace was slowing. The sheriff stood up. "Eddie, you stay right here. Just relax. Have some water. I'll be right back."

Eddie kept his head down on his arms as his crying subsided. He heard the door close as Sheriff Thurow left the room. Silence. He now felt like he was floating. He had just relived the awful time with Krueger, as he had on so many sleepless nights. Taking a deep breath, Eddie sighed and gathered himself. He sniffed and then wiped his cheeks, nose, and eyes with both his sleeves. Lifting his head up, he gulped down two glasses of water. Then Eddie sat back, stretched out, and just rested his head on the back of the chair. He stared at the ceiling like he had stared at the wall that awful night. But now he felt safe.

With his eyes closed from exhaustion, Eddie did not know how much time passed. He must have dozed off. Sometime later, he heard a soft rap at the door. "Eddie, are you feeling better now? You okay?"

"Yes, sir. Oh yes, I feel much better now," Eddie said and thanked the sheriff for his time.

"That's good. That's good." The sheriff paused. "Eddie, could I ask just one more question?"

"Yes, sir. Sure," he said calmly, relief in his voice.

The sheriff sat down. Eddie sat up.

Sheriff Thurow placed his elbows on the table and clasped his hands in front of him. "Eddie, lean forward. Look me in the eye."

Now more relaxed, Eddie sat up, put his elbows on the table, and looked Sheriff Thurow directly in the eye. "Yes, sir?"

"Eddie, did you tell me exactly what happened? The complete 100 percent truth?"

Without hesitation or blink of an eye, the boy said, "Absolutely. The truth, just the way it happened. I promise you on my life I'm tellin' the truth. Every word. Scouts honor. Although I wasn't a Boy Scout, I always wanted to be one."

"I know you are, Eddie. I believe you. I'm so sorry this has happened to you. Look at me. I promise this man will never touch you again."

"Thank you, sir." Eddie brushed his hair to the side with his left hand. Sheriff Thurow detected a slight smile on his face.

With that, the sheriff stood up. "You've been very helpful, Eddie. We're finished. You can go now."

He walked around to Eddie's side of the table and opened the door for him. He saw Wolfe standing behind Miss Gardner's desk as if he was waiting for a verdict he did not want to hear. Sheriff Thurow put his left hand on Eddie's shoulder and proceeded to walk in front of Miss Gardner's desk. Her nose was not in her Corona. She looked with concern as the sheriff and Eddie passed her desk. Wolfe stood there and said nothing. Sheriff Thurow walked to the door that led into the main hall. He stopped and turned back. Eddie stood next to the sheriff with his head down.

"Miss Gardner, could you please ask Mr. Duncan to take Eddie back to his room?"

"Sure, Sheriff. Whatever you need," she replied with a friendlier attitude, hoping to gain the sheriff's approval. The atmosphere that afternoon had changed as the meeting had progressed. She sensed that the visits were not supportive of Mr. Krueger.

Clarence Wolfe turned and walked into his office. He quietly closed the door. Before Miss Gardner even lifted the phone, James Duncan advanced toward the sheriff and Eddie Small. He halted a few paces behind the boy.

Sheriff Thurow said, "Now, you are going to be okay, Eddie. You're safe. I will be staying in touch with you."

"Sheriff, you told me earlier that you met my dad. How is he doing? I know he has his troubles, but he wants to be a good dad. If you see him again, tell him I really do miss him. Tell him I'll be okay. And … and tell him someday I'll be home."

Sheriff Thurow looked at Eddie and said, "I did see him. He's very concerned about you, Eddie. I just suggest you continue writing those letters. He said he keeps them all."

"Thank you, sir. Thank you so very much." With that, Eddie stepped forward, put his arms around the big man's chest, and gave him a hug of relief and gratitude. Sheriff Thurow was touched and thought, *Eddie really needs someone.*

"Let's go, Eddie. I'll take you to your room."

Not another word was said. Together, Duncan and Eddie walked down the hall. As they passed an office before ascending the stairs, Eddie glanced at the closed door: *Phillip Krueger, Director.* He just kept on walking.

Having finished his last interview at the reform school, the sheriff made his good-byes. He stopped at Miss Gardner's desk. "Is Mr. Wolfe behind that door by any chance?" he asked, bringing his right hand up close to his face and pointing at the door.

"Yes, sir, he is."

"Could you ask if I can have a few minutes?"

"Yes, I can, sir. Please wait just a few minutes."

The sheriff again remained standing at Miss Gardner's desk. He imagined he could see steam curling from beneath her trusty typewriter.

"Yes, Sheriff?" Clarence Wolfe said, now standing in his office door. "I hope everything went well."

"May we have a word in private?" the sheriff asked, looking away from Miss Gardner. While waiting for Wolfe, he had also noted that Duncan's door was wide open. He imagined radar signals.

"Sure, come on in," Wolfe stepped back, standing at the front of his desk, not wanting the sheriff to sit down and make himself at home.

"I'll get right to the point," the sheriff started off. "I am convinced that some very serious mistakes have been made out here. I'll begin with what's top on my list now without investigating further. Mr. Krueger raises a very high degree of suspicion. I am going to review my notes from today's inquiry. I will be giving you a call tomorrow. Do you expect Krueger to report to work?"

"No, I don't. I've given him the rest of the week off. He'll be back next week."

"That's good to know. What about Bernard Bednar?"

"Oh, he's always here, although he does alternate shifts."

"Thank you, Mr. Wolfe. I will leave now. I'll be in touch," Sheriff Thurow informed him. "I'll be in touch real soon, as a matter of fact. I don't like what I see out here," he added in his blunt style.

Sheriff Thurow closed the door and walked by Miss Gardner's desk. She was focused on her Corona.

"Well, Miss Gardner, thank you for your hospitality. The water you serve is truly top of the line."

"Thank you, Sheriff. Only the best for our men in uniform."

"Good day, Miss Gardner."

She nodded and gave a slight smile. As the sheriff turned and walked away, she wondered, *What all did he learn about this place?*

The next day, Sheriff Thurow anxiously skipped up the steps to the back door of the courthouse. He enjoyed his reserved parking space, second only to the county executive. After checking his phone calls and mail, he buzzed for Alice Whitehouse, his personal secretary.

"Good morning, Mrs. Whitehouse. How is everything going today?"

"Good morning to you too, Sheriff. I'm just feeling wonderful today. Here's your coffee."

"But, Mrs. Whitehouse ... you say that every day."

"Oh, Sheriff, I know I do. That's just how I feel. Do you need anything else?"

"I do. Would you have Sergeant Bauer come in as soon as he can?"

"Why sure. You bet I will." The slightly short and portly lady turned in pursuit.

She was as noticeable from the back as she was from the front. Her knee-length silk dress swayed back and forth, and her black heels clicked when she walked across the oak floor. Within two minutes, Mrs. Whitehouse returned. The bun in her hair always gave her a happy but down-to-business look.

"Sergeant Bauer is here," she announced.

"Hello, Morry. Come right in," the sheriff said, appreciating his prompt appearance.

"Good morning, Sheriff. What can I do for you?" A former sergeant in the marines and a WWII veteran, the sergeant was dutiful, disciplined, and most dependable. Always wearing the crispest of white shirts and best polished shoes, the ex-marine was the finest officer on Sheriff Thurow's county force.

"Sergeant, I need for you to bring a man in for some serious questioning. His name is Phillip Krueger. He's an administrator at the reform school."

"I know, Phillip. Very active around the city. Civic-minded kind of guy. He's a member of our Lion's Club. Always very helpful. He's also the scoutmaster at our troop from St. Thomas Moore."

"Good to hear he's such an upright citizen," the sheriff added.

"You know, I am very active there, Sheriff. Me and Esther both spend lots of time volunteering. Anyway, where's he live? Should I go to the school?" The sergeant was always ready to serve the sheriff and the county.

"No, he should be at his home today ... Here." He handed the sergeant a slip of paper with Krueger's address. "Go there this morning. Tell him to report to me at exactly one o'clock this afternoon. If he resists, tell him you'll be back within an hour with a warrant. He won't risk that."

"Yes, sir. I'll leave right now. Sir, may I ask?"

"Go right ahead, Sergeant. What is it?"

"If he's done something wrong, I would find it most surprising. Phillip is known all over town, a good person, a model citizen."

"Yes, I know. So we'll keep this quiet. Don't want to arouse the *Plain Dealer*. Just keep it low. Okay, Sergeant?"

"Sure will, Sheriff." The sergeant left with almost a full about-face.

Sheriff Thurow looked at the Seth Thomas clock on the wall—8:20. *Tick tock.* He loved that steady sound. Five hours and forty minutes. *Krueger's gonna catch his lunch.*

CHAPTER 37

CRITICAL MEETING ·

Phillip Krueger—April 23, 1958

RETURNING from Phillip Krueger's house, Sergeant Bauer walked directly to Sheriff Thurow's office.

"Well hello, Sergeant Bauer. You weren't gone very long," the sheriff's secretary said.

"That's right, Mrs. Whitehouse. Got a job to do, get it done," Sergeant Bauer replied.

"I see you have someone with you," she said in return, noticing Phillip Krueger and his wounded state of appearance. "Hello, Mr. Krueger. What brings you here?"

He mumbled something in return.

"Mr. Krueger, I just have to tell you my son, Charles … you know, Charlie Whitehouse, Sioux Patrol? Well, he loves the Scouts. Said he really likes you as scoutmaster," Mrs. Whitehouse said, complimenting Mr. Krueger, trying to offset his obvious embarrassment.

"Good scout that Charlie," Krueger responded with minimal enthusiasm.

"Oh hello, Sheriff," Sergeant Bauer said as Sheriff Thurow opened his office door. Fit and proper and a big man in his mid-fifties, the sheriff always portrayed himself as a stately politician or successful businessman when out of uniform, which was his usual manner.

Sheriff Thurow stepped away from his office. "You can follow me," he said to the obviously apprehensive Krueger.

Krueger was determined to be cooperative. He knew he was in deep trouble and wanted nothing to do with an arrest.

"Thank you, Sergeant Bauer. Well done." Sheriff Thurow acknowledged in a military sort of way, as he was very aware of Sergeant Bauer's disciplined manner. "That will be all for now," he added.

"Yes, sir. Thank you. Call me as needed," Sergeant Bauer replied. He turned briskly and proceeded to the door. *Mission accomplished. Well done*, he thought.

"Mrs. Whitehouse, I'll be down in the quiet room at the end of the hall. We'll be a while, I'm sure."

Krueger rolled his eyes behind the sheriff's back. *Not good*, he thought. He felt his own stress level spike.

"No disturbance unless there is an emergency," the sheriff said as he turned and led Krueger down the hall. "Follow me!"

Without a word, Krueger followed the sheriff down the hall to the last door on the right. Windowless, the room was about twelve by twelve feet. Two chairs sat on one side of a rectangular table, and a single chair sat on the other. The rest of the room was stark. All walls were covered with soundproof board. One fan hung from the center of the ceiling, decorating the room.

"Have a seat over there," Sheriff Thurow said, pointing to the solitary chair on the far side of the table.

Krueger noticed the large eight-foot mirror on the opposite interior wall of the room. He did not like seeing himself, so he kept his head down. He had noticed the sign on the front door: *Interrogation*. He did not have a warm and fuzzy feeling.

"First of all, Mr. Krueger, I'd like to thank you for telling me what happened at the reform school."

"That's okay, Sheriff. You know, I've thought about it, and well … I don't want Bernard to get into too much trouble. It was wrong … you know, what he did to me. But … but I just don't want Bernard to lose his job. Maybe it was a fit of passion, even rage."

"I'd agree with that assessment, Mr. Krueger. This is about rage, passion, and violence. Then I would add perversion, immorality, and criminality. That's thoughtful of you, Mr. Krueger. I mean, your consideration for Bernard. You know, I hear many good things about you around town. You are very civic-minded. I've been told you are active and popular in the chamber. What else?"

"Oh, the Lions Club, and of course the Scouts."

"Understand you are the scoutmaster. You must like being around boys."

Krueger did not want to respond to the obviously baited statement. "Yes, that's right, Sheriff," Krueger said, referring to the original question. "I do believe in giving back to the community, and well, Sheriff, I also have a good position at the reform school."

"Yes, I understand all that. Some might say you're a model citizen."

"Well, thank you, Sheriff. So hopefully you see why maybe you and I can kinda … maybe dust this little situation under the rug. Let's say for the good of the community and for the sake of Bernard, of course." Phillip Krueger's confidence started to build as he got a feeling that the sheriff was understanding him. *Maybe this isn't going to be so bad after all,* he thought.

"That could be a possibility," the sheriff said, lulling Krueger into a trusting position. "So let me summarize. You're an outstanding citizen in the community. You love your job. You forgive Bernard … and maybe it's best to make all this go away," he said, giving Krueger more line as he boosted the man's confidence.

"Exactly, that's it. I want to continue to do good for the community and the reform school, which is, I might add, an excellent detention and educational system. We really work closely with the boys," Phillip Krueger said as his confidence that he was winning the sheriff over raised even higher. Krueger was beginning to feel safe.

"Oh, before I forget … Did you remember to bring your wallet? You know, just a routine formality."

Krueger reached for his back pocket and then the front. He stood and patted all four pockets. "You know, Sheriff, I must have forgotten it again. That captain didn't give me much time to get ready. He was pretty insistent on *now*!"

"Oh sure. I understand when you lose things. Can't remember when you had it last. Same thing happens to me. My wife is always helping me find my keys. I understand."

"No, no, Sheriff. It's on my dresser. Saw it there this morning. Just too much in a hurry."

"You know, Mr. Krueger, it's illegal to drive without a license, but we aren't here to be concerned with trivial matters. Okay, let me get this straight. Are you saying your wallet is on your dresser right now as we speak?"

"Yes, sir, it's there. Absolutely. I wouldn't lie to you."

"I said nothing about lying," the sheriff responded in a sterner voice. "You sure you saw your wallet this morning?" he asked, giving Krueger another chance. "As I recall, you forgot your wallet when you met with me at the reform school. That's twice now. You're pretty forgetful there, Mr. Krueger."

"I have a lot of responsibility. I have a very important position at the reform school. Sometimes, I do forget things."

"Well, are you saying everything you have told me then and today is true, Mr. Krueger?"

"Yes, sir. Oh yes, sir. One hundred percent of everything is true. I stand by that."

Krueger was unaware that Detective Spelling was standing behind the one-way mirror, assisted by a secretary, who was taking down every word in shorthand.

"Yes, yes. What's this about?" Krueger asked, feeling a little more threatened.

"One more question. You said you had all your clothes on the night of April 14 when Bernard Bednar roughed you up."

"Sheriff, of course I had all my clothes on. I'd just run down from my office."

"Did you have a suit on?"

"Yes, ah, but my jacket was upstairs."

"Mr. Krueger, what's your middle name?" the sheriff asked.

"What does this all have to do with Bernard Bednar?"

"Nothing. Just answer the question."

Krueger stopped. "I don't like this. Do I need a lawyer?"

"Mr. Krueger, I'm not accusing you of anything. What's your middle name?"

"Karl. Phillip Karl Krueger. There!"

"Now that's more like it," the sheriff said approvingly. "Now, Mr. Krueger ... did you wear your suit home that evening?"

"Why of course I did, Sheriff. Oh yes, after I went back upstairs and got my suit jacket and briefcase."

"Do your trousers have pleats? What color is your suit?"

"Sheriff, where are you going with this?" Krueger asked with a puzzled look on his face.

Sheriff Thurow responded, "I will tell you when I get there. Answer the question."

"Two. All my suits have two pleats, except for a couple of old ones that have three. My suit was gray, I recall."

"One last question, do your shirts have monograms?"

"Just a few. Monograms are expensive."

"Were you wearing a monogramed shirt on April 14?"

"I have no idea. What's this got to do with anything?" Krueger asked in total confusion.

"I'm asking the questions. You answer them."

"Can you repeat the question?" Krueger asked.

"I said were you wearing a monogram shirt on April 14?"

"I can't remember."

The sheriff didn't say another word. He reached down and pulled up a box from beside his chair. He set the box on the table so Krueger could easily see the label on the end: *Evidence*. Krueger stared. Sheriff Thurow opened the top, reached in, and pulled out a pair of trousers.

"Are these your trousers?"

Krueger recognized the slacks immediately. He was stunned. His eyes bulged, and he could feel his heart throb and begin to race. "Well, I don't know. Don't know for sure."

The sheriff slowly reached into the right pocket of the trousers, pulled something out, and hid it in his hand. Slowly, he put his closed fist in front of Krueger then turned it over so Krueger could see sheriff's open palm and the exposed coin. "Do you recognize this?" Sheriff Thurow handed Krueger a gold coin the size of a silver dollar. "Recognize that, Mr. Krueger?" the sheriff asked proudly.

"Hmmm. Let's see." *I'm in some deep shit*, Krueger thought.

"Let me help you, Mr. Krueger." The sheriff reached over and set the coin on the trousers. Now Krueger was leaning forward, his hands folded below the table. The sheriff turned the coin over. "Now does that help remind you? Does that ring a bell? Can you read that to me?" he asked calmly.

"*Hmmm.* Now, Sheriff ... " Krueger pulled his hands from under the table and leaned forward. His elbows were now on the table. He ran the fingers of both hands through his black oily hair. He was unshaven that day.

"Don't you 'Now, Sheriff' me. I'm asking the questions."

Picking up the coin, Krueger read, "*Congratulations, Phillip Krueger. Class of 1933.*"

"Is that your coin?"

"Yes." Krueger paused. "Yes. That's mine," he said a defeated tone.

"It came from inside these trousers, did it?" the sheriff asked.

Phillip Krueger nodded. His blood pressure went up while the expression on his face went down.

"I asked you a question. Yes or no?"

"Yes," Krueger said, quietly lowering his head.

Sheriff Thurow pointed. "From those trousers?" Then the sheriff reached into the back pocket of the two-pleated trousers. "Does this billfold belong to you?"

Krueger looked up in alarm. "Yes." He paused again. "Yes. That's mine," Krueger almost barked back at the sheriff.

"Did you lie to me when you said your billfold was on your dresser?"

Krueger knew he was trapped.

"Answer me. Did you lie?"

"No!"

"No?" the sheriff said. "Now you are lying to me again. Where was it?"

"I don't know."

"Well, I'll tell you, Mr. Krueger. These suit trousers have been in this evidence box, along with the coin and the wallet." Sheriff Thurow leaned over again and pulled a white shirt from the box. "Do you see a monogram on this shirt?" the sheriff asked, pointing to the three initials.

"Yes, I do," Krueger said almost inaudibly.

"Read them to me," the sheriff directed.

"PKK," Krueger said, disgusted.

"Is this your shirt?"

"Yes, that's mine. Yes, yes, yes, yes, yes—all of it."

"Did you wear these clothes the day of April 14?"

"Yes, I did!"

"Did you wear them home?"

"No, I didn't."

"Were you naked in the room with Eddie Small?"

"I can't answer. Please don't make me answer. I think I need a lawyer."

"Mr. Krueger, you are far past that," the sheriff said. "Were you naked? Answer me."

"*Stop!*" Krueger shouted. "Yes, I was. Yes, yes, I was naked."

"Did you fondle and attempt to perform an act of sodomy on Eddie Small?"

"Yes, for the last time, yes! I was *naaakeeed*! There were three boys. I did it!" With his right hand, he swept the trousers and the shirt onto the floor. Burying his head in his hands, he screamed, "Yes, yes, yes, to all of it! Oh my God!" Krueger broke down, laying his head on his arms and sobbing uncontrollably.

With that, Sheriff Thurow calmly said, "I'll be right back. Just relax, Mr. Krueger. Get control of yourself." The sheriff stood. There was a knock on the door.

Detective Spelling stepped inside. "Good job, Sheriff. You nailed him," he said in a low voice so Krueger could not hear.

Sheriff Thurow then left the room. Krueger sobbed. He tried to catch his breath. With the absence of the sheriff, he began to calm down. A few minutes passed. Krueger sat up. He saw Detective Spelling standing by the door, arms folded, staring directly at the washed-out Krueger. *A broken man*, the detective thought. Then Krueger stood and walked around the table, stepping over his trousers as he walked to the other end. Palms down, he braced himself, leaning on the table. He lowered his head again and looked down between his straight arms. *He's got me. I'm done. Everything will be over for me.* Phillip Krueger returned to his chair and just bounced his head on his arms. *This is bad … real bad.*

Krueger sat at the table alone for ten minutes, twenty minutes.

Detective Spelling didn't move. The quiet was now deafening. Finally the door opened, and the sheriff calmly walked in.

"Here, you might like this." He set two bottles of Coca-Cola on the table. Krueger took the first bottle and gulped it empty. Sheriff Thurow laid a pad of paper on the table and placed a pen on top. "Now, take all the time you need. Tell me everything that happened that night in the storage room. Everything. Then I want you to do the same regarding our visit at the reform school. Lastly, write down everything you told me today. This will take a while. Do it right. Every word, every incident. Write it just as it happened."

"If I do that, will I be able to go home?" Krueger asked pleadingly.

"We'll see. Depends on how good a job you do with that pen and paper."

Krueger looked hopeful and conceded.

"I'll be back in an hour. Take your time." Then the sheriff placed his palms on the table, braced himself, and bent over right into Krueger's space. "You listen to me. You write everything. Nothing but the truth," he said in a low, slow, and deep voice. Then his voice became almost a hard, firm whisper. "Do exactly what I said or I'll have your ass in front of the judge faster than I can move your nose to the other side of your ugly face. You hear me?" Sheriff slammed his fist on the table, "You hear me?"

"Yes, sir. Yes, sir. I will. Just take me home"

"Don't you dare cross me, Phillip Karl Krueger. Now write!"

Phillip definitely got the message. He knew he had no choice. Looking at the paper, he slid it across the table to rest in front of him. Krueger grabbed the pen. Sticking the end in his teeth, he started to think. At the same time, the sheriff walked to the door. Grabbing the knob, he slowly turned around.

"Oh, one more thing, Krueger," he said, looking directly at the flawed man. "See that grill by the mirror? There's a stenographer behind it. I recorded every word you said in this room. Now back it up. Get writing."

The sheriff turned and exited through the door. The jarring slam startled Krueger. Now he was alone, jailed in the cell of his own mind. Phillip Krueger knew there was no escape.

He sat with pen in hand but no words on the paper. Like a driver in a rolling car, flipping end over end straight into an oncoming trailer truck, his life flashed across his mind. Now reduced to a pen, paper, and tormented thoughts, Phillip Krueger was left alone. Alone to write his own death warrant in his journey through this life-changing event.

Flashes of his childhood, parents, and civic life vividly appeared like the oncoming truck. He thought of the family he never had. Immediate reflections of the boys were all too fleeting. So many years, so many boys—he could barely remember their names. At forty-four years old, he had spent twenty-plus years transforming secret fantasies into the reality of unscrupulous deeds in hidden places, inflicted on the innocence of youth.

The pen was like a knife. Each word, each victim, each deed was a cut into his very being. Slowly and with self-inflicted scorn and anguish, Phillip picked up the pen and began to write. He labored over every sentence. The more he thought, the more his mind raced to the past. *Put it on paper. Get it out. Stop, stop,* he said to himself. *Write about now. This one deed. Don't confess your entire life.*

The rush of full disclosure in his mind was like a self-serving cleansing. From the dark closet of his mind, he brought the real Phillip Krueger into the light. He didn't like what he saw, but the images kept racing, so many, like a thundering herd. He had the urge to get them all out. Cleanse himself. Faces, so many faces he could see. Like a kaleidoscope manipulating the scared, tormented, painful, and hurt faces, Krueger felt their disgust, their sorrow, their shame, and their rage. His hand continued to write with speed and force. He kept writing nonstop. Time had no meaning.

Get it out. Get it out. All of it. It's over. You're done. The more he wrote, the more disgusted and ashamed of himself he became. Drop by drop, beads of sweat fell upon the paper. A few words blotted. He stopped, leaned back, and wiped his forehead, smearing the beads of sweat upon his brow. His breathing was heavy. He threw down the pen. It bounced on the table, spun, and came to a halt at the table's edge. He had written more than he should, self-incriminating himself over and above what the sheriff had asked for.

I did it. It's all here. Unaware of time, Krueger breathed a sigh of relief. His disgusting life had come forward from behind a dark hidden door inside him. *Take me. I'm through. Do with me what you must.* The confession, he would remember afterward, was the climax of his tortured life.

An unknown amount of time elapsed. Krueger reflected on all that was closing in around him. Lost in his tormented world, he jumped backward in his seat, startled by the twist of the doorknob when Sheriff Thurow returned to the interrogation room. The sheriff was not alone. A middle-aged man who was balding in the front and had a stern, official look on his face accompanied him. The man reminded Krueger of an ex-marine. The man's crisp white shirt and wide striped tie portrayed the look of a defense lawyer, detective, or prosecutor. Whoever—Krueger didn't even care. The two sat down at the table opposite him. Sheriff Thurow reached over and picked up the pen at the table's edge. He handed it to Krueger.

"Let me see it," he said in an almost whispered command as he looked at the papers in front of Krueger.

Krueger pushed the disheveled papers in front of the sheriff. After picking them up, the sheriff straightened them by dropping the edges against the table. *All square.* Thumbing each page, he counted five sheets. He read each one carefully. Silence. When finished, he said, "Lots here. Should be enough. Makes me sick, all that you've done to these innocent boys."

Krueger looked down with overwhelming embarrassment and sorrow. He looked up and said, "Sheriff, I am sorry."

Showing no empathy toward the admitted predator, Sheriff Thurow looked Krueger in the eye. "Well, that's not going to cut it with the judge. Moreover, I can assure you that when victims come forward, you'll only begin to see the destruction you've brought on so many lives. I refer not just to the victims. Did you ever in your depraved mind think of their families, little brothers and sisters? Sick, sick, sick." Handing the papers back to Krueger, the sheriff said, "Now sign and date the last page. Initial all the pages in the bottom right. Date by your name. Mr. Callaway here will sign as witness. I will gladly do the same."

Slowly, Krueger picked up the pen. He began to write under the last paragraph.

For the above named deeds and harm caused for the victims, I, Phillip Krueger, am totally responsible. I have written this confession of my own free will. Phillip Krueger, April 23, 1958.

"Let me see that." The sheriff turned the sheet on the table. He paused. "That's good. That's good," he said, nodding. "That's really good. Thank you, Mr. Krueger."

After witnessing and signing below Krueger's name, Sheriff Thurow and Mr. Callaway stood up. "You stay here," the sheriff said, pointing at Krueger. "We'll be back." They turned and left the room. The door closed quietly.

Phillip Krueger was alone. All alone. He knew his life was over. With the sheriff and the signed confession, Phillip Krueger's self-serving will also left the room.

Krueger was later taken to a private cell. His night was sleepless. The next morning, he was served a tray of mushy scrambled eggs and greasy bacon. The coffee was drinkable. At 10:00 a.m., a sergeant came to his cell.

"Come with me." The burly sergeant escorted Krueger through a double set of sliding jail doors.

After walking down a long hall with several turns, Krueger and the guard arrived at a small room hidden by a green metal door. Inside was a table, a phone, paper, and a pen. *This place looks familiar.* However, there was no large mirror in the room.

"The sheriff said you have an hour. You can make calls to your attorney, work, home, wherever. At three-thirty this afternoon, you will appear before the circuit judge."

"Will I have a chance to post bail?" Krueger asked.

"The judge will explain that. I'll be waiting outside the door. See you in an hour," the guard said matter-of-factly, showing no concern for Krueger's plight.

His first thought was to call Clarence Wolfe. *Who else? What will I say? He'll explode,* Krueger thought. Picking up the phone, he dialed the school.

Ring, ring. "Good morning, Wabash Reform School. Miss Gardner speaking."

"Miss Gardner, this is Phillip Krueger. Can I speak with Mr. Wolfe?"

"Well, he's not here. He left for a meeting. Should be back soon. So are you getting better, Mr. Krueger? Is your face healing? When will you come back?" she asked knowingly, putting him on the spot.

Why does she always have to rub me the wrong way? "Thank you for asking, Miss Gardner. You always have a way of making people feel so much better," he answered with heightened sarcasm. "I'll call back in fifteen." He hung up immediately. Knowing he would need an attorney, he decided to wait for Wolfe's advice.

Twenty minutes passed. Krueger called again.

"Hello, Miss Gardner speaking."

"Phil Krueger again for Mr. Wolfe. Has he returned?"

"Yes, he's back," she taunted.

"May I speak with him? That's why I called, Miss Gardner. What other reason would I call back? Do you think it's to hear your sweet melodious voice? What else?"

Miss Gardner did not reply, but did put the call through.

"Mr. Wolfe, this is Phillip. I'm ah … I'm … I'm in some serious trouble."

"Well, isn't that a fine hello? What do ya mean serious trouble? Explain now," Clarence Wolfe ordered.

"Sheriff brought me in yesterday for questioning. It ah … it ah didn't go well. I couldn't defend myself. He had me."

"What do you mean he had you? Did you have a lawyer?" Wolfe asked angrily.

"No, I already told them too much, so I just spelled it all out."

"Now that's smart, you idiot. What did you spill? Is it in writing? Did you say anything about the school? What you do here? Anything about Zilbar's connection?"

"No, no. Nothing about Zilbar. I don't want to die that soon. I told them all about me. Me and the boys. That's it. Only me. I'm done. Can you get me a lawyer?" Krueger grew quiet.

"Anything else?" Wolfe asked.

"Yes, there is one more thing."

"Do I need to brace myself?" Wolfe asked, expecting another surprise.

"I wrote out everything. Put it all on paper. The sheriff forced me."

"You mean you signed a confession there? You absolute idiot! You need a lawyer," Wolfe said. "Might be a little late. Let me make a call. Krueger, you are sure you talked only about you and the boys? Nothing about anything else? I need to know before I call Randall Zilbar."

"Don't worry, don't worry, I didn't say anything about the fourth floor or what goes on in the locker rooms. Nothing about Cicero. Nothing, nothing. Don't worry. Just talked only about me. Nothing about you and Zilbar."

"Did you say anything about visitors or about … about … ?"

"No, I said nothing about visitors or Cicero. Nothing, for Christ's sake."

"Yes, but you could have written down anything—"

Krueger cut Wolfe off. "No. Again, nothing about you, Mr. Wolfe, or the visitors from Chicago. Although I'd like to implicate your Miss Gardner. *Bitch.* Just kidding, Mr. Wolfe, just kidding."

"That's good. You keep your mouth shut. I'll call for a lawyer. Don't talk to anyone till we get you a lawyer." Wolfe slammed the phone down.

Randall Zilbar—April 24, 1958

Clarence Wolfe immediately called Randall Zilbar. He anticipated Zilbar's reaction. Being at the receiving end of Randall Zilbar's quick temper, and sometimes rage, was worse than walking over hot coals with bare feet … even if only over the phone.

Ring, ring. "Hello, Mr. Zilbar's office."

"Yes, this is Clarence Wolfe. Is Mr. Zilbar there?"

"One moment … " Silence. "Yes, Mr. Zilbar will take your call."

"Hello, Clarence. What's going on?"

"Good afternoon, Randall. Remember a week ago when it happened? I told you about Sheriff Thurow snooping around. I hate to tell you this," Wolfe said, clearing his throat. "Sheriff's got Krueger down at the county jail. Guess he spilled out all his involvement about what went on at the school."

"What the hell! He's in custody? Goddamn it, Wolfe! I told you to keep this all under wraps. You ask for my advice, and then you don't follow through. We don't need that kind of attention at the school. It's

a quiet place. That's why I use you. Now you've got this goddamn eruption. You've got to get him a tough lawyer. We've got to shut him up. He
knows too much. You both should take the fall for this. I can't have it."

Randall Zilbar's temper was about to hit full throttle when he said
to himself, *Settle down. Think this through.* "All right, Wolfe, I've got it.
You call Gino Moretti. He's a defense attorney. He'll shut Krueger up.
His office is down at the Parker Building, top floor. He's got a good prac-
tice. Defended the Riverside murder case last year. He's the best lawyer.
Practiced in Cicero for twelve years. My secretary gave you the number.
He'll be expecting your call. Get it right this time. Hear me? And don't
use my name anyplace!" Randall Zilbar slammed the phone down before
Wolfe could reply.

No sooner did Zilbar hang up with Wolfe than Zilbar was on the
phone to Moretti. "Gino, Randall Zilbar here."

"Hey ya, Randall. How's it go?"

Not responding to Gino's greeting, Randall said, "Listen, Gino,
you're gonna get a call from a Clarence Wolfe. He runs the reform
school. They've had a little problem in their office with some of the staff.
Bangin' around with the boys if ya know what I mean. This one guy,
Phillip Krueger, needs a little of your persuasion. I want you to shut him
up. He knows a little. A little too much. He's a nobody, but I want him
handled."

"Yeah, yeah, heard little bits and pieces about that school over the
years. Some guys just get off on those young boys. Don't get it myself.
Now an all-girls school … that's another thing. Ha. Just kidding. Just
kidding."

"Listen up. Clarence Wolfe, the director, will be disclosing some
information to you about this Krueger guy. Go down and see him. Keep
him quiet. If he's done it, just keep him from spreading any other poison
that we don't want out. Ice it. Box him in. Know what I mean?"

"Gotcha, gotcha. I can handle it just the way you want. As you say,
I'll box him in," Gino confirmed to Randall, always seeking his approval.

"Don't use my name anyplace. I have a reputation to uphold in this
town. I won't have a small-time queer messing with me," Zilbar made it
clear to Gino.

"You bet, Randall. You can count on me. Don't you worry. Ol' Gino will handle it all for you."

Phillip Krueger—April 25, 1958

Phillip Krueger was surprised the next morning when he received a call from Gino Moretti. *Seems he knows all about me.* Gino made an appointment to be at the jail at 1:30 p.m. However, at precisely 11:30 a.m., Sheriff Thurow walked into Krueger's cell. Krueger was sitting on the side of his bed, despondent, hunched over, with his head hanging low between his knees. He was focused on the ants marching in and out of the crack in the discolored gray floor. *That's me in prison.*

"Phillip, I am placing you under arrest based on witness reports, along with your signed confession. Now you are going to pay. I'm taking you down," Sheriff Thurow warned, describing his own personal vendetta.

Random thoughts of despair flashed through Krueger's mind. *Why? Why? Why did I do this? Not worth it. I want to take it all back. I'm sorry. Jesus, I'm sorry.*

"You will never touch another boy again. Stand up," the sheriff told him, showing his power over Krueger. "You are being charged with seven counts of lewd and lascivious behavior and three counts of sodomy against minors. Your confession alone will convict you, in addition to two witnesses. Come with me. We're going to book you now. You'll appear before the judge at three thirty today. Did you talk with a lawyer?"

"Yes," Krueger said in a low, shamed voice. He was shocked with the decisiveness of the sheriff's words. He felt flush. His heart raced. *Is this real? Can this be happening?* Cold steel snapped around each wrist. At least he had not been cuffed from behind.

The sheriff's large hand clasped around Krueger's upper left arm as he led Krueger from the cell and guided him down the hall. The hard squeeze conveyed the inner emotion of disgust from Sheriff Thurow.

Random thoughts kept rushing through Krueger's mind: *This isn't me. Jesus, say it's not me. I died. I want to be young again. Back in school.* The silence of the cell block was eerie. As they approached the end of the hall, the only sound was the footsteps of the sheriff. His heavy leather shoes echoed on the cracked concrete floor. Phillip's heart pounded. He felt as if the end was near. Trying to stop at the end of the hall as if he was defying the sheriff, he felt a sudden jerk on his left arm.

A stone-faced uniformed officer opened the main cell door. The neighboring cells were empty, with the exception of one. A gaunt-faced, whiskered old man occupied the first cell; he was snoring, sleeping off a long night of booze and more booze. The hall reeked with the smell of cheap gin. The cell guard, tall and gaunt, sat leaning on the back two legs of a straight wooden chair, tilted against the brick wall next to the steel-clad door. Not moving, he reached around with his left hand, turned the key of the hall door, and pushed it open for the passing sheriff. The sheriff looked down. The guard nodded in return as if this was a simple routine.

Sheriff Thurow and Krueger walked the long hall to the booking chamber. "Sit right here," the sheriff said, pushing him down onto a brown wooden captain's chair. Then he let go.

Krueger reached his right hand around and rubbed his upper left arm. He felt the impressions of the big man's hand on his upper arm. He waited. An officer sat in a chair a few paces away against the wall. He was staring directly at Krueger as if he was looking for an excuse to hit him on the side of the head ... or even pull a trigger. *Hate*. Krueger stared at a wooden-case wall clock on the far side of the room—11:52. The pendulum swayed in a slow, steady motion. Krueger waited. *That clock's my future.*

A little after noon, a second officer came to the desk. *Fingerprints. Yes, this is happening. Why even see a lawyer?* After the fingerprints, Krueger signed more papers. The officer then stood up. Borrowing the sheriff's tactic, he clasped Krueger's sore arm and guided him into a room. "Stand here." *Flash!* Now he knew his mug would forever live within the confines of this jail. It would not change. Permanent. He didn't want to see his own picture. Never.

Within another thirty minutes, Krueger found himself alone again in his private cell, sitting in despair on the side of his bunk. He thought he could feel a broken spring through the thin gray mattress.

"Here's your lunch," groused a man in a green uniform as he slid a tray into Krueger's cell.

He looked at the green and gray Mass upon the plates dismissively.

Throwing himself back on the stained mattress, he lay prone, staring at the blank ceiling. He felt comfort on the bare mattress. There was pain in his head, pressure on his heart, and despair in his mind. Phil Krueger dozed.

"You have a visitor. Wake up," the tall, gaunt cell guard ordered.

Krueger felt the eeriness of the cell block every time he looked at the guard. The length of his long, thin face was only exceeded by the length of his neck. His gray uniform and placid color disappeared into the gray walls of the cell block.

"Mr. Krueger, I'm Gino Moretti. We have an appointment for one thirty," a man said from beside the guard.

"Yes, yes, I believe we do, for whatever good it will do," Krueger said in a most negative tone.

The officer let the attorney into the cell. Pulling up a chair, Attorney Moretti sat at the side of the bed. Having turned the straight chair around, he rested his arms on the back of the chair. He looked directly at Krueger.

An enthusiastic soul, Gino was spry and lively, with a head of wavy black hair with just enough oil to spell *Italian*. "I'm here to get you out of this trap," he said, looking around at the dingy, dark cell. No place I'd wanna be," he informed Krueger. "Now, tell me everything that's happened these past few days. When was that?"

"Yesterday morning. A sergeant came to my house."

"Did he have a warrant for an arrest?"

"No," Krueger said while the attorney jotted notes on a pad.

"Did he ask you questions?"

"No. He just said 'Come with me—now!' Made me think I was a prisoner of war."

"When you got to the station, did they question, interrogate you?"

"Yes. You bet they did. For hours. Excruciatingly."

"Who?" Moretti asked.

"That big asshole, Sheriff Thurow. The one who thinks he's Matt Dillon. Here, look at my arm," Krueger said, pulling up his sleeve.

"Looks pretty black and blue."

"Black and blue? That prick gave me permanent tattoos," Krueger said, exaggerating.

"Did you sign anything?"

"Yes, I wrote it out. I'd guess you'd call it a confession. Signed it and all. Glad I did. Just told all that's happened. I've had it. I'm done. I just want out of here."

"You've got to be kidding. You told them? Then you signed?"

"Look at me, Mr. Moretti. My closet is black, hidden with pain, terror, and broken bones. I'm tired, worn out, disgusted, and ashamed of living this hidden life. I want it all over. There's witnesses. They'll testify against me. No no no! I don't want to go through it all. I'm guilty! Look at me. I did it all! Years and years. Looking back, I know I hurt boys. I wrecked lives. I was wrong! All I want from you is to get me out of here. Now! Today!"

Moretti didn't respond. He twisted his lips while he gathered his thoughts. "You sure? You know now that Clarence Wolfe and Mr. Zilbar want no implications from you. This was all your doing. You are the only one. Do you get that?"

"Yes, I do. Assure them for me. I'll take all the blame," Krueger said. Then he leaned backward and sat erect. He paused and then leaned forward again. "Mr. Moretti, listen." Krueger was close enough to see Moretti's face and the glistening sheen of the lawyer's curly black hair. "Let me put it this way. I did wrong. I hurt boys. Scores and scores of times. I can't count the years. I'm done. It's over. No more. I want to plead guilty. No trial. All I ask is to get me the lightest sentence you can. I want to die old … and at home."

"I see. I understand," Gino assured him.

Krueger leaned forward even farther. "One more thing. I know a little about what's going on out there. There, at the school. Wolfe talks tough, but he's a puppet. That Zilbar's got his hook in Wolfe. Zilbar can't be trusted," Krueger explained to Moretti in a low, quiet, convincing voice. "I warn you, don't turn your back on him. I'm not saying anything about either one, but I know enough dirt on the bastard Zilbar to send him to Terre Haute before me. Dirty rich prick."

"Guess we're before the judge at three thirty." After closing his notebook, Moretti slipped it into his briefcase on the right side of his chair. Standing up, he returned the chair to its place against the wall and turned as the guard opened the door.

"Mr. Moretti," Krueger called as Gino started to walk down the hall. "Mr. Moretti ... this is—I know this is what I have to do."

"I hear you. It's your call. Plead guilty, accept your sentence, and do your time. I'm sure that will also please Wolfe and Mr. Zilbar. See you at three thirty." Moretti gave an understanding nod of acceptance. Then he was gone.

Phillip Krueger lay back down. *Another step,* he thought. *I just want this over. Over.* He closed his eyes to enjoy the temporary solitude. Little did he know the true definition of solitude. That would all come later.

Randall Zilbar—April 25, 1958

Meanwhile, Randall Zilbar was steaming over the bungled mess at the reform school. He was now second-guessing why he had first gone out there so many, many years ago. He knew that all had been long forgotten. He couldn't recognize his own weaknesses. Trusting in Clarence Wolfe had been the real mistake of Zilbar's dealings and connections with the reform school. Once Wolfe allowed Krueger to become aware of their business, Randall Zilbar had known a day would come that he would have to eradicate him.

CHAPTER 38

TIME IS ETERNITY

Phillip Krueger—April 25, 1958

THE three thirty hour was fast approaching. Reality was setting in. *My choice. Only mine. No real advice. Any influence from Moretti, Zilbar, or Wolfe can't make me overturn my will. Give up. No fight. Should I? Forever behind bars may be hell itself. Could I beat it? Nothing was really terribly wrong. Didn't hurt anyone. It's not bad. Love. Help them. They were all deprived boys anyway. I made them feel wanted. Love. Yes, so much was showing love.*

He clenched the bars of his cell with both his hands. He noted the one stationary guard in a chair, leaning against the wall at the end of the hall. A custodian was wiping the gray floors—back and forth. A black-and-white metal clock was noticeable from both corners of the cell— 2:56 p.m. *There is still time. Moretti will soon be waiting for me. Together we will stand in front of the judge. There's time. I can change my plea. I can. My past life ... I can't give it up. I couldn't handle life in prison. Oh, the horror of time in prison. If I go to prison, I may be on the other end of the horror.* At that very moment, Phillip Krueger's decision was made.

At 3:10 p.m., Krueger heard the door open at the far end of the hall. The guard's chair tipped forward from the wall. Shaking his head as if he had been awake and alert the whole time, the unsuspecting guard watched the Sergeant Bauer head straight to Krueger's cell. The guard lumbered behind him with the keys.

"Mr. Krueger, it's time to proceed."

The tall, gaunt guard unlocked the cell.

"Your attorney is in the judge's courtroom at the other end of the courthouse. I'm taking you there now." The sergeant placed the cuffs on Krueger. "Come with me," he said in a commanding voice as if to coax Krueger to defy him.

Sergeant Bauer walked Krueger through the corridors of the courthouse like it was the defendant's last walk before an execution. As they approached the double doors to the courtroom, the sergeant opened the right door and guided Krueger through first. *Honorable Henry Seiler, Circuit Court* was painted on the front of the courtroom door. Moretti was waiting in the second row of dark wooden seats. Several others were being arraigned.

"We have at least fifteen minutes. The judge is running a little late."

The sergeant removed the cuffs and took a seat inside the rail. He waited without expression.

"Listen, we gotta talk," Krueger whispered with purpose. "I can't do this. I'll be in jail forever. I know what will happen in there. The prisoners will make my life hell for me. You know what I mean?"

Gino nodded in agreement. "No, no, Krueger, listen to me. You plead no contest. This judge'll have some mercy. No more than ten years. Promise."

"Ten years! You've got to be kidding. That's like forever. Ten years? Hell, if I'm still living, I won't be able to walk, let alone take a shower. If I plead not guilty and go to trial ... can you get me off, convince the jury of my innocence? I want a *not guilty* or at least a hung jury. God knows I don't want them to hang *me*."

"Who do you think I am? Perry Mason?" Gino asked Krueger. "Look at the evidence. Hell, they found your clothes and ID in the trash bin. There were witnesses."

Krueger pleaded to Gino first, "Just get me bail."

"Okay, okay, I'll get you bail, but if we go to trial, the hammer of justice is coming down. The judge'll give you twenty years. Maybe twenty-five years. Like I said, they've got witnesses. No telling how many more of your boys, victims, they can get to come forward. My God, they've got your entire confession."

"Confession, that ... from that sheriff. It was forced. I had no choice. For Christ's sake, I had no lawyer."

"That's for sure," Moretti replied. "But you wrote and signed it."

"The sheriff threatened me. I was scared, under emotional stress. I had no choice. He was threatening."

"Witnesses. They say they've got them. How could we build a defense?"

"The confession!"

"*Shhh.* Not so loud, Krueger," Moretti said, as he could see Krueger was getting excited. "Quiet, *shhh.* Let's step to the back of the courtroom and keep it down."

Moretti looked at the sergeant sitting in the back row, engrossed in surveillance. He pointed to Krueger, himself, and three rows back, indicating a move. The sergeant gave one nod and held up five fingers. *Must be for time*, Moretti thought.

Once they were alone, Moretti deliberated and decided. "We can fight the confession. The judge might not let the prosecutor submit a coerced confession," Moretti suggested but did not confirm.

"Yeah, yeah. That could be. You could make it happen. Let's do that," Krueger said with newfound enthusiasm.

"Then there's the jury. You're in conservative Midwestern Wabash County. They don't even know about abuse. What's that, they'd ask. Then they'd think firing squad. The prosecutor would paint this horrific picture of you and the boys. Every minute detail. The jury would be appalled. I'd have no chance at cross-examining, and then the jury would call the firing squad."

"Firing squad?" Krueger asked with alarm.

"Just making a point. No way, of course. These people are all about family, kids. I don't want to know what you did. It's all about the jury, jury and witnesses. You told me this Bernard fellow caught you. Is that right? Any more?"

"Look, there's just Bernard and the custodian, but he didn't see anything happen. He just found me."

"Found you. What do you mean?"

"Bernard found me with the boys, like I told you yesterday. The custodian, well you see, he found me early the next morning. You know, after Bernard had worked me over real bad. Why do I have to say this again? This Bernard guy just stampeded me."

"Okay, stop. Stop now! Listen!" Moretti heard a knock on wood. Looking toward the sound, he saw Sergeant Bauer holding up two fingers.

"Two minutes, two freakin' minutes. Now let me talk. I met you a few hours ago. You were holding a white flag, hands in the air, finger pointing at yourself, so I went along. Hey, this guy did it. So I'm thinking ten years … at most … plus maybe some time off for good behavior. You're known around town. Civic-minded, good guy. You plead no contest, so no trial. Seven maybe eight and you're out."

"Well, I wasn't thinking straight. That sheriff, he—"

"Quiet. We're out of time." Gino saw the sergeant move his left index finger in a circling motion. "Okay, time's up," Moretti told Krueger. "Okay, Sergeant, we're almost done," he said and held up one more finger. The sergeant gave a nod.

Moretti said to Krueger, "Now you want to fight. We'll be in front of Judge Seiler in a few minutes. I know him. I'm going to ask for a continuance on the plea. Maybe he'll give us till Monday. We'll go for bail now. Maybe get you home tonight. He'll give us a day, maybe two. The court won't convene again until Monday anyway. Now not a word. Listen to me. You hear? Look at me, Krueger. Let me handle this. Let's go. Don't say a word unless I ask or give an okay. Yes or no answers. The judge hates rambling."

Moretti stood up. Krueger followed. As they walked in front of Sergeant Bauer, Moretti leaned down. "Thank you, Sergeant. Thank you."

The sergeant just nodded. They returned to the front row and waited ten to fifteen minutes more and then twenty minutes.

Time was eternity.

"Phillip Krueger," the bailiff finally called out.

Moretti leaned over. "Not a word till I say."

After opening the gate next to the defense table, Moretti walked through as Krueger followed. Sternness waved like a flag over the judge's bench. His combed-back gray and white hair was thinning over his high protruding forehead. The judge's wire glasses were anchored at the end of his nose by wide nostrils. His white mustache was still peppered with a little black, but was trimmed tight. Moderately heavy set, Judge Henry Seiler was the epitome of a not-to-be-messed-with "it's my courtroom, my way or the highway" type of authority. Minutes passed.

Moretti and Krueger approached the bench.

"Step forward, gentlemen," Judge Seiler said, peering over the top of his spectacles. "I have before me a charge. Serious, really serious 'round this neck of the woods," he stated, getting right to the point. "You are charged with seven counts of lewd and lascivious behavior and three counts of sodomy against minors. How do you plead?"

Immediately, Gino Moretti stepped forward. "Your Honor, I would like to have placed for the record that my client was arrested yesterday and detained the day before. He did not have counsel till this morning. I first met him at eleven. We have had only an hour or so to discuss this charge."

The courtroom door suddenly opened, allowing the spread of some sunlight. Judge Seiler looked beyond counsel and noticed a large man in a dark suit step in and take a seat in the last row. He was alone. Staring forward, the man first noticed Sergeant Bauer on the opposite side of the center aisle. The sergeant scrutinized the man in the dark suit and then nodded.

"A serious charge, I might add," the judge spoke, looking down his nose and over his wire glasses directly at Phillip Krueger. "Is this fact, Sheriff Thurow?" the judge asked the sheriff, who sat near the prosecutor's table.

"Yes, Your Honor, correct."

"This is an arraignment, you know, Mr. Moretti. How is your client going to plead?"

"With all due respect, Your Honor, I would like to ask for some more time to meet with my client. Justice would be better served—"

"Don't lecture me on justice, counsel," Judge Seiler said firmly.

"Yes, Your Honor," the slight Italian lawyer answered with a firm hold on meekness.

"Now, what were you asking, counsel?" Judge Seiler asked, giving Moretti another opportunity to plead his request for more time.

"Your Honor, we would like for some more time to discuss this plea. My client has no previous record. He is recognized as a giving, civic-minded citizen in and around Wabash County. He's a member of—"

"Yes, yes, I know. I am very aware of all of your civic contributions, Mr. Krueger. I read the *Wabash Plain Dealer*. I know people. You do have a reputation and have made a name for yourself contributing and doing good works around our community. I will refrain, however, from commenting on this wayward departure from—what shall we say—wayward departure from civic responsibilities. All that said, counsel, Mr. Krueger, you have until three thirty on Monday, April 28. No excuses. I'll expect your plea."

"Judge, one other thing. I request, with great respect to your judgment, that based on Mr. Krueger's previous record and outstanding recognized position within—"

"Get to it, counsel."

"Recognizance, sir. Would you ... would you please—"

"No, I will not. Thank you. Mr. Krueger is under arrest. He will remain in this house until Monday, at which time, based on your plea ... if bail becomes a question, I will set it then and not an hour sooner. Do I make myself clear, counsel?"

"Yes, yes, Your Honor. Thank you, Your Honor."

"Recess!" The judge pounded the gavel, stepped down, and proceeded toward his chamber. Stopping at the side of the bench, he looked back at the man in the dark suit. The man was still sitting in the back row. *I recognize that man. I've seen him before*, Judge Seiler thought.

Sergeant Bauer stepped forward. Approaching Krueger, he pulled the cuffs from his polished black belt. *Click, click.* "Back to the cell."

"I'll be back tomorrow, Phillip. We'll figure this all out. Be prepared. You really have to weigh the risk of not guilty," Gino Moretti advised his client.

"Thank you, Mr. Moretti."

The sergeant gave a tug, clasped Krueger's left forearm, and walked toward the rear door of the courtroom. Krueger noticed but did not acknowledge Clarence Wolfe sitting alone in the back of the room, his dark brown suit blending into the paneled wall. He thought, *He'll have to contact me.*

CHAPTER 39

A HEAVY HEART

Linda Singleton—May 4, 1958

MORE than a week went by. Linda was distraught about her meeting with Father Sullivan. Her heart was heavy. All she could remember was his caring, melodious voice and the feel of his arms around her as she was leaving. It was imprinted in her mind. Answers were absent as she thought about Father Sullivan daily. Linda knew in her heart of hearts that she could have love, but she would never be able to share love with the good priest. She wondered, *What can it all mean, and where will it all go if I can't conquer that love and lust in my heart for this wonderful man?*

Selfishly, Linda's mind was consumed with her own struggles. She knew Joey was her priority. Her job at the courthouse was important as well, as she was their family's only means of support. As always, her religion and her faith played such an integral part in her life. Her divorce had impacted her forever. Linda Singleton felt she lived with sin. Her life was full of concerns and challenges, but her deepest thoughts and desires always came back to him—Father Sullivan. That night, however, she knew she must be there for Joey, comforting him more directly.

It was 9:00 p.m. on Sunday. Linda knocked on Joey's bedroom door.

"Mom? Come in."

Linda saw Joey sitting at his desk, reading. "Hi, Joey. Have a few minutes to talk?"

"Sure, Mom. What is it? I'm just reading *Huckleberry Finn*. You know, that had to be a great time to live. Carefree, fishing, living on the Mississippi. What a day," Joey said with a smile. "No worries."

"Well, you live on a river, Joey. The mighty Wabash," his mom said, smiling back.

"It's not exactly the same," Joey responded, still smiling.

"I know. Life is always changing. Times are different now compared to those days that Mark Twain describes. I can assure you, though, Mark Twain had his troubles too."

"I know, Mom, but some things never change," Joey said as if he was so experienced in life.

Linda decided not to pursue that. "Okay," she said, folding her hands and setting them on her lap, atop her flower-patterned apron.

"Oh, the fried chicken and the mashed potatoes were great for dinner, I must say," Joey added as if he wanted to delay what he assumed might be the true purpose of their conversation.

"You're welcome, honey. I know it's your favorite. Now ... " she said, taking a deep breath, her hands still folded. "We have to talk. It's about you and your friend Father Jaeger and the priesthood."

"Sure, Mom. What are you concerned about?" Joey asked hesitantly.

"Joey, you and Father Jaeger, how good of friends are you?" Linda cleared her throat. Her hands were clasped.

"Really good, Mom. I really like him," he said, trying to answer in a relaxed manner.

"I understand." Linda nodded. "Well then, if you like him a lot, do you love him?"

"Mom. Love him? Love, that's for girls. We are ... we ... " Joey paused, now feeling on guard. "Mom, that's sick. Sick," he said defensively, raising his voice.

"Now, Joey," she interrupted, "men can have feelings for one another. Men can love one another. People love one another. Love is not divided by whether you're a man or a woman. Don't you see that? I didn't say it's wrong when men love one another."

Joey just listened.

"Men, you know, there are men who love each other, live with each other. Instead of having wives or girlfriends, they can have another man in their lives. Most people just are not aware of that."

"You think so, Mom?" Joey looked at her, seeking approval.

"Joey, I know that kind of friendship—you know, between two

men—can be frowned upon. As a matter of fact, most of these men live secret lives. They conceal who they are. And, Joey, in most cases I think these men have no choice. Like it is who they are, how they were born. The way I once loved your father is the same way two men can love one another."

"Really? Really?" Joey replied as if he was hearing, *It's okay.* But he thought, *I can't tell Mom the way I feel though.*

"Could you ever ... have you ever felt this way, Joey?"

There was a pause. Then silence.

Joey looked down at his book and then said, not lifting his head, "Well, maybe. I don't really know, Mom. I can't figure it all out."

"That's okay, Joey. You're thirteen. You are at an age when you're trying to better understand yourself. You have a lot going on."

Maybe she understands, Joey thought.

"However, Joey, let's just suppose you had these feelings for a man. It could be the beginning of something natural, but if it was with an older man, that just might not be what's best for you. I'm saying if it was this kind of love for a priest, that would be sinfully wrong for him because of his vows and then your age. You are still thirteen."

"Love a priest? Gosh no, Mom. That would be wrong ... a sin. Priests love Jesus. They love God. Not men. Not boys. But, Mom, what if it's with another boy, not a priest?"

Linda wasn't anticipating that question, as she had been so totally focused on Father Jaeger as the perpetrator. "Well then, Joey, I'd say if that's who you are, then give it time. You both would have to wait to show your love in a certain way, just like boys and girls have to wait until they can bear children. They must wait for marriage." Linda felt Joey was listening. "Now I have to say, if—and I'm not accusing you—but if you are close or even being intimate with ... "

Joey took a deep, deep breath. His eyes were welling up. Linda could see the tears.

"Joey, can you talk about your friendship with Father Jaeger? Have you asked yourself what kind of friendship you have?"

Joey gushed forward with tears. He stood and knelt over in front of his mom, burying his face in her apron, sobbing uncontrollably. She held her arms over his shoulders.

It was then that Linda knew. She thought of Joey. She thought of her own dilemma. They cried together.

CHAPTER 40

DOUBLE JEOPARDY

Father Warren—May 5, 1958

FATHER Warren was awake late into the night on Sunday. He was still stressed with Ralph Smith's news about the abuse at the hands of Father Jaeger several weeks ago. Father Warren had put off any decision to call authorities. This evening, Father Warren came to a decision.

Monday morning as he waited for Father Sullivan to come to breakfast, he stared at the morning paper.

"Good morning, Father," Father Sullivan said.

"Good morning to you, Michael," Father Warren replied with a look of concern. "Actually, it's not a good morning," he clarified. "Michael, I've decided that you and I should meet with Ralph Smith. We are the three who are aware of the actions of Father Jaeger that night. I believe it all happened as Ralph described. There is no way he would be making that up. I know it is all true. I called Ralph about an hour ago, and he'll be here to meet with us at seven o'clock this evening, after he's home from work. I'd like you here."

"Of course. Fine with me, Father. We can't put this off any longer. We've waited too long. Actually, Father," Father Sullivan said point-blank after hearing Father Warren's decision, "I still think the police should become involved."

"Let's not jump too quickly."

"Father, enough time has lapsed. I have since learned that Father Jaeger may be involved with another boy, except this time the boy could be a willing to be with the priest."

Father Warren shook his head, "Please no."

"Yes, Father. Confidentially, Joey Singleton."

"My dear Lord, Michael. Tell me this is not true. How far can this go? Are you sure about Joey?"

"Yes, pretty sure. His mother approached me. She's distraught to say the least. I believe I will be meeting with Joey."

"Oh good. That's good. Let's address what's before us, but you keep me informed about Joey." Father Warren rubbed his forehead with his fingers. "Joey, Joey Singleton, and his mother is such a good person. Does so much for the parish."

"Please forgive me, Father, but we should call the police. We should go to the bishop and our Cardinal Cullings. Father … " he hesitated. "With all due respect, Father, our Holy Father should be aware. This abuse problem has to be solved. If it is beyond our parish, which we both know, then our Holy Father, John Benedict, he's the one. Our directives must come from the leadership in the Vatican."

Father Warren widened his eyes and gently patted Father Sullivan's hand. "Michael, Michael. I appreciate your passion, but all in due time. We're not ready to call the pope."

Michael took a deep breath, "Okay, Father Warren. Okay."

"We'll talk all about that this evening when Ralph is here." Father Warren had strong feelings about handling the abuse within the parish and not involving the police.

Both priests understood one another. Their growing difference of opinion on whether or not to expose the abuse to the authorities had not dissolved their trust and respect for one another. Both were appalled. Together they planned to address and eliminate the severe problem caused by Father Jaeger within their parish.

Not finishing his breakfast, Father Sullivan gathered his napkin, stood, and said, "Excuse me, Father. I've got to leave. Talking to the eighth graders at 9:15 about the importance of love and friendship. We will work this out together. You know I will do whatever you ask."

Father Sullivan—May 5, 1958

Father Sullivan's day passed slowly. He was anxious for his meeting with Father Warren and Ralph Smith that evening. He went directly to the front parlor. As he was about to enter the room, he heard a knock at the front door. He passed the parlor and from the corner of his eye saw Father Warren waiting in his favorite chair. Opening the front door, Father Sullivan greeted Ralph Smith. Together they entered the parlor.

"Good evening, Ralph. Come right in," Father Warren welcomed both Ralph and Father Sullivan. "Thank you for coming on such a short notice," he said while standing and reaching out to shake hands. "I'm glad you're here," he continued in a low, calm voice. "Have a seat." Ralph Smith sat on the couch, while Father Sullivan took the chair at the other end, opposite Father Warren.

Father Warren spoke first. "Gentlemen, we all know why we are here, so let's begin. Ralph, why don't you begin and refresh our memories? Give us a brief summary of what happened that Saturday evening."

"Sure, Father. I will."

"Oh, one other thing before we begin," Father Warren said. "I spoke with Father Jaeger this afternoon. He's been gone over a month. Now he wants a couple more weeks. He will be on vacation with his family in Chicago. We have been keeping this quiet within the parish, but we cannot any longer. Too many tongues wagging. We need a formal announcement from the pulpit. Too many rumors and innuendos passing around the parish. I should have done this weeks ago. I plan on informing the parish of Father Jaeger's time off at next Sunday's Mass. Meanwhile, Father Sullivan, if anyone asks, just say he's visiting family."

"Excuse me, Father, giving us time for what?" Father Sullivan asked, leaning forward in his chair. "We have to do something now. Look how long it's been. The boys deserve at least that. We must contact their parents now and then the police."

"Go ahead, Ralph. I want to hear," the elder priest said, not acknowledging Father Sullivan's comment.

Ralph Smith could feel some tension between the two priests. "Well, as I said, I found Father Jaeger in the woods with three of the scouts."

"Excuse me, Ralph. Was Peter Goodnar one of the boys?" Father Sullivan interjected.

"No, no. Peter was safe in the cabin with the other scouts. Phillip

Krueger was with them. No, it was Paul Woodward, Mark Salisbury, and Henry Langley."

Ralph continued, "Father Sullivan, I knew Father Jaeger was camping all night with three of the scouts. Phillip Krueger had informed me earlier. They were completing requirements for their camping merit badge. There was another group with two of our Eagle Scouts, Bob Wilkus and Gene Stephens. They were camping at the opposite end of the woods, far from the other side of the cabin. I had told Phil I wanted to take a walk and that I would check on them. I recall him telling me it would not be necessary. Kinda had the feeling he didn't want me to go searching. I went anyway," Ralph said, now looking at Father Warren.

"As I recall, Father, you asked me to keep an eye on Krueger. I was just taking a nice walk. There was almost a full moon. The woods were cool and still. Not a bit of wind. Eventually I could see the light from a campfire and could smell the aroma of the smoke. As I approached Father Jaeger and the boys, I stopped short of the light of the campfire. They didn't see me. I could not believe what I saw. As I said, Father, I found them all naked around the campfire."

Father Sullivan shook his head, sat quietly, and listened, as Ralph Smith reconfirmed the story he had previously shared with Father Warren.

"You'll recall, Father, Father Jaeger had taken Paul into the woods, leaving two of the boys around the fire. I demanded, I called for him to come out. He did wearing only a blanket. I did everything to control my rage," Ralph said, his face turning red.

Father Sullivan sat still, absorbing every word. He did not say anything as his mind filled with disgust, concern, disbelief, and outrage. Quietly controlled, he avoided responding emotionally to what he was hearing from Ralph Smith. *We must inform the parents and police now*, he thought.

"And then I told Father Jaeger to go back to his car. Don't stop at the cabin. Leave now. I just had to get him away from the boys, out of their sight. I felt it was very important that I talk to the boys right then around the campfire. I explained as best I could to them how wrong, how terribly, terribly wrong Father Jaeger's actions were. The boys were scared, but I knew they felt relieved after he left. I asked them to keep this between us until I spoke with you, Father Warren. Let's not forget that we need to talk to these boys and their parents. All parents must know."

"That's how I found out. Henry Langley's dad called. I said I would be back after conferring with you, Father," Father Sullivan said looking at the pastor.

"After we finish this evening, would you like for me to talk to the three boys?"

Father Warren thought for a moment. "Yes, Michael. That would be a good idea. Talk to the boys first. Get their reactions and then see me about approaching the parents. Learn more. I want you both to know I called Bishop Powers this afternoon and asked for a meeting. Unfortunately, he is busy tomorrow, but he will meet with me in South Wayne on Wednesday morning at 11:00 a.m. I'm going to tell him all that has happened. Seek his advice. As you both know, this parish is responsible to the diocese. The bishop will make the final decision as to what is to be done with Father Jaeger."

Father Sullivan was astonished. "Yes, Father, but what about the police? This should be reported. This man is an abuser. He is a molester. Father Warren, the way I look at it, this hideous act is a felony. We have waited too long."

Ralph Smith sat listening. He agreed with Father Sullivan. When their eyes met, their expressions confirmed their mutual concern that Father Warren would be making a mistake by not alerting the police.

"Ralph, Michael. Excuse me, Ralph. I often call Father Sullivan Michael when we're together," the elderly priest said in his calm, soothing manner. "First we need to talk to the bishop. What needs to be done will be the bishop's decision. I am responsible for this parish and everything that happens within it, so I must report this to Bishop Powers. And the bishop? He reports directly to Cardinal Cullings in Indianapolis. And all three of us know that the ultimate decision, the final voice on the disciplining of priests, lies in Rome with the Vatican. We are all ultimately responsible to Pope John Benedict. It is not our place to supersede any of the structure of our church," Father Warren explained.

"That's right, Father. That's where the responsibility should be. I'm sure we aren't the first. I have read about Ireland. Abuse has been closeted for decades. What has Rome done to stop this? Why don't we hear from Pope John Benedict? Why, Father? Please, for these boys' sakes, tell me." The volume of Father Sullivan's voice rose as he spoke.

Ralph looked at Father Sullivan sitting on the edge of his chair.

"Now, now, Michael. I appreciate your passion for these boys, but we have to address it in the right order. That begins with Bishop Powers."

Ralph sat back. He didn't say a word.

Father Sullivan began again, "With all due respect, Father Warren, I know my responsibility. My obedience lies with you. But what if the bishop decides he is going to handle this within the diocese, keeping it within our parish?" He paused, then again questioning the older priest. "Then this will never get to the desk of Pope John Benedict. That's where it should be. If I were running—"

Father Warren cut Father Sullivan off. "Michael," he said sternly yet with a calming effect. "Michael, you are not running this parish or diocese." He paused. "At least not for now." He gave a slight smile. "We are not there yet. Keep in mind that Father Jaeger is away for two more weeks. I am meeting with the bishop on Wednesday. I have already made the arrangements. That's in two days. I have confidence that Bishop Powers will do what is right for our church, our parish, and Father Jaeger." Father Warren paused and looked at his folded hands. "Yes, I know the bishop quite well. For me, I think he will do exactly what is right."

Father Sullivan noted an inquisitive look on Father Warren's face. "Yes, Father, but what about Paul, Mark, and Henry? What about Peter Goodnar? How many more could there be? You told me the other day that you had some concerns regarding Father Jaeger and his transfers from one parish to another. Didn't you say he was in Crawfordsville? At St. Michael's? Where was he before that? Did this problem start here at St. Thomas Moore? Is this the first time? We all three know that can't be."

"Michael—" Father Warren cut him off again.

"Please, Father. Please let me finish. I'll stay calm. It seems to me that if we did not know about Father Jaeger before he came here, if we were not told about this man, then why was he transferred here? I think you said he was in several parishes for short times. What, less than two years each? This transfer is not a coincidence. After looking at everything I have learned these past several weeks and months when this problem was assigned to us, I believe the bishop transferred Father Jaeger to our parish after whatever he did in Crawfordsville. Now look where we are. Look what's happened to the lives of these boys. They will be affected forever, and I bet their families don't even know. You might have faith in Bishop Powers, but I question him and, as a matter of fact, all the hierarchy of the Catholic Church. Yes, as I said, especially Pope John Benedict."

Ralph Smith just sat there. Still not a word. He was stupefied at what he was hearing.

"Michael, I understand your concern, your passion, and even your outrage, but we don't know for sure. I have to ask some hard questions of the bishop," Father Warren said in his defense.

Michael replied, "Father, I do know for sure. Ralph caught him in the act. A perverse act with these innocent boys, naked in the woods. The boys were terrified. Boys in our own parish whom we are to protect. I have questions I want to ask of Father Jaeger."

"Michael," Father Warren said with a stern voice.

"Yes, Father. Sorry." Calming down, Father Sullivan lowered his voice. "I am not without sin. Our dear Lord did not make any of us perfect. I do not want to accuse Father Jaeger falsely. However, we have to look at the facts. As I see it, Father Jaeger has come to our parish and passed a cancer onto some boys. Boys we know. God only knows if there are other abused boys I haven't even mentioned hidden within our parish and, for heaven's sake, probably in other parishes. The way I look at it, Father Jaeger has been passed on by Bishop Powers. The bishop must know the reason for the litany of transfers."

"Father Warren, I would have to agree," Ralph Smith said, commenting for the first time. Ralph knew Father Warren quite well. Something had to be done. They needed to act.

Father Sullivan continued, "I believe he has probably been an abuser in other parishes. If this is true, I think Bishop Powers has a lot of questions to answer. The bishop has been in South Wayne for what, twelve, fifteen years? He became bishop sometime around when Father Jaeger was ordained. That begs the question, was Father Jaeger involved with this abuse in the seminary? Father, what I see is a giant cover-up within our church. That even begs another question. Father Jaeger is not the only priest doing this. Abusing children. I'm sure there are more priests in this diocese involved in the same, what should I say, the same sickness?"

Father Warren interjected, "Michael, hold on. You are making a big leap here. Do you have reason? Now you are mentioning other priests." He raised an eyebrow, looking at the younger priest.

"There have to be other priests in other parishes in Indiana, Iowa—all over the country. I think there may be many priests who are abusers, hiding underneath the protective cloak of our church. This isn't just here in Wabash. I have read. I have talked to others. The same thing is happening all around Europe, other states. If we look deeply, we become aware that the abuse has been around for thousands of years. Father, we both know. If I recall, you are reading a book about *Abuse in Ireland*. Others can be doing the same thing, abusing our youth. Sadly, in my heart of hearts, I worry that this is probably the truth. There are probably more, maybe many more immoral priests." Father Sullivan voice's was much lower and more controlled.

Father Warren did not respond.

Father Sullivan went on to say, "Please, let me say I respect you. I admire you. You are not only a good priest, but you are a great man, Father Warren. I would do anything for you, and I don't want to see your sparkling career tarnished."

Father Warren was still listening, as was Ralph Smith, who in his own mind agreed with everything Father Sullivan was saying.

"Father, I think this is a cover-up by Bishop Powers for sending him to us. We have been duped. We were not prepared for what has happened. We were not even told of his past, his history. We simply had no way of expecting this. Bishop Powers should have told you. And in reality, Father Jaeger should simply not have been assigned to this parish, or to any other. If he did these things before, then he's a criminal. He has broken not only moral laws, but he has broken the laws of our society, the laws that are there to protect our children."

Father Sullivan leaned back in his chair. "I'm tired. That's all I can say now. I will trust your good judgment, Father. But please, something has to be done and done now." Father Sullivan hung his head, rubbed his eyes, and folded his hands. "We need to go to the parents and the police," he said as if to quietly demand action.

The clock on the wall struck 9:30 p.m.

He then added, "Time to call it an evening."

The three men sat quietly for a few moments, digesting all that had been said.

"Ralph, Michael, thank you both. I am going to South Wayne Wednesday. I will explain everything that has happened directly to our bishop. I will ask him some tough questions. Michael, what you say does have validity. There is truth, and we need answers. First of all, we need answers for these boys. I welcome your thoughts. You both have given me more insight." Father Warren said, "I am very appreciative for all the passion and concern you have shown." Father Warren put his hand on his knee, and with a low groan, he stood, as did Ralph.

Father Sullivan remained in his chair and said, "Father, I want to say one more thing. I have a request, a favor."

Father Warren listened. "Sure, Michael, of course. What is it?"

Father Sullivan looked at Ralph and directly at Father Warren. "Father, I would like to go with you to meet with Bishop Powers. Please, Father, this is very important to me."

Father Warren sat back down in his chair. Ralph Smith stood quietly between the two priests. Feeling awkward, he sat down. Both he and Father Sullivan looked at Father Warren.

Father Warren was quiet. Father Sullivan could tell he was considering. "Please, Father. I can help," Father Sullivan interrupted Father Warren's thoughts.

Father Warren rubbed his forehead. He looked down. Silence. "Frankly, yes, I think that might be okay. It may be a good idea, Michael."

"Thank you," was all the younger priest needed to say.

The three men quietly bid their farewells. Clasping Ralph's hand in both of his, Father Warren looked Ralph directly in the eye. "Thank you, Ralph. I know you are as concerned as I. And we both ... " Father nodded. "We both know this should be in the hands of the law." Ralph nodded.

As Father Sullivan walked Ralph to the door, Ralph turned and reminded the priest, "I'll be here whenever you need me."

"We know that, Ralph. We know that." Father Sullivan patted Ralph's left shoulder.

Ralph nodded and stepped out into the cool spring evening.

Father Warren remained in his chair. He thought and prayed. *I know Michael and Ralph are correct. I must act now.* Glancing out the window, he watched as Ralph Smith walked by the post light and disappeared into the darkness.

CHAPTER 41

REVEALING THE TRUTH

Phillip Krueger—April 25, 1958

THE night was long. The cell was cool. Phillip Krueger struggled and fought with the decision. He weighed his options over and over. A no contest plea would save having a trial, and hopefully the judge would grant some mercy. A not guilty plea would erupt the inner sanctum of the school and demand a trial that could send him to prison for a much longer term than a no contest. Zilbar and Wolfe, along with other staff members, would be dragged into the fight. If no contest, he could depend on Clarence Wolfe to be a character witness and focus on this one singular incident.

Across town, Wolfe was having trouble sleeping. He knew he could speak up in Krueger's defense without damaging his own administrative record. Wolfe could confirm how well Krueger worked with the boys, although Wolfe didn't care about him. He knew Krueger could be sacrificed. Krueger knew some but not all the aspects of the Wolfe-Zilbar association. Wolfe knew Zilbar would do whatever necessary to keep Krueger quiet … at all costs. Wolfe especially knew that Krueger was self-serving, but Zilbar had no conscience when it came to his own power and glory. He would stop at nothing.

Phillip Krueger had disclosed in their first meeting what Bernard had witnessed. Bernard Bednar could be his downfall. Wolfe could keep the boys quiet. Fear would conquer them. Phillip Krueger's only concern was Bernard, as the man had seen him with all three boys. Naked with all the boys. Caught in the act. The prosecutor would define premeditated. Bernard was the problem.

Then next day at 10:00 a.m., Krueger heard the sounds of footsteps on the cold concrete floor.

"You have a visitor," the thin, gaunt-looking guard informed him.

"Oh, Mr. Moretti, you're right on time." Krueger decided he would be upbeat for Moretti.

"Did you expect any less? I'm always on time. I always win," he said with confidence.

"No, no, I'm just glad you are here. I don't know what to do. There is no way I am going to that state prison. Half the felons in the state are imprisoned there. I've heard that's one of the toughest penitentiaries in the country. The prisoners are predators and will do anything to anyone. You know … satisfying their needs on the weaker ones. You know where that will put me."

"You sure get right to the point. Must be really bothering you." Moretti sat down in the straight chair. Bent over, putting his elbows on his knees, he responded, "You plead no contest, you're going to prison for sure. Judge Seiler will have you there in less than thirty days. Now, I've checked out this witness, the one who caught you. Bednar … Bernard Bednar? Right?"

"Yes, he's the one. He'll tell it all. I'll have no chance."

"He's been working at the school for more than twenty years. No record. No problems at the school. Understand he's a little slow. So tell me what he saw."

"Oh dear, I hate this. Okay. I was with these three boys. They were on a bench."

"How? What do you mean on a bench?" Moretti asked.

"They were kneeling."

"On a bench, they were kneeling?" Moretti asked. "Oh, oh, okay. You mean like in church? Of course. Were they dressed?"

"*Hmmm*. Well … " Krueger didn't like the question. Pride or shame was in his way.

"Look, you gotta tell me. I'm your only hope," Moretti threatened.

"Okay, yes, they were naked. This is so awful. Embarrassing."

"You should have thought about that when you unbuckled your pants," Moretti fired back. "Naked? So you had three boys kneeling *naked?*" the attorney asked, shaking his head. "Where were you? I suppose behind them?"

"Yes," Krueger answered as if too ashamed and embarrassed to say it.

Moretti then asked, "I suppose you were naked?"

Krueger knew there was no denying it. A flash raced across his mind. *Why? Why?* he asked himself.

"Answer me. I must know. Answer me," Moretti commanded, controlling Krueger.

"Yes, I was! Okay? Yes, I was! How else could I … ? Oh nothing. You know what I mean."

"Then that begs only one question," Moretti stated.

"What's that?" Krueger asked.

"Did you rape those boys? Did you sodomize them?"

"No, no! I didn't. Really, I didn't."

"What do you mean you didn't? You were naked. What else could that mean? You weren't there to be photographed for some skin magazine," Moretti said, really giving Krueger the first degree.

"Yes, I must admit I was ready to."

"Then what stopped you? If you were ready, why didn't—"

Krueger looked Moretti in the eye. "Because he stopped me! Bernard grabbed me from behind. I didn't do it that time. He stopped me!"

"That time you didn't. That's good. Other times aren't relevant!" Moretti shouted back.

"Quiet down there!" They both heard from the far end of the hall.

Moretti stood up, pushing the straight chair away. Walking to the back wall of Krueger's cell, he looked up at the small barred window. He ran his fingers through his black wavy hair. Turning around, he stood facing Krueger, who was still sitting on the side of the bed. Stepping back one step, Gino Moretti leaned against the solitary wall-hung sink.

"Now, listen to me. Let me summarize. You have no record. You are involved in the Lions Club and Boy Scouts. You have a respected position in the reform school. Your boss will back you up. So there is this one time you are caught in a compromising position … but there was no crime. There was simply a crime of stupidity. This witness actually saved you from committing a crime. You are just dumb, if not dumber than your actions. You are lucky he stopped you."

"Yes, that's it. That's all that happened," Krueger responded with almost a sigh of relief. *Maybe this guy can get me off.*

"We're not done. What about these seven counts of lascivious behavior?"

"The sheriff just thinks that. He thinks he has some boys who will come forward. Oh, maybe I did a little grabbing and patting but nothing serious—no crime, no rape. No rape ever."

Now Moretti knew Krueger was not telling the truth, but that did not matter. "There was no crime this time," he said aloud to Krueger. Moretti was feeling a little more confident. "Okay, we have some time. The plea is Monday. I'll be here in the late morning, eleven o'clock. We'll have a few hours till we go before the judge. I have to think this out. I must have all questions answered in my mind. I have to know before we step in front of that judge if I can get you out of this. Understand?" he told Krueger.

"Yes, but if I plead not guilty, can you ... can you get me off? Keep me out of the state pen?"

Moretti looked at Krueger. Leaning over, he picked up his hat and black-strapped briefcase. Krueger looked up. Moretti put his hat on and tugged the front brim downward.

"Let me put it this way. If I tell you Monday to plead not guilty, then I assure you that you'll never see the inside of that prison."

Krueger stood up and extended his hand. "Thanks. Thanks, Gino. That's all I needed to hear."

"Guard, guard," Moretti called.

Krueger watched as the cell door was opened and Moretti turned and proceeded down the hall.

Eleven o'clock Monday ... we'll have our plan. If he can get me out of this, I'll be okay. Everything I know about Wolfe and Zilbar will stay behind closed doors. Oh God, I can't go to that prison. Moretti's going to handle this. I just know it.

CHAPTER 42

SECRET FILE

Randall Zilbar—April 26, 1958

GINO Moretti knew to report to Zilbar about his visit with Krueger. He hustled up the stairs to his second-floor office, room 232—*Gino Moretti, Attorney-at-Law*. The black letters on the opaque glass on the top half of the door were as bold as the man himself. Throwing his briefcase on the side chair, he immediately called Randall Zilbar. Zilbar's secretary took the call, as Zilbar was away, but due to return within the hour. She said he would call back. Moretti sat at his desk and sorted through the mail. He was at a loss with his secretary, Rosemary, out sick.

Practicing law alone gave him a little extra cover and independence. Moretti liked it that way. Originally from Cicero, Illinois, Gino Moretti had been convinced to move to Wabash ten years before. Randall Zilbar had assured Gino that the move would be lucrative. So far, Zilbar had been right. Moretti enjoyed the frequency with which he could go back to Chicago, either for business—usually at the hands and request of Randall—or for his own personal reasons. Wabash was just too small a city for any kind of personal action. Zilbar, however, kept him quite busy.

About twenty minutes before the hour was up, the phone rang. "Hello, Mr. Moretti. I have Mr. Zilbar on the line for you."

"Gino, what's the status?"

"He'll plead Monday."

"How?" Randall asked hurriedly in his direct, impersonal manner.

"Let me explain. There's really only one viable witness, the guy who caught him in the act. Bednar, Bernard Bednar. I'll be able to handle him in cross. The kicker is, Krueger said he's not going to prison, no matter what. That's easy to figure. We both know what would happen to him there."

"How's that?" Zilbar asked.

"Think about it. Look how he's hooked on young boys. If he goes to the slammer, those animals will look at him as a boy. He'll become their prey. You know, what goes around comes around. Even dark justice prevails," Gino explained to Zilbar.

"I'm not concerned about justice. I just care about what this bastard Krueger could spill. You know, Krueger is aware of some but not all of what's going on out there with Wolfe and all. Gotta watch that bastard. That's for later. Besides this small-potato 'joy-boy' stuff that Krueger gets his kicks on could pull in the other project."

"Yes, I know, Mr. Zilbar, but that's why you've got me here in this godforsaken farm town. I'll take care of all this for you. Don't worry," he assured him.

"Will Krueger talk?"

Moretti went on to explain, "Let me put it this way. If he pleads not guilty, then we've got to get him off. But he might talk if the prosecutor probes into the school. No tellin' what he'll say. He'll sing like a choir boy. Krueger's holding a trump card on you. If he goes no contest and he knows he's going to the pen, then he has no incentive to keep his mouth shut. You know, Krueger's not fond of Wolfe. As far as you go, I don't know his thoughts. Either way, if he goes down, he could spoil the whole setup."

Gino went on, "This may be a delicate question, sir, but as your attorney, I should ask. Now remember this is, of course, all privileged. It's all confidential between you and me. Let me be sure I understand. You told me that several years ago Krueger came across a file on Wolfe's desk while Wolfe was on vacation."

"Yes, that stupid buffoon Wolfe left it on his desk," Zilbar said. "Inside, Krueger found a letter of request, a request to purchase. The name on the file was Bellini, Vito Bellini."

"Is that correct?" Moretti asked for assurance. "Do I recall that correctly, Randall? And Vito is your father-in-law?"

"Yeah, yeah. That's it. Vito is family," Zilbar confirmed. "My wife's father."

"So when Wolfe was giving Krueger a little static about finances, a raise, Krueger didn't like what Wolfe was going to give him. So Krueger made Wolfe aware of the letter in the file. Let's call that a little protection for Mr. Krueger."

"Yes," Zilbar replied.

"That letter, if exposed, could screw things up for you," Moretti said.

"Well, no kidding, Dick Tracy. Thanks for tellin' me the obvious. You're a genius, Gino. A real goddamn genius," Zilbar said, humbling his attorney. "Yes. That letter haunts me every day." He shook his head.

"Now I understand. Some people call that blackmail. You know that, Mr. Zilbar," Moretti said.

"Yeah, some would call it smart. Dangerous for Krueger but smart," Randall Zilbar acknowledged. "This is enough. Keep him quiet. You think he's gonna talk, call me immediately," he demanded.

"Got it. It's all handled, Mr. Zilbar. You can count on ol' Gino."

He better be right. He better be, Zilbar thought while slamming down the phone. *Arrogant bastard!*

Randall Zilbar often hid his true character. However, even friends quietly questioned his personal and business sincerity. Most thought he was devoid of any character. When it came to deals, he was unscrupulous. Zilbar would smile to your face, talk of all he would do for you, and then behind the door he would orchestrate deception for personal gain. He would leverage, control, and cause pain as needed. Moretti was his go-to guy. Zilbar always demanded, "Cut where it hurts!" He'd take from his mother to gain the upside of the deal. To him, a good deal was a deal that hurt the other guy. That meant he got more for himself.

One hour's time was all he needed. Once he made the decision, Randall Zilbar placed a call to a friend in Cicero. "Mario, this is Randall."

"Hey, guy. How's it go?" Mario responded in his deep, raspy voice. "What can I do for you?" Mario ruled from the back corner office of his concrete and trucking company. Most late afternoons, he could be found in the back room corner table of Vinny's. Randall loved Mario because Mario always wanted to help—or as Randall Zilbar would say, *take care of things*, kind of in a Sicilian way.

↑ RACIST COMMENT

"I'm going to need a little help down here for a couple days. Got a talker. Need him handled. Taken care of for good. All the way. Need someone I can really trust."

"Got yourself a little situation?" Mario asked gleefully, imagining he could do a little favor. A *little favor*, he thought, *can always receive one in return*.

"You might say that," Zilbar replied, "but nothing a little help from you can't handle."

"Hey, Randall, that's what ol' Uncle Mario is for. When do you need him?"

Randall replied, "Tuesday, Wednesday next week. He's out on bail Monday. I've been assured of that."

"Then you can be assured. I'll have my man, Lucco, make a little trip south. Consider it done, Randall."

"Perfect, Mario. Just have Lucco check into the Wabash Inn out on the south side of town on Highway 13. Tell him to use an alias ... let's say, John. Yeah, Johnny Turner. Tell him to wait and lie low, and I'll call Tuesday evening at seven o'clock. This work for you?"

"Of course, Randall. Ol' Uncle Mario handles all." Mario always liked to help a friend. He never knew when he would need a favor in return, though Randall was doing quite a bit for Mario in their business relationship. "Say hello to your lovely Elenore for me. And of course the same to Vito. He still doing good work?"

"Nothing but the best. I guess he's better with age, so fastidious, so perfectly detailed. A real craftsman. What a perfectionist ... but that's what we both want. Mario, I know I can always depend on you. I'll meet Lucco, I mean Johnny, Tuesday evening. This means a lot to me. I want to keep our project going well for both of us."

"You got it, Randall. Be in touch."

Randall Zilbar heard silence. He could leave nothing to chance, especially knowing his plans for the years ahead.

CHAPTER 43

MEETING THE BISHOP

Father Sullivan—May 6, 1958

FATHER Sullivan and the two altar boys waited for the exact time to begin Mass. Paul and Joe were servers that Tuesday at the 6:00 Mass.

"All right, Paul, it's time," Father Sullivan directed him to ring the bell. Then they walked into the sanctuary.

Father Sullivan followed the two eighth graders to the front of the altar. Genuflecting in unison with the servers, he prayed in perfect Latin, "*In nomine Patre, et Filii et Spiritus Santus. Amen. Introibe ad altare Dei.*"

"*Ad deum qui laetificat juventutem meam,*" the two servers responded.

Paul enjoyed the Latin ritual, even if he didn't understand all the words. Serving at low Mass was fine, but high Mass on Sunday with a full church, the choir, the organ, and all the candles was the highlight of the week. He especially loved holding the paten while the priest distributed Holy Communion.

Joe was a server and an even better Catholic. His parents had taught him well.

Several times Father Sullivan's mind wandered intermittently during Mass with thoughts of his trip with Father Warren to visit Bishop Powers. "*Misereatur vestri omnipotens Deus, et dimissis peccatis vestris, perducat vos ad vitam aeternam.*" *May almighty God have mercy on you, forgive you your sins, and bring you to life everlasting.*

Paul and Joe responded, "Amen."

"*Indulgentiam, absolutionem et remissionem peccatorum vestrorum tribuat vobis omnipotens et misericors Dominus."* May the almighty and merciful Lord grand you pardon, absolution, and remission of your sins.

"Amen."

Forgive you your sins, Father Sullivan thought, thinking of Father Jaeger. *So terrible, my Lord, but just how can he be forgiven?*

Paul rang the bells three times through the consecration of the Mass. Soon thereafter the priest stepped down from the altar and proceeded to the communion rail. *"Corpus Domini nostri, Jesu Christi"—the body of our Lord Jesus Christ*—he said to each communicant.

Paul devotedly held the paten under the recipient's chin as he preceded the priest, who placed the Host on the tongue of everyone receiving communion.

Startled, from his right periphery Father Sullivan recognized Linda Singleton as he approached the last of the communicants. Head down, she waited. *Father, forgive me for all my sins,* she thought as she was next to receive Holy Communion.

Father Sullivan stood before her. Lifting the Host from the chalice, he said, *"Corpus domini nostri Jesu Christi."*

Linda lifted her head, eyes open, and looked at Father Sullivan, and he at her.

Placing the Host on her tongue, he said, *"Custodiat animam tuam in vitam aeternam. Amen."*

Linda bowed her head, made the sign of the cross, and proceeded away from the communion rail—a fence she felt between them. After walking back to her pew in the back of the church, she bowed her head and said a prayer of thanks and contrition.

Having finished passing out communion, Father Sullivan stepped back up to the altar. He purified the chalice with wine. Wiping the chalice and his lips, he covered it and placed it in the center of the altar. Kissing the altar, he turned to face the congregation. As he said the final prayer, Father Sullivan consciously scanned the church, looking for Linda. A sparse number of parishioners attended the early Mass. He could see her kneeling alone in the back of the church. Her head was bowed in prayer.

"Dominus vobiscum." The Lord be with you.

"Et com spiritu tuo," the servers responded. *And with thy Spirit.*

"Ite Missa est." Go, you are dismissed. *"Deo gratias."* Thanks be to God. As Father Sullivan turned toward the altar, Linda lifted her head. Lost in prayer, she had not seen his face as he turned toward the back of the church.

He said, *"Ite, Missa est."*

After walking back into the sacristy, Father Sullivan stood and solemnly took off his Mass garments. Standing there in his long black cassock, he did not speak with the servers as they went about their post Mass routine. The candles were put out.

He walked to the entrance to the sanctuary. Standing in the doorway, he could smell the smoke of the extinguished candles as it circled in irregular paths above the altar. Peeking out, looking toward the back of the church and the empty pews, he could see one person—a lady still kneeling, her head in her folded hands, praying. Linda. He paused and looked at her for a few seconds. She did not see him. With the thought of Linda in his mind, Father Michael Sullivan turned and walked back to the rectory.

That Tuesday was a long day for Father Sullivan. Anxiously awaiting his trip with Father Warren to see the bishop, he remained around the church and school. That afternoon, he worked his way through three religion classes—fourth, sixth, and eighth grades on Tuesdays and Thursdays. In the late afternoon, he spent a significant amount of time in St. Michael's Chapel.

Dear Heavenly Father, help me do what is right for You, our church, and our parish. Most of all, help me do what is best to find and secure safety for the victims of these bad deeds. Let me be fair and strong and persevere with good purpose. Let me not forget that we are all sinners and we must resolve to do good as You have taught us. Allow me to 'seek justice but not revenge.'

Solemnly kneeling alone in the chapel, Father Sullivan thought about the difference between justice and revenge. He could not find the words or intentions to hate Father Jaeger, but his being was filled with the need to bring justice for the boys harmed at the hands of Father Jaeger.

On into the evening, the next day was a priority on his mind. He resolved to assist and not lead Father Warren during the visit with Bishop Powers. He spent far more time in the chapel that evening. As light grew dim, he made the sign of the cross, stood, genuflected, and made his way back to the rectory. Later on, he slept sporadically. Father Sullivan prayed and thought of the troubles and conflicts in his life.

The next day, the usual one-hour ride to South Wayne was encumbered with the stress of anticipation. Father Sullivan planned on driving west on Highway 24 from the north side of Wabash and then straight north on Highway 15 to South Wayne. Neither Father Warren nor Father Sullivan had much to say to one another. Both were focused on their own thoughts about the upcoming meeting.

As Father Sullivan drove the older priest's car, Father Warren sat quietly, staring at the road ahead. Father Sullivan could almost feel the elder priest's concern ... and his pain. He waited for Father Warren to initiate conversation. About halfway through the ride, Father Warren asked how his dad was doing since the death of his mother. Father Sullivan replied, but the conversation didn't last. He knew the elder priest was thinking about how he would approach Bishop Powers while at the same time praying and asking help for what lay ahead.

The flat Indiana farmland was freshly plowed and planted. Knowing they were ahead of schedule, Father Sullivan suggested stopping for a cup of coffee.

"I happen to know of a little diner on the north side of Warsaw," Father Sullivan offered.

"That sounds good, Michael. Thank you," Father Warren said agreeably.

"Also, they are known for their special banana cream pie," Father Sullivan said, trying to lighten the moment. He turned off the highway.

Inside the Big Four Diner, Father Sullivan picked one of the wooden booths directly next to the front windows. "Two coffees please," he said to the waitress.

Sixty years old with red hair, the waitress looked as if she enjoyed the Big Four's hamburgers and fries frequently. Noticing the two collars, she greeted the priests with an extra friendly smile. "You guys must be priests," she said, more an obvious statement than a question.

"Yes, we are, ma'am. We are just driving through from Wabash,"

Father Sullivan responded, looking directly at her name badge, which was proudly displayed beneath her left shoulder. "Jackie?" he asked.

"Yep, named me that. Just Jackie. No middle name. Guess Mom forgot that, but Jackie's just fine. Say, would you like some of our banana cream pie? My husband, Richard, makes the best."

Father Warren looked up. "Why, thank you. Sounds good, but I'll pass for now. Maybe another time."

"That's okay, but you'll be sorry. Ah, ha-ha ... bet you priests all know about *sorry*." The waitress chuckled as she walked away.

"Well, she's a speck of sunshine on this gloomy day," Father Sullivan said, smiling.

During coffee and a little casual talk about their impending visit, Father Warren suggested with a slight smile, "Well, we better head up the road, Michael. Don't want to keep the bishop waiting. I know a little bit about him. Not all good."

Father Sullivan was inwardly surprised at Father Warren's comment about Bishop Powers. But he knew this was not the time to ask what he meant.

A little while later, as Father Sullivan drove into South Wayne, the rain began to pick up beyond mere sprinkles. "Don't worry, Father, I have an umbrella for us," Father Sullivan assured his friend.

The wipers swept back and forth on Father Warren's 1953 black Ford. Ahead, they could see the twin spires of St. Leonard's Cathedral.

"What a magnificent and beautiful church!" Father Warren exclaimed.

Built in 1909, St. Leonard's had just been named a cathedral in 1957. Constructed with cream city bricks railed in from Milwaukee, Wisconsin, the church had taken on an aged hue, making it look much older than the year its cornerstone was laid.

"Yes, Father, it is beautiful ... and large. The cathedral's twin spires and all, but remember our St. Thomas Moore's still has the tallest spire in northern Indiana."

"You're right, Michael. We'll always have that to brag about, or should I say to be proud of. We do have a good parish, and we're keeping it that way!" Father Warren exclaimed with determination in his voice.

Father Sullivan drove right up to the curb in front of St. Leonard's.

"Michael, we still have twenty minutes. It's 10:40. I want to first go inside the cathedral for a visit," Father Warren said.

"Of course. Good idea," Father Sullivan agreed.

They parked the car and approached the entrance to the cathedral. After walking up the high span of steps, Father Sullivan reached around, pulled the giant walnut paneled doors open, and held them for Father Warren. Once inside, they both removed their wide-brimmed black hats. As they stood in the high-ceilinged vestibule, both priests looked around at the heavily paneled walls.

"Wow," Father Sullivan said. He then opened the door leading into the main church.

Together, they stood. Their eyes were immediately drawn to the painted ceilings supported by round fluted granite columns that ran up the side aisles to the altar, dividing the church into three spaces.

"You know, Father, this church reminds me of Holy Hill in Wisconsin. Remember, where I went on retreat two years ago?" Father Sullivan said.

"Yes, yes it does. Although Holy Hill was built a little earlier than St. Leonard's," Father Warren agreed. "Milwaukee has many, many grand and wonderful old churches," he said as he dipped his hand into the holy water. After making the sign of the cross, Father Warren proceeded slowly down the center aisle.

Father Sullivan stayed back, genuflected, and knelt in the back of the church. He watched Father Warren slowly walk up the center aisle, genuflect by the front pew, and then walk over to the right side in front of the statue of St. Jerome. There he lit a candle and then knelt. Ten minutes or so passed. Father Sullivan watched and waited. Then Father Warren stood, walked to the center aisle, genuflected, and slowly returned to the back of the church where Father Sullivan was kneeling.

As they left the church, Father Warren asked, "Michael, do you know who St. Leonard is the patron saint of?"

"No, I don't."

"Well, he's the patron saint of prisoners. Think about the meaning of that, Michael." Father Warren walked down the front steps with Father Sullivan at his side, holding the umbrella over the two of them. "The rain's coming down more. Hope that's not a bad sign."

Father Sullivan didn't reply, but he did think about the meaning. *Patron saint of prisoners*. They walked over to the rectory, which stood just beyond the cathedral. Father Sullivan rapped the heavy knocker on the front door twice. The door opened.

A young sister said, "Good morning, Fathers. You must be Father Warren and Father Sullivan from St. Thomas Moore?"

"Yes, we are, Sister. This is Father Warren, and I am Father Sullivan." Father Warren acknowledged her with a brief smile.

"Please come in. Looks like the rain is coming down much harder," she said. "I'm Sister Joelda. Please follow me. Bishop Powers is waiting for your arrival. He'll be with you in a moment."

After she said that, a studious-looking priest walked around the corner from the main hall. His black-rimmed glasses made him seem much older than his thirty-eight years. He politely nodded, extended his hand, and said, "Good morning, Fathers. I'm Father Schmidt, Bishop Powers' administrative secretary."

"Pleased to meet you, Father. I'm Father Warren, and Father Sullivan here is one of my two assistants along with Father Jaeger, who is not with us today."

Father Schmidt seemed eager to tell them about his position and responsibilities. "I oversee the daily operations here at St. Leonard's. I deal with all personnel issues within the diocese, mainly with the priests from all the parishes, assignments, transfers, and retirements."

Father Sullivan's ears turned right into the words *assignments* and *transfers*.

"We have a large diocese, so we are very busy. Please follow me. Bishop Powers is waiting in the library. "

The rectory was very stately. The high ceilings in the hall were crowned with double moldings of fifty-year-old aged wood. An oriental runner covered the narrow oak flooring. The walls were lined with original portraits, paintings, and photo portraits of bishops who had served the diocese. On one side of the wall hung a series of original photos of the cathedral's construction.

"Amazing how they built these churches without all the mechanical cranes we have today," Father Sullivan said.

An etching of St. Peter's hung solitary in the middle of the hall just off the entrance to the library. To the other side of the library entrance hung a portrait in an early 1880s frame of Pope John Benedict. The double doors to the library were open. Floor-to-ceiling shelves abound with leather volumes bordered the room. On the far side, opposite the double doors, two tall leaded double-pane windows opened to a stone courtyard on the back eastern side of the rectory.

"Well, Father Warren, good to see you again. It's been a while," Bishop Powers said as he walked toward the visitors, extending his hand.

"Yes, Bishop, it has. Not to give away the bishop's age, but we were together in the seminary. Though I was two years ahead of His Excellency."

"Now, let's not get too personal, Father Warren," Bishop Powers said with a pleasant smile.

"This is my assistant at St. Thomas Moore, Father Sullivan."

"Father Sullivan, I'm sure you are doing well if Father Warren is your mentor," the bishop said.

"It's my honor, Your Excellency. Thank you."

"I see you've already met Father Schmidt." Just then another priest in his early thirties walked into the library. "And this is Father Holtz, who assists Father Schmidt in personnel."

A large dark mahogany conference table stood in the center of the room. Wooden chairs graced the sides and ends of the table.

"Here, gentlemen, let's sit down and be comfortable," the bishop said graciously as he took his seat at the far end, his back to the floor-to-ceiling bookcases.

With perfect timing, Sister Joelda turned the corner and walked into the library through the center double doors.

Father Schmidt asked, "Oh, Sister, could we have some coffee along with a pitcher of water?"

"It's already brewed. I'll bring it right in," she responded. The sister left in pursuit of the coffee, prepared rich and black just like the bishop preferred.

"Please catch the doors when you leave," Father Schmidt directed.

"Sorry you didn't have better weather driving up. But you are here, so let's begin." The bishop paused, setting the agenda and tone in his mind.

A relatively large man at six-foot-one and a generous 250 plus pounds, Bishop Powers had a passion for good food and wine, which one could note by his ample girth. He wore wire eyeglasses hidden by the background of his rather round face and reddish complexion. His hair was gray and thinning and always combed back. Bishop Powers could be likeable upon first impression if he wanted.

"Now how are things at St. Thomas Moore? You know I just love your beautiful church. It's definitely one of my favorites. I know, I know … you have the tallest spires this side of Indianapolis," the bishop said with a big smile. Bishop Powers was an outgoing, gregarious man—quite political to say the least.

Father Warren responded, "Everything is going quite well. Our finances are all in order. The school addition capital fund is ahead of projections. And of course you'll be coming down next month for confirmation."

"Oh, yes. Yes, I look forward to that."

"There is one problem, however, which has prompted our visit. As I explained earlier on the phone, we have a situation with our assistant, Father Jaeger. You know him, of course, as you assigned him to our parish about two years ago … early in 1956," Father Warren explained.

"Yes," Father Schmidt added. "We thought your parish would be just the right environment to use his many talents. The parishioners in a previous parish really loved him. He's most affable, loves to teach, and is very good with children."

Bishop Powers half nodded with approval after Father Schmidt's glowing yet exaggerated analysis. Father Sullivan thought, *Let's get real.*

"Bishop, Fathers," Father Warren said as he looked directly and separately at both Bishop Powers and Father Schmidt. "Getting to the point, we have two known verbally documented situations in which we have reason to believe that Father Jaeger has taken advantage … you know, sexually taken advantage of young boys in our parish."

That's well stated, Father Sullivan thought of Father Warren's introduction.

"Are you sure? Do you have witnesses? Has Father Jaeger admitted to this?" Father Schmidt asked immediately. As the first line of defense for the bishop, Father Schmidt handled all complaints, reassignments, psychological evaluations, and disciplinary action when needed.

"Yes, I have, Father. I am sure. One of our parishioners, a Ralph Smith, found Father Jaeger with three boys on a camping trip. Father Jaeger and the boys were standing around the campfire and ... " Father Warren paused.

Bishop Powers said, "We all know there's nothing wrong with standing around a campfire." Trying to lighten the situation, he gave a half chuckle.

"Well, you see, Bishop ... they were all naked. Completely, I am told, and ... and that ... well, that includes Father Jaeger. Mr. Smith happened upon the group just as Father Jaeger took one of the boys—he even took a blanket—and they disappeared into the dark of the woods."

Bishop Powers furrowed his brow and pursed his lips. Father Warren continued to talk as the bishop sat listening, hands clasped and both index fingers covering his lips. Father Schmidt did not respond immediately.

Then Father Schmidt slowly inquired, easing over the first revelation. "You say there is a second situation?"

"Father Sullivan, you are directly involved ... Why don't you tell?" Father Warren asked, wanting to include Father Sullivan.

"Well, sir, there are a couple of incidents to bring up. A young student, sixth grade, asked to talk with me. He said Father Jaeger enticed him to his room. While there, he abused him in bed. The boy thought he had sinned even though it was against his will. He shared the incident in detail."

"Excuse me, Father. Can you say, was this an accusation of fondling, or was there more? To be specific, I refer to penetration. There is a difference, you know," Father Schmidt clarified.

"Yes, he told me there was both," Father Sullivan said with a look of disgust.

Bishop Powers then responded, "Let's see. If this is exactly as you explained ... then I would describe this as a serious matter. Do you think, Fathers"—the bishop looked both at Father Sullivan and Father Warren—"that some exaggeration might be a part of this boy's story? You know how young boys can fantasize and things can be blown out of proportion."

Father Sullivan responded, "I can assure you that this boy did not have the imagination to describe rape without experiencing the act itself."

"That's pretty explicit and a very strong accusation," Father Schmidt said to Father Sullivan in an almost defensive manner. "Let me ask. Where is Father Jaeger in all of this? He has a right to give his side of the story."

"Yes, he does, but the detailed accusations speak volumes. His conduct speaks for itself," Father Warren responded immediately. "The second incident took place at the camping trip. This was at about eleven o'clock in the evening. Father Jaeger was told to leave camp. In fact, he fled. Father called me from his parents' home in Chicago. He's been there for about five or six weeks now. We've agreed to say he's on a vacation. We wanted your direction, Bishop, before we take any action. If he was not guilty, I believe he would not have left. He would not have fled to Chicago without even stopping at the rectory. It all kind of adds up," Father Warren explained.

"Let's hold it right there. When you say *action*," the bishop's secretary said, actually raising his right hand as if to say *stop*, "yes, we need to deal with this cautiously and with patience. We're dealing with a priest's life and reputation," Father Schmidt explained. His focus was on Father Jaeger and concern for Bishop Powers. He did not seem to consider the boys.

"Yes, Father, Bishop, with all due respect, if these accusations are true—and I think they are—then this is a criminal act. This should be handled by the authorities outside of our parish," Father Sullivan explained. "We are dealing with boys, young boys not yet familiar with the ways of the world. They are being affected for the rest of their lives."

"No no no ... wait a minute. If this is true, we handle our own priests within the diocese," Father Schmidt explained emphatically.

In a very soothing voice, Bishop Powers added, "Yes, if something like this does happen, we keep this within the diocese and within the parish. Unfortunately, we do have some experience in these matters. It works out best that way for all involved."

Father Sullivan did not say a word. He remained calm although he was beginning to boil inside. *Cover-up*, Father Sullivan thought. *Quiet, just listen. Cover-up*.

Father Warren prepared to ask a question, intentionally not directing it to either the bishop or the secretary. He observed that Father Schmidt was doing most of the talking, but the elder priest sensed that it was under previous direction from the bishop.

"Let me ask this," Father Warren continued. "Father Jaeger is completing his second year at our parish. He has worked hard. He is dependable, and overall he seems to be liked by the students and parishioners alike. However, his performance cannot conceal these dastardly deeds, if true. Might I ask, where was Father Jaeger before he was assigned to our parish?"

Father Schmidt rubbed his chin. He was silent for a moment and then replied, "He was an assistant at St. Michael's down in Crawfordsville."

"Would it be fair to ask why he was reassigned? How long was he there?"

Father Schmidt looked at the bishop as if saying, *Would you please answer this one?*

Picking up on Father Schmidt's uneasiness, Bishop Powers said, "Let me respond this way." He put his hands together as if he was going to pray and propped his chin on the end of his fingers. Calmly and deliberately, he said, "Because of some stressful health reasons Father Jaeger was experiencing in Crawfordsville, we thought it would be best to transfer him to a more established parish like yours. St. Thomas Moore is an example of a most substantial religious, educational, and financially secure parish. Of course, that's the result of your leadership, Father Warren, and I assume the same of your assistant," he said, nodding and looking over at Father Sullivan.

"We wanted him to be in a parish in which his best talents—communicating and being involved with the people of the parish—could best be utilized. So maybe everything did not work out according to our plan. That's why you are here, it sounds like to me. Father Jaeger was in Crawfordsville for a little over one year. For now, that's all we'll discuss about his previous assignments," Bishop Powers said, setting a different tone for the meeting.

The whole time Bishop Powers was speaking, Father Sullivan watched Father Warren, who was listening and focusing directly on

Bishop Powers with a suspicious look on his face as if to say, *I know you better. You're not fooling me.*

Father Warren did not reply, as he could tell Bishop Powers had said everything he was going to say about Father Jaeger's previous assignments. Saying not a word, Father Sullivan wanted to ask, *What were the health reasons? Why didn't he get along? Where was he assigned before that?*

"Excuse my question, Father Warren. Speaking only for myself, I wonder was Father Jaeger involved in any situations in which young boys were abused? Had he been accused by one or more boys? Had he been caught in any sexual situations with any boys?" Father Sullivan asked, trying to stay calm.

"Michael, that should be enough," Father Warren said, placing his hand atop Father Sullivan's forearm.

Father Schmidt responded, "I appreciate your concern, Father Sullivan, but these matters are all private and confidential, especially for the privacy of the victims."

"Oh, the victims. Are you saying there are victims, Father Schmidt? Then there is an abuse history with Father Jaeger? Then why did you send him to us? Why didn't you make us aware?"

"Enough! Enough!" the bishop said. "Let good minds cool. These are private cases, and we will no longer discuss them. The matter is closed."

Father Sullivan sat back. An unconscious suspicion of Bishop Powers immediately entered his mind. *This man is definitely covering for himself. I wonder how much more there is.*

Father Schmidt, knowing they had another problem with Father Jaeger on their hands, decided to add, "We considered the aspects of the mental stress Father Jaeger was under. After his counseling, evaluation, and time off, we had every reason to believe he would not have issues while at St. Thomas Moore. Maybe we were a little premature. Where did you say Father Jaeger is now?" Father Schmidt asked, looking directly at Father Warren and trying to shift the subject.

Father Warren brushed his hand through the side of his full head of white hair and said, "Father Jaeger is on an additional two-week leave, and as far as I know he's in Chicago with his parents. I asked him to call at the end of this week."

Father Schmidt looked to the bishop, hoping for a recommendation.

Bishop Powers leaned back in his chair. "Gentlemen, our options are few. We accept your word as truth and fact," he said, looking directly at the two priests. "However, before there are conclusions, we will meet with Father Jaeger. An evaluation in your parish would be to no avail, but I do agree that something must be done." The bishop paused. Gathering his thoughts, he then said, "Upon Father Jaeger's return from his vacation, I want him to come and meet with us. Then we will make our decision as to his situation, future, and innocence or guilt."

Father Sullivan chimed up again and said, "But what about calling the police? What about the victims? We can't overlook the legal rights of these victims. This can't be covered up."

"Now, Michael," Father Warren said.

"Cover-up. That's simply out of order," Father Schmidt said. "We will handle this. We will address this internally within the diocese. I can assure you, Father Sullivan, this situation will be addressed. As the bishop said, we are experienced in these matters."

"Thank you for reaffirming. I assume by experience that you mean this issue goes beyond our visit today about Father Jaeger?" Father Sullivan asked.

"That is not relevant to the issue at hand, Father Sullivan," Father Schmidt replied, immediately correcting him.

"Well, I think we all know where we stand. Wouldn't you agree, Father Warren?" Bishop Powers asked.

"Yes, why yes. You and Father Schmidt have explained very clearly your position. We will wait to hear from you after you meet with Father Jaeger. Meanwhile, Father Sullivan and I can cover for Father Jaeger back home. We can say his Masses. We both teach classes and hear confessions. Ah, ah, all we ask is that you let us know as soon as possible your decision about Father Jaeger and the action you are going to take."

The tenseness of the meeting somewhat subsided, although Father Sullivan was not at all satisfied. Father Holtz sat silently at the end of the table. He listened, observed, and concluded. He observed the dynamics of the meeting. He understood reality.

Bishop Powers stood first. "Gentlemen, we thank you for taking your time to make us aware of your concerns about Father Jaeger. You did the right thing turning this issue over to us. We will do what is right and handle it within the diocese. We will make sure Father Jaeger receives all the proper assistance to help him overcome his … " Bishop Powers paused. "We'll call it his condition."

Condition my … Father Sullivan thought. *How do I respond to this cover-up? Later.* Calmly he said, "May we ask … what about the boys?"

"We recommend that you should meet with them individually within your own parish. Explain that Father Jaeger will be away for a while. He's been under a lot of stress. They should understand. Tell them to keep everything quiet and confidential. Tell them to discuss with you and maybe not bring their parents in at this time. It wouldn't be good for this to get out," Father Schmidt replied as he glanced at Bishop Powers for confirmation.

Father Sullivan asked, "So as I understand, you are saying keep this all confidential. Don't tell the authorities. Don't tell the parents. You will take care of it all."

"If you are putting it in those words, then yes. That's the way it will be," Father Schmidt confirmed.

Bishop Powers summed it up by saying, "Good afternoon, gentlemen. Thank you both for bringing this to our attention. This meeting is over." He stood, nodded, traded glances with Father Warren, and then left the room.

"I'll walk with you to the door." Father Schmidt moved toward the door and then added, "The bishop is very knowledgeable and experienced and knows what's best for the priests at heart in these matters. Sometimes we find that these situations are, well, that the priests are just lost souls. Our job is to assist them to overcome their problems. We aren't here to persecute them."

Father Sullivan walked ahead toward the door. *Let's get out of here.*

Just as he was leaving, stepping out on the front stoop, Father Warren said, "Thank you, Father Schmidt. We appreciate your and the bishop's attention to this matter."

"Thank you. Have a safe trip home. Good day to you both," Father Schmidt said dismissively.

Father Warren and Father Sullivan donned their black hats.

Out of courtesy, Father Sullivan started to say thank you but immediately dismissed the idea.

The ride back to Wabash was quiet. Considering the emotions of the moment, both priests needed time to think ... and not speak. Father Sullivan waited for Father Warren to begin the conversation, but nothing happened. Father Warren sat stoically as Father Sullivan gripped both hands tightly around the steering wheel. He waited, fuming inside.

Father Warren knew. He reached over and patted Father Sullivan on the forearm. "There'll be the right time, Michael. Please just trust me."

The two priests didn't take time to stop for banana cream pie. It just didn't seem the right thing to do.

Father Schmidt—May 7, 1958

Pulling back the drape in the window of the front parlor just enough to watch the two priests without being seen, Father Schmidt watched them slowly drive away. The rain was now a steady downpour. *How could Jaeger have done this again?*

Time to think ... no time to pray. Father Schmidt walked over and sat in the big easy chair in front of the fireplace. Time lapsed. The priest was lost in thought, knowing this was going to come down on him to handle, just as before.

"Father Schmidt, I was looking for you. Thought you might be in here." Bishop Powers stood in the archway to the parlor, not wanting to take a seat and commit any more time. He said in a low methodical voice, "This needs to be addressed ... carefully. What do you recommend?"

Father Schmidt was thirty years the bishop's junior. Bishop Powers had known him since Father Schmidt's days in the seminary at St. Matthew's in western Ohio. Bishop Powers had offered him the secretary's position about ten years after Father Schmidt was ordained. He felt a bond.

Bishop Powers liked Father Schmidt for his keen intellect, his experience in parish work, and his attention to detail. Father Schmidt carried out orders. A slight, bespectacled man, he had dark hair with graying highlights. He looked older than his years. Most of all, Father Leonard Schmidt made it his business to know the right people in the diocese. The diocese was specifically linked to civic and business leaders in South Wayne who made things happen. Bishop Powers was the face of the Catholic Church in South Wayne. Father Schmidt made sure it all worked.

Bishop Powers had higher ambitions. Archbishop and then hopefully cardinal. He knew the right people in the curia in Rome.

"First and foremost, I am concerned, troubled to say the least," Father Schmidt responded. "Father Jaeger has been assigned now to … let's see … Crawfordsville at St. Michael's, St. Peter Paul's, St. Benedicts … shall I continue?"

"I know. I know. This has to stay here. Absolutely, I do not want this to go to Cardinal Cullings's desk. You stay clear of Indianapolis. I do not want my name associated with this. Cullings, you know he is acquainted with Pope John Benedict."

"The others we've had and transferred around have kept low profiles, under the radar," Father Schmidt reminded the bishop.

"Leonard, you're from Iowa. You did parish work in Urbana Falls. Isn't that the biggest city?"

Father Schmidt replied, "Yes, but what does that mean?"

"You have friends, roots. Aren't you familiar with a lot of the parishes, or how about a high school? Better yet, a seminary? A seminary would be quiet, out of the way," Bishop Powers suggested to his secretary. "A good place for Father Jaeger."

Father Schmidt spoke up, "But remember, Bishop Powers, St. George's Seminary didn't work."

"Yes, yes. You're right. Too much temptation," Bishop Powers agreed.

Father Schmidt thought, *How out of touch this man is*. Father Schmidt was in a quandary. He just wanted to retire someday in peace, maybe at a little parish in the country. Meanwhile, knowing Bishop Powers was his superior, he was aware that the bishop had higher ambitions. His place was to accommodate the bishop. Father Schmidt knew he had no choice but to execute the bishop's demands to control these abusing priests, keeping them quiet and contained within the diocese. Psychological testing, transfers, and containment were the only options. Cover-up was their strategy. Bishop Powers knew this approach was being used in other parts of the country.

"I do stay in contact with two priests I met while I was in seminary. One I am really close to … Father Arnold. He is a blessed, holy man. If anyone can help Father Jaeger, Arnold could. Sometimes he can work miracles."

"That would be good. Very good," the bishop replied with a nod and slight smile. "Take it upon yourself to take care of this situation. Get back to me next week. Jaeger should still be in Chicago."

"Yes, sir. I will be right on it, Your Excellency."

As Bishop Powers walked away, he stopped midstride, turned, and said, "Leonard, you tell your friend Father Arnold ... *maybe we need a small miracle.*"

CHAPTER 44

A CRIME AGAINST YOUTH

Father Sullivan—May 8, 1958

FATHER Sullivan was a little apprehensive as he walked down the stairs on his way to breakfast. Conversation had been very light on the way home yesterday from their visit with Bishop Powers. Father Sullivan knew Father Warren had not liked some of the direct questions Father Sullivan asked the bishop.

"Good morning, Michael," Father Warren said, his nose still in the paper.

"There's an interesting editorial in the *Plain Dealer* this morning. You should read George Griffin's column about unsolved murders in Wabash. He mentions a mysterious death of a young boy at the reform school. A Gordon Yoder back in 1934. Are you aware of that?"

"Heard rumors, innuendos, but not really. When I say Mass there, I am usually gone afterward. I do know Father Jaeger spent more time there than me."

"I'm sure you saw that article about Phillip Krueger being arrested. And, of course, we have our Father Jaeger. You know what I mean? At least these two are not involved in murder."

Father Sullivan looked at Father Warren and asked, "Did the reporter mention the lady who was murdered in her home? Where was it?"

"Oh, yes, out on Mill Creek Road," Father Warren replied. "Let me see ... Gretchen? Yes, Gretchen Streater. They found her murdered two months ago." Realizing he had brought up the subject before finishing the article, he thought a moment and set the paper down. "Yes, I do remember that one."

Reaching for the pot of coffee, Father Sullivan said, "Oh yes, Gordon. That name came up when Sheriff Thurow met with you, me, and Father Jaeger." Michael looked at Father Warren. "Yes, Yoder. I recall the word *murder*. Hard to believe."

"This is not a pleasant subject. Why'd I bring it up?" Father Warren pushed the paper aside.

They were sitting in the small breakfast room off the kitchen. The area was separated by a swinging door. Quiet, comfortable. Father Warren looked up at Michael and changed the subject.

"Back to what's really on my mind. Michael, I've been thinking a lot since we arrived home yesterday. It's the only thing on my mind. I have to begin by saying I'm very disappointed in you."

Father Sullivan felt an immediate surge, an emotional jolt. "What did I say wrong?"

"On our ride home I thought for sure you'd stop for that famous banana cream pie," the elder priest said with a relaxed smile.

"Don't do that to me, Father," Father Sullivan responded with relief. He appreciated Father Warren's sense of perspective, but his timing was far from perfect.

"Seriously, Michael, we can talk now if you have the time. I know you understand. Too hard to talk in the car on our way back from meeting with the bishop." Father Sullivan looked at the closed door. "She can't hear us," Father Warren said. "Just a minute."

Sister Agatha appeared, ready to take Father Sullivan's order for breakfast. "What'll you have for breakfast this morning?"

"I'm not really hungry. Maybe just coffee and toast."

Sister Agatha nodded, left, and then brought a pot of coffee and toast almost immediately.

"That'll be fine for this morning, Sister. Thank you. Father and I are going to visit for a while," Father Warren said. Then, turning to Father Sullivan, he said, "Michael, let me begin. I believe I understand your feelings about this matter with Father Jaeger, wholeheartedly believe you and Ralph Smith. Father Jaeger's self-inflicted departure really confirms that he probably does have something to hide. If he was wrongly accused, he would have beaten a path to my door and defended himself. That's not reality, unfortunately. He left. An obvious sign to me."

Father Sullivan took a sip of coffee, listened intently, and didn't say a word.

"Now this begs the question: What do we do? First, I'm going to address the obvious concern." Father Warren paused. "Michael, we cannot go to the police, at least not for now. I am responsible to our bishop. He has the final say. After that, it would be Cardinal Cullings." He paused again. "Then of course, only the pope can ... Well, I'm sure this won't go that far, but the pope does have the final word. It's highly unlikely this will go that far. You know, defrocking a priest is only at the discretion of the pope. Bottom line is, Michael, I must go along with the recommendation of our bishop. And for certain, we can't get ahead of ourselves. Defrocking? That's extreme."

Father Sullivan immediately said, "His actions are extreme. Priesthood is not for an abuser like Father Jaeger." Father Sullivan took a breath. "You know I think this is a crime. A crime against our church, a crime within our criminal system, and most of all, a moral crime, actually a felony, against innocent youth."

"Yes, Michael, I agree. I do respect and empathize with you. However, I can't go against our bishop. For now, this is my decision. This may take some time. Remember, I said I know the bishop from before. I need your support. At least until we have the bishop's evaluation and decision."

Father Sullivan focused on his quandary. He poured another cup of coffee and said, "The bishop and that Father Schmidt are going to contain and cover this up. I can just feel it. Look how many transfers Father Jaeger has already received. To me that ruins more lives. A little counseling, say you are sorry, and start all over again. Give me a break. That just won't work. Father Jaeger will be transferred to another parish and repeat the abuse. The vicious circle continues. The priest says he's sorry, receives some psychiatric treatment, and then the devil is transferred. Sorry, Father, but this is wrong. So very, very wrong."

"Michael, we know Father Schmidt will call us by the end of next week. They might invite us back to South Wayne. Father Jaeger will meet with Father Schmidt and the bishop. The decision will be the bishop's. We must be patient. Can you and I agree to have patience for another eight, nine days, Father?"

Father Sullivan put his forehead in his hand, rubbed his fingers back and forth, and nodded. "Yes, of course, I will support you, but this can't go on forever. Of most importance though, what about the boys we know of? They need to be talked to. We have to ask about and observe the effects on each and every one of them." He took a sip of coffee. "Father, may I ask? Were you and Bishop Powers ever involved in a situation, you know, about abused boys before, similar to Father Jaeger?"

Father Warren raised his eyebrows but did not reply. He ignored the question and went on to say, "Michael, I couldn't agree more. May I suggest you be the one to meet with the boys who have been abused?" he asked.

"With your approval, I will definitely do that, Father."

"Okay then. I'm going to call Ralph Smith and explain our position. I will tell him all about our meeting with Bishop Powers. Ralph can be trusted," Father Warren assured the younger priest.

Father Sullivan lifted the pot of coffee. "Empty. Guess that means the meeting's over. Right, Father?"

"Yes, Michael. It's over for now. I think we've covered everything." Father Warren stood and walked to the hall with Father Sullivan. Raising his hand and placing it on the taller priest's shoulder, Father Warren said, "You're a fine priest, Father Sullivan. And you are a good, good man. We'll get through this together. May God bless you."

Father Sullivan responded with a smile. They walked off in separate directions. As Father Sullivan headed for the chapel, he thought, *I hope you are right, Father … for everybody's sake.*

Father Warren—May 8, 1958

Surprisingly, Father Warren received a call that afternoon. Sitting at his desk, he picked up the phone. "Good afternoon. St. Thomas Moore's rectory. This is Father Warren."

"Hello, Father … " There was a pause. The caller cleared his throat. "Father, Father Jaeger here. I felt I should call you. Can you talk? Are you alone?"

"Yes, Jerome. I'm here. I'm listening. You must be going through a terrible time." Father Warren could only imagine the emotional trauma Father Jaeger was experiencing.

"Yes, I am. Very bad," Father Jaeger said in a low monotone. "If I were there, I'd ask you to hear my confession," he said, almost pleading.

"When you return I will do just that, Father Jaeger. I'm sure you are truly sorry. Now you are having to pay the heavy price of guilt while searching for remorse."

"No, Father, no. That can't be. You see, I'm not going to return to St. Thomas Moore. This morning I received a call from Father Holtz at South Wayne."

"Oh, I see. Yes, Jerome. You must know that Father Sullivan and I met with Fathers Holtz and Schmidt and Bishop Powers."

"You mean Father Sullivan was there too?" Father Jaeger asked. He paused. There was silence. "That even makes it worse. What about Ralph Smith? Did he tag along?"

"That is a poor use of words, Father." Silence.

"As a matter of fact, I'm meeting with Ralph tomorrow, but he's the least of your worries," Father Warren said.

Still in a low monotone, Father Jaeger asked, "What about the police, the sheriff?"

"No, not at this time. Right now, it's all in the bishop's hands. Authorities could be called in later. You know that, don't you?" Father Warren asked. "Father Jaeger, your sins and your admissions are very serious in the eyes of our Lord and God and I'm sure you know, Father, also in the eyes of the law. If you are accused, go to trial, and are found guilty, then I must say you would go to prison."

"Yes, Father. I do know that now. I think I've gone too far this time. I really am sorry, Father," Father Jaeger said, regret clinging to every word.

Father Warren thought, *Considering the facts, how can I as a priest even believe Father Jaeger?*

"Anyway, I am to meet with Father Schmidt the Wednesday after next."

"Well, I guess the bishop is addressing this right away," Father Warren added.

"No, Father, no."

"What do you mean, Jerome?" Father Warren asked.

"The meeting is with Father Schmidt, his secretary. It's not with the bishop. Father Schmidt takes care of these matters. The bishop stays back. I know how this system works. I have been through this before, as you might know. Schmidt is in control."

"Oh, I see. Well, Father, if you say you aren't returning, then you are shedding new light on the subject. I guess we'll wait to hear from the bishop. No, I mean Father Schmidt. Could you please call me after your meeting?"

"I will, Father. I will." Father Jaeger hung up the phone as soon as he could. He respected Father Warren and felt remorse, ashamed of his actions.

Father Warren was in disbelief. *How could I ever have imagined this in our parish? Our wonderful St. Thomas Moore parish.*

CHAPTER 45

FULL DISCLOSURE

Joey Singleton—May 13, 1958

LINDA Singleton was enjoying the evening and preparing dinner. She wore a very comfortable blue cotton housedress that hung below the knee and had white piping around the neck and sleeves. A small blue flowered apron hung over her shoulders, neatly tied with a small bow in back. The smell of pot roast, potatoes, and carrots hit Joey as he bounded through the front door. He could hear the tune his mother was singing in the kitchen. Linda loved to cook. Joey always rewarded her efforts, continuously reminding his mom of how much he appreciated everything she prepared.

Joey sauntered into the kitchen.

"Hello, sweetie," his mom said. "Hmm, you look … "

Joey hung his green waist-length sweater on the back of the chair. He plopped down. "Hi, Mom. Can we talk?"

"Sure, of course," she said, placing the lid back on the roaster.

Joey sat down at the table. "Smells like pot roast."

"One of your favorites." She wiped her hands on the front of her apron and then sat across from him at the kitchen table. "I'm all ears," she said, trying to relax Joey with her full attention.

"Remember our talk … our talk a few weeks ago about … about … ?" Joey hesitated as he tried to frame the right words. He rubbed his hand across his forehead and into his curly brown hair. Joey was a handsome boy. "Let's see. You know, we talked about love. You told me that real love … " Joey nervously hesitated, "could be between two men. You even said—and I can remember—you said like it was once between you and Dad. You know … a man and woman."

"Yes, we did talk about that. And of course I still feel the same. Nothing changes the truth," she reminded Joey. "Although I must say, Joey, considering all the challenges in life, it is better if it is romantic. Let's say physical love is between a man and a woman."

He stammered a bit and then went on, "All right then, Mom … " Silence. "Oh, how can I say this?"

"Just say it, Joey. I'll understand. You know I'm always here for you, no matter what."

Joey raised his head and looked into his mom's beautiful green eyes. *Just say it,* he told himself. "Mom, I love you … " He paused. "Mom, I really do, and I never want to hurt you. You know that? You know … " He paused again. "You believe me?" Tears began to well in his eyes.

"Of course I do. Always," she said, reaching across the table and clasping her hand around his.

"Mom, I love Father Jaeger. Please, please … I really do," Joey said, his voice rising an octave. "He's so good to me. I don't care if I'm thirteen. I love him. I love him all the way."

Before Linda could respond, he buried his face in his folded arms on the oilcloth-covered table. Linda took a couple deep breaths.

"Oh, my Joey." Linda scooted her chair closer to his. Pulling his right hand from under his arms, she protectively clasped his hand between hers. She patted the top of his hand, gently brushed his hair, and pulled him closer to her. Joey kept his face buried in his left elbow. He whimpered slowly. "Joey, did something bring this all on?"

He lifted his head, replacing his right hand with his left. She held on tightly.

"Yes, today at school. Mom, I was in the hall by myself. I had asked to leave class to go to the lavatory. Then I went … It was so quiet in the hall. No kids." Joey wiped his eyes with his sleeve. "I got a drink of water at the water fountain, and then I heard. I heard, Mom. It was terrible. Tell me it's not true. How can I know? They were around the corner whispering, but I could hear them. They didn't see me."

"Who were they, Joey? Just calm down. I'm listening to every word," she assured him.

"I heard Sister Elenora and Sister Anders talking quietly about Father Jaeger. She said he's never coming back," Joey explained. "I know who it was. I recognized their voices. They didn't know I was around the corner. Then Sister Anders said it's all about the boys. She heard he's been doing … doing … Sister then said, 'Oh my dear God in heaven. He's been doing sex acts with some of our boys?' She said something like that. Best I can remember. She then said, 'No, no, I can't believe it.' The other sister said, 'Yes, it's true.'

"Then Sister Anders asked who told her, but a door slammed down the hall. I didn't hear the name. The door scared me. It was another sister leaving a room and going the other way, so I just left. I had to go. I walked around the corner toward the lavatory as if I didn't even see them. This afternoon was terrible. Then I came home to see you. Mom, please tell me. I didn't tell a soul. Mom, could it be true? Could it? Father Jaeger is gone? Gone forever?"

"Joey, Joey, first what you overheard … it could be just gossip between two sisters who heard the same from another sister. Words can get twisted."

Joey hung on every word between his intermittent sobs and whimpers.

"But, Mom." He looked up. "I heard every word exactly. Sister Anders said it's true. Nuns don't lie, Mom."

"On the other hand, what you heard could be very true. You know Father Jaeger. You know … Well, I'd say, Joey … Look at me. You know this man's inclination. You might know better than anyone," Linda said, immediately realizing she might have chosen the wrong words.

"What does that mean?" Joey said in a sharp tone.

"It only means that it seems you may be his best friend. That's all I meant." Creasing her brow, she looked at Joey and tilted her head as she looked at her son. "Aren't you? Aren't you his closest friend?"

"Well, maybe. I guess so," Joey replied.

"What concerns you the most? Tell me," she said, reassuring Joey of her understanding.

Joey stared at her with a blank look. He breathed heavily. "Ever since he came here, he's been … been so nice to me. Father Jaeger's always there. He makes me feel good about myself." Joey paused and then said, "Mom, I just can't live without him here. He means so much. He's got to come back."

How do I say the right thing? Linda thought. "Joey, I don't know. This is so troubling for you … and for me. Remember, I told you that a man can love a man … " She paused. "But a man can't love a boy. I mean, love him like, you know, the way we talked. Joey, his being a priest makes it all that much worse. If it were to be true, a priest being intimate with a minor, Joey … that's just wrong. Father Jaeger would know that." As soon as she uttered those words, Linda knew they were a poor choice to say to Joey at this critical time.

Joey froze. His face turned red, and he shouted, "No, no … it just can't be! It's not wrong. He loves me! He has to come back!" He jumped from his chair, shouting, "Mom, you just don't understand … No, no!" The chair fell backward onto the floor. Joey charged from the kitchen.

All Linda heard was the front door. *Slam!* She thought she heard the glass rattle. She didn't move. Rubbing her hand across her mouth, she fixed her eyes on his books. Arithmetic, English … religion. *Joey's catechism? Religion? What does it all mean?*

Time lapsed. Linda remained at the kitchen table. Lifting her apron, she wiped her eyes. Joey hadn't returned. *What concerns you the most? Tell me*, she remembered her exact words. Joey hadn't mentioned the boys. Joey didn't see the wrong. He only talked about Father Jaeger leaving, leaving for good. Nodding, she knew. She knew the truth, the hard truth about her son and a priest—the unthinkable. Then Linda thought of her own situation. *And a priest. My God, how can this be?*

Linda Singleton—May 17, 1958

Saturday came not too soon. Linda Singleton had been consumed with worry about Joey. He had never been in such a frame of mind. Linda had stayed up late the evening of their talk, waiting. Sometime after midnight, Joey came home. He did not say a word as he passed her in the front room and headed for the stairs. Joey quietly closed his bedroom door. Linda decided to let him be. *He's home.* The next morning, Joey insisted he was sick. For two days, he stayed home from school.

As much as she wanted him to, Joey wouldn't talk or confide in her. The week passed slowly. Saturday was the day for afternoon confession.

Linda decided she must go to confession, although maybe not for the right reason.

The sun was shining brightly. Linda remained around the house all morning and early afternoon. Joey left the house midmorning. He told his mom he would be back in the afternoon. Where he went, she did not know. Her attempt to clean the house was futile. She skipped her regular routine of grocery shopping at the corner Sunnyside Market. Linda was determined to go to church late that afternoon.

Joey was not home yet. Linda waited as long as she could, hoping Joey would arrive before she left for church. *I'll walk. I have the time.* After she closed the door, she walked down the porch steps and headed in the direction of St. Thomas Moore. The ten blocks she always traveled by car would provide exercise and time to think and reflect. Her short heels echoed on the gray concrete sidewalk. The smell of the green grass along the front walk punctuated the freshness of spring. Linda looked ahead through the elms that lined both sides of the street. Traffic was always light on Church Street. She could hear the sounds of boys in the vacant lot, yelling and playing baseball on this glorious Saturday afternoon. *Where can my boy be?* she kept wondering.

Halfway to church, Linda heard the sounds of traffic increase. She turned left onto Hill Street and saw the spires of St. Thomas Moore come into view. Arriving at church, she passed the historic cornerstone and climbed the steps to the tall dark front doors. Pulling her scarf from her purse, Linda walked inside. It was 4:50. *Perfect timing.* She knew where Father Sullivan would be.

"In the name of the Father and the Son." Linda dipped her hand into the holy water. She blessed herself and genuflected at the third pew from the back.

Checking the light above the confessional door, she glanced at the name card below the cross: *Father Sullivan.* Four people were in line against the side wall. Edna Samolski looked over. Linda returned a simple smile. After hearing the confessional door open, Edna stepped inside. Linda walked over and took her place in line. She prayed to herself before she entered the confessional, her rosary reminding her of the past—the repentance, the guilt, but never regret. Time lapsed. The left side door opened. An elderly gentleman stepped out and held the door open for Linda.

"Thank you," Linda whispered, stepping inside.

"God bless you," he said in a kind old voice. Linda noticed his well-worn suit and the large knot at his collar. He had dressed for the occasion.

Darkness. Linda knelt, prayed, and focused on the moment, not wanting to hear the slightest whispers of the priest hearing Edna's confession on the other side. Her hands, still clutching the rosary, now rested on the shelf below the black veiled sliding door. Linda could hear the pace of her heart. She waited for the sound she knew so well. The black veiled door slid open on the priest's side. Still separated by an ever-present black cloth screen, Linda could not see, but she knew he was near.

"Bless me, Father, for I have sinned," she began with the confessional request. "Father, this is Linda."

A moment of silence passed. "Why, Linda, I know it's you. Your melodious voice I never forget. I'm glad you're here."

"Oh thanks, Michael. Excuse me, I mean Father. I just had to see you. I mean talk with you. I felt that this would be the easiest for both of us."

"You are probably right. I concur. Linda, it's fine. Don't worry. What is it?"

"Michael." *She felt comfortable using his name.* "Is that okay?"

"Of course. That will be fine. Go ahead. What's troubling you?" He wondered if it was about him.

"This won't take long. I have just one question."

He listened.

"It's Joey. Can you tell me? I hope this is okay to ask. If you can't answer, I'll understand. Is Father Jaeger leaving the parish?"

Surprised somewhat by the question, Father Sullivan waited a moment and then said, "Yes, Linda. Yes, Father Jaeger is gone. He's gone for good. We will be announcing his resignation during the sermons tomorrow."

Linda's first thought was of Joey. "Father, can I ask? I need to know. He's gone because of ... because of the boys. You know what I mean?"

"Yes, Linda, I know. And yes ... it is about boys ... and his relationship with them. We don't know exactly to what extent. Father Warren decided to tell our parishioners that Father Jaeger is on leave ... on leave for health reasons. He will be recognized and thanked for his positive contributions. From the pulpit, Father Warren and I will wish him well. That's it. Now you know. You understand I just can't say any more." Father Sullivan paused to

307

select the right words. "Linda, remember—and I trust you implicitly—we must honor the confidence and secrecy of this confessional."

"I know. I understand. Of course. You know you can trust me. Father, you can trust me always."

"I have a question," Father Sullivan said to Linda. "Is Joey ... has Joey been involved? Involved with Father Jaeger?" He already knew but wanted to hear it directly from Linda.

"Yes, Michael. I know he has."

"Oh, I was hoping so much that you'd say no."

"I don't know what to do." She tried to hold in her emotions and tears. "I'm so scared. I think Joey's been involved very much with Father Jaeger. And, Father, it's so hard to say, but I can tell you ... I can tell you, can't I?" she asked as she groped for words. She knew, of course, she could tell him. "Father, I think he was involved because ... No, please hear me ... I think Joey was involved because he wanted to. He actually told me that he loves this man. That he won't be able to handle it if Father Jaeger leaves the parish. Father, that just can't be. Joey's hardly talked to me since he found out."

She did not hear an immediate reply from the priest on the other side of the curtain. Startled, Father Sullivan didn't have a response.

"Linda, what if you asked Joey to talk with me? It would give him someone else to maybe open up to. It would be tough for him. However, Father Jaeger is not coming back. I can assure you that it's best for everyone, including Father Jaeger."

"I know you're right, Michael. Seems you always have an answer, always know best." Linda waited a moment. "You always did." She hesitated while raising her handkerchief to her nose. She wanted to say more but couldn't. "Time for me to go. Good-bye, Michael."

Linda was out the door before Father Sullivan could even say, *Linda, please come back again.*

Unfortunately, she thought as she walked back home in the darkness, *Joey may be the only one to think Father Jaeger's leaving was not for the best. I know I went to confession to talk to Michael about Joey, but I also really needed to be close to him.*

Part III

Meetings and Leaving

CHAPTER 46

COUNSELING AND REASSIGNMENT

Father Schmidt—May 12, 1958

FOR three years, Father Schmidt had been dealing with abusive priests for Bishop Powers. His assistant, Father Ben Holtz, had been assigned to the diocese as a special secretary for internal affairs. Father Schmidt scheduled the counseling sessions, made arrangements for boarding between assignments, and worked with local parishes for future reassignments. All recommendations for assignments and transfers were presented to Bishop Powers for approval. Bishop Powers made all final decisions.

Father Schmidt asked Father Holtz to meet in the conference room on Monday morning after the 8:30 a.m. daily Mass.

"Good morning, Father," Father Schmidt greeted Father Ben, as he liked to be called.

Father Holtz pulled up a side chair next to Father Schmidt, who was already sitting at the head of the table. Getting to business, Father Schmidt opened his leather binder and produced a file—Father Jerome Jaeger.

"Do I assume Bishop Powers will be attending the meeting with Father Jaeger?"

"Yes, he will," Father Schmidt replied.

"How many cases will we be hearing next Wednesday?" Father Holtz asked.

"Let me see … Father Metzger is up for his three-month review of progress, but we will postpone him until next month. No hurry."

"Father Beechem, I visited him last week and will give an oral progress report," the younger priest added. "Also, Father Atticus Albright will be here for his reassignment. I believe he's made substantial progress. Frank Benders, he's one of our counselors, will give the one-year report after his visit with Father Gordon, who will begin his second year at Holy Trinity. Father Gordon has been at Holy Trinity for one year, and there has not been one reported incident. The counseling worked well."

"Our main concern is our Father Jaeger in Wabash," Schmidt mentioned. "We both know this is more serious this time. There is a witness. Think Father Jaeger really pushed too far. He'll be here at 3:00 p.m. Here's a copy of his bio and workup." Father Schmidt handed three sheets from within the file to Father Holtz.

Picking up the cover sheet, Father Holtz immediately began reading the front copy page.

"This one requires an immediate decision. I don't know if it will be a transfer or one year at the seminary. Ralph Smith, a parishioner and the supposed witness—remember what Fathers Warren and Sullivan said—confirmed the incident. Says he was there and saw Father Jaeger with the boys."

"How many priests do we have in the diocese that are, let's say, receiving counseling or ready for transfer? As I see it, this continues to get worse. What's happening to all the children?" Father Holtz asked with deep concern. "You know, Father Schmidt, if we were seeing a rise in vocations, we could just push to permanently remove them, these bad apples."

"Yes, I know, Ben. That's not the case. As Bishop Powers says, 'We must keep our parishes staffed.'" Father Schmidt went on, "Most of these situations are nothing more than accusations. No witnesses. Nothing proven. We still have to address each case one at a time. I assume the parishes counsel the boys. We just … you and I have a job to do. We must be prepared for Wednesday. Bishop Powers always wants concise reports, a recommended plan, and then execution. We both know he doesn't like idle chat or spiritual or psychological ramblings."

"Yes, Father. Guess we have a plan," Father Holtz agreed.

"Good. That will be all," Father Schmidt said dismissively.

Father Holtz left the room, thinking, *This is not the reason I became a priest.*

Father Warren—May 17, 1958

On Saturday at 10:35 a.m., Sister Agatha rapped twice on Father Warren's study door.

"Yes, who is it?"

She opened the door slightly but did not step in. "Excuse me, Father, but someone's waiting for you in the front parlor. It's Father, it's Father Jaeger."

Father Warren felt a rush. He took a breath. "Tell him five minutes. Offer him some coffee. Then I'll be right there." *Why did he not call? I must listen. Just let him talk ... if he will. Maybe he'll open up. Father Sullivan shouldn't come in. Better tell the sister. That wouldn't be good. Okay now, just listen first.*

Father Warren slowly stood up from his desk. He walked to the single wooden kneeler at the side of his room. Kneeling down, he made the sign of the cross, bowed his head, and prayed. Five minutes passed.

Father Jaeger could hear familiar footsteps advancing down the hall. Then there was quiet as Father Warren walked across the rug in the foyer. Father Jaeger felt his heart pounding in his chest. Standing in front of the fireplace, he was nervous, anxious ... and ashamed. Then he saw Father Warren in the doorway.

"Hello, Jerome," Father Warren said in a very low voice. Turning, he closed both doors. Father Jaeger immediately sensed the elder priest's comforting voice.

"Father Warren, thank you for seeing me without notice. Coming here today to see you has taken all the courage that ... Well, Father ... I'm just so ashamed."

"Of course I would see you, Father. I do have empathy, and I'm very concerned for you. Very concerned," Father Warren said, extending his open hand to the sofa.

"Thank you, Father," he said timidly as he seated himself on the comfortable sofa.

Father Warren took his usual brown and deep red tapestry wingback chair. "Well, Jerome, let's talk. You can say anything to me," the elder priest said in an inviting voice.

Father Jaeger smiled nervously. "This feels like confession." He paused. "You know, like the other side, like I'm going to confess to you."

"Maybe that's what you need."

"I'm sure I do," Father Jaeger said, ashamed. "Father, I guess this is as low as it gets. I've never felt worse in my entire life. My personal struggles have been almost uncontrollable. When I'm alone, my heart goes out to the boys. Then somehow the demons inside me take over. I lose control. Nothing else matters." Father Jaeger could tell that Father Warren was really listening. "When this happens, I … I forget everything that is right. I just … Father, I don't know how to say it. I focus on my own satisfaction." He placed his head in his hands and closed his eyes. "I don't even think of right or wrong. I simply don't stop until the desires, the lust, the urges are gone. I know it's all so wrong."

Father Warren listened intently to every word—the sorrow, guilt, and what he hoped to believe was real remorse. He even detected a desire to change, to repent. *Can Father Jaeger overcome this enormous hurdle in his life?* Father Warren thought while listening to every word of the younger priest.

"What about your parents? How are they doing, Father?"

"My becoming a priest was all they ever wanted. All they ever talked about, even way back before the war. I can remember when Dad left in '41. The last thing he said was, 'Son, I'll come home for your ordination.' My becoming a priest meant everything to my parents. They know I have some time off, but please understand, Father, I can't … I just can't tell them the reason, about my sinfulness. These awful acts. They'd be crushed. They're such good people, such good parents. Mom and Dad deserve so much more than what I have offered. I don't deserve them. I've let them down … "

He paused. "Father, I just can't tell them." He fell quiet. Silence followed. Father Jaeger leaned back and rested his head against the sofa. He stared at the ceiling. His gaze followed a jagged serpentine crack in the plaster as if he was the snake himself.

Father Warren took advantage of the silence. "Father, you've let your

Lord and God down. You've let these boys down." Then he said in a distinct whisper, "Jerome, you've let yourself down, your parents down. Imagine all these hurt people in your life. Then what about our Holy Mother Church, the priesthood, the very collar you wear?"

Pulling his hand down over his face, Father Jaeger leaned forward. "Yes, Father Warren, I've let you, this parish, and everyone down." The forlorn look on his face made it seem as though he had finally met reality head-on. His self-indulgent ways had brought him to a place from which he could see no escape. Father Jaeger felt cornered and alone and wondered if there was even a future for a fallen priest.

"Yes, you have. Yes, you really have," Father Warren said with a clear dose of reality. He looked at Father Jaeger. "I should say *this time*, Father. I'm sure this is not the first?" Father Warren commented—half statement, half question.

Without lifting his head and in a weak voice, almost a whisper, he said, "You are right, Father. Not the first or the second, third, or forth."

"You've let everyone down. But, Jerome, that's all in the past. You must repent, change your ways, and move forward, thinking of others to help … not hurt. You must think of yourself *after* helping others. You can't think of yourself in your past sinful ways."

Father Jaeger leaned forward. Elbows on his knees, head down, he said nothing. He just shook his head. Time passed. Father Warren said nothing, just leaned back as if saying, *Shame, shame, shame*. Father Jaeger was a man facing despair.

The good priest calmly asked, "Jerome, do you have contrition? Do you have regret? Can you repent?"

Leaning back, Father Jaeger looked up again at the ceiling and at the serpentine crack, becoming almost life-like. The priest choked on his own misery. He felt lost with no end in sight. Except for the dim table light to the left of Father Warren's chair, the room was dark on a dreary day. Father Jaeger saw his world only before the light would go out. He pressed his lips together. His eyes welled with tears.

"Father, I see nothing but darkness. Sins too grave to be forgiven." His hands shook. "I am sorry. I do apologize to you." Taking a deep breath, he looked at Father Warren and said, "I don't know how to conquer the demons. The darkness is a place I don't want to go. But, Father" —he looked up at the concerned priest—"I don't know how to stop."

Father Warren responded unusually. Putting his elbows on his knees, he leaned forward and clasped both of Father Jaeger's hands. "Father, all I can tell you is that only you can decide. It's up to you to seek forgiveness and control the desires, urges, lust, and actions. You must pray for help from our Almighty Lord. He will help you, but you have to ask.

"For now, however, you have other challenges you must immediately face. Yesterday afternoon I received a call from Father Ben Holtz. He's the assistant to Father Schmidt in South Wayne. After your last transfer to St. Thomas Moore, Bishop Powers granted you another chance. Now you must go to them again and admit your failure. I understand you are meeting with them next Wednesday. Father Jaeger, you need to be there," Father Warren said with firm authority.

Father Jaeger's face was a picture of alarm. "I don't know how I can do that now. It's almost … it's too … it's just *too much* right now." Staring toward the fireplace with a blank look, he couldn't find the words.

Father Warren looked at the despondent man. "Jerome, you should have thought of that before. It was your indiscretions with those boys that put you in this unholy state. Now you have to ask where you are now. What are you going to do?"

Father Jaeger looked at Father Warren and said, "I've lost everything in my life. I see—" He took a deep breath. "I see no reason to live." Without another word or any hesitation, Father Jerome Jaeger stood, turned, and started to leave.

"Jerome, wait one minute," Father Warren walked up to him. "You mentioned confession earlier. That would be the right thing to do. Confession will not alleviate your problems. However, our Lord listens, he forgives, and he looks for goodness in each one of us." Father Jaeger listened. "Now, my son, I will be in the confessional in fifteen minutes. I look forward to your visit."

"Thank you, Father. I need that. See you soon."

Father Warren looked the dejected, despondent priest In the eye. "This is good, a start."

Father Jaeger turned and walked down the hall and headed for church. *Please, God, show me the light.*

CHAPTER 47

LONG JOURNEY HOME

Father Jaeger—May 17, 1958

THAT afternoon, Father Jaeger spent time alone in his room, packing his personal items. He had asked Father Warren not to inform anyone that he was there and not to mention their visit. *Just pack, load, and be gone.* There were a few friends he wanted to say a last good-bye to, but he decided not to take the risk. He thought about Sister Johnelda, who had always been an understanding friend. She knew he had issues but not the full extent of them. He had talked about loneliness, his vocation, and even about not having a family of his own. *Never about the boys.* Sister Johnelda was a good listener.

Peter Goodnar and Joey Singleton also came to Father Jaeger's mind. He hoped to have had a positive effect on Joey's life, hopefully influencing him to become a priest. But Father Jaeger dismissed good-byes in favor of avoiding shame and having to explain. The loss of the ease of familiarity with the boys to satisfy his own selfish desires, pleasures, and passions created a deep depression. The deep-seated desires would not be easy to suppress in his heightened moments of thought and anticipation. At least not until he found others to conquer his lust and passion.

Father Jaeger stood up from his chair. He knew he must force himself to pack the empty boxes he had hauled from the back of his car. Only the antique table and tapestry-upholstered armchair would require space in the backseat. Luckily it was a four-door sedan. The table and chair had been a gift from his grandfather. He carefully packed the Tiffany lamp that stood atop the table, along with the pipe and blue delft ashtray. He had many pleasant memories of his grandma and grandpa on their small farm in central Indiana. Those were the days of summer he would never forget.

Opening the closet, Father Jaeger removed a couple of sport shirts to pack in his suitcase. Two black suits and two cassocks hung together in plain view. Looking at the top shelf, he stared. He noticed a couple crisp white collars sitting there. He reached up, slowly took hold of the collars, and carefully set them on the bed. The bed. How ironic. *How polar*, he thought. The bed. The collar. One so good. One so bad. Focusing, Father Jaeger looked directly at the collar. *The symbol of my vocation*, he thought. *My long journey.* He pictured his parents, then all the boys. The past raced through his mind. The room began to swirl. Reaching for the foot of the bed and placing both hands on the footboard's crossbar, Father Jaeger braced himself. *Why? Why? Could it have ended another way? No, not this. I'm not bad. I want to do good. I loved them. Dear Lord, You know how I loved those boys.*

Heart racing, taking deep breaths, the torn man now found himself on his back. The ceiling, that familiar ceiling. *Is someone there? Am I alone? Hello, hello. Yes, I'm here. Who's there?* Father Jaeger felt a presence. He thought he heard voices. Was it Peter? Joey? Gene? No! He closed his eyes in hiding. He waited. Silence. *Don't want to know.* As he lay on that very bed, a place of sin, guilt, and shame surrounded him. Then he knew. Opening his eyes, Father Jaeger saw the crucifix straight above his head. The wounded Jesus was looking down. Father Jaeger knew he was not alone.

He knew this was another solitary good-bye, just like two years ago, and then a year and a half before that. *How many times? This must end.* Shaking his head and wiping the perspiration from his brow, he sat up, looked around, and then fell back on his board of shame.

Time lapsed. He did not know how long he laid on the bed. The afternoon was getting late. He would load his car without being detected. He forced himself to make several trips. Then Father Jaeger went back to his solitary bedroom for one last look, one last time. As he opened the door, the stark plainness of the room mirrored the horrible loneliness and feeling of one more loss. The single window shed little light on that late Saturday afternoon. One empty dresser with a cracked frameless mirror hanging above sat against the wall. The mattress was stripped bare. Soiled and gray—the home of dark, regrettable deeds. He looked around the barren, worn plaster walls. Laths showed through several gaps where pieces of plaster had fallen away. Looking up above the bed, his eyes focused once more on the crucifix. He felt the presence of the crucified Lord. He identified with the suffering Savior.

Placing his right knee on the bed, he reached up and removed the universal symbol of suffering and forgiveness. He carefully placed the crucifix atop his clothes inside an old leather suitcase. A collar lay next to the crucifix. Both reminded him of his place in life.

After closing the old suitcase, he buckled the leather straps. A paper pennant was adhered to the side—*ST. AMBROSE SEMINARY*. That was where it all had somehow started. *Only if I could go back.* He had almost forgotten about the seminary. Father Claude Cranowski, his first encounter with another man, his superior, much older. He remembered in detail how it had all begun. A friendly smile, a touch to the shoulder, a roving hand, a place to recline. All so new then. All so familiar now. *Predisposition* was a word that always conflicted his mind. Forty-four years old and he had yet to fully understand his inner self.

Maybe they'll send me someplace far away. Far, far away. States away. A sudden feeling of relief at the thought of a new life rushed through his veins. *If only … if only I could.*

Ready to leave, suitcase in hand, Father Jaeger was stopped in his tracks by a knock at the door. "Who is it?" He was not prepared to see anyone.

The door opened slowly.

"Hello, Jerome. Father Sullivan here." Father Jaeger felt a rush, startled, unprepared to see the visitor. *Oh, God, no.*

"Yes, ah yes, Michael. I wasn't expecting you. Maybe you should," Father Jaeger paused. "Michael, sorry this is not a good time."

Awkwardly, Father Sullivan stepped into the room.

"Last time here, I guess," Father Jaeger acknowledged.

"You all packed? Need some help?"

"No thanks, just this one last suitcase," Father Jaeger looked away. "There's a couple suits and cassocks yet in the closet. Lucky to have loaded the car before the rain."

"Driving back to Chicago tonight?" Father Sullivan asked, trying to make conversation.

"Oh, no set goal. Just as far as I can get till I'm tired. Depends on the rain. Some of those motels are five to six dollars a night. Maybe I'll just wait until tomorrow to see my folks. Maybe in time for Sunday dinner, " he said, setting his suitcase back on the bed and continuing the light banter.

Father Sullivan engaged, "Do they know?"

"*Know* is all relative, Michael. Depends on what they need to or should know. Better yet, it's what I want them to know. I think I told you we live in a working-class German neighborhood on the south side of Chicago. After the first war, Dad worked as a meat packer. Been there for thirty-eight years now. Worked in a cold locker all that time. Tough man. Worked five and a half days a week. Knights of Columbus every Thursday. Confessions once a month. Routine. Every Sunday—suit, tie, Ma, and us three boys. Seven o'clock Mass. Always arrive at 6:45 sharp. Sunday paper … Ma's fried chicken for afternoon dinner and then take a nap. That's life. Six more years, he retires. Then what? Hang around the house, play cards at the K of C, nag Mom?

"My oldest brother, Frank, works in a machine shop. Joe, my younger brother, was always in trouble. Never married, no family. That leaves me. All Dad wanted since I could remember was for me to be a priest. Now look. If I left the priesthood, it would literally kill him. Mom would be there for me. Him? No!"

Father Sullivan was touched by Jerome's remarks. He could only imagine. Alone at a cheap motel somewhere between Wabash and Chicago. Where would all this take him? Opinion about his disgust for Father Jaeger seemed pointless. He had a sense of pity for the poor man. Rage did not step forward in this small dark room late that gloomy Saturday. Alone together. It didn't seem right. Father Sullivan searched for forgiveness as he listened to Father Jaeger, but even now forgiveness did not come.

Father Sullivan did say, "Father Warren said Father Schmidt called. You're to go there next week?" he asked, already knowing the answer.

"Yes. I just don't know how I can handle that again." Then he paused. He walked over and looked out the window as the rain ran down the windowpanes. Not turning around, Father Jaeger continued to stare out the window. "You know, Michael, I need one more chance. One more chance to prove to all those I hurt, to all those I let down, that I can beat this.

"All I really wanted in life was a family. When I knew that couldn't be, I just wanted to be a good priest. Never had an aspiration to be a bishop, not even a pastor. Just a good priest—say Mass, hear confessions, teach the kids, wear the—" Then he stopped. "Wear the collar. Make our Lord and my parents proud. That's all. Not asking too much. Now this. Now this whole dastardly mess. Just can't believe what I've done. Just can't believe it." The rain was letting up. "Maybe this is the right time to go," he said as he noticed his watch—4:40 p.m. Pulling the suitcase from the bed, he walked toward the closet.

Father Sullivan reached in and took the two suits and cassocks from the closet pole. "Here, I'll carry these for you." Father Sullivan noticed something white toward the back corner of the shelf. Standing up on his toes, he noticed a collar Father Jaeger had left behind. "Here, Father, you almost forgot this." Carrying the suits and cassocks over his left arm, Father Sullivan handed the collar to Father Jaeger. "Here, Father. It's a little tarnished, but maybe you'll…" Father Sullivan stopped what he was about to say and simply handed the collar to Father Jaeger."

Father Jaeger placed the collar in his left hand, in front of the suits and cassocks he also took from Father Sullivan. He picked up the suitcase and left the room. Father Sullivan stood alone as Father Jaeger walked out the door.

"Take care, Jerome. I will be thinking of you and praying for you."

Father Jaeger stopped, turned around, and simply said, "Thank you, Michael. I'm sure I'll need all the prayers I can get."

Father Sullivan watched as Father Jaeger disappeared down the hall. Those were the last words spoken between the two priests. Both their worlds were about to change.

Although Father Jaeger wanted to be unnoticed, a need to go into the church seemed appropriate. He quietly entered through the side door. Having left his suitcase, suits, and cassocks in his car, he walked across the front of the church toward the chapel. It was 4:55 p.m. Lines had formed in the back of the church for confession. The sun shone through the stained glass windows on the west side, having peeked through the cloud cover. He walked carefully and genuflected at the center aisle only, avoiding being seen by the few in the back of the church. His steps broke the silence as he walked toward St. Michael's chapel one last time. Opening the wooden door, he stepped into the room, which was lit only by two candles to the side of the front altar.

Kneeling in the front pew and burying his face in his hands, he closed his eyes. Again he asked for forgiveness and strength to press on. He knew not what lie before him. He could only pray for strength and courage. Thinking of his parents, he knew leaving the priesthood was not an option.

CHAPTER 48

THE ANNOUNCEMENT

Father Warren—May 17, 1958

FATHER Warren stayed up late that Saturday evening, alone in his study. He had not said a final good-bye to Father Jaeger. Confessions had come first, but all things considered, maybe that was for the best. Father Warren and Father Sullivan did not share supper together that evening, as they both sought time alone after Father Jaeger's departure. Father Warren spent the time praying in his study. Kneeling before the crucifix, he prayed for hours, hands folded, head bowed, lost in deep concern for the matters at hand.

Sometime around 11:00 p.m., he moved over to his desk. Pen in hand, Father Warren wrote a letter to the parishioners that he would read the next day at all the Masses. Placing a sheet of carbon paper between the St. Thomas Moore letterhead stationery, Father Warren rubbed his forehead, thought for a moment, and penned his most sincere, understanding, and empathetic letter.

The next morning, Father Warren said the 5:30 and 8:30 Masses. Father Sullivan celebrated the 7:00 and 10:15 Masses. A visiting priest from Huntington said the 11:30. Father Warren read the letter announcing Father Jaeger's departure at each of the five Masses. A letter of this importance, he wanted to share in person with the entire parish.

Gene Kowolski sat in church with his family for the 5:30 early Mass, as they were planning to visit Gene's mother's parents in Covington, Indiana, a long day trip.

Father Warren hesitated as he looked across the congregation, about to begin his sermon. Reaching under his chasuble, Father Warren pulled out a sheet of paper, laid it before him, and read, "My dear friends in Christ. Today, I am announcing that Father Jaeger is leaving our parish as an assistant priest effective today, May 18, 1958. When Gene heard Father Warren say Father Jaeger's name, his mind snapped to attention. He noticed his father look across the pew at his mother as if they knew something he didn't.

His heart raced in anticipation to hear Father Warren's letter. He listened intently.

Father Jaeger is departing for personal and health reasons. Although his sudden departure was not foreseen, I understand and support his reasons. I am thankful for all the positives Father contributed to our parish. Let us not pass judgment or question his personal decision or motivations. Of most importance, we must all remember him in our prayers … and wish Father Jaeger a future in the continuation of Our Lord and Savior's mission on this Earth. May God give him eternal guidance. Sincerely, Father Thomas Warren."

Few had attended the 5:30 Mass. After reading the letter, Father Warren looked up. The startled faces were few, as most of the attendees were older and not as involved with parish activities or in personal contact with the younger assistant priests.

Gene quietly celebrated to himself. *He's gone. Thank you, God, for answering my prayers. Please help me to rid him from my mind.* Then he thought, *May his soul burn in hell forever.* Gene closed his eyes. *Thank you, Dear Lord. I will be forever grateful.*

The 8:30 Mass was a contrast to the 5:30 Mass. Parents, parish volunteers, students, and a cross section of the entire parish represented the vast majority of attendees. Rumors about Father Jaeger's departure had not filtered to most of those in attendance. Most knew Father Jaeger. Almost all liked him. Only a few knew or had any reason to be suspicious of the man behind the collar.

Father Warren knew idle talk, rumor, and innuendos would engulf the parish this coming week. He elected, however, to let the letter speak for itself. More explanations, opinions, or sermonizing would not stem the tide. A parable would not be apropos. The looks on the faces of those he saw said it all. Father Warren knew the weeks to follow would be nothing less than a stern challenge for him and many within his parish.

After Mass, Father Warren hoped Ralph and Grace Smith would stop by. They did. They waited for the priest to exit the sacristy. The four altar boys had left. Soon after, Father Warren emerged from the church.

"Good morning, Ralph, Grace," Father Warren said with a smile and polite nod.

"Hello, Father. I know that was difficult," Ralph commented. Grace smiled, standing at his side.

"Yes, it was, Ralph. Thank you for saying so. Any chance you could come to the rectory tomorrow? I'm going to ask Tim Brennan and Randall Zilbar to also join us. I think it would be helpful to have Sister Christopher and Sister Mary Michael to represent the school. Of course, Father Sullivan will be there. I will be informing everyone of our role in the diocese's and our parish's response."

"May I ask, Father? What about the police?"

"Ralph, it's not the direction the bishop wants to take at this time."

"That's what I expected," Ralph said, disappointed.

"I know you have other ideas. We'll talk about that tomorrow."

"Father, you know we'll support you. Whatever is best for the parish and, of course, these kids. I'm afraid they may be lost in all of this."

"That's what frightens me also. Okay then. Tomorrow at seven o'clock."

Father Jaeger—May 18, 1958

The rain had finally stopped by the time Jerome Jaeger arrived at his parents' home late on Sunday afternoon.

"How was your trip, Jerry?" his mother asked as soon as he walked through the front door.

"Where's Dad?" he asked, passing on commenting about the trip.

"Ah, he's tending to his garden, planting those tomatoes. You know how he loves them. Take your things upstairs. I'll go get him."

By the time Jerome returned downstairs, his parents were already sitting at the kitchen table in the center of the room. The narrow gabled house was a typical white clapboard circa-1920s structure with a parlor, a center dining room, and a kitchen in the back. The three bedrooms and one bath upstairs provided wonderful space for the family. The working-class neighborhood was neat and safe and provided a great family environment.

Mr. Jaeger had already opened a bottle of his favorite beer, Pabst Blue Ribbon. His mother poured coffee.

"Beer, Jerome?" his dad asked.

"Sure. Thanks. I could use that about now."

"Tell us about your trip," his mother directed.

"Yes, do. And why all this time home? Your school year hasn't ended yet. Has it?" Father Jaeger's father asked with a confused, inquisitive look on his face.

"No, no. Another few weeks, Dad." Father Jaeger knew there was no way out. He would have to address the issue. *Well, not all of it,* he thought. "You both know how I've been fortunate these past ten, twelve years. The bishop has really been accommodating transferring me around. He's allowed me to experience different parishes, different people. Working with so many fine priests and nuns, he knew I'd probably like to be a pastor, but I need more time. More experience."

"Well, do you like St. Thomas Moore? You always spoke well of your pastor. Wasn't his name Father Warren? Very pastoral, I think you described him."

"Oh yes, Mom. He's been great, so helpful to me. And Father Sullivan, the other assistant, he's been a good friend. I liked everything about the parish."

"Why aren't you down there then? Don't they need you?" his dad asked quite matter-of-factly.

"Sure, sure, but I just need some time. You both know I love the priesthood. We've all three talked about me being a priest since, gosh, since back in, wasn't it the sixth grade, Mom?"

"No, it was the fifth grade," Mr. Jaeger said emphatically.

"Yes, precisely. You became inspired around Easter. You just loved the whole Easter experience … Holy Thursday, Good Friday, and then Easter Sunday. You couldn't wait to receive your server assignments. That's the year you became a server."

"I remember it like yesterday. Your first Sunday Mass. We were both so happy to see you there. All in black and white. That clean, starched surplus. Yes, that was it. Saw you in that black cassock. I knew you'd be a fine-looking priest. Now you are, so you should be down there now," Mr. Jaeger said with sternness in his voice.

"Let's have another beer, Dad," Father Jaeger said, trying to fend off the tension. "Mom, Dad, I'm just telling you I've asked for a couple months off. I've gotta ... "

"A couple months off?" his father shot back. "A couple months off? I haven't had a couple months off total during the last eight, heck, the last ten years!"

"That's right, Jerry. You know your father gets one week of vacation, and paid at that."

Father Jaeger did not want to stoke the fire of his dad's German temper.

"You take two months ... then they'll ... then the bishop will send you someplace else. That's not the way it's done. I've been at the shop ever since the end of the war. What's this modern world coming to? A couple months!" Jerome's father pounded his square fist on the oilcloth atop the kitchen table, almost leaving a print.

"Arthur, Arthur, not now. We have to respect Jerry's decision. I'm sure he knows what he needs to do," Jerome's mother said, trying to smooth things over, as was her usual routine.

"Jerome, is there something you're not telling us? Something else bothering you?" his dad asked, raising his bushy, unkempt eyebrows.

"No, no, of course not. I just need some time to think. Need to make sure this is ... " He paused. "Well, need to make sure this is what I want to do for the rest of my life."

"Well, Judas Priest!" his dad said, using the name to emphasize his concern about what he had just heard.

Jerome stood up. "Please, just believe in me. I need a little time to myself."

The firm set of his dad's jaw required no response. "I'll be in the backyard." He reached over, opened the refrigerator door, and took out another cold Pabst. He didn't say another word, as he stomped out the door.

Father Jaeger's mother stepped over and placed her arms around Jerome. With a comforting hug, she said, "I'll be here for you, Jerry. You'll never disappoint me, son."

Father Jaeger hugged her back, left the room, and thought, *There's probably disappointment ahead for all of us. Much more than we'll ever want to know.*

CHAPTER 49

NOT ALONE

Peter Goodnar—May 18, 1958

PETER Goodnar learned the news about Father Jaeger's sudden departure while attending Sunday Mass with his parents. Sunday began as usual, no different from last week or two months before. Together with his parents, older brother, older sister, and his two younger sisters, Peter attended the 8:30 Mass at St. Thomas Moore. Arriving at exactly 8:15, the family sat together, all seven of them, always in the middle of church on the left side. For fifteen minutes, the family prayed in quiet as they waited for Mass to begin.

Once every six weeks, Peter served Mass. Prior to this Sunday, he had heard rumors around school about Father Jaeger that said he was never coming back. That morning, Peter prayed the rumors were true.

At 8:29, Father Warren and the four altar boys waited in the sacristy. The lead server rang the bell signaling Mass was to begin. The congregation stood. Father Warren and the altar boys entered the sanctuary. Immediately, Peter noticed Henry Langley and Paul Woodward were serving Mass. Peter's mind wandered. He held his St. Joseph missal as if he was following every Latin word.

Previously, Henry, Paul, and Mark Salisbury had spent time with Peter one day after school. They had ended up at Gackenheimer's Drug Store, where they talked about baseball, breasts, Fords, and Chevys. Talk had become serious when Henry said, "Father Jaeger is a perv." Peter remembered the day a couple months ago vividly.

Peter was walking home from school alone. It was a cool gray day in March. He heard someone call his name, "Hey, Goodnar, where ya going?"

Peter turned toward the voice from the other side of the street near the bus stop. He saw Henry, Paul, and Mark walking in the same direction.

"Just headin' to Gackenheimer's for a cherry Coke. Meeting someone there!" Peter yelled back from across the street.

"Well, that's where we're going too!" Mark Salisbury bellowed back.

The three boys crossed the street to Peter's side. Henry, Mark, and Paul were all eighth graders, two years ahead of Peter. *These guys seem so much older*, Peter thought. They crossed Wabash Street, just up the hill from Market.

"Hi, guys. How's it goin'?" Peter tried to say nonchalantly.

"We're all great. Just looking for chicks," Mark said with a kidding laugh, slapping his knee at the same time.

"You're such a cornball, Mark," Paul said, pushing on Mark's back.

"Hey, Paul, I saw you staring at Diane Woodbury today. I think the whole class was watching you. There was drool comin' out of your mouth," Henry said, trying to belittle Paul.

"Well, yeah. Did you see that sweater she had on? She's gotta be a double D," Paul shot back.

"Right, Casanova, as if you'd know. All you know about *D* is its the fourth letter in the alphabet, stands for dumb, and it's all over your report card. Duh."

"Hey, I might not know, but I sure got good taste. Not like you, dork head." Paul pushed Henry's shoulder, knocking him off step.

"Not like me, pea brain. I've already been hands-on with Peggy. I know for sure. See this?" Henry opened up his hand and stretched his fingers as if to palm a basketball. "Couldn't even get this around either one. They're so big," he said, talking like the experienced one of the bunch.

"Either one, meathead? They're both the same size," Paul slapped Henry's back, trying to counter Henry's experience.

Now Peter Goodnar was really feeling like one of the older guys, hearing all this sex talk.

"Hey, we're here." Mark opened Gackenheimer's front door for Henry but then dashed in first. "Gotcha!" They all heard the jingle of the bells above the door.

"Better tell us the rest of your two-hand palm jobs," Mark said.

"Okay. Get a booth and I will," Henry replied.

"Hi, Miss Alice. We're here. Throw a nickel in the jukebox. How about 'Peggy Sue'? Better line up four cherry Cokes. Okay with you, Peter?" Henry asked as if he owned the place.

"Don't worry about Henry," Paul said, nudging Peter. "He's always gotta be the big shot."

"Sure thing. That's my usual," Peter said like one of the guys.

"Make mine a Schlitz. You guys know, the beer that made Milwaukee famous," Mark said, throwing a quarter on the counter.

"Get real, big shot. You couldn't handle the first swig," Henry shot back. The four guys slid into a corner booth. "Okay, everybody, chalk up," Henry demanded. Mark and Paul slapped their nickels on the table. Peter soon did the same.

"Here's twenty cents. You be our waitress, bucko," Henry directed Paul. Soon Paul was back with four cherry Cokes.

"Okay, Henry, you two-handed Peggy? Any more to tell?" Paul asked.

"Yeah, over at the park, right on a picnic bench. She even lifted her blouse for me."

"You mean you saw 'em?"

"Yeah, both of 'em. She had her bra on, of course, but she still let me feel inside." Showing them the open palms of both hands again, Henry said, "My hands needed to be twice this size to get all the way around. Then I pushed and lifted them up."

"Bet that's not all that was up," Mark said, slapping the table as he laughed at his own joke.

"You guessed it, buddy boy. You're just jealous. Course, your Sally still has a training bra," Henry belittled Mark.

"Yeah, plus lots of Kleenex," Paul added.

The booth erupted in laughter. Peter went right along.

"Hey, you guys, show a little civility over there. I've got other customers," Miss Alice said sternly with a half smile.

Peter thought this was tons of fun. He wished he had a girl to cup. The horrid image of Father Jaeger cupping flashed across his mind. Daily,

Peter remembered the filth around his body. He couldn't get the priest's image out of his mind.

"Okay, you two book freaks, get serious if your pea brains can get off of sex for a minute—"

"Hey, we can sure get off on sex," Henry goaded and then roared again with laughter, as if imitating Lou Costello.

Mark followed by slapping the table. "Hey, that's a good one," he said, siding with Henry.

"*Shhh*, you two morons. You're both crazy sex hounds," Paul said seriously.

Mark stood up, strummed an imaginary guitar, and began singing, "You ain't nothing but a hound dog!"

"Kid thinks he's Elvis." Henry pulled Mark by his belt. "Quiet there, Exlax."

"You just wish your two hands could feel the real thing, Paulie boy." Henry wouldn't let up.

"Listen, guys, we all wanted to ask Peter about what we heard, so be serious," Paul said. Mark and Henry looked at each other.

"Okay, ten minute break for Bishop Sheen. No sex. No fun. Let's just talk about the pervert priest Then back to boobs, sweaters, tits, and more sex talk. Mark, you keep time," Henry said with a big laugh.

Paul began, "Peter, we heard a rumor."

Peter looked startled, as if they were going to ask about his experiences with girls.

Henry added, always taking control, "Peter, we heard Father Jaeger got you up to his room and then did it to you."

Adrenaline shot through Peter's body as he felt his face go hot. "What are you talking about?" Peter frowned and sat back in the booth, not playing it very cool. He could feel the goose bumps up and down his back. He could not stop his blush. His first thought was Jaeger and then dashing out the door. "No way did he—"

Henry cut Peter off, "Don't freak out, man. Be cool. We just heard that prick got to you. We're on your side. Look at the three of us. We've all been there with that cocksucker. He got us all."

"Hey, Henry, mighty big words there, but don't include me in his room."

"You bet. That queer likes 'em big. Course that leaves you out, bucko."

Henry shot back at Paul. "That's right, I've never been there like you two sisters. Yuck!"

"Yeah. He just felt you up in the cassock closet," Henry explained seriously. "Don't dodge the bullet, buddy boy. How many times in the cassock closet? Fifty-two was it?"

"Yeah. Once a week for a year." Mark slapped the table and laughed knowing that fifty-two times was an exaggeration.

"Wow, didn't know you could count, moron," Paul shot back.

"Remember the time we were in his car?" Mark reminded Paul.

"Yeah, sure, but at least I had my clothes on. Not like you two naked jailbirds," Paul reminded Henry.

"Don't forget, Mark and I saw his arm between the two front seats. We know where his hand was," Henry said, looking straight at Peter to see if he was taking in all the barbs.

"That's why Henry and I jumped in the backseat first," Mark explained to Peter. "We gotcha, buddy."

"Buddy, my ass. I had to push his slimy hand away, as he tugged at my zipper," Paul said, wrinkling his nose and whipping his hand downward, palm open. Then he said, "It was awful. Couldn't wait to get out of that seat, rush home, and take a bath."

"Hell, when that slimy prick gets his hands on you, you need a garden hose," Mark said, slapping Henry's arm. "Right, Hank?"

"Hey, that's a good one," Henry replied. "Garden hose. Get it? Like a hose job. Course that's a little advance for you, Mark. You think a hose job is like working in your grandma's garden."

"Bingo! Gotta him again, Henry," Paul added. "So I never asked. Which one of you had to get in the front seat after I jumped?" Paul asked, looking at Henry and Mark.

Mark turned toward Henry, and Henry looked back at him. Then they both gagged with laughter. Henry said, "Neither one of us got in the front seat. When he told one of us to jump in the front, I said, trying to make a joke, 'No way, Father. We're staying back here. We want you to be our chauffeur.'" He slapped his knee then laughed.

"You know what this crazy dork head said to Father Jaeger?" Mark asked. "'Book on, James. Take us to our front door.' As if the dorky priest was our chauffeur. And Father played along like one of the guys. He didn't get it. Stupid fool. What a perv."

"We tried to muffle our laughter in the backseat, watching the slimy creep driving us down Main Street in his long black Studebaker. Creepy car like the driver. You know, the Studebaker has that bullet thing sticking in front between the two fenders, just like the dork. The guy's queer as a three dollar bill. Get it? What a sight it must have been." Henry said, cracking up again. "Wish I could have seen us. Why can't he be cool and drive a Chevy?"

"Nah. Drive a Ford. Now that's cool!" Paul exclaimed.

"Yeah, with mud flaps and pipes," Mark added.

"He likes pipes all right," Henry said seriously. "Get it, Mark? Pipes? Like he likes your pipe?"

"Yeah, wish I had a little black hat. You know, like the Rochester wears for Jack Benny. Yes, sir, Mr. Benny," Mark said with a guffaw.

"You two guys are such dork heads. Why didn't you tell me that before?" Paul asked. "Jaeger probably thought you were serious. What a fool. I thought all along one of you was in the front seat with the good father havin' a real hold on you."

"He's gotta a hold on you," Mark crooned again, swaying side to side on the bench. Henry gave him a shoulder.

Peter was kind of stunned. Here they poked fun at each other, yet he could tell they hated what Father Jaeger had done to them. Peter felt better knowing he was not alone. He loathed the priest even more.

"I can tell all you guys one thing, maybe ten or twelve years, whenever," Henry said, his suddenly straight face turning red with anger. "Someday I'm going to find him. Don't care if he's a priest or not. I'm going to pay that man back for all the terror, for all the sleepless nights, and the torment he caused me. I promise you all, I will. I'll bring justice to that slimy bastard."

Mark and Paul both looked at Peter. "And he means it," Paul said. "Henry will."

"Yeah, I'd love to be there when that happens," Mark added. Leaning across the table, Mark lowered his voice to a whisper. "How ya gonna do it, Henry? Tell us. We'll keep it quiet."

"Listen, you all swear never to repeat this."

"Promise. I promise I won't tell a soul," both Paul and Mark said. Peter just listened.

"Well, I'm gonna fess up. Listen. Not a word to anyone. Promise?"

Paul and Mark both nodded while crossing their fingers in front of Henry and then crisscrossing their hearts. "Promise on my mammy's grave." They looked straight at Henry.

"So I said, 'Take me home, Father. Mom will be waitin' up.' 'Sure. Sure, Henry, I'll take you home.'"

Paul looked over at Mark. "Then what, Henry?"

"Well, he headed for my house and then turned left instead of right onto my street. 'Where you goin', Father? Take me home,' I told the fruitcake."

"Father said, 'Sure,' but he drove up the hill to Hannah Park and pulled down to the end of the street. Holy shit! I was scared."

"What'd he do? What'd he do?" Mark looked directly at Henry.

"Well, I stayed in the backseat and yelled at him to take me home. He said, 'Sure, sure, I will.'" Mark and Paul couldn't believe their ears. "The prick got out of his creepy car and took off his shirt and then his pants."

"Holy crap! He what?" Mark shot up from his seat. "His pants? You mean you saw it? There in the park?"

"Next thing I knew, he was all over me, that son-of-a-bitchin' queer! That's it! That's it! Tellin' you guys no more." Henry's face was white. Peter couldn't believe, although it sounded so familiar.

"What'd he do then?" Mark asked eyes wide open.

"That's it. You guys know what he did. I blanked out. Next thing I can honestly remember was runnin' up my steps. It was … it was … it was terrible. I'll get him though. You know, Father Warren or Sullivan won't do anything to Jaeger. He's off scot-free. My parents love the priests, but now listen here. I told Duke. He's got this friend doing time in Terre Haute. Beat up a guy real bad. Almost killed him. Sent away for ten years, so I'll be about twenty-two. Duke will be thirty."

"Who's Duke?" Peter asked.

"That's my brother. He's a mechanic. Tough guy. Been in the slammer a few times." Lowering his voice again, Henry said, "Duke and this Spencer, Harold Spencer, they'll take me, and we're gonna find Jaeger."

"Then what?" Mark asked, his mouth open, his eyes wide. "Tell us in spades. Gonna cut 'em off?"

"We're gonna show Jaeger real terror. He may be a priest, he may have power, but he just hides behind that collar. When I told Duke how Jaeger stripped me naked and then wrapped me with his sweaty slimy body, my brother went ape shit."

"No. Really?" Paul asked.

"Yeah. He wanted to go after Jaeger right then. I cooled him down. Said I want to be a man first. So Duke says ten years. Then Duke, Spencer, and me, we'll get him. We'll bring justice."

"You mean kill him?" Mark asked as if he was listening to an Al Capone story.

"No. No way. We're not gonna kill him. That would be letting the pervert off too easy. He didn't kill us."

"Yeah, and that's a mortal sin," Paul said. "Killing."

Henry looked at Paul, Mark, and Peter. "We're gonna get him, bring justice for all he did to me and to you guys. Terror for justice."

"But how?" Paul asked in wild curiosity.

"This. This right here," Henry said, pounding his right fist in his hand. "Duke said, 'I'll take a bat or pipe straight to his … ' You guys know," Henry described.

"You mean straight to his balls? A bat to his balls?" Mark asked as if he was challenging Henry.

Henry said, "I'll stand back ten years, but then times up for him. He'll face me because … " Henry paused. "I'll never forget. Ten years, he'll have to face me."

"Wow!" Paul said.

"Yeah, I'd do the same. Just like you, Henry."

Mark pounded his fist on the table. "I'd hit as hard as Sugar Ray," Mark said.

"You're just a wannabe. First Elvis now Sugar Ray Robinson," Henry said, nudging his buddy.

"Don't forget Bishop Sheen," Mark responded.

"That was Paul, you dork."

"Oh yeah."

"One more thing. Duke said Harold has a gun, and he's used it before. 'Just shoot him where it hurts … but never, never kill.'"

Paul, Mark, and Peter just sat back in the booth. They could not even drink their Cokes. One thing they all agreed on that unforgettable day in Gackenheimer's Drug Store was that Jaeger deserved every bit of pain and horror, and they all wanted to be there.

For the first time in months, Peter Goodnar felt that he was not alone. Four guys from St. Thomas Moore's grade school in 1958 with one common bond, horrific and terrible. Together they talked tough, laughed a little, and verbally beat up on the man and the acts of his depraved mind. But when alone in the dark late at night, they all knew how to cry, as their minds drifted on into the darkness.

CHAPTER 50

FACING THE TRUTH

Father Jaeger—May 19, 1958, Monday morning

MARY Jaeger hurried from the kitchen to pick up the ringing phone. "Jerome, it's that Father Schmidt calling again. It's a person-to-person call. This is the third time he's called. Would you like to take it?" She couldn't understand why Father Schmidt kept calling. Then she thought, *For whatever reason, maybe I don't want to know.*

"Okay, Ma. Okay. I will. Tell him I'll be right there."

"Operator, yes, he'll take the call. Can you give him just a minute?" She could hear his footsteps slowly coming downstairs. He walked into the middle room.

"Thanks, Ma."

As his mother returned to the kitchen, she closed the swinging door separating the kitchen and the dining room. Jerome heard the squeaking hinge come to a halt. "Hello."

"Is this Jerome Jaeger?" the operator asked.

"Yes it is."

The operator connected the call.

"Hello, Father Jaeger, this is Father Schmidt from the bishop's office in South Wayne. Hope I didn't call at a bad time." Father Jaeger was at least pleased to hear the somewhat friendly greeting. "Father Holtz gave me your number. I understand you are at your parents' home in Chicago."

"Yes. That's where I am for now," Jerome answered as he awaited the next question to drop the bomb.

"I'm just calling to confirm your appointment. We are going to talk about your current situation at St. Thomas Moore. It's been almost two years since we last discussed your future. It's time again. You'll be here Wednesday, May 21, at three o'clock."

"Yes, I told Father Holtz I'd be there. But do you think ... oh, I mean, could we delay for another week? I'm not quite ready now. This has been very trying. Could maybe next month work? It'd be better for me," Father Jaeger said, hoping to buy himself some time.

Taken aback by being put off, Father Schmidt said with conviction, "That will not work. I can assure you that your presence here this week is of major importance to your future. You will be here," he said with deliberate emphasis on *be here*.

"Yes, Father," Father Jaeger paused. "Yes, I can. I guess I can make that work," he responded unenthusiastically, knowing the purpose of the meeting.

Not appreciating Father Jaeger's lax response, Father Schmidt said, "We'll all look forward to seeing you this Wednesday at 3:00 sharp. Thank you. Good-bye."

"Good-bye." Father Jaeger's heart thumped in perfect time as he slammed the receiver down. Within two seconds, he heard the squeak of the swinging door.

"Is everything all right, Jerry?" his mother asked.

He stared through the lace-curtained window at the frame side of the neighbor's house. *Everything is all right. Everything is just fine.* "Yes, Mother. Everything is hunky-dory," he replied, adding to his mother's concern. "Just an educational meeting in South Wayne." She gave a puzzled look and returned to the kitchen as he continued to stare out the window at the blank wall just a sidewalk away. Turning around, he did not look in the direction of the kitchen. He proceeded to carry his blank look upstairs. Ascending past the second step without looking toward his mother, he asked in stride, "Will Dad be home at the usual time?"

"Oh yes, dear. Of course, always. Tonight's the K of C monthly meeting."

I know. He never misses, Father Jaeger thought.

"You know he never misses the Knights of Columbus," he heard his mother say.

Some things in my life never change.

As could be expected, the Wednesday of his meeting in South Wayne was overcast with a steady drizzle, casting an even more gloomy look on the day. Jerome had plenty of time to drive to South Wayne even though the rain was supposed to increase. The trip would take three hours, more or less. He was glad he wouldn't have to leave in the wee hours of the morning.

His mother was busy fixing breakfast in the kitchen. As a child, Father Jaeger could remember her ever-present self in the kitchen, cooking, or in the basement, tending to the wash or canning.

"Good morning, Jerry," she greeted as he entered the kitchen just before 8:30 a.m. "Can I make you some breakfast? I have some good ham."

"Nah, Mom. Just coffee will be fine. Dad's gone?" he asked, already knowing the answer.

"You know him. Two eggs over easy, ham or three strips of bacon, juice, and coffee. Then, 'See you dear,' a peck on the cheek, and out the door between 6:15 and 6:20 a.m. every day except Sunday."

"How long's it been now?" Father Jaeger asked.

"Let's see, 1958 … He started in 1922. That's thirty-six years except for the two years during the war. Says he wants to go nine more. You know your father; he sets a goal, makes up his mind, and then always straight forward."

"I know. Never any detours. Doesn't use crossroads. Obeys every traffic sign."

"You're right, Jerry. He's a true old-fashioned German just like your grandfather was."

Father Jaeger did not respond to the obvious statement.

"So what's your day?" his mother asked, hoping to prod him into talking about what was on his mind.

"Oh, haven't really decided. Few friends I'd like to see. Gonna be leaving around nine thirty or so." Not wanting her to know about his trip to South Wayne.

"Well, wherever you're going, take your umbrella."

Father Jaeger laughed lightly at himself. *Yeah, I'll probably need an umbrella with all that's gonna come down on me.*

Driving through Gary on his way to South Wayne, Father Jaeger could see nothing but a sea of dirty black and gray steel mills, heavily sooted homes, and rows and rows of 1930s and 1940s black cars. He thought how fortunate he was to not have to work in the mills.

Within less than two hours, Father Jaeger was gaining ground on South Wayne. He felt no inclination to hurry. The meeting with Father Schmidt would come all too soon. After a couple stops along the tollway, he pulled off at the first stoplight into South Wayne. Immediately, he spotted the twin spires of St. Leonard's and carefully followed the well-known landmarks. Once he arrived in front of St. Leonard's, he could see the sign to park at the side of the church. It was 2:45; he had fifteen minutes. The rain had stopped. *Is that a good sign?*

Cranking the window down, the priest leaned his head back on the seat. *Just five minutes,* he thought. *Five solitary minutes.* Remembering back to the summer of '56, he recalled that the experience wasn't as bad as he had expected when he was assigned to St. Thomas Moore. There had been questions about the "incidents," as Father Schmidt referred to them, that had taken place at his previous assignment … but fortunately they weren't too specific. The discussion had leaned more heavily on willingness to repent and understanding the psychological reasons for the "moral discrepancies," as they were called. Most specifically, Jerome Jaeger remembered the focus on counseling and confidentiality. He hoped today would be a carbon copy of two years ago. Checking his watch, he saw it was 2:53—time to go in.

Slowly, Father Jaeger made his way to the side door of the rectory. He recognized the small sign, "office." He rang the doorbell and then waited. The rain had stopped, but the clouds were still ominous.

The door opened. "Father Jaeger, I presume? Please come in," the sister said politely.

"Yes, yes, thank you." Removing his hat, Father Jaeger immediately noticed the picture of *Christ at the Door*—a picture he had seen so many times at his Aunt Marie's house in St. Anne, Illinois.

He heard footsteps approaching. "Good afternoon. I'm Father Holtz, Father Ben Holtz. I was not here during your last visit two years ago. I'm

Father Schmidt's assistant. Please follow me. We are running ahead of schedule. Father Schmidt is waiting."

Oh, that's just great, Father Jaeger thought. *His sword is probably drawn.*

As they entered the room, Father Schmidt stood up and walked over toward Father Jaeger, extending his hand. "Hello, Father. Hope the rain today didn't hinder your trip."

"No, quite fine. Thank you. It was a pleasant ride. Actually, I'm looking forward to our visit."

"I'd like for you to meet Father Kessler, who is here in the bishop's absence."

That's good news. Father Jaeger was relieved to hear the bishop would not be present. Father Kessler reached across the table and shook hands with Father Jaeger.

"Also, I'd like for you to meet Dr. Samuel Bloomberg, our visiting psychologist. And of course, you've already met Father Holtz." Taking the lead, Father Schmidt sat down, and the rest followed. "Father Jaeger, take a seat on this side of the table, as it will be more efficient if we speak directly facing one another."

Father Schmidt began with the written agenda before him. "Thank you for coming this evening. There have been rumors, questions, and innuendos about Father Jaeger's departure. We thought best to explain and clarify to you, Father Jaeger's situation. As I briefed you earlier, Father Jaeger met with us back in the late winter of 1956, almost two years ago. At that time, with the support of Bishop Powers, of course, we decided to assign Father Jaeger to a very fine parish in Wabash. That would be St. Thomas Moore, which is under the guidance of Father Thomas Warren." The priests and Dr. Bloomberg listened as if they had heard this line before. "For the record, we did meet with Father Warren and Father Sullivan the week before last. Our purpose today is to discuss a specific incident that took place at a ... let's see ... the scout camp. Is that correct, Father Jaeger?"

"Yes, it is. It is, unfortunately," Father Jaeger added, trying to show some remorse. "Although I might assume the experience may not have been correctly portrayed by my two colleagues."

Father Kessler was the first to ask a question. "Were you involved with one boy that evening, and if so, how old was he?"

"There were three boys, Father. I believe they were all eighth graders, so that would make them thirteen."

"Were you active with all three?"

"No. I just spent time, really a short time, with just one."

"Why so?"

"The reason is simple," Father Jaeger said, ashamed. "A parent happened upon us as we were around the campfire. He found that to be inappropriate … and he created an embarrassing situation. I did not want to have a confrontation in front of the boys … so, well, I left the campsite."

"*He* created an embarrassing situation? Don't you have that reversed?" Father Kessler said, correcting Father Jaeger.

"Yes, sure. Sorry. That was a poor way to phrase it. It was embarrassing, but we were only acting out what we thought to be Indian rituals. No more, no less," Father Jaeger said, correcting himself.

"Was there sexual contact with any of the boys?" Father Kessler asked.

"No, not really," Father Jaeger replied. "Maybe we did get a little too close as we were acting out. Nothing really serious."

Father Schmidt immediately took over the questioning as he tried to evade graphic detail that could be used as automatic guilt. "Did you see the boys again?"

"No, I didn't. I just left," Father Jaeger explained.

"Could I ask a question?" Father Schmidt asked. "Did any of the parents come forward after this incident?"

"No, Father. I've never had a parent bring a complaint. As a matter of fact, I have a very good rapport with the parents, and the sisters, I might add. The experience, and I might say my progress, has been very positive these past two years."

Father Holtz sat quietly, listening, though he had a most stern look on his face.

"Father Jaeger, were you involved with any other boys at St. Thomas Moore?" Father Kessler asked.

"Well, yes, yes, I was involved," Father Jaeger answered as briefly as he could. "Some whole classes, and that includes the girls. I have devoted my life to teaching. I love those kids."

"Father Schmidt, may I ask further?" Father Holtz said, asking for clarification.

"Of course, Father."

"Father Jaeger, I find your answer to be evasive. You know why we are here. Were you involved with other boys in an abusive nature?"

Raising his left hand to his forehead, Father Jaeger paused and then said carefully, "Yes, maybe two."

"What do you mean *maybe?*" Father Holtz asked.

"Now, Father Holtz, let him answer. He says two, and that's what it says here in the file according to Father Sullivan."

"Yes, he's right," Father Jaeger replied in response to Father Schmidt's interjection. He hoped the file did not indicate any more. "I would add that with those two, it was not as significant as the night at the campfire."

"Then let me ask it this way—" Father Holtz said.

Father Schmidt interrupted and said, "Now, Father Holtz, please. This is not an inquisition. Let me add some perspective. We've established that Father Jaeger has made progress during this assignment at St. Thomas Moore. He has admitted that he experienced a setback. There have been two others but not to the degree as before. We must first admit that we do believe in forgiveness. Now, that said, Father Jaeger, your indiscretion was a serious matter. Do you agree?"

"Yes, I do, Father. That evening was uncalled for," Father Jaeger agreed.

"I'd like to then ask, Father, do you feel that you can overcome this frailty? That if you spend a time, a length of time with Mr. Bloomberg, you could end this once and for all? Please tell us."

"Yes, I would like to comment," Father Jaeger responded, very forthright and positive. "I do admit to some sins. I also know that this problem is one that—with your guidance, support, and prayer—I can beat." He went on to say, "I love being a priest. I love working for the honor and glory of Our Lord and Savior Jesus Christ. Now, I am not without sin. I ask for His forgiveness. I do want to continue being a priest. I would like to do whatever it takes to gain your complete confidence. Fathers and Dr. Bloomberg"—using his thumb and right forefinger, Father Jaeger most reverently clasped his collar—"I do want with all my heart to continue to wear this most sacred collar. It is my life. My life's work."

Father Kessler looked at Father Schmidt as if to gain his support. Dr. Bloomberg looked at everyone in the room. Father Holtz looked only at Father Jaeger.

"Before I make a suggestion that we recess, are there any more questions?"

Dr. Bloomberg spoke up first. "I have questions, but it would be more informative and helpful to discuss them one-on-one with Father Jaeger during our sessions."

"I don't have any other questions," Father Kessler added.

Father Holtz did not respond either way. He knew he needed to keep a distance from being too critical of the bishop's tribunal.

"Well with that, I suggest we take a break. We will meet back in session in about thirty minutes. Father Jaeger, thank you for coming for this meeting. We will be making a formal written response. You'll receive it by next Wednesday. I'd like for you to continue to realize the seriousness of this matter. Then with God's help, I hope we can work together with you to resolve this issue for the good of our church and all the needy souls who look to us for help. May God bless you, and may you have a safe journey home."

CHAPTER 51

DEALING WITH FATHER JAEGER

Father Warren—May 19, 1958

FORTUNATELY, the end of the school year was fast approaching. It was a week until Memorial Day. Father Warren had decided it would be important to pull together some parish leaders and two of the sisters for the purpose of discussing the Father Jaeger situation. The meeting was scheduled for Monday evening in the rectory conference room.

Father Warren invited Walter Welsh from the Knights of Columbus and Ralph and Grace Smith, Tim Brennan, and Randall Zilbar from the parish. Sister Mary Michael and Principal Sister Christopher would represent the school. Father Warren and Father Sullivan would conduct the meeting.

After everyone arrived, Father Sullivan asked them to be seated. He began with a prayer to St. Michael. Sister Agatha had prepared iced tea and homemade sugar cookies, which were presented on an antique side server against the interior side of the meeting room.

"Thank you, everyone, for coming this evening," Father Sullivan said after the prayer. "During the course of the evening, I will ask for your input and questions about the challenge that has arisen in our parish. I refer to the unfortunate situation with Father Jaeger. Father Warren, would you like to begin? Please keep in mind we seek your advice in confidence."

"Yes, Father Sullivan. Thank you. Let me begin by saying that I am saddened about what has happened in our parish. As you all heard in the letter I read Sunday, Father Jaeger will no longer be an assistant at St.

Thomas Moore. I ask each and every one of you to keep everything that is discussed this evening *confidential*. We will be discussing some private matters. The subject is tough. I hope it is isolated within this one parish. You are all important to me. You are leaders in our parish. I need you. I will begin by rereading Sunday's letter: *My dear friends in Christ … "*

All eyes were glued on Father Warren as he read. He spoke in a monotone voice.

" *… may God give him eternal guidance.*" After setting the letter down, Father Warren folded his hands and rested them on the table. "Tonight, I will go beyond the letter. I remind you of confidence." Father Warren cleared his throat. After taking a deep breath, he began, "For the past two years, from everything we have learned, Father Jaeger has been molesting and sexually abusing boys in this school. Hard to believe, I know." Father Warren paused and cleared his throat again. "We know of six, maybe seven situations."

"How could this happen?" Tim Brennan asked. "Where did this happen? Father, wasn't someone watching for this?"

"How could we monitor for something we didn't know existed?" Father Warren asked. There were no replies. "We did not know any of this until the boys came forward. Initially we found out when a young boy came forward to Father Sullivan. Now, I do not plan on going into many details. The idea, the act itself, raises questions, which bring many more. Presently, the matter is In the hands of the bishop."

Randall Zilbar said, "Father, if this gets out of control, it could become public and damage the reputation of our parish. It could affect financial contributions. This needs to be kept quiet. Shut down. We don't want authorities delving into a parish matter. Some of our wealthiest contributors would shy away from the parish if they thought their personal reputations could be affected."

Father Warren cut Zilbar off before he went too far. "Financial matters and wealthy donors are the least of our concerns."

"I agree wholeheartedly," Father Sullivan chimed in. "Finances have no place in this discussion."

The Brennans, Smiths, and the sisters said nothing, but the expressions on their faces reflected their disapproval of Zilbar's arrogant and repugnant remark. *Investment advisor, finance man, how insensitive, Ralph*

Smith thought. The rest of those in attendance could see through the self-serving Randall Zilbar.

Though he loathed the flagrant, callous remark of Randall Zilbar, Father Sullivan continued, "We have assessed that we have two primary focuses. First and foremost, what about the victims? We will be there for them," he clarified.

"Yes," Father Warren added. "I have asked Father Sullivan and Sister Mary Michael to address any situations that arise regarding any of the boys. They will meet with each and every one. Now, I believe we all know the basis of this unfortunate situation. My main purpose for meeting is to ask for your advice. I respect and trust all of you, so please speak up regarding our options."

Ralph Smith wasted no time. "Father, may I comment?"

"Yes, of course," Father Warren replied.

"As I see this, if roles were switched, we might see this differently. For a moment, let's set aside the fact that Father Jaeger is a priest. If he committed these acts, then they are no different than rape of one of the girls in our parish. If that happened, the police would be all over this. Jaeger would be jailed for statutory rape. This is no different. This man has raped and sodomized, and we have sent him to the bishop?"

Ralph was in total control of all that he was expressing. His passion was contagious to some. He knew Father Sullivan agreed. "And to what? Counseling and then transfer to another parish? I understand your dilemma, Father Warren, but if he gets away with this, he'll do it again. Then another priest is accused, and the bishop handles it the same way. Before we know it, the pattern is in cement. Then the cancer continues. I say to each one of you, just wait until the parents of one of the abused steps forward in the courts, or worse yet, if a parent comes forth and confronts Father Jaeger directly, even physically."

What he says could be true, Sister Mary Michael thought.

"It might sound far-fetched, but they could sue. Who would they sue? The priest? Yes, and at the same time they'd sue the employer, the church—this very parish! Just imagine this parish being sued for tens of thousands of dollars. The attorney fees alone would cripple us financially. We must address this now with the proper authorities."

Even Father Warren could understand Ralph Smith's reasoning, which Sister Mary Michael also supported.

"No, no, you're wrong," Randall Zilbar spoke up as he pushed off any rebuff of his earlier remarks. "I concur with Father Warren. We don't need the police involved. We must wait for the bishop's decision."

Randall Zilbar was very cognizant of Father Jaeger's connection with Masses at the reform school and, even closer, his friendship with Phillip Krueger as scoutmaster. *Too close*, he thought. Randall Zilbar's thoughts or concerns did not lie with the abused, with the victims; he just didn't want anyone making a connection to Phillip Krueger.

Ralph Smith spoke up, "Father, what about Father Jaeger? What's going to happen to him? Are we going to finally report him to the police?"

Father Warren had known the question was coming. He had to hit it straight on. "I answer to Bishop Powers directly. He's handling this directly within the diocese. Ralph, everyone in this room … I can't over-rule Bishop Powers. He is the supreme authority within our diocese. I just can't. I might handle this differently, but that is not my decision. This is the way our parish will respond—according to the decision and direction of Bishop Powers."

Tim Brennan asked, "Who does Bishop Powers answer to? Of course, Cardinal Cullings." The room was quiet. "Then by gosh, the cardinal answers to the pope himself. That's where the ultimate power lies. If this problem is beyond our parish, beyond our diocese, then the pope should be involved. He is the shepherd." Tim's emotions were taking hold.

"We understand, Tim, but there is a chain of command within the Catholic Church," Father Warren said.

"These boys don't understand the chain of command. They just know pain, guilt, hurt, and terror. Yes, terror," Father Sullivan interjected.

The room grew quieter. A few moments passed. Father Warren sat back in his chair. He knew he had made his point. Based on previous discussions, he had known there would be differences of opinion. Father Sullivan had thought they might even grow further apart. Father Sullivan knew Tim Brennan would continue undying support of the victims and what needed to be done. Only Randall Zilbar was ambiguous.

Father Sullivan had never quite trusted Zilbar. Although Zilbar was wealthy and successful, Father Sullivan could not feel sincerity or depth in the man. He knew Zilbar would always do best for himself before he considered others. He thought Zilbar was a man without soul. He clapped to himself after hearing Tim Brennan's impassioned remarks.

Father Sullivan asked Father Warren if he could comment again and went on to say,

"Lastly, I am assuming it may be a while before another priest is assigned to our parish. There is one thing I do know: for the first time since just before the war, we are seeing a downward trend in the enrollment in our seminaries across the country. We need our young people's vocations. If there was to be a decline in the number of new priests—and I might say the same is true about our good sisters—then this would be very concerning to me. So we must act now in order not to add a mortal wound to our church."

Father Warren closed the meeting by saying, "Thank you all for being here this evening. We have much to do for the good of our parish, our church, and these boys. There is lots to pray about. Thank you all."

After everyone left, Father Sullivan asked Father Warren, "Why did you have the meeting? Why involve these parishioners?"

Father Warren folded his hands. "In case this situation becomes more public and our parishioners are made more aware as this hits the papers. I want the people here tonight to know they were informed before the public."

Father Sullivan responded, "With all due respect, Father, you mean this was more of a defensive measure for you and me, especially you?"

Father Warren looked Father Sullivan directly in the eye. "Yes, Michael, it is. That is exactly why we met. I think this situation is going to become more public."

Father Sullivan did not respond. He appreciated Father Warren's candor and directness.

Those involved that evening were not prepared for what was to follow.

CHAPTER 52

BELOVED PASTOR

Father Sullivan—May 24, 1958

SINCE he had first become aware of the abuse by Father Jaeger, Father Sullivan's first concern had always been the boys. As each day passed, he saw the attention and focus on Father Jaeger, his problems, and how it was going to affect the church. Father Sullivan had mixed feelings about the intentions and decisions of his beloved pastor, Father Warren. In moments of confusion, Father Sullivan even experienced doubt about Father Warren's concern.

Father Sullivan knew Father Warren was mindful about the boys and how they had been victimized. *Father Warren is concerned about the boys. That's why he took me to South Wayne. I know that.* Most disappointing, Father Sullivan felt absolute shame in the way the diocese, specifically Father Schmidt in the name of Bishop Powers, was addressing the situation.

Father Sullivan agreed with Ralph Smith; the authorities should be involved. Then there was Randall Zilbar. He could not place his finger on it, but he did not trust Zilbar. The successful businessman that Zilbar was, Father Sullivan simply had a sixth sense about the man. Oh, he could see the trust Father Warren had for him. Money? Yes. Power? Yes. Zilbar could pull strings if needed—politicians, city hall, businesses, even connections in Indianapolis and Chicago. Father Warren, as pastor, easily needed the help of both qualities of Randall Zilbar. *It's what doesn't meet the eye about Zilbar that troubles me,* Father Sullivan thought. *Never turn a blind eye to that man.*

Father Sullivan knew Sister Mary Michael would be there for him. The boys would always be first for her. Then, lying heavy on his heart, there was Linda Singleton. Her cross was double. He wondered how he could address either one. He realized that the six boys he knew to be abused would all have hidden issues to deal with as a result of these most unnatural of realities. Father Sullivan's commitment would always be to the boys first. On Monday, he felt a visit to Sister Mary Michael should be the priority of his agenda.

Sister Mary Michael—May 26, 1958

That afternoon, Father Sullivan approached Sister Mary Michael. She personified all that was good about a nun. She was kind, caring, and devoted to the children, parents, priests, and her fellow sisters. Most of all, she was devoted to her Lord and God. Her continuous smile was welcoming to everyone with whom she came into contact.

"There you are … always correcting papers," Father Sullivan said as he gently knocked on her classroom door at 3:20 p.m. and peeked his head inside.

The sister's classroom was a warm, pleasant learning atmosphere. Six rows of stationery wood desks lined the length of the room, and colorful art hung on the walls. Colored chalk letters, numbers, and images covered the blackboard. The students sometimes called her Sister Palmer for her steadfast insistence on good penmanship.

"Oh, Father Sullivan, so good to see you. Come on in. You are a welcome sight after a long day." Setting her red pencil down, Sister Mary Michael walked around her desk and took a place in the front desk. She watched as the handsome priest, dressed in his long black cassock, walked up the aisle. Father Sullivan squeezed into the desk in the next row.

"Glad you don't teach second grade, or we wouldn't have a place to sit," he joked.

As she held the side beads of her ever-present rosary, they talked.

"What have been your thoughts, Sister?" he asked.

Moving the beads, she looked down at her gentle hands. Father Sullivan noticed the gold band on her finger—a reminder of her marriage to Jesus.

"Father, I think a lot about these boys. Like you, I am deeply affected by this horrific abuse. Do you have time? Time for a story? I believe it would be most appropriate."

"Sure, I do. Should we go someplace else to talk?"

"This is fine. Everyone's gone. As long as you're comfortable in that desk." Sister Mary Michael smiled. "Back in 1921, when I was ... " she began hesitantly. "Let me see, I twelve years old, would you believe? We lived down state in Salisbury, Indiana, a little town of fifteen hundred just south of Terre Haute. We were a good family, a good Catholic family. Eleven children. I was the fifth. Six boys, five girls."

"Real good Catholic family. Irish, of course?" Father Sullivan asked.

"Sure and proud of it there, Father Sullivan." She raised her eyebrows as if to ask how many in his Irish family.

"Just three."

"I'm sure they were all good like you."

"Any other vocations? Brothers or sisters?" he asked.

"Oh yes," she said proudly. "My second oldest brother, Lawrence, became a priest. I think that was the happiest day of my parents' lives. Then my sister, Elenore, a year older than me, joined the convent."

"One priest, two sisters. Pretty good ratio," Father Sullivan noted with a smile.

"Yes, it was. Unfortunately, all was not good and happy. My third brother, Arthur, was six years ahead of me. He too wanted to join the clergy. Of course, my folks were so supportive. Let's see. Arthur was thirteen at the time. He was a good kid, although a little different, not like my other brothers, who were more outgoing, athletic—ruffians sometimes. But Arthur was so kind and loving. A real gentle soul. From the time he was about ten to thirteen, he always seemed troubled, Mom said, though he'd never talk about it. Never. Dad couldn't understand. Mom tried. Oh, she tried.

"We belonged to St. Phillip's. We had this one little Catholic parish in our small town. Lots of farm families though. Came from far and wide. Well anyway, we had such a wonderful pastor, a kind, sweet man. Didn't have an assistant in those days. Just too small. Anyway, everyone loved the elderly priest. I recall Father O'Malley coming over to the house for Sunday dinner. Mom invited him quite often. She would always prepare his favorite—fried chicken. Of course, Mom's pan-fried chicken was always our favorite. This man was a saint. As I said, he was older. I remember him as if he was sitting here today, right here with you and me."

Father Sullivan noticed Sister Mary Michael move the beads a little faster. *Where is this story going?* he wondered.

"Okay, I digress. It was 1921. A flu goes through the parish. The good Father O'Malley was not spared. He caught the virus, so I was told. His fever was high, very high. Then about three days later, the housekeeper found him in his room. He had passed away during the night. All alone. Everyone knew, or should I say assumed, it was the fever. Yes, our parish was devastated. We had lost our beloved pastor. I was only twelve, but I can remember that funeral. I think the tears in that church could have flooded Main Street. He had touched the lives of so many." Sister Mary Michael stopped.

Father Sullivan could see tears in her eyes. "He must have been such a blessed man," he said, giving her more time. "An elder pastor is the heart and soul of every parish."

"He was a father. He truly was. Kind, giving. He loved everyone. Everyone loved Father O'Malley."

"You okay, Sister?" Father Sullivan asked, placing his hand on top of hers. He could feel the rosary.

"Yes, yes. Should I continue?"

"Sure. I'm listening to every word."

"I might add, Father, that Father Warren does remind me sometimes of Father O'Malley. White hair, kind manner, and fatherly figure. Although you know, Father, nothing replaces the good memories of our innocent youth."

Father Sullivan half chuckled, shaking his head. "You are so right, Sister." He then nodded and said, "Please, go ahead."

"After the funeral, we were without a priest. I think it was two months or so till we received a new one. Of course, we all knew Father O'Malley could never be replaced. Father, I don't know if I should be telling you this story. I've only shared this with my older sister. She's such a good person. Sister Emma John. She took both my mother's and father's names. Father Sullivan, this is a long story, but I think you'll understand. I keep thinking of Gene Kowolski. Gene and those other boys. Father, I don't know if you can truly understand the effects. Not only on the boys, but also on their families. Abuse can harm a family in so many ways. Both directly and indirectly."

"Sister, I'm trying to understand, but you mentioned Gene Kowolski. The connection. I'm confused."

Sister Mary Michael took a breath and continued. "Three days after Father O'Malley's funeral, some ladies of the parish gathered in the rectory to care for and pack the father's personal items. He was from Boston. He really didn't have a family left. Just a couple of nieces, we were told. They couldn't even be found. Poor man. He was buried in the parish cemetery. Mom was one of the three ladies who volunteered to sort his personal items. While in his room, she was packing up his desk. Sitting in his chair, she noticed a stack of unmailed bills. I remember her telling me that it was like lightning from the sky. There was this unmailed letter that was addressed to Arthur Delaney. Delaney was our family name."

Father Sullivan could feel his pulse elevate. He watched as tears streamed down the sister's cheeks. She reached inside her habit and pulled out a white handkerchief. "Mom said she knew it was wrong, but she just slipped the letter into the pocket of her dress and kept on packing."

By this time, Father Sullivan knew he might not want to hear the end of the sister's story for what he concluded might be a tragic ending. He listened intently. "Well, what happened, Sister?"

"Father, it's so hard to talk about. But you see these priests, they don't seem to think of the consequences of their actions. Father, in the name of God, it's all so self-centered. Sad, so very, very sad. These good priests can become so self-indulgent."

"I still don't understand, Sister."

"That night, after everyone went to bed and all the lights were out, Mother sat in the front room by herself. The family all rose early, but she was always the last to bed. Elenore and I shared a bedroom with our younger sister Rose. Our room was at the top of the stairs. We were asleep, and then I heard, 'Martha, Martha, wake up.' That's my given name, Father. Elenore and I crept to the door and tiptoed to the stairs.

There was a dim light on in the lower hallway by the stairs. We could barely see Mother in the chair in the front room, but we could hear her crying quietly. More like a whimper.

"Together, we walked down the steps. Mother looked up. Elenore asked her if something was wrong. I'll never forget. Mother stood up and slowly walked over to the two of us as we stood at the bottom of the stairs. She put her loving arms around both of us. I can still remember her crying. I could feel the love in her arms around us. She hugged us both so tightly. The three of us didn't move. We just held our arms around each other.

"Then she said, 'Girls, we sometimes have sadness in life. For me, this is one of those times. It's private, and I'll be fine. You two go back up to bed. Don't wake Rose.' She kissed us both on our foreheads and said she loved us both very much. We were puzzled and concerned for her. Arriving back at our room, we looked at each other, both thinking the same thing: *Why? Why was she crying? So sad. What could it be?*"

Father Sullivan continued to listen intently.

"We never talked about that night again. Seventeen years passed. Then it was 1938. By then, Elenore and I were both in the convent. My older brothers and sisters were scattered throughout the state, most still around Salsbury except for Arthur. After the summer of 1921, let's see, I was twelve, plus six years, so he was eighteen. He did finish high school and then went off to Indianapolis. Never held a real job. He was in and out of halfway houses. We know there was alcohol. Never a woman. Of course, now we know."

The sister's face was flushed. "Just a minute. Can you wait here? I won't be long." She got up and left the room. She checked the clock— 3:59. Within a couple minutes, she returned with a letter in hand. She didn't say a word. She sat back in the small desk, her rosary at her side. She pulled the letter from the envelope. Father Sullivan noticed no post-mark, just a penny stamp. The letter had never been mailed.

"It was in 1921 that Mother read this letter that night by herself. Alone. The night Elenore and I came down the stairs." Sister Mary Michael handed the letter to Father Sullivan. He saw a forlorn look across her face. Pulling the letter from the envelope, he looked at her as if to ask, *What is this?* He then read it.

The Tarnished Collar

Dear Arthur:

*By the time you read this letter, it will all be over. The flu that is
affecting our parish provides the perfect timing. Please accept from me my apology.*

*I am so sorry. I will never ask for forgiveness. Considering the suffering I've put
you through, only God could forgive me.*

*You were so young when it started. Even then you were so handsome, so gentle
and kind. You became more so these past three years. The advantage I took of
you was so wrong, so sinful, so selfish. Even though you wanted to be left alone,
I continued.*

*You were scared, I know. I tried to convince you it was love. Now that I look
back, I know it was all focused on me.*

*From the time I left Ireland as a young priest, I tried to run away from
the secrets in my past life, my youth, the seminary. I thought in America I could
start over. Yes, I left many sins in my homeland.*

First Boston, then Pittsburgh, and now here at St. Phillip's.

*You have been wronged. I'm so sorry. I hope you do recover and find
happiness in this world. For me, now is the time to end it all. Once and for good.*

May God bless you,
Father O'Malley

Father Sullivan leaned back, speechless. He waited for Sister Mary
Michael to speak.

"Mother gave the letter to me. I assume for safekeeping. It seems she
couldn't contain the sorrow. For me, the letter answered so many questions about Arthur. For our dear Mother and Arthur, Elenore and I share
our secret to this day. My heart still breaks."

The sister looked at Father Sullivan. "Maybe sorrow is easier to bear
when the pain is shared with someone. We never told our daddy. Never.
He left us, a quiet man, back in '46, just after the war. Our younger

brother, Michael, gave of himself at Normandy. Dad never recovered. Mom passed away in 1954. I still think she too died of a broken heart, just like Daddy. After his death, she lived with Agnes, our oldest sister. Agnes never married. You see, Father … "

Now the sister's face was red, tears still flowing. Father Sullivan stood up, walked to the back of the room, and closed the classroom door. He returned. Sister Mary Michael had pulled out another handkerchief, along with her rosary. The letter was tucked back in the envelope, hidden away he was sure within the pockets of her black habit.

"You see, Father, Mother waited those seventeen years with purpose. Arthur died alone in an upstairs flat in Indianapolis in 1938. Our family could never figure all the reasons for his troubled life. It was like he was in and out of our lives. Sometimes at family gatherings. Other times, we wouldn't see him for more than a year. Sometime after the war, Jimmy Langley came to visit our family after he arrived home from Okinawa. He was Arthur's best friend. Arthur had made him promise to keep the secret about his, his … well, you know, Arthur and Father O'Malley. However, the war had such a profound effect on Jimmy. He saw so much suffering. He remembered all the suffering, shame, and guilt Arthur carried and how that priest had wronged him.

"Jimmy knew Arthur and I were close, so he simply told me all that he knew about my poor brother. He said Arthur couldn't live with the guilt. We never found out how he survived alone. We never really knew the exact details about his death. I did see the certificate … natural causes. Arthur was buried at home in our family plot. Ironically, Father O'Malley was but a few gravesites away. All such tragic deaths. I'm convinced to this day, Arthur's troubled life was all because of what happened to him as a boy. The gentle pastor was a good, beloved priest to his parish, but then I have to ask, what about to Arthur and how many others?" Sister Mary Michael shook her head, squeezing the beads tighter. *That wicked Father O'Malley.*

"Sister, there's something I don't understand. The letter made it sound like Father O'Malley didn't die from the flu."

"That's right. The man was a good priest but a weak, troubled man with demons, and he inflicted those demons on Arthur. I don't want to know if there were others." Sister Mary Michael paused and then looked at Father Sullivan. "You and I both know there were others. Maybe many. Maybe just a few. Father, he left his home country. Why? Then Boston, then Pittsburgh, and then my hometown. Always moving on. I once heard a parishioner say that Father O'Malley served in seven, maybe eight parishes. Now we can see he was moved on by others, bishops and the like."

"Are you saying Father O'Malley died of guilt for his sin?"

"Yes, I am, or maybe his life was so tormented that he … yes, I believe he ended it all because of the guilt."

Father Sullivan nodded but with a question.

Sister Mary Michael then said, "Remember in the letter, he said, 'For me, now is the time to end it all'? The flu was the perfect excuse. He could have even faked the fever," she explained. "The letter was sealed. Just never mailed. Mother said it was on the left side of the desk. She thought he wrote the letter and acted quickly. Maybe he assumed someone would find and mail it. Maybe he forgot. Who knows. Arthur never knew. Mom said she couldn't bring herself to give it to him. Elenore and I felt she should have given it to Arthur. Then I think she spent the rest of her life suffering from a horrible guilt after Arthur died. She took the secret to her grave, or so she thought she did."

"Again, how? Maybe it was the flu," Father Sullivan said.

The sister continued while patting her eyes with her handkerchief, "As I said, in the letter to Arthur, Father O'Malley wrote, 'Now is the time to end it all.' You see, just above the papers and the letter was an empty bottle of barbiturates. The lid was off. To the right was a pitcher of water. On the table were two empty glasses." Sister paused, "Father O'Malley did die of guilt along with the help of those pills. Then Mother knew. She just kept the secret inside for all those years. The mystery, of course, was buried with her. She never told us why she didn't give the letter to Arthur."

Sister Mary Michael looked at Father Sullivan. "I still live with this tragedy every day of my life. These sinful priests not only affect the lives of the victims, but they bring heartbreak and sorrow to the families. So often parents do not know the problem, but they see the horrific effects on the victims. It's life-altering. It was for me," she said despondently.

The sister took a breath and dabbed her eyes. "Father, I had to share this story. The reason? I think it shows us that we really don't know priests. No matter how kind, how good, they may have a dark closet. I keep asking how this good pastor, loved by so many, could damage and affect so many lives. Cover-up, betrayal. It's all so horrific. Their lives, just like Arthur's, affected forever. And my mother … "

Father Sullivan could tell the sister had said all she cared to. He stood, bent over, and held both her hands. "You are a good person, Sister Mary Michael. A very good person." He nodded, turned, and left the room.

Sister Mary Michael spent time alone that evening, first in St. Michael's chapel. Then later after supper, she knelt at the side of her bed for hours.

Later the same evening, Father Sullivan was haunted by Sister Mary Michael's story. He immediately thought back to his own brother and all the sorrow his father still harbored. After he left Sister Mary Michael's classroom, Father Sullivan felt internal rage toward Father Jaeger, who had committed so many deplorable deeds. *If only I could* … Father Sullivan stood and looked at the clock—2:12 a.m. Needing to resist temptation, Father Sullivan closed his eyes, prayed for the boys, the demon, and her. Soon he drifted on into the darkness.

PART IV

CITIZENS AND POWER

CHAPTER 53

DECISION TIME

Phillip Krueger—April 28, 1958

ELEVEN thirty AM. Phillip Krueger could hear the jangling of keys. He had anxiously paced in his cell all morning. *Today determines the rest of my life.*

"You have a visitor, Krueger," the guard announced. His drawn face was always absent of expression. "Now I want you to keep it quiet down here," he said with exaggerated self-imposed authority.

Unlike the other day, Gino Moretti wanted to pop the guard right on his protruding Adam's apple. Right above his buttoned collar would be perfect. Even though he was a fiery Italian, Moretti knew better.

He gave the guard a "yes, sir" and a military salute. The guard broke into a faint smile.

"Good morning, Mr. Moretti. Good to see you. Really good. This has been a long night. Didn't sleep," Krueger informed his attorney.

"We all have our needs," Gino said to Krueger.

The guard locked the cell door behind the attorney as Moretti reached for the chair. "Thanks again, officer. Good job," Moretti said with heightened sarcasm.

Krueger just sat at the bedside, elbows on his knees, wringing his hands.

"Here's the plan, Mr. Krueger. As I see it, pleading no contest will get you about ten years at Indiana State Prison," Moretti said, flipping the steel straight chair around and positioning the back between Krueger and himself. "Maybe eight if the judge had a good night before at his K of C's poker game. Not guilty and we go hard against your number-one obstacle, this Bernard Bednar guy. My plan would be I'd tear him up, rip him apart on the stand. If the prosecution brings up the clothes found outside, we'll have to risk it by showing that Bednar took them off you while you were delirious with pain from the fight. Now let me explain. I'll show the jury that it was you trying to save the boys from Bednar. Unfortunately, he overpowered you. Took your clothes and simply set you up as the perpetrator. His strangeness will itself inflict enough damage on the stand to create the doubt, overwhelmingly. Then they'll have no choice but to acquit."

"Really? That sounds to me just like it happened. Yes, Mr. Moretti, that's it. That's what happened. Bernard set up the whole thing and blamed me."

"Now, I know what you're thinking, Mr. Krueger," Moretti said in anticipation of his client's question. "The answer is no! You will not take the stand. You just sit there. Not a word. Not a grimace. No emotion. My job is one thing, and one thing only: doubt! Look those twelve jurors from across all parts of this county straight in their eyes, and they will be confused. They won't be able to figure how you, Phillip Krueger, committed the dastardly deed. All's won. You're free, and most of all, Zilbar will be happy. That's our plan. Just leave it to ol' Gino. Meanwhile, I'll go for bail today. Do you have five thousand in cash?"

"Let me see. I have two savings accounts. Sure, maybe six, seven thousand. I know it's a lot, but I've got a good job, and I save," Krueger assured him.

"Perfect. I'd say the judge will set a high bail, probably fifty thousand. With no record and your civic resumes, he'll allow bail. However, this judge takes no prisoners. I know it's going to be fifty or higher. You'll need 10 percent cash. Own your house?"

"Sure I do," Krueger said proudly. "Paid for too. No debt. I'm a responsible person," Krueger said, trying to create credibility with his attorney. *Now's the time. D-day.*

Gino Moretti looked straight into Krueger's eyes. "How are you going to plead?" he asked.

Without hesitation, Krueger responded, "Not guilty. I didn't do anything wrong—"

Moretti stopped him immediately. "No explanation. Just 'Not guilty, Your Honor.' That's it." Moretti stood and placed the straight chair back against the wall. "I'll see you before the judge at three thirty sharp. You'll be there fifteen minutes before. Guard! Guard!" The rattle of keys was almost immediate, as if he had been close enough to overhear the attorney-client discussion. "Yes, officer. Sorry to bother you. I know how busy you are. If it works for your schedule, would you please unlock this flea-bitten cell of yours, as I have a date."

"A date?" the guard asked, picking through the ring of keys.

"Yes, a date with a certain judge up on the second floor."

"Ah ha, you fooled me," the gaunt-faced guard said like he now got it.

"Naw, just funnin' with you, Chester."

Taking Moretti seriously, the guard looked at him and said, "Shut up."

"Well, well, aren't we a little touchy this morning? Not enough sleep, or did your old lady say no?"

The guard did not respond. He locked the cell door after Moretti walked out. Then he walked back, sat down on his chair, leaned back against the wall, and thought to himself, *Little wop lawyer*. He watched the well-dressed Moretti confidently walk down the hall.

For the first time in days, Krueger could see his newfound future at the end of the tunnel. He took every word of his attorney as fact. *Just think, I'm going to get out of here*. Soon the threat of the state pen would be a distant and needless bad memory.

Phillip Krueger thought it had been only a few minutes. Time had lapsed. He immediately looked at the black steel clock at the end of the cell hall: 1:22 p.m. *Soon*, he thought. The routine continued. The keys rattled as the guard approached the cell door.

"Time, Krueger. Now I want no problems from you," the guard said, obviously trying to impress the man following him. Right behind the guard stood Sheriff Thurow.

"This is it, Krueger. Don't want to miss your encounter with the judge. Judge Seiler's going to make you pay for your devious deeds. That'll be it, Roger. I'll gladly take him from here," the sheriff said to the guard, who was unwittingly dismissed from his duty.

Once in the courtroom, Sheriff Thurow reached for Krueger's arm. *His clasp feels even tighter than before*, Krueger thought. *God, I dread this. Prick sheriff showing off his authority.*

"Phillip Krueger, number PK-WBH-766!" the bailiff called out.

Krueger stood and followed Moretti up before Judge Seiler.

"Well, Mr. Moretti, I'm pleased to see you and your client here on time," the judge said, putting forth an unusual personal observation.

"Yes, Your Honor, always on time for you."

"Now don't try to placate me, counsel." Moretti didn't respond. "Let's see here. We discussed the charges, as noted on 3:30 p.m., April 25, 1958. So, now time for a plea. Have you reached your decision, Mr. Krueger?" the judge asked sternly, looking directly at the defendant.

"Yes, we have, Your Honor," Moretti said, immediately answering the judge.

"Well, Mr. Krueger, do you fully understand the charge against you … or does it need repeated? Mr. Showers, would you please read the charge against Mr. Krueger?" The judge nodded to his trusty bailiff.

Sheriff Thurow, sitting behind the prosecutor's table, looked on with focused anticipation.

"You are being charged with seven counts of lewd and lascivious behavior and three counts of sodomy against minors."

"Mr. Krueger, how do you plead?"

Phillip Krueger, overtaken by the moment and the decision that would keep him out of Indiana State Prison, did not respond. Gino Moretti looked at him and nudged his left elbow into Krueger's side.

"Ah, I plead … " He paused. "I plead not guilty."

"Now, you're sure of that?" the judge asked based on Krueger's hesitation.

"He's just a little nervous, Your Honor," Moretti added, raising his eyebrows a couple times to the judge.

"So I see."

"Yes, not guilty, Your Honor. Absolutely," Moretti said as if seconding the motion.

"Okay, okay, enough. We've established that. Do you have his plea, Miss Turner?" the judge asked the clerk.

She nodded.

"Your Honor, we'd now like to ask for bail based on Mr. Krueger's outstanding civic contributions and lack of any previous record."

"You can make the request, but no editorializing, counsel. In anticipation of the request, I am prepared to set bail at seventy-five thousand dollars."

Gino erupted inside without showing any exterior response. "May I have a word with my client, Your Honor?"

"Considering the gravity of the situation, yes, you may. Five minutes." The judge slammed the gavel.

"Back here. Step away," Moretti said, moving back to the defense table. "This is huge," the attorney informed Krueger. Then he thought to himself, knowing what Zilbar's response would be.

Krueger said, "You gotta do something. I just want out of here."

"Yes, yes, I can make it all happen. Let's go. The judge is waiting." They moved back to the defense table and faced the judge. "Your Honor, it will take one more day. We'll post tomorrow."

"That will work. One more night for Mr. Krueger till bail is posted in full. Trial will begin in sixty days." Judge Seiler looked down over his glasses. "Mr. Krueger, I'll see you in sixty days. In addition, you will report to this court at exactly 10:00 a.m. every Friday up until your trial date. You will remain, and you will not leave the city limits of Wabash through the term of your bail. Do you understand me, Mr. Krueger?"

"Yes, sir. Yes, sir, I do," Krueger said with a look of fear on his face.

"Furthermore, Mr. Krueger, if you fail to report on Friday, seven days from today, we will come and bring you into the county jail, and you will be incarcerated seven more days. Do you understand the seriousness of breaking your bail?"

"Yes, sir, I do."

"Break it a second time and you're here until your trial date. Now, Mr. Moretti, will you confirm to me that Mr. Krueger not only understands that he is to report to this court but also that he will appear? Do you understand me, counsel?"

Moretti responded with clarity to the judge, "Yes, Your Honor, I do understand, and I will make sure Mr. Krueger reports per your directions."

Judge Seiler pounded the gavel. "This hearing is closed."

The sheriff stepped forward. He gladly recuffed Krueger as a matter of procedure. "At least I've got you for one more day," the sheriff said begrudgingly to Krueger. "They're gonna fry you like chicken liver."

Moretti asked the sheriff if he could have a few moments with his client. The sheriff nodded and then stepped back and waited by the courtroom entrance. Moretti explained the bail procedure. Krueger agreed to sign the papers the next day, releasing his bank accounts. Anything, he told Moretti, just to get him back home.

Moretti whispered to Krueger before the sheriff led him away. "All according to plan. We'll post bail tomorrow, and then you'll sleep in your own bed at least for sixty days."

Krueger's face was a visual for mixed emotions. One more night in the hellhole cell along with the creepy guard and rotten food. Then freedom for sixty days. Of course, his main concern was post trial and its outcome. Krueger remembered the warnings about leaving Zilbar out of this whole circus. *Not a word. Not one word about Zilbar.*

"Sheriff, any chance you can hang loose of my arm? I'm not going any place."

"Quiet, Krueger. You're still in my custody."

That damn Bernard Bednar, Krueger thought as he was led back to his cell. *Damn him anyway. If it wasn't for him, I'd be*—Krueger's thoughts were interrupted by the sheriff's tight grasp and threatening words.

"I'm gonna make sure the judge throws the book at you. Snakes like you deserve the max." The sheriff pulled Krueger to a halt, leaned over, and threatened with a whisper, "Those guys in Terre Haute are going to do it to you. One after the other, you'll know what hell is all about."

All that night, Krueger shook with sweat, and fear dripping from every pore. The side of his face pressed against the cold concrete wall of his cell. Krueger's fear was only exceeded by the sheer terror at the thought of being alone and at the mercy of the animals waiting for him in prison. His dreams were filled with vultures and hyenas fighting over raw meat.

CHAPTER 54

NEW ASSIGNMENT

Father Jaeger—May 30, 1958

A week after his meeting in South Wayne, Father Jaeger walked into the house after a midafternoon walk. From the kitchen, he heard, "Hello, Jerry. There's a letter there on the desk for you. Do you have a friend at the diocese in South Wayne?" his mother asked in her natural inquisitive manner.

"Oh yes, I have a priest friend there," Father Jaeger said. *She wants to know everything.*

He took the letter and headed directly to his room. Then he stopped, slipped the letter into his trouser pocket, and stepped back to the kitchen. "I think I'll be upstairs for a while. I need a little time. Maybe to catch up on some reading. Oh, what's for supper? Smells good," he asked, wanting her to know he was not thinking about the letter.

"Meatloaf and mashed potatoes. One of your favorites. Baked a cherry pie also."

"Sounds great. Call me when it's ready." He turned away before she could start to inquire about the letter. Upstairs, he sat in his old brown upholstered chair next to the only window in his room.

Dear Father Jaeger:

After due consideration, it has been decided that you will begin a weekly series of psychological testing and counseling under the direction of Dr. Samuel Bloomberg. The term will be for thirty days and will begin on July 1, 1958.

An apartment will be provided for that period of time. The location is two blocks from St. Leonard's. Once your sessions have been completed, and anticipating satisfactory results as determined by Dr. Bloomberg, you will be assigned to report to St. Vincent in Eastville, Indiana, just west of Terre Haute. A small parish, St. Vincent will have an opening for an assistant as of August 1, 1958.

We look forward to your return to the ministry.

Sincerely,
Father Leonard Schmidt

Jerome Jaeger felt a surge of relief. He could begin anew. Therapy would satisfy and cover the bishop. The small parish in Illinois would give him a feeling of the resolve of a fresh start. Now he just had to get through the next two months.

The time he spent at home with his parents always presented Father Jaeger with challenges. His father just could not understand or accept his son's time away from his parish or the responsibilities of being a priest. He continually reminded Jerome that priests said daily Mass. They heard confessions. They taught in school. His strong-willed father just couldn't accept a priest just hanging around the house. The casual short sleeved shirts, replacing the collar every day, did not add up to the father of the priest.

Continuously, his mother—although well-intentioned—tried to pry and needle into everything he was doing. All along, the environment created a forced state of abstinence that tormented his mind, body, and heart. Even to himself, Jerome Jaeger tried to understand the reality of his passion, lust, and desires. He thought of the boys who had been in his life the past couple of years at St. Thomas Moore. Father Jaeger would even pray and ask if the love was real or just a self-induced camouflage he used to justify his physical acts. When in a relaxed state of mind, he realized that his thoughts, desires, and urges were wrong.

Dear Lord, I know I have committed deeds against others that are immoral, unnatural, and sinful. Please understand that I have no desire now and have never had desire for sex or physical contact with women or girls. I never have had a choice. My choice was to serve You by becoming a priest. For that, I will always be grateful to you, for my vocation, Dear Lord. I do ask for Your forgiveness. I do ask for Your help to overcome my plight. Indeed, I do want to be a good priest … and even more, a good person.

Father Jaeger's prayers were also a torment in his mind. He believed in the truth of his intentions. However, when alone in the darkness of the night, the struggle within his mind and body overwhelmed his good intentions. The desire and urge for closeness, intimacy, and gratification totally overwhelmed his rational being. He could think of only one thing; the inducement was like a drug, and his only desire was a fix. Unfortunately, in his innermost mind, Jerome Jaeger knew he could not outlast the next month. His good intentions were paralyzed with the conflicts within his physical being. *Somehow I have to make this all work.*

The end of June arrived but not too soon. Not that he did not want to spend more time with his parents. *God love them.* Father Jaeger did find comfort in their home. On the other hand, he might not have recognized his procrastination to the upcoming therapy sessions. He explained to his parents that he was going to be in South Wayne for a summer course regarding continuing renewal of vocations. He explained to them that it was like a retreat. They were pleased to hear about his new assignment at St. Vincent's to the south in Eastville. He was happy. No one would know him there. His future would begin again.

Father Jaeger - June 30, 1958

The end of June did not come too soon. After packing his few personal belongings, Father Jaeger bid a fond farewell to his parents. They both shared their appreciation for his visit and wished him well during the retreat. His mother reminded him that retreats were good for the soul. His dad told him to do good work at St. Vincent's and not to take too many days off.

"You're a priest, you know. Have to be there for everyone."

Father Jaeger gave them both an obligatory hug, threw his suitcase in the trunk, and drove away to South Wayne. His mom shed tears when she saw him waving out the window as he drove away. *Whatever will happen to my boy? May he find peace, Dear Lord.*

Upon arriving in South Wayne, Father Jaeger first stopped at the rectory. It was late in the afternoon that Monday. The weather was warm and sunny. A good day to begin a new life. Another chance. Father Jaeger rang the doorbell of the rectory. He was greeted by Father Holtz.

"Good afternoon, Father Jaeger," Father Holtz said.

"Same to you, Father. I'm reporting for duty," Father Jaeger joked. Immediately he knew he had misspoken, considering Father Holtz's serious demeanor.

Father Holtz explained that the bishop and Father Schmidt were both away that afternoon. He asked Father Jaeger to drive over to the apartment and park in the private parking area in the rear. One of the four spots belonged to him for the month he was to stay there. Father Holtz gave directions for the two-block trip.

"You can't miss it. The house is old cream city brick. We own it. There are four apartments. You'll be in the front second floor. Here's the key. Use the back door. You can drive over now and begin unloading. You'll be in number 4. I'll be over in about an hour to explain the agenda for next month. See you there," Father Holtz said, delivering all instructions as if talking to a stranger he did not want as a tenant.

Father Jaeger said, "Thank you," and left not feeling overly welcome. He found his home for the next month on the second floor of the turn-of-the-century brick home just a few blocks from the cathedral. It took only a short while to carry in his personal items. Just as he finished carrying in the last load, there was a knock at the door.

"Everything unloaded?" Father Holtz asked as he knocked and walked through the open door just off the front hall.

"Oh yes, I live pretty simply. Don't have much beyond clothes, books, and … well, not much really. Little warm, though, trudging those stairs."

"You'll be okay. The ceilings are high, and you have cross ventilation with those windows. Oh yes, there's a GE fan in the back closet off the kitchen. Otherwise, you can burn off energy using that hand fan there on the couch," Father Holtz said, watching Father Jaeger's expression to see if he caught the intended sarcasm.

He continued, "Hopefully, this month will offer you time to reflect. The bishop would like for you to say Mass daily. You'll be able to have complete exposure to the side chapel. You can make out your schedule weekly, alternating weeks between the seven and eight o'clock Masses. We have a seven and nine o'clock daily Mass in the main church. Of most importance, you'll be meeting twice a week with Dr. Bloomberg. I have arranged for Tuesdays and Thursdays. Should total eight sessions, 1:30 p.m. each day. Here's the address of his office. It's close enough that you can actually walk. Every Thursday at four o'clock, you'll meet with Father Schmidt and me. We'll have time to discuss your progress. Father Schmidt predicts it will take a month for your rehabilitation. From what I know about your past, you'll have a busy month. By month's end, you should be ready for your new assignment. A chance to start over. This all seem clear, Father?"

Father Jaeger said, "Yes, absolutely. I plan on doing well. Thanks also for this apartment. Really feels comfortable. I think I'll like it here."

"As I said, by month's end you should be ready for your new assignment at St. Vincent's in Eastville. Father Schmidt is friends with the pastor. He feels this small parish and school will be just the right environment for you. There should be a lot less stress than what you experienced at St. Thomas Moore. Here's the rectory's number. Call me with any questions." Father Holtz turned to leave. "Oh yes, don't forget our meeting Thursday. Father Schmidt will want to discuss a few more things with you."

"Sure. Thank you, Father Holtz. I look forward to meeting with both of you."

Father Holtz looked directly at Father Jaeger. "I feel badly for you, Father. Not only for your digressions, but the infliction, the harm you have done to those boys and their families. As a priest, I am here to help, and hopefully, forgive as our Lord forgives."

"Thank you, Father Holtz. That means a lot."

Father Holtz stepped forward, almost in the face of Father Jaeger. "However, as a parent, If one of those boys were my son, and I knew of your transfers, your continuing abuse of these poor boys, this thirty day slap on your wrist, then I would not turn my cheek. I would have no mercy on you."

Startled, Father Jaeger stepped back, jolted by the words, almost a threat from the younger priest. Neither of the priests said another word. Father Holtz made a quick sign of the cross and turned, leaving Father Jaeger speechless. *Forgive me, Dear Lord, but as a man I simply spoke my convictions.* Father Holtz walked away, thinking to himself, *Who do Father Schmidt and the bishop think they are kidding? Rehabilitation in a month and then back to work with new kids? What's this church thinking?*

The two front windows of the apartment opened to Market Street. There was a strong lock and wood box manufacturing company across the street. A large black-and-gold sign faced the street—*Kobel Locks and Box Company.* Farther down, three blocks beyond the cathedral, closer to downtown, the sign for the YMCA was highly visible. He noticed a diner on the corner two blocks from the cathedral. Father Holtz had informed him of the twenty-four hour diner as a place for good food and cheap prices. *What was that name now?* he asked himself. *Hmmm, Blue Plate … Blue Plate Diner.* Knowing he would have Mass tomorrow at 8:00 a.m. per Father Holtz's instruction, he figured a blue plate special for this evening would really hit the spot.

Father Jaeger enjoyed the short walk to the diner. Once he arrived, the YMCA sign was much more noticeable. *Maybe I'll check the Y out after supper*, the priest thought. *It's been a while.*

CHAPTER 55

KRUEGER EXPOSED

Randall Zilbar—April 28, 1958

ONCE back in the office, Gino Moretti immediately called Randall Zilbar. Unfortunately, Zilbar was busy in a meeting.

"Mr. Zilbar told me for you to be patient. He'll call within the hour," his secretary instructed Moretti.

"Fine. Just fine. I've plenty of paperwork. I'll wait. Thank you, ma'am."

One hour passed … then two. At about 4:35 p.m., just before Gino's happy hour meeting, the phone rang. He heard Rosemary answer and then a pause.

"Mr. Zilbar is on the line for you, sir."

Great. About time, arrogant prick, Moretti thought.

"Gino, Randall here."

"Hello, Mr. Zilbar." Before Zilbar could ask, Gino said, "Everything went well. I handled it. Never a mess up."

"Stop the bullshit, Gino. Describe what happened," Zilbar demanded.

"Plead not guilty. He'll be out tomorrow on bail. Unfortunately, it's for seventy-five thousand."

"Does he have it?"

"Oh, it's covered. He has 20 percent. Bondsman will handle the rest."

"Think Krueger will flee, skip town? I don't want him loose, shooting off his mouth. Don't want him coming back at me."

"No way. He's not the type. Too weak. I explained how I'm going to get him out of this. I have a plan. It comes down to one witness. One witness who I can handle. Don't you worry about a thing, Randall."

"Better not let me down," Randall Zilbar said convincingly. "Gotta go. You keep me posted. Want that bastard Krueger shut down. Just get it handled." Zilbar hung up the phone without another word. He thought to himself, *Great. Everything is going as planned. Moretti thinks he's the one handling Krueger.*

Phillip Krueger—April 29, 1958

Everything broke loose on Tuesday morning when the *Wabash Plain Dealer* hit the street. For a small town, the story was huge. *CIVIC LEADER ARRESTED IN ABUSE CASE.* The guard brought the paper to Krueger's cell. Thought it would be fun to slip it to him. He pushed the paper under Krueger's cell door, sliding it perfectly with the headlines face up so Krueger would read the words even before picking up the paper. "Here's yer paper, Krueger. Thought you might enjoy catching up on all the local news, you being so civic-minded."

Krueger, lying prone on the bed in his cell, heard the paper sliding on the rough concrete floor. He picked it up. The words *abuse case* jumped off the page. Flopping back onto his bunk, he tried to catch his breath before he read it. *How? How did I ever get into this situation? I meant no harm. Moretti will get me off. Never, never again will I expose myself to this.* The story read like a reoccurring *nightmare. Bastards, all I've done for this city.*

Later that morning, Gino Moretti returned with bail papers to sign. Phillip Krueger gave power of attorney to his trusted counsel. With that, Moretti was able to withdraw the funds from Krueger's savings for posting bond. Then he met with the bondsman. The seventy-five thousand was made available to Wabash County Circuit Court.

Precisely at 2:00 p.m., the jingle of the keys could be heard. This time, the sure-handed guard left the cell door open for Krueger to leave without the steel wristbands. As Krueger exited the door at the end of the hall to freedom, he calmly looked at the guard and said, "Thanks for your hospitality ... *you long-faced jerk!*"

He understood his responsibility for the posted bond, but he also knew he had the best lawyer, who would get him out of this legal conundrum.

That evening, Phillip Krueger spent the night in his own friendly confines. Little did he know, his ordeal had just begun.

That's my answer. I'll simply write a letter to Sheriff Thurow. No he hates me. Sizemore? Na, too weak. Somebody. Who? Like a bolt of lightning… *Of course, Detective Peterson. Know him for years.* Elated with his idea, Phillip Krueger concluded, a letter to Peterson and he would expose all the bad between Zilbar and Wolfe. *The perfect plan.*

CHAPTER 56

THE CONVERSATION

Joey Singleton—April 26, 1958

TIME for reflection passed slowly since Father Jaeger left for good. Heartbreak and sadness permeated Joey Singleton's every waking hour. His personal reaction to the priest's departure even gave Joey doubts about becoming a priest. He felt so let down by Father Jaeger. The hurt was personified by the absence of his friend and lover. Most of all, Joey could not understand why. Why, he wondered, hadn't Father Jaeger even seen him before he left? A simple explanation, a good-bye, and a "let's stay in contact" would have been the least the priest could have done. Joey wondered daily if he would ever hear from Father Jaeger again.

Joey sat with his mother for supper. For the first time, his appetite seemed to return somewhat. As he picked at his food, Linda could tell Joey wanted to talk. She waited.

"Mom, do you think Father Jaeger cared about me?"

Linda knew her true feelings but couldn't risk being too direct with Joey. Raising her eyebrows, she waited a moment and said, "I think Father Jaeger liked you very much. You are a good person. You are kind, and he saw that in you. Everyone likes you, Joey."

"Then why did he leave without telling me? I had to mean more to him than that."

"Joey, I'm sure Father Jaeger saw the reality he faced. For his own personal reasons, he couldn't stay here. Maybe he felt good-byes would be too difficult for both of you."

"Mom, kids at school were calling him queer. I know he wasn't like that. He loved us. Really, he did. He loved other boys. Just like he said how Jesus loved all his apostles."

Linda knew that there was something deeply wrong with the priest. His convincing Joey that it was all right to be with these boys, more than one, made her even more thankful he was gone, not only for Joey's sake but for everyone's. *He's really a bad priest and a bad man*, Linda thought.

She decided to be more direct. "Joey, what he was doing with all the boys was wrong. Actually, it was sinful, immoral. Joey, look at me … It was unlawful. He could go to jail if caught. Yes, he may have cared for you more than the others, but that didn't make it right."

Joey did not respond. He didn't look defensive. Linda could only think about his hurt and confusion.

"Think about this, Joey. A man loving a woman is for marriage. Physical acts are a part of that love. Do you think it would be right for a man to physically love more than one woman? From one perspective, he may have liked and loved you. However, Joey—it may hurt to hear this—but he could have been using you."

Joey frowned as he tried to figure this out. "But it's so hard, Mom. How could he leave without a good-bye? Seems so wrong. Father Jaeger told me so many times how nice I was. He told me how he wanted to show his love." Joey put his head down on his folded arms. "No, no, I just can't go on."

Linda's heart hurt almost as much as Joey's. "Joey, please listen to me. I know you feel pain, loss. There will be more times in your life when you won't understand. You might be hurt again. Joey, you might even hurt someone, even though unintentionally. Now I just want you to know I'll be here. I also say maybe you might talk to someone else."

"Like who, Mom? Nobody can replace Father Jaeger."

"What about Father Sullivan? He likes you, Joey. He is a good man," Linda suggested very cautiously. "Father Sullivan could be the right person. He knew Father Jaeger. Father Sullivan would listen to you. Just think. Think about talking to him."

Joey looked up and rubbed his eyes. Linda thought she might have said the right thing for the moment. Joey sniffed and looked at his mom. "Maybe. Not promising but maybe I could talk to Father Sullivan," he said with a tone of relief … maybe hope.

"You think about it. You don't have to decide now. Father Sullivan would be more than happy to listen to you. I know that. I know that for sure," Linda said in a reassuring manner.

Joey looked at his mom. She detected a faint smile. "Are you sure? How well do you know Father Sullivan?"

Linda didn't respond immediately. "Well, I've met with him a couple times. Let's just say I have a sixth sense that he is not only a good priest, but also a caring and kind man."

"Do you mean a kind man like a father you wanted me to have?"

How observant. "Yes. Yes, Joey, that's a good way to put it. The kind of father I wished you had.

"Maybe I will, Mom. Maybe I will." Joey stood up, leaned over, and kissed her on the forehead. Then he turned and walked away.

Please, God, nothing would make me happier right now than for Joey to be helped by this good man. Nothing at all. If only we…Linda stopped her thought. I just can't go there.

Joey thought long and hard about his mom's words and advice. Deep down he knew she was probably right about Father Jaeger, but it was still so difficult to forget about his friend. He thought about how Father Sullivan could help. Joey did think that maybe his mom was right and Father Jaeger would forget about him. Now Joey began to realize that all the boys were eleven and twelve years old. He thought, *Guess I am the oldest, at least that I'm aware of.*

A week after his conversation with his mother, Joey decided to talk with Father Sullivan. After the 8:00 Mass on Tuesday morning, Joey gathered his nerve and walked into the sacristy.

"Good morning, Father Sullivan."

"Hey, Joey. Good to see you. It's been a while."

"Yes, it has been, Father. Well, I'm here," Joey said, trying to break the ice. "Actually, Father, do you think you'd have some time to talk with me? There's something I want to ask you. My mom suggested I contact you."

"Your mom. How is she? What a fine lady," Father Sullivan expressed.

"She's doing okay. Really helping me with a few things. Thanks for asking. I'll tell her you asked."

"Tell her I send my best. Okay, you mentioned a visit," Father Sullivan said before responding about a meeting. "Oh yes, you asked about a meeting. When? The during the week or on a weekend?" the priest asked, giving Joey a choice.

"Whenever is best for you, Father."

"How about four o'clock this afternoon?" Father Sullivan suggested, not wanting to give Joey time to change his mind.

"Sure, Father. That would be great."

"Just come to my office. Ring the bell at the front door of the rectory." Reaching over and patting Joey on the shoulder, he said, "I look forward to our visit."

"See you then, Father." *That wasn't so bad. He really is a nice guy ... like Father Jaeger ... Maybe Father Sullivan can give me the right advice just on what to do.*

CHAPTER 57

TAKING CARE OF MATTERS

Randall Zilbar—April 29, 1958

LOOKING at himself in the mirror that Tuesday, Randall Zilbar knew this was the day. In spite of the way he used and treated people, the mirror reflected his perceived image. *I feel good. I have money, power, and control.* Aside from his family, Randall Zilbar's love in life started with his wealth and all he derived from it. Using people and taking advantage was just a part of the game. A means to an end. Empathy, understanding, and concern for others were not words in Randall Zilbar's vocabulary.

Aside from that, the mirror spoke to him about his good looks.

Mario, Lucco "the Wire," Gino Moretti, and Phil Krueger were all pawns in his life game of chess. Using and hurting others were always trumped by his arrogant and self-serving ambition.

At 7:00 p.m., Randall Zilbar dialed as planned.

"Hello, Wabash Inn. May I please help you?"

"Yes, please connect me with Guest Turner, Johnny Turner."

"One moment, please … " the front desk attendant said. "Now you can go ahead."

"Yeah?" Randall heard a gruff voice on the other end of the line.

"Mr. Turner, this is Randall Zilbar. You're expecting me?"

"Yeah, seven o'clock," Lucco responded.

"I'll stop by your room at nine when it's dark. What's your room number?"

"Room 122. Park out around the side. No need to go through the lobby. See you then." Lucco hung up on Zilbar before Zilbar had a chance to hang up first, which Zilbar did not appreciate. *Let it pass this time. He's doing me a favor. Plan's working,* he thought.

Zilbar waited in the office. Coat off, he loosened his tie and stylish suspenders. He was a tall, slim man. Despite his wealth and confidence, his facial features looked average. In his early fifties, his brownish black hair was always perfectly groomed. Every so often, he compared his looks to Clark Gable, which was totally in touch with his narcissistic personality.

Having plenty of family money, Randall Zilbar had reached out on his own. Wise investments gave him capital he had never dreamed of having. Zilbar even had his own private four-engine plane and personal pilot. The only one in Wabash. He often flew to Cicero or for meetings in Chicago. However, Indianapolis was far more frequent in his flight patterns. Occasionally he flew to New Orleans or Omaha. Sometimes he drove alone. Either way, his trips were frequent. Other times, he received a visitor from Cicero. That connection was always made at the reform school.

It was now 8:45 p.m. After tightening his tie, pulling up his suspenders, Zilbar slipped on his suit coat. He walked over to his desk and reached down opening the bottom drawer. Zilbar picked up a large envelope, thick with its content and tucked it securely inside his breast jacket pocket. *All's ready.* Randall Zilbar left the office. *Time for the connection.*

Randall always felt special driving his brand new 1958 black Cadillac with fins, chrome, and full white sidewall tires. He looked at the chrome-covered car as the final touch of class. In a few more years after the big deal, he planned on buying a brand new Rolls Royce from the dealer in Carmel, Indiana. He was very much noticed being the only one in town owning a brand new Caddy. It was important to be recognized, but not this evening. He did not want anyone to see him.

Heading south out of town, Zilbar drove over the Wabash Street Bridge. He soon approached the Wabash Inn on the edge of town. The two-story motel was new and modern. The pool made it even more luxurious. Randall pulled in on the far side of the lot, hopefully unnoticed. Following the numbers on the door, he tracked 118–120 and then 122, second from the end. As it was a weeknight, there were few cars in the lot. After driving by 122, Randall parked in the back. He noticed a black 1956 Buick with Illinois plates parked along the back fence. He parked his car at the end of the south wing, totally out of sight and hidden in the darkness.

Zilbar sat for a moment, then tapped his breast pocket. *Cash talks, time to go.*

Zilbar approached room 122. He knocked on the door and waited. From inside he heard a voice say, "Name?"

Randall replied, "Mario sent me."

The door opened. Randall saw nobody. "Step out before I enter," he commanded.

A large man of about 360-390 pounds with suspenders over a white T-shirt appeared from behind the half-open door and stared at him. In his right hand, he held a gun pointed at the ceiling. "Makin' sure," Lucco grunted in a low voice. "What can I do for ya?"

"Exactly what Mario told you. As I say ... " Zilbar said, establishing his authority in spite of the force in front of him. "I'll sit. Let's talk."

"Sure, have a chair. I'm Lucco, Lucco Gagliardi."

"Pleased to meet you, Lucco," Randall said with a nod.

Lucco sat on the side of the bed. Randall sat in the brown fabric chair in front of the closed drapes. He looked directly at Lucco, even wondering if the bed would hold the bulk of the man. Lucco's neck draped over onto his shoulders.

"Whatcha got?"

Randall reached into his suit coat pocket and pulled out a piece of paper the size of a business card. It was blank on both sides. He wrote down an address—1722 Pike Street—and handed it to Lucco.

"One man, Phillip Krueger, lives alone. He's on bail. He's to never return to jail. Tomorrow morning, drive by so you are familiar with the exact location, maybe around nine o'clock. Then in the evening, late after midnight, show up. Enter through the back door. It's hidden inside a small back porch. No harm, no shot, no noise. Want no blood, no scuffle. Leave everything as you found it. On the way back to Cicero, do what you have · to do. Back at Cicero, dispose of the body the way in which Mario is accustomed. Whatever Mario says. Most importantly, no gun, no knife, no blood. Mario's told me they call you Lucco 'the Wire' Gagliardi for a reason."

"The Wire, that's right. That's all I ever use. Quiet, clean, and fast."

"Painful?" Zilbar asked.

"Wouldn't know. I never feel a thing," Lucco responded. "Wouldn't recommend it if you happen to like to breathe air."

Zilbar nodded. "Tomorrow after midnight. Not a sound." Zilbar stood and walked to the door. "Oh yes." He reached into his jacket pocket and pulled out the thick envelope. "Almost forgot. A reason to meet." Zilbar threw the envelope on the bed. "Take your half and give the rest to Mario." He nodded and walked back to the door. "See you, Lucco." Zilbar looked at Lucco's hands. They were the size of a catchers' mitt. *I wouldn't want those pulling around my neck*, he thought as he closed the door. Randall Zilbar, his mission accomplished, walked to his car and disappeared into the darkness.

Driving back into town, Randall Zilbar felt in total control. He was confident Krueger would be handled systematically, clean and professional. All would be quiet at the school. Randall imagined the huge man—dark suit, black hat pulled low over his brow, leather shoes—slowly stepping up the walk to Krueger's porch. Once Lucco entered Krueger's house, Zilbar could only imagine the sheer fright that would overtake Krueger. He felt impressed with his power to control and make this happen yet keep his hands clean. As he drove home, Zilbar thought only of Lucco Gagliardi and Phillip Krueger. *Soon it will be over.*

Slowly, Zilbar turned left and then took a right past the school. He approached Pike Street. He thought of turning west and slowed his car, but then his better judgment steered him to the Carroll Street Bridge. Memories immediately flashed back. He recalled his many late-night trips on Mill Creek Road past the reform school to the house on the hill just before the bridge. He thought of the frequent visits south on Pike, west of town. He thought of the farmhouse, reform school, and the secrets of both. Zilbar's mind wandered back, and he thought of the stops at the reform school he'd rather forget, especially during the years before the war.

Zilbar knew it wouldn't be a good idea to drive through Krueger's neighborhood in Monkey Town or those two other locations farther south on Pike and Mill Creek Road. Instead, he drove that night through the quiet downtown. Lucco and Krueger were now out of his mind. Randall Zilbar was confident that his plans were in motion. He drove down the hill toward the river and the Carroll Street Bridge then disappeared into the darkness.

CHAPTER 58

MISSION ALONE

Lucco Gagliardi—April 30, 1958, Wednesday morning

THE day was long for Lucco. He knew he would take care of business late that night. *Just a job*, he thought as he waited to commence his mission. Not interested in being seen by any of the locals, Lucco remained in his room for the day. He hung the *quiet* sign outside his doorway. Hunger began to take over. Noticing a menu on the bedside table, he searched for pasta. Past breakfast, he immediately recognized a simple description of his favorite—spaghetti and meatballs in red sauce. He was sure it would not be Sicilian, but hopefully it would be edible and a large serving.

Ring, ring. "Good afternoon. Wabash Inn."

"Room service? I'd like to order."

"Yes, sir. May I help you?" the front desk clerk asked enthusiastically.

"Spaghetti and meatballs. Two orders. You got garlic bread?"

"Yes, sir, we do."

"Deliver to my room."

"Sure thing. Thirty minutes," the desk clerk answered as if he was bent on service for his guests.

"Listen, place my order, and you bring it to me."

"Well, sir, I have to stay at the front desk."

"Listen, sonny," Lucco said to the middle-aged little man at the other end of the line. "You and me are friends. I have two extra dollars for you. I need my spaghetti in twenty minutes. No, make it in fifteen. Haven't had breakfast."

"See you in fifteen minutes, sir."

"Room 122," Lucco demanded.

The Wabash Inn was new and modern. Air-conditioning and a TV were in all the deluxe rooms. Lucco read one of his Western paperbacks. *The Guiding Light, Search for Tomorrow,* and *The Garry Moore Show* provided some entertainment on TV. Late afternoon, before the manager left his shift at the front desk, Lucco again ordered another double order of spaghetti. Still hungry, he added a loaf of garlic bread. Within fifteen minutes, the clerk knocked on the door. Startled again by the big man, he nervously stepped in and set the tray on a small table next to the chair. "That'll be $1.80. Ninety cents per order. Same as your first order today. Please sign."

"Nah. Here's five. That'll cover your two dollars."

"Thank you. Thank you, sir." As the clerk turned toward the door, he noticed a gun and shoulder holster hanging from the desk chair. "Thank you again," he said, hoping the big man didn't hear the gulp in his throat.

As the clerk reached for the door, Lucco said, "Hey, sonny, need some wine." He handed him another three dollars. "Bring me a bottle of Chianti. What's your name?"

"Russ. Russ, sir. I'll be back in fifteen minutes."

As the door shut, Lucco smiled to himself. *Like he never saw a gun before.*

When Russ returned and handed the bottle to Lucco, the big man asked, "How late you here today?"

"Six o'clock, sir."

Lucco reached in his pocket and pulled out a twenty dollar bill. "Here, bring me another double order, some extra meatballs, and make that two bottles of Chianti. That should cover my room. Check me out. Will be leavin' early tomorrow."

Without hesitation, the clerk said, "Sure. Sure will. You can count on me, sir. Hope to see you again."

Lucco nodded and closed the door. The clerk tucked the twenty in his pocket and walked away, thinking only of the extra money he had earned that day.

Rested and satisfied, Lucco was ready for the long night ahead. He stood, gave a loud belch that vibrated off the headboard. Lucco tightened his tie and brushed his white shirt. After strapping his gun and holster under his left arm, he put on his black striped suit jacket. Lucco straightened his wide lapels, pulled out his thick wad of cash, and flipped an extra three dollars on the table. After pulling the bedspread back over the pillows, Lucco flipped the lights off and walked to his waiting black Buick.

On the way, he reached into his right suit coat pocket. He checked for the long metal wire, making sure all was ready. He felt inside his left pocket for his leather gloves. As he approached the car, Lucco walked directly to the trunk. Inside, he untied and rolled out a dark brown leather tool kit. Neatly tucked in their slots were screwdrivers, pliers, a small chisel, black tape, a hammer, wire cutters, a knife with a five-inch blade, and an extra roll of wire. The head of the steel hammer was bound and taped with a rubber pad and machine cloth fabric. The hammer silencer worked as well as the silencer for his handgun. After rolling up the tools of his trade, he picked up the tool kit, closed the trunk, and placed the kit under his front seat.

Quietly, Lucco drove around the quiet side of the building and exited out the far south exit, avoiding the front door of the motel. Knowing the exact location of the house, Lucco planned to park his car in the school parking lot, where it would not be seen during the early hours of the morning. His car would easily be lost when he parked near a large oak on the edge of the lot. Cautiously driving toward the tree, he could see a night-light at each end of the 1930s Deco style school. Parking near the oak tree, he knew he would be unnoticed as he walked a few blocks to Pike.

Lucco threw the car into park. He pulled his trusty tool kit from underneath his seat. After picking up his fedora from the front seat, Lucco stepped from the car and placed the wide-brimmed hat on his head. Once it was situated perfectly, he gave the front brim a final tug over his heavy brows. Patting his gun underneath his left arm, he tucked his tools under his right arm. Then, hands in his front pockets, Lucco Gagliardi began his slow walk to Pike Street.

The streets were quiet. The moon was half full. A few floodlights sat atop some poles at cross corners. Pike Street did not have lampposts. The light in the neighborhood depended on the random use of the front porch lights. The silence of the neighborhood was broken by the sound of the big man's shoes on the sidewalk.

Lucco heard a rustle in a bush. He stopped to watch a raccoon scurry across the street. Now just one block away, he could see his final destination. Random lights shined from a couple houses. Lucco felt secure in his approach. Suddenly he heard a barking dog that could have detected his presence. Looking down the drive, Lucco saw a German shepherd tugging at a chain that looked like it was tied to a back garage. There were no lights in the house where the dog was barking in full attack mode. Lucco kept walking. Fortunately, the Krueger place was only five doors away—1722 Pike.

Lucco looked at his watch—11:35. *Perfect.* A lone exterior light hung over the front of Krueger's porch. Lucco walked down the gravel drive on the side of the house. He stepped onto a small covered stoop and tested the screen door. To his surprise, the back door was not even locked. Slowly, he stepped into the kitchen. Conscious of the sound of his leather shoes, he stepped down perfectly without a sound. He had practice. Making his way through the dining room, Lucco saw the entrance to the bedroom hallway.

The house was furnished tastefully in a style of the prewar era. The kitchen cabinets were white. A large oval oak table stood in the dining room, the leaves obviously missing. The furnishings and lace tablecloth gave the house a 1920s look. The dining room wallpaper was a deep pattern. A dark blue-and-green oriental rug covered most of the wood floor in the dining room. The bedroom doors were open. Lucco saw Phil Krueger asleep, conveniently on his back. A tall oak headboard overwhelmed the bedroom. Lucco scanned the room before approaching the bed. Within seconds, the huge bear of a man stood over Phil Krueger. Lucco pulled a small green machinist towel and a roll of black tape from his left pocket. He held the towel in his left hand. With perfect aim, he squarely placed the towel over Krueger's mouth.

Startled, Krueger awoke and immediately gasped for air. While his arms and hands reached for the hand over his face, his legs immediately kicked and thrashed as he tried in vain to free himself from the smothering grasp of the massive intruder. Terrified in instant horror, Phillip Krueger looked at the man's face and only saw the whites of his eyes piercing through the darkness.

"Quiet, quiet." Lucco eased off, allowing Krueger to catch his breath. "Not a word. Don't resist, and you won't be hurt. Do exactly as I tell you," he ordered in a low, hushed tone. "The gun under my arm can easily be engaged. Not one word."

If this man doesn't kill me, my beating heart will, Krueger thought.

"Now sit up."

Krueger obeyed. Lucco pulled the roll of black tape from his left pocket. After laying the folded towel across Krueger's mouth, leaving his nose free to breathe, Lucco could feel and hear the man's muffled gags. With his left hand behind Krueger's head, he wrapped the black tape around and around, totally covering the gag. Krueger discontinued his needless efforts to free himself from the grasp of the overpowering hulk of a man. Lucco placed his finger beneath Krueger's nose, making sure he could still breathe. Then, taking Krueger's right arm at the elbow, Lucco pulled him from his bed.

"Do as I say," Lucco said, looking straight into Krueger's terrified eyes.

Standing in his long pajamas, the man's body shook in sheer fright.

Lucco pulled Krueger into the hall. "Need the bathroom? You may be more comfortable. We're going for a ride."

Krueger moved his head up and down, and Lucco allowed him to use the bathroom.

"Nah, nah, door stays open." When Krueger was finished, Lucco told him to get his clothes and shoes. "You're gonna be gone for a little while."

Krueger tried to talk through the taped gag. Useless. He was at the big man's mercy. Krueger gathered clothes from the chair and took off his pajamas. On went his underwear, shirt, trousers, shoes, and socks. When Krueger was dressed, Lucco clasped his upper arm and pulled him into the hallway.

"Stand right here," Lucco commanded.

Keeping his eye on the frightened man, Lucco pulled a side chair from the dining room table. After closing the bedroom door, Lucco set the chair in front of the door but in the short hallway. He loosened his suit coat and then pushed Krueger down onto the chair. With that, he once again pulled the black mechanic's tape from his pocket. Beginning with Krueger's feet, the big man taped the frightened man's ankles to the chair. Then he pulled Krueger's hands behind the chair. He double wrapped his crossed wrists and then secured them to the chair. With big loops, Lucco wrapped and bound Krueger's chest. Within minutes, the chair and Krueger were one.

"You wait here. I'll be back in twenty minutes, maybe thirty at the most." Lucco could hear loud *hmmms* from Krueger's bound face as he twisted and turned, trying unsuccessfully to free himself. "You rest. Save your energy. You're gonna need it."

Lucco Gagliardi retraced his footsteps on the sidewalk. He walked to the far side of the street to avoid the German dog. Not even a raccoon interrupted his walk this time. Suddenly he saw a car up toward the end of Pike Street. Despite the distance, Lucco detected a bulb atop the oncoming car. *Police.* Calmly, he stepped toward a very large well-positioned oak tree between the sidewalk and street and leaned his back against it. Even the big man found visual protection behind the massive tree.

The police car advanced down the street in Lucco's direction. The spotlight was not on. The officer was driving slowly as if he was looking for something. Most likely he was just killing time on a quiet spring night. As the car went by, Lucco—protected by the tree—saw the car's red taillights. If the cop had seen Lucco, he surely would have stopped. A large man walking down a quiet street in Wabash in a black striped suit, tie, and hat at this time of night would look like an elephant through a barnyard.

Within a few seconds, Lucco saw the red glow of the brake lights engage. Lucco wondered if the policeman might have seen his silhouette frozen tightly against the tree. He waited. Immediately he could hear the chained shepherd barking at the cop car.

Displaying a play of authority, the cop shined the spotlight down the drive. The dog howled even more. Soon the lights went on in the house. A man came to the front door. The policeman did not get out of his car.

Lucco could hear, "Any trouble in there?"

"Nah, nah. Is that you, Fred?"

"Yep, it's me. Just keepin' your neighborhood safe."

"This shepherd, he'll bark at every squirrel, car, or walker passing by on a quiet night like this." The man clad only in boxer shorts and T-shirt looked normal, as normal as a man stepping into the night in his underwear could look.

"Well, there's no walkers, and I'm the only car. Guess all is well," the policeman said. He beamed his spotlight into the surrounding darkness to no avail. *All's quiet on the western front,* he thought.

"Thanks, Fred. See ya next week at Dyes."

The lights soon went out. The dog let out a few more yelps. Then quiet. Slowly the cop car continued its nightly trek. Still leaning against the tree, Lucco watched the red lights disappear. He continued his walk back to the school parking lot.

Within a few minutes, he approached the black Buick, opened the door, and sat behind the wheel. Leaving the key in his pocket, Lucco glanced at his watch—2:16. He decided to wait an hour, giving the cop a chance to clear the neighborhood. Lucco could only imagine Krueger frantically wondering where his intruder was. Lucco didn't worry. Krueger wasn't going anyplace, at least not for another hour or so.

Lucco looked up at the half-moon partially covered by darker clouds. Over an hour had passed. He was ready. He straightened his tie, felt the pack under his left arm, and tugged the brim of his hat. He also checked the wire inside his left suit coat pocket.

After turning the key in the ignition, Lucco shifted the black Buick slowly into drive. He circled the parking lot and then drove along the outskirts darkened by bordering trees. The visitor from Cicero pulled into the street, drove to the corner of Pike, and turned left. Lucco's plan was to back up to the rear door of Krueger's house and then load him into the car trunk. No dog, no cop car, no nighttime walkers would be able to see him. The shadows of the house and trees along the gravel drive blanketed the car in darkness. Lucco pulled in front of Krueger's white frame house, stopped, shifted into reverse, and slowly backed down the drive to the rear door.

Lucco entered the house. He could see Krueger still gagged and bound to the chair. While Lucco was away, Krueger had managed to tip the chair and slide himself into the center of the dining room. He looked exhausted. In the process, he had managed to knock over two dining room chairs, but his efforts to free himself had been futile.

"Sorry I took so long," Lucco Gagliardi said in a gruff voice. "Thought I needed a little nap before our trip." He bent over and easily pulled Krueger's chair to an upright position. He took out a large pocketknife and slit the black tape binding Krueger to the chair. Slowly, he eased Krueger into a standing position. "We're leavin'." That was not what Krueger wanted to hear.

The gag in his mouth allowed only sounds of guttural, frantic, muffled words. *Can't talk. Can hardly breathe. This bastard has no mercy.*

Lucco packed up the loose tape, straightened the chairs, and semi-made the bed. "Anything you want to take from your room?" Lucco asked. "Don't worry, you won't need extra clothes."

Krueger's heart almost froze. He was beginning to understand, this was no pleasure trip.

"Stand here." Lucco walked back into the bedroom and picked up one of Krueger's pillows. "You may need this."

Phillip Krueger raised his eyebrows in confusion. *A pillow?* he thought. Lucco led Krueger into the kitchen, reached into the cupboard to the left of the stove, and pulled out a glass. Taking a twist of the black tape from behind Krueger's head, Lucco ripped the tape around and around, ungagging Krueger. "Wha-whaaa-whaa—?"

"Quiet. I'll give you some water. One time you make a sound, just once, and I'll send the sharp end of this blade right into that black heart of yours," Lucco said, touching the end of Krueger's nose with his oversized pocketknife. A man of few words, Lucco added, "Know why I'm here? You hurt young boys. You sick prick." A few small drops of blood fell from inside Krueger's nose.

"Sure, sure, not a sound. Please no knife. Promise," Krueger replied with the frantic plea of a terrified man.

"We're goin' for a ride." Reaching into his pocket, Lucco pulled out three pills. "Take these Librium. You'll sleep like a baby."

"Never had these, but if you say so. Where you taking me? You know I'm on bail."

"On a little ride. Don't worry. Judge won't know." Lucco took Krueger's elbow. "This is your last chance," he said, guiding Krueger back toward the bathroom.

"Thank you."

Lucco waited in the dining room with the bathroom door open.

"Let's go," he said to Krueger as they walked back toward the kitchen.

"You bet I'm ready. Anything you say, big guy." The Librium was starting to kick in. "We going anyplace fun? I could use a little getaway. You and me. Big fun. Get it?"

"Quiet, shit face." Lucco retaped Krueger's wrists. He wrapped one round of tape around Krueger's mouth. Lucco guided Krueger out the back door, holding the smaller man's upper arm in the grip of his giant hand. He motioned Krueger to get inside the trunk. Krueger saw only the silhouette of the large man hovering over him. Lucco saw the terror in his eyes. From under his arm, he threw the pillow into the trunk. Two blankets awaited Krueger's arrival. The large trunk of the big black Buick was spotlessly clean.

Krueger first resisted Lucco's invitation but to no avail. With one push, the large brute of a man secured Krueger's position inside the dark cavern.

With one last look at the terrified passenger, Lucco said, "Now you just rest. Leave the drivin' to me. I'll watch out for bumps." Krueger nestled his head onto the pillow. "If I hear any sound or cries for help, a slug will find its way through the backseat, creating a hole someplace in your body. So quiet!"

With one slam of the trunk, Krueger was captured in darkness. Lucco heard a few kicks from inside the trunk and then quiet.

With the first phase of Lucco's mission now complete, he was ready for the trip ahead. Little did Krueger know where the end of the journey would lead.

Phillip Krueger abided Lucco's command about any sounds from within the trunk. He adjusted the gag to breathe better but did not remove it. The total blackness within the trunk relieved his sense of place. He really did not care. Along with Lucco, the pills were now in control of Krueger.

Once his companion was hidden away, Lucco walked around to the front of the car. The stillness of the night remained. He could hear the sounds of the gravel drive crushing beneath his feet as he stepped to the grassy middle area of the driveway and followed it to the sidewalk. Lucco looked a few houses back up the street. He didn't hear a sound from the

German shepherd. The houses were as dark as Krueger's coffin. The sidewalks and tree-lined street created an enclosed feeling. *All's quiet. Time to go.*

Lucco heard the hoot of an owl hidden somewhere above in the darkness, informing him that he was not totally alone. He walked back to the car and tapped on the trunk lid. Not a sound. Krueger had already checked out, the pills having done their deed.

Slowly Lucco pulled his black Buick to the end of the drive. A solitary streetlight shed a faint flow across Pike Street. He turned north on Pike and headed across the Carroll Street Bridge and toward the downtown. Driving across the tracks in the heart of Wabash, Lucco saw a hobo with a knapsack over his shoulder walking the rails, looking for a train. He paid no mind. The tramp stopped and took notice of the big black Buick. Lucco turned east on Wabash Street and drove on through the downtown. He only noticed a stray dog sniffing around a flowerbed by a tree on Market, just beyond the courthouse. Then he headed north out of town in the direction of Cicero. Lucco turned west on 24, headed straight out of town about ten miles, then turned north on Highway 31. There was hardly a car or truck on the road during the wee hours.

A couple of hours north of Wabash, Lucco remembered on the way down from Cicero he had noticed a dilapidated farmhouse with a falling barn in the back. Checking the miles, he watched for the abandoned farmhouse. He remembered a rusty gray mailbox. Soon he saw the mailbox ahead. Turning into the drive, Lucco was barely able to drive through the overgrown underbrush. Once by the house, there was room to turn his car around facing the highway from which he came.

Lucco got out of the car. For a moment he thought he saw a glimmer of a light from inside the house. He noticed the glare of the moon reflecting off the glass window in the back. Lucco detected the smell of smoke. He walked around to the trunk and heard a *rahhh, screech.* Startled, he reached for his gun and then noticed a rat scurrying from behind the house lickety-split, followed by a mangy old gray cat.

Placing his gun back in his holster, Lucco started to open the trunk when he heard, "Don't you dare move, sonny." Looking to the back door, he saw a decrepit old man with a full-face beard, a few dark teeth, dirty brown long johns, and bib overalls that were hooked only on one shoulder. Lucco did not like staring down a two-barrel shotgun that had a shaky finger attached to the trigger. "Whatcha looking for?" the old man asked.

"Just a quiet place to park my car and take a little snooze."

"Where ya from?" the old man asked.

"Chicago. Been down in Indy. Mom died, and I'm heading home from Gary, just up the way."

"Home?"

Lucco lied in response. He could hear Krueger. *Must be kicking the trunk lid.* "Would like a little coffee if you could spare some for a weary traveler," Lucco said to the old man, wanting to get him away from the noise.

"Oh, you seem all right. Come on in. Got some on the stove from yesterday."

Pushing some papers and tin cans from the table, the old man cleared a place for Lucco to sit and rest.

"Thanks, pal, I'll stand. Those chairs might not support me."

"Yeah. Looks like you don't spare any meat and taters. You look pretty road weary. You'll like this. Stronger than a mule's kick," he said, chuckling, exposing his dark gapped, split, and stained teeth.

Lucco smiled back. "Funny."

They waited a couple minutes as the old man stoked the fire under the wood-burning stove, heating the hearty brew. Touching his finger to the blue porcelain pot, the old man said, "Oh. Plenty hot now, sonny. Here, try this."

Having set his shotgun against the table, the old man leaned over and poured the coffee into an old chipped porcelain cup. Lucco was not pleased with his dilemma. The location was perfect, off the main road. The old man could not be a witness left behind. Although it was not of his liking, Lucco was left with only one choice. As the old man poured, steam rose from the cup. He turned his back and set the pot back on the stove. In an instant, Lucco, having not yet taken off his black gloves, reached into his left pocket, wrapped the wire around both hands, and reached from behind the old man's neck.

"*Ekkkk*," the man gurgled and then gagged.

Krueger could hear the ruckus from inside the house. *What the hell?*

Krueger couldn't figure it out, but he was instantly terrified. The pills were wearing off.

The coffee pot rolled to the floor, and cans scattered across the table. The old man's arms flailed. He grabbed for the wire around his throat. He kicked and thrashed with his feet. His nails tore at Lucco's throat and then his face. One of the scratches tore the flesh of Lucco's cheek. Blood. The old man was helpless, overwhelmed by the wire and the bulk of the big man.

Lucco stood almost stationery, totally overpowering the old man. With his knee now secured against the old man's back, the flailing subsided. The old man's gasps for air diminished. He went limp. With one last twist and tightening of the wire, the giant gave one last jerk, ensuring death. He loosened the wire and withdrew it from around the old man's neck. The man dropped to the floor. Lucco Gagliardi stepped over him, closed his mind, and proceeded out the back door.

Without hesitation, he walked to the trunk, wire still in his gloved right hand. Krueger could hear his traveling companion's heavy breathing. Lucco opened the trunk and immediately saw the frantic terror in Krueger's eyes.

"I'll make this quick," Lucco said, moving at an unfamiliar hurried pace.

With his left hand, he pulled Krueger up, dragged him from the trunk, and threw him to the ground. Krueger saw his fate in Lucco's right hand. He pleaded in unrecognizable words as saliva slipped from beneath the tape. *The beast is gonna kill me. No! No! God, please!*

Lucco moved behind Krueger and wrapped the wire around his neck. Before he unleashed his strength, he whispered in Krueger's ear, "This one's from Randall Zilbar. He sends this wire with vengeance." Lucco pulled the wire with the unleashed strength of both his powerful arms. Krueger followed his neck upward.

Kicking skyward, Krueger fought in desperation, hands clawing, trying to dislodge the hold of the thin steel wire that grew tighter and tighter. His eyes bulged at the sight of the moon. He gave all the strength he ever possessed to one last moment in his unrelenting quest for air, for life. As the wire cut off the air to Krueger's windpipe, Lucco stopped. Holding the wire in place, he pressed his lips close to Krueger's right ear.

"And this twist is from me. You think of every time you inflicted those innocent boys with your slimy ... "

"Ahhh." Krueger gagged, as Lucco unleashed his entire might. In his closing seconds, Krueger felt a throb, thrust, and push from behind as if a giant boulder was crashing into his back. Higher and higher his feet flew into the air, while his head was pulled into the mighty man's chest.

Krueger saw his deplorable life. A life of forty-four years flashed by in an instant. He saw his uncle strip him naked and overpower his entire body. Again, *oh no*, he remembered the muffled yell and the sweaty body of his camp leader. The look of his seventh grade teacher's lustful eyes from the darkness of the cloakroom, the seminary, the old priest. Abusive scenes flashed their terror across the screen of his mind in his last moments of life. Boys he abused, every single one—their horrified, distorted faces all yelled back pleas for help. Crying, stench, excitement, and deplorable acts. In a last split second there was sorrow, remorse. Krueger cried inside with nobody to hear. *I'm sorry, sorry. Oh no, not me.* Blank stares. *I'm dead.* Nothing. Like slow motion, his feet floated. His hands went limp.

The wire unleashed. Krueger's entire body fell lifeless to the ground. *Nothing but darkness.*

Over to the side of Krueger's body, the old man's firewood pile was neatly stacked. The blade of an ax was buried deep into the chopping block. Overwhelmed with fatigue, Lucco's body was devoid of energy. He staggered to his car. He stumbled in exhaustion and then caught himself with his hand against the car door. Opening the door, Lucco pulled a previously opened bottle of red wine from the glove compartment and popped the cork. He sat down on the chopping block to enjoy his reward. His first gulps consumed half the bottle. *Well earned*, he thought.

Suddenly Lucco gasped for breath. His chest was wracked with pain. Bent over, he tried to brace himself as he fell forward. He threw his hands to the ground, breaking his fall. He turned over and lay prone on his back, glaring at the starlit sky above.

Two men dead. Lucco didn't know how long he lay motionless. Time passed. Stars lit the sky. Eventually, he could hear the birds of dawn begin to chirp. The sun had yet to break the darkness of night. The wine had passed. Lucco felt his hand scraping the ground as he tried to gain his bearings. He felt the broken glass of the discarded bottle. *The old man should not have gotten in the way.*

Lucco blinked hard as he slowly turned to push his hulking frame up. Reaching for the chopping block, Lucco pulled himself to his knees and wobbled to a standing position. He turned and tried to remember the hours before. To his last days, Lucco Gagliardi would never be able to figure out how with his deteriorating heart condition he had been able to clean up the site and get back on the road to complete his mission.

CHAPTER 59

DOUBLE COVER

Randall Zilbar—April 30, 1958, mid-afternoon

NOW that Phillip Krueger was out on bail and the Cicero connection had been made, Randall Zilbar thought a meeting with Wolfe would cover any connection he had with the unknown state of affairs of Krueger. Behind the closed door of his private office, Randall dialed Wolfe.

"Good afternoon. Miss Gardner speaking."

"You connect me with Wolfe," Randall insisted in his usual arrogant manner.

"I will, but who is me?" she asked smartly, not appreciating the caller's command.

"Tell him Randall's on the line. He'll know."

"Oh yes, Randall. And the last name?"

"Zilbar. Randall Zilbar. Get Wolfe."

"Mr. Wolfe, Randall's on the line," she said, smiling to herself. Not seeking a second verbal rebuttal, Miss Gardner connected the caller to Mr. Wolfe.

"Hello, Randall."

"Your secretary puts me through an interrogation every time I call," Zilbar said, scolding Wolfe.

"Oh sorry, sir. I will say something to her." Even though Wolfe was five years older than Randall Zilbar and had a strong demanding personality in his own right, Zilbar still had the upper hand in his manner of speech. Although Randall Zilbar was very impressed with his own importance, he still needed Wolfe.

"Meet me late afternoon for thirty minutes. I'll be at the Indiana Hotel. It's about Krueger."

"Sure, sure, Randall. What time is best?"

"Five o'clock sharp. I'll see you then." Zilbar put his phone down in a half slam without acknowledging a good-bye.

He didn't even ask if I had time, Wolfe thought. *Had to be spoiled as a child.*

No matter when they met, Clarence Wolfe, with all of his gruffness, rudeness, and dominant personality traits, always felt anxious and edgy before meeting with Randall Zilbar.

Zilbar could be smooth in manner if he felt the need. He did not always display the demanding presence that was more standard with Clarence Wolfe. Zilbar's passion for control and arrogant demands could not be trumped. Ten minutes early for the appointment, Zilbar preferred to select his own seat and position before any meeting he was to hold or attend. He loved this time of day.

Armond, the bartender, gave a respectful welcome to Zilbar when he entered the Green Hat Bar in the Indiana Hotel. Zilbar walked unescorted to his favorite corner booth. After hanging his tailored fedora and suit jacket on the bracketed brass pole at the end of the booth, he sat back, relaxed, and waited for his cocktail to arrive. Within one minute, the barmaid appeared with a vodka martini—his drink of choice.

The attractive brunette in her early forties said, "Good afternoon, sir," placed a napkin on the table, and perfectly set his martini before him.

The Green Hat Bar was a place that embraced dignity and class. The stately bar, with its stylish wood columns, framed the beveled glass back bar. The Green Hat was the place to be seen in Wabash. On rare occasions, when looking for a little diversity, Randall Zilbar would drop into the utterly sophisticated Club Royal next door. Usually the Club Royal was reserved for later in the evening.

The whiskies, bourbons, and scotches were all top-shelf at the Green Hat. The wine selection was extensive and housed in a perfectly tempered cellar in the lower level. Even the tap beers were pulled with distinction and flair. In late afternoons, when many a day's work was complete, the Green Hat was a special place for those who enjoyed the finer luxuries of life. Randall Zilbar appreciated the Green Hat more than any place he patronized in Indianapolis or Chicago. After the first couple sips of his martini, he relished in his taste for only the best.

"Good afternoon. What's your name?" Zilbar asked the waitress in a most polite and friendly manner.

"Sally Brown," she replied.

"Oh, you must be new," he stated.

"Well, kind of. I started just a few weeks ago, right after … " Then she paused. "I'm replacing Gretchen Streater. She passed away. Maybe you haven't seen me because I work a swing shift," Sally said to the well-heeled patron.

"Oh yes," he said, nodding, not taking his gaze off Sally. Her remark aroused his curiosity about Gretchen. "Yes, I remember. Of course, Gretchen Streater. She was a nice lady," he said in a more too-bad-it-happened voice. "You know, I haven't seen anything in the paper lately regarding who her murderer was. What a tragedy."

"Oh yes, our staff all liked her. They still talk about her." Noticing another customer walk in, Sally changed the subject. "Excuse me, sir. I have another customer," she said, not wanting to talk about Gretchen. "It was nice to meet you, Mr. Zilbar."

"Oh, Sally, I do have a friend who will be joining me soon."

"I'll be right back for you, Mr. Zilbar." Sally turned and walked over to a newly occupied booth on the far side of the room.

Randall Zilbar watched her as she walked away. A young man and an elderly gentleman had just seated themselves.

Sally looked over at the elderly man with a bashful yet teasing smile. As she walked back to the bar with their order, she noticed a gentleman walk in and join Randall Zilbar. Hurriedly turning in the elder gentleman's order, she walked back to Zilbar's booth. "Good afternoon," she said to Clarence Wolfe. "What can I get for you?"

"Make mine a Manhattan," Wolfe said abruptly. "Make it a double," he said with a kind of dirty old man smile.

"Yes, sir. Thank you." Sally walked back to the bar, leaving Wolfe alone in the presence of Randall Zilbar.

In his usual curt manner, Zilbar addressed Wolfe. "Now here's the situation. Krueger's out on bond. He pled not guilty. That means a trial, witness stand, you know. You've just let him know too much."

"Yes, but, Randall—"

"Don't *but* me. When you left the papers on your desk and allowed him to meet the runner from Cicero, he became too wise. He knows just enough that when on the stand if the prosecutor—and I think it will be McMann—asks the right questions, he could implicate us. That can't happen. You hear me? Can't happen."

"But how do we control him?"

"I have that handled," Zilbar said.

Not aware of Zilbar's real plan, Wolfe thought Zilbar might have a discussion with the prosecutor.

"You go see Krueger. He works for you. Call him. Go to his house and then make him a deal," Zilbar commanded Wolfe.

"How? What kind of deal?" Wolfe asked, wondering what Zilbar had in mind.

"Give him two options. First, tell Krueger to get out of town now. Leave the state. He'll be provided a new ID, a new social security number, a two-year lease on an apartment in Chicago, and fifty thousand dollars in cash. Now that means this week."

"What's the second option?"

Randall Zilbar looked directly at Wolfe. "Same as the first. Get it? I want him gone."

Wolfe nodded in acceptance of Zilbar's offer.

"Considering what he's done, the sicko, he should take the fifty and run. Young boys for God's sake. Remember, he's weak," Zilbar added.

Remember? I can remember back before the war also, Wolfe thought, but he dared not mention that to Zilbar.

"You go see him tomorrow. Get back to me by Saturday. Hear me? Any questions?"

"Daytime or nighttime should I see him?"

"Makes no difference. You know the bastard best. Just get it done this week. Make it happen," Zilbar directed.

"Just let me ask, what if I can't do this? What if I can't convince him?"

Randall Zilbar leaned forward. He waited, thought, and then said, "How much money do you owe me?"

Wolfe thought. "Twenty, twenty-five thousand."

"That's right. Now you are aware, I have friends."

"Of course, I know. Do I take this as a threat?" Wolfe asked timidly.

"No, I wouldn't threaten you, Clarence. You just need a reminder every so often. Now you have one option."

"What's that?" Wolfe asked, knowing there would be no option with Zilbar.

"Get it done now," Zilbar said convincingly. "Of course, you know what to do. I assume you don't want any visitors. Does that make good sense to you, Clarence? Then do exactly as I tell you."

"Yes, Randall. I totally understand. Agreed. I'll make the deal."

"This is good. Your thirty minutes are up," Randall Zilbar said to Clarence Wolfe.

After standing, Wolfe took his jacket, slipped it on, and properly situated his fedora.

Zilbar stood, straightened his jacket, reached over, and patted Wolfe on the shoulder. "I can depend on you. Now just get it done."

As Randall Zilbar was leaving, he stopped in front of Sally, who was standing at the end of the bar. He handed her a crisp five dollar bill. "Thanks for the service … " He paused. "You know, Gretchen was a good lady. Too bad they haven't caught the guy."

"No, they haven't," Sally said, shaking her head. "But I think they will."

As he exited the hotel and disappeared around the corner, he thought smugly to himself that Wolfe's attempt to find Krueger would be futile.

CHAPTER 60

BACK TO BEFORE

Father Jaeger—June 30, 1958, early evening

FATHER Jaeger felt satisfied after leaving the Blue Plate Diner, a popular stop in South Wayne. Turkey, mashed potatoes, and gravy had really hit the spot. He stopped at the corner of Tenth and Market. As he crossed the street, heading back to his apartment behind the cathedral, the red flashing neon sign of the YMCA caught his eye.

Only a block away, Father Jaeger turned and strolled back over toward the three-story pre-WWI building. After walking up the granite steps, he opened one of the double doors. The familiar smell of chlorine from the pool hit him immediately. *Y's all smell the same.* Just thinking of the blue water, the thought of a cool swim on a warm night excited him.

He noticed a group of older boys playing billiards on one side of the lobby. The lighting was fairly dim. The far side of the main room had an array of worn upholstered chairs, some old worn leather. Two large sofas looked deep and welcoming. All looked very old and used. A few elderly men sat reading newspapers at a table. A middle-aged man was dozing in an easy chair, a book resting on his chest.

The center of the lobby housed a circular registration desk. A portly man about forty to forty-five years old greeted Father Jaeger as he walked through the door. "Good evening, sir."

Father Jaeger noticed the man's tie was open at the top. The humid evening air was stuffy and very warm. Sweat beaded on the clerk's forehead and upper lip. His white shirt was graying. Father Jaeger was sure the man did his own laundry.

"Can I help you with anything?" the man asked from his position behind the high circular counter.

"Oh, just checking things out. Staying in town for a few weeks. Do you have weekly or even daily passes?" Father Jaeger asked. He was glad he had made sure not to wear his collar that evening.

"Sure. We can accommodate you either way. Daily pass is thirty-five cents. For $1.25, you can purchase a weekly. That includes full use of the gym, running track, weight room, and pool. You can use up to two towels per day. Ten cents for extras."

"Oh, that sounds reasonable. I'm mostly interested in the pool."

"Let's see now, the facilities are open seven o'clock every morning till ten o'clock at night. Have you ever belonged to a Y before?" the clerk asked, reaching out to shake Jaeger's hand. "Bill's the name. Bill Myers. Ask me anything. I know everyone in town," he bragged with a huge gregarious smile.

"Yes, sure. Belonged to the Y as a kid back in Chicago. We had one in our neighborhood. The Y was my second home."

"Then you should be familiar with our rules. No street shoes past the locker room. Smoking only in the front lobby and the locker room. Of course, we enforce the common practice of most Y's in the country: trunks are not worn in the pool. You know everyone swims in the nude, including our instructors," the clerk said, winking at the priest and looking for approval from his new guest. "It's all about cleanliness and sanitation. Shower before and after entering the pool. Hot and soapy. We promote good hygiene."

"I'm very familiar with nude swimming at the Y. That's the way it was in Chicago," Father Jaeger said agreeably.

"You could use the facilities this evening. Gym and pool are open for one more hour."

"I might just do that. A refreshing swim would be perfect on this warm June evening. Maybe I'll buy a weekly pass. When is the pool less crowded?" Father Jaeger asked a baiting question.

"Late mornings and early afternoons during the school year, but now during the summer we have boys all day."

"What ages do you allow?"

"To be a member, they must be ten. Otherwise, they need a parent."

That sounds routine, Father Jaeger thought, finding out exactly what he wanted to know. Just the thought of a clean pool, freedom, and boys swimming naturally enticed and even aroused the priest.

"Your name, sir?"

"Jerome Jaeger," he said, deciding not to complicate things by announcing *Father*. He knew he would have to remember not to wear his collar. After paying his $1.25, Father Jaeger followed the clerk's directions down the stairs to the lockers. At the bottom of the stairs, a large window provided a full view of the pool. A middle-aged man was swimming laps, and another was practicing dives.

Father Jaeger saw a group of three boys horsing around. They were handsome, built well. *Built well all over*, he thought as he watched them play around in the water. They were older. Two boys were probably thirteen, but by the looks, he thought one was fourteen. Anxiously, he walked into the locker room. The room was square and lined with full-length steel lockers with long dark wooden benches in front.

The walk-in showers were at the far end of the room. Wasting no time, Father Jaeger undressed and hung his clothes inside the locker. Picking up his white towel throwing it over his shoulder, he walked toward the showers. After hanging his towel on the metal pegs outside the shower, Father Jaeger followed directions by taking a good, hot, soapy shower prior to entering the pool. *Hygiene, of course.* A feeling of freedom came over his body as he opened the door and entered the exposed pool area.

Not paying attention to the two gentlemen at the far end of the pool, Father Jaeger's mind blanked as he focused on the three boys frolicking, jumping … just fooling around as boys will do. The sight of the three nude boys affected his pulse and aroused his desire. Father Jerome Jaeger knew he would enjoy his month's stay in South Wayne. *How convenient, the Y is so close to my apartment.*

A few months had passed since Father Jaeger had said Mass. That first morning in South Wayne, he looked forward to fulfilling his most important priestly duty—daily Mass.

Last evening had been filled with arousing thoughts and desires he experienced during the forty-five minutes he spent in the pool. He had put on a good front of swimming and exercise in case anyone had noticed him alone in the pool. However, his main focus had been elsewhere. Exercise had not been his priority. The Y had always been a favorite hangout ever since he was a boy. In his mind, the Y was an immediate association with water, naturalness, and young boys in the nude. He thought of the Y often.

That first morning, Father Jaeger was again visually overwhelmed when he stepped into the cathedral, just as he had been during his first visit more than two years ago. The high arched ceiling was crowned and supported by half-beveled rafters. Chamfered vertical columns running parallel with the center aisle supported each rafter. Additional pews and side aisles were outside the columns. Ornamental gold leaf lined the columns, crowns, and rafters. The sanctuary was spectacular in both size and décor. The altar, along with its three spires, were made of white marble. Within the larger center spire, a gold crucifix hung in solitary splendor. The cathedral was a work of art, splendid and spectacular in design, color, and grandeur.

Father Jaeger slowly walked up the center aisle. Gazing all around, he felt a closeness to his Lord. Upon approaching the marble communion rail, he stopped. Turning around, he felt the glow of sunlight beaming through the multicolored hexagonal stained glass window above the choir loft at the very end gable of the church. Below, the colossal pipes of the organ stood silently like soldiers lined at attention. Father Jaeger could only imagine the triumphant sounds the magnificent organ would echo through the canyon of this spectacular cathedral. He was in awe of his surroundings. He reached up and tugged at his collar as if searching for proof that he really was a priest. *Yes, I am a priest. My Lord's messenger on this Earth. I'm here to save souls.* For a few moments, Father Jaeger was lost in thoughts of all the good he did as a priest.

From the sacristy, where the bishop was preparing for his morning Mass, Father Holtz noticed Father Jaeger approaching. He raised his finger as if saying, *Stop. Halt for one minute.* "I'll be right there."

Father Jaeger stopped and stood by the pulpit in front of the communion rail, accepting the command from the younger priest. He noticed the back of Bishop Powers through the doorway to the sacristy where he was preparing for Mass. He understood why Father Holtz did not want him to come in there. *Let dead dogs lie.*

Almost immediately, the young priest walked over. "Good morning, Father. Let's go over to the side chapel. Come this way," Father Holtz said, walking past the priest standing in front of the railing.

Father Jaeger had yet to endear himself to Father Holtz. Walking in front of the communion railing, Father Jaeger followed him around a main corner column. About a quarter of the way down the aisle, Father Jaeger saw the entrance to the chapel. A gold metal bracket hung out from the wall, and a sign hung below it: *Holy Innocence Chapel.*

Father Jaeger followed Father Holtz into the chapel. It was small but very conducive for more private Masses or just visitations. The center aisle separated two sides and marked off the ten rows of pews, eight seats per row. The chapel was unique from the main church. A simple wooden altar and crucifix presented a more intimate, private space for Mass. The chapel seemed much older than the main church. Father Holtz walked into a small almost closet-like room to the side of the altar. Inside, he could see a chest like a counter with ten drawers below its top. "All the vestments you'll need are here."

"This is beautiful. What a solemn, peaceful chapel," Father Jaeger told the younger priest, trying desperately to make a connection with him.

"Yes, it is. Thank you. I just love to come here to be alone, pray, and meditate," Father Holtz said with a slight smile. "A few people may drift in and out during your Mass. Pay no mind, as most aren't attending Mass. They may just want to light a candle and pray. That's quite common." With that, he said, "Enjoy saying Mass. I'll be in contact with you later, and we'll discuss your first visit with Dr. Bloomberg."

"Thank you, Father, for setting me up. This will be most enjoyable. I could use some quiet downtime. An occasion to pray."

Father Jaeger had a sense of piety during his first Mass in the chapel. How simple and beautiful. During Mass, his mind drifted a couple times to his parents. Then later he thought of Father Warren. Shortly after, he felt a twinge of stress when he thought of Ralph Smith ... and then the bishop. Father Jaeger prayed for many. After communion, he thought of Joey Singleton. He prayed with deep conviction. *Forgive me, Oh Lord, for sometimes I know not what I do.*

After Mass, Father Jaeger walked ten blocks to the heart of the downtown. South Wayne was a lively, bustling place. Even on Tuesday, sidewalks were filled with businessmen and shoppers. He walked into Pete's Cigar and Magazine Shop and enjoyed perusing the magazine section, but he was careful which magazines he thumbed through. He did not want to be seen. A few blocks away, he walked into Woolworth's five and dime. He noticed a group of boys at the soda fountain. He sat down a few stools away, ordered a Coke, and spent about fifteen minutes eavesdropping on their conversation. Nothing interesting. The priest felt uncomfortable and walked back uptown to the rectory. He never wore his collar while away from the cathedral.

After a small lunch and nap, Father Jaeger drove his car to the corner market about six blocks from his apartment. He knew he could not afford to go to the diner every day. Knowing the swim schedule at the Y, he decided to catch the 5:00 p.m. free swim and then maybe he would go to the diner afterward.

At about 4:30 p.m., Jerome headed for the Y. He took two steps at a time up to the front door. Feeling like a regular member, he showed his weekly pass and took a towel and locker key from the end of the counter. Down the stairs he flew. He quickly undressed and showered, but he still had to wait until 5:00 for free swim.

Lessons for ten- to twelve-year-olds would be over at 4:55, the locker attendant informed him. Having ten minutes to wait, he stood at the window and watched the boys swimming their last laps before the end of class. There were about twenty young boys in the class. He could not help but look and admire their form and developing young bodies. Standing at the window in his natural state embellished his uninhibited state of mind.

The whistle blew. Father Jaeger heard, "Everybody out!" from the well-built thirty-something instructor.

The pool door banged open. Most of the class came running through. Trying to look uninterested in their activity, he watched each of the naked boys run to the showers. Once they were all through the door, he casually sauntered into the pool area. A group of three boys remained for free swim. A few adults followed him into the pool area and immediately headed for the deep end.

Father Jaeger walked to the shallow end first, bent over, twisted his back a few times, and shook his arms as if he was going to jump in and swim a few laps. Scanning the pool, he glanced from the corner of his left eye at the three boys resting at the side of the pool. *Are they looking at me?* Their arms lay spread-eagle against the side of the pool as they rested after their last laps. He watched closely as they began to kick and float with their arms still resting on the poolside. The boys did not pay any attention to the lone swimmer. How free and invigorated he felt.

Energized, Father Jaeger swam four laps. During each lap, he glanced at the boys as he passed. By the end of the fourth lap, he was gasping for air. He noticed one of the boys looking his way. Boldly while trying to regain his breath, he asked, "Any of you guys racers?" He wondered if they might respond and maybe accept his challenge. Wiping water from his eyes, he could see two of the boys look at each other as if to say, *Who is this guy?*

"You look pretty fit," Father Jaeger said as if to challenge the third to a race.

Suddenly, one of the boys jumped up. "Sure, I'll take you on." The boy swam over to the priest. Father Jaeger felt a rush.

"You're on." Father Jaeger hoisted himself out of the pool. "Come on out," he said, trying to get his opponent out of the pool. "We'll start with a shallow dive."

"Of course," the kid said.

Suddenly they were standing side by side.

"Name's David. Yours?"

"Jerome."

"Okay, Jerome, get ready for a lickin'. Two laps up and two laps back."

Father Jaeger liked the sound of that. "You're on!" he said, accepting the challenge while taking in a full view of David's young, lean body. By now the two other boys took notice of them. While they stayed waist deep in the water, Father Jaeger could see the reflection of their naked bodies waving below the surface.

"On your mark, get ready ... go!" Father Jaeger counted. He felt an exciting current run through his body.

On the signal, David dove a split second ahead of Father Jaeger. Halfway down, Father Jaeger could see the splash of David's feet. Briskly, he stroked and stroked, gaining on David. David made the turn a full body length ahead. Father Jaeger was behind but feverishly tried to catch up.

By the end of the first lap, Father Jaeger was still behind. A quick flip and David raced ahead, now two body lengths in front. With a deep breath, Father Jaeger kicked off in chase of the younger swimmer. He could imagine David's body flowing beneath the blue water. Exhilarated, he caught a second wind. With one length of the pool left after the final turn, the priest pushed off with all his strength. Halfway home, Father Jaeger was within a body length of the boy.

Faster and faster David stroked as he saw the end in sight. Only thirty yards left, and Father Jaeger could see David's shoulders getting closer and closer to the end of the pool. *I've got him … I've got him.* Father Jaeger felt the surge. With a final thrust, David kicked. Reaching for his three strongest strokes, David hit the end of the pool just an arm's length ahead of the panting priest.

Exhausted, gasping for breath, Father Jaeger saw the other two boys leap into the air as they cheered David. Their bodies and limbs raised up and then back down. Jerome immediately threw his arm around David. "Great race," he said breathlessly.

He intentionally turned his body, brushing up against David's side. In the same motion, Father Jaeger kicked away, making sure David did not notice any miscue. Backstroking, he kicked away while taking a full glimpse of the excited boys. He noticed their bodies in different stages of development. Turning his head, he caught the full back view of David raising himself from the pool and then leaning his full body against the wall.

David was joyous in his victory. He raised his fists high in celebration, and Father Jaeger took in the full frontal view of what he thought to be about thirteen, maybe fourteen years of explosive virility. The priest's mind was on far more than losing a race.

"I'm zapped, finished, out of here," David announced.

Father Jaeger could tell he was the leader as the other boys followed, all heading for the door to the lockers.

"Great race. What did you say your name was?" the boy called back.

"Jerome," he shouted, still in the pool. As much as he wanted to exit and go shower with the boys, Father Jaeger caught control of himself. *Not ready yet to exit the pool. Just wait. Shower with the boys later.*

Excited, anxious, and lusting for more, Father Jerome Jaeger got a grip. Not yet. *There'll be another time. Hope they take a long shower.*

CHAPTER 61

VISIT WITH FATHER

Joey Singleton—July 1, 1958

AT 4:00 P.M. later that day, Joey rapped on the rectory door. He was glad to see Father Sullivan when the priest opened the door and greeted him.

"Hi, Father," Joey said enthusiastically.

"Come on in, Joey."

Following the priest through the foyer toward the back hall, Joey noticed Father Warren sitting alone in the front parlor. "Good afternoon, Father," he said, passing with a slight wave.

Walking ahead of Joey, Father Sullivan asked if he would like a pop while they visited.

"Sure, that would be great."

"Sounds good to me too," Father Sullivan said, looking back at the boy.

Joey followed him into the kitchen. Father Sullivan popped the tops of two RC Colas. "Take a swig, Joey." *Good and cold.* "Let's go sit in my study."

They walked down to the end of the hall. Opening the door to his study, Father Sullivan invited Joey in. "Sit over here," he said, looking at the two upholstered wooden armchairs in front of the desk.

Joey took the chair where, unbeknownst to him, his mother had sat back in April. "Joey, before we begin, two things. Tell your mother hello for me. You know how fortunate you are to have her as a mom. And I know she says you're such a good son to her."

Joey smiled. "Yes, Father, I do know how good she is to me. Sometimes too good."

"Secondly, Joey, I want you to know that I like you," he said, looking Joey directly in the eye. "I'd like to help you any way I can.

"That would be great, Father. Times have been a little tough lately."

"So let's just focus on you. Joey, what is the main thing you are concerned about?"

Joey thought about how he could tell the priest about Father Jaeger.

"Let me ask this way, Joey. Could I ask what your relationship was with Father Jaeger?" Father Sullivan asked, giving Joey the much-needed opening.

Joey's shoulders raised as if to tense up. "You know, Father Jaeger and I were pretty good friends. Spent a lot of time together. I felt older when I was around him."

"That's fine, Joey. So he was a friend."

"I guess it's the way he left. Never saying good-bye. I thought we were really close friends, and good friends wouldn't do that." Joey wanted to say more. He wanted to talk about how he loved Father Jaeger, how close they really were, but he could not bring up the subject to Father Sullivan.

"Do you want help? Do you want straight answers?"

"Yes, Father, please. I'm old enough. I can handle it."

"Okay. You see, I think he genuinely liked you. I also know this may be difficult to talk about."

Joey assured Father Sullivan, "Go ahead. We need to."

"Did Father Jaeger ever … did he ever touch you inappropriately? To be more specific, did he sexually touch you?"

Joey looked down and thought for a moment. "Is this between just you and me, Father?"

"Absolutely. I promise, Joey."

"I trust you, Father," he said with conviction. "Yes, he did," Joey said without hesitation. "In the beginning, he would come up to me in the sacristy after Mass. He'd give me hugs. Say how handsome I was. He never touched me those first times. I thought he cared for me like my dad would hug me." Joey caught himself. "Or I guess like I would want my dad to hug me. Father, I have no dad."

Father Sullivan just nodded as if he understood, but of course, he already knew.

"Soon, after a few hugs, he touched all around my back and then … then … " Joey squeezed his eyes tightly shut, and tears poured out.

Father Sullivan waited for Joey to continue. Joey blew his nose on the tissue he offered.

"Then … one time he put his hand in my pants. The next time he took me up to his room."

"That's enough. You don't need to describe more. I get it. I can imagine," Father Sullivan said, relieving Joey. "Joey, I have to ask you a very important question. Did you try to force Father Jaeger away? You know, like say no when he approached you?"

Joey replied, "Yes, oh yes, at first." He sounded as if he wanted to say more. "Then things started to change. The first time he took me to his room, he made me take all my clothes off. That's … that's when it was different. It all seemed more natural. He called it love. But Father, I have to tell you, gradually I didn't mind. I kind of got used to our times together."

Father Sullivan was taken aback by Joey's straightforwardness.

"A few other times, Father, he took me out to this old farm. The house was secluded, empty, way back off the road."

"Yes, I probably know which house that is. It belongs to the parish. Father Jaeger looked after the old place."

"We had complete privacy. We stayed all afternoon. Even into the darkness. He loved the darkness." Joey looked at Father Sullivan. "No, Father, I didn't say no. I actually welcomed him." Joey paused for a bit. "I didn't say anything. For the past year, I had been feeling different. Seems I felt ahead of the other guys. I knew something was different. Something was happening to me. I had no interest in girls, had no desire or feelings for any of them, although I do have girls who are friends. For boys it was different. Then Father Jaeger came along. He helped me get to know myself. He made it happen."

Father Sullivan said nothing. He listened to Joey's surprising frankness and honesty.

"I enjoyed it. I loved him. I still love him." Feeling comfortable talking to Father Sullivan, Joey said, "Father Jaeger taught me who I am.

I don't want girls. Don't want a family. And Father Jaeger encouraged me to become a priest, Father, for all the good reasons. We went to the old farm a number of times, whenever we could."

Father Sullivan knew this was so wrong. The vows of a priest, sex with a minor. However, he proceeded cautiously with Joey, wanting to maintain his confidence. "Joey, I think it's wonderful that you want to become a good priest. I know how you care for people. You are also the leader type."

Joey felt a connection with Father Sullivan. He felt comfortable talking with him. He trusted the priest. He took a long swig of his RC Cola. "One other thing, Father."

"What's that, Joey?"

"I don't want to say anything against Father Jaeger. However, I know what he was doing to the other boys was wrong. I know it even if I was the only one. Worst off, I was the one who wanted the time with him because … because that's who I am. Yet, Father, I know my age and that it was wrong for both of us. Father Sullivan, it's important that you know, I deeply want to be a priest and devote my life to God. However, Father, I know I don't want to be a priest like Father Jaeger. You know what I mean?"

"Yes, I do, Joey," Father Sullivan said, now with a much better understanding of him. Most of all, he was learning more about Father Jaeger. *This man has to be stopped.*

CHAPTER 62

ANOTHER CHANCE

Father Jaeger—July 3, 1958

ANOTHER chance meeting at the Y arrived just a few days later, but it wasn't too soon for Father Jaeger. He arrived at the pool at midafternoon. Hurrying, he undressed and headed for a hot, steamy, soapy shower. Already he could feel excitement racing through his body.

Ten minutes remained for swimming classes to end. Just like a few days before, the priest watched from the window overlooking the pool. He enjoyed seeing the boys lunging in and out of the water, jumping up and down, and trying to keep limber before diving back into the pool. He took delight as he watched their bodies form like arrows while diving back into the clear water. Lusting, he stared as they grabbed the side of the pool and lifted themselves out of the water, exposing their posteriors to the onlooking eyes of the man looming outside the window.

Soon the instructor blew his whistle, signaling all out of the pool. Their feet slapped the wet tile as they exited for the lockers. "No running, boys!" the instructor yelled.

Luck was with Father Jaeger. David and his buddies decided to stay for free swim like before. *Maybe David saw me in the window and wanted to stay for some more action.* Anxiously, Father Jaeger flashed through the door and made a perfect running dive into the cool water.

"Hi, Jerome. How's it goin'?" Father Jaeger heard as he emerged after touching the bottom of the pool.

Father Jaeger thought David was hinting for a rematch.

"No racing tonight. I'm pooped," David said.

"Oh, I know. You're afraid you'll get beat this time," Father Jaeger said, egging him on.

"No way. Next time I'll beat you by half a lap. Just not tonight. I'm too tired," David replied.

Disappointed, Father Jaeger countered, "How about some alley-oop, headfirst?" he suggested.

"What's that?" one of the younger boys asked.

"Here, I'll show you." Moving out into the waist-deep water, Father Jaeger pulled the little guy over in front of him. "First, turn around. Your back to me." Father Jaeger took him by the waist, turning the boy's back toward him. "Now, you place your left foot in my hands below the water. On *go*, I'll bend down, raise you up, and flip you into the air. Thrust yourself as high as you can, and then you dive way out as far as you can. Of course, don't dive for the floor. Not deep enough here."

"Okay, I'm game," freckled-faced Lenny Smith said, accepting the challenge.

Father Jaeger knew this would be easy, as Lenny could not weigh even a hundred pounds. He put his hands around the boy's waist, pulling his back close to his chest. He then slid his hands down the boy's legs. All in one motion, he cupped his hands to catch the boy's left foot. "Hold back tight first. Balance. Ready?" Father Jaeger felt the expected touch beneath the water. "Ready, *go*."

With all his might, he raised both hands together, thrusting the boy high. Then Lenny dove ten feet out front for a smooth, shallow entrance into the water.

"Hey, my turn," Johnny Crocker said. "Looks fun."

With that, Father Jaeger enjoyed a whole thrust, heave, touchy-feely clashing of bodies. Fortunately but unfortunately, his lust for more was creating all kinds of bodily changes.

After the first round, Johnny knew exactly what to do. Turning his back to Father Jaeger, Johnny placed his hands backward on the priest's shoulders.

"One, two ... " *Another perfect flip.* "David, your turn."

"Nah, I'm too heavy."

"Oh, let's try."

With that, David came over close to Father Jaeger. Turning his back to the priest, David yelled, "All ready!"

As Father Jaeger slid his wide, open fingers down David's torso, he knew David could feel him close. Father Jaeger clasped his hands together in front of David's legs, creating a stirrup in which David could stand before he raised and flipped the boy high into the air. The intentional touching was a thrill for Father Jaeger, but to David it was an accident underwater.

In a swift motion, Father Jaeger thrust David upward but could not lift him high out of the water. In the failed toss, David fell backward. Father Jaeger reached to catch him, his open arms touching and grabbing David in the flurry under the water. David lunged forward, not liking the encounter.

"See, I told you, Jerome. Too heavy," David said, turning around and now facing his launch pad. Quickly, he backstroked away. "Enough for me. I'm out of here."

"Me too," replied Father Jaeger. The other boys followed. Carefully, the priest exited the pool, checking as he heaved himself up and turned to sit at the side of the pool. *Okay, stand up. Not too obvious*, he thought. *Quick shower will take care of it. Think of blowing snow.*

Father Jaeger hung out at his locker for a moment, sitting on the bench. The boys headed for the shower. Timing it right, Father Jaeger also headed for the shower. David was at the end. The other three guys were already out snapping towels at each other.

"You're just a little heavy, David. Strong though. How about a cold soda after the shower?"

David thought to himself.

Then Father Jaeger said, "What grade you in?"

"I'll be a freshman this fall."

"No wonder. I thought you were older. Well then, would you prefer— *dare I suggest*—a cold beer at my place? It's safe," Father Jaeger said before David could answer, referring to underage drinking.

David raised his eyebrows twice. "That might be cool. I said I had to go home, but heck. I can be a little late. Went to the library, Mom," he said, as he had been prepared to say no to the soda. David and Father Jaeger proceeded to their lockers. David decided to give Father Jaeger another chance. The other boys were still flicking towels and horsing around when David was ready to leave. "See you dorks tomorrow."

"Bye, Dave."

"Yeah, see you, big guy." They continued with their horseplay, not noticing David and Father Jaeger leaving together.

Walking down the front steps, Father Jaeger pointed the way to his apartment. Knowing it had been a while, he tried to control his elevating anticipation before it would soon become full throttle and body ready.

"What sports you like, David?" Father Jaeger asked, trying to switch his mind and body off—but only temporarily.

"Baseball. I'm an Ernie Banks fan, Cubs."

"Oh, too bad. For me, Minnie Minoso is better."

"Ah, Jerome, he's past his prime. Ernie's even better than Mays."

Lost in baseball banter, Father Jaeger was glad to see his apartment just a block away. "It's that house across the street," he said, pointing to the gabled cream city brick building. "My apartment's on the second floor, but we've got to use the back stairs."

As they walked through the door, David said, "Cool place. Just you here, or do you have a roommate?"

"No, just me. All alone," Father Jaeger suggested. "At least for now." He kept talking while he searched for anything recognizable or associated with being a priest. "Excuse me," he said, stepping into the bedroom.

Immediately he noticed his missal and collar on the bedroom dresser. Quickly, he stuffed them into the drawer. That was everything. *Oops*, he thought, immediately reaching for the crucifix above the bed. Taking it down, he placed it in the empty bottom drawer of his stark, almost empty dresser.

Upon returning to the front room, Father Jaeger walked to the refrigerator. "Well, David, pop or I've got some beer. Ever try Pabst Blue Ribbon? I have a couple bottles of Schlitz."

"No pop now. Let's have a beer. As a matter of fact, make mine Pabst Blue Ribbon, just like you, Jerome, seeing you have a couple of Schlitz. Save that 'till later," David said, trying to accommodate.

Father Jaeger liked David's response. *No hurry here.* He reached for the opener and popped the lids while he held both bottles in the same hand. He handed David the Pabst. "Here's to good times," he said, lifting his bottle toward David.

"Back at you, Jerome. You know Schlitz is the beer that made Milwaukee famous. I'll have that next. Maybe both bottles," David said, overzealously throwing in his beer jargon, which he had heard around his house from his dad and older brother.

Each impressed the other with long swigs. Talk of baseball continued in earnest, an easy topic. Ten minutes later, Father Jaeger took another long swig and said, "I'm hot. Let's have another." He went to the refrigerator and pulled out two more beers. "You ready for another one, David?"

"Sure," the boy replied. "Don't forget, Schlitz this time," he said, feeling a little buzz. David looked at him and said, "Here's to us."

Father Jaeger followed in unison as David took a long slug consuming half the bottle.

After a couple more long swigs, David finished his second. Father Jaeger thought, *This is easy, but I better not take everything out of him.* Within minutes, David was experiencing a good buzz. Soon the priest returned for a third beer for his blond-headed friend. David took one large swig and then two more all within minutes.

"Hold on there, David. You're too fast. There's no hurry. You'll take the fight out ... I mean you won't be able to walk home."

"I'm a ... a ... me? I fine." David tipped the bottom of the bottle toward the ceiling, emptied it, and slammed the bottle on the table. He plopped back on the sofa with a huge refreshed sigh. He unbuttoned the top of his shirt.

"Sure is hot in here," he said, not knowing what his statement could lead to. "How about one more, Jeeerooome?"

"Okay, but take this one a little slower, David. I want you to be able to walk home. As a matter of fact, this one is going to be our last." Father Jaeger walked to the refrigerator, not yet having finished his second Pabst. When he returned, he handed David a cold Schlitz. *My god, this is his fourth. Better stop or David will ruin it for both of us.*

David reached up for the bottle and lifted it back, exposing his open shirt and square shoulders. For an instant, Father Jaeger thought, *Oh, he so much reminds me of Joey.* Then he immediately switched his thoughts back to his handsome new friend. The topic of baseball was waning. Father Jaeger was wanting something, and it wasn't beer.

A small sip slurred every word David spoke. Blinking while trying to hold his head erect, he took lighter swigs of his beer. "Yeah, it's hot in here," he said, innocently unbuttoning the rest of his shirt. The heat and beer were both affecting him.

Father Jaeger could see more of his developing muscular body. Noticing the intended progress, Father Jaeger followed by removing his shirt. Like tough guys, they both took deep breaths and expanded their chests. Father Jaeger smiled as he watched David becoming a little silly with his talk.

"I haven't felt—*hiccup*—felt like this good since I ... I ... mean I—*hiccup*—felt up sweet Mary. You know, I mean I know what really feels good ... ah ... ah now mean, I ... you'd like Maaary, Jerome. Maybe, maybe be baby, I could ... oops ... fix you up with her. Ha-ha."

Although Father Jaeger did not care for David's inebriated suggestion about Mary, he realized his new friend was in an I-don't-care kind of mood. With that, Father Jaeger said, "David, before another beer, let's have total comfort." Taking his pants, boxers, shoes, and socks off, he felt the full sensation of nature taking over.

"Sure, why—*hiccup*—why not?" David tried to follow, though he was a little shaky, not able to get his pants beyond his knees. "Little far for me," he said as he plopped back on the sofa.

Father Jaeger helped David steady himself. "Enjoy the freedom." With that, he reached over and grabbed David. "Here, I'll help." Once he had slipped off David's pants, no more beer was needed. Father Jerome Jaeger was in full control and began to physically overpower his helpless, waning prey. All was completed to his satisfaction.

At night's end, David was totally unaware of what had taken place in the second floor apartment on Market Street that steamy summer evening. The next day, however, he knew there was something wrong about the previous afternoon. Although David felt a little discomfort, he couldn't remember anything after walking upstairs.

CHAPTER 63

NIGHTMARES

Peter Goodnar—July 7, 1958

KNOWING he was not alone after palling around with Henry, Mark, and Paul at Gackenheimer's Drug Store weeks before, temporarily brought a semblance of relief to Peter Goodnar. The nights, however, never stopped engulfing his mind with nightmares about distorted figures, crying faces from hell, and merciless wolves chasing, chasing, chasing him through burning flames.

The image haunting him most was the wide eyes, horns, long fangs, and smile of glee coming from the dastardly priest. Peter squinted his eyes every time he imagined the priest's naked body, "No! No! Not again!" The form of a collar floated and twirled without gravity, ever moving closer to his own neck like a choke chain. No longer white, the collar was tarnished with rust-like dark dried bloodstains in the shape of teardrops. A tarnished collar dripping with tears would suddenly cry out in the night for forgiveness. Weeping for all the lost souls, the collar would turn and float down as if to strangle Peter. Then all Peter could see was the unbearable vision of the priest's grotesque face, his neck encircled by the collar of tears, with protruding glaring eyes.

First the lustful smile, then a call for Peter, "Peter! Peter ... it's me again! Come here!" His outstretched arms, open hands, and gnarly fingers would lunge at Peter.

Suddenly Peter awakened, sat up in bed, grabbed his knees, slapped his own face, and then stared at the wall, realizing it was his own reoccurring dream of terror. He knew it was the goodness of God that had brought him back to reality. Oh, the nights were the terror of Peter's young life. The deep effect of the unnatural acts tormented his very being.

Peter continually reminded himself that priests were supposed to be all good. They were our Lord on Earth, doing His work to save souls. Peter thought of how he was losing his soul. His mind was overwhelmed by confusion. *How can this be? God, how can this be?*

During the day, Peter would go to church alone. Kneeling in a pew off to the side of the church, he always prayed to St. Joseph, a good man. Peter prayed to God to help him be free from the monster priest. Even though Father Jaeger was gone, the nightmares continued. Peter could not escape the priest's strangling reoccurring presence. Could life ever be normal again? Could he ever have a girl in a natural, loving way?

Oh God, how can I live with this haunting secret? Will it last forever? Can I ever get him out of my mind? Peter's mind was consumed with the image of Father Jaeger. He hoped and dreamed of the day when he could be there with Henry and his brother, both bringing justice to the wicked man. Together, both having been abused by the same man, Peter and Henry would bring harm to Father Jaeger in a way the priest could not imagine.

CHAPTER 64

SEARCHING FOR A CURE

Dr. Bloomberg—July 8, 1958, mid-afternoon

FATHER Jaeger was anxious about his first meeting with Dr. Bloomberg and talking to a strange man about his hidden life of desire, searching, and fantasy. He vividly remembered their meeting two years before. He even thought this time it would be easier talking with the doctor about his desire for young boys.

Walking into Dr. Bloomberg's office, Father Jaeger felt very stressed. The receptionist took him into Dr. Bloomberg's office and offered him the chair immediately across from the doctor's desk. He waited just a couple minutes. Upon hearing the door open from behind him, Father Jaeger turned, stood, and shook hands with Dr. Bloomberg, who proceeded to his desk.

"Well, Father Jaeger, we meet again. What's it been? Two years?" he asked with a slight tone of sarcasm.

"Yes, about that," Father Jaeger answered.

"Well, tell me about where you are now. I mean, which parish? Let's see, where was that?"

"St. Thomas Moore in Wabash. I had been doing quite well. No major conflicts until ... until I had a setback."

"What about minor conflicts?" Dr. Bloomberg asked, not letting the priest off the hook.

"Oh, couple times, just wrestling around with some boys ... just horsing around."

"Horsing around? You're a priest," the doctor shot back.

"You're right. Poor choice of words," Father Jaeger answered the correction.

"I'm not concerned about that, although horseplay, as you call it, can lead your mind beyond just play. Remember, like I told you two years ago … where the mind goes, the body wants to follow. Your own desires and fantasies are the toughest to control. You can go or stay in a certain place. Control your body, control your life. You tell your feet where to take you. Back to the incident, the one you called, what was that again? A setback? Tell me about it."

"Actually, I really have followed your advice from two years ago. Now, I must admit my mind does wander. I still have occasional desires and lusts. Seems natural to me but not like before. So now I do know I'm better. Of course, I want to be perfect. I am dedicated to my Lord and my Catholic faith."

"Well, explain why you are here. I mean your setback. Tell me, Father Jaeger. Explain to me your definition of better, perfect. Still sounds like you are a far cry from either, as your chart here reads."

"I'm really trying. Made headway in my mind."

"Then convince me of that, Father Jaeger."

"Okay, I will. During my second year at St. Thomas Moore, I became active with our Boy Scout troop. I would attend a troop meeting maybe once a month. I tried to attend all camping outings so I could say Mass for the boys on Sundays. We were at an overnight camp outing a couple months ago. While most of the troop slept in the main cabin, I volunteered to take three boys to camp out in the woods for a camping badge. It was only for one night."

"What happened?" Dr. Bloomberg asked. "Did you keep your pants on?" he replied putting the priest on the spot to seek the truth.

"Can't remember exactly, but one thing led to another, and we got a little carried away. Actually, we ended up naked around the campfire."

"Unfortunately, Ralph Smith was out walking, oh, around ten o'clock, and he happened to come upon our campfire, and the rest is history. I'm no longer at St. Thomas Moore, but I learned so much, and I'm anxious to be transferred to a smaller parish," Father Jaeger said, trying to cut off the dialogue.

"Were you suppressing any other stress or hardship in your life for which this dancing naked was becoming an outlet? Maybe the dancing with the boys was merely a way to act out what was really bothering you."

"No, no, Doctor. I just wanted to be with the boys. Touch, be close. It comes from within. Hard to explain. I'm not about men, not post adolescents, never women ... just ten-, eleven-, twelve-, thirteen-year-old boys. They are so innocent, clean, untouched, virgins in their own right."

"How do you interpret that?" Dr. Bloomberg asked.

"I find it clean, loving, innocent. So pure."

"No, Father, let's examine this more clearly. Do you first feel the sexual urges and desire to be with these boys and focus on your own fulfillment, your own gratification? Then after your own personal satisfaction has been attained, you feel a more gentle, compassionate feeling of love and tenderness? Could that be happening, Father? Let's you be honest with me."

Father Jaeger thought to himself. He didn't respond immediately. Rethinking his time with Joey, Peter and others, he readily agreed and admitted to it himself. "Yes, yes, the sexual urges came first, but I feel a closeness to the boys. Once the desires are satisfied, a soothing feeling of relief and wanting to be close overcomes me. I really love these boys."

Dr. Bloomberg raised his fingers to his chin. "For you to state that is positive and very good. That means your conscious mind sees your desires in reality. If you place love first, you are more than likely to allow your subconscious to fool your true instincts."

"You make it sound so clear, understandable," Father Jaeger agreed.

"You were born with these desires. Sometime during your own sexual evolution, you were drawn to a desire for men, and your outlet became preadolescent boys. You had no choice as to your preference for men. However, you elected to abuse these boys. There is no justification," Dr. Bloomberg stated abruptly. "This has to stop cold. Eventually, you are fooling with a crime, a felony, if convicted. You have no choice. You could have been affected by a relationship with a parent, a classmate, an aggressive uncle. We talked about that a couple years ago. Who knows, but this is who you are. Do you think your affection for young boys is okay morally, ethically, legally?"

Father Jaeger thought. "I believe we were put on this Earth to love as our Lord Jesus Christ has shown to us. I see no wrong for me. My church sees wrong. Parents see wrong. The police see wrong. For me, it is natural and beautiful."

"What about the victims, Father? Do they see wrong?"

"Doctor, I must admit, I have yet to confront a parent. I'm just showing the boys how to love."

"You're showing me how to rationalize, justifying your actions," Dr. Bloomberg responded. "However, these boys are underage, so you are under the jurisdiction of the state, and as far as the church, you have taken a vow of chastity. In our society, your actions are unacceptable to all. As real as your desires are, all your justification for them, is false nothing more. You have taken a vow of chastity. I tell you, my friend, this must be harnessed. This must be curtailed. You must think first of the victim and then direct your desires and ambitions elsewhere. We all have things in our lives that we want. Most recognize what they cannot have. Does any of this make sense to you?"

"Yes, yes, I get it," Father Jaeger said, knowing he had no other option.

"Let me share this. If you ever get too involved with a boy, you might find one who cannot hold his reactions inside. He'll go straight to his parents, and they may bypass your pastor and go straight to the police. A psychiatrist will do you little good then. You would be talking jail time, twenty years. The aggressors in those cells would make your life living hell. You don't know how bad those prison animals can be. They can do a lot more to you than what you do to your young boys. Sometimes it can be not just one but two, three at a time. Think about that as a fact of life. And have you ever thought about a parent bypassing the church, police, and taking his own hands to you? No telling what an enraged person would do for justice or revenge. You would be at their mercy."

In the environment of the doctor's office, Father Jaeger could very well understand the logical advice and agree to adjust and change his behavior to avoid a more costly personal tragedy.

"I must admit, Doctor, you have my attention. You have made me more aware of the risks, not only for myself but also for the church, our parish, and the victims themselves."

Dr. Bloomberg leaned back in his chair. Looking at Father Jaeger, he said, "You've been given plenty of chances. The bishop could be running out of places to transfer you. He could run out of patience. If you don't make this new assignment work, you may face the unimaginable."

CHAPTER 65

COVERING CLOUDS

Father Holtz—July 16, 1958

BISHOP Powers called for a 10:00 a.m. meeting with Father Schmidt and Father Holtz. He poured coffee for them as they took their seats in the conference room. Father Holtz detected a slight tension and apprehension coming from Father Schmidt.

"Tell me about Father Jaeger's progress with Dr. Bloomberg. We must decide what to do. He's been here what ... two weeks now?" Bishop Powers asked, looking directly at Father Schmidt.

Father Schmidt spoke up, "He's been meeting with Dr. Bloomberg twice a week. The doctor said progress is being made. Actually, he said he's seen a marked change in Father Jaeger since their first session two years ago. This time, Dr. Bloomberg said he believes Father Jaeger sees and admits he's wrong. He wants to change for the better. To be a good priest."

"You tell Dr. Bloomberg that Father Jaeger needs to be in his new assignment before month's end. I want a positive report on Jaeger's progress. I want to hear that Jaeger's ready for parish work. I do not want a cloud over this diocese. Cardinal Cullings will be making his annual visit this fall, and Jaeger's not to be here. I've been told there are other cases in the diocese. I want a clean report. Ready or not, Jaeger's in the field by the beginning of August. Has Jaeger been keeping clean here?" the bishop asked.

"Oh yes, Bishop, we haven't had one problem. We'll have him ready, hopefully by the end of this month."

"Make sure I have all the proper paperwork from Dr. Bloomberg to support everything we will be doing with Father Jaeger. Now, where are we sending him this time?" the bishop asked.

"He'll report to Father Arnold, the pastor in Eastville, Indiana. You were there a couple years ago, remember? St. Vincent's. Should be the perfect place for Father Jaeger," Father Schmidt said to assure the bishop of his decision.

"Well, your report should say he's being transferred for health reasons. Stress or his sessions with Dr. Bloomberg will not be reported to the new parish. Father Schmidt, I'm holding you responsible that he stays clean. He's a priest for Christ's sake. He's to be celibate. For the next six months, I want Father Holtz to make a trip to see Jaeger every other month. The two of you report back to me. Are we all clear on this plan?"

"Yes, Bishop. Father Holtz and I will execute your plan as stated."

"That should be it. Any questions? It's time for my lunch."

"Consider everything handled. I assure you, Bishop, this will not erupt again," Father Schmidt said.

Father Holtz withheld his skepticism.

Later that evening, Father Holtz was out for a late-night walk. It was about 9:05 and getting dark. As he walked by the Kobel factory, he happened to notice Father Jaeger's apartment. He stopped and watched.

Father Holtz detected the priest leaving by the back side door. He was walking with a young boy of maybe twelve or thirteen years old. Not noticing Father Holtz, Father Jaeger and the boy continued walking down the block. *Suspicious? Yes. Proof?* Father Holtz thought. *I know. No.* For the rest of the evening, instinct told him what Jaeger would be up to. Father Holtz concluded that evening that he could not stand idly by. Somehow, someone needed to step forward and expose Bishop Powers' cover-up. The question in his mind was who? He felt he was the one.

The next afternoon, Bishop Powers and Father Schmidt left on a trip to Indianapolis to attend a conference meeting the following morning. Late in the afternoon after their departure, Father Holtz went to the office to check on a specific file, that of Jerome Jaeger. He had perfect access.

The door to Father Schmidt's room was unlocked as usual. He went directly for the small file. Top drawer ... A–K. Paging through to the middle, he came upon Father Jaeger's file. He tucked it under his arm and planned to return it the next morning before their return. That night, he carefully read the entire file. He took notes of relevance:

Rev. Jerome Jaeger

- Ordained 1945
- Assistant pastor 1945–1947, St. George's, Kokomo, Indiana, reassigned for health reasons
- Transferred 1947–1950, St. Dominic's, Milton, Indiana ... reassigned ... stress related
- Transferred 1950–1954, St. Peter Paul's ... physical and mental exhaustion
- 1954–1956, Assistant pastor, St. Michael's, Crawfordsville, Indiana
- 1956, January, February, leave of absence
- 1956–1958, St. Thomas Moore, Wabash, Indiana
- 1958, May, Father Warren, Father Sullivan (St. Thomas Moore)
- Father Jaeger accused of physical abuse, four boys
- Discovered by Ralph Smith, layperson
- Father Sullivan adamant about reporting to police authorities
- Father Sullivan very aggressive in pushing to handle out of diocese
- 1958, July, returns to South Wayne for thirty-day psychological analysis
- Reassigned St. Vincent's, Eastville, Indiana

Father Jaeger had already been reassigned before the end of his thirty-day evaluation. Holtz reviewed the file again later that evening. The written statement in the file referenced the May meeting with Bishop Powers, Schmidt, Holtz, Warren, and Sullivan, In which Father Sullivan was adamant about bringing the police into the investigation. He knew something had to be done, even though Father Jaeger would be in his new position at St. Vincent's soon.

For the next two days, as carefully as he could, Father Holtz observed

Father Jaeger's daily pattern … dinner, the Y, his apartment. Over the course of three different days, he had seen the priest with at least two different boys. That night, Father Holtz tried to figure out his options. He knew he could not confront Bishop Powers. Family pressures and the security of his own career prevented him from exposing the cover-up of abusive priests.

He thought long and hard into the night. The words *Father Sullivan was adamant* kept nagging his brain during the sleepless night. Father Holtz knew he had access and was involved in all the abuse cases. He knew who had been reassigned and who was working along with Father Schmidt. He knew the names of all the priests who had been accused or were under the supervision of psychologists and psychiatrists. Father Holtz knew there was a cover-up. Now, behind the back of Father Schmidt and the ambitious Bishop Powers, he had to disclose the cover-up scheme hidden within his beloved Catholic Church.

Sometime after he had looked at his clock … 2:00, 4:00, 5:00 a.m., the idea struck him. Father Holtz had the access. Father Sullivan had the commitment to expose the scandal. That morning, Father Holtz decided he would contact Father Sullivan. Nobody could know.

CHAPTER 66

FINISH THE JOB

Lucco Gagliardi—May 1, 1958

HAVING staggered to his feet, Lucco reached deep for newfound energy. Putting his gloves back on, he picked up the broken bottle and tossed the other broken glass pieces into the bushes at the side of the house.

Now the messy work. He reached in his trunk, pulled out a ten-by-twelve green canvas, and spread it on the floor of the trunk. He easily picked up the old man and forced him toward the back of the trunk. Krueger followed. Like wrapping a package, Lucco pulled the back flap over the top of the two bodies, encircled the canvas with black tape, and then tightly bound both ends. The canvas easily encased both bodies. For a moment, Lucco stood at the open trunk. Looking toward the front of the bundle, he visualized the old man. *Too bad.* He shook his head and then securely closed and locked the trunk.

Lucco checked the house before leaving, as if anyone would ever notice. Picking up the cans, papers, and coffee pot, he displayed them as well as they had been before the thrashing had begun. He tightened his tie, straightened his jacket, and then tugged the brim of his hat toward his eyebrows.

He kept the headlights off as he pulled out to the end of the driveway. It was 4:45 a.m., not a car in sight. Turning right, he headed north for Cicero. The last leg of his journey had just begun. He had until 6:30 to be at the pay phone at the Standard Oil Station just thirty-five miles up the highway.

Lucco Gagliardi was distressed about the old man. He did not like the outcome. No choice. Within seconds, he noted a flashing light in his rearview mirror. He immediately swore but otherwise remained calm. He pulled to the side of the road but did not want to get out of the car. He set his hat on the seat. The officer approached the passenger's side door.

"Happened to see your back left brake light is out. What a shame on this big beauty of a Buick," the skinny officer said as he baited Lucco. "Where you headin', mister?"

"Up north to visit my mom in Kenosha."

"Kenosha? Hear they got a lot of you degos in Kenosha."

Lucco bit his lip. This whole thing could backfire. He didn't have enough room for a third passenger in the trunk.

"Well, I gotta figure out what to do," the officer said like he was hunting for the right reply. "Sure have a safety hazard here. Anything in the backseat or trunk?"

Lucco knew this could be serious. With that, he pulled a wad from his left pocket and slipped a fifty between two fingers on his left hand. "Here's for the backseat," he said, passing a fifty dollar bill to the officer.

"Gosh, I don't see anything back there." Then the officer said, "What about the trunk?"

Another fifty came from inside the car.

"Guess that trunk's empty too. You should be all set. Let me check that brake light. Hit 'em. Well, I'll be darned. They're working perfectly. Must have been a short. Free to go, mister. Drive safely."

Lucco knew a shakedown when he saw one. At this juncture of the journey, it was worth a hundred bucks. Lucco smiled to himself. *Small-town cops. Well, for one hundred bucks, I'm back on the road.* From the left side mirror, Lucco saw the officer get back into his car. *Guess his work's done for the week.*

About sixty miles north, Mario wrestled in his sleep, wondering if Lucco had pulled everything off as planned. It was important to Mario that Randall Zilbar was given the best of service. Mario always fulfilled his promises ... especially to such a rising and powerful man as Randall Zilbar. Mario knew where future projects with Zilbar could lead, and if successful, he could reach no higher level. Knowing it would take years, maybe even a decade to set all the pawns into place, Mario just wanted to be alive to see it all come together.

During the early hours of the morning, Mario needed just one phone call. Tossing and turning, he waited for Lucco's ring. *I shouldn't worry. Lucco always completes his mission.*

Lucco hit the ignition. He loved the hum of the powerful V8 in his '56 Buick. After straightening his tie and tugging the brim of his fedora downward, Lucco slowly slipped the gearshift into drive. The load did not feel any heavier. Leaving his lights off, Lucco turned north on 421. *Damn small-town cops.*

Glancing at his gold watch, which was tightly secured around his large, hairy wrist, Lucco noted 5:24 a.m. With daylight emerging after the long, grueling night, Lucco looked forward to coffee when it was time to stop and call Mario. He knew it would be about forty-five minutes to Crowne Point. Lucco was not fond of playing truck driver to combustible cargo, but he knew it was part of the job. Emptying the bodies into a hole and then covering them with five yards of concrete—it worked every time.

Lucco could see and almost feel the light from the east entering his trusty Buick. He could smell the aroma of a fresh brew swirling around his head. The thought of finding real espresso in northern Indiana was beyond his wildest imagination. *These farmers would think espresso was a fast-moving freight train.*

When he pulled up behind a semi-truck and trailer, the driver signaled a right turn. Lucco slowed, knowing he was probably approaching a blue-collar, flannel-shirt truck stop. *Wonder if they'll like my tie*, he thought. As the truck slowed down, the Buick followed closely. Immediately, Lucco read the bold letters on the back door—*Hall Freight Lines.* Then he saw the Standard Oil sign. Flashing back ten years, he remembered a job he had down by the truck terminal in Danville, Illinois. Even more so, Lucco recalled his reward for a job well done. He had spent a long evening on Green Street just behind the terminal. There the ladies of the night could be propositioned right on their front porches.

Parking the Buick on the outside perimeter of the lot, Lucco backed into the parking space, tight against the cyclone fence. Out of his element, he sauntered into the truck stop. He waited in line for luke-warm coffee and burgers to go. At the end of the counter, he noticed a line of about six phones, all occupied. Fortunately, the burly trucker with the motorcycle hat at the end of the line slammed his phone down, retrieved his nickel, and left, leaving a line of four-letter words behind him, all familiar to the man from Cicero. After dropping in a nickel, Lucco placed a person-to-person collect call to Mario.

"Yes, I'll accept," Mario replied to the operator. Rubbing his eyes as he leaned on his elbow in bed, he heard the familiar craggy voice.

"Mario, Lucco here. Directions?"

"Yeah, glad ya called. Change in plans. Concrete job too risky. Had incident at the yard yesterday. Too many strangers will be there today. Ya know what I mean? Follow this. You go to Delmote, Indiana, on 421. North of town five miles, you will find Torino Brothers Quarry surrounded by a cyclone fence. You can't miss it. Yard opens at seven o'clock. You be there at 6:45."

"Where's Delmote?" Lucco asked.

"Eight miles south of Crowne Point."

Aware of his present location, Lucco responded, "Gotcha, boss. I'm there."

"You'll see a large front-end loader waiting for you just inside the gate. My friend Rocco will open up for you. He owes me couple favors. Follow him. When safe, he'll stop and lower his bucket. Back your Buick up and unload it. Wait there till 7:15, and then when all's safe, leave and head back to Cicero."

"What about the concrete?" Lucco asked, surprised.

"My friend Rocco will take a ride to the bottom of the quarry. He already dug the hole. He will make the drop and then add two buckets of crushed limestone on top. He'll level it out. All done. Cleaner and easier than concrete. No extra truck needed. In a couple years that quarry becomes a lake. Our friend will be swimmin' with the fishes. Know whadda mean? All set, Lucco?"

"All set, Mario." Lucco decided not to mention the old man. *Ah, it's just one big bag.*

"By the way. Rocco doesn't talk much. Gotta job, do it."

Lucco heard the phone disconnect. *Swimmin' with the fishes,* he thought. Within two hours, Krueger would be gone forever. Within a couple days, the judge, Gino, and the sheriff would all wonder about Krueger's whereabouts as if he had disappeared into thin air. Little would they know, some things are gone forever.

CHAPTER 67

DISCLOSURE

Father Holtz—July 21, 1958

FATHER Holtz took a late-afternoon walk. The weather was warm and humid. He did not wear his collar. He placed a lot of change in his pockets—nickels, dimes, and quarters—which he had set aside from the collection and replaced with his own dollar bills. His slacks jingled as he walked up the street toward downtown. He knew of a public phone booth in the back corridor of the city hall, just four blocks from the rectory. There were two booths. The location offered privacy.

At 2:30 p.m., the priest made himself comfortable in the phone booth and shut the door securely. He set a handful of change on the ledge below the phone. Then he picked up a nickel and dropped it in the slot.

"Hello. Operator."

"Yes, ma'am, I'd like to make a person-to-person phone call to Wabash, Indiana."

"Yes, sir, the number please."

"Wabash 420-7900," Father Holtz said distinctly.

"And who are you calling?"

"Michael Sullivan," he replied, not using *Father* as part of his name.

"Just one minute."

Father Holtz was anxious to talk with the other priest, having no doubt that this was the right thing to do.

"Hello, sir. I have Michael Sullivan. Thirty cents please."

He dropped in the coins and heard the connection. "Hello, Father, this is Father Ben Holtz calling from the diocese in South Wayne.

Remember, we met in May when you and your pastor, Father Warren, came to see Bishop Powers?"

"Oh hello, Father. What a surprise. What can I do for you?" Father Sullivan asked with interest.

"I've been reading the file of Father Jaeger, who was an assistant with you."

Father Sullivan raised his eyebrows and said in a curious tone, "Oh yes?"

"Father, we need to trust each other. This is a highly unorthodox call that I should not be making. Please, may I have your confidence, your complete confidence? This call cannot go beyond the two of us."

"Why, of course. Yes, absolutely about such a serious matter. Totally confidential."

"I'm glad you understand. This is very important, especially to the victims, the children, if you know what I mean."

"Yes, I know. It's good to hear someone else is thinking of them. I thought I was the only one."

"Father, talking on the phone is not good. Would you be willing to meet me face-to-face? Alone, away from the church?" Father Holtz suggested.

"Sure, why of course. Where?" Father Sullivan asked.

"There's a Checker's Truck Stop on the north side of Warsaw on the corner of Highways 15 and 30, northeast corner. Could you meet Wednesday afternoon, say two o'clock?"

"Let me see. Sure, sure, 2:00 to 2:15."

"Wear sunglasses," Father Holtz instructed.

"I can do that. I drive a '53 green Chevy," said Father Sullivan.

"Me a '52 black Ford. Confirmed. Oh yes, once again, Father, this is totally confidential. Nobody can know. Nobody. I am going way out of bounds on this. Our meeting will never have taken place once we meet. We never talked. Father, like the seal of confession, *always*."

"You bet, Father. Thank you for calling me."

Maybe I have finally found someone who is as concerned for the boys as I am, Father Sullivan thought.

Father Sullivan—July 22, 1958

With Father Sullivan and Father Warren saying all the Masses, their weekly breakfast had been interrupted over the past weeks as a result of Father Jaeger's departure. Father Sullivan stopped in the sacristy to see Father Warren after the older priest completed the daily 8:30 Mass.

"Morning, Father Warren."

"Hello, Michael," Father Warren said as he watched a young server extinguish candles. "How are you doing?" he asked.

"Oh, okay I guess," Father Sullivan responded in a hushed voice. "I'd like to talk if you have some time."

"How about at breakfast this morning? I'll be up there in about ten minutes," Father Warren responded.

"That's good. Works for me, Father," Father Sullivan replied appreciatively.

Father Sullivan walked directly to the kitchen. "Good morning, Sister. Sure smells good in here."

"Just baked your favorite blueberry muffins, Father Sullivan," Sister Agatha said, looking for his approval.

"You spoil me more than my own mom, Sister. Father Warren and I would like to have breakfast this morning in the dining room. Would that be okay?"

"Why, of course. Whatever suits the two of you best. The usual this morning—two eggs over easy, ham, and one piece of whole wheat toast? I'll spread the butter?"

"Perfect. As I said, you spoil me, Sister."

"That's what I'm here for, Father Sullivan. I'll bring you some coffee before."

Father Sullivan walked into the dining room, sat down, and opened up the *Plain Dealer*, having brought it from the kitchen table. *They still haven't discovered where Krueger went after he skipped bail. The trial was supposed to be last month.*

This is just terrible and all at the same time as Father Jaeger. What's this world coming to? Reading on, he noticed the article said, "Clarence Wolfe, director of the Wabash Reform School, did not return calls." Skepticism mounting, Father Sullivan knew other abusers could be on the loose at the noted reform school. *Local papers*, he thought, *always mixing feature stories with the editorial page.*

"Hi, Father," he said as Father Warren walked into the dining room and took his place at the head of the table.

With lots on his mind, Father Warren did not even ask why they were having breakfast in the dining room instead of the breakfast room off the kitchen. "What was it you wanted to discuss?" he asked, getting right to the point.

"Father, we are sitting here waiting on word from the bishop. I'm just concerned that the bishop is going to pass Father Jaeger to another parish and cover-up all that happened here."

"Michael," Father Warren said, shaking his head. He coughed then coughed a second time, Father Sullivan noticed. "Excuse me, Michael, It's out of our hands. I'm as concerned as you that he might fall into old habits." His kind face looked troubled under his neatly combed hair.

"Are you okay, Father?"

"Yes, I'm fine. Thank you for asking. Maybe just a little stressed. That just goes with the job, pastor, you know. But, Michael, understand, I can't go around the bishop. He has the authority, the final say. Then beyond him it could be Cardinal Cullings and then, God forbid, Pope John Benedict."

"Yes, I do know, Father, that the Vatican, the pope, makes all the final decisions. Don't tell me that's what has to be done. Think of the lives he'd affect all the while."

"Michael, I'm not saying that," Father Warren answered abruptly. "I just don't want it to go that far."

"I know you don't, Father. Our Bishop Powers has to do the right thing. Father Jaeger should not be sent anyplace around children. Father Warren, we both know the police should be informed."

"No, Michael, no," Father Warren said emphatically. "Not in my parish. He's gone. He's gone. He's in the bishop's hands now. We are not calling the police."

Father Sullivan paused, reflected, and then asked, "If the supreme authority in our Catholic Church is the pope, the Holy See, then he should know of these problems. This is so serious; I think the pope should set a firm policy to handle these abusing, cancerous priests."

"Now, Michael, let's not get ahead of ourselves."

"I hear you, Father. What if this problem grows? What if priests have their hands slapped and are then rewarded with a reassignment to other parishes? What if a parent comes forward, goes to the police, and then to a lawyer? These boys are victims. This problem could get so out of hand that in ten, fifteen, twenty years, the church could have lawsuits for damages … for money. It could be millions. Now is the time, before it's too late."

There was a lull in the conversation. Sister Agatha walked into the room. "Two hot plates from the sister's kitchen just for you two hungry gentlemen," she said with a break-the-ice announcement. Father Sullivan thought she could have been listening even though they had moved to the dining room. "More coffee?"

"No thank you, Sister." Father Warren replied.

She set the hot plates down and returned to the kitchen. Then there was silence.

Less passionately, Father Sullivan continued, "Father, listen please. I've talked to Peter Goodnar and Joey Singleton. I know what Father Jaeger has done. It is sickening and immoral, and he is damaging these boys for a lifetime. Some men would be put in prison for life if they did that to a woman."

"Michael, we've gotten rid of a very bad apple. It's all up to Bishop Powers," Father Warren said, not accepting the true essence of what Father Sullivan was trying to say.

"Sorry, Father, I disagree. We've not gotten rid of a bad apple. We've gotten rid of a sack, a big sack of cancer, so *our* parish is safe. Now, he'll be passed on to do it all over again. Worse yet, our holier-than-thou, almighty, good Bishop Powers, leader of our diocese, our link to Rome … is … is going to spread the sack all around for more children to wallow in. This is wrong. Sorry, so sorry, Father. I don't mean to be disrespectful, but we need to see an end to this."

His face drooping in sadness, Father Warren looked up at Father Sullivan and said nothing. Father Sullivan wiped his mouth with the napkin.

"Sorry, Father. Sorry." Father Sullivan stood, turned, and left the room. He had much to think about before tomorrow's meeting in Warsaw.

WABASH, INDIANA
... circa 1958

Indiana Hotel

The Sheriff   *Joseph Leonard Stouffer*

WABASH, INDIANA
first electrically lighted city in the world

Wabash County Courthose

Sinclair Station

Gackenheimer's Drug Store

CHAPTER 68

CLOUD OF MYSTERY

Randall Zilbar—May 1, 1958

H AROLD Weakman was a mentor to Randall Zilbar. There had been a closeness, a father-son type relationship over the past twenty years that had proven very lucrative for Zilbar. Although schooled as an attorney at Loyola and licensed in Illinois and Indiana, Randall Zilbar had not made law his long-term career.

Harold had inherited all his wealth, including the Wabash State Bank, from his father, who had chartered the bank back at the turn of the century. Harold was successful in everything he undertook. Honor student, class president, and a graduate of Notre Dame in South Bend, Harold was a civic leader and a pillar of the community. His early teenage years had been good years. His father had included him for summer, after-school, and Sunday jobs at the bank. He had immediately begun learning the organization, functions, and structure of a growing financial institution. Accounting, posting transactions, and learning the functions of the various departments, commercial lending, and home mortgages had all been a part of his father's plan to indoctrinate Harold into the banking business. Eventually, Harold's father brought him into the bank full-time but only after he graduated from Notre Dame. Harold had been destined for success.

Randall Zilbar was president of the bank, and Harold Weakman carried the title of chairman of the board, which he totally controlled. In 1956, Randall had hired a young man named David Booth as an assistant comptroller, but he had only done so at the direct insistence of Harold Weakman.

For some years, even as far back as grade school at St. Thomas Moore, David had been a mysterious, sometimes secretive part of Harold's life. Harold Weakman was an extremely private man. Not married, no brothers or sisters, Harold's main focus was his banking business and caring for his elderly mother, Martha. She still lived alone in a large brick Victorian house on Grand Avenue. Her wealth was more than likely the largest in town, if not the entire county.

A cloud of mystery hovered over David, including his relationship with Harold Weakman. Rumor and reality were twisted in fate. Innuendo encircled David, as the man had no family. Although born in Wabash, he had ridden a circular train from distant relatives to friends, even foster families. David never knew his father, although some confirmed he lived in Wabash.

Somehow, David's name had surfaced in association with Gretchen Streater, a good lady who was prone to hard times and mystery. Never married. Gretchen had been murdered a little over a month ago.

Her father, Max, lived a life consumed with alcohol. He was eventually found alone, dead in the alley behind his house. Her mother lived an equally sad and tragic life.

No one really understood the relationship between Harold and David. Their relationship was seen as distant, strange, or even clandestine. David, as a youth, had been known to be seen with Harold, driving around town, visiting the Sweet Shop, and even walking together around Harold's stately Victorian home.

No matter what their relationship, Randall Zilbar had not been pleased to see David join the bank as an assistant comptroller at Harold Weakman's instance. Zilbar had his own agenda and goals. Along with Randall's other investments outside the bank, he had a master financial and organizational asset plan. That, however, did not include the likes of David Booth.

Randall Zilbar did not like the connection between Harold Weakman and David Booth. He saw Harold's affection for David. Years down the road, Randall Zilbar could envision David Booth as a detriment to his financial plan relative to his holdings in the bank. Harold and his mother owned the majority of the bank stock by far. Even though Zilbar held some eighteen to twenty percent, he did not have what he enjoyed most—control. With control came power. The remaining fifteen percent of shares were owned by board members and a few other well-to-do's around Wabash.

Randall Zilbar knew that eventually the control of the bank he coveted had to change hands. Over a three-year plan, if carefully executed, the bank could be totally in his control. David Booth was an unknown. Randall maintained growing confidence that his Cicero connection would continue to pay dividends. Only Randall didn't know just how big they could be, how far they could go, and whose lives would be crossed. But to attain his goals, he didn't rightly care what it took, what he had to do, and who he had to move out of the way. The means were always justified by the end result, no matter who was hurt along the way. David Booth, Zilbar thought, could be a factor he would have to deal with in gaining his control.

CHAPTER 69

FIRST MEETING

Father Sullivan—July 23, 1958, 11:45a.m.

DRIVING north to his meeting with Father Holtz, Father Sullivan maintained a heightened state of anticipation. Not knowing Father Holtz, other than in the meeting last spring with Bishop Powers, Father Sullivan knew he would initially have to be guarded and cautious in his conversation. He knew, however, that the meeting could be an important turn of events if Father Holtz was truthful, knowledgeable, and reliable. Father Sullivan's gut told him he would have no doubt in Father Holtz's credibility.

Ahead, he could see Checker's Truck Stop, where they had agreed to meet. Down shifting his Chevy, Father Sullivan drove into the parking lot and easily found an open space. He backed into the last row, just like he had when he was in high school. *Oh, those days,* he remembered with fondness. Walking toward the front door, he noticed a plain all-black '52 Ford. *Has to be him, I'm sure.*

Looking like just another traveler—untucked shirt, brown penny loafers, and sunglasses—Father Sullivan casually walked into the diner side of the truck stop. Among the work shirts, double clutching diesel boots, and billed hats, Father Holtz could only pass for someone lost and totally out of his environment. *That's him, there in the corner booth,* Father Sullivan concluded as he glanced across the entire room.

Even though they had previously met at Bishop Powers and Father Holtz's meeting, Father Sullivan asked, "Father Holtz, I presume?"

"Yes, that's me. How did you ever figure that out?" Father Holtz returned with good-natured sarcasm.

"Well, your black shirt and white collar sort of says, *I'm a priest, not a truck driver,*" Father Sullivan replied.

"Guess this black shirt in 90-degree heat gives me away," Father Holtz said with a smile and good-natured self-deprecation. Immediately both priests knew they were going to like one another. "I'm having an iced tea. Would you like one?" Father Holtz asked.

"Unsweetened tea will be fine," Father Sullivan responded.

"We both might want something a little stronger after this meeting," Father Holtz said, trying to dispel any nervousness.

After their congenial introductions to one another, each priest gave a little background about his life, where he was from, his family, and so on. Although about ten years older than the younger Father Holtz, Father Sullivan could already tell there was a likeness between them.

Looking very serious, Father Holtz began, "Father, let me—"

"Excuse me, Father, let's make this a little easier. Make it Michael."

"Fine then. Ben for me."

Both priests confirmed with a nod.

"Michael, let me begin by saying this meeting today never took place. You simply cannot repeat our conversation. Never. I know Bishop Powers. I know Father Schmidt. They would not approve at all about what I'm about to tell you. By nature, I do not like to talk negatively about people. I'm not perfect myself. However, what I'm about to tell you is well-intentioned for the good of our church and these boys. I have no other agenda." Father Holtz was fully engaged. He leaned forward. "Michael, all these poor abused boys. I've been observing this for two years. Two long years now since I arrived at the diocese."

"Excuse me, Ben, may I ask specifically ... observed? Observed what for two long years?"

Without hesitation, Father Holtz said, "The cover-up—yes, *cover-up*—as unbelievable as it may sound."

Father Sullivan jolted back in his seat, not expecting those words to be spoken so directly. "How can our church hide all this abuse? Ben, I don't understand. You mean there are more? There are more than Father

Jaeger?" Father Sullivan asked with a look of astonishment yet inside knowing this went beyond just Father Jaeger.

"Let me clarify. There are two things I want you to know. I have to tell someone. Hopefully, you are the right person. Someone I can completely trust, Michael, and I think that is you," Father Holtz assured him. "We shouldn't even say *Father* in front of Jaeger's name. He doesn't deserve to be called *Father*. He degrades the priesthood."

"Ben, Jaeger shouldn't be allowed to wear the collar. He's tarnished his beyond recognition. It's like blasphemy," Father Sullivan said with conviction.

"I know. I agree. He's been at this a long time," Father Holtz said. "So many reassignments. Anyway, I want you to know. I have to tell you, the bishop is going to transfer him again. He's being assigned to a small parish in Eastville, Indiana."

"What? What the hell?" Father Sullivan exclaimed, excusing his language in front of his fellow priest.

"*Shhh*, better keep it down. I know it's hard. Makes you want to scream. Honestly, Michael, I was in a meeting the other day, a meeting with Father Schmidt and Bishop Powers. When I heard this, I wanted to reach across the table and pop Father Schmidt. Dear God forgive me," Father Holtz said, his face turning two shades of red. "Michael, there's so much going on. I want you to know. I want you to work with me."

"Excuse me, gentlemen," a curly haired waitress in a checked dress said. "Would you like to order? Our blue plate today features half a fried chicken, mashed potatoes, gravy, and—"

"Sure, sure, we'll each have one," Father Sullivan said quickly, dismissing the waitress. She stomped off, unable to engage with the priest and his rude friend. "Yikes! Guess I was a little short with her. Sorry."

"Do you know that he's at it again?"

"What do you mean?" Father Sullivan asked. "At it again?"

"Jaeger's in South Wayne for one month, meets with a counselor weekly. Then as I said, he'll move to his new assignment in Eastville. He'll prey again. Wish I was saying *pray*. Meanwhile, I've been keeping my eye on him. During the first two weeks in counseling, I saw him with two different boys, taking them to his apartment. Seen it with my own eyes. Michael, can you believe it? Besides that, he goes to the Y almost every day. You know the Y policy as well as I do, which is the same all over the country. They all swim in the nude, and that's where he's been spending his time."

Father Sullivan was speechless. He felt a lethal combination of rage and nausea sweep through his body. *Cover-up ... how? How?* He stood up, "Excuse me, Ben."

The coffee counter was lined with men in denim, plaid shirts, and sweat-spotted T-shirts. Their conversations about the price of fuel, stagnant home life, sex, and whiskey were not heard by the priest dashing for the door. Outside the diner, Father Sullivan felt the blistering heat. He was boiling; the humidity and the heat of the day were only exceeded by his disdain for the news delivered by his newfound friend. He just had to get fresh air and composure. Father Sullivan wished for a cigarette, but he had given them up while in seminary. He walked to his car, leaned over, and put his hands on the burning metal. "Judas priest!" he cried out, his hands scorched. He kicked the tire, his Irish getting the best of him. Then he took a breath and walked back to the diner.

Returning to the booth, Father Sullivan slid across the seat, right past his just-delivered fried chicken and potatoes.

Father Holtz asked, "You okay?"

"No, I'm really not. I am overwhelmed with all this." Then he added, "With all I've seen at St. Thomas Moore and now to hear the result. Transferred. What'd you say, reassigned? He'll do it all again," Father Sullivan replied.

Father Holtz, seeing the alarm on Father Sullivan's face, said, "Father, that's not all. This goes beyond Jaeger. The cover-up is bigger ... much, much bigger. There's something else I've got to tell you."

Father Sullivan closed his eyes and rested his forehead in his palm. "What is it, Ben? Tell me. I need to know it all if I'm going to help these boys ... I need to know everything."

Father Holtz continued, "Michael, you're not going to like this."

Father Sullivan leaned over, elbows on the table. "I'm sure I won't. Go ahead. I'm all ears." Neither man touched his blue plate special.

"Several weeks ago I received a call."

Father Sullivan listened but could not imagine what Father Holtz was about to say.

Father Holtz continued with a somewhat ashamed look in his eye, as if he did not want to disclose the awful truth. "This unexpected call has torn at my gut ever since." Father Holtz took a large drink of his cold iced tea. "I didn't recognize the caller's voice."

Father Holtz took a deep breath and began to relay the tale. "I received this call, and the voice at the other end quietly said, 'Father, I need to see you. See you now.' I asked who it was and if I knew him. He then said, 'You don't know me, although you might have seen me around the cathedral. Just meet with me. I'll explain to you then. I've heard about a priest from Wabash. Don't know which parish. I heard he's here in South Wayne. He's an abuser. You know, boys. I'm one who knows all about abuse, pedophiles, rape, the whole thing.'

"His voice was getting louder. I then asked what he meant by abuser, as I was looking for the credibility of the person on the other end of the line. He went on to say, 'I know something you need to know. I have heard rumors about what's happening. Do you work for Bishop Powers?' I did not answer; I was looking for some verification. I then asked if he belonged to the parish. He said no but that he attended Sunday Mass maybe once every month or two. He does not attend if Bishop Powers is celebrating Mass. He told me he would explain everything face-to-face, and then he asked to meet that day.

"Sensing his urgency, of course I agreed. I suggested meeting at the cathedral at 2:00 p.m. He emphatically said, 'No, not there. No way. Somewhere else. Can't be seen.' He asked if we could meet at the little diner on Clark Street. I would recognize him. He described himself as six feet tall, dark hair, and twenty-two years old. He would be wearing a blue shirt, sunglasses, and a New York Giant's baseball hat. I agreed to meet with him. Michael, it was a hot day. Electric fans were at a premium. Two movie theatres, a couple restaurants, and one hotel provide air-conditioning in town. Unfortunately, air-conditioning has yet to be installed at the diner."

"Kinda like here," Father Sullivan said as he looked up at the fans above them.

"At exactly 2:05 p.m., I walked by a man in his early twenties sitting in a far booth, wearing a yellow New York Giant's baseball hat and sunglasses. As I made my way to the booth, I could feel the refreshing air from the ceiling fans. Lunch hour had ended; there were few patrons. He recognized my collar, so he stood up as I approached, and we shook hands. He mentioned that he appreciated me meeting him on short notice. He said he had attended my Mass on several occasions. He thought my Latin was inspiring. I thanked him. He smiled and then began with, 'I won't waste your time,' while placing his glasses in his hat on the bench. 'My name is Ned Thornbauer. I was twelve while attending St. Ambrose Academy in South Wayne back in 1948. Bishop Powers met me at a seminar here at St. Leonard's.'

"After their second class, Bishop Powers asked Ned to stay after. He explained that he needed some extra help correcting papers and other favors. Having checked his records, the bishop knew Ned was a bright student. Truth is, he wanted more than records to be taken care of, Ned later found out. The bishop explained to him that he had a grant for out-standing altar boys to give each semester. One hundred and fifty dollars! Ned jumped at the chance. I interrupted Ned by asking what kind of favors. He went on to say, 'Sexual favors. Goddamn sexual, abusive favors, Father.' He then apologized and continued.

"Michael, I hope I don't leave any of the conversation out. For the first couple of sessions, Ned simply met bishop in his apartment. They discussed class, and Ned corrected papers, just the objective tests. About the third session, something unexpected and strange happened. Bishop Powers said he could extend the grant through the 1949–1950 academic season. Ned told him that would be great, as he could use the money for high school. Then the bishop told him about his little cabin on a lake in southern Michigan. He invited Ned to go along with him on his day off. There was fishing, boating, and swimming.

"Can you believe this, Michael? This Ned is telling about sex with the bishop. Bishop Powers wanted to go on a Thursday and stay over for one night. That's how the bishop set Ned up. Once they got there, the first thing the bishop did was show Ned around the cabin and grounds. Then they went for a swim. That's when it all started. When it was time to swim, the bishop looked at it as a sexual experience more than physi-cal exercise. Everything started there. Ned was very uncomfortable. The bishop told him while at the lake, 'We swim in the nude, just like at the

Y.' Ned was astonished, but the bishop persisted. While swimming, the bishop began his move. Ned couldn't wait to get out of the water.

"Once they got back to the cabin, the bishop wasted no time, and they ended up in his bedroom on the second floor. Bishop Powers told Ned how much he enjoyed the swimming. He kept telling Ned that the water was so clean and natural. He wanted to know if Ned thought it felt good. Ned told him it was a little awkward swimming with him. The bishop said Mass, had been to Rome, listened to confessions, and now had swum with Ned. Didn't seem right to him. He simply didn't know how to respond. He had been shocked to feel the bishop's groping hands under the water. Ned had also detected that the bishop was very excited during that experience. Most awkward was having to climb the ladder onto the dock when they exited the lake. Ned moved fast to be the first one on the deck.

"Michael, I couldn't believe what he was telling me. Ned went on to say that the bishop walked from the pier up the hill to the house … naked. His towel and trunks hung over his shoulder. He told Ned he had too much sand in his trunks. Ned had already tightened his string."

Father Sullivan continued to listen in shock and amazement.

"Apparently, the cottage spared no luxury with its rattan furniture, colorful drapes, a big new television, a full kitchen, and lots of windows. The screened porch overlooked the lake. Ned said the whole cabin was comfortable and inviting. The bishop was most anxious to show him his room upstairs. Within a few minutes of entering the guest room, Ned heard the bishop say, 'Come see this view.' Ned wanted to go home, but he was only twelve at the time. There were windows overlooking the lake from the top of the hill. Then he saw the bishop standing, looking out over the lake. Ned said all he could see was his big—excuse me, Father—'fat ass' and thought, *Please don't let him turn around.*

"He asked Ned to come and look at the view. He didn't know how to say no to a bishop. Standing behind and to his side, Ned saw bishop's hairy back. He noticed a patch on the right side of his waist, just above the towel. Looked like a patch on an inner tube. Some kind of a birthmark. Ned still sees the patch in his sleep. The bishop wanted him to stand close to him to look at the sunset. Bishop Powers placed his right arm firmly around Ned's shoulder and then pulled him to his side.

The bishop said, 'That's God's sunset. He created it to show us his love.' What's that supposed to mean?

"All of a sudden Bishop Powers dropped his hand from Ned's shoulder along his side, tucking his thumb into Ned's trunks then pulled them to the floor. Ned froze. He started shaking. Mustering the courage to stop this most unforeseeable, sick situation, Ned told the bishop that this didn't seem right and he wanted to go home, but the bishop told him to relax, as this was God's work, the beauty of nature, and we are a part of nature. The next thing Ned knew, they were both on the bed. His trunks were off. Ned did recall saying *no*. He said *no* many times. Bishop Powers was more than twice Ned's size, all of 250 pounds. Ned couldn't physically resist. The bishop was all over him. Then Ned felt this horrible pain. He couldn't see the bishop because he was behind him. Ned said the pain hurt so bad. The breathing was heavy with all kinds of noises.

"Father Sullivan, that was ten years ago. Ned is twenty-two now. He is haunted every day. Every day Ned sees the bishop, but it borders on hate for him and all he represents. Ned then asked me, 'Father, do you know what it's like when someone does something unjust to you or your family? It never goes away. You continually think of how to bring justice. I vowed to do just that. Bring justice to that selfish, sick, arrogant pig of a man. I will never end my quest. Someday, Bishop Powers will wish he had never done it. I will get him. I will!'

"Ned finished by saying the bishop did everything to him that night. He said he must have been in there for well over an hour. At one time, the bishop got up from the bed to go to the bathroom and then went down to the kitchen. He could tell by the sounds of the toilet flushing and the refrigerator door closing. He heard two pops of a bottle. Fortunately, they were Cokes. By now, the sun had set, and then he came back upstairs and almost dove on the bed, all over Ned. They lay in bed, still watching that view through the two open doors. Ned prayed. Wanted to get up and run. His mind ran rampant with guilt and sin."

"Why didn't Ned run?" Father Sullivan asked.

"He was scared. One other thing, knowing that this was against his will, the bishop suggested that he go get a good night's sleep, like he was trying to be nice or something. Ned remembers shaking and crying in his bed that night. He was terrified the bishop would come back into his room, but he didn't.

"The next morning, Ned asked if they could skip their swim, as he wasn't feeling well. The bishop understood, so he suggested Ned nap in his room while he swam. Ned watched the bishop from the deck as he walked down the hill, already naked. His fat body was probably already in heat. I'm sure he didn't enjoy swimming by himself.

"Their ride home was very quiet. Ned couldn't say anything. The bishop did say that this may have been difficult for Ned. He wanted Ned to know that he appreciated that he came along. He said it as if his awful, sick deeds hadn't even happened. Bishop Powers did tell Ned, 'Let's keep everything just between you and me.' That's exactly what happened according to Ned. He will never forget. The horror stays with him.

"I was glad we talked. I told Ned I was exhausted and sickened by his story. Then I told him I had a couple questions. I asked if there were other times with the bishop. Ned paused before answering. 'Yes, I'm ashamed to say. Lasted the whole summer. Maybe three trips to the cabin alone.' Then I asked if there had been anywhere else. He said, 'Yes, in the fall he had me come to an apartment in town. I think it was a guest apartment now that I look back. He never chanced the rectory. He was smart and coy. He carefully planned every meeting.'

"Then I asked if anyone knew about all this? Had he told his parents? Then Ned confided, 'I didn't tell my dad.' They lived with their grandmother until Ned got his own apartment. She raised them and does a lot for Ned and his little brother. He told a good friend, who he lives with, about the bishop. He keeps telling Ned to come forward. Go to the newspaper. Tell the world. Ned looked directly at me and said, 'Now I've come forward because of Danny.' Ned paused, and I asked why. Bishop Powers is now doing the same thing to his little brother! Can you believe this, Father? The same wretched hands of that wicked man have taken Danny to his cabin. Ned never told Danny before. Then he finds this out.

"I asked Ned one last thing. I asked him if he swore all this happened. That it was all true. He said, 'Just ask the bishop to see his back. Look for the reddish-brown birthmark above his waist. You'll find the truth. Give me a lie detector test. There's so much more to tell you, but I've said enough.'

"I encouraged Ned to go forward and said he would be helping other boys. He hesitated and looked a little flustered, but there was one other thing he wanted to say. Something important he had held back. He hadn't known how this meeting would go. I believe in what Ned was saying, but I wish it wasn't true.

"Ned went on to say, 'On our way home the last time, the bishop started to talk. I remember it vividly. I think he could have been concerned that I'd tell what happened. He went on to say that the night was beautiful. He reminded me that as a bishop and a priest, he needed to show God's love. Men, women—we should all love one another. He said he represents our Lord on this Earth. I am His shepherd among men. Shepherds not only look after their sheep, but they also love their sheep. He said I was like a sheep, and he was the shepherd sharing his love. All I could do was agree with him.'

"Ned went on to say that the bishop told Ned that their time together was covered by the code of the Catholic seal. Under the threat of mortal sin, Ned could never, never disclose what had happened between the bishop and him. Just in case Ned were ever weak and tempted by the devil himself to break the Catholic seal, Bishop Powers reminded him of something the bishop knew about Ned. Bishop Powers said, 'And you wouldn't want me to tell. Remember the collection baskets? I know where you are getting your spending money.' Ned knew it was a lie, but the bishop had the power and the authority."

CHAPTER 70

GONE FOREVER

Lucco Gagliardi—May 1, 1958

LUCCO checked his watch. Ten minutes. After driving around the gravel pit a few blocks, he returned to the main gate at 6:44. Just as he threw the big Buick into park, Lucco heard the roar of a huge yellow loader. The bucket on the front was about the size of his car. The machine pulled up to the gate. High on the seat, he could see a thin muscular man dressed in a flannel shirt and bib overalls. He wore an engineer's hat. The cigarette dangling from his lips was full-length. *This has to be Rocco.*

The man waved for Lucco to follow. Lucco watched as Rocco jumped down from the loader, open the gate, and climbed back on the loader. He waved for Lucco to follow. Down a gravel road, dust flew. Lucco held back trying to avoid the flying dust and debris landing on his black car. Through the cloud of dust, Lucco could see the machine pulling behind a high fence. Suddenly, the large yellow loader stopped. Lucco waited for the dust to settle. Then he pulled his car forward alongside the high loader. Rocco was lighting another cigarette. He stayed anchored to his seat. Lowering the bucket, he signaled Lucco to drive forward. Then he drew his hand back.

Seeing the crushed stone on the bottom of the huge bucket, streetwise Lucco understood the signal immediately. After pulling the car forward twenty yards or so, Lucco threw his right arm atop the back of the seat and looked over his shoulder—a hard maneuver for a big man. He loosened his tie and then backed the car up perfectly square to the bucket. He watched

460

Rocco's hand waving him back. Rocco put up his palm, signaling Lucco to stop. Then he waved Lucco out of the car.

Lucco took his suit coat off, neatly laid it in the backseat, and closed the door before dust infiltrated the inside of his black Buick. Two feet of gravel lay between the car's back bumper and the front of the bucket. Lucco looked up at the signal caller, expecting him to get down from the loader. All he got was a signal to open the trunk.

A powerful musty smell escaped into the dusty air. "Ah, shit!" *I got 'em in … I'll get 'em out.* This time the package was stiffer. With the weight of two men, it took both of his arms to roll them out of the trunk. With a loud thump, the canvas-covered bodies landed almost square in the bucket. Then with his feet, Lucco pushed the wrapped bodies to the back of the bucket. With a second push, the canvas was square. No sooner had he escorted Krueger and the old man into the bucket than the loader moved back two more feet. The big bucket revolved back toward the machine, engulfing both of the bodies inside. The bucket then soared high above Rocco.

Rocco sat there for a moment with the bucket high overhead. Lucco could only see the exposed bottom of the steel coffin. Rocco lit another cigarette, took a long drag, nodded and gave a half salute signaling a good-bye to Lucco Gagliardi. Dust hovered high overhead. Lucco watched as Rocco drove away. About one hundred yards down the road, he observed the loader turn right toward the quarry.

Lucco got back into his car and followed the same path as the loader. He pulled up to the spot where Rocco had turned and entered the quarry. From his car, he could see into the mouth of the giant pit, maybe fifty acres in size. The time was 6:58 a.m. Lucco watched far in the distance as the yellow loader headed across the back of the quarry. He waited and watched—6:59 a.m. Suddenly he saw the loader stop. The bucket tilted forward over what, from the distance, looked like a hole or a pit.

Barely detecting the wrapped tarp, Lucco watched the bucket roll over and its load disappear into the grave. Immediately, Rocco backed up and then pushed a nearby pile of gravel into the pit one bucket at a time until the pile was gone and the hole was leveled flat. Phillip Krueger's journey had come to an abrupt end, along with his uninvited companion.

As Mario Molinaro had said, they'd swim with the fishes. *Some things are gone forever.*

PART V

YOUNG BOYS AND VICIOUS MEN

CHAPTER 71

MISSING

Sheriff Thurow—May 2, 1958

CONCERN about Krueger's whereabouts surfaced when he didn't show up at the courthouse that Friday. Sheriff Thurow did not know where he could be. He was confident that Krueger would not dare skip bail. Late Friday afternoon, the receptionist led Sheriff Thurow to the judge's chambers.

"Judge, do you have a minute?" he asked.

"Yes, of course. We let you in, didn't we?"

"Krueger failed to show for his bail report."

"What? Nobody skips bail on me. Check it out ... Find him!" the judge responded abruptly.

"Yes, your honor, I will." Sheriff Thurow knew better than to make excuses. He left and went back to his office in the courthouse.

The sheriff was fuming. "Find Sergeant Bauer."

Within minutes Bauer appeared. "Yes, sir?"

"Come with me, Sergeant. Krueger didn't report for bail. We're going to check it out." Both men quickly headed to the sergeant's car. "Go to his house on Pike. He's got to be there."

After pulling into the side driveway of Krueger's house, which had last been traveled by a big black Buick, the sheriff and his trusty Sergeant Bauer exited the car. Sergeant Bauer knocked on the back door. No response. He called out Krueger's name but was met with silence.

"Open up," Sheriff Thurow instructed. Testing the knob, he found that the back door was unlocked. "Go ahead. We'll check it out. He's on bail. This is our jurisdiction," he said.

Sergeant Bauer and the sheriff walked in the house as if they owned the place and checked all the rooms. All were vacant. The bed in the front bedroom looked slept in. The bedspread was pulled back as if someone had half attempted to remake the bed. Nothing else in the house was askew.

"Hey, Sheriff, look at this," Sergeant Bauer said, picking up the wooden chair that was still tipped over by the side of the dining room table. Bauer looked the chair over.

"Call Detective Peterson and have him come over right away," Sheriff Thurow said, his sixth sense telling him something was wrong.

The front parlor and back bedroom looked all in place. The sheriff tested all the windows, looking for forced entry. There was none. A couple of the windows were painted shut. Within twenty minutes, Detective Hamilton Peterson arrived. A big guy, the detective had graying hair, wore a plain wide lapelled suit, and was missing his left hand, which he had lost during the war. Peterson was all business.

"Sheriff, Sergeant, what do we have here? Real crime scene, no doubt. Seen this before," Detective Peterson said.

"The subject, Phillip Krueger. This is his house. This Krueger guy's out on bail. A huge one. He is accused of sexual abuse at the reform school."

Detective Peterson shook his head. "I always said there is some no good going on at that place. Have suspected that for years. Remember back in '34? Never found out the real cause of that boy's death. Should've had me on the case except I wasn't here then. Most unfortunate."

Sheriff Thurow told Detective Peterson that they had checked out the entire house. Nothing had been disturbed. "Peterson, see this?" the sheriff asked, holding up a chair.

"How could I miss it, Sheriff? You got it right in my face."

"Oh sure. Sorry. What do ya think?" sheriff responded.

Peterson took the chair, walked over to the window, and examined it closely, holding it by the back rung. Peterson detected residue of glue or something sticky. He pulled the chair within two inches of his eyes. "Ah ha … residue, glue, sticky glue. Absolutely. Black threads."

Immediately, he thought of tape … black tape. Setting the chair down, Peterson thought a few seconds. "Hmmm. Of course. No two ways about it. Someone was bound and tied to this chair. Obvious to anyone with a trained eye." *Now,* he thought, *where are they?*

"How do you know that?" Sergeant Bauer asked.

"Keen eye, analytical mind, just my gifted sixth sense. Won at Indian poker every time when I was a kid."

Detective Peterson showed the chair to the sheriff. Then he thoroughly checked the top, underneath, and the legs. Sliding his hand over the back right leg, he felt a crack. Examining it still closer, he tried to separate the crack. It opened easily. Releasing the pressure, he asked, "Could Krueger have been bound to this chair? Then he tried to free himself. As he rocked the chair, the back leg cracked. If so, then someone had to stop him. Sergeant, let's check the place for any other signs," Detective Peterson said as he checked the chair more carefully. Then he asked, "Where's the green paint in the house?"

The sheriff and the sergeant looked at each other, puzzled. "Why's he asking that?" Sergeant Bauer asked the sheriff.

"Yes, green paint," Peterson said again. "Something wood. Furniture. Woodwork that has green paint. Obvious if you know what you're doin'."

The three began to look around.

"Why green paint?" the sergeant asked Sheriff Thurow.

"Wanna paint the chair, Sergeant. Let's just find it and see," Peterson said. "Obviously, this hallway and the doors to the bedroom and bath are green. Turn those lights on," he said as he began to check the woodwork. "Bring that chair to me."

The sheriff was not used to being bossed around. Sergeant Bauer lifted the dining room chair and handed it to Peterson.

"Okay, let's say you have a reason to tie me up, bind me to a chair. Where do you set the chair?" No answer from the sheriff or the sergeant. "You set the chair where it can't be seen, like in this hall back from the archway, which leaves only in front of this bedroom door. Assume you have tape. " He set the chair down about a foot in front of the door. "Why not against the door, you ask? He could bounce and make noise … wood on wood," the detective said to the two men in uniform.

"Right! And if you move it forward, the chair's in the archway and could be seen from the window."

"Makes perfect sense to me," said the sheriff, agreeing with Peterson.

"Watch this. Assume I'm bound and taped in this chair. What do I do? I rock it. Now, if I rock this chair back against the door, what happens?" Not giving them a chance to answer, Peterson said, "This. He tips the chair back like this. See the scratch and scuffed green paint on the door? Krueger pushed the chair back, scratching the door and cracking the back leg of the chair."

"Yeah, you're right," said the sergeant. "How'd he figure that all out?" Sergeant Bauer asked, looking at Sheriff Thurow.

"I didn't just get out of crime school, Sergeant." Peterson looked up. "Now look at the back of the chair." Tilting the chair forward, Peterson showed them the green paint smudge against the stained wood.

"Now I see it," the sheriff said.

"Very good there, Sheriff. Now you're learnin'. Here's what happened. It's obvious to the well-trained eye. Now listen here, you two Boy Scouts. Oh sorry, no disrespect, Sheriff. I think the sergeant here is still a Cub."

Sergeant Bauer looked up at the sheriff, "What's he mean?"

"Listen to him. You'll learn something."

"During the night, someone broke in, probably just picked the lock or the door might have left open … small town. He finds your Krueger asleep. He overpowers him, probably a tight gag, and then tapes him to the chair. The intruder either wanted to search the house, or maybe the intruder didn't want to leave right away. Other business. *Hmmm.* Let's see. There's no blood here. No indication of a physical tussle. I'd assume Krueger just cooperated under duress. He had no choice."

"Okay. I get what happened, but why was he bound to the chair? Why not just tie him up and leave him on the floor?" Sheriff Bauer asked.

Peterson replied with a look of distant, "'Cause he was a thoughtful intruder. Wanted Krueger to be comfortable. What else? This may have been a burglary. Gave the intruder time to loot the house. Or someone doesn't want him to go to trial … and … he's simply gone."

"All sounds plausible. Think you've got it all figured out?"

"But who could have done it? Who comes to mind?" Peterson asked.

"The only one I can think of is Bernard Bednar," the sheriff said.
"Who's he?"

"Just a worker at the school. He is the guy who caught Krueger and pulled him off the boys."

"Well, that could very well be the case. One thing we do know, this Krueger guy did not skip bail. Think about it," Peterson said. "Someone maybe didn't want him to go to trial. On the witness stand, he could expose and implicate others. I have always been suspicious about that school."

"We sure know what they were hiding," Sheriff Thurow said to Peterson.

"What's that?" Peterson asked. "This guy and the boys? An abuser?"

"Yes, that's his gig. Boys. The boys they were fooling with. They didn't want anyone to know," sheriff said.

"You're probably right. However, maybe there's more than meets the eye. Maybe, just maybe, they were hiding something else. Look beyond the obvious. We know about the boys, as you say this guy's on bail," Detective Peterson said.

Sergeant Bauer looked at Sheriff Thurow. "What's he mean the obvious?"

"He means this Krueger could be screwing around with more than just these boys."

Detective Peterson looked at the sheriff and sergeant, his hat resting back on his head and his tie ajar. He bent his knees into a crouch, looked again at the green paint on the chair, and moved his head up and down. "Yep, this is beyond the obvious." Peterson stood. "Ol Hammy here's got it figured out. Okay, gentlemen. Have another investigation that needs my attention." Peterson turned and left the scene.

Gino Moretti—May 2, 1958

Gino Moretti received a phone call from the sheriff's secretary, informing him of Krueger's disappearance. Gino responded by immediately calling Judge Seiler. "Connect me with Judge Seiler."

"Judge Seiler here."

"Judge, this is Gino Moretti. What's this about Krueger?"

"He flew the coop. Gone. Vamoosed. Bye. He's out of here. You have any ideas? I warned you, Moretti. The sheriff's over at his house now. Do you know anything about this, counsel?"

"He's my client. I have no idea. I haven't seen him since we posted bail," Gino said to the judge. He knew immediately that he had better call Randall Zilbar. "I'll check this out and get back to you, Judge."

Gino immediately called Zilbar. "Hello, Gino Moretti here for Randall."

"One moment please."

"Randall, Gino. Listen up. Krueger's gone, skipped bail. Now what? What do you want me to do?" Gino asked.

"Play it out. Just let it play out," Zilbar said and then hung up the phone.

What the hell's that mean? Gino asked himself, puzzled at the lack of reaction from Zilbar.

Randall Zilbar—May 2, 1958

Anxious to hear about the results of Lucco's trip, Randall Zilbar gave Mario a call. "Hey, Mario, this is Randall. Checking back to hear about Lucco's time in Indiana."

"Randall, my man. Always good to hear from you. I know you wanna know if Lucco has returned. All's handled for you. He arrived back yesterday afternoon. I can assure you on my mama's grave in Sicily, your friend doesn't exist anymore. No strings, no loose ends. Gone. Done. Forever"

"That's good to hear. So good," Randall said, knowing Mario's word was gold.

"It's our way. We take care of each other. Ya know what I mean?" Zilbar heard across the line.

"Another subject, Mario. I want to send a couple of your runners down here. I'll make sure Wolfe has two briefcases for you. Have them arrive Thursday afternoon, August 14. That should be enough time. Wolfe will be waiting. Tell them to be careful." Randall liked how his operation was adhered to and handled between Mario, Vito, and Wolfe. He preferred just pulling the strings.

"Always do, Randall. You know that. Say, how's my man Vito? How's he doing in that small berg? I'm glad he likes being close to his daughter. Bet she's a great wife to you, Randall."

Randall replied, "She's a great wife and mother, and Vito is just remarkable. Totally focused in his world. As you can expect, I'm very fond of Vito and all he does for me. He is very talented. A true craftsman and artist. Again, tell those guys to drive carefully. Important cargo, you know."

"Never worry, Randall. Keep it hummin' down there."

"You bet. Oh by the way, Did your big guy give you the envelope, Mario?"

"Sure did. Remember, Randall, one hand washes the other."

"See you, Mario. Thanks again." Randall Zilbar sat back in his chair. *All's going well.*

CHAPTER 72

LONG FRIENDSHIP MADE

Father Holtz—July 23, 1958, mid-afternoon

FATHER Holtz and Father Sullivan had been meeting for more than three hours by the time Father Holtz finished his story about Ned. Their uneaten chicken was now room temperature, which meant warm.

"What did the bishop know about Ned?" Father Sullivan asked.

Father Holtz took another drink of iced tea and said, "When the bishop was Ned's pastor, he knew about the private and personal lives of his parish. Bishop Powers told Ned that there were things about his father that he need not know. He told Ned there was an incident Ned's dad had with the law, and of course, the bishop's treatment of Ned taking money from the collection. Ned was caught in the bishop's unscrupulous trap. Although he did not disclose to Ned the exact details about his dad, he made it clear that he would hold the secret as long as Ned would never tell about the trips to the cabin. The ten-year secret about his father was always in the back of Ned's mind, just like the night at the cabin he could never forget." Father Holtz looked at Father Sullivan. "I'm trying my best to tell this just as Ned told me."

"I'm following okay," Father Sullivan replied.

"Father, I want to tell you more about Ned's family to understand his plight. Ned's father was a strange fellow who never knew his own father. He never graduated from high school. He had minor scrapes with the law and was divorced twice. When Ned was eleven years old, he and his infant brother went to live with their grandmother, Ida Thornbauer. She was in her early sixties. Ben said she never talked about her own son,

Ned's father. Ned did know he'd had a very difficult childhood. Ned's father disappeared just after Ned moved in with his grandmother."

"How do you know all this?" Father Sullivan asked.

"Ned was very open. I don't know him well, of course, but he seems to have a very level head. I'll tell you this, he adores his grandmother. He also said he came forward because of his little brother."

"Sounds like he's had quite a challenging life, and I have a hunch that you're about to tell me more," Father Sullivan said as if he were asking a question.

Another hour passed. Father Holtz could tell the waitress wanted to know what their long meeting was all about. He could tell she was a little aggravated, as she kept eyeing the uneaten fried chicken every time she filled up their iced tea glasses.

Father Sullivan looked absolutely perplexed. "I would have never dreamed all this about Bishop Powers. I don't even know how to respond," he said to Father Holtz. "I thought you would be telling me something else about Father Jaeger."

"Yes, I say there's more than meets the eye. Jaeger is one of the growing number of abusive priests we've dealt with since I've been working with Father Schmidt. There have been six others … all moved on to other parishes. Yes, it's a cover-up. No two ways about it."

"Then you tell me about the bishop. Logic tells you that Ned wasn't his first. You'd think there may have been others before. Makes it easier to understand why he covers Jaeger and the other priests. He's also covering himself. As you said, Bishop Powers is very ambitious despite his horrific sins. What are you going to do, Father, if this sickens you like it does me?" Father Sullivan asked.

"Michael, considering my position on the inside, I mean working directly for the bishop, I can't chance exposing their wrongdoings. At least not yet. I'm on the inside. Observing, I journal everything. If we could totally trust each other and stay in complete confidence, we could fight this together. These are crimes against minors. Police have to be told," Father Holtz informed him.

"How do you mean, fight this together?" Father Sullivan asked.

"We begin with Father Jaeger. When I learn what is happening from my communications with Father Schmidt or Bishop Powers, I will keep you informed. You in turn can come back against the bishop by going to Cardinal Cullings or even the police. This has been kept very quiet. That's the way the bishop wants it. We need to make the authorities or, like I said, the cardinal aware. You can help me expose this before a scandal develops in the church," Father Holtz said.

"What if we begin by me going to the bishop and asking him to take definitive actions against this?" Father Sullivan suggested. "If that doesn't work, I'll go to Cardinal Cullings in Indianapolis. Isn't there a saying, Father? All roads lead to Rome?" He paused. "We have a pedophile priest being transferred to another parish with children. We have a cover-up. I have to talk to Bishop Powers. I don't need to confront him yet, I mean challenge his own abusive ways. He can't send Jaeger to another parish." He continued, "Ben, what about the police?"

"We had one case. It was close to South Wayne, and the boy's father went to the district attorney," Father Holtz said.

"And ... what happen?" Michael asked.

"It went nowhere. Not enough evidence, the DA said. Then I find out it's all political. The DA is a parishioner at St. Leonard's. Didn't stand a chance. The DA and the bishop knew one another. For one thing, I'm going to keep my eye on Jaeger while he's here," Father Holtz promised.

"It will be more difficult for me, being a hundred miles away, but somehow I will," Father Sullivan promised.

"I'm sure you will, Michael. I can tell where your heart is," Father Holtz added. "I called you based on trust." He paused a moment, "I may sound paranoid, but please agree that my name will never come up? I'm just the source for you," Father Holtz asked. "If I stay at St. Leonard's, they'll keep me involved if I'm quiet. I'll learn more ... and, Michael, I'll keep you aware. Do you have a private post office box?"

"No, I don't," he replied.

"Then get one. Better than over the phone. Someone could listen. We can meet here again when needed. I want to fight this. It's bad. Real bad. We must stop it ... before it grows and goes further. Remember, everything is confidential. We never met today ... or ever in the future."

Father Sullivan looked at Father Holtz and assured him they could work together confidentially. Before the waitress returned with more tea, the two priests agreed it was time to go. After paying the bill, they walked together to Father Holtz's car.

"I'm glad I called you, Michael," Father Holtz said.

"Me too," Father Sullivan responded. He placed his hand on the younger priest's shoulder and said, "If you'll keep me informed, I will bring Jaeger to justice."

Thus began a long and trusted friendship. Both priests wanted to help the victims and save their church. *Who knows how far this can go*, Father Sullivan thought as he headed back to Wabash. *Who can possibly know?*

CHAPTER 73

TIME HAS COME

Father Warren—July 24, 1958

WALKING through the rectory in the late evening, Father Sullivan saw Sister Ann Marie. He asked if she knew of Father Warren's whereabouts. Sister Ann Marie told him Father Warren had just left for church. Father Sullivan knew where he would be.

Walking through the side door of the church, he could see the elderly priest kneeling in his usual solitary location, rosary in hand. Twelve rows back from the front of the St. Joseph's statue, always three spaces in, Father Warren felt comfortable, peaceful, and alone. Usually he was left alone. He saw Father Sullivan approaching.

Stopping at Father Warren's pew, Father Sullivan leaned over and said, "Sorry to bother you, Father."

"That's okay, Michael. Quite okay," he said with overflowing peacefulness.

"I'd like some time to talk," Father Sullivan said.

"Right here." Father Warren patted the wooden pew. "Late afternoon, we're all alone. So peaceful. Sit down and join me. Take in this special place." He looked at the concern on Father Sullivan's face. "Now tell me, what is it?" he asked, giving Father Sullivan an open invitation.

"Thank you, Father. I've been doing a lot of thinking, talking to some of the right people, learning more. Father, I can't let this pass. Don't you believe that sometimes in life there are times when we are faced with injustice, when others are hurt? You can't think of yourself; you have to bring the perpetrator to justice. It's the right thing to do,"

"Yes, there are times when justice must prevail. You, Michael, are the only one who knows if that time has come. Nobody else can tell you. As a matter of fact, you may be hearing what you don't want to hear: *Hold back. Forget the injustice. You can't do it alone.* Yes, Michael, only you know when the time is right."

"Thank you, Father, for the insight. I know you understand that I have to do what is right for these boys."

"I do, Michael. I do."

There was silence between the two men. They were engulfed by the comforting quiet within the beautiful church.

Father Sullivan looked at Father Warren. "My time has come. I can't sit back. Trust me, there's a lot more going on in our church than just Jerome Jaeger," he said to Father Warren. "There's more. Much more. I know I must expose the wrongdoers. I must bring those twisted souls to justice."

Father Warren responded, "I know you are going through frustration, agony. I respect that. Your intentions are good. And Michael … " He paused. "I think you are justified. I know you, your conviction, integrity, and passion to do what is right. You love our Lord and God. You love our church. If you need to pick up this torch … then it is your choice, your crusade." The older priest reached over, took Father Sullivan's hands, and cupped them in his. Squeezing tight, he said, "Michael, you have my blessing. Do what you have to do, my son." Nodding, Father Warren knelt back down and began his rosary again. Twice again, he coughed. Father Sullivan noticed the elder priest take a deep breath. Almost a gasp.

"Father, I worry about you and that cough. Have you been checked lately by your doctor?"

"No, not really. Little time, but I will make note. Get a physical."

Father Sullivan stood in the vacuum of silence of the grand church. Looking down at his good pastor, he bent over and placed his hand on the priest's shoulder. With his index finger, he gently touched his white collar. He felt strength reverberate deep into his soul. "Thank you, Father. Thank you. May God bless you."

Father Sullivan leaned over and kissed the top of the white-haired priest's head. The moment was touching for both priests. Neither said a word.

Father Warren continued to look straight ahead … *Who art in heaven. Hallowed be thy name.*

No more words were spoken.

Father Sullivan genuflected and walked to the back of the church, blessed himself with holy water and disappeared into the darkness.

CHAPTER 74

SCHEDULED PICKUP

Clarence Wolfe—August 14, 1958

A black '57 Buick pulled up in front of the reform school. One black suit stepped out. The driver waited in the car, the motor running. Carrying two black briefcases, the man with a pug nose and deep-cut scar over his right eye climbed the steps and walked through the front door, straight to Miss Gardner's desk.

"The name's Sam, Sam Baretti. Mr. Wolfe's expecting me."

Miss Gardner eyed him up and down. She knew those shoes were not from Wake's Shoes on Canal. "I'll be right back, sir. Have a seat over there by the wall," she said, pointing to the empty row of wooden banker chairs.

"I'm fine, ma'am. Thanks. Will stand right here."

"Sir, our procedure is to wait over there, sitting in the chair."

"Will stand right here," he said again.

Okay, if you insist, she thought. *Can't follow rules.* As Miss Gardner walked into Wolfe's office, Wolfe could see Sam through the door.

"Just send him in," he said, not giving her a chance to play her role. "Mr. Baretti, please come in. Close that door behind you."

"Got the packages, Mr. Wolfe?" Baretti asked once the door was closed, as he knew the routine.

"Right over here." Wolfe walked over to the table on the windowless side of the room.

"Good." Baretti could see the packages. Setting his two briefcases on the table, he unlocked them and carefully placed four packages, about eight by eleven by three inches each, in one of the two cases, locked the latch, and spun the combination. Repeating the action, he moved to fill the second black case. Looking at Wolfe, he asked "There only three more?"

"Yeah. That's right. All there."

Baretti placed the three packages in the second case, locked it, turned with both cases securely in hand, and said, "Thank you, sir. Till next time." He then left, walking past Miss Gardner without a word.

"Thank you, sir. Please come again," she said as if she had any influence on their visits. "We enjoy having out of town guests."

Wolfe knew Randall Zilbar would be pleased when the packages were delivered to Mario in Cicero. There, Mario would expedite them to their final destination.

Randall Zilbar—August 14, 1958

Randall Zilbar's life was in a perplexing state of limbo. His personal finances in real estate, stocks and bonds, and other lucrative under-the-radar investments were thriving. Greed for money, power, and control had no limitations as far as he was concerned. Growth beyond Wabash was becoming more a way of life. His financial tentacles now reached to Indianapolis and Chicago. Meanwhile, his two main concerns—Wolfe and Booth—both presented obstacles. While Wolfe held a trump card on his past, David Booth could be a barrier in Randall's pursuit of control of the bank.

Randall Zilbar did not like surprises. He was concerned that one was on the horizon. A plan had to be executed. At fifty-two, he foresaw a long prosperous financial future ahead. Nothing could be in his way. His money, power, and self-centered arrogance had cultivated an assumed power beyond his own worth. Randall Zilbar's narcissism continued to grow like thorns on a dry bush in the desert.

CHAPTER 75

DECEPTION

Father Jaeger—July 31, 1958

THE day was another sultry one. Clouds hung low, trapping humidity over the city. Father Jerome Jaeger was elated to have his last session with Dr. Bloomberg. Knowing he was concealing his non-acceptance of all that the doctor was saying or trying to do for him, Father Jaeger went along with the well-intended doctor like a fox. *One more session in this small, plain four-corner office and I'll be out of here.* The form-fitting plastic chair was more than moderately uncomfortable, and he detested the constant tick of the cheap wall clock.

Dr. Bloomberg heard the knock on the office door. "Come in! Father Jaeger, good afternoon."

"And to you, sir."

"Have a seat, Father. As you know, this is our last meeting. Hopefully our time together has been helpful. I thought today we could pull together our sessions and analyze our progress."

"First of all, thank you for your insight," Father Jaeger said. "I tried to open up the best I could to you, sir. You know I love being a priest. I want to … I really want to do better. You have been most helpful."

"Maybe you can tell me where you are today compared to a month ago when we first started," the doctor suggested.

"Sure, I sure can. I'd have to say, you have helped me look at myself and figure out why I have … you know, why I have strayed and become involved with a couple of boys during these past few years," Father Jaeger said trying to minimalize his discretions.

"That's good. You have to recognize your own faults first before you can change and become a better priest."

"As I see it, my problem goes back to childhood, to my dad. He is a good man, a good Catholic. I have to admit that his toughness, his strictness makes him … thinking back when I was a kid … it makes him cold. Cold and unapproachable. Did I tell you he never once hugged me? Not once. Let alone ever kissed me?" Father Jaeger explained. "I always felt alone. Sometimes even unloved. Then on the other hand, my mother hovered over me … too close. She loved me. I'm sure they both still do, but I was stifled."

"I commend you, Father, for being able to admit that," Dr. Bloomberg said. "I do think you have been making progress."

"You helped me open my eyes and look back at my childhood years. Once I realized I was not attracted to girls, admittedly, I know I tried to hide that. I felt ashamed. What I can't understand, though, was my vocation, my wanting to be a priest. What did it? I mean is that why I decided to become a priest? Did I want to hide my true sexuality? I don't know, Doctor. I haven't figured that out yet."

"A way to look at it is that maybe you wanted to be a priest, do good to help others, and truly be Christlike. At the same time, you knew you could hide your sexual preference. Even for a priest, chastity is a huge hurdle in life."

Father Jaeger listened intently while keeping an eye on the clock. "Then why the physical attraction to boys?" he asked.

"Think about it, Father. You were young. Your own father didn't show you love and affection. That wasn't a part of your life. With your kind heart, I think you didn't want to see others suffer as you did when you were young. You were acting out your own natural physical drive, and well, we might say, simply the lust for gratification. It is natural, you know," the doctor explained.

"And that is?" Father Jaeger asked, the question written all over his face.

"Affection, Father. Your father didn't show you affection as a boy. Now you are replacing, trying to help other boys, but then you do go too far. Way too far, obviously."

"How can this make me understand why I did what I did? What

happened during the last twenty years? Why didn't I learn?" Father Jaeger asked in self-examination.

"As far as your sexuality, you must ask yourself ... did I make a choice? Maybe, just maybe, it's because you cared about the boys and at the same time you were fulfilling what you missed," the doctor explained.

Father Jaeger sat back in his chair. Searching for how to respond, he waited a moment and then said, "Dr. Bloomberg, if I'm honest with myself, I never had a choice. I didn't choose my sexual preference. It was just there. I think you are right." The priest nodded. "I think you are right."

"The real question now is do you think you can forge ahead without having boys in your life? I mean sexually in your life?"

Knowing the session was about to end, Father Jaeger agreed, "Yes, I can. I believe I can move forward and do only what is good for the boys in my life. I will beat this."

"This is good. Good. I really can see your progress. Father, I will be finishing my report tomorrow and giving my recommendation to Father Schmidt, and of course, he'll share it with Bishop Powers." Dr. Bloomberg stood and placed his left hand on the priest's shoulder. Then they shook hands. "I wish you all the success in your new assignment in Eastville. I have confidence that you'll do right for yourself and for your church."

"Thank you. Thank you, Dr. Bloomberg. I will always be appreciative of our time together this past month."

As Father Jaeger approached the door, he stopped, turned, and said, "I know this time all is going to go well. I don't plan to return for another session with you. I'll make this work. Take care," he said. Then he closed the door and left. Walking down the hall, Father Jaeger admitted to himself, *It's good to be out of jail.*

Now that the month of therapy was in the past, Father Jaeger had a reason to celebrate. Knowing he would be leaving the next day, Father Jaeger thought about this evening, his last meal at the diner, and a final swim at the Y. But he had one more hurdle before the evening arrived.

Later that afternoon, Father Jaeger met with Fathers Schmidt and Holtz for the last time. He shared the conversation between himself and Dr. Bloomberg. He told the fathers all that had transpired in great detail.

"Thank you for your observations. I know Bishop Powers will be anxious to read Dr. Bloomberg's full report," Father Schmidt said while Father Holtz sat and listened, taking notes as they talked. "As you can expect, the bishop takes these situations, accusations, and assignments very seriously. Mostly, he's concerned for the abused victims. At the same time, he doesn't want this sort of thing associated with our diocese. He's a good man, and you never know, he might become an archbishop someday," Father Schmidt said, portraying Bishop Powers as a good man with ambitions.

"Yes, I know he is," Father Jaeger replied. "Tell him that I appreciate his kindness and understanding. Most of all, tell him I won't disappoint him this time. I've learned so much thanks to Dr. Bloomberg. I'm really looking forward to going to St. Vincent's in Eastville.

"We believe you, Father. I think this has been a special month for you. A month you'll never forget," Father Schmidt said. A slight smile broke across Father Schmidt's face.

"You're right about that. I've enjoyed the solitude of the apartment. Spending a month by oneself offers plenty of time to reflect about the past and plan for the future. Daily Mass in the chapel, my sessions with Dr. Bloomberg, and meeting with the two of you has been … well, I'd say enlightening to say the least. Honestly, I feel like a whole new person. I'm revived and ready to get back with the people. This has been like a retreat."

"We know you will do well this time, Father," Father Schmidt assured him.

Father Jaeger looked at Father Holtz, who had a very nondescript look on his face.

"Thank you, Father Schmidt. I plan on leaving tomorrow sometime after Mass. I'll drive to Chicago and spend the weekend with my folks. Actually, I look forward to being with Dad. We have some … Well, I'll just say, I look forward to visiting with him. Then Monday I'll drive to Eastville." Smiling, Father Jaeger said, "I plan on this being a special assignment." With that, he said good-bye to the two priests. "Please remember to give my best to the good Bishop Powers." As Father Jaeger walked down the hall, he thought maybe he did get more out of this month of counseling. *Just maybe I did.*

Father Schmidt responded, "Take care, God bless, and good-bye."

During the entire conversation, Father Holtz had remained silent. He had a different insight into Father Jaeger's one-month session. An insight he hoped would never come to fruition.

CHAPTER 76

STAYING IN TOUCH

Linda and Joey Singleton—August 31, 1958

A cloud of gloom hovered over the dinner table that Sunday evening. Tuesday would be the first day of public school. Joey was nervous about beginning high school. He still carried lingering feelings for Father Jaeger. Temporarily his mind wandered as he smelled the comforting aromas of his mom's pan-fried chicken. Joey helped her set the table. Both sat down together, immediately bowing their heads.

"Bless us, oh Lord, for these our gifts," she began.

Joey looked at her during the blessing and thought, *What a good mom.*

"Amen," they said together while making the sign of the cross.

Linda reached for the plate of golden fried chicken and passed it to Joey.

"Mom, you know this has been a difficult summer. I hardly saw anybody. I know working at the flower shop took thirty hours a week ... but I didn't want to see kids. Father Jaeger helped me know who I am. I felt confident about that."

Linda listened intently, as she had not been expecting such a serious conversation.

"Mom, all I can say is I still miss Father Jaeger. I really want to see him. I can't help it," Joey said with affection. "He was everything to me, besides you of course."

"Thanks, honey. I'm glad to hear that."

"Another thing, Mom. I wonder if I should have gone to the seminary this year. I'm convinced for sure I want to be a priest, a good, loving priest like Father Jaeger."

That's not a lofty model, she thought. "We can talk about that in the spring, toward the end of your freshmen year."

"Yeah, I know. That's probably best. I'll just have to have a good year." After supper, Joey thought, *Now if I can just figure out a way to see Father Jaeger.*

Joey Singleton—September 2, 1958

The first day at the public school was uneventful. Joey tended to himself. It was tough enough getting from one classroom to another in the eight-minute intervals between classes. He knew the first day that he would like this freer structure compared to St. Thomas Moore's one grade per room.

Later that afternoon, Joey bounded into the house. "Hi, Mom! Home!" He flew up the stairs.

She followed over to the base of the stairs. "Joey, Joey, come down. There's a letter here for you. Don't know who it is from."

He went ahead and unpacked his books, changed clothes, and even took time to feed the fish. Soon Joey bounced down the stairs.

"It's on the desk by the telephone."

Reaching over and picking up the sealed envelope, Joey immediately recognized the distinctive handwriting in scripted black ink. Not even opening the letter, Joey raced back upstairs to read it in the privacy of his own room. Slowly, he used his letter opener, neatly slicing to preserve the envelope.

August 24, 1958

Dear Joey:
Please accept my apology for the absence of a good-bye to a friend this past May. It was a stressful time. My mom was not well, and I needed to get back to Chicago immediately.

At the same time, I was called to the diocese in South Wayne, as the bishop needed an assistant in a parish down in Eastville, Indiana. The pastor is elderly. They were without an assistant, so I was transferred for the overall good of the parish. School begins next week.

I was assigned to spend a month in South Wayne for the purpose of taking two additional theology classes. I will be teaching more at my new parish.

By the way, the parish is St. Vincent's in Eastville, Indiana, just west of Terre Haute. I'm looking forward to the change and will begin next week. I still will miss all my friends at good ol' St. Thomas Moore. I will always have wonderful memories of my days in Wabash. Joey, I miss you in my life. Never met anyone like you.

Thank you for being such a good friend. I think of you often.

Wishing you all the best.

God bless,

Rev. Jerome Jaeger

Joey studied the letter and then tossed it onto the bed. He stared at it. At first he felt the urge to just tear the letter up. He picked up the letter to read it again. *"I think of you often." What does that really mean? No invitation to visit. He didn't say we'd see each other again.* Joey had an empty, sick feeling. Father Jaeger's letter reinforced that which would never be. Stretched out on his bed, letter at his side, Joey clasped his hands behind his head on the pillow. He stared at the ceiling.

So far away, I'll never see him again. "Think of you." Yeah! No mention of we'll see each other again. "Miss you in my life. Never met anyone like you." What was your purpose, Father Asshole? Never said good-bye. Never heard from you all summer. Now this letter out of nowhere. You shouldn't have ever written. Just makes it worse. Never want to hear from you again. It's all your doin'. All your loss. Go to hell, Father Dipshit! Never want to hear from you again!

Closing his mind, Joey turned over, threw his head facedown on the bed, covered his head with a pillow.

When it was time for supper, Linda called to Joey. No response. She knew who the letter was from. She decided to just let Joey have his space. Linda didn't hear from him the rest of the evening.

CHAPTER 77

A NEW START

Father Jaeger—August 4, 1958

DRIVING south on Route 1 on the eastern side of Illinois, Father Jaeger was full of optimism. After his sessions with Dr. Bloomberg, he had gained a clearer understanding of himself. He felt keenly aware of the reason for the transfer, the new parish, the new pastor, the sisters, and of course the children. Staring at the road ahead, his thoughts reverted back to his overwhelming desires deep within the dark side of his soul.

The tall green corn and bean fields of central Illinois flashed by. The closer Father Jaeger drove toward Eastville, Indiana, the more he focused on his inner being, his lust and desires, and how they could be conquered. He felt the exultation and desire to be a good priest. But in moments of darkness, Father Jaeger's mind was conquered by his physical thirst for the pleasure of being close, the excitement, and the antici-pation that would result in his own gratification. During moments of reality, he imagined the risks he had taken without ever being caught. Then he thought of that dreadful night by the campfire. As Father Jaeger drove into Eastville, he was plagued with self-doubt and concern for who he was.

Eastville was a small town of 1,850, featuring turn-of-the-century buildings on Main Street and tree-lined streets of white clapboard houses. St. Vincent's was easy to find. Father Jaeger drove south on Main Street through the friendly little burg. The downtown featured a hard-ware store, bakery, shoe store, cafes, and a pharmacy. The corners of the main block were anchored by the Farmer and Merchant's Bank and Latoz

Hardware Store. As Father Jaeger turned right on First Street, the IGA grocery store was in plain view. Two blocks left off Main stood the quaint 1890s brick St. Vincent's Catholic Church and rectory. The grade school was a two-story brick and located across the street.

Activity was heavy in the downtown on this early August afternoon. A few cars were parked in front of the church. Father Jaeger slowly drove his black Studebaker around the corner and pulled up in front of the rectory. Walking up to the front door, he knocked and was surprised to be greeted by a much older pastor than he expected.

"You must be Father Jaeger," the elder priest said with a welcoming smile. He extended his hand. "I'm Father Arnold. Please come in."

"Thank you, Father Arnold. I'm pleased to be here. What a nice-looking church and school."

"Yes, we are fond of this place. We have many fine parishioners who truly make the church and school their second home."

"This is good. This is real good," Father Jaeger said, supporting the proud priest's statement.

"That's what I like to hear," Father Arnold said thankfully. "Father Schmidt didn't tell us much about your background. By first meeting you, I can tell you must have a liking for people." Father Arnold turned and walked into the small, quaint rectory parlor. "Sit here. Let's visit awhile. You must be tired from your trip."

"Oh, maybe a little tired, but I enjoyed the drive. Good to be out alone on the open road."

"Do you enjoy teaching?" Father Arnold asked. "We not only have the grade school, but we also offer classes for the Catholic students who attend the public schools. Lots going on in our parish."

"That's great, Father. I like all facets of parish life: daily Mass, fund-raisers, visiting the sick—all parts of the job. I especially enjoy children."

"Well, I'm sure you'll fit right in," the elderly priest said. "I need some young blood around here. My last assistant was suddenly transferred. Nice guy. Health reasons, they told me. Up and gone in about a week." Hearing that, Father Jaeger thought to himself, *Transferred.*

Father Jaeger relaxed and felt very comfortable around his new pastor. They sat and talked for a while. Father Jaeger tried to keep the conversation all about the church, school, and Father Arnold himself.

He avoided bringing up his past and background and was relieved when Father Arnold didn't inquire much.

As they were ending their conversation, Father Arnold said, "May I suggest I show you your room? Then you can unpack and make yourself at home. You and I will have dinner together in the dining room. Would that work for you?"

Father Jaeger was more than pleased with his quarters. He had three rooms all to himself, completely furnished and located at the end of the hall just inside the side entrance door. *How convenient.* He checked his watch—3:25 p.m. Plenty of time before supper to unpack his clothes and put a few belongings away. Downstairs, just outside the side door, he saw the door into the sacristy. As he opened the door and peeked out, he was met by a group of boys coming out of the church.

"Oh hi, Father. You must be the new priest ... ah, ah, Father Jaeger. We're all altar boys. Just finished some practicing for the first all school Mass. Gotta go. Hope to see you around, Father."

"Oh, you will," he said as he watched them hustle down the walk. *Hope to see a lot of you.* Father Jaeger already had good feelings.

Later that evening, after a pleasant meal and visit with Father Arnold, Father Jaeger took a slow walk around the church and school and then walked two blocks to scout out the downtown. He was delighted to see a fine hardware store, a bakery, a shoe store, and other primary business establishments in the downtown. To his amazement, Father Jaeger saw a small Boy's Club at the far end of Main Street, just four blocks from the parish church. He hadn't expected to find this in such a small town. He hoped it would have an indoor pool. Walking back to the rectory, he felt a comfortable ambiance about the town. *I believe I'm going to like this place. Imagine there will be lots for me to do.*

CHAPTER 78

THEN THERE WAS GENE

Sister Mary Michael—September 3, 1958

FATHER Jaeger had left St. Thomas Moore, but he left turmoil, frustration, and shattered lives in his wake. Gene Kowolski came into Sister Mary Michael's classroom and approached her desk right after recess began. The class was scurrying to the lunch room. "Sister, could we talk after school? You know, about Father Jaeger?"

"Sure, why of course. Any time, Gene. I'll be here in the classroom."

"Thank you, Sister," he said timidly.

"Oh, Gene, remember I said I'd help you. And by the way, you know Father Jaeger is gone?"

"Yes, I know. He's been gone all summer. Sister, I need some advice. Okay? I'm having a, well, really hard time."

"Sure, Gene. I'll see you after school. I'd like to invite Father Sullivan. You know he's a good man. He can help also," Sister Mary Michael said to Gene as if she was asking a question.

Gene put his index finger to his mouth. "If you say it's okay, Sister, I'm fine with that. I trust you and Father Sullivan also." Time passed very slowly for Gene that day.

After the fire drill that afternoon, the students were standing in line outside, waiting to be called back into school. Sister Mary Michael saw Father Sullivan standing in front of the church just thirty yards away. She immediately scampered across the lawn, holding her habit up at the knees with both hands. The sounds of her bouncing rosary beads alerted Father Sullivan: nun on the grounds, nun on the grounds!

"Wish I had a picture of that dash," he said, smiling at the sister as she approached.

"Oh Father, you're just funnin' me." Then she said seriously, "Gene Kowolski asked to see me after school. I'd like you to be there. It's important. He needs both of us, I'm afraid."

"Yes, Sister, absolutely. I'll be there."

"Thank you, Father." Sister Mary Michael turned to leave.

"By the way, I bet you'd fly if you wore tennis shoes."

"Oh come on, Father. Don't embarrass me," she said awkwardly, not used to a man's comment.

The bell signaled the end of the school day at exactly 3:15. Father Sullivan arrived at Sister Mary Michael's classroom ten minutes later.

Knock, knock.

"Oh hello, Father. Gene just got here. Good timing."

"Hi, Gene," Father Sullivan said as he walked up the aisle.

"I saved your favorite desk," she told the priest. Father Sullivan squeezed in, and Sister Mary Michael started the conversation. "Gene and I have been very confidential about a problem. A serious problem. Gene, please tell Father Sullivan."

"Gene, you can trust me," Father Sullivan assured the boy.

"So is this like confession?" Gene asked.

"Well, sort of. What you say can be between the three of us."

"I don't know if I can say this in front of both of you. It's … it's like … embarrassing."

"Gene," Sister Mary Michael said. "Truth may hurt. Just tell the truth, and you'll never have to cover yourself. You can trust both of us."

"Okay, I'll do my best. Father, I'm just going to say it all. Like I told you, Sister, it all started before Christmas. Father Jaeger came into the cassock room after Mass." Feeling so uncomfortable, Gene put his head down. "Let's see. He first put his hands on my shoulders. No, maybe he grabbed me first. Can't remember exactly. Sometimes it's a blur. It felt awful. He moved his hand all around slowly. He said, 'This feels so good. It's because I like you. Like a private way friends shake hands.' Then a week or so passed. He came in the closet again. This time it was much worse. He actually loosened his belt … and … and then he, well he unzipped his pants and—oh this is so bad. I'm a sinner. He put my hand inside. He made me do it. Please, Sister, Father made me. I didn't want to commit a mortal sin."

Sister Mary Michael grimaced.

"How many times did this happen, Gene?" Father Sullivan asked.

"I'm not sure. I think nine, maybe ten times." Gene paused. "Seemed like a hundred, but not always there. Other places. One time he had me come into his room; that time was the worst. He handed me a towel and said we were both going to honor Jesus."

"Honor Jesus? What do you mean?"

"Father Jaeger pointed to the crucifix above his bed. He said we were going to honor our Lord and dress like Him, so I had to take all my clothes off and cover up with the towel just like Jesus."

"All your clothes?" Father Sullivan asked with disgust, his blood pressure rising.

"Yes, except I kept my socks on. The floor was cold."

"How did you feel, Gene?" Father Sullivan asked.

"I was terrified. I just wanted out of there."

"What did Father Jaeger do?"

"Well … well, Father … " Gene looked at Sister Mary Michael.

"It's okay, Gene. Tell Father Sullivan," she said with calm assurance.

"Father took his towel off. I tell you, he wasn't terrified. I became more startled 'cause I didn't know what to do. It was ugly. Then he said while standing at the front of the bed, he said, 'Now, Gene, like Jesus, get down on your knees and pray.' Father Jaeger sat on the bed next to the discarded towel. While I was on my knees, he pulled me close to him. I can't bear to think of it. He started to bounce a little on the bed. Not high, only a few inches. Just enough. He pushed on top of my head. I closed my eyes, and I did pray. I prayed for Jesus to get me out of there. I was shaking. Then he said, 'Kiss me. Kiss me if you love me.' Startled, I screamed 'No, no!' and I jumped up."

"What happened, Gene?"

"He grabbed my shoulders and pulled me close and hugged me. That didn't feel good. You know, Father, what I mean?" Gene said, looking for approval from Sister Mary Michael.

"Then what happened?" Father Sullivan asked, wanting to know if Jaeger had sodomized young Gene. It was an awful thing to pursue, but authorities would have to know eventually.

"Father Jaeger told me love is shown in many ways. Jesus loved us. He even died for our sins because he loved us. I looked at him and said, 'Father, can I please go now? I'm scared. This is a sin.'"

Father Sullivan stayed calm but raged inside just thinking of Jaeger in his state of lustful focus.

Gene went on. "Then he said, 'Let's just lie here on the bed. I'll show you what Jesus meant.' Then he took my towel, threw it on the chair, and lay on his side behind me. He started groaning, scarylike. Then I

495

felt something. It hurt. 'Please no, please no.' I closed my eyes. 'It hurts, Father, please stop'. He didn't hear me cause he was moving a lot."

"Okay, Gene, that's enough. We need to hear no more about that," Father Sullivan assured him, as he was also sensitive to the sister having to hear this. "Can I ask you one more question? Was this the only time?"

Gene put his head down again. He was quiet. Then he looked up at Father Sullivan and Sister Mary Michael and said, "I said nine, ten times. For sure, I was in his room three times."

Father Sullivan rested his forehead in his palms, shaking his head. "Gene, to bring justice, to stop this from happening to others, could you tell someone else? Someone of authority?"

Looking a little taken aback, Gene said, "I already did."

Father Sullivan looked at Sister Mary Michael. Both had an unexpected surprised look. "You did?" the priest asked to clarify.

"Yes, I told my dad and mom."

"What did they say?" Sister Mary Michael asked.

Gene looked a little sheepish. "That's why I came to tell you."

"What do you mean, Gene?" she asked.

"Well, Sister, Father … " Gene was hesitant. "My dad said he's going to kill Father Jaeger."

Sister Mary Michael looked terrified. Father Sullivan understood.

"That was a week ago. My mom and dad have been fighting ever since." Gene's eyes filled with tears. "I love my dad. He's a good man. He works hard down at the tannery. Mom said he started working in that dirty slaughter house right after the war. I know little. All I know was that he was at Iwo Jima. Lots of killing. My dad's a tough man. Oh, Father, I wish I hadn't told him. I'm glad Father Jaeger's gone. I hate … I'll hate forever what he did to me, but my dad is very tough. Father Jaeger would not want to see my dad coming at him." The tears on Gene's face overwhelmed his freckles. He wiped his nose on his shirtsleeve. His red hair was a mess, now hanging straight down on his forehead. He kept nervously tapping his black tennis shoes.

Father Sullivan looked at Gene. "I just have to ask. This happened last year. Why did you wait to tell us now?"

Gene put his head down. Rubbed his eyes. Without looking up, a whimper-like response, "Be … be … because I thought nobody would believe me. Then the nightmares were so bad ... I had to ask for help. Sometimes, a lot of times, I just want to die. I hate him." Gene sniffed, "I ... I hate myself."

Sister Mary Michael looked at Father Sullivan, who was shaking his head. "Oh, my dear Gene," she said, pulling him over and giving him a hug.

Gene felt awkward. She didn't even mind his smudged eyes on her white bib.

"Gene, look at me. Would you like for us to talk with your parents?"

Without hesitation, he said, "Oh yes, please. Please do. It's awful in our house. My younger sister and brothers are scared of the constant arguing and fighting. Could you call my mom? She would like that."

"Yes, we will," Sister Mary Michael reassured him as she offered him her handkerchief. "You go on now. Father Sullivan and I will talk. We'll call your mom this week."

Gene stood up. He awkwardly hugged them both and left the room. Sister Mary Michael and Father Sullivan sat speechless. A few moments passed.

"Let's think all this over. That lecherous man behind that collar. Oh, Father, oh how he has tarnished that collar for all you good, good priests," Sister Mary Michael said, now with passion in her voice.

Shaking his head, Father Sullivan agreed. "But, Sister, he has tarnished more than the white symbol of our priesthood. Just look at what he's done to this good little boy and his struggling family."

"Father, I think it best that it be you, a priest, who calls Gene's family."

"Yes, Sister, I know. I know. I should. And, Sister, I am already thinking of the daunting task ahead." Father Sullivan also wondered if there could be a real safety concern for Father Jaeger. He placed himself in Mr. Kowolski's shoes for a moment and could understand Gene's father's reaction and what he might do if he had a son that had been abused without consequences to the priest.

Linda Singleton—September 6, 1958

The silence in the church on the late Saturday afternoon offered a warm feeling of serenity. Linda noticed the center door of the confessional with its elaborate carved woodwork, including the cross on the triangle above the center of the door. His name was on the door. Her heart swelled. She entered the confessional. *Quiet.* Linda felt the surround of silence until the interruption of the priest sliding the small confessional door open. His closeness floated through the black cloth screen.

"Bless me, Father, for I have sinned. Well, it's been a few months. I hope you don't mind, Father. I just have, you know, I just want to hear your voice. Please, I hope you don't mind."

"Why of course, Linda. I don't mind ever," Father Sullivan said, feeling a surge of inner warmth.

"Michael, does anyone ever tell you they love the confessional?"

"Well, I must say, Linda, that's one I don't believe I have ever heard before."

"Let me explain. By the way, I was last in line. Don't want to hold you up, Father."

"You're okay," he replied, trying to comfort her as best he could.

"You see, Father, just the quiet, the silence in this beautiful church gives me a feeling of peace. At the same time, I feel melancholy, as I'm reminded I'm alone. Now, Michael, that's not a complaint, just reality, just the state of my life. Then I stepped into this deep dark inner sanctum. It's quiet. I can't see. I only hear your voice. Between us a wall, a small sliding door that's now open … yet we're shut off from one another by this dark cloth, a veil of division. Like open … yet closed. And then I wrap my arms around myself. I pull you close. I feel your presence. I feel only for you." She paused, and silence filled the confessional. "I'm sorry, Michael. Oh, forgive me. I shouldn't have told you my feelings. That's my life. I'm going too far," she said hesitantly.

"Linda, it's okay. You're fine. I have feelings too. I heard every word you said." Then there was silence. "Linda, my dear Linda, I still have emotions of wanting to be with you. I yearn just to touch you, look in your beautiful eyes, and hold you."

Linda could feel the passion in his voice. Her heart raced as she savored every word.

"Linda, my feelings for you are always there. I live with them daily. I fight with my own passions." Then he paused, wondering if he had said too much. Father Sullivan could hardly hold back his emotions. He longed to share these words of intimacy. "Without saying, we both know my situation. I do wear this collar. I am a priest. And, Linda, that's … " Pausing again, he thought while Linda hung on to every word, yearning for just a little hope. "That's not going to change. I've taken vows."

Taken aback by Father Sullivan's unexpected words of sentiment, Linda said, "Yes, Michael, I know so much." With his last words, she had to check her emotions. "Please, you know … I have to go. Your words are so … are so … good-bye, Michael."

"Linda, one more thing. You are always welcome to come to this confessional. I might not see you or touch you, but Linda, I love the sound of your voice and … and I can feel your presence, so close."

"Thank you, Michael," she said as tears ran down her cheeks. She made the sign of the cross, stood, and left the confessional.

Father Sullivan sat alone in his private solitude for a while. Linda was the last repentant of the day. As much as he loved listening to her, the difficulty and frustration he experienced from not having her in his life was sometimes overwhelming. However, he knew he could not share his complete feelings with her. He knew it would be too much. Too much for both of them. Alone, Father Sullivan sat for awhile in the stillness … in the darkness.

CHAPTER 79

CONFRONTATION

Father Sullivan—September 7, 1958

FATHER Sullivan was anxious and restless late Sunday evening. He could not get Linda off his mind after yesterday's visit in the confessional. Then he thought and worried about Father Jaeger, who he knew had begun his next assignment at St. Vincent's in Eastville.

As he sat in his favorite chair in the study, Father Sullivan's mind was focused on Bishop Powers. After his visit with Father Holtz, he had concluded that a cover-up had been orchestrated. He especially thought about Ned Thornbauer. *Ned Thornbauer.* An idea flashed across his mind. He thought about Ned and the abuse by Bishop Powers.

The bishop, Father Sullivan thought, *was actually blackmailing Ned.* He had warned Ned not to say anything about their time together in the cabin or else he would disclose the secret lie about Ned stealing money from the church and reveal troubles his father had with the police. Although it wasn't true, Ned had been affected by the bishop's threat. *That's it,* Father Sullivan thought. *I have to meet Bishop Powers.*

Immediately, Father Sullivan penned a letter:

Dear Father Holtz:

I have decided to confront Bishop Powers about the transfer of Father Jaeger. I feel Father Jaeger will continue his insidious conduct at St. Vincent's. More victims, more hurt families.

Something must be done. I have an idea. Keeping your confidence,

I would like to talk with Ned Thornbauer. Would you be willing to contact Ned and ask if he'll meet with me or at least call? Tell him you'd like his permission to give me his name. I will take it from there.

Please send his contact information to my private post office box.

Hope to hear from you. Thank you so much.

Rev. Michael Sullivan

Father Sullivan felt a rush of enthusiasm as he walked to the post office that evening after supper. *Time to get things started.* Father Sullivan thought if he could get Ned to come forward and expose the bishop for his crimes, he could put an end to the cover-up of the abusing priests.

"Hello, Father Sullivan. This is Sister Mary Michael," Sister spoke over the phone a few days later. "I'm calling from our convent's phone. It's private in the room off the parlor. Nobody can hear. Do you have a minute?"

"Yes," Father Sullivan replied.

"I want to tell you something, Father. Gene is lost in his life, his school work, and interaction with the other kids. I happened to be over in the park yesterday and saw Gene by himself on the big swings, doing nothing. He's not mixing with the other kids. It's like he's in his own private world. I just worry about the long-term effects, even though Father Jaeger is gone."

Father Sullivan replied, "That is most concerning. The effect on the boys and their families is devastating."

"Yes, Father. I'm really concerned."

"I've been wanting to talk again, Sister. I called Gene's dad. Left a message. He called me back this evening. He works the seven-to-three shift over at the tannery. Said he'll go home after work, clean up, and come see me around four thirty. I have to know if he's blowing off steam or if he is serious. I'll find out and call you tomorrow. Sister, I'm going to get to the bottom of this. Right now, I'm also concerned about Father Jaeger and what he may do in his new parish."

"Do you know where he is, Father?" Sister Mary Michael asked, knowing he might not be able to tell her.

"I heard he was in South Wayne, taking some classes at the diocese," Father Sullivan held back the whole truth. "I'm just concerned he'll keep on repeating his past if he is assigned to another parish."

"That's my concern also. The man scares me. How anybody could do those awful things to Gene? He has to be a sick, sick man," the sister said, confirming Father Sullivan's belief. "It's just so sad, Father Sullivan. Gene's fortunate to have you on his side, there for him."

"I'll do my best for Gene and ... " Father Sullivan didn't want to mention the other boys, Joey and Peter, to her. "I have to go now, Sister. I will call you after my meeting with Mr. Kowolski."

Heat consumed the study in the rectory as Father Sullivan awaited the arrival of Gene's father later that day. It was an extraordinarily hot September day. He was even concerned that the humidity could disfigure the pages of some of his favorite books. Straightening his forefinger, he ran it along his sweat-covered neck inside his white collar. His full-length black cassock compounded the uncomfortable feeling of trapped perspiration.

Sister Agatha gently tapped on the open door. "A Mr. Kowolski is here for his 4:30 appointment."

"Please send him in, Sister," Father Sullivan said, wiping his forehead with his handkerchief.

Within seconds, the priest heard the sounds of a man's leather shoes approaching. Standing up, Father Sullivan walked around his desk. "Hello, Mr. Kowolski. I'm Father Sullivan," he said with a welcoming smile.

"Hello, Father. Glad to meet you," Mr. Kowolski said, extending his hand as he bent toward the priest. A middle-sized man, he looked fit, as one would expect from a former marine and a blue-collar worker.

Before the conversation began, Sister Agatha said, "I have some cold iced tea. May be just right on a day like this."

"Oh yes, that would be great. Thank you, Sister," Father Sullivan said, speaking for both of them.

He could see Gene's face in his dad. His hair combed neatly to the side, Mr. Kowolski had a nervous, awkward look in the priest's presence.

Father Sullivan recognized the man's respect for their meeting; he had dressed in a short-sleeve button-down shirt and a wide blue-and-white striped tie. His worn black belt was pulled tight around his waist. His firm handshake told Father Sullivan that Gene's dad was a working man, a person of conviction.

Sister Agatha returned with a tray supporting two tall glasses of tea, as well as sugar and a small bowl of extra ice cubes.

"Thank you, Sister. Please pull the door closed as you leave. Mr. Kowolski, please have a seat. Make yourself comfortable. That's if you can in this humidity."

"No concern, Father. Comfort is not important as I work in the tannery. This is a very nice office," he stated looking around at the books, desk, and furnishings.

Father Sullivan gestured toward the chair. "I have the floor fan facing that direction. This is a hot one," he said, noticing the beaded perspiration across Mr. Kowolski's forehead.

"Thank you. I'm just fine. I left the tannery about an hour ago. They said it was 118 degrees on the floor today. Big ceiling fan. Heat's not that bad."

Father Sullivan could easily detect the man's nervousness. Even though he was a parish member, they had not previously met.

As if he needed to get something off his chest before talking with a priest, Mr. Kowolski announced, "I'm not much of a churchgoer, Father, but we really like St. Thomas Moore. The school is such a big part of my family's life. You know, Nancy and the kids are very active in the parish, especially the wonderful school. Nancy knows every one of the sisters."

"Yes, I know, Mr. Kowolski. All your children do well. I especially have gotten to know Gene. Fine young boy."

"Thank you, Father. I know we are proud of him. His mother does a great job. A great job with all five of the kids."

"Yes, it's unfortunate that we must meet about such a situation with Gene. I can assure you, Mr. Kowolski, I feel confident that this is nothing of Gene's doing," Father Sullivan said, trying to set the man's mind at ease. He knew it was a warm day, but he was sure the perspiration on Mr. Kowolski's forehead was more a consequence of nerves. Father Sullivan reached over and turned the tin-bladed wire-cage fan up to high.

"Maybe you could share with me what Gene has told you," he suggested while at the same time gesturing to remind Mr. Kowolski of the cold tea. He could hear the dryness of Mr. Kowolski's mouth even over the hum of the fan. "Try some of those cubes," he suggested, trying to relax the anxious father.

"Yes, thank you, Father," Gene's dad said as he took a generous drink. "That's better. Sorry, I'm a little nervous."

"You're fine. We're just here talking about someone we both care about," Father Sullivan said with calm kindness in his voice.

"Gene has always lacked … lacked confidence. He's not a big kid … and for the last couple of years … " Father Sullivan could see Gene's dad's growing irritation. "Those big guys, Herbie Ratski, Jack Downer, and Marvin Finch, always give Gene a hard time. I'd love to … "

"Yes, I can understand that," the priest cut him short immediately, noticing Mr. Kowolski turning red and moving forward in his chair as his voice became quite threatening.

"Father, sir, I just keep seeing that guy all over my Gene. You know, that priest … Jaeger. He's like a … I don't know … like a … a snake sneaking and slithering around." He shook his head. "I'm gonna get him, Father. Can't help it. Don't care if he is a priest. Damn him anyway! Goddamn him!" Wiping the sweat from his brow, he threw himself back in the chair.

Father Sullivan could see that the man was extremely irritated as they began to discuss Father Jaeger. Trying to break the tension, he said, "Mr. Kowolski, I'm disgusted and ashamed also. I'm going to end this, but I need … " Father Sullivan then tried to diffuse the subject by talking about Gene's participation with other kids but to no avail. Mr. Kowolski was focused only on Father Jaeger. "Yes, Mr. Kowolski, I believe he has violated your son and he needs help. I assure you…"

"Assure me? He needs help. Look what this priest has done to Gene."

"Yes, I know, sir…"

"Don't 'sir' me. This man should be in jail. Yes, jail. He's a lecherous rapist," Mr. Kowolski said as his emotions continued on fast-forward. Suddenly he stood up. "I knew it. I knew it. You priests are all alike. Think you're so holy … while this … this other priest preys on my boy. Sorry, Father," he said, still showing some respect to Father Sullivan, "but I can't take this. I'll say the wrong thing. I've gotta go. I'm leavin'. No more!" Heading for the door, Mr. Kowolski turned and pointed his finger at Father Sullivan. "Hear me ... You haven't heard the last of me. I'm gonna get him." From down the hall, he shouted, "I'm gonna get that ... that—"

The slamming of the door muffled the last words from the enraged parent.

CHAPTER 80

TOO HARD TO HANDLE

Gene Kowolski—September 11, 1958

THE next morning, Gene Kowolski's dad had already left for work and was unable to see his kids off to school. Gene's two sisters were dressed in their new school dresses. His two little brothers, third and fifth graders, were bouncing around, teasing one another while supposedly getting ready for school. His mom was busy fixing breakfast and trying to coordinate everyone in getting ready.

"Okay, everybody down here! Tell Pops his coffee is ready!" Gene's mother called from the bottom of the stairs.

Gene's grandfather had been living with the family for almost a year, ever since his wife, Gertrude, had died of heart failure the previous Christmas. Since then, Pops had not been the same. To make matters worse, he had been diagnosed with pancreatic cancer in July. He enjoyed and cherished every minute with his grandchildren. The only thing that equaled his love for them was their love for him in return.

"Everybody here?" Mom called out. "Dad left for work a half hour ago. I need to see six hungry faces for breakfast. Includes you too, Pops," she said, pouring his coffee as he took his place at the table. She then kissed him atop his thinning white hair.

"Want me to cut those pancakes for you, Billy?" Pops asked in his caring voice.

"Sure, Pops. You always help a friend," Billy said, repeating one of Pops' favorite lines.

"You bet, little guy. All five of you are my special friends. Wait a minute ... one, two, three, four. One's missing. Where's Gene?"

"Oh, he said he's not going to school. Says he's sick," Diane announced to everyone.

"What's that?" Mom asked. "Here, Jane, you dish out the pancakes. Make sure everyone has milk. I'm going upstairs."

Gene, the middle child, had his own bedroom. It was small, just enough room for a bed, dresser, and a small desk and chair. Pegs on the wall substituted for the missing closet. The door was closed. She knocked lightly on the door.

"Not going to school," Gene said, muffling his voice in the pillow.

"Gene, you're a seventh grader now."

"Mom, please, I don't feel good. My stomach's killing me. I'm not going to school," Gene said emphatically.

"Then you'll have to take this up with your father tonight." As she was closing Gene's door, she thought she heard, "I'm never going back."

Gene's mother checked on him several times that day. He never left his room.

Later that afternoon, there was a *knock, knock* on the door. "Gene, it's Dad. Can I come in?" Not a sound. He cracked the door open. "Gene?" No response. He could see him covered in the bed. Not a move. "Hey, big guy. Checking on you." Silence. "Gene?"

Then Gene spoke up. "What do you want?"

"I just want to know how sick you are. Do you need to go to the doctor?"

"No, no! I don't need a doctor," Gene replied.

"Then what's wrong? I'm concerned about you. Is there something you want to talk about? Any way I can help you?" Gene's dad asked.

"Really want someone to listen to me," Gene said from beneath the covers.

"Then why don't you sit up. I'm a guy. You know I'll listen and help."

"I know, Dad, but I've gotta another problem though. I'm hungry."

"I would hope so," Gene's dad said, patting him on the back. "Listen, Gene, why don't you get up and have supper with the family? Then after a healthy plate of Mom's good cookin', you and I will go for a walk. Maybe together we can sort things out. Just talk. Deal?"

"Okay, Dad," Gene said, sitting up in bed, his hunger and need for help overcoming his self-imposed isolation.

His dad leaned over and gave Gene a hug. "Wash up now, guy. Put some clothes on. See you downstairs in ten. Supper's almost ready."

"Okay, Herb," Gene said with a slight smile on his face. Every once in a while, Gene kidded around by calling his dad by his first name. Dad opened the door. The smell of chicken and noodles floated into Gene's room. "Be right down. Thanks, Dad."

Although Gene was quiet at the table, he enjoyed being with his family. Taking his place next to his granddad, Gene felt a hand patting him on his knee underneath the table. Gene looked up at his Pops and smiled.

After a dessert of apple pie, Herb Kowolski said to his wife, "That was a great meal, honey. Gene and I are going for a walk."

Pops was on the front porch, sitting on the swing when his son asked if he wanted to also take a little walk. With a wink, Pops said, "Walk with Gene? Sure enough."

Gene and his dad were both close to Pops. They knew he had a good ear and a kind heart.

"Good. I'll get Gene," Herb Kowolski said.

Gene, knowing he wanted to talk privately with his dad, thought for a moment about Pops. "Sure. Good idea."

"You know, Gene, with his illness, we don't know how much longer Pops will be with us," Gene's father said.

Gene didn't respond. He didn't want to think about it. Gene and his dad walked down the steps and waited for Pops at the front sidewalk.

"He's coming. Had to get his sweater and cane."

"All ready, guys?" Pops asked, adjusting his sweater as he stepped out onto the porch.

Gene loved walking with Pops. The sound of the cadence of Pops' wooden cane gave Gene comfort knowing he was near.

"Great supper. This is good to walk it off," Dad said, initiating the conversation.

"Yeah, thanks for making me come down. I was getting tired of my room," Gene said.

Gene's dad brought up the subject on both their minds. "Wanna tell me what's bothering you?"

Gene hesitated and then said, "Nightmares. Every night. I keep seeing him, that … that … I call him the greasy monster," Gene said, describing the departed priest.

Pops was two steps behind and to Gene's right. *Click, click.* The wooden cane tapped the sidewalk. As soon as Pops heard *greasy monster*, his ears perked up.

"I didn't want to go back to school today because I thought he might be there."

"Gene, he's not. He was transferred to another parish. I don't know where, but I heard far away."

"For sure?" Gene asked.

"Yes, I know. I even called the rectory and asked. Father Sullivan told me directly that Father Jaeger is not coming back."

Gene, being especially frank, said, "You're sure, Dad? I cannot get him out of my mind. I see him every place. Then it makes me think of all those horrid times, you know, when he was all over me."

By now, Pops was putting two and two together. For the first time, he spoke up. "What do you mean all over you? A priest for Christ's sake?" Pops said, astonished.

Having forgot Pops was there except for the click of his cane, Dad said, "I'll tell you all about it later. But yes, a priest has been very bad, very wicked to Gene."

"Judas Priest! Why didn't anyone tell me? All over my Gene? Why … I'll … I'll … "

"Now, Dad. *Later,*" Herb said.

Silence. *Click, click.*

"I just don't know how to … how to. I'm scared. What if another priest comes and he's the same?" Gene asked his dad.

"Now, Gene, one step at a time. Father Jaeger is gone. I know you've had an awful summer. I've hardly ever seen you with friends. I know it's difficult, but you have to move on. Get beyond him."

Gene was silent for a few moments. Then he said, "Dad, there's one other thing. I … I always … " Gene paused.

"What is it? You can tell your dad."

"I'm tired all the time. I just feel lousy and weak, sad. I'm … I'm scared," Gene stammered. "You see, there's this … "

"There's this what?" his dad asked.

"Pain, Dad. Ever since the last time I was with him. You know what I mean? Last time, I was with him, pain in my … " Gene didn't say. He kept walking even faster, like he wanted to escape the truth.

"Pain? Tell me." Gene's dad put his hand on his shoulder. They stopped walking. "Look at me. What pain?" The cadence of the cane fell silent.

"The … the … Dad, the pain in my rear." Gene put his hand behind him. "Right here. Almost all the time. It hurts."

Gene's dad's face turned red.

"I found blood."

"Blood? You have blood? Does your mom know? Gene, that was last year, sixth grade, and you still have pain?"

"Yes, Dad." Peter put his head down. "Had the pain all summer. Couldn't tell anyone. I was just too embarrassed."

Now that Gene had opened up and admitted he needed help, his dad said, "Why that dirty son of—" He stopped from talking. *God, he's a priest.* "We're gonna get you to the doctor. That I promise. I promise, Gene."

"It hurts so bad, and it's getting worse," Gene told his dad. "But how is he gonna examine me?" he asked.

"One thing at a time, Gene. Let's get the appointment first. Dr. Curtis will know what to do."

The walk that evening was painful for Gene's dad to hear. By talking openly, though, Gene felt closer and knew his dad would help. He felt as if someone cared and understood his emotional and physical pain. He also felt comfort that evening knowing Pops was there. Pops did not say much, but he took it all in.

Later in the evening, after all the kids were in bed, Gene's dad noticed

Pops sitting alone on the front porch swing. Opening the screen door, Herb stepped out. "Need some company?"

"Sure, son. Sit, enjoy the swing."

At first they said nothing. The cadence of the chain of the swing reminded him of Pops' cane on the sidewalk. *Steady, soothing.* After a few minutes listening to the comforting late summer sounds of the cicadas and an occasional car passing by, Pops spoke up.

Looking straight ahead, he said, "I couldn't believe my ears. My God, Gene, a priest. I would never have thought I'd live to hear such a thing. Even with my short time left, this reminds me of the evil I will leave behind." Then he paused for a minute. "Your son ... my grandson. Look what he's done to our Gene."

"I know, Dad. I went to see Father Sullivan," Herb said to Pops.

"Who's he?"

"Sullivan is the other assistant. Good guy. This Father Jaeger, I guess, was assigned to St. Thomas Moore from another parish as a second assistant about two years ago."

"What they doin' about all this?" Pops asked.

"Best I know, the bishop up in South Wayne's handling it. That's what Father Sullivan told me."

"*Hmmph*, thought all priests were good," Pops said with disgust. Then it was quiet. The swing continued back and forth. "What about the police?" he asked, trying to understand the situation completely.

"That's what I think. The police should be on this, but they're not," Herb said.

"Far as I'm concerned, I'd take care of it myself," Pops said emphatically. "When I think about Gene, I just wanna kick Jaeger's ass across the county and strangle him," he said, the tension in his voice mounting.

Herb told Pops, "I said that and more to Father Sullivan. Pops, if I got my hands on him, don't know if I could stop. It's all so wrong. So very, very wrong. This is so unjust. Somehow, don't know how though, justice has to be served. He's no priest. He's a damn animal. You know what they do to bad animals?"

"Yes, bet I know, and I could do it," Pops responded to his son.

The light flipped on in the front parlor and shined right onto the swing through the window. The door opened. "You guys both out here?"

"Yes, Blanche. Just enjoying the evening," Herb said.

Pops was too revved up to respond.

"Kids are in bed. I'm going up," Blanche said as she leaned out the screen door. She walked over and gave them both a kiss on the cheek. "Now don't you guys be up too late," she said jokingly, not knowing what they were talking about.

The screen door swung closed. The light went off. Tranquil was the night.

"Sometimes, Dad, it's all I can think about. This so-called priest and what he's done to Gene. He's gone, and Gene still suffers. Somehow I wanna get him. Somehow I gotta do something." There was a pause. The only sound was just the squeaky chain above the swing. "My children are the most important part of my life. I have to protect them, Dad. Sometimes, I feel ... I actually feel, Dad, like I could ... that I could ... "

"Shoot him," Pops said, finishing his son's sentence.

"Yeah, shoot him ... or, or strangle him for what he's done ... or just cut it off," Herb said. "This haunts me every day. Every single day. I can only imagine how Gene feels."

"Even more, this will affect Gene all his life," Pops said to his son. By this time, Pops was ready to use his cane for another purpose. "If only I could meet that wretched man. A priest. Ha."

"Yes, Dad, I understand, but he's far away now," Herb said to Pops.

Little more was said. Together, father and son sat and swung back and forth on the porch swing. Soon some raindrops spattered on the porch railing. All was quiet. The lights were out except for the Tiffany lamp on the telephone table in the hallway. In silence, they thought of Gene. One of them, however, thought far more about Father Jaeger.

CHAPTER 81

STEPPING FORWARD

Father Sullivan—September 12, 1958, mid-morning

ALLOWING for a four-day turnaround of Father Holtz's letter, Father Sullivan walked two blocks to the post office on Friday morning. The postal boxes were positioned to the side of the lobby. The clerk's desk was in a room off the front lobby, opposite the front entrance. The clerks could not see the boxes from the postal counter. Father Sullivan anxiously walked to the stand-up desk in front of the boxes and unlocked PO Box 404. Father Holtz's letter was there, right on schedule.

Opening the letter, he read:

Dear Father:

I contacted Ned Thornbauer. He was reluctant at first but agreed to meet with you. Ned lives here in South Wayne. You have his phone number. He will decide if he wants to give you his address.

When we first met, I found Ned to be open, direct, and credible. Give him a call. Hope it works out for you. Please let me know the results.

Respectively,
Rev. Benjamin Holtz

That afternoon, after three tries, Father Sullivan was able to connect with Ned Thornbauer. After a brief conversation, Ned agreed to meet. Actually, Father Sullivan thought Ned was quite receptive. The priest explained that he had received Ned's name in confidence from Father Holtz only after Ned and Father Holtz talked. Ned thanked Father Sullivan for first calling Father Holtz. He and Ned agreed to meet on Monday, September 15 at the same truck stop where Fathers Holtz and Sullivan had first met.

A few days later, Father Sullivan traveled north to meet Ned. Father Sullivan's imagination provided vivid pictures of Bishop Powers falling like a mighty oak for all he had covered up. Each main branch symbolized an abusive priest and his victims. Father Holtz had shared the names of six known accused priest pedophiles. Bishop Powers had authorized their reassignment to other parishes. Father Sullivan was about to learn more about the master of the cover-up—an abuser himself. Father Sullivan thought that as a result of the bishop's high position within the church, the crime would not be able to be glossed over, transferred, or even kept from civil authorities.

Walking into his favorite truck stop, Father Sullivan looked for a twenty-two-year-old man in sunglasses and a white short-sleeve shirt. The priest appeared to have arrived at the truck stop first. He walked in and found a corner booth. The Formica tabletop hosted an array of dirty plates, empty soda glasses, and wadded-up used napkins. Father Sullivan was now accustomed to the cracked fake leather seats moistened by another day of heavy humidity. *Nothing describes the open road in 1958 better than an eighteen-wheeler truck stop*, he thought. The temperature was much more bearable than several weeks ago. The air was filled with the smell of burgers on the grill, fried eggs, bacon, and hot coffee. He thought of the pan-fried chicken he had reluctantly left on the table last time.

Within minutes, Father Sullivan observed Ned walking through the front door. Ned surveyed the counter, booths, and tables from behind dark sunglasses. Father Sullivan stood and waved his hand until Ned caught notice. He immediately walked toward the priest's booth.

"Hello, Father Sullivan ... Ned Thornbauer." He was a handsome man, five ten with brown wavy hair and a generous smile.

"Good to meet you, Ned. Thank you for agreeing to visit." Within seconds, a connection was made.

"Been here long?" Ned asked politely.

"Not really. I like this place. I enjoy watching the people. You know, these tough guys and their big rigs. Part of America," Father Sullivan said.

Ned began. "Father, honestly, I'm glad you called."

Father Sullivan could tell Ned really wanted to talk about his abuse. "Just go ahead, Ned. Say whatever you like. I'm a good listener."

Accepting the open invitation, Ned said, "My life's been haunted for many years. Of course, I assume Father Holtz told you about what happened. What the bishop did to me."

"Yes, he did, Ned. The whole story. Can I ask how you happened to call Father Holtz?" Father Sullivan asked.

"Sure. I had heard through a friend that the bishop and a priest at the Catholic Church were dealing with some abuse cases. Of course, I immediately thought of mine, so I found out the name of the priest. I called the rectory. Glad I didn't get Schmidt. I hear Father Schmidt is Bishop Powers' protector."

"What do you mean, Ned ... the bishop's protector?"

"Let me explain my horrid experience. Then you will better understand how he threatened me. I don't like to talk behind people's backs, Father. And I'd say this directly to Bishop Powers." Ned looked at the priest and said, "Bishop Powers is an evil man!"

Just the way Ned said it, the inflection of his voice, gave Father Sullivan a slight chill. "Ned, may I ask why you contacted Father Holtz?"

"Sure, absolutely. Earlier this summer I could tell something was bothering my little brother, Danny. He still lives with our grandma. She raised us both, you know."

Without saying a word, Father Sullivan nodded, as Father Holtz had already told him.

"That evening, Danny and I had a long talk. I was shocked when he told me about Bishop Powers. Danny told me about this cabin in Michigan and how he went there with the bishop. Swimming in the nude, alone in the cabin, the porch, the bed, everything. Hearing all that, I wanted to strangle the bishop. After all my years of suffering ... now my little brother."

"So what did you do?"

"I confronted the bishop."

"You confronted him? How?" Father Sullivan asked.

"The day after hearing this from Danny. I went directly to the rectory. Rang the bell. A young priest answered. Later, I was to find that it was Father Holtz who answered the door. I asked for the bishop. Father Holtz said, 'The bishop is out for a walk. By now, he should be up by Hannah Park.' I thanked the priest and walked straight to the park. Immediately I saw him. Bishop Powers was sitting alone in the gazebo in the middle of the park. There were some kids playing catch at the far end. I walked directly up the brick walk. My pace grew faster the closer I came to him. A few yards away, I said to Bishop Powers, 'It's me. I'm back.' The day was warm. He was wearing a short-sleeved black shirt. No collar. A gentleman's straw hat covered his head.

"As I called his name, he turned. 'Bishop, it's me, Ned. Remember me?' I could feel my pulse racing. I stepped into the gazebo. He remained sitting. Just seeing him, I was already hot under my collar. The bishop said he didn't know me and that I needed to lower my voice. I said again to him, 'It's me, Ned, Ned Thornbauer. Remember your cabin? Summer 1949?' I did lower my voice while I tapped his chest with my closed fist. I told him, 'Now you listen to me ... you immoral bastard. Don't you ever, ever touch my brother, Danny, again or we will both go to the police.' Bishop Powers didn't say anything. His face was red ... in a state of shock.

"I also said, 'One last thing. The Thornbauers have suffered enough. I am going to get you. You will be served justice. I recommend you keep an eye out over your shoulder.' Bishop Powers was defenseless. He knew everything was true. 'One more thing,' I said. "I didn't take one nickel from the collection basket. Don't ruin our lives any more than you have already, or I will ... It will be the biggest regret of your *pathetic life*. You ... you Bishop Powers are a fat, unscrupulous, arrogant imposter. A no-good man hiding behind your collar. You don't deserve to wear your collar. Now remember, I'm going to get you. Justice will be served.' I was breathing so heavily I could hardly talk. I told him he better understand why I was there. He looked at me with apparent alarm. Then I said, 'I'm bringing you to justice.'"

Father Sullivan said, "I've lost my breath just listening, Ned." He knew Ned was telling the truth without even asking. He had added to Father Sullivan's conviction about the guilt of Bishop Powers.

"Just kept thinking of these kids, so many abused."

"Yes, that's what I'm learning," Father Sullivan said with disgust in his voice.

"Trust me, Father, there are lots, lots more." Ned leaned across the table. "You know, I know two more guys who were abused by the bishop himself, just like me. They are willing to speak up. They too want to stop these predator priests. They'll come forward if you need them. Meanwhile, I'll help any way I can."

"Are you telling me all three of you would speak up if you were asked?"

"You bet. We'd love to. Give us the chance. Heck, one of the guys is actually a homosexual, and he hates the bishop for what he did to him. He thinks the guy is crazed. Of course, he was just like me at the time."

"Ned, this sheds additional light on the bishop. First thing's first. Would you sign an affidavit drafted by an attorney that discloses all the sexual encounters and abuse you suffered at the hands of Bishop Powers?" Father Sullivan asked very seriously.

"You bet. I'll even prove I was with him because I know of his reddish-brown birthmark."

"Reddish-brown birthmark?" Father Sullivan asked. "Oh yes, I remember. Father Holtz mentioned that before."

"Yes, right on his waist, just above his ugly fat ass."

Father Sullivan shook his head. "Second question, would you present the affidavit and read it in front of the bishop?"

"Father Sullivan, please give me the chance," Ned said with enthusiasm. "Father, I've had nine horrible years because of this man. I'll help any way necessary to keep him from other young boys. I stopped it for Danny."

"What about your friends?"

"I'm sure they'd do the same. The three of us have been discussing this quite a bit these last few weeks. The memories are so horrifying. Even now, I can't forget ... pictures of his fat, panting body, hungering for his own satisfaction," Ned said with conviction in his voice. "There's something else I'd like to tell you, Father. I hang out at the K of C quite a bit. I was active in the youth hall when I was in high school. Well, now

I go to the bar area every so often. There's a pool table in front, plus lots of euchre tables. In the back rooms, they have two poker tables that are behind closed doors. Always a game going on. Not a problem though. Many local cops are Catholic. The K of C's is a real hangout for Catholic men like me."

"Yes, go on," Father Sullivan said.

"About a month ago, I was havin' some beers with Paul. He's one of the guys I told you about. Paul hates the bishop. Well, there's these three guys in their thirties—families, kids, you know—sitting next to us at the bar. They're talking about these two priests. One priest is an assistant. The other is a visiting priest not assigned to a parish, but he comes to the church and school regularly. Paul and I were just eavesdroppin'. Anyway, one of the guys was tellin' his two friends about the problem in their family. He was tellin' about his son and this priest."

"You mean the priest fooling around with the son?" Father Sullivan asked.

"Lots more than foolin', Father. He did some bad things, real bad things," Ned said as if he were cautioning Father Sullivan.

"Father". Ned looked directly at Father Sullivan, "I know there's more out there. That's all I'll say."

"How'd you know?" Father Sullivan asked with questioning eyes.

"Father, I'm twenty-two now. I'm becoming more open about this. In the past, I've kept this hidden in the closet. Now I have to speak up."

"Ned, yes. That's why we're here," Father Sullivan assured him.

Father Sullivan and Ned were lost in conversation. Suddenly a high, shrill voice spoke up. "Well, well, you're back."

Father Sullivan immediately recognized the checked dress, white apron, and stiff flipped-up hairdo.

"Never forget a face. Specially a handsome one like yours," she said to the priest with a fun, teasing smile. "Let's see, iced tea and fried chicken. We have that special again today."

"You had lunch, Ned?"

"No. Sounds good."

"Okay, two. Make 'em large teas, lots of ice."

"Chicken?" she said, kind of swiveling her shoulders in temptation.

"Fine, fine. Tea first. Then can you wait twenty, thirty minutes on the chicken?"

"You bet. Just the best for the two of you," she said, smiling back at Father Sullivan as she turned away.

"Go on, Ned," he said.

Ned continued, "The guy looked serious yet friendly enough for me to say, 'Excuse me,' but then I heard him say, 'Priest, your son' ... something. They looked a little taken aback, like *who are you?* So I immediately said to pull down their guard, 'Happened to me nine years ago when I was thirteen.' The one guy's eyebrows went up as if he wanted to hear more. He asked me things like 'Can a priest do this? What'd you do?'"

"Did you get his name?" Father Sullivan asked hopefully.

"Actually, he wrote down his name and phone number. He belongs to St. John's over on the other side of town. I don't have his name with me."

"Well, okay. Ned, if this goes any place, I'd like his number."

"Sure, no problem with that, Father. I have nothing to hide anymore."

Father Sullivan sat back and thought, *Father Jaeger and six other priests transferred. Now Ned tells all about the bishop. Where will this all go?*

"Here's your chicken."

Father Sullivan was immediately pulled from his thoughts. "Okay, thanks," he said, not showing her any attention. "Ned, let's eat while we visit," he said, not wanting to miss the meal this time. "Father Holtz told me about your experience with Bishop Powers, but now I understand it so much better. Actually, I find it almost hard to believe."

"I assure you, Father, it's all true and more."

"Ned, what I want to know is how have you been affected. Watch it there," he said, pointing to Ned's mashed potatoes and gravy. "You've got to whisk those flies away. Food's good though."

"You bet I've been affected. I spent two summers goin' to his cabin. It was seven trips total. Every time we stayed overnight. He was always nice to me, but when he was ready to go, he couldn't stop. One time he did it to me out on the front porch. He loved to walk around naked. Since then, my life has been horrid."

"Why didn't you tell your grandmother?"

"Father, she adores priests. Mom left a few years after Danny was born. Dad's always traveled. Our Grandma Ida is the one who raised us. Now, she didn't know the bishop, but priests could do no wrong. My grandmother sees a collar, and she thinks she's seeing Jesus Christ himself. "

"You have to tell her though," Father Sullivan said.

"One time I told her about a priest—I couldn't say the bishop—just to see what she'd say. I told her that after Mass two weeks before, the father bumped into me and I felt him grab me where he shouldn't. I couldn't say another word. She stopped me cold. I was scared, but she wouldn't hear of it. Then of course the bishop threatened me. It was about me stealing from the collection basket, which of course I didn't. To her, priests do no wrong."

"Ned, you don't need to tell me about that," Father Sullivan explained.

"Oh good. Father, here's the deal. The bishop wasn't just an F and G. That's what we called fondlers and grabbers. Rape, sodomy, oral sex— that was his thing. I can give a detailed written report. Awful, awful. I can't bear thinking of it. At thirteen, it was painful in so many ways, if you know what I mean."

Father Sullivan just nodded. His mind was in a whirl, learning so much so fast. He felt even more determined to confront Bishop Powers. "Ned, is there anything else you want to tell me?"

Ned leaned back. He looked long and hard at Father Sullivan. Father Sullivan could feel the vibration of Ned's knee bouncing under the table. The gravy on Ned's uneaten mashed potatoes was forming waves like an oncoming hurricane.

"Okay, you asked. Yes, there is one more terrible thing. It's the main reason I want to speak out. Father"—a deep concern overtook Ned's expression—"yes, there is something else."

"What is it? What is it, Ned?" Father Sullivan's voice raised in anticipation.

"I didn't know if I could share something else with you. Another reason I want to step forward is all about the money. I think you should also know that I routinely saw the bishop ask for the collection baskets before the ushers counted the money. He'd have us bring them to him. I'd see him set the baskets on his dressing table in the sacristy. You know, the one that has all the shallow drawers where he stores all the garments. I first saw him from the cassock closet. He took the bills. Not all, of course. I watched him quickly count. How much, I don't know. Danny says he still sees the bishop do the same thing. After all these years, I'm sure he has quite a stash."

"Ned, I can't believe it." Father Sullivan looked Ned directly in the eye. "Ned, assure me you are telling the truth. If I move forward against Bishop Powers, you will be an integral part as an accuser and victim."

Ned replied, "It's true, Father. I swear. He accused me of stealing, but it was him. I saw it happening several times. Father, everything I said is the factual truth. I swear to God Himself."

Father Sullivan leaned back and took a deep breath. "Ned, I believe you." The priest then paused. "My next meeting will be with Bishop Powers. Once we go there, Ned, there will be no turning back."

Leaning his left elbow on the table, Ned rested his chin in his palm. He paused. Making sure he said exactly what was on his mind, he said, "Father, I have never been so sure of anything in my life. I will support you all the way. If it's the last thing I ever do, I will bring this horrific man to justice. So help me, Father, I will."

"Okay, Ned, I respect that. I believe you." Father Sullivan could tell that signals were racing through Ned's mind. "Next week, same time. Here. I'll have a plan. If something comes up for either of us, call. Otherwise, see you in a week."

"Yes, this is a good place to meet, Father. I look forward to hearing your plan."

CHAPTER 82

THY EYES SHALL SEE

Bishop Powers—September 15, 1958, late afternoon

"FATHER Schmidt, we need to prepare for the Chicago conference in two weeks. This whole issue of birth control is going to be
the main topic. I must make sure I'm on the right side. Along with the
majority of bishops and cardinals, I support the position that the church
must not change our universal policy. Birth control is wrong."

"Yes, Bishop, I agree, but have you read the article written by Cardinal Albinio Luciano of Venice? He has been ruffling some feathers in
Rome."

"I know, I know. He's listening to all those couples who can't control
themselves. They want birth control so they can take God's intended use
of the sexual act beyond procreation. Don't you agree, Father?" Bishop
Powers maintained an aura and a way of asking questions that implied he
was always right and others had better agree.

"Bishop, I do. The conservative approach of our church I support on
most issues. Like sex, for example. Look at these priests in our diocese
that you and I are burdened with. We're left with cleaning up the mess
... priests like Father Jaeger. I'm sickened. You can't have a scandal in
this diocese if you are looking toward being archbishop or even possibly becoming a cardinal." Father Schmidt chose every word to show his
undying support of Bishop Powers.

"My ambitions are not paramount," the bishop stated with half-
hearted conviction. He walked over to the side bar in his study. Looking

at the small array of cognacs and whiskies, he selected a twenty-one-year-old McCallan. "Would you like one, Father?"

"I usually don't. Maybe, yes, maybe this time I will."

"Straight up with a splash? That's the way to drink it. No ice," Bishop Powers confirmed.

"Yes. I'll enjoy it that way. Just like you, Your Excellency."

After handing a snifter to Father Schmidt, Bishop Powers walked over and sat in his overstuffed easy chair. Taking a sip, he rested his forearm along the arm of the chair, the scotch in his hand dangling over the end. He looked up at the fireplace mantel, which was fixed with an array of family pictures and candles from his first Mass. "The last picture closest to the chair is one of my favorites. That's me with my parents on ordination day." To the right was a smaller frame. The bishop posed with his arms around two young altar boys taken after Christmas service. Of most importance, however, Bishop Powers prized the photograph with Pope Pius XII taken in the Vatican in 1954. He proudly displayed it for all to see in the center of the mantel. Overhead, a gilded-edge gold frame encased an oil portrait of himself he had commissioned in 1956.

"I'm looking forward to going to Chicago actually. I usually enjoy the bishops' conference. Especially since it includes our brothers in the Midwest. Good to get away from O'Brien in New York and those other two liberal fat cats in Boston and Philly," Bishop Powers said to Father Schmidt.

Father Schmidt, sitting in the matching chair opposite the bishop, separated only by a small table, listened intently, having taken his third sip of scotch.

"Father, you sip good scotch. It's not like drinking a beer."

"Oh sure, sure," Father Schmidt agreed, not wanting to expose his lack of knowledge of how to drink scotch.

Bishop Powers took his second sip and then said low, almost in a whisper, "I hope to spend some alone time with Bishops Moore and Stanski. I'd like to hear their views on a few other matters not on the agenda."

After finishing his drink, Bishop Powers stood up, took his collar off, and walked over to pour another scotch. He lifted his empty glass first in question to Father Schmidt, but Father Schmidt shook his head. *Keep coherent*, Father Schmidt shook his head *no*, as he knew he had other matters to take care of.

Father Schmidt stood. "I need to go, your Excellency."

Bishop Powers said, "One more thing. You are to be at every session of the conference twenty minutes before. Talk with the other secretaries. Listen to them. Listen, Father, listen."

"You can depend on me. Always."

The quiet solitude of the study, which was filled with antiques and books, gave the bishop a feeling of comfort and serenity. The single malt lent a helping hand. The bishop thought to himself. He hoped Father Schmidt noticed his feeling of contempt for those wicked abusing priests. The bishop felt confident that Father Schmidt could see his disgust for any priest who would ever touch a young boy.

Father Schmidt—September 15, 1958

The hallway on the second floor of the rectory housed seven bedrooms. The bishop's apartment was at the far end, while Father Schmidt's two rooms were at the opposite end, closest to the downstairs entrance and across the walk from the cathedral.

After leaving the bishop's study on the first floor, Father Schmidt walked from the side entrance of the rectory, across the walk, and into the sacristy of the cathedral. He knew Billy Donovan and Russell Jones should be finishing cleaning and straightening the sacristy.

"Oh, Father, good evening," Billy said at the same time Russell was throwing on his jacket and leaving.

"Hi and good-bye, Father Schmidt," Russell said, dashing out the door.

"Did you guys finish everything, Billy?"

"Yes, Father. Time now to go home and do homework. Yuck. Sister's giving us a huge English test tomorrow."

Father Schmidt hesitated before his planned question. Billy finished hanging the last of the cleaned and pressed surpluses in the cassock closet. "*Hmmm*, say Billy, before you go, would you have time to help me move my sofa upstairs? I'm moving it to the back wall."

"Oh sure, Father…ah, if it won't take too long," Billy replied.

"Let's do it now if you can. Should only take a few minutes," he assured the boy.

Billy followed Father Schmidt upstairs. Walking into the room at the far end of the second floor, he noticed the couch against the side wall.

"Catch the door there, Billy. Throw your coat and books on the chair. This couch weighs a ton." Each took an end. "Lift with your legs, Billy." Father Schmidt could hear Billy straining.

Suddenly Billy's end hit the floor. "Sorry, Father." Billy breathed deeply. "Okay, I'm ready."

Father Schmidt said, "Now, step-by-step to your left. That's it. One more. Drop. Here, I'll scoot this end." With that, Father Schmidt flopped down on the couch. "Whew! That was heavy." Patting the cushion next to him, he said, "Sit here a minute. Rest."

Billy firmed up. "Oh, Father, please no. You said that the last time, and look what happened. Please, Father, I don't feel like doing that again," Billy pleaded.

"Now, Billy, you like being an altar boy. Come on. You enjoy getting that five bucks extra per week. You're the only one that takes it. Remember the other boys don't. Just you. We won't take too long. Ten minutes, Billy. I want to show you. You're getting older."

Without hesitation, Father Schmidt leaned over and pulled Billy's shirt over his head like a parent undressing a child. Before Billy could blink, he was uncomfortably being stripped by the relentless priest. Father Schmidt took his own shirt and slacks off in one continuous motion.

"I want to show you a new way to pray. Praying between friends. It's loving," he said anxiously with lust in his eyes. Standing in full figure in front of Billy, who was now seated on the sofa, Father Schmidt then knelt down in front of him and slid off the boy's pants. Placing both hands on Billy's knees, Father Schmidt said, "I'll pray first. Then it will be your turn. You hold the crucifix."

As Father Schmidt bowed his head, he was startled by the twist of the doorknob. The door suddenly opened partially. Jerking his head up, Father Schmidt looked at the two piercing eyes of Bishop Powers through the six-inch opening. Billy immediately put his hands over his eyes. The opening stayed stationery. Not a word was exchanged. Father Schmidt froze. His entire priesthood flashed before his eyes. *I'm done.* The bishop's two glaring eyes sent a jolt through his body. A few seconds seemed like an eternity. Then, with a half-crazed smile, Bishop Powers gently closed the door and walked back down the hall.

A few moments before, Father Holtz had been walking down the hall, heading for the stairs and sacristy. Rounding the corner of the hall, he froze in his tracks as if ordered by an overzealous staff sergeant. There, he could see Bishop Powers' back, his head half into the doorway of Father Schmidt's room. Something looked fishy. Father Holtz knew something was not right. He immediately did an about-face and stepped back ten feet to the door of his room. Silently, he turned the knob, walked in, and closed the door with the same degree of care.

From inside, he kept his ear flush to the door. He took a deep breath and held it, drowning out any sound. Five seconds, six, seven—he heard footsteps heavy upon the floor. Louder and louder. Then he heard breathing softer, softer. Five more seconds, then quiet. Father Holtz knew the bishop had passed back in the direction of his own room. The closing of Father Schmidt's door had been unmistakable yet not out of character of the prying bishop, who cherished control along with his other self-serving vices.

After waiting a few minutes, Father Holtz quietly opened the door and stepped into the hall. He took a few steps and then peeked around the corner. He could see Father Schmidt's door still closed. Quietly and softly, he walked down the hall past Father Schmidt's door. A slight hesitation, Father Holtz heard, "I told you 'no'. Now look what … " He then proceeded down the hall. He opened the back door, stepped across the walk, and entered the side door of the cathedral. Without turning on the light inside the small foyer, Father Holtz sat down on the step by the paned window just above the foot of the stairs.

A half-moon shown through the window, but the stairs remained in darkness. There he sat perched on the third step. With his hands on his knees, Father Holtz waited anxiously. The rectory door was in full view. The outside light right over the door simply lit a crescent around the sidewalk between the two buildings. Father Holtz was sure he had verified a hunch that someone was in the room with Father Schmidt. Why hadn't the bishop stepped in, and why hadn't he heard any words from the bishop? *I'll wait.*

Billy had hoped the bishop's short unexpected appearance in the door would stop the advance of the lusting predator. Although he had been with Father Schmidt several times before, this time seemed unfamiliar, as the priest was far more aggressive. Billy trembled before succumbing to the distastefulness of the act. Moments later, he awkwardly tried to push the demon away but to no avail.

After an undetermined length of time, the priest slumbered by Billy's side, keeping a grip around the boy's shoulder. Billy squeezed his eyes shut. *God, Almighty Father, please, please, help me.* Moments later, his own cries of, "No, no. Please, no more. Father, no," eclipsed his unanswered prayers. Surrendering, Billy endured the moment. With his eyes closed, the passage of time became only an afterthought.

As the priest released his grip, Billy stood up and quickly jumped into his clothes. Father Schmidt was still sprawled out on the sofa, cradling a couch pillow across his waist. Pointing his finger at Billy while sitting up on the couch, Father Schmidt watched the boy streak for the door. "Not a word, Billy Donovan. Not a word. You understand?" he said.

Billy was already halfway out the door. He only heard *not a word*, which really did not register as he focused only on getting away. As he dashed in the direction of the stairs, he heard again the muffled words of the priest's demand, "Not a word!"

Billy jumped down the stairs two, three at a time. Catching his balance before almost falling headfirst to the bottom stair, he swung around the corner and lunged for the door handle. The flash of a locked door pierced his mind. As his right thumb hit the knob, Billy's adrenaline spiked. He pushed the door. It opened. Instinctively, he jumped the step onto the sidewalk. His leather shoes skidded as he pivoted on the concrete walk. Lifting both arms for balance, Billy raced toward the front walk. The unnoticed figure sitting on the steps behind the window of the cathedral recorded the entirety of the surreal events, as Billy Donovan disappeared into the darkness.

CHAPTER 83

TIME TO CONTACT

Father Holtz—September 15, 1958

BILLY Donovan running away from the rectory was fixed in Father Holtz's mind. *What took place? What happened in that room with Father Schmidt? Lord only knows. Stands to reason, Father Schmidt is just like the bishop. Two of the same. Of course, that's why the bishop let them be. More of the same. Cover-up, cover-up. The snakelike bastards. Sorry, Lord, sorry,* Father Holtz thought as he made two quick signs of the cross for his language. *Sorry.*

That evening while sitting at his desk in the privacy of his room, Father Holtz reached for his fountain pen, which neatly rested in a leather tray of small personal items. Dad's K of C tie clasp, a small unframed 1920s photo of his parents, and his deceased grandfather's 1932 driver's license nostalgically sat by the side of his favorite fountain pen. Father Holtz treasured his pen—a present from his parents when he was ordained in 1948.

Dear Father Sullivan:

I have new information that I must share with you. Hopefully, you'll receive this letter before you approach Bishop Powers via Father Schmidt. New revelation. Can't put in writing. Call me at 5-5339 at 5:00 on Friday, September 19. I'll be waiting in a phone booth three blocks from the rectory.

Remember, please destroy all my letters, or at least keep them hidden in a secure place.

Respectfully,
Ben

Father Sullivan—September 17, 1958

After meeting with Ned and learning more about what he was up against with Bishop Powers, Father Sullivan felt confident that now was the time to contact Father Schmidt in South Wayne to schedule a meeting with Bishop Powers. *Should I write, call, or show up at the front door?* Father Sullivan asked himself. Concluding the latter was too chancy and writing might negate a reply, Father Sullivan decided to call Father Schmidt.

"Operator, I'd like to place a person-to-person call to Father Schmidt at St. Leonard's rectory in South Wayne."

"Is this a collect call?" the operator asked.

"No, please charge to this number. Thank you."

Father Sullivan waited. Person-to-person calls were often like a day in limbo. "Yes, I have Father Schmidt on the line," the operator said in a high-pitched voice. "Thirty cents please."

"Good morning, Father, this is Father Sullivan from St. Thomas Moore. Thank you for taking my call."

"I hope all is well with you," Father Schmidt said, forcing himself to greet Father Sullivan politely.

"Thank you, I'm well," Father Sullivan responded. "I'd like to speak with you on an important matter. I am very concerned about why you transferred Father Jaeger to another parish where he will be around children once again. You are aware of what happened at St. Thomas Moore. Father Warren and I told you ourselves."

"I can assure you, Father, you have nothing to worry about. Father Jaeger went through a thorough psychological evaluation this summer with Dr. Bloomberg. We were all pleased, including the bishop, with the results we observed. Bishop Powers and I were also able to work directly with Father Jaeger. Both the psychological and theological advancement he displayed have prepared him well for his new assignment."

"I assumed that is how you would feel, considering your past history of reassignments."

Father Schmidt ignored the implications from Father Sullivan. "He is not without sin. We all have sinned, but Father Jaeger is a priest, a man of the collar. He is needed to carry out the good works of our church. He deserves to have the opportunity to do the work of our Lord, just as you and I do, Father," he said, trying to convince Father Sullivan to drop any further questioning.

Those last words reek with exaggeration, naivety, or insincerity. Maybe all three, Father Sullivan thought. "I understand. You have worked closely with Father Jaeger this past summer," he agreed. "With all due respect, Father, I request the opportunity to meet with you and the bishop."

"I am afraid that will not be possible. Bishop Powers is quite busy. In any event, he has delegated these responsibilities to me. You can see, as I have outlined, we have made tremendous progress with Father Jaeger."

Being more direct, Father Sullivan added, "I'm sorry, Father, but there are a few more issues I would like to address, such as notifying the legal authorities."

"Now wait one minute, Father. You're out of your territory. This is an issue of the diocese, not your parish. So let's discontinue this conversation. Please give my best to Father Warren. Have a good day, Father Sullivan," Father Schmidt said, trying to get the last word in before he slammed the phone down.

Better check the post office box, Father Sullivan thought while making a late afternoon trip to the bank the next day. The short ride downtown did not keep his eyelids from fighting to stay open. The last few nights had been basically sleepless. Cranking the car window down more, he hoped to shock his system enough to keep him out of the way of any oncoming traffic. After turning left on Maple, Father Sullivan parked in back of the building. He walked around to the front and into the post office. The terrazzo floors, high ceilings, plastered walls, and ceiling fans created an area cooler than the outdoors.

Father Sullivan felt the coolness as he entered the building. He panned the post office boxes—398, 400, 402, 404 ... *bingo*. He inserted his key and clicked the box open. One solitary letter. He speared his right thumb into the envelope, tearing the paper, and piercing the silence in the lobby. *Have new information ... Please ... Friday, September 19, 5:00.*

Today is Thursday, Father Sullivan thought, glancing at his watch ... *Hmmm. Only twenty-five more hours.* Two key words jumped off the paper: *new information.* Upon arriving back at the rectory, Father Sullivan immediately headed to his room. He locked the door behind him. Suddenly, he threw his head down in disgust and put his hands on his hips. Friday couldn't come too soon.

Peter Goodnar—September 19, 1958

The school year had begun quietly for Peter Goodnar. Concerned about how he was doing, that Friday morning Father Sullivan sent a message to Sister Mary Michael. He asked her to have Peter stop by the rectory that afternoon after school.

"Thank you, Sister," Peter said when she handed him the note.

During lunch hour, Sister Mary Michael, Peter's former sixth grade sister, saw Father Sullivan standing at the edge of the park, across the street from the school. He was just watching kids as they ran off their noon meal. Kids ran by and said, "Hi, Father Sullivan," but didn't stop. Two or three boys came up to him to ask if he thought the White Sox could still win the pennant. All the students liked Father Sullivan. They sometimes even talked him into pitching a few innings of baseball—his favorite sport.

In the distance, on the edge of the playground area, Father Sullivan saw Peter swinging alone, barely moving. He sat with his arms wrapped around the chains, hands clasped, feet dragging, head down.

As the priest watched, he heard a soft voice from behind him. "Hello, Father."

Half turning, he said, "Oh hi, Sister Mary Michael."

The boys standing around talking baseball with Father Sullivan said, "Gotta go, Father," as they saw her approaching.

"I let Peter know about seeing you after school."

"How's he doing this past week?" Father Sullivan asked.

"Well, Father, you know Peter's in the seventh grade, not in my class anymore," Sister Mary Michael said.

"Oh, Sister, too much on my mind. Of course, and here I passed the note to you," Father Sullivan said as he hit his forehead with his open palm.

"Father, don't worry. I talk to Sister Joaugustus every day, not only regarding Peter but also Gene Kowolski and a few others. Peter and Gene though have been affected the most. Sister told me some things she's observed, even during these first few weeks, especially with Peter." Not knowing what she meant, Father Sullivan did not comment about Gene. "We think Peter's an altogether different person compared to the beginning of sixth grade. Sister Joaugustus said he's so quiet, inward, more than just shy, and he never takes part in class. She said he just keeps to himself … morose. Like he has no interests in life. You can tell something's bothering him. Sister Joaugustus noticed it right away."

"Well of course we both know what that is," Father Sullivan assured Sister Mary Michael. "Sister, what do you think if I call his parents and talk to both of them? He's begged me not to. Actually, Sister, I'd say I've been negligent not doing so. I should have done it last school year. Can you believe, Father Jaeger is gone, but just look at the long term effects on these boys."

"Yes, probably," Sister Mary Michael answered. "We can all second-guess despite our good intentions. Father, I must say. It's not only Peter and Gene. I'm concerned there could be more boys we don't even know about."

"You're right, Sister. You want to know what worries me just as much?" he asked. "Father Jaeger is with kids in another parish while the two of us are standing here talking."

Resting her elbow on her left hand, which was positioned across her waist, Sister Mary Michael propped her chin on her right hand and shook her head. "Oh my dear Lord." She closed her eyes and then said, "I'll remind Sister Joaugustus again this afternoon, just to make sure Peter comes to the rectory."

"Thank you, Sister."

"God bless you, Father," she said, turning and walking back to school.

Father Sullivan, too, was at a loss for words … but he knew exactly what he had to do.

When he arrived for his meeting with Father Sullivan after school, Peter greeted the priest when he saw him through the open door, sitting at his desk. "Good afternoon, Father Sullivan,"

"Come in, Peter. It's so good to see you," Father Sullivan said as he stood and walked around the corner of his cluttered desk.

Peter pressed his lips together but didn't respond. Setting his books on the side table, he sat in the chair at which Father Sullivan pointed. Father Sullivan took the adjacent chair. Both could feel a gentle wind drifting through the screened window on the side of the desk. Father Sullivan's sixth sense detected Peter's apprehension.

"Peter, I really am glad to see you. How was your summer?"

"Oh, it was okay, I guess."

"What all did you do?"

"Nothin' much," he replied without conveying any expression.

Father Sullivan waited. He didn't say anything, wanting to see what Peter would say next.

Peter looked up. "Still hate him. Still hate that priest," he said, referring to Father Jaeger.

"Pretty tough words. Hate. Hate a priest?"

"He's just a bad man. No priest to me. You're a priest. You care. He's a … he's a … just a … Sorry, Father. I can't say the bad word."

Father Sullivan waited without a response.

"My dreams are the worst. Dreams, horrid dreams. A couple of times I even screamed. Maybe more. This one night, my mom rushed into the room. 'What is it? What is it,' she asked me."

"What did you tell her, Peter?" Father Sullivan asked, eager to know.

"Oh nothing, just a bad dream. No way can I tell her or my dad. They wouldn't believe me."

"You know, Peter, maybe you should consider telling your parents, although it may be very difficult for you—"

Peter interrupted, "No, no, Father, I can't. They love the priests. They wouldn't believe this. Priests do no wrong in their book." Then Peter muttered, "That dirty son … Oh sorry, Father. I did tell someone."

Father Sullivan raised eyebrows and furrowed his forehead. *Is this progress?* He waited.

"Well, I was talking to someone else. Someone else Jaeger got."

Father Sullivan didn't say a word.

"Do you know who? Do you want to know, Father?" Peter said, sounding like he needed to release a secret. Maybe to prove he wasn't the only one.

"That's up to you, Peter. If you'd like to tell me, of course it's confidential."

Peter leaned back in his chair. His chin poked the bottom of his neck. Father Sullivan knew the boy was thinking. Patiently he waited as Peter contemplated. Father Sullivan felt new waves of breeze gliding over his neck as he waited for Peter to disclose the name. He heard the chirps of robins on the windowsill, and then he waited longer ... Not a word.

Then suddenly Peter said, "Gene. I told Gene."

"You mean Gene Kowolski?" Father Sullivan asked intently as if he didn't know.

"Yes, Father, and Gene told me Jaeger did the same things to him. Actually, more times than me ... " He paused. "One thing different though."

"What's that, Peter?"

"Gene told his dad."

"He did?" Father Sullivan asked, pretending to be surprised and that he didn't know Mr. Kowolski. He, of course, had already met with him.

"And you know what Gene told me? Gene told me his dad was gonna get him. Get Father Jaeger," Peter said, thinking he was disclosing a huge secret.

"What'd he mean ... get him?" Father Sullivan asked.

Peter leaned forward as if he was going to disclose something terrible, very terrible. He paused and looked over his chair, making sure the door was closed and nobody had silently entered the room. Whispering, he said, "Gene's dad said ... he said he's gonna kill that GD priest. You know what GD stands for, Father? I can't say it."

"Yes, I know what it means, Peter."

"Said he's gonna kill him," Peter said with almost glee in his voice. He leaned back in his chair as if he had just told the secret of the Lone Ranger's identity.

Although he understood the passionate statement, Father Sullivan did not approve of the threat. He was glad, however, that Peter had opened up and shared a big secret and had spoken with emotion and passion. Peter knew what Father Jaeger had done to him and Gene was wrong. He also knew it was wrong to kill.

"Father, can I ask a question?"

"Sure, Peter, anything."

"Is it a mortal sin to say you're gonna kill someone? Even if you don't do it?"

"Peter, the intention is very wrong. It is wrong to desire to kill."

"Yes, Father, but Gene said his dad really means it. Know what though, Father? I don't think he's gonna kill him. I think Gene's just doing big talk."

"I'm sure you're right, Peter. Very observant."

"Can I tell you another secret, Father?"

"Yes. I won't tell a soul."

"Father … " He paused. "Father, three times I've said the intention."

"Peter, intention to what?" Father Sullivan asked.

"Yes, Father, I've said three times that I'd like to kill him, but really I don't mean it. I was just mad. Talkin' big. I do wish something bad would happen to him, just like he was bad to me. Think I need to go to confession?" Peter asked with remorse in his voice. Then he asked, "Father, can a priest commit a mortal sin?"

Father Sullivan nodded. "Yes, they can, Peter. Yes, they can." He looked at the boy. Even though he knew Peter would not kill Father Jaeger, he was glad to know Peter was so conscious of right and wrong. "Peter, I think it's good for you to go to confession. Confess and talk with a priest regularly. Cleanse your soul. One last thing, Peter. You don't have to answer today. I just want you to think about something. Someday I may ask you to be with me and tell someone else about what has happened to you. You know what I mean? What Father Jaeger did to you all those times. It would be to help keep Father Jaeger from ever doing these bad things again to someone else just like you."

Peter sat up. Father Sullivan could tell he was surprised and maybe even alarmed.

"Father," Peter said, "Father, I'd really have to think about that. This has always been a secret between you and me. He still scares me. Scares me what he might do to me again. I have all these bad dreams."

Father Sullivan replied, "It still is a secret only between you and me. I just want you to think about it." There was silence. "I may need your help someday, Peter. You're a good person. I just may need your help."

Peter long remembered his visit with Father Sullivan that day in September 1958. So did Father Sullivan. He felt confident about his visit with Peter. The boy had opened up, saying what bothered him, and how he was doing his best to deal with his terrifying secret.

Father Sullivan—September 19, 1958

A little while later, at 5:02, Father Sullivan approached the open phone booth. He immediately placed a call to Father Holtz.

Father Holtz's right hand grabbed the phone. "Hello, Michael. Good to hear that ring."

"Sorry I'm a couple minutes late. But I'm anxious to hear what you have to say. All's well?" Father Sullivan asked.

"This is going to explain more about the cover-up."

Father Sullivan pressed the phone more firmly to his ear.

"I have to tell you, this was most shocking for me to learn," Father Holtz disclosed.

"Yes, yes, what is it?"

"The other night as I was walking down the hall, I turned the corner and saw Bishop Powers leaning into Father Schmidt's room. He was standing in the hall, mind you, but his head was inside the doorway. Only lasted for a few moments. I immediately went back to my room, closed my door, and listened from inside. Then I heard the bishop's footsteps as he walked by in the direction of his room. That's not all. I had a hunch about Father Schmidt. I left my room and quietly walked down the hall, stopped, and listened at Father Schmidt's door. Thought I may have heard two voices. A moan? Wasn't sure. Then I heard, "No! I told you no!" I hurried down the stairs and over to the sacristy. I waited inside by the window. The lights were out. Then about twenty, maybe twenty-five minutes later, I saw Billy Donovan dash out the side door and disappear. I'll never forget the look of alarm on his face."

"What's it mean, Father?" Father Sullivan asked.

"It means Billy was who the bishop saw when he peeked into Schmidt's room. What the bishop saw was Father Schmidt together with Billy," Father Holtz said.

Father Sullivan thought and then replied, "Yes, the circumstances would lead you to believe that."

"Unfortunately, you are right, Michael. Billy was with Father Schmidt. Only one thing at this hour, the noisy moans. As I look back, I know I should have ... should have ... " Father Holtz paused. "But I didn't know."

"If we assume the bishop knows about Father Schmidt, then that explains even more about the cover-up, and that begs a question. We both know about the bishop. However, does Father Schmidt know about the bishop and the Thornbauers? Maybe more?" Father Sullivan asked. "Think about it, Ben. The bishop could have known about Father Schmidt and Billy before that night. Surely it wasn't the first time for Schmidt ... being with Billy or some other boy. These guys usually have hidden pasts. I'm sure Bishop Powers hung that over him. No wonder Father Schmidt does everything the bishop tells him to do."

"I see it every day," Father Holtz said. "On the other hand, maybe Bishop Powers first found out about Schmidt when he peeked in the door. Or you're right and he could have known before."

"Ben, this is all so surreal, so unbelievable to me. Could one be covering the other to cover himself? Like I know but don't tell? Hold like blackmail?" Father Sullivan paused, thinking about what he had just said. *Surreal!* "I've got to tell you, Ben, I did call Father Schmidt this week. Bottom line, he would not consider meeting with me. He was very definite and protective of Bishop Powers when I said I wanted to meet with the bishop."

Suddenly, Father Sullivan saw an anxious-looking woman in a very stylish dress. She was standing outside the phone booth about ten feet away by the curb. Frowning, she looked at Father Sullivan and pointed with her index finger toward her watch several times. Obviously she was waiting to use the public phone. Father Sullivan nodded and held up two fingers.

"Ben, I've got to go. I have to figure out how I'm going to meet with Schmidt and the bishop. Somehow I'll make it happen."

"I know you will. Remember, leave me out. Never use my name. And one more thing … " Father Holtz waited.

"Yes?" Michael asked.

"We never talked today. Never, ever."

"Of course, Ben. Never. Take care. We'll stay in touch."

Father Sullivan looked west, startled by the directness of the sunlight. He took the long walk back to the rectory. *Need some time alone. I have a lot to think about.*

CHAPTER 84

FOOTBALL

Father Jaeger—September 14, 1958

THE first two weeks of school at St. Vincent's started off well for
Father Jaeger. He fit right in with the teachers, parents, and especially the students. Father Arnold enjoyed standing near the sidelines
and watching Father Jaeger take charge. The elderly pastor could feel
the weight of so many parish responsibilities being lifted from his shoulders. The previous assistant, Father Yates, had developed issues with
some of the parents regarding his relationship with a few of the students.
Although a group of parents had previously met with Father Arnold about
his previous assistant's relationships with several of the boys, nothing was
brought out into the open. Father Jaeger was informed that two of the
boys had withdrawn from school with no apparent explanation.

The parents' visits, the boys dropping out of school, and the transfer
of Father Yates had all transpired in fewer than ten days. Prior to Father
Jaeger's arrival, Father Arnold had been in Columbus. His ninety-six-
year-old mother had not been well. He had taken advantage of July to
spend time with her. It was fortunate that he had; she had passed away
just two weeks before the start of school. With the hectic July and August
behind him, Father Arnold felt revived. He could focus on the new year
and his bright young assistant.

The noon Mass on Sunday ended. The church emptied quickly. Terry
Groves and Butch Rector were the servers for the low Mass. They closed

539

the sanctuary. Smoke from the candles drifted, curled around, and snaked into the sacristy.

Father Jaeger initiated conversation. "You guys football fans?"

"You bet, Father. We're both Bears fans. Someday when we can drive, we're going to ask for the ol' man's car and go see a game at Wrigley Field," Terry said.

"Yeah, but how we gonna get tickets, meathead? You know how much they cost?" Butch asked, jabbing his elbow into his friend's ribs.

"Well, maybe let me know when you have a license and car," Father Jaeger said. "My uncle happens to work in the ticket department at Wrigley Field. Maybe I could help you out."

"Really, Father? That'd be cool. Real cool. Any chance you know how to get Elvis tickets? Ah, just kidding, Father," Butch said, giving Terry another jab.

"Time to finish up, boys. It's almost one o'clock," Father Jaeger said, anxious to hurry on.

Terry and Butch headed to the cassock closet, having finished their post Mass ritual. They were close friends. As they both stood inside the closet room, removing their surplices, Butch heard the door close. Turning around, Terry saw Father Jaeger standing with a sly, unsettling smirk stretched across his face.

Squatting down with his arms outstretched, Father Jaeger blurted out, "You know why I like football? Tackling!" With that, Father Jaeger lunged forward and wrapped his arms around Butch's waist. In the same motion, his open hand made a full clasp six inches below Butch's belt. Butch immediately let out a shrill yelp and then screeched. So surprised by the blind side, Butch reacted instinctively in sheer pain.

"See you gotta get 'em so they don't move. That's called control," Father Jaeger said, thinking he was showing them a real football tactic.

"That's called broken balls, Father. That hurt like hell. Back off!"

"Ah, come on. Just showing you some tactics," the priest said, brushing off the remark. "Then there's the simple version." Having let go of Butch, Father Jaeger moved, his arms outstretched as if in slow motion. He opened his hand with spread fingers and thrust it directly into Terry, undercutting his groin with a gentle lift from underneath, between his legs.

"Ahhh," Terry yelped.

"Father, we don't like your football moves. We don't play football like that. God, that still hurts," Butch said, still bending over, hands on his knees. "Back off, Father, or I'll tackle you with an illegal hit. My knee to your belt, and you'll be speaking Latin with a squeaky voice."

"Oh come on, I'm funnin' you guys. We'll have to get together for a little sandlot game some Sunday afternoon," Father Jaeger said, blowing off the incident, disguising his true intention.

Butch reached for the door past the priest. "Bye," he said without stopping. Terry followed like a flea on a dog.

"Don't be so serious, you guys!" Father Jaeger shouted as he quickly stepped out of the closet after them. He stood there, hands on his hips, watching the boys. "Just kidding, guys!" he shouted, but they were already out of sight.

The incident in the closet was still on Father Jaeger's mind later in the week. *Maybe I went too fast.* He remained edgy. Father Jaeger jerked backward when he heard Father Arnold down the hall.

"Hello, Father Jaeger. Have a minute?"

Turning, Father Jaeger proceeded back toward Father Arnold, who was standing in the doorway to his room. "Yes, Father, what is it?"

"Come on in. Here, have a seat," said Father Arnold with a serious look on his face.

Immediately, guilt raced across Father Jaeger's mind. He thought about Butch, Terry, and the cassock closet from a few days before. He sat down. "Sure, Father, what is it?" he asked, instinctively leaning forward in his chair.

"I need to talk to you. I received a call this morning from a parent. They are quite disturbed. Actually, extremely upset regarding their son, one of our altar boys."

Father Jaeger shifted in his seat. Wringing his hands, he hoped Father Arnold did not see a look of alarm. *The closet, the grab—why did I?*

"The parents insist on seeing me this evening. They won't wait."

Now Father Jaeger realized he was probably going to meet Butch or Terry's parents. *How will I explain?*

"Father, I must say you are involved," Father Arnold said.

Oh God, no. Not again. Father Jaeger felt a rush through his body.

"Seems you've been getting real close with the students."

"Yes, but Father, I can explain. I was just showing—"

"Showing them what, Father?" the older priest said, interrupting Father Jaeger.

"Football. Just showing them where to grab."

"Grab? Grab who? Grab what? I don't understand."

"You see, Father," Father Jaeger felt immediate perspiration on his forehead. "If you squeeze their—"

"Wait a minute," Father Arnold interrupted again. "Are we talking about the same thing? Grabbing? Squeezing? I need you to substitute teach my CCD class tonight. There are about fifteen students from the public grade schools who have a religion class with me every Thursday," Father Arnold explained.

Trying to look calm, Father Jaeger slowly sat back in his chair. He felt the perspiration on his back soaking into his shirt. "Of course, Father, I'd be happy to help," he said with hidden relief, knowing he had almost said too much too soon.

"My class outline is simple. The subject this session is confession, the forgiveness of sin, heaven, hell, and purgatory. You'll do well," Father Arnold assured his assistant.

"If you don't mind me asking, Father, what's the problem? Who are the parents you are going to see?" Father Jaeger asked just to ease his mind that Terry and Butch hadn't told their parents.

"There's a boy, Johnny Rafferty, in the eighth grade. Comes from a troubled family. Anyway, he had an altercation with Sister Benedict. Parents say it's all the sister's fault. I couldn't put this off another day. Have to meet tonight."

Not only did Father Jaeger feel relieved, but he felt exonerated from his mischievous act with Terry and Butch. His fun in the closet was now justified in his mind. *Just having a little fun.*

Father Jaeger arrived at the recreation room in the church basement about fifteen minutes before the seven o'clock class. The room was sparsely decorated. The far wall contained a series of posters, all painted in different styles by eighth graders. Each poster depicted the Blessed

Mother and Jesus. The back end of the room was lined with stacks of folding tables and chairs. Additional chairs were set up in the middle of the room, forming a meeting type setting with chairs placed around four tables pushed together.

"Good evening, Father. Where's Father Arnold?" asked an exuberant young man bearing a crop of hair as red as the countless freckles stretched across his nose.

"He had a special meeting to attend," Father Jaeger explained.

"Special meeting? Ha! We're the special ones," Kenny Heiser said and then laughed as he looked around for applause.

Within a minute, small groups of two or three students walked in and threw their Baltimore Catechism books at their usual spots on the tables. Another minute passed, and Father Jaeger counted heads … twelve, thirteen, fourteen. He stood alone, reviewing his outline.

Noticing the movement of the hands on the electric clock on the far wall, Father Jaeger said, "Good evening, everyone. Let's all find a seat."

"Found mine just where I left it last week!" Kenny blurted out. Ignoring Kenny, Father Jaeger waited for them to settle down. "My name is Father Jaeger. Father Arnold isn't able to be here tonight. I'm taking his place."

"Ah, shucks," a voice sprung from the far table. "We like good ol' Father Arnold. He always tells us stories. Did you know he was a chaplain in France during World War I? Boy, does he have the tales. Scary war. They even used poison gas."

Father Jaeger replied, "No, I didn't know that. I'll have to ask him more about his past. Sounds interesting." Continuing his effort to begin class, he said, "Let's go around the table." Immediately Kenny stood up and walked toward the priest. "And what are you doing, young man?"

"I'm just going around the table like you said," Kenny responded, bending over and slapping his knee.

"Okay, just take your chair."

Kenny turned and threw his hands in the air. "Just doin' as I'm told," he muttered in a voice everyone could still hear. The class was glad to see the priest smile.

"Okay, everyone. Now that Red Skelton has his seat, state your name and tell me something about yourself. I don't know any of you. Let's begin." Father Jaeger pointed to the young lady immediately to his left.

"My name is Betsy Flanner. I'm in eighth grade at Eastville Grade School."

"Yeah, and she's my girlfriend," an overweight kid with a buzz haircut said from the back table.

"You wish," said the little guy next to him.

"Two more of you. Guess we have the Three Stooges here tonight."

"Oh sorry, Father. I meant she's my friend. We're all good Catholic boys."

As if she did not hear their remarks, Betsy smiled sweetly, her hands neatly folded atop her *Baltimore Catechism*. Around the table they went. Everyone stated his or her name and school. A few more cutup remarks were tossed about. All was in fun. It was very light humor, and Father Jaeger went along.

"Say, Father, where you from? What did you do during the World War I?" Knowing Father Jaeger's much younger age, all the kids laughed in unison at Kenny Heiser's remark.

"Maybe I'll have stories, but mine would be from the Civil War. I'm older than I look."

"Ha! That's a good one, Father. You got us there!" Kenny blurted from the far side.

"Where you from, Father?"

"Actually, I'm from Chicago, south side. My parents still live there."

"Cubs or Sox? Level with us," Bruce Young said, trying to test Father Jaeger.

Not wanting to trap himself, Father Jaeger said, "Being from the south side, White Sox, of course."

"Luis Aparicio and Nellie Fox are the best. Can't argue that," Bruce responded.

"Before you start class, any tricks, jokes, or stories? You know, get our attention?" Kenny asked.

Father Jaeger leaned back against his front table, half sitting, half leaning. "Let me see ... " He paused. "Here's one. You all be quiet, and I'll go around the table and say your complete name and what school you are from."

"No, no way, Father. You can't."

"Here goes." The room became quiet. "Betsy Flanner, Eastville Grade School. Mary Anne Carpenter … " He paused. "Ah, ah, Don Crawford, Eastville Grade School. How am I doin'?"

"Great, Father, but you can't get all fifteen."

As he went through to the fourth and then to the ninth student, his memory was perfect. At number ten, he said, "Randall."

"Wrong. Gottcha, Father."

"Excuse me, Andy, Andrew Charles." Father Jaeger quickly rattled off the next four and then the final—the fifteenth. "Davey, Davey Morgan."

In unison, everyone clapped. Being the last one, Davey stood up and bowed to everyone. Davey seemed like a nice kid. They all did.

The hour-and-a-half class whizzed by. Father Jaeger definitely made a positive impression with the students. They liked him and thought he was cool. After about twenty minutes of talking about confession, Joe Smith popped up and said, "Five, four, three, two, one … Your time's up, Father."

Father Jaeger looked up at the clock just as the secondhand hit the number twelve. Waiting to see the priest's reaction, they all laughed after screening his smile.

"You be here next week, Father?"

"That's up to Father Arnold. We'll see."

"You come back. You're cool. You have our blessing," Kenny said as he looked around for applause about his blessing joke. Palms up, he lifted his hands, but no laughs.

With that, Father Jaeger made the sign of the cross, said a prayer, gave his blessing, and said, "Thank you, class. Hope to see you again. Before I forget, does anyone need a ride home?" Half the class was already out the door. Quietly, Davey Morgan said, "Father, we live about ten blocks. Joe lives one more block beyond me."

"That's fine. My car's in back. You guys get the lights. Meet you at the top of the stairs."

Davey and Joe followed Father Jaeger to his car.

"Nice car," Davey said, referring to Father Jaeger's black 1950 Studebaker. "Looks almost brand new."

"We call it 'the Chief.' Know why?" Davey asked, testing the priest's car moxie.

"The chief on the hood of course, but that's on a Pontiac."

"You're cool, Father. Thought I'd catch you."

"This is a '50, commander. See the bullet on the hood, not a chief. Hey, both of you jump in the front. Nobody sits in the back by himself."

"Heck, this car even feels new. My dad's Pontiac is a 1950," Davey said. "This is a cool car."

Father Jaeger had never received a compliment like that. *These boys seem friendly*. On the way toward the edge of town, Father Jaeger saw the A&W Root Beer stand. "You boys have time for a cold root beer?"

The boys looked at each other. "Sure, that would be great."

Father Jaeger zipped into the A&W stand, right under the awning that stretched across the front. A cute young waitress flew right up to the car, roller skates and all. "Hello, boys. My name's Susie Lynn Walters. Oh excuse me, Father. Didn't see your collar." Standing by the driver's door, she tugged and pulled her skirt down. "Root beer, boys? Large?"

Davey and Joe stretched their necks to look past the steering wheel at Susie and nodded in unison.

"Okay, Susie Lynn, three large ten-cent root beers."

As they waited for their root beer, Father Jaeger turned to his right, parking his knee sideways on the seat. He rested his right arm across the top of the bench seat while leaning back against the car door. He teasingly pulled at Joe's hair; he was sitting in the middle. Davey frowned.

"You guys come here often?"

"No, not much. No car. Every so often we'll bike up here. How come you don't have a radio, Father? Don't you like Elvis or Buddy Holly?"

"Holly's my favorite," Joe added. "*If you knew Peggy Sue …* " he began to croon.

"Just a simple car for a priest. Nothing extra. Runs well. Gets me where I'm going. You guys like baseball, the Y? What's your interests outside of school?"

"I'm into sports, Father," Davey said. "All of 'em—baseball, basketball, and football."

"Not me, Father. I'm a swimmer. Love to swim. Hold a couple of records," Joe bragged.

"I agree. Swimming is my favorite. Don't you have a pool in town?" Father Jaeger said, already knowing the answer.

"Oh yes, the Boy's Center. We go there all the time."

"Great. Will have to meet there sometime," Father Jaeger informed Joe.

"Not me," Davey said. "I got football practice. You guys take that easy sport. I'll take football, rough and tough. Oops, here's our beers."

"That will be thirty-one cents, please."

"Here's fifty cents. Keep the change. You give good service, Susie Lynn. Like your skates."

"Thank you, Father."

Davey leaned forward. "Heck with the skates, I like your whole outfit."

Susie respond, "Don't get fresh with me in front of the good father."

"Sit back, Davey, and enjoy your root beer," Father commanded.

"Okay, okay, but I'll have to go to confession this week, Father. I just committed a venial sin."

"That's a good one," Joe said giving an elbow to Davey.

"All right, boys, I've heard worse."

Susie smiled, as if she didn't hear a word, took her tip, and happily skated away. "Hope you guys come back again."

Father Jaeger and the boys sat and chatted for another ten minutes. Joe and Davey had already downed their root beers. Father Jaeger took his last drink and said, "It's probably time to get you guys home. You'll have to tell me which way to go." He turned on the ignition and shifted into gear. Soon they were heading down the road.

"I live at 1218 Oak," said Davey.

Father Jaeger kept watching for 1218. Looking, looking …

"Here it is, the white one with the small front porch. There's my dad's '50 Pontiac. See the chief? Thanks for the root beer. Maybe see you next week, Father?" Davey asked as they pulled up to his house.

"We'll see what Father Arnold decides. Can only do what he tells me, but I'd like to teach your class again."

Davey got out of the car and was immediately attacked by his little black spaniel. "See you guys."

Father Jaeger turned the car around and headed back two blocks to

Joe's house. After they passed the first block, he reached his right hand across the seat and placed it on Joe's knee. As he approached Joe's house, he maneuvered his hand halfway up Joe's thigh. Joe froze.

"That's my house," Joe said, pointing to the two-story white frame house, ready to immediately jump out of the car.

Stopping the car in front of the house, Father Jaeger patted Joe's knee and then rested his hand on the steering wheel.

"Good time. Say, Joe, let's go to the free swim tomorrow. Wanna go?" he asked, knowing he'd already been there several times.

"Sure, maybe I can," Joe answered hesitantly, only wanting to get out of the car. "Oh, I guess I could tomorrow," he said as he thought about swimming while suppressing the memory of the priest's hand on his knee.

"Sounds fine. Meet you there?" Father Jaeger asked.

"Oh yes, I'll walk," Joe said. "Meet you there about 6:45. Free swim is seven to eight o'clock tomorrow."

"Maybe a ride home if you need one. Might be getting dark," Father Jaeger replied.

"Thanks, Father. Thank you for the root beer. Maybe a ride home tomorrow would make it easier. Thanks a lot. See you tomorrow."

Driving back to the rectory, Father Jaeger thought it had been a really good day. *Maybe Father Arnold will have me substitute with the same class next week. This could be fun. Real fun.*

PART VI

GOOD AND EVIL

CHAPTER 85

LIFE IN SHAMBLES

Gene Kowolski—September 19, 1958

A S the school year approached the end of September, Gene withdrew further into himself. Normal thoughts occurred in his adolescent mind. *Gosh, I'd love to hug Cindy. Her tight sweaters and lovely boobs.*
Wanna play baseball, but they probably won't pick me today. You guys should
see my arm.

Gene looked like such a normal kid. He loved Jerry Lee Lewis and
"Great Balls of Fire." Mickey Mantle was his favorite baseball player.
He thought he might have singing talent. He practiced imitating Elvis
Presley in front of the mirror in his bedroom. That, of course, he did not
share with his entire family.

Sister Joaugusta's seventh grade class was a typical assembly of boy-
friends and girlfriends hanging out at the drug store, seventh grade basketball, too much homework, and the forever longing to get into high
school. Every class in public and Catholic schools had a small contin-
gency of bullies. Usually a group of three but no more than five misfits. In
1958, they were easily identified by their turned-up shirt collars and their
greasy hair combed back on the side like a duck. Kids called them DA
haircuts—duck's ass. Collars were turned up and jeans hung low. Herbie
Ratski and his two buddies, Jack Downer and Marvin Finch, were the
hoods in the class. Sister Joaugusta fought their identity on a daily basis.

"Herbie, collar down, pants up." Cooperation was always short-lived.

Bullies preyed on the defenseless. Jack and Gene represented both
ends of the spectrum. Silence permeated the room as Sister Joaugusta

walked up and down the aisle, head bobbing back and forth to each side, her piercing eyes making sure all heads were down and all pencils were in hand as her students solved each arithmetic problem.

Jack found time to write a note. An idea had sprung into his insensitive and mischievous mind. One morning he had followed Gene down the hall and noticed a new stride in his walk, as if he had a wad in his pants. *Queer*, he thought.

Jack pulled out a piece of paper from under his wood-top desk. Diligently, he printed the message, smearing the lead as he wagged his tongue in unison with the hand holding the dull yellow lead pencil. Once finished, he folded the paper into a square and penciled *Gene* on the top. "*Psst, psst.*" Jack tapped Mary Lou's shoulder. "Give this to Gene." Seat by seat, the note passed up to Lewis Mason, who then reached across the aisle.

"*Psst, psst,* Gene." Gene looked up from his textbook, saw Lewis, and reached over to accept the note. Hoping it was from Cindy, Gene quietly opened the four squared paper. His heart sunk, and his adrenaline rushed. Gene slid down in his seat. Across the paper, the most hated and feared word stared back at him: *homo*. Below the word read, *Gene, Gene, the homo machine*. Nothing could have been more crippling to a boy's ego than being called a homo, queer, or fag.

Immediately Gene wadded the paper and stuffed it into his pocket. *This is the worst. How could he? Could they know? Did someone say something about Father Jaeger? Can't take this.* Forgetting his arithmetic test, Gene put his head in his folded arms atop the desk.

"Mr. Kowolski, are you finished early?"

"No, Sister, no. Just trying to figure the answer," Gene replied, not concerned in the least about the test. All he wanted to do was hide from those torturous words. *Do other kids know? Is the word out? God help me!*

Time was up before Gene was able to finish the test. *Another notch in my drift to a bad report card.* Gene had bigger concerns now. The school bell rang. With trepidation, he got up and dropped his arithmetic paper on the sister's desk. Subject to the hands of fate, Gene arrived at the door just before Jack. Gene walked faster. As he rounded the corner, he heard, "See you tomorrow, homo man."

Gene knew everyone at both ends of the corridor heard *homo* echoing down the hall. *Why's he so cruel?* Gene asked himself as he made his way down the stairs. Fortunately, Cindy was walking in front of him—a pleasant distraction from the wrath of Jack. All Gene wanted was to escape the confines of school and rush home to the safety of his own room. However, he knew he had to go home for his doctor's appointment. His mother was waiting to take him to see Dr. Curtis. Walking too fast was not in the cards, as discomfort accompanied Gene with each stride of his rather short legs. He was not fond of the idea of going to the doctor, though he knew he needed relief.

The doctor's office was housed in a large old white Victorian home. As Gene walked up the steps with his mother, his body cringed in fear as he thought of Dr. Curtis's long, sharp needles. When he entered the office, the nauseating cocktail mixture of alcohol and chloroform immediately hit his nose. He first thought of the doctor inserting a six- or seven-inch needle into where the pain was harbored. Gene could imagine no worse pain for any human to endure. This could be like the nails on Jesus's cross, only worse considering the rear end location.

Miss Aggie, the nurse, handed Gene's mom a card to fill out. No sooner had he sat down than Dr. Curtis walked out from his office. "Hello, Mrs. Kowolski."

"Hello, Dr. Curtis."

"Got a little problem, young man?" Dr. Curtis always got right down to business. "Let's go into the examination room."

Miss Aggie followed. Gene felt twice as short since Dr. Curtis and Miss Aggie were both tall.

"Please close the door," Dr. Curtis said to his nurse.

"Take your shirt and pants off, Gene," Miss Aggie instructed. "You can sit up here," she said, patting the examination table.

Gene's mother could hear every word from the waiting room. *My poor Gene.* She was as anxious as him. Ten, maybe fifteen minutes passed. The quietness in the waiting room was interrupted when she heard, *"Wee-oo ouch!"* She only heard that one time. *Brave little boy.*

Within about ten minutes, the door opened, and Miss Aggie stepped out. "Doctor's still with him," she said as she walked to her desk.

Within a few more minutes, the door opened, and Gene slowly

walked out. Dr. Curtis remained inside the doorway. "Mrs. Kowolski, could I have a few minutes?" He motioned her to come into the room.

"Glad it's over," Gene said softly, looking at his mom as she stepped toward the exam room. He was glad to just stand near the couch. He didn't say anything to Miss Aggie. *Gosh, all in front of a woman.*

"Have a seat, Mrs. Kowolski." Dr. Curtis leaned back against the exam table. "Gene has an infection, a rather bad infection. Now I will give you a prescription for an antibiotic, a strong one for him to take for ten days. Then come back when he has taken the entire regimen."

"Yes, Doctor. I'll make sure."

"Now, there's this issue of bleeding. From my exam, I detect some lesions, as if there's been some … some … well, foreign penetration. This is sensitive," Dr. Curtis said, trying to comfort Mrs. Kowolski.

"I try to understand, Dr. Curtis. You see, my husband, I think he knows more about what's happening … a lot more. He tells me someone may have taken serious advantage of Gene. Says he's checking into it. He hasn't totally shared what he knows with me. I don't understand. We just don't know what to do."

With a stern voice and a serious look, Dr. Curtis said, "Your son is a minor, underage. If someone took advantage, we need to report it. This is very serious. We can't end this here. This concerns me greatly, Mrs. Kowolski."

"Thank you. I understand, Doctor. I will tell my husband. Everything you say, I'll tell him."

"That's good. He's to call me," Dr. Curtis said, giving her extra assurance of his concern. "I'm going to give you an antibiotic ointment for Gene to use. The instructions will show him how. You may have to help. At the same time, I want him to take the penicillin for about ten days. Hopefully, that will clear it up."

"Oh thank you, Dr. Curtis." She stood.

He clasped her hand with both of his. "I want to hear back from you. Promise? After the medicine's gone, you make an appointment, Mrs. Kowolski. Meanwhile, you need to talk more directly with your husband. Consider the police. Something has to be done."

"Police?" Now she was even more startled.

Dr. Curtis and Mrs. Kowolski walked out of the office and into the reception room. "Miss Aggie, make sure you call Mrs. Kowolski in ten days. If anything unexpected comes up, Mrs. Kowolski, then you contact us. Understand?"

"Yes, Doctor," she said, thanking Dr. Curtis and Miss Aggie again.

"Thank you. Thank you, Dr. Curtis. You too, Miss Aggie," Gene said.

Waiting for Gene and his mother to close the front door, Dr. Curtis looked at Miss Aggie. "I don't like what I saw. I'm a little suspicious. Something doesn't add up, but I'm not sure."

"I'm totally with you. I thought the same thing when you were doing the examination," Miss Aggie said, noticing Dr. Curtis's serious demeanor.

"Miss Aggie, we have to keep a close eye on Gene. A very close eye." Dr. Curtis hoped Gene's condition was not caused by what he thought it could be. *No, that just can't be.*

Gene and his mom talked very little on the way home. *My life is in shambles. I hurt. I'm not a homo. Where can I go?*

Blanche eased the Plymouth station wagon onto the drive, the double cement tracks straddling the grass strip between the wheels. "Gene, would you please open the doors to the garage?"

"Sure, Mom." Gene opened the wooden garage doors like wings on a plane. Off to the left side, Gene saw his favorite possession in the whole world—his red twenty-four-inch Schwinn bicycle. Already two years old, the red bike looked like new. Not a scratch.

Before she pulled in, Gene scooted the bike out onto the grass. As he kicked the stand down, the bike beckoned him to hit the road. Red, white, and blue plastic streamers hung from the black handle grips. Two twin lights were mounted on the handlebar. He stepped back as his mother drove slowly, making sure she stopped exactly two feet from Dad's tool bench, which spanned the width of the back of the garage. A single three-paned window was centered above the bench. Two single windows at each side of the garage provided enough light for when Dad was working at the bench or Gene was polishing his bicycle.

As his mom walked toward the house, Gene dutifully closed the garage doors. Then he charged into the house and flew upstairs despite his continuous discomfort. Fifteen minutes later, he yelled to his mom, "Goin' for a ride!"

"Be back for supper, five thirty sharp. I have a couple of chores for you!" she hurriedly yelled as Gene flew out the front door.

"Okay, Mom!" he answered back as he ran alongside his bike before hopping on. Gene wanted to get away. He headed for the Big Four Trestle. There he could be alone. Just a half mile away on the east edge of town, the train's trestle—a giant erector set of wood beams and columns—had been carrying abundant loads of coal, lumber, and grain across the mighty Wabash River since 1908.

Gene pedaled standing up, subconsciously burning energy and targeting his frustration and sadness in life. Pedaling standing up was far more comfortable than pumping sitting down. He pulled his yellow wool baseball cap tight to his brow. Across town he raced, right on Spring Street. The trestle was in sight, perched high in the air. The biggest dare of any boy in Wabash was to walk the bridge full-length to the south side. Although twelve, Gene had yet to accept the challenge, but he thought today he would.

He didn't lose speed as he traversed the gravel road toward the river. Giant six-foot-high concrete footings carried the weight of the daunting skeleton. Parking his bike down toward the river, Gene charged up the embankment to the tracks. He bravely stepped onto the railroad ties on the trestle. Carefully, he stepped on each railroad tie that secured the shiny steel rails. First railroad tie, then second ... twelfth ... thirtieth. He stopped and looked ahead toward the fiftieth tie but could go no farther. Carefully, he turned and walked back the way he came.

Off to the south, thirty yards from the track and high above the banks of the Wabash, Gene spotted his special solitary hideaway. A large rock, maybe two feet wide, made a dandy rest area next to a giant hundred-year-old oak. Secured by the rock, Gene would often hear the mighty roar of the powerful locomotive in the distance. Then suddenly from around the bend on the far side of the trestle, he would be able to see the thundering Iron Horse roaring closer and closer. As the train hit the entrance to the trestle, the sound would thunder across the tracks and down through the river valley below. The engineer sounding the steam whistle, sent a cadence through the valley as the locomotive roared across the trestle.

Some days, passenger cars were included along with the countless coal, wheat, and box cars. Gene often waved to the travelers, wondering about their far-off destinations. Chicago? Cleveland? Minneapolis?

Sometimes, he remained at the base of the trestle and sat on the giant concrete footings. There he would lean against the wooden beams. High overhead, the Wabash Cannonball would send vibrating waves to the very base. Gene could feel the train and all its power.

Legend had it that the Big Four Trestle provided a place of daring for those encountering troubles in life. Some said that a few had ended it all there above the mighty Wabash River. One story had it that back in 1932, while at the center of the bridge, three boys misjudged the distance of the mighty horse racing down the tracks. Running desperately for the Wabash side, the first two boys got to the very end and leaped to safety. Turning around, they saw that their pal had fallen in the middle of the track. Trying to get back up, he failed to move, stuck in the tight fist of fear. The other two stood helpless; it was too late to run back and help. In horror, they watched the oncoming locomotive.

As the legend went, the two boys were never the same after that day. Ten years later, they enlisted in the army, just after Pearl Harbor. They remained in the same platoon, side by side, right up to June 6, 1944, when they stormed the beaches of Normandy. Neither ever returned to Wabash.

Every day, the events of the past year engulfed Gene in deep sorrow and sadness. Today was no different. He sat alone beneath the great trestle. Looking up at the sheer height, his mind wandered to the story about the despondent lover he read about in the paper only two years ago. *The Plain Dealer* had run a story about a man who walked to the middle of the mammoth trestle and leapt to his fate, deep into the current of the Wabash River ninety feet below.

Today, Gene enjoyed peace and solitude—his place to be alone. For Gene, the mighty Big Four Trestle was a place to dream his problems away. Considering the horrors in his mind and the ever present vision of the priest, Gene thought to himself, *Could I ever jump from so far up above?*

When Peter arrived home on time for chores and supper, he was mired in sadness as he envisioned his thoughts while alone at the Big Four Trestle.

After supper that evening, Herb Kowolski spoke to his wife about Gene. "Blanche, let's talk. I want to hear about what Dr. Curtis had to say about Gene."

They both stepped into the dining room and sat at the table. The kids were all upstairs doing homework.

"Herb, I'm very concerned. Wait. Pops is in the parlor. He'll hear us."

"That's okay. He knows," Herb said.

Blanche went on and told him the entire conversation she'd had with Dr. Curtis, almost word for word. She explained how the doctor had been especially worried about the bleeding.

"Did you tell him I went to see the priest?"

"No, not really. I told him I didn't know everything."

"Okay, go on," Herb said.

"Then he mentioned … he mentioned … oh, I hate to hear myself say it. Dr. Curtis said *penetration*. Herb, how can that be? Explain what that means."

Sitting alone in the parlor, Pops took in most of the conversation. His trusty cane was between his right leg and the arm of the chair. Without paying attention, he soon heard the muffled sound of his right hand tapping the cane into the rug with a firm grip. The more he heard, the faster the cane tapped.

"Dad, could you hold on to that cane?" Herb asked curtly without turning around to look at his dad.

The tapping stopped. Pops didn't say a word. He just listened.

"Herb, what are we going to do? On the ride home from the doctor, Gene didn't say a word. Well, he did say one thing when I mentioned the bleeding. He said it does hurt all the time, it's hard to sleep, and it's embarrassing. Then he said one day the blood went through right to his jeans. It was after school. He was home in the backyard. I told him I knew. I do the wash. It was so urgent, Herb, that you called Dr. Curtis. 'What if that happens at school? Kids might see,' Gene said to me with anguish on his face. My heart breaks for him. Herb, what are we going to do?"

Pops was having a hard time containing his comments. He was furious inside. *That damn priest! He needs to burn in hell!*

Blanche continued, "Anyway, when we got home, Gene went straight to his room. About fifteen minutes later, he came back down. Said he was going for a bike ride, and out the door he flew."

Herb didn't say anything. Blanche just sat there. Pops shook his head and tapped his cane. Herb looked down at his clasped hands, which were folded and resting on the oak dining table. He squeezed hard, exposing his white knuckles. The lace doily provided little comfort. Herb and Blanche Kowolski were at a loss for words.

Herb reached over and placed his hand on Blanche's. "One good thing, the priest is gone. Meanwhile, we have to figure out what to do. Let's think on it."

Blanche responded, "Yes, let's think on it and pray."

Herb looked at her and said, "Together we must help Gene."

"Yes, we will … together." Blanche paused. "Let's pray that medicine works."

Pops laid his head back on the chair. The comfortable easy chair engulfed him. The doily across the back protected his head from the itch of the upholstery fabric. The continuing thought remained jailed in his mind: *What can I do? What can I do?* Pops' medicine for his cancer didn't help his slowing failing body. He thought of Christmas coming soon. Despite his illness, Pops wanted to be with family for the holidays, one last time. Again, he thought of the priest. Soon he surrendered to the power of sleep.

CHAPTER 86

TIME TO MEET

Father Sullivan—September 22, 1958

"**G**OOD afternoon, operator. My name is Michael Sullivan, and I'd like to place a person-to-person phone call to Leonard Schmidt."

"Just one moment please. Stay on the line." A couple of minutes passed. "Mr. Sullivan, I have Leonard Schmidt on the line. Go ahead."

"Good afternoon, Father Sullivan. I was not expecting a call from you."

"I would assume you weren't. I imagine you hoped you'd never hear from me again. However, I do not give up easily."

"So I see," Father Schmidt responded.

"I'd like to add a little more information for your files. As a matter of fact, you will need to add two more files."

"What's this all about?" Father Schmidt asked rather tersely. "I told you last week—"

Father Sullivan cut in, "And I'm telling you this week. Here are the facts. I'm going to meet you and Bishop Powers next week. That is for sure. You and I are going to find a convenient time for all three of us. I'll make sure I'm there. I want an hour and fifteen minutes set aside. Minimum! You'll be interested in what I have to say. That I assure you, Father Schmidt."

"I can hardly believe that." Father Schmidt's words were laden with sarcasm.

"Any time that's convenient to you," Father Sullivan said.

Then Father Schmidt replied, "I'm afraid this meeting will not be possible."

"If that's so, I will play by your rules. If you are going to be hostile to my visit, then I will now level the playing field."

"Father Sullivan, are you threatening me?"

"No. I'm just trying to make this as easy as possible for you because you are not going to want to hear what I have to say. Understand?" There was silence on the other end. "Father Schmidt, you have three options: One, grant me a meeting immediately. Two, grant me a meeting after I disclose the names of two boys I know have been personal with you and the bishop."

Father Schmidt didn't respond. There was silence. Father Schmidt knew he was had. Taking a deep breath, he said, "What is option three? Dare I ask?"

"Father Schmidt, I will oblige. I want you to have a choice for the time of our meeting. Yes, option three. If you do not select options one or two, I will not come alone. I will be accompanied by the two boys I referred to, along with the district attorney. In addition, I will invite reporters from the *Indianapolis Star*, the *South Wayne Tribune*, and your local TV station. I have their names and phone numbers. If I call and tell them about our little gathering, I'm sure they will be more than happy to attend … and look into the scheme you and the bishop have going. Do I make myself clear?"

"Yes, quite clear."

"Oh, one more thing to jar your memory. Think of the name Billy. He may have hurt his back lifting the couch. Know what I mean, Father Schmidt?" No reply.

In a complete about-face, Father Schmidt suggested they should talk and work together. "So let's go ahead and meet tomorrow at one o'clock. I will make sure the bishop has the time. I prefer your first option."

"Oh, I was sure a reasonable God-fearing priest like you would choose the first option. I commend you for your clear thinking, Father Schmidt," Father Sullivan said, emphasizing his command of Father Schmidt. "Don't forget that other priest. Forgot. What's his name?" Father Sullivan asked.

"Father Holtz? Why would—"

Father Sullivan cut him off. "You might need him to take notes. I don't want you to forget anything. Thank you, Father Schmidt. I look forward to our meeting," Father Sullivan said in closing. "Make sure both the bishop and Father Holtz are in attendance. Let me know the time."

"One o'clock tomorrow. See you then," Father Schmidt said, slamming his phone down.

A meeting was one thing, but Father Schmidt thought, *How do I inform the bishop about what Sullivan might know? These priests have caused the bishop so much trouble. Now all this, and Sullivan's including me. God help us all.* Father Schmidt walked back into his room. He sat down on the couch, leaned back, and sighed. *I have to protect Bishop Powers. He's my salvation.* The priest dozed off, hoping to relieve the pain of reality.

The next morning, Father Sullivan sat down with Father Warren for breakfast. "You seem a little tense this morning, Michael."

"I'm thinking about my visit with Bishop Powers today. Hope to see you after I return home, probably late afternoon. So yes, I am a bit excited. We meet at one o'clock in South Wayne. Speaking of tense. In all due respect, Father Warren, I've been a little concerned about you. You seemed stressed and that I keep noticing your cough."

"Michael, I'm fine. You do have to know though that I do, just like you, tend to keep much inside."

"Yes, Father, that must simply come with the territory; stress, tension, priesthood. They all roll into one."

"Very well put, Michael, I would concur. That's quite understandable that you are tense." Father Warren said, not looking up from his plate. "You know I'll be praying for you."

"Yes, Father, that will help, I know," he said, nodding. "It may be unconventional, but I'm doing the right thing … " He paused. "The right thing for these boys." Father Sullivan stood up. Looking down at Father Warren, he placed his right hand on the older priest's shoulder. "I will represent these children, our church … and this … and this collar well," Father Sullivan said, running his finger between his neck and the crisp white starched collar.

"I know you will, Michael. Travel safe and God be with you."

"Thank you, sir." Father Sullivan turned and walked away. He always felt blessed and inspired when around the good pastor. He hoped to have positive news for Father Warren upon his return from South Wayne.

The thought of confronting Bishop Powers motivated Father Sullivan as he steered his green Chevy north to South Wayne later that morning. Dark clouds hovered overhead, mirroring the heaviness of the situation. Having truth and morality on his side gave him the confidence to continue his journey to bring justice.

No need for banana cream pie. Too much on his mind, he thought as he passed the road to the Big Four Diner. A cup of coffee would be welcome, but it would have to wait until the next stop. Within no time, Father Sullivan was pulling into the side parking lot of St. Leonard's rectory. As per the previous trip with Father Warren, he first stepped into the spectacular cathedral. He noticed an elderly couple kneeling together in one of the forward pews. What looked like a homeless man sat alone in the back. All three, he was sure, were seeking quiet and solitude and were surely praying for their own special intentions. Father Sullivan found his space at the side altar of St. Jerome. There he prayed.

Father, give me the strength to do what is right, to say what is right. Let me speak only the truth and without malice. I care not to hurt anyone involved. I just want this horrid plague to stop within our church. We need more leadership, more advocates. I commit myself to do what is right for you and the victims of abuse. Please help me do the right thing always. Amen.

Father Sullivan stood up and exited the pew. He bowed his head toward the large crucifix hanging above the altar in the distant front of the church. He respectfully genuflected, blessed himself with the holy water, and exited through the great gothic doors in the front of the cathedral. He eagerly bounded down the granite stairs. *Time of reckoning,* Father Sullivan thought as he tapped the door knocker of the rectory. Calmly, he waited. Within a few moments, the door swung open.

"Hello. Good afternoon, Father Sullivan."

"Same to you, Father Schmidt," Father Sullivan said politely.

After pleasant greetings, he followed Father Schmidt to the main conference room. The door was open. Bishop Powers, a big man, stood at the end of the table. He extended his hand to Father Sullivan. Father Holtz quietly sat with his back to the wall about six chairs from the bishop. Father Schmidt walked around the bishop and took his seat halfway between Father Holtz and the bishop.

Passing over any need for small talk, Father Schmidt began, "We are here today at the insistence of Father Sullivan relative to Father Jaeger. Bishop Powers wants to comment about his concerns regarding Father Jaeger's new assignment."

Placing Father Sullivan on notice, the bishop added, "I'm sure Father Schmidt has explained the diocese's position. We are handling the situation very well, I might add, thanks to Father Schmidt," he said, ignoring Father Holtz.

Father Sullivan responded without hesitation. "As a priest in this diocese, I would like to see all the files on all the priests who have had one or more accusers come forth. Then I would like to review their transfers to their present locations. Lastly, I'd like to know exactly what the diocese did to correct these problems."

"Hold one minute, Father Sullivan. I am the bishop here. Nobody has appointed you judge and jury. You are way out of line."

"I totally agree with you. I am not judge and jury. I am a priest who is working for young boys who have been grossly and permanently affected by Father Jaeger. I know him. I know what he has done. Well, not all," Father Sullivan said, correcting himself. "He may be up to his old pattern of behavior as we speak. No way was he ready to be reassigned."

"Father, let me again remind you, I am in charge and will make all the decisions. This is final," the bishop said as Father Sullivan watched his face flush red.

Father Schmidt sat quietly. His nerves tangled inside. He was focusing on option three: two boys and reporters. *This Father Sullivan is serious and determined.*

Father Sullivan leaned back in his chair, waiting for the bishop's blood pressure to normalize. "Bishop Powers, might I—with your permission—make something clear?"

Father Sullivan leaned his elbows on the table very slowly and clasped his hands together gently. He looked at Father Schmidt and then to the bishop. At first he was quiet. He confidently rested his chin on his folded hands.

Then in a low whisper, he raised his right hand, pointed at the bishop, and said, "Let me make myself very clear to both of you. We all three know that harm and abuse has come to numbers of young boys in our parish. I might add, I am confident that abuse has taken place here in South Wayne. Now I am going to mention two more names. Are you ready, Father ... Bishop Powers?" With the slow edge in his voice, he sensed he had their full attention.

Father Holtz thought, *Michael isn't holding back.*

His voice became quieter. "Now each of you think really hard. You will not only recognize them, but you will also feel internal turmoil after I mention the names. You will then try to not show me any self-incriminating reactions."

Father Holtz nervously shifted in his chair as he observed Father Sullivan going straight for Father Schmidt and Bishop Powers' jugulars. It took all his self-control to not react with a grin and stand up. He knew he would want to applaud. *Hallelujah! Calm. Calm. Bite your lip.*

"What are you talking about, more accusations?" the bishop interrupted. "I've had enough of this, Father Sullivan. You're wasting my time. Do you know who you are talking to?"

"As a matter of fact, yes, I do. I'm talking to an abuser of boys."

"That's enough!" Bishop Powers slammed his fist on the table.

"That's quite a reaction, quite a display, and I haven't even said their names."

Bishop Powers took a deep breath as he tried to regain his composure. Internally enraged, he sat back.

Father Schmidt was feeling queasy. Father Holtz just sat back and watched the show. *Bring it on, Michael.*

"Specifically I am referring to—you both know their names—Ned Thornbauer and Billy Donovan. Now, I recommend you hold your reflexes and emotions in check. Stay calm. Pretend like you don't know who I am talking about. You need not react or defend now. Everything will come out when you are exposed ... or should I say indicted? You see, I've done my homework. Internally you are about to erupt, Bishop Powers. Your language, you are screaming inside 'cause you know that I know. That's why you are trying to act calm." Father Sullivan looked over at Father Schmidt. "Father, Father Schmidt, you are toast, or should I say milk toast. I know about Billy Donovan, you know the furniture mover? You know the bishop knows. Those glaring eyes piercing through the door at you was not some random raccoon walking down the hall. Remember? Could that have been the bishop saying, 'Father Schmidt, I see you. Naughty, naughty.' I bet you about tossed your cookies about then, except you were having too much fun with Billy boy."

Father Sullivan continued. Father Holtz kept a straight face. *He's really pouring it on.* "We all know you're an abuser just like the priests you transfer. Hmmm, so do you transfer yourself to run away and hide in another parish? No, no, you don't want to run to another parish. Right now, Father Schmidt, you want to run out of this room and straight to the toilet down the hall."

Bishop Powers didn't move. His face flush in crimson red. Father Holtz could hardly contain his glee watching Father Sullivan crucify Bishop Powers and Father Schmidt. Bishop Powers' eyes became the size of silver dollars. He did not say a word. He wanted to go to the bathroom.

Slowly, Father Sullivan sat back comfortably in his chair as if he had just thrown a winning touchdown pass. *A real Hail Mary.* He again clasped his hands and rested his forearms and elbows comfortably on the arms of the tapestry-backed wooden chair. Silence. The height of uncomfortable silence. Father Sullivan knew. They all knew.

"These two, ah, these two names mean nothing to me," said Bishop Powers.

Father Schmidt still had not moved. He knew the bishop knew. Father Holtz coughed twice.

"Are we done with this charade?" the bishop asked.

"No. Just one more thing. If I conclude you are not planning to work with me in this matter, I want you to know that I will not stop here," Father Sullivan paused. Then in a low whisper, he looked directly at Bishop Powers. "You know. I know. We all know. Now let's sum this up. If you will not cooperate, I will continue to move forward within the hierarchy of the church and civil authorities. This is my mission. Nothing will stop my pursuit of justice. Would you like to tell me anything else, Bishop Powers?"

"No, I think we've covered it all, Father Sullivan." Bishop Powers paused and then continued with authority, "One more thing. Hear me.

The audacity of your actions are inappropriate, untrue, and I will deal with you directly. That I guarantee."

"Covered it all? Covered it all?" Father Sullivan asked. "I'm sure you have, Bishop Powers. You used the right word ... *covered*. I think you have accomplished just that. Covered ... covered up ... until now." He closed by saying, "You have not heard the last of me. Thank you for your time. Good day to you both. Oh yes, you too, Father Holtz. I can find the door."

Father Sullivan, aware of his abruptness, did not turn around as he walked out of the rectory. Driving home to Wabash, Father Sullivan's mind raced with ideas and plans for his next move. By the time he arrived home, he wanted to immediately meet with Father Warren. Father Sullivan wanted to keep his momentum and credibility with the good priest.

Bishop Powers—September 23, 1958

"What was that all about?" Bishop Powers asked Father Schmidt ten minutes after Father Sullivan's departure, referring to Father Sullivan's accusations and brashness. He glared directly at his secretary. "What the hell? The arrogance of that son of a bitch! Excuse me, Father Holtz."

"Bishop, Father Schmidt, maybe I should leave the room?" Father Holtz asked.

"Yes, Father, thanks for your help," the bishop replied.

"Good afternoon, Bishop. Father Schmidt, please call if I can be of any further help." Father Holtz wanted to stay and listen to the impending comments and reactions. He left the room and walked outside, wishing he could talk with Father Sullivan about Ned and Billy. *My dear Jesus, Michael, you knocked it out of the park*. Father Holtz took a deep breath, bent over, hands on his knees trying to muffle his laughter. He envisioned Bishop Powers and Father Schmidt yelling and screaming while they pick each other up off the ground. *Oh, Dear Lord, wish I had a tape recorder*.

Father Schmidt sat in his chair, praying that he could evaporate into thin air. *Will the bishop bring up Billy's name? God, if he does, what do I say?*

Bishop Powers, knowing he was in quicksand, realized he could not be associated with Ned Thornbauer. He felt safe taking the high road.

"Well, now you've done it, Schmidt. How the hell did Sullivan know about Billy Donovan? Do you think Billy would have told him?"

"No way, Bishop. Sullivan doesn't even live here," Father Schmidt tried to explain. "Sullivan's in Wabash."

Bishop Powers knew there would be no denial, no defense, regarding Billy Donovan. Father Schmidt remembered the two piercing eyes looking through the cracked door.

Bishop Powers said, "I never expected this of you, Father Schmidt. With all we're going through, now my most trusted secretary is going where the bad boys go."

Clenching his teeth, Father Schmidt asked, "What exactly are you referring to, Your Excellency?"

"Don't *Excellency* me. Whose eyes do you think were peering through your door that night? Jesus Christ's?"

Father Schmidt knew he was trapped. He could not deny it. Bishop Powers had seen him sprawled out with Billy. Quickly, he decided he had to appeal to the bishop's mercy. "Oh, I see," he said sheepishly, not knowing what else to say.

Bishop Powers stood up and walked around the far side of the table. Pointing his finger straight across the empty table at Schmidt, he said, "How could you? How could you? No self-control and right here in the bloody rectory! Have you no shame?" The bishop's face grew red as his voice screamed louder. "Have you no class? Now you are in this. If this gets out, am I to cover for you? You're supposed to act like me, to emulate me. You're here for me and not for your own selfish gratification. Damn you! Damn you, Schmidt! I should have charged into your room that night."

The bishop walked over and stood next to Father Schmidt, who was still nailed to his chair. He leaned down into Father Schmidt's face, spittle flying. "How long have you been balling around with this Donovan kid? How many more are there? How many? Tell me now."

"Oh maybe, maybe about ... " Schmidt whimpered.

"I want to know exactly. Hear me?"

"Five, six, seven times. What's the difference now?" Father Schmidt asked, throwing his face into his folded arms on the table.

"My God, I was hoping that night was the first. Now you listen, who was that Ned kid? Thorn or whatever? Was he another one of yours? Tell me!"

"No, no. Don't even know him," Father Schmidt said, defending himself in the face of his own lies.

"Did Sullivan just make that name up? You listen here. You do exactly as I say. I'm going to have to figure what to do with you. I own you. You hear me? I own you. For now, this whole episode with Sullivan didn't happen. I'll see you tomorrow."

Taking a deep breath and gathering his composure, Bishop Powers stood erect, turned, and left the room. He walked straight to his quarters. *Now I have Father Schmidt right where I want him.*

Father Schmidt concluded that Bishop Powers was not only a liar but also delusional, as he knew well and good that Bishop Powers had ordered him to set meetings up with boys. *Does he think I thought the meetings were for altar boy practice at his cabin on the lake?*

CHAPTER 87

FALLING INTO PLACE

Randall Zilbar—August 18, 1958

"RANDALL, Mario calling here. Got a little time?"

"Sure, Mario, whatever you need. What's going on?" Randall replied as he nestled the phone on his shoulder while continuing to sign some documents.

"My friend, my friend who I trust like my own son, I have this problem."

"What is it, Mario? Tell me."

"Like ya know when the boys came back from the last trip? Ya know, on da packages? She got some missing parts. Know what I mean?"

"Missing parts? You mean paper?"

"Let's put it this way. Enough missing to make Mario not happy."

"You're not expecting me to have—" Randall asked, already knowing the answer.

Mario answered most emphatically, "No, no, course not. You're my source, my friend. From you, I want to know who. You wouldn't do anything to Mario."

"There's only one handler, Mario. From Vito Bellini to Wolfe and then to your guy. So on this end, it can only be one. Wolfe," Randall concluded.

"You trust him?" Mario inquired.

"Yes, kinda … but not when the heat is coming down. Here's the deal. This guy owes me. Couple ways. One is twenty-five thousand dollars, which he doesn't have. I've gotta leash on him, even a chain," Randall explained to Mario, who knew Zilbar could yank his own chain any time. *No, I won't yank Wolfe's chain now*, Randall thought, not wanting to remind himself of years long past.

"Maybe someone unhooked his leash, Randall. Maybe he's in trouble. A woman? Needs money? Ya know what I mean?"

"I know the Krueger deal really has him worried that … that … He thinks Krueger could come back and talk. He'd be in big trouble. Krueger has a couple handles on Wolfe."

"Now, Randall, we both know Lucco handled Krueger."

"Yes, we know that, but Wolfe doesn't. Maybe we'll think about it, Mario. Maybe he thinks he might need to raise money to quiet Krueger when he returns," Randall said. "Maybe it was least of two evils. The paper or having Krueger talk. Let Wolfe think that."

"You're right, Randall. Smart thinking. He knows too much. Maybe we need a … like a different structure. New way to move things around." Mario knew Randall was listening.

"You're probably right, Mario. Wolfe does know enough to … to what do ya call it?"

"Blow the cover, blow the cover," Mario confirmed.

Randall waited. Even over the phone, he knew what Mario was a thinking.

"Tell you what we're gonna do," Mario said. "You talk to your friend. Tell him we're gonna step up the operation in a few months. Tell him I'll want to talk with him. I'll call and invite him to see me. If he did pull something, then I'll know if I'm lookin' him in the eye. He won't fool ol' Mario. So then maybe I have something on him. Let's say he'd then owe me. Then he'll do whatever I say. He can be of help to me and more to you, my friend," Mario explained to Zilbar in his own unique way. "Will give it some time. Eventually, I know we'll have to address this Wolfe guy. You keep me posted, Randall."

"You're right, Mario. That makes sense. We'll have him right where we want him," Randall said with glee in his voice, knowing Mario would handle it.

"Control. In a business, it's all about control. You remember that, Randall. Now you keep an eye on this guy, Wolfe. We may need him in other ways. Patience. Give him time. No hurry for now." *This is good. Randall agrees.*

Randall replied, "Sounds like a plan. Works for me." *This one hiccup by Wolfe works perfectly for me … Control. Absolute control.*

Homer Atkins—October 23, 1958

The dogs howled late into the night, but that's not what kept him awake. The nights grew longer, and the days were starting to become cooler. Sometime after midnight, awakening from the same recurring nightmare, Homer Atkins was soaking wet. He suddenly sat up in bed with a yell of horror. Sweat had absorbed into his grimy gray sheets. The haunting memory of the killer on a night decades ago, back in 1934, forced Homer Atkins's decision that he had to confront the murderer. *This nightmare must end.* Decision made, he planned to rise early and drive west to Wabash.

Homer lived with his two brothers on a family farm located on an unmarked country road off Highway 24, just west of Huntington. He moved in with them back in 1938 after he left the reform school. Quiet and solitary, Homer worked hard tending the farm's nine head of cattle and array of chickens, sheep, and pigs. Most of all, he loved the long days he spent in the fields, plowing, planting, and cultivating the crops of corn, wheat, and beans. Quiet and intelligent, Homer also loved to read.

The approaching fall harvest was Homer's favorite time of year. However, the nighttime wreaked havoc with his mind. After the morning feeding, Homer left the farm at about nine thirty. His 1948 green Ford pickup was meticulously kept. Peering over the steering wheel, eyes glued to the road, Homer held both hands steady on the wheel. Having driven through Wabash and then out Pike Street, he took the curve beyond Friends Cemetery and then drove another mile. He could see the daunting brick edifice of Wabash County Reform School looming ahead.

As if in slow motion, Homer remembered himself in the dingy cafeteria and the long gray halls with the stern teachers and tough guards. He remembered the peace he had when he escaped to the shelter of his own bed. Most of all, his memory was dominated by that one dreadful night in the room with Gordon and the killer. Despite a disadvantaged childhood, a solitary life, and unforgettable nightmares, Homer had succeeded in developing confidence in himself. More self-assured, he deemed the time had arrived to conquer the mystery of who killed Gordon Yoder.

The green pickup truck pulled up in front of the reform school. Homer turned his green pickup truck right then slowly up the drive, the brick building looming large ahead. Memories returned. Many nightmares. His breathing was heavy. His life flashed before his eyes. Homer parked the truck and remained inside for a few minutes. He glared out the window from the comfort of his truck, delaying the harsh task ahead. He jumped at the sound of an elderly man tapping on the passenger side window.

"Need any help there? Lookin' for someone?"

Homer relaxed seeing the slight smile on the whiskered man's face. "Nah. Just lookin'. Comin' to see a friend." Homer looked again, as the old man's face looked familiar. *Twenty-four years. No, couldn't be or could it?* The man tipped his hat and headed back toward the side of the school. Homer opened the door, buttoned his coat, and walked up the sidewalk. Everything looked the same except for the maple trees, now more than a generation older. Not used to entering by the front door, Homer felt strange and out of place as he walked into the lobby. He took the first right directly in line with Miss Gardner's desk.

"Good morning, sir."

"Hello. Is that you, Miss Gardner? You're still here. I remember you. Yes, yes, I do."

"Well, I guess you could. I started working here in '32, let's just say few years after high school. I don't remember you. Who are you?"

"I'm ... I'm, ah, you wouldn't remember me. Never mind. I'm here to see the ... to see ... " He couldn't think of the name. Miss Gardner gave him a strange look. "To see the principal, the head man."

"Oh, that would be Mr. Wolfe, but he's busy in his office. You can sit over there and wait. Of course I don't know how long that'll be."

"Yes, ma'am, but I drove a long way to get here."

"Well, so did Mr. Wolfe. He lives on the far side of town." Miss Gardner turned sideways and continued typing.

"Excuse me, ma'am. I think Mr. Wolfe will see me. Tell him it's about the murder of Gordon Yoder. I'm sure you know the name, since he was murdered at this school in '34. That's two years after you started."

"Excuse me," Miss Gardner swiveled around, extended her open hand across her chest. "That, sir, does not happen in this fine school."

Gordon's name sparked an immediate internal response in the secretary. Without saying a word, and somewhat befuddled, she flipped the typewriter carriage with contempt, turned, and calmly but without hesitation walked into Mr. Wolfe's office.

Five minutes seemed like an hour. Homer looked around. Nothing had changed. He stepped out onto the terrazzo floors. The hall and rooms had the same wide heavy woodwork. He could see the cross hall at the far end that led to the room. Nausea erupted within him. He coughed. Returning to Miss Gardner's desk, he saw Clarence Wolfe standing in the doorway. Passage of time had no reference as the face of the big mustached man in the room twenty-four years ago was the first image that came to Homer's mind. *Can't be. No. Think straight.*

"Mr. Wolfe, this gentleman wants to see you." Miss Gardner looked harshly at the visitor, as if Homer was an intruder.

"Sir, it's about Gordon Yoder. Can we talk?"

"Never knew him. Before my time." Wolfe gave an unyielding glare as he saw James Duncan looking from beneath his visor in the office on the far side of the room. "Step in here." Wolfe turned and walked into his office. "I'm busy now, so what's this about? Why are you asking about Gordon Yoder? Besides, he died of the flu back in 1934. Weak little kid."

"Thought you said you didn't know him."

Wolfe paused and deliberated, caught in his own lie. "Read the school records. We have files, you know."

"Well, look at mine." Homer said. Wolfe passed off the remark. "I'd like to see my file."

"Just one minute. What makes you the authority? Why all these questions? My god, man, that was twenty-four years ago. You're not much older than that."

"Please stand corrected, Mr. Wolfe. I am thirty-six years old, the same age Gordon would have been if he hadn't been murdered here in your school."

"Beg your pardon. My school? I wasn't here in 1934." The more Wolfe talked, the more Homer noticed something strange—the quick temper, the protruding forehead, and the mustache. *Nah, can't be.* Homer kept observing Wolfe's features.

"Sir, let me make something clear. I have lived with the memory of that night for twenty-four years. I am one of the three people who knows what happened in that dingy dark room. I can still remember the lamp with the dim light. I'm stepping forward. You, sir, are the first person I am contacting. My next call will be to the sheriff's office unless you decide to cooperate."

Wolfe didn't say a word but knew he needed to learn more about Homer Atkins' intentions. "Have a seat. Maybe you can tell me something I don't know about this. What did you say his name was?"

"Yes, sir. Gordon Yoder."

Casually, Wolfe sat down at his desk and pulled out and lit a Lucky Strike. Homer watched as Wolfe inhaled deeply. His cheeks pulled inward to the ends of his dark mustache.

"His name's Gordon Yoder. He was a good kid."

"Sure. I'm sure he was. We're a reform school, we get the cream of the crop, the first boys of our generation. Senators, businessmen, even priests and ministers," Wolfe said sarcastically. "Now, how did you happen to be here, Mr. Atkins, future bank robber?" Wolfe said trying to put Atkins in his place.

"I was there, sir. I saw him murdered."

"You what? How can that be?" Immediately Wolfe asked, "Did you see who did it?"

"So now you believe me? You're right. It wasn't the flu like you said before," Homer informed Wolfe. Wolfe knew not to respond. "Take me to the room. I want to see. I want to see if it's still the same."

Wanting to appear unalarmed, Wolfe stood almost nonchalantly. "Follow me."

He's good at giving orders, Homer thought. *I didn't think he'd show me the room.* There was no conversation. Homer followed, listening to Wolfe's footsteps on the terrazzo floor, echoing down the hall. *Seems like he knows where he's going.*

At the end of the hall, Wolfe turned left, walked several paces, and then opened the first door on the right. The sight of the black leather couch on the back wall horrified Homer. He stood frozen. He blinked.

His mind played games. He remembered the feel of the leather on his bare skin. His eyes watered when he recalled Gordon naked and motionless.

"What's wrong, Mr. Atkins? Here, sit down."

The picture in his mind was as vivid as the present. It all came back to him. He spoke as if in a trance. "There were two of them. One tall, distinctive face and brown hair. The other, square jaw, mustache, and piercing eyes. I'll never forget the tall one. Over six feet. There were wine bottles on that table," Homer said, pointing to the low table in front of the couch. "That lamp was there between the couch and chair. I remember three leather pillows. Now I see two. They both wore suits and white shirts—well, until they took their clothes off. They stripped us both naked. The man with the mustache took me over to that chair." Homer pointed to the leather chair next to the lamp. "He sat down. He made me kneel. The other man was rough. I can remember Gordon's plea, 'No, no.'"

Wolfe listened intently to the detailed description.

"I'll never forget," Homer said. "The big man with me moaned." Homer looked directly at Wolfe with piercing eyes. "He moaned until … until, well, until it happened. I heard him say—I'll never forget—'Yeah, easy.' Then he said, 'Randall, stop over there. Back off. Back off. You'll smother the kid.' I turned around. Couldn't even see Gordon underneath the tall one. When the guy in the chair, that chair right there, stopped his moaning, he pushed me away. I was sick with vomit. He stood up. I buried my face in that chair, gagging. Rushing, he put on his clothes.

"I remember him saying, 'We better get out of here. You hurt that kid. Look, he's not even moving.' What I remember most was the tall man standing right there, tall and naked, his chest heaving, looking down at Gordon lying on the couch. The last thing I remember, I saw him reach over and take the blanket from back of the couch, turn Gordon over on his back, and then cover him up. The two men raced out the door. For a moment, I stood horrified at the sight of Gordon. I dashed out of the room, carrying my clothes as I ran, and met head-on with a man coming straight from the other side of the hall. I saw the startled look on his face. I didn't know the man, but I knew he worked at the school. I saw him again weeks later after Gordon died, but he never said a word. I know he knew who I was. Never a word."

Clarence Wolfe memorized every detail of Homer's story. "Who did you see? What was the man's name who saw you in the hall?"

"I don't know. I never asked. Never said a word." Homer continued to stare at the couch. He shook his head as if to wake himself from a gruesome dream.

Wolfe knew he had a problem. He knew who else had a problem. "That was quite a story. Are you sure it happened as you described?" he asked cautiously. "Could you identify them?"

"I can remember the face of the one who killed Gordon. You never forget horror like that. Not so much the one with the mustache. My eyes were closed."

"Well, Mr. Atkins, I will write this all down and make a full report. I'll make sure it's documented and filed. That's a ... well, that's quite a story. Are you sure it's not just that? A story?"

"Documented and filed?" Homer asked with contempt. "I'm here, sir, with purpose. I want justice for Gordon Yoder. I want to rid my mind of this ghastly daily torment."

"What are you saying?" Wolfe asked as he noticed a dark mole to the right of Homer's right nose.

"I'm saying I want to confront this Randall."

"Do you know Randall?"

"I'll never forget that name. The man with me said, 'Randall, stop over there. You'll smother the kid.'"

"Randall ... Let me see." Wolfe raised his hand to his chin. "Not right off hand. No, I don't really know a Randall."

Homer was surprised by Wolfe's response. "Well, let me help you. I just learned two weeks ago. There are two Randalls I have located in Wabash who would be the right age. Randall Glaser works over at Ford Meter Box. He's short, a little overweight. Then I learned and checked this out. There's a Randall Zilbar, big shot over at the Wabash Bank. He's tall and I understand quite wealthy. Very prominent in town. Actually, I'm surprised you don't recognize the name, a man of his stature in the community. I was sure you'd know the important people in Wabash." Having baited Wolfe, Homer waited for a reply.

"Yes, oh yes, I do recognize that name. Don't know him. Guess he is quite wealthy," Wolfe said. The image of Homer's mole now jarred Wolfe's memory.

Wolfe felt relief when Homer said, "Seen enough." He turned and walked out of the room.

Wolfe locked the door of the room of terror and followed Homer down the corridor to the front door. Although Wolfe wanted to dismiss the disclosure Homer Atkins had just made, he waited to see what Homer would say. Wolfe walked up to Homer, who was waiting at the front door.

Homer nodded. "Yes. This is what we'll do. I'm not going to the sheriff for now. You can breathe easier, Mr. Wolfe."

Wolfe interrupted, "I can promise you, Mr. Atkins, I have no reason to breathe heavy."

"You and I are going to meet this Randall Zilbar. Right here. Same room and very soon."

"Mr. Atkins, I can assure you that Mr. Zilbar is not going to meet with you, no matter how hard you try. For you to accuse him of murder? Come on. Don't be foolish. The only way he'd talk with you would be through his attorney. I suggest you forget this whole wild story. Zilbar is powerful. You don't want to mess with him. He'd step on you like a bug."

"Well, Mr. Wolfe, I may be small, a nobody, but I can assure you his power will be defused. Thank you for your time, Mr. Wolfe." Homer started for the door and then stopped. "Thought you didn't know Zilbar."

"Well, I don't. But he is well-known, now that you mention it. Guess I know of him."

"Sure. Sure, Mr. Wolfe. I bet you do. I will call you by the end of the week. You'll arrange the meeting right here. The three of us. Good day, sir." Homer turned and walked out the door. Suddenly he stopped and walked back inside. "Oh, by the way, Mr. Wolfe, how did you know which room I wanted to see?"

"I just—"

Homer didn't listen to Wolfe's reply. He closed the door and left. *Lot more than expected.*

CHAPTER 88

URGENT

Father Sullivan—September 26, 1958

A slight rain fell on Friday morning. Banking day, a perfect time for a walk. Hovering under an outstretched black umbrella, Father Sullivan walked with a feeling of peacefulness and solitude. Time to think. He enjoyed the pitter-patter of random raindrops on the umbrella above his head. *Maybe check the post office.* It was only six blocks away. The rain continued to dance in a light shower.

Walking up the stone steps of the post office, Father Sullivan noticed the water collecting in the imprints that had been worn into the stone over time. Year after year, decade after decade, the steps reflected the lives written on paper, the letters passing through the aged building. He thought of the letters mailed to soldiers overseas. Christmas greetings reminding families and friends of joyous times. Love letters from those separated by distance.

Father Sullivan was perplexed by his next move and what to do about his continuing crusade to expose the deviant priests. Bishop Powers and Father Schmidt had their cover.

Hoping to discover a letter from Father Holtz, Father Sullivan walked over to the post office boxes, went straight to box number 404, and unlocked the small metal door. He saw not one but two letters in the same hand.

Opening the one with the oldest postmark, he read his counterpart's words: *I'll call 3:00 Monday, same number. URGENT.* It was the last word that raised Father Sullivan's alarm. Without a pause, he opened the second letter, which was a duplication in case the first letter did not arrive. *Father, this letter backs up the first, just in case the first one did not arrive. IMPORTANT.*

Leaving the post office, Father Sullivan tilted his umbrella slightly forward; the slow, comforting rain had progressed into more of a wind-blown downfall. His black leather shoes splattered the puddles on the steps as he began to scurry back to the rectory. *What could urgent mean?* he wondered.

Three days later while waiting at the phone booth for Father Holtz's call, Father Sullivan reflected on the word *urgent*. He could not imagine.

At 3:03, the phone rang.

"Hello, Ben. Thanks for being on time. All I could think of for the last three days was the word *urgent*."

"Sorry, Father. Maybe I overstated it. I should have emphasized *important*."

"That is not a problem. Don't worry. Just good to hear your voice," Father Sullivan assured him.

"Actually, Michael, I have some good news. We really need to meet in person."

"Sure, of course. What about tomorrow?" Father Sullivan immediately suggested. "Maybe in the morning at 10:30 or 11:00."

"Works for me. Maybe 11:00 would be best though. I have Mass and then a short meeting with Father Schmidt. That'll only be a half hour or so because I know he's leaving in the morning for a two-day meeting in Chicago. If I'm a few minutes late, don't worry. Just go ahead and order your fried chicken."

"Ah, funny guy," Father Sullivan responded with an unseen smile. "What's it about though? Why so important?"

"Michael, it's about a friend of mine. I think he can help us. Maybe he can really help us."

"Okay. I won't ask any more over the phone. I'll live in suspense for another day."

"I look forward to our visit, Michael. See you tomorrow. Bye."

"Oh, oh, Father, one thing."

"What's that?" Father Holtz asked.

With the most sincere words, Father Sullivan said, "Thank you so much, Father, so very much. I couldn't do this without you."

"You're most welcome. I respect so much your passion and conviction. See you tomorrow, Michael."

Father Sullivan heard the click. *What a friend,* he thought as he turned and walked back to the rectory. He looked around for the impatient lady, but she was nowhere to be seen today.

His mind was continually focused on the boys. Thoughts of them and the abusing priests were part of his daily routine. He always found time to think of Gene Kowolski, Joey Singleton, and Peter Goodnar. Of course, the other boys were not far from his prayers. He even prayed daily for those of whom he did not know. Ones he was sure were still hidden in secrecy in the dark shadows. Then he thought of Linda.

Later that night, Father Sullivan slowly turned his green '53 Chevy off Pike and onto Carter Street. Just beyond, the slight scent of decaying leaves filled the air with the familiar smell of the approaching autumn. Father Sullivan knew the house, of course. It was past dusk. The front porch light was on. He parked along the curb, just short of the drive. The white-sided craftsman style house was familiar. Dressed in his cassock, he bent over and buttoned the garment below the knees. The black garb had not been designed for driving a car.

The full moon above cast light across the small front yard. Even the cracks in the sidewalk were highly visible. As he approached the steps, he heard the whisk of a cat running across the yard behind him. Somewhat confused by his motives, he slowly climbed the five steps leading onto the wooden porch floor. The porch swing hung empty in front of the parlor window. Two wicker chairs still remained on the bedroom side of the porch.

The milk box to the side of the front door was lidless, exposing two empty quart jars for pickup in the early hours of the morning. The house was a picture of tranquility in the quiet neighborhood of Wabash. The man dressed in black felt slight apprehension about his unannounced visit. Gently, he knocked on the front door. He hoped she would answer. She did.

Opening the door, Linda was first startled to see the unexpected caller dressed in black standing on the front porch. Then she recognized him. "Why, Father Sullivan," she said, placing her hand against her chest in surprise.

"Good evening, Linda. Ah, please ... please accept my apology for this unannounced call. I was just in the—"

"Of course. That's fine. Step right in. Good to see you, Father," she said with a most pleasant smile across her face, trying to hide her heightened emotions. *Oh God, how good to see him right here in my house.*

Father Sullivan stepped across the threshold and took off his hat. "I hope you don't mind the cassock. I was just out for an evening ride. This was kind ... this was kind of a spur of the moment thing," he said apologetically.

"Yes, perfect, that cassock and your white collar. You look just great. You know I'm delighted to see you. Come in and sit down," Linda said as she untied her small floral apron, slipped it over her head, and laid it across the back of one of the dining room chairs.

Father Sullivan took a seat in the big easy chair in front of the sofa. A radio, lamp, and table stood to the side of the chair. An upholstered rocker sat to the other side. He noticed she still did not have a television. "Where's Joey?" he asked, raising his voice to her somewhat as she sat down on the sofa.

"Oh, he's out. Some practice. He just left a few minutes ago."

Oh, good, Father Sullivan thought.

"Would you like something to drink? Coffee, tea, pop?"

"Oh, don't bother. I'm fine," he said, hoping she would make some coffee.

"Michael," Linda said, blushing a little. "I'm so glad you're here. Please let me show a little hospitality. I know you love your coffee."

Linda immediately walked into the kitchen to put some coffee in the pot. She turned on the electric stove. "I'll be right out!" She knew she had no time to run upstairs. She looked in the small wall mirror to the side of the kitchen door and fluffed her fingers through her hair, pressed her lips together, and straightened her dress. *Can't believe he's here.* Taking a deep breath, she casually walked back into the front parlor.

Sitting at the end of the sofa, across from Father Sullivan, Linda said, "I'd be remiss, Michael, if I ... I mean, Father, if I ... "

"Linda, Michael is fine. That's my name. I know your respect," Father Sullivan said, noticing her slight nervousness.

"Thank you, Michael. As I was saying, I'd be very remiss if I didn't say it's good, so good, to see you."

"Same here," he said in a sincere but reserved response. "I have been thinking about Joey. It's been quite a while since he and I talked."

A smile came across her face. "Now that Father Jaeger is gone for good, Joey realizes, I think, the mistake. Ever since his talk with you, he's like … well, almost like a different person. Maybe that's not the word. More like a changing person."

"That's very good to hear," Father Sullivan replied.

"Actually, he is talking more and more about becoming a priest. He does want to help people. Joey cares." Linda looked down at her hands, which were folded across her lap. "You know, Michael, this is even difficult to say, considering what he endured. Joey, I believe, is a better person. He loves the church and really wants to be a part. Do good for others. The older he gets, the more I realize how kind and giving he is."

"I think you're right," Father Sullivan said, continuing to allow her to talk.

"Joey knows, well, at least he's learning who he is and what he wants to do. He feels that a family just isn't in the picture. You know what I mean, Michael? No family and all that comes along with it. I'm okay with that. Joey being an only child, maybe God doesn't want me to be a grandma."

Father Sullivan looked down at his folded hands and sat forward in the chair, elbows on his knees. "Linda, I know all too well the sacrifice it takes. We priests do so much for so many." He hesitated. "But think back. You and me. I think about all I gave up. Oh, I'm sorry. Shouldn't have said that. I'm here about Joey." Father Sullivan sat back in his chair.

Linda dabbed her eyes. "Oh, Michael, that's all right. I know what was in our hearts, but my dear friend, I know you made the right decision. You are a wonderful man and a caring and loving priest. Just look at all the people you help."

"Please stop there. Thank you, Linda. I know. We know." With a slight chuckle, he said, "You're too young and pretty to be thinking about being a grandma." Looking very serious, he then said, "I must admit, every so often I have thought about the fact that I'll never be a father or grandpa."

"Michael, you're a father every day. Maybe that's one of the reasons you care so much about all these boys," Linda said, trying to reassure him.

Father Sullivan thought, *There's truth to that. Yet there's so much more.*

"Oops, better check that coffee," Linda said, breaking the serious talk. As she walked to the kitchen, she had a brief thought of grandma, father, their relationship, what could have been. "Cream or sugar?" she asked from the kitchen.

"Black for me," he replied. "How else can a priest drink his coffee except black?" he kidded.

Linda didn't respond, as his comments reminded her that he was a priest. *Oh stop it. Grow up, Linda,* she said to herself. Walking back to the parlor, she carried a tray with two cups, cream, sugar, napkins, and a small plate of homemade cookies.

"Well, isn't this nice?" Father Sullivan said, taking a cup and saucer.

"Now have a cookie," Linda insisted. "I baked them just for you since I knew you were coming," she teased with a pesky smile on her face.

Father Sullivan smiled. "Back to our conversation," he said in a polite yet serious tone. "Linda, how are you? Joey's doing better, but how are you?"

Looking directly at him, she paused and then said, "Thanks for asking. I'm doing pretty well, pretty well considering everything. I'm especially happy about Joey's progress. That's good." *Where's this going?*

Not totally understanding his real intentions, Father Sullivan just instinctively said, "How are you feeling, Linda? How are you doing? I'm not asking about Joey."

The thought of the confessional flashed across her mind. Linda looked down. She bought some time by taking a sip of coffee. Then she said, "It's tough sometimes. I have a good job. Then I must admit, there is the loneliness. I still have the feelings. The emotions. So much of the longing for … for … I can't say, Michael."

"Well, don't force yourself. I'm asking because I'm concerned. I know there is our past. We both know what can't be. We do our best," he said.

"I know. We both do our best. I try so hard, Michael," Linda said, appealing to his understanding of her real plight. She almost broke down when he said *our past*. She had felt as if time were in slow motion between *our past* and *can't be*.

Linda took a deep breath rather than retreating to the kitchen. "Your words are thoughtful and kind, Michael, so I just have to say ... I'm ... " Linda now felt more free to express her feelings. "My feelings are still wrapped around you." She took another breath. "So there. There, I said it. I know that which can't be. I accept that. But feelings. They are private. They are mine. My actions I can control. My feelings I can't control," she said, slightly shaking her head. "To be perfectly honest, I've been thinking about maybe moving."

"Moving?"

"Yes, Michael, I think best. Here, you are so close, yet so far," Linda said, standing behind the couch, "I simply love you too much." She turned and walked to the kitchen. Father Sullivan was startled by the unexpected revelation. Leaving the door open, "Joey's been talking about going to the seminary for high school. That would leave me here. Here alone. You know my dad passed away. It's been ten years now. Remember?" she reminded him, as she walked back into the living room.

"Of course, 19 ... 1948?" Father Sullivan replied.

"Yes, 1948." Linda went on to say, "Mom lives with her sister now. I have two brothers. They both have large families. Then my sister, she and her husband don't have any children yet. She's the youngest, and they all live in Lafayette, so I'd be with them. Nothing has been decided. I'll wait and see what Joey does about the seminary. The real reason, though, is I think it best to be away from you. There are too many reminders here."

"Well, I must admit that's a surprise. I can understand. You have to do what's best for you and Joey," Father Sullivan said, trying to reassure her. *Oh, how can she move away? No.* He then said, "Linda, I—"

Suddenly the front door swung open. "Mom, I'm here! Oh, excuse me. Hey. Hi, Father Sullivan."

"I know you didn't expect to see me here," Father Sullivan said to Joey. "I was driving nearby and just decided to stop by and see how you're doing," he said defensively as to why he was there, alone with Joey's mom.

Joey did not think a thing of it. "Oh, I'm fine, Father."

"That's what your mother says. That's really good, Joey. I'm happy for you both."

With enthusiasm in his voice, Joey said, "Yeah, everything's better. Your talk really helped me … made me think. Now with Jaeger, excuse me, Father, I meant Father Jaeger … With him gone out of my life, I kind of see how dumb I was. You know, like really stupid, but I want to be a priest just like you, Father Sullivan."

"Gosh, thank you, Joey. You're kind to say that."

"Hey, Father, why not? You're a good guy. I want to help people the way you do." Joey looked at his mom. "Say, I think I'll have something to eat then do my homework."

"There's fresh cookies in the jar." Joey shot into the kitchen.

"*Wooo*, guess he's really up. You know, Linda, I must confide—confidentially, of course—that my mission continues. I have learned so many bad things about these priests. Even more. It's not just Father Jaeger; it's numbers more. I don't even know how many right here in our diocese. Besides that, it goes beyond into other states. I don't even know how many. What I do know is that I'm going to uncover it all. I'm going to bring justice. It's all so immoral, so unethical. The whole thing is so unjust."

"I don't know how you do it, Father," she said, suddenly noticing how the topic of conversation had changed. She could see his passion for his advocacy.

"So with that, it's good to hear a positive report about Joey."

"Thank you, Michael," Linda said, although she did not like the immediate change in conversation to the topic of abusive priests.

Still thinking about Linda possibly moving, and not knowing what to say next, Father Sullivan stood. "This has been a good visit. I'm really pleased to hear that Joey's doing so well. Seeing him, I feel much better about his future, his vocation."

As Father Sullivan walked to the door, he turned, reached out, and touched Linda's arm. He could feel her yearning for a hug good-bye. Joey was still in the kitchen. "Good-bye, Joey!" he said from the front door.

"You too, Father!" Joey yelled from the kitchen table, focusing on his milk and cookies.

Linda was glad Joey did not show manners and come to the front door.

She didn't want Father Sullivan to leave, but she knew she shouldn't make too much of it. Feeling his steady hand on her arm, she looked directly into his eyes. She felt as if she was saying good-bye to someone for the last time. Linda knew that was exactly what she was doing.

"Goodnight, Linda."

She opened the door. As he turned to leave, she reached out to him with one hand. Father Sullivan looked at her and squeezed her hands in both of his. He held tight for a few moments. Then he let go, turned, and walked down the porch stairs.

"Goodnight, Michael. Thank you so much for stopping by. I hope I didn't…"

"Stop, Linda. You didn't do anything wrong. I, too, have intense feelings." Father turned to walk away, stopped then stepped back giving her a small kiss on her cheek. He immediately turned and walked to his car. Inside, he leaned his head downward to wave to Linda standing on the porch.

Her arms folded, Linda looked up to the light of the moon. She walked back into the house and peered out the window at the priest still sitting in his car. Linda watched his headlights appear. She turned off the living room light and walked upstairs to the loneliness of her room. *I love that man more than life. How can I live without him? I may never see him again.* Darkness filled the room. Father Sullivan, sitting in his car, thought of Linda as the lights went out. He drove away and disappeared into the darkness.

CHAPTER 89

NEW REVELATIONS

Father Holtz—September 30, 1958, 12:10p.m.

FATHER Sullivan arrived at the truck stop on a cool picturesque September day. Driving through the gravel lot, he cautiously tried to avoid the water puddles. Each pothole was at the mercy of the monster eighteen wheelers. Inside the truck stop, disheveled truckers went about their business, drinking coffee at the counter and perusing the magazine rack overloaded with *Car and Truck*, *Hunters and Wildlife*, and a wide array of so-called skin magazines.

Walking by the cash register, Father Sullivan noticed his usual booth was occupied, but he detected an empty booth in the opposite far corner. Walking over, he saw a small army of donut crumbs, burnt ends of French fries, and coffee rings. He sat down and cleaned the table with a wad of napkins as best he could. A cup of coffee mysteriously appeared. He soon wanted to move and separate himself from the conversation blasting the back of his head from the booth behind him. He had no interest in listening to a flannel-shirted, leather-vested trucker with a three-day growth of whiskers trying to coax a local nineteen-year-old waitress with dyed blond hair to come out and see his new tandem truck.

Looking up, Father Sullivan noticed Father Holtz searching for his companion. Raising his hand, Father Sullivan immediately dashed to their now-empty regular booth even though it was still cluttered with plates of uneaten navy beans and burnt fries. As they sat down and pushed everything to the middle of the table, the dying embers of a half-smoked cigarette caught a new breath of life.

"Still love that smell but haven't had one since seminary," Father Sullivan said, admitting his guilt of an earlier vice to the younger priest.

"Good to see you, as always, Michael," Father Holtz said, giving a friendly greeting to his friend. "Did you order your chicken yet?"

"Let's wait till they clear this mess. Just having my coffee," Father Sullivan said. "*Important ... urgent*, the words of the day, Ben. You've got to tell me."

"Right to it then, okay? When I was in the seminary, I became friends with Ronald Girouard. Just a great guy, quite an athlete and an all-state in football and basketball. Anyway, we met in seminary and became best of friends. He was *summa cum laude*, fluent in Italian and German. After ordination when I went off to parish work, Ronald applied for a position in advanced theological studies in Rome. His goal was to work inside the Vatican. He was always intrigued by the mystery of the Holy See. Ronald is very ambitious."

"Sounds like quite a guy," Father Sullivan said, stating the obvious.

"You're not kidding. Ronald was everything. Like I said—student, athlete, and with a great sense of humor. Michael, he could have had any girl he wanted. Came from a working-class neighborhood, good parents, family with ten kids. Most of all, Ronald was deeply religious, principled, a real man of integrity. I know it sounds like I'm really building this guy up, but he really is this and more."

"Well, yes it does, but, Ben, I believe you," Father Sullivan responded. "Although I don't know what this has to do with us, Rome and all."

"Patience, Michael, patience. I'm getting there. You'll see in a minute."

"I'm with you, Ben. Move on."

"So of course, Ronald was accepted at the Vatican. He studied during the reign of Pope Pius XII. They were making changes in the church. Pius XII especially ended the majority of Italian cardinals. He called for reform and the sanctification of priests and religion. I remember Ronald saying priests were encouraged to be living examples of the love of Christ and his sacrifice, as the pope wanted to make the church more universal."

"Now here we are faced with this corruption and scandal. Examples of Christ's love. Give me a break," Father Sullivan said, leaning back against the bench. "Oh, not you, Ben. I mean the church and the pope. Does the pope even know what's going on?"

"Ronald assisted Bishop Colasante who reported directly to Pope Pius. The bishop knew how to gain information within the inner circle of the Vatican. Officially, he oversaw the Vatican art collection. However, his network within the Vatican from the kitchen staff to Bishop Bellini of the Vatican Bank proved to be most helpful to the pope himself. Ronald had become a trusted assistant; however, he wanted to work in a parish in Italy. He thought the training and experience would be beneficial for his future work in the Vatican, so he applied for a transfer. Within a couple months, he was sent to the province Belluno in northern Italy. There he worked with Albino Luciano, who Ronald thinks is a saint. Like Ronald, Luciano came from a large family. Ronald learned so much. He thinks Luciano will soon become a bishop. Actually, Ronald says this guy is so good, he could someday become pope."

"Ben, how does this all help us?"

"Ronald and I stay in touch. Couple letters a year, some years more. A phone call at Christmas. Actually five years ago, I spent a week with him in Rome. So here's the good news." Father Holtz leaned his elbows on the table. "Last Friday, I got a letter from Ronald, Father Girouard. His father is gravely ill, terminal. He requested a transfer so he can be with his father here in Indiana. His folks live in Zionsville, just north of Indianapolis. Last month Ronald was transferred to … Are you ready? Indianapolis. Yes, he's an assistant to Cardinal Cullings, who was appointed by Pius XII. Ronald told me the cardinal was close to the pope. Of course, now we have a new pope, John Benedict. I'm sure Cardinal Cullings might not know him as well. John Benedict did spend his last ten formative years in the curia before becoming pope. Plus, can you believe the cardinal was a friend of Pope Pius and we hope Pope John Benedict as well? Ronald learned that he goes to Rome at least once a year."

"Wow, I'm impressed. So now I get it," Father Sullivan said enthusiastically, anticipating a connection that could seriously aid his mission.

"You see, Michael, I can continue to work under the radar in South Wayne. Schmidt and the bishop have no suspicion about me and these secret meetings of ours. I just listen, go along, remain quiet, and do what I'm told. However, I feel we could have access to Cardinal Cullings and, if ever necessary—God forbid—access to Rome. Nobody in the world knows we are talking. We are 100 percent confidential. No phone, visual, or paper trails. You are hiding my letters in a safe place, aren't you?"

"Oh, to be sure, Ben. In fact, I have destroyed them."

"So far you've gotten nowhere with the bishop. He's stonewalling you. The good thing is we've learned not only about cover-ups, but also about the corruption of and abuses by the bishop and Schmidt. From cover-up to, well, you know … Ned. Then Schmidt is right there. Ronald says Cardinal Cullings is so much like Monsignor Luciano. Michael, this could be your key. As you learn and uncover, you could then pass the information to Cullings and maybe even to Rome."

"Yes, Ben, Rome. That's where this abuse has to be addressed."

"Now get this. Ronald asked me to come and visit. Said he's going to introduce me to Cardinal Cullings. He's a real holy man. Bet he wouldn't tolerate any of these shenanigans and perversions … injustice."

"This is the best news ever. If I could just get an audience with the cardinal, he could totally expose everything to Pope John Benedict. The question is, however, will the pope take action against these pedophiles?"

"I'm going to see Ronald next Tuesday. He wants me to be there when the cardinal has a light schedule."

The two fathers' excitement was contagious. They agreed to talk by phone next Wednesday. Walking back to their cars, feeling two feet off the ground, they stopped.

Father Sullivan looked at Father Holtz. "I'll never be able to thank you enough, Ben." He put his hand on Ben's shoulder. "I couldn't do this without you." Truly a bond had been created between the two good priests.

Driving home that late afternoon, Father Sullivan could see a dim light at the end of this long, long dark tunnel.

CHAPTER 90

GAINING CONFIDENCE

Father Jaeger—September 19, 1958

"**G**OOD morning, Father," Father Jaeger said to Father Arnold when he first saw him the day after the Catholic Christian doctrine class he'd filled in for the night before. "How was your meeting?"

"Just like the last one. Nothing ever gets accomplished. Can't believe the parents and the sisters sometimes." Scratching his head of thinning white hair, Father Arnold said, "I became a priest to do the work of Christ." Then he shook his head as he sat down to his first cup of tea. "You need to try this instead of that black coffee. That stuff can really perk you up, but it's not for me. Guess it just gets you younger guys up for the day," Father Arnold told him.

"That's why I like it, Father Arnold," Jaeger said with a slight smirk on his face.

"Oh, I should ask you, how was the CCD class last evening? Nice group of kids, aren't they, Father?"

"Father, it was just a pleasure. What a fine group of young men and women. Mature for their age. Too bad they aren't getting a full Catholic education. Would like to see them around our parish more."

"All the kids in Eastville, for all sorts of reasons, just can't go to Catholic school," Father Arnold said, speaking from experience. "Family, money, mixed marriages—there are all kinds of reasons."

"I understand," Father Jaeger said.

Father Arnold poured his second cup of tea. "Sure you won't try this? Tea soothes the soul."

"Then that makes it a good Catholic drink," Father Jaeger kidded. "For you, I'll try some." Then he added, "Another day though."

As Father Arnold enjoyed his tea and English muffins, he read the morning paper. Father Jaeger calculated how to ask the next question without looking too anxious.

"Excuse, me, Father, I was thinking. I'd be glad to help out with CCD class. I could take one night a month. You could still handle the other three. Better yet, we could alternate every other week."

Father Arnold set down his cup of tea and pressed his lips together as if he was contemplating some big idea. "*Hmmm.* You know, Father, that could give me one Tuesday a month off. I have to be honest: then I could first watch our beloved Bishop Sheen and Red Skelton on television. Did you ever see him?"

"Red Skelton? Yes, Father. I like Freddie the Freeloader best."

"The best comedian I've ever heard or seen. Say, he's funnier than Laurel and Hardy. He does this character, Clem. Clem Keddlehopper. I just laugh and laugh."

"That should be good for you. A little more humor in your life," Father Jaeger said, encouraging him to consider the idea.

"That sounds reasonable, Father Jaeger. Let's do that. I can make that decision right now. You teach that class first, beginning next month. We'll see how it goes. That's a good idea. Of most importance, working with those public school kids will provide an excellent experience for you. 'Cause you know what I think?"

Father Jaeger didn't respond, just raised his eyebrows.

"Someday, Father, I see you becoming a pastor." Then he paused. "Maybe even here."

"Why thank you, Father. You know, I'd like that." Father Jaeger paused for a minute and then said, "My dad would be very proud if I became a pastor. Very proud."

The end of September arrived quickly, though not quickly enough for Father Jaeger. There was so much to learn about his new parish. He continued to involve himself in all facets of parish life. Father Arnold's words about becoming a pastor proved very motivational, even inspirational. As his past grew farther away, Father Jaeger felt a new beginning.

He felt a higher sense of spirituality. The little things of the priesthood brought more satisfaction. Father Jaeger was focused during Mass. Giving blessings and saying prayers were part of his daily life. He was proud of his collar and all it represented. Sometimes in his most glorified perception, Father Jaeger felt like he was Christ on Earth.

However, the dark shadows of reality still reached out and encircled the darkness in his soul. Blackness was a hidden closet in his mind. Late at night when he was all alone with just himself, his body, and his soul, Father Jaeger would open the door of darkness. Peering inside, he would see glimpses of devious exploits of the past. Embedded desires, passion, and lust would engulf his mind. He could not free himself from the bondage. Father Jaeger, despite his pursuit of goodness, found himself turning back to what was so engrained in his body and soul—the carnal lust for the pleasures of the flesh.

The weeks flew by. The first Thursday of October, Father Jaeger anxiously waited by his desk for his religious youth class to arrive. The young boys and girls meandered into the evening class one and two at a time. For some, class was a chore. For many, it was an excuse to leave the house on a weekday evening.

"Good evening, everyone. Seven o'clock, time to begin. Let's take our seats."

"That means you too, Father," someone kidded.

Father Jaeger immediately recognized most of their faces and remembered their names. He looked over the class, hoping Davey and Joe were in attendance. He recalled the good time they had at the Boy's Club a few weeks ago.

Father Jaeger began, "I will be teaching class every first and third Thursday for the rest of the year. Father Arnold made the decision."

A few kids clapped, most smiled and gave positive one-word responses. At the end of the applause, they all heard a voice from the back of the class say, "Ah shucks, we want Father Arnold back. Oh just kidding. Just kidding you, Father. We all like you," Joe said, hoping Father Jaeger could take the joke.

"Oh, that's you, Joe. Actually, I was hoping you had dropped out of class," he said, throwing back a zinger. Everybody laughed and liked that the priest could take a jab and then throw one back.

Father Jaeger deepened his bond that evening with the entire class. Well, most of them. Davey liked Father, but he could not understand what kind of priest he was. He thought Father Jaeger wanted to be liked and accepted while making himself too familiar, like when he gave them a ride home after that first class.

Eight o'clock arrived quickly that evening. Father Jaeger soon dismissed the class. A couple kids approached his desk, asking about what hell was like. Joe walked up and interrupted, "Ride home, Father?" he asked, secretly hoping for a root beer stop.

"Sure, sure. See you outside also, Davey?" he said, looking directly at the boy. Father Jaeger said goodnight to a couple of stragglers, turned off the lights, and headed for the car. Davey and Joe were waiting outside, leaning against the front fender of the priest's black Studebaker.

"What took ya so long, Father?" Joe asked. "Ya wanna give Mary Beth and Polly a few extra minutes?"

"Always a wise guy. Get in the car."

"Shotgun!" Davey called, staking his claim on the passenger seat.

As they pulled into the A&W, Joe said, "This is probably our last visit. They're closing for the season." Joe covered his face with his hands and faked sobbing. "Oh, wo is me."

"Don't worry, Father. We'll take you to Susie's. That's the soda fountain shop downtown. They have great doughnuts. You can watch 'em right there, flipping in the grease. Hot doughnuts with chocolate icing and cocoa. You'll love it, Father."

Father Jaeger enjoyed his acceptance among the boys. *They seem to like me for just who I am.* "Next time, we'll try it. Your turn to buy, so save your nickels, Joe."

Driving home, Father Jaeger knew right where to go. First he stopped at Davey's.

"Thanks again, Father," Davey said as he jumped from the car.

"Say, Davey, want to go to the Boy's Club again soon? Firm up your muscles?"

"No thanks, Father. I have all the muscles I need," he said as he raised his right arm and flexed even though it was hidden by his jacket.

"Your loss," Father Jaeger said. "See you in a couple weeks."

Joe scooted over as close as possible to the door, not saying a word. Unexpectedly, he intuitively felt a little apprehensive. Something was in the air. "Gotta get home to finish homework," he reminded Father Jaeger.

"Oh, it's only 8:40. Something I wanna show you."

Joe didn't respond, not feeling funny anymore. He gripped the door handle. Father Jaeger drove east and up the hill toward Douglas Park. The road grew narrow. Brush and woods lined the gravel road. Ahead, Joe could see the gray weathered posts that encircled a turnaround at the road's end.

"Father, we have to turn around. It's dark. I gotta get home." Joe's heart began to race. He could hear his own breathing. Father Jaeger gripped with wheel with both hands, driving with careful determination.

"That's just the end of the road. Look, there's a path into the woods."

Joe saw nothing more than a wide dirt path. The blackness of the night served as a stage for the full moon. Joe could hear Father Jaeger breathing heavier. The car bounced over potholes as it followed the crooked trail. He noticed perspiration beading on the priest's forehead. There was focused excitement in the priest's eyes.

"Up and down we go, Joe. You'll love what I found out here."

"Maybe during the daylight would be better. I can't see anything but coal and black cats," Joe said, trying to lighten the moment.

"You will, Joe. You will. Watch for the moon. It will be beautiful."

Driving about a hundred yards beyond the end of the gravel road, Father Jaeger followed the path, which was bordered on both sides by thick, dense brush. The moon grew faint, and then the black car turned sharply to the left and stopped. Shifting into reverse, Father Jaeger backed up and pulled forward in the direction from which they had come. With a jerk and a push on the brakes, he stopped the car.

"Now turn around, Joe. Look through the back window."

"I don't see anything but black. We better go home, Father. I'm gonna get in trouble."

"No, no. Tell your mom I had to check something at the sacristy. Yes, you can see. See that giant oak at the crest of the hill?" Father Jaeger asked.

"No, no, I don't."

"Here, jump in the backseat," Father Jaeger said as he immediately placed his outstretched hand under Joe's buttocks while extending his fingers in a far reach forward.

"Father!" With that, Joe went over the front seat and headfirst into the back.

Father Jaeger reached over and pushed the lock on the passenger's door. "Joe, take off your clothes. I'm gonna show you how friends have fun, and nobody will know."

While his prey was hostage in the backseat, Father Jaeger opened the driver's side door in one motion. Out of the car, he jumped. His shirt and trousers hit the ground at once, along with his shoes and socks—everything. Joe pushed himself into the corner of the backseat.

"Now your turn, Joe. Off with everything." Father Jaeger was in full view, naked and running on high.

"Oh, Father, no. Please no." Joe could see the priest's outstretched hands reaching for him.

Father Jaeger reached into the car and pulled off Joe's sweater. After taking the boy's shoes off, he pulled Joe's pant legs both at once. Joe coughed. He started to choke. He wanted to vomit. The craving in the lustful man's eyes was like a large cat in the night. The panting predator tugged at Joe's pant legs again. The tight waist enclosure prohibited the priest from pulling the pants off by the ankles. Father Jaeger's fingers gripped Joe from behind, clasping the terrorized boy's waist and twisting him around until Joe saw only the light of the moon through the back window.

"*Noooo!*" Joe screamed. "Get away from me! Please, Father!"

Joe's shouts were all for naught. His frantic calls were heard only by the creatures in the darkness of the night. His screams accelerated the priest's excitement. Joe could feel the older man's heated body all over his naked backside. He could feel the pain. The finality of the hideous, deranged, and carnal act drained the beast of all his energy. Father Jaeger collapsed in heaving gasps for air. With a powerful twist, he spun Joe around.

Father Jaeger fell back against the seat, panting, exhausted, and covered with sweat. Joe tucked himself into the far corner of the back-seat. He was numb.

"It's okay, Joe. Nobody will ever know. You're a man now. This is our secret. Not a word, Joe. Not a word … " The priest's words drifted from Joe's consciousness as he hid in shame in the corner of the backseat, curled up like a cat. His world went dark. He felt himself falling into an abyss, a dark world of fire and teeth.

Joe didn't remember the trip home. Suddenly he saw the front porch light. Once the car stopped, Father Jaeger leaned across and pushed the door handle down. Joe stepped out of the car.

"Here's your books. Can't forget them," the priest said as if nothing had happened. "See you in class."

Joe didn't even hear him drive away. He stood on the walk and straightened his clothes. *Mom can't know. Oh God, she'd never believe me.* Climbing the steps onto the front porch, Joe could only remember the haunting words of the monster in his mind: *This is our secret. Not a word, Joe, not a word.* As he opened the door, Joe immediately heard the chime on the wall clock. It was nine thirty.

From the kitchen, he heard, "You're a little late, honey. Better get upstairs, wash, and do your homework. Your father's out at the K of C's meeting. He'll be home later. I'll be up to kiss you goodnight."

Fortunately, the only bathroom in the house was empty. Joe dashed up the stairs, locked the door, and ran hot water at full throttle into the tub. He poured half the shampoo bottle into the rushing water, which overflowed the tub with suds. As he stripped off his clothes, the hot water racing at full force, Joe suddenly started to gag. He bent over the toilet, only to throw forward dry heaves at first and then everything else. He hoped the running bathwater would overpower the sounds of his gagging.

As the tub filled, Joe lay sprawled out on the bathroom floor mat. *Oh God, Mother, Mary full of Grace, tell me it's over. I didn't mean to sin. I ask for Your forgiveness. Please, Lord, forgive me.*

He reached for the toilet scrub brush and scratched his bare skin, ridding himself of every hair, every drop of sweat from the lecherous priest. Joe pulled himself up over the side of the bath and into the exceed-ingly hot water. *I deserve this. Burns like hell! But forgive me, my dear Lord.* Joe felt the soothing enamel and hot water as he sat, especially where it hurt the most. *Oh, the pain.* Joe gagged some more. Time lapsed. He tried to discard the darkness of the last two hours. The panting, hovering body flashed in and out of his mind. The sweaty, slimy smell made him gag more as he pictured the white clammy monster. *Damn him to hell!* he thought. *God, please damn him to hell!*

"Joe, Joe, you all right?" He heard his mother knocking at the locked door. "Finish up. Your sister's turn to use the bathroom, and then your dad will be home."

"Okay, Mom. Be right out. Just taking an extra long bath tonight. Don't have homework. I'm just tired." After his bath, Joe retreated to the safety of sleep as he escaped deep down under the privacy of his own covers. *Oh, if I can only sleep without thinking of the horrid nightmare of reality.* Then he heard again, *This is our secret. Not a word, Joe. Not a word.*

Who would believe me anyway? he thought as he turned out the light. The intense pain throbbed. *No one. Nobody would believe what happened tonight,* Joe thought. Somehow, his eyes closed. Somber, his mind finally drifted into darkness.

CHAPTER 91

A CHANCE TO MEET

Judge Seiler—October 23, 1958

JUDGE Seiler called Sheriff Thurow to his chambers. It took the sheriff no time to report.

"Have a seat, Sheriff. I want to know the status of our lost soul, Phillip Krueger. What's the latest?" the judge asked, expecting straight answers.

"Judge, we've had an all-points bulletin posted throughout the state for months. The state police have been very cooperative, although there are no leads. Our department has followed up on everyone in town who knows him. Some we've questioned twice."

"What about the Bernard character?" the judge asked.

"Nothing. Absolutely nothing. We think he's clean. As you know, I interrogated him. He's the one who helped the boy when Krueger attacked him. Judge, we have the right man."

"Well I beg to differ with you, Dick Tracy, with no disrespect," Judge Seiler said shaking his head side to side. "You had the right man. Now he's gone." Judge slammed his fist down.

"Right. We couldn't find any other clues except the turned-over chair in Krueger's house. No fingerprints. No sign of a break-in. It's only a hunch, but after seeing the chair, scratches on the door, and some black tape adhesive on the chair, I would still conclude that he was tied up for whatever reason and abducted. Maybe he knows something, and someone wants him gone. There were no signs of burglary or breaking and entering. That's my best professional hunch. Sorry, Judge, but there's not much more we can do."

"How'd you figure that all out? Sounds pretty sophisticated detective work there, Sheriff."

"Detective Peterson came over and helped us a little."

"Well," Judge Seiler responded. "That's a different story. Hamilton Peterson. That man's the best. He could figure out the hangman in a gang of hooded KKKs. Wish we had more like him. Sheriff, it begs the question, what was going on out at that school? Then you wonder if something is still going on."

"You're right, Judge. I do wonder. But there's no reason to bring anybody in."

"Then I ask you, what about the director? Could you be questioning him about Krueger's disappearance? He could know something."

"The director is Clarence Wolfe," the sheriff informed Judge Seiler. "And not really, Judge. No complaints. No reason to."

"Do you trust him?"

"There's something about him that doesn't add up. He's kind of a fishy character. Doesn't make you feel comfortable when around him."

"You go out there and check things out with this Wolfe. Make up a reason. Ask about Krueger's friendly work performance."

"Will do, Judge."

"Something just doesn't add up. Now listen here, Sheriff Thurow, you have twenty-four days to bring this skumbag or, Sheriff, hear me, I'm going to bring in your worst nightmare."

"Nightmare? What do you mean? Already is."

Judge pointed his finger, "Twenty-four hours or I'm turning this entire case over to Detective Peterson. He'd find the fox in the chicken coop with one hand tied behind his back. Get it there, Sheriff? One hand tied?" *Bang!* Judge slammed his gavel. "Good day, Sheriff."

CHAPTER 92

OLD FRIENDS

Father Holtz—October 7, 1958, early afternoon

FATHER Holtz paid a visit to Father Girouard on Wednesday as planned. Father Girouard set aside the entire afternoon, hoping Father Holtz would have a chance to meet Cardinal Cullings. The two priests would be glad to see each other, as it had been two years since they were last together.

Arriving at the rectory, right next to the cathedral on Meridian Street, Father Holtz was totally immersed in anticipation of seeing his old friend and possibly meeting Cardinal Cullings. *Meeting a cardinal in person for the first time*, Father Holtz kept thinking.

He was first taken by the grandiosity of the four-columned stone cathedral of Saints Peter and Paul. He walked to the rectory and knocked just once. The door opened, and Father Holtz was immediately greeted by his old friend. Hugs were automatic after such a long time. At six foot two, Ronald Thomas Girouard was a striking figure.

"Good to see you, brother," they said in unison and then laughed at the timing.

"Come in, come in. We have so much to catch up on," Father Girouard said as he lead Father Holtz into the parlor. Looking around, Father Holtz saw so much beauty in the rectory. Art, paintings, traditional furniture, and the most beautiful wood floors and oriental rugs.

"I suppose you'll say this is a letdown from the Vatican?"

"Let's just say each place has its own character," Father Girouard said. Father Girouard was first to ask Father Holtz about his family and his position at South Wayne. Father Holtz proceeded to give Father Girouard a status report, but he did not mention his newfound friend, Father Michael Sullivan, or the cover-up at St. Leonard's.

"Okay, Ronald, you've heard all about my ecclesiastical adventures over this past decade." Both priests had been ordained during the war in 1943, though Ronald had by far landed at the top in achievement of their ordination class. "Now you can tell me, have you set your sights on becoming pope?" Father Holtz asked, only half kidding.

"Stop that," Father Girouard said to his good friend. "I'm just enjoying the present. Rome and Italy are beyond compare. Well, you know. You visited."

"Yes, the grandeur, antiquity, and mystery of Rome is a world unto its own," Father Holtz added.

"Let me tell you about my new work with Monsignor Luciano," Father Girouard mentioned. "He is the most wonderful, caring, and loving human being I have ever met. He's so humble. Like me, he came from a large family. His father was a bricklayer. Right now he is the vicar general to the bishop in the province Belluno in northern Italy. However, word has it that next month Luciano will become bishop. He's already told me that I can return at my will. Considering the downturn in Dad's health, Ben, I think it will be rather soon."

"Your bishop, or soon-to-be bishop, sounds like a great man."

"Oh, he is. He does not like the ostentatious riches of the church. He actually rides his bicycle to visit hospitals and parishes in the province. Ben, he rides a bicycle! I've been privileged on numerous occasions to ride with him. Trust me, bikes over there are not red Schwinns like we have here."

"I'd love to meet him someday," Father Holtz said.

"That just might happen, Ben. He would enjoy meeting you."

Father Holtz responded with a smile and a gleam in his eye.

"Like I told you before, Father Luciano is a saint here on earth. I really see a day when he could become pope. For now, I want to be there and enjoy his mission, work, and be close to him."

"Whoa, Ronald, I can sure feel your passion." Father Holtz put his head down. He paused and then said, "You speak so well of this saintly type priest. It reminds me of how good our Catholic Church is to be represented by priests of that caliber." Father Holtz paused again. "Ronald, your story brings me to Earth. Good priests like your soon-to-be bishop inspire us to dedicate ourselves to do good. I'm happy for you," he said, empathetic and pleased for his friend's success and passion.

"Yes. But, Ben, are you close with the bishop? What's his name?"

"Bishop Powers. Yeah, Bishop Powers." Father Holtz looked around as if to make sure there was no one else in the room. "Ronald, don't repeat this. My bishop, I'm sorry to say, is … well, he is the exact opposite of your Monsignor Luciano."

"What do you mean?" Father Girouard asked.

"Not now," Father Holtz said, shaking his head. "Time for that later."

"Ben, fate and faith sometimes come together." Leaning forward in his chair and talking in a lower voice, Father Girouard said, "Cardinal Cullings is so much like Luciano. It's … it's almost like they are brothers. Listen, the cardinal is very humble. He's a little softer spoken. He listens to you like you're the only person in the room. The cardinal goes around and visits hospitals and orphanages. Last week, he visited Christamore Settlement House on 16th Street. Lots of poverty there. We met this college student, a volunteer. Name was, let me see, Bob Lang. He liked working with those poor kids. He introduced Cardinal Cullings to the kids. They gravitated to the cardinal, of course. He even drove himself. Can you believe that? Just like Luciano riding his bike.

"Right now, the cardinal is speaking out on the whole issue of birth control. He doesn't come from a big family like Bishop Luciano—well, soon-to-be Bishop Luciano. He is also a strong advocate for the option of Mass being celebrated in English. I've heard him say he would like to see this change while still offering the option of Latin Mass for our traditionalists. I can't wait for you to meet, hopefully this afternoon."

"I've been thinking about meeting him all week," Father Holtz said. Then he chuckled. "Of course, I was anxious to see you too, Ronald. You know, I'm so proud of you."

"Nice of you to say. We've both come a—" Father Girouard stopped and then said, "Oh why, Cardinal Cullings."

Peeking his head in the door, the cardinal said, "Excuse me, Father Girouard. I knew your friend was coming. My meeting ended early, so I thought I'd stop in and say hello."

Father Holtz jumped up from his chair. Stunned, he didn't know what to say. The cardinal looked majestic, even regal, in his red cassock. The smile on the cardinal's face looked gentle. Father Holtz felt his heart race. *I've never met a cardinal,* he thought.

"Cardinal Cullings, I would like to introduce my friend, Father Ben Holtz."

The cardinal extended his hand. "Nice to meet you, Father Holtz."

Father Holtz replied, "I am honored to meet you, Your Eminence." Then he was at another loss of what to say.

Fortunately, Father Girouard picked right up. "I've been telling Father Holtz all about you, Your Eminence."

"Now, Father Girouard, not too formal. Cardinal Cullings will be fine. Just don't get too friendly and start calling me Gus," he said, nodding and chuckling.

"Here, Your Eminence, please have a seat." Father Girouard stood, giving his chair to Cardinal Cullings. He walked over by the desk and brought a side chair for himself. "Gus?" he then asked.

"Yes, that's what my family always calls me Gus … Gustav Anthony Cullings. My sister calls me G.A."

"Now that's a real shortcut. Where are you from, Your Eminence?" Father Holtz asked inquisitively.

"I'll have to correct you too, Father. It's Cardinal Cullings."

Father Holtz smiled and nodded. *He's really a nice guy.*

"I'm a Hoosier. Born and bred. My hometown is Terre Haute. All my family's from there. My mother came from a farm family. Kasameyer's their name. She and my dad were both born just after the Civil War. We were members of St. Benedict's. Have family who still go there. I try to get there a couple times a year." Sitting back in his chair with his elbows on the chair arms and his hands folded, he said, "What about you, Father Holtz? Where are you from?"

"Wisconsin. Actually, Waukesha."

"What's that?" the cardinal asked.

"Waukesha. Indian name. We have them up there. Mukwonago, Oconomowoc."

"I won't even try to say or spell those."

"So yes, that's where I'm from. Went to grade school and high school there and then on to Marquette University."

"Now that's a good school. Named after a priest," the cardinal acknowledged. "Father Girouard said you are now with Bishop Powers in South Wayne. I know him. We both have been in attendance at a number of bishops' conferences. How do you like it up there, Father?" the cardinal asked.

Father Holtz hoped his pause in answering the cardinal was not noticeable. "I've really been learning a lot—administration, working with the priests in our parishes around the diocese. Then of course there is learning how the bishop works, along with his secretary, Father Schmidt. I'm there to assist them." *I hope I scooted around that answer okay. Learning a lot,* he thought. Trying to change the subject, Father Holtz continued, "Do you mind if I ask, when did you become a priest ... and bishop?"

"*Ahhh,* smart questions. You just want to find out how old I am," Cardinal Cullings said with a laugh. "You won't have to figure. I'll just tell you. Born in Terre Haute, of course, like I said previously. I was ordained in 1914, became a bishop in '42, and fortunately Pope Pius made me an archbishop in 1950."

"When did you become a cardinal?" Father Holtz asked.

"That was 1954. Just think, four short years ago."

Father Girouard asked, "How many parishes have you served, Cardinal?"

"After ordination, let's see ... I spent four years as an assistant at St. Mary's in Westville, Illinois. From there, I was fortunate enough to become pastor close by in Danville, Illinois, at St. Patrick's. That church was one of the most beautiful parish churches I have ever seen. I was there for ten years. Although Danville was a small town, they have some outstanding parishes. Father Mottset is pastor at St. Paul's. Guess he's quite a character. Loves horses almost as much as his parishioners. Oh yes, Father Seisel in St. Mary's. He was after my time, I heard. They have a wonderful Catholic high school called Schlarman. New since, I believe, 1950."

"You sure have a good memory, Cardinal."

"Thank you, and if you are a good Bear's fan, Zeke Bratkowski is their quarterback. He's from St. Mary's and Schlarman High. Now that man can throw and even kick farther. Okay, boys, enough of that back history."

"Cardinal Cullings, I'm really interested to hear about your experience in the Vatican. That's if you have enough time," Father Holtz said with consideration.

"Thank you for asking, Father Holtz. Like Father Girouard, I also had an opportunity to study in Rome," Cardinal Cullings said. "How that happened is fate, luck, and a story from another time. That was '38 to '42.'"

"I'd like to hear that story," Father Girouard said.

"I was a theological administrator for the Conference of Bishops in the office of the pope's secretary. It was a worldwide responsibility. My Italian, Spanish, and German helped. It was during the reign of Pope Pius XI, but that was only for one year. Then our next pope was Pius XII. That was my good fortune. I worked in his office from '39 to '42. A good man. Remember, that was during the war. It was Pope Pius XII who sent me back to the states then as a bishop, and—still hard to believe—I became archbishop here in Indianapolis in 1950. Then this red cassock in '54."

"Excuse me, Cardinal Cullings," they heard the voice of a sister from the doorway. "Your appointment is here."

"Thank you, Sister. I'll be right there. I'd love to visit more with the two of you, but I've taken enough of your time. Maybe again someday before this good father heads back to Rome. He'll be pope someday," the cardinal said to Father Holtz about Father Girouard.

"I wouldn't bet against him," Father Holtz responded.

Cardinal Cullings nodded, patted Father Holtz on the shoulder, turned, and walked to the archway from the library. Then he stopped. "The two of you have a good day. Maybe the next time you might be interested in hearing about my last trip to Rome and my meeting with Pope John Benedict," he said with a playful smile on his face. "I really enjoyed meeting you, Father Holtz."

Knowing the cardinal was out of hearing range, Father Girouard put his hand on his good friend's shoulder. "That, my friend, was Cardinal Gustav Cullings. He and the soon-to-be Bishop Luciano are the most blessed priests I have ever met. Equally so, they are the two best men I've ever met. If my priesthood ended today, I would be the most fortunate of priests to have worked with both of them."

Father Holtz fell backward in his chair. "I will never forget meeting him. Never. He's so nice, humble, and personable."

"You are right, Ben, and he's a most blessed man. I've heard only parts of the story. Do you realize he just returned from Rome? He was there for almost a month," Father Girouard said, his voice rising in amazement. "And we're here talking to him like, I don't know, like a friend next door. Like a favorite uncle. Back in the seminary, we would never have imagined this," he said in almost exhausted enthusiasm.

"I agree. Thank you so much for making this possible, Ronald. This has been one of the most memorable experiences of my life. Hopefully someday we'll be able to hear more about the conclave he was a member of when they elected Pope John Benedict. Unbelievable," Father Holtz said. "And right here in Indianapolis."

"You know, Ben, Cardinal Cullings does not talk about our pope. Something tells me they are not of the same cloth."

"What do you mean, Ronald?"

"It's like they are so different in character. I don't really know the pope, but I do believe they may have different views regarding the ... let's say the 'openness of our church.'" Then, changing the subject, Father Girouard asked, "Would you like to go get a sandwich? There's a Steak 'n Shake just a few blocks away. Not fancy."

"Sounds great," Father Holtz responded. "That will give me some time to ask a favor of you. A really serious favor."

"Anything for you, Ben."

"Well, you won't believe this when I tell you."

Father Girouard wondered, *What could that possibly be?* The two friends took a break from their memorable meeting with the cardinal to go and celebrate with a quick dinner.

CHAPTER 93

WITHOUT YOU

Linda Singleton—October 11, 1958

LINDA could not help but think of Father Sullivan after his surprise visit the week before. She felt consumed by thoughts of the priest. Joey was away for the weekend visiting his aunt Rosalie in Huntington. Linda looked forward to two days alone. No work, no parent-teacher meetings, no St. Thomas Moore parish activities. She had much to do around the house—mending, washing curtains, playing handyman with a short to-do list that could only be attended to by herself. *The plight of a single mom,* she often thought. Joey, when around, would always lend a helping hand, but he was away. She even thought of taking a Sunday ride on the roads of Wabash County.

The sky was a bit overcast early that Saturday morning. Linda was busy with the nagging chore of replacing screens with storm windows before the winter winds blew. As she walked through the living room and approached the staircase, she stopped. A two-tone green Chevy was slowly driving by. She took a few steps toward the window. Linda squinted, focusing on the rear of the car as it stopped and then turned right in the direction of downtown. *Couldn't be,* she thought. *It was just a week ago. My mind … no, just wishful thinking. Couldn't be him.*

The sun played hide-and-seek. Drying the clothes on the backyard line was a chance Linda took, figuring the gentle breeze was a sign that the wash would dry quickly before any raindrops visited that morning. A half glass of milk, a ham sandwich on rye, and chocolate chip cookies made the night before offered a welcomed break. Once finished, Linda remained at the table and glanced through the *Plain Dealer* from a few days before. She noticed an article about the Wabash Reform School. Young boys and abuse sent a cold chill down her spine.

Concerns about Joey raced through her mind. Although troubled by the article that reminded her of Joey, Father Jaeger, and the doubt she harbored daily, Linda erased the thoughts about the dastardly subject when she heard a distant crack of thunder. After looking out the kitchen window at some ominous clouds, she stood up, rushed out to the backyard, and quickly pulled the clothespins that held the sheets, shirts, and pants on the line. Raindrops started to bounce on the last sheet. Linda quickly carried the last three storm windows to the basement through the exterior cellar door.

Back inside the house, Linda sat on the down-filled couch in the front room with a cup of hot coffee and stared out the window. She could hear the pitter-patter of raindrops bouncing off the newly hung storm windows. Joey, Father Jaeger, and the priesthood consumed her thoughts for some time. A black car drove by. Linda's mind reflected on the green car she had noticed earlier that morning. Stretching her neck, she looked outside at the corner and thought, *Yes, it was him. Had to be.* The street was very quiet with little traffic; it was really only used by those living in the neighborhood.

It's Saturday. The rain will let up. I'll finish my chores. Then go to confession. I must. Can't wait any longer to see him. Linda walked back into the kitchen and checked Sunday's bulletin to see who would be hearing confessions this day. *Father Warren? Father Sullivan?* Pleased to see the right name, Linda glanced at the white kitchen wall clock hanging to the left of the door. *Four hours. Perfect. Plenty of time.*

Later that afternoon, Linda took a deep breath, squeezed her rosary, and closed her eyes in anticipation of the mumbled whispers on the other side of the sliding confessional door. She heard a slight ruffle of the thin black curtain, as Father Sullivan slid the small confessional door open.

"Bless me, Father, for I have sinned. My last confession was … " Linda hesitated. "Michael, I'm not here for confession. I just need to hear your voice."

On the other side of the curtain, Father Sullivan braced his hand against his forehead, his finger and thumb spanning his brow. Surprised, he paused and then said calmly, "Hello, Linda. It's good to hear your voice again."

The suddenness of his presence caused a rush of excitement inside her and an immediate longing for the priest. Linda felt his closeness in her own dark, quiet closet.

She sensed a welcoming tone from the other side of the confessional. "Michael, my dear Michael, please forgive my sin before it is committed."

"Linda, let there not be sin. Just to have you here, well, it's ... maybe it's good for both of us, but no, not a sin."

"Oh, thank you, Michael. I pray daily. I do all I'm supposed to do. I work hard. I care for Joey." Linda felt the heaviness of her breath, the desire to just burst forward and tell him all. She wanted to tell him of her desires. Everything that was hidden in her heart. She wanted to reach out and hug him, to give of herself completely, but she first held back, paused, and then said, "Michael, please understand, and I know this is wrong, but I need to see you. I try, but I'm weak. I long for you. I dream about our cherished times together an eternity ago. Last week was not enough." She took a breath, not giving him a moment to respond. Linda sensed her entire being, her body, reacting to the freedom of telling him. "Michael, please understand—"

Father Sullivan cut her off. "I hear you, Linda. Every word. Yes, I do understand. I too have thought of you since our visit." Then there was silence.

Linda waited, giving him a chance to tell her.

"This can't be. We both know. Maybe this is the right time. I'm a priest, but every day, I am a man. And yes, I continuously long for you. Right now, I can't think about sin. Only you, close to me, quiet, darkness, together, the closeness of your body next to mine," Father Sullivan said, speaking from the heart.

Linda closed her eyes, her head dropping to her hands in relief. For a moment, Linda Singleton and Father Sullivan listened in silence.

Enclosed in the darkness of the confessional, Father Sullivan made the sign of the cross. "But where? When? How can we?" he asked.

"Michael, it's Saturday. Joey's away at his aunt's in Huntington. I'm alone. Our street is quiet. The alley behind the garage is hidden by the neighbor's trees. Maybe you can go for a walk. Tonight. I'm home and alone. I will have the back door unlocked. Let's just see. No plans. Just be together. If you can't, I understand."

"I rarely see Father Warren after dinner on Saturdays. He usually retires early before his Sunday Masses. He will not notice my absence."

"Michael, nine or nine thirty? Will that work for you? I will have the kitchen light on. There is a gate by the garden at the back corner of the garage." Linda waited. Then with hesitancy she whispered, "If you change your mind or are unable to come, I will understand."

"The time is perfect. I will see you this evening, Linda. I want to be with you so very much. Go in peace."

The small door of the confessional slid closed. Linda made the sign of the cross, immediately left the church, and walked home. Her only thought was wondering whether they would spend time together that evening.

Later that evening, shortly before 9:00 p.m., the rectory phone rang in the first floor hall. Father Sullivan was heading for the stairs to his room on the second floor before leaving for an evening walk.

"Hello. This is Father Sullivan." He listened. "Yes, yes, I understand. Yes, I want to. Thirty minutes." He hung up the phone and went directly to his room.

Linda couldn't help but watch the clock on the kitchen wall. In her mind, everything was set. *Is this really happening? Will he show up?* The coffee was on the stove ready to percolate. More importantly, she uncorked a bottle of merlot and set two wine glasses on the dining room table. Linda anxiously waited in anticipation. Minutes seemed like hours. She spent time walking back and forth between the living room, dining room, and kitchen. Noticing the dim street light through the front windows, she walked over and pulled down the shades.

After paging through *Life Magazine* for the second time, Linda walked upstairs to check her room just in case. It was 10:08 P.M.. She moved to stand in the dining room. The wait too long, Linda poured her first glass. She knew it was Michael's favorite. Swirling the wine, Linda watched the red liquid move around inside the glass. After a long slow sip and then two, she felt a slight rush and then drank some more. At 10:24 P.M., she poured her second glass. *He's not coming.*

Ten minutes later, Linda poured more wine into the half-filled glass, stood, walked into the kitchen, and turned off the light. She then headed back to the dining room, living room, and started to walk upstairs. The wine took the edge off her disappointment as she turned and took the first steps up to her room.

The rap on the back screen door was hardly audible. Linda stopped. *It's him. Please.* Returning to the kitchen, she flipped the light on and immediately saw a dark figure standing outside. Quickly opening the door, Linda stepped onto the porch. "Michael, I'm s—"

He did not wait for her to finish. "I'm so sorry. Forgive me," he said.

"Sure, sure, that's okay. You're here."

As he took off his black fedora, she thought, *How handsome.* He unbuttoned his jacket. His dark gray casual shirt was a perfect contrast to his black trousers.

Following Linda into the kitchen, he said, "I know I'm late. I'm so sorry. About eight thirty, I received an urgent call from one of my troubled parishioners. Health problems, money, and now her husband. I won't go into it, but she really needed me to stop by her house. By nine o'clock, I was there, not here. I should have called, but—"

"Michael, that's fine. You know I understand that so many need you. You're here. That's all that matters."

He looked directly into her eyes, "Yes, Linda, you always did understand." He took her hand and gently put his arms around her. Linda took in all of his embrace.

Taking a deep breath, she looked up at him, "Some wine? Your favorite." Linda poured a glass of merlot.

Father Sullivan looked down. "That sheepish little smile. I'll bet you've already had yours."

Linda rolled her eyes. "Come on." She took his hand, and he followed her into the front room.

Only the Tiffany lamp between the chairs on the window side was turned on. The illumination created a softness to the room. Linda sat down in the middle of the couch, leaving just enough room between herself and the high stuffed arm at the far end for Michael to sit. He sank into the down-filled cushion. "I always loved this couch."

"My grandmother's when she was married in 1918. Mom never had room for it, so she gave it to me when she moved into the Mattern Apartments up on Fisher Hill."

"Oh yes, Mattern Apartments. I still take Holy Communion to Mrs. Boyd. She's about eighty-eight now. Linda, come on. Let's talk about you."

Linda looked up over her left shoulder. "No, let's talk about you."

"How about us?" Father Sullivan replied as he placed his right arm completely around Linda's shoulder.

"Oh, Michael, I always feel so good, so relaxed when I'm with you. Daily, I remember our times together. I remember, Michael," Linda said as she rested her head on his shoulder.

He tilted his head toward hers while stroking her right arm. Linda felt her body naturally move closer as she placed her left arm on his leg. Michael flinched. Placing his hand on hers, he lifted it while standing up.

"Michael, what's wrong? I didn't mean to—"

"It's okay, Linda. I just need to … " He stood up and walked around the side of the chair across from the couch. He stared out the front window. Linda remained on the couch and waited.

"No, no," he whispered from across the room, still staring out the window. "It's not you. I'm just torn. I've thought about you every day since we last met and now this evening and … " He stopped and turned around. He saw her alone, almost unprotected between the arms of the old couch. "It's like I know this is wrong. My vows, my life." Taking a deep breath, he said, "Yet, it's you I want to be with. So much, I want to take your hand and walk you up those stairs. Like, like … "

"Like before, Michael?" she whispered.

"Yes, yes. Like before."

Linda reached out her hand. "Come here. Come back here."

Michael walked back to the couch. He stood in front of her and took her hand. Instinctively, she pulled him down beside her.

"It's been so long," he whispered softly.

"That's for both of us." Linda could feel his warm breath. "*Shhh*. Let's enjoy this time, these moments together. There's no hurry. Nobody in the world knows we're here," Linda said, trying to relax the priest.

Michael reached over, picked up his glass of wine from the side table, and held it in front of Linda. Slowly, she took a sip from his glass and tasted the glorious red bouquet. Michael took a sip and then set the wine aside. Michael turned and looked Linda directly in her brown eyes. He saw her innocence. He felt her longing.

"Please understand, my dear Linda, so much to say. I need to tell you, but … " He lifted his finger to her lips. "You are more dear to me, Linda, than ever."

Placing his left hand on her cheek, he gently leaned over, and their lips met. Linda felt some restraint.

"Linda," he whispered. "My heart beats. I must make the right choice."

"Together, we will make the right choice, Michael."

Linda felt her whole body wanting to give up to him. "As we must, Michael."

Michael felt the unrestrained rush and his affectionate desire for Linda. The couch was comforting. Time passed. Together, they sat, each engrossed in their own thoughts and desires for one another. Linda knew what was right for her. Father Sullivan looked into the eyes of Linda as he knew what must be right for him.

CHAPTER 94

CLOSING IN

Clarence Wolfe—October 23, 1958

CLARENCE Wolfe felt a rush of panic as he watched the green pickup truck slowly drive away from the reform school. Wasting no time, he immediately went back into his office, lit a Lucky, picked up the phone, and dialed Randall Zilbar. Zilbar answered.

"Randall? Wolfe here. We've got a big problem. I mean really serious."

"Hold on. What are you talking about?" Zilbar asked.

"I'm talking about our worst nightmare. Twenty-four years ago."

Zilbar reacted internally, his pulse heightening. "Explain," he demanded.

"You know the other boy? The one who was with me in the chair? He walked into the school this morning. I couldn't believe my eyes. He said he's looking for you because you were the one who did it. You know what I mean. This guy is looking for you. He seems really serious. I don't like this at all, Randall."

"Hold on there," Zilbar replied. "Don't say that kid was with me. You were with two boys. I wasn't even there. You just told me the story. I can't cover for you."

"Wait a minute, Randall. You were there with me. That's when he stopped breathing. You were all over him. On top. You know you were totally naked. Remember? I can still see you leaning down and picking up the wine bottle, taking another swig. It's all coming back. So vivid. Yoder kept screaming, 'Help, please help.' That's when you reached down and put your left hand over his face. I said, 'Stop, you'll smother him!' Remember?"

"Didn't happen, you lying bastard!"

"Yes. Yes, you kept pushing down with your left hand with the wine in your right. That's how he died! It wasn't from you pumping him! You smothered him, killed him with your own hand, with that big left hand! Remember, you screamed, 'Goddamn, he bit me. Holy shit, he took a chunk out of my finger'? You had blood all over. That's when you took the pillow, put it on his face, and held it tight. He stopped breathing. I remember seeing your blood all over the pillow. Then you turned him over, slapped him, and jumped down on his back. Zilbar, he was already dead! You smothered him! Sick! Sick! Then you turned him back over and covered him up with a blanket. You frantically yelled, 'Ah, my finger!' You got blood all over your white shirt. When we got in the car to drive away, you said, 'Look, the little bastard took a hunk from the bottom of my middle finger.'

"You might think I'm your lackey, but you aren't pinning that one on me." Wolfe couldn't believe his own ears, hearing himself talking to Zilbar that way. He was even more shocked when Zilbar failed to respond to his insubordinate words. "Better think twice. You're not lying yourself out of this one, Randall. This kid's pretty smart. He wants to see you."

"No way am I going to talk with him. Kid's a liar. Screw that little son of a bitch. It's your problem, Wolfe."

"He's not little. Name's Homer Atkins. He's the one who ran out of the room. Remember? I talked with him. He's thirty-six now. That's twenty-four years ago, Randall. Twenty-four goddamn long years. Now he shows up. Somehow he found your name. Lives over in Huntington. This kid's got the goods, Randall. If you don't meet him, he's going to the authorities. We've got just a couple days."

"He's not cornering me. Little bastard!" Zilbar slammed the phone down and began pacing.

Son of a bitch. Goddamn that Wolfe. Mario's gotta handle him. After about an hour of no calls, no interruptions, Randall Zilbar's first thought was to call Gino Moretti. He picked up the phone and dialed. *Ring, ring.* Then without hesitation he slammed the phone down. *No, can't involve him yet. I'll take care of this without Gino ever finding out. Money will trump a lawyer*. Randall figured out in his own mind that power could over-whelm finesse.

Wolfe called Randall Zilbar back but to no avail, as he was now out of the office until early afternoon. The entire morning was quite wrench-ing as he checked the clock every five minutes. Wolfe was finally able to get through to Randall. Again, he explained the seriousness of the problem. Subsequently, Zilbar agreed to meet Wolfe late that afternoon at the Indiana Hotel for a brief thirty-minute session.

After hanging up the phone, Clarence Wolfe took a triple drag, buried his cigarette, and then lit another. Reaching into the bottom drawer, he pulled out a bottle and glass and poured a double. *Zilbar thinks he can control everything. Not this time. Stupid arrogant bastard. Atkins is in control.*

Sitting alone, Wolfe emptied the bottle. Smoke filled the room. In the distance, he heard a knock at the door.

"Mr. Wolfe, you okay? You've been in here alone since before noon." Miss Gardner waved her hand back and forth as she walked into Wolfe's office. She tried to clear the smoke blocking her path to his desk.

"Time is it there, Garner girl?" His voice was groggy.

"Almost three, sir. You need to cut back on those cigarettes."

"Cut who? Back who?"

"Those cigarettes, sir. You're gonna kill yourself."

"Kill myself? You should, should. Let's see. Me? Look who's talkin', Missus Garner. You puff more than a … than me," he said, the whiskey slurring his words. "You're like a smokestack all day. Your breath smells like limburger cheese."

"That's enough, Mr. Wolfe. Yours doesn't smell like spring flowers. You've got a bad case of monkey breath. Cigarettes and booze."

"He pointed his finger at her like a gun. "Hey, that's a, let me see, that's a … an idea. Bingo. Gotta gun?"

"Sir, I'm making a stiff pot of coffee."

"Stiff, did you say? Why, Missus Garner, shame on you."

"Be right back." Gardner turned and quickly stepped out of the room. *Smoking, drinking. May be the boss, but he's a fool. Something's bothering him for sure.*

Clarence spent the next hour with his head buried in his folded arms on the desk, hoping the coffee would bring him back to his senses. He had to be in good condition to meet Randall Zilbar at the hotel. *Couple hours yet*, Wolfe thought.

Miss Gardner returned an hour and half after serving the coffee, which was untouched and cool.

Trying to figure out how they'd escape the claims of Homer Atkins, Wolfe concluded, *Yes, it'll come down to money. Zilbar will just pay him off. Yeah, that's it.*

"Mr. Wolfe, you have a call. Says his name is Homer Atkins. He's that guy who was here earlier today."

"Thanks for reminding me. Close the door!" He pulled out a Lucky and picked up the phone. "Clarence Wolfe here. Yes, Atkins."

"Mr. Wolfe, hope you've had time to inform Mr. Randall Zilbar about our meeting. I want to meet next Friday night at 7:00 p.m. at the reform school."

"Wait. Wait, Atkins. He said he won't meet. He's a tough guy. Control guy."

"I can understand that. However, this time is different. He'll be there or I'm going to the police. You both be there at seven o'clock sharp, Friday."

"I'll do my best to get ahold of him, but I ah, I have to tell you, I can't promise. Zilbar doesn't like people telling him what to do."

"Is that so. Mr. Wolfe? You tell Mr. Zilbar that this time after twenty-four years, I'll be glad to tell him what to do."

"Okay, okay. I'll get him. I'll get him here."

Homer Atkins added, "Oh, I almost forgot. I have another witness. Now there's two of us. Only thing I don't have is … is, ah … "

"What don't you have, Atkins?"

"Just don't know who the big guy with the mustache was, but I think Zilbar will tell us. Don't you? You know Zilbar better than you let on. See you Friday. Don't forget now." *Click.*

Later that afternoon, Zilbar walked past the doorman of the Indiana Hotel without acknowledging his presence. The doorman tipped his hat. "Good afternoon, Mr. Zilbar." *Rich snob.*

Zilbar walked into the lobby. Taking off his topcoat, he proceeded toward the bar. The receptionist kept her head down, pretending not to see him.

Not expecting a response, the bartender Armond said, "Good afternoon, Mr. Zilbar."

Randall gave one nod. Armond reached for the vodka on the top shelf. Zilbar hung his hat and coat and proceeded to his usual place in the corner booth. He liked the service and the fact that Armond respected his privacy.

Within three minutes, the bartender set a perfectly prepared martini in front of him. "Someone be joining you, sir?"

"Yes, in a couple minutes." He took one soothing sip and heard the clock in the foyer bong five times. *There he is. At least on time.*

Wolfe slid into the booth and motioned to the bartender. "Hello, Randall. Thanks so much. This is serious. Extremely," Clarence Wolfe spoke in an anxious voice. His hand tremored slightly.

"I'm listening. Explain," Zilbar commanded.

"You have to meet with this Atkins. Deny all you want, but we both know what happened. Now this guy says he was the other boy, and … " Wolfe leaned forward. "He has a witness."

Zilbar listened and hid his concern. "This martini is excellent. Would you like one?"

"No, no. My whiskey is on its way."

"There was no witness. He can't prove a thing." Zilbar sipped his martini slowly. "*Ahhh.* Clarence, you are overreacting."

"This kid, I mean this guy, was there. Hell, he's the witness, as I was. I saw what you—"

Zilbar pointed, cutting Wolfe off. "Wolfe, shut the fuck up! I wasn't even there!"

Wolfe shot back, "Damn it, Randall, listen to me." Wolfe leaned forward with his elbows on the table. In a low whisper, he said, "We meet with him or he's going to the police."

"Just bluffing. Probably wants money."

"Yeah, yeah, that's right."

"Well, he's not getting a dime from me. Nothing to hide." Randall spoke in his usual narcissistic, arrogant tone.

"Okay, okay, but meet him. See what he wants."

"When?"

"Next Friday at 7:00 p.m. or he's going to the police on Saturday. He wants only you."

"What about you, Clarence?"

"He doesn't know who the other guy was. Just found out it's you, Randall."

"My lawyer will take care of him. Anyway, if he doesn't know the other guy and we meet, then he'll find out you were there."

"Hell no. Leave me out or … or I'll … Leave me out or I'll tell him the truth. It was you who killed that little kid. I know. I saw you do it. Then you covered him up, and we both left. That's when … that's when you ran into that freak Bednar. Bednar has known it was you all this time. He's been waiting. Your ass is grass. No telling what that Bednar will do, Randall."

Randall glared at Wolfe and raised his finger again. "Don't you talk to me like that, you sick son of a bitch, or I'll have you—"

"Have me what? Killed? Just like Krueger? I've got you figured out, Randall. Krueger didn't just jump off a cliff. Well, maybe he did with not so friendly a push."

Calmly, Zilbar raised two fingers to Armond. He nodded. "Damn this martini is good." He took the last sip. "Tell you what, Mr. Wolfe," Zilbar said with a current of sarcasm. "Seven o'clock next Friday it will be. I'll meet Mr. Atkins," Zilbar said, keeping his motive to himself.

"Good. Now you're being reasonable. You can take care of him. Little money. That's all. Everyone does what you want, Randall. You always figure it out. Always get your way."

"Tell me now, who'd he say the witness was?" Zilbar asked.

"He didn't, but I know. I figured it out. It's Bernard Bednar. Remember the guy who came running down the hall that night?" Wolfe jarred Zilbar's memory.

"No, didn't see anyone that night. We just left out the side door. You weren't even working there in '34."

"Yeah, I know. I know. Now I ask myself, what the hell?" *What the hell was I thinking going back and accepting that job?* Wolfe thought after Zilbar's acknowledgment that he was there.

"That's appreciation," Zilbar replied. "You come back from war.

'Randall, I need a job.' I knew who owed you. I made the call. Made this job happen for you. More than you are worth. One favor for another, and you ask why?" he reminded Wolfe. "Now look how you screwed it up. All this." Zilbar shrugged.

Having calmed down, Wolfe said, "I know it was after the war, but I didn't forget his face for twelve years. Within a week, I saw that ugly Bednar face. Should of gotten rid of him then." Clarence wondered if he should spill the rest. *Now's the time.* "Yes, this Bernard is the same guy who messed up Krueger. Also been told he's roughed up a couple bullies on the floor."

"Why the hell didn't you get rid of him?" Zilbar asked.

"Couldn't. He saw us that night in '34."

"Who is this son of a bitch?"

"Bernard Bednar. I told you he's been working here since the early '30s. Hard worker. Keeps to himself. He's not retarded, just slow. Doesn't even have a car. Lives with his folks over someplace off Pike Street."

Randall Zilbar lifted his second martini as if to toast. "You know, Clarence, you're dumber than I thought. You kept him here? All your goddamn fault. Now we've got this mess. I wanna see him."

"Atkins?" Wolfe asked. "Bednar?"

"Yes, I want to see both of them. Atkins and Bednar. I want to know what I'm dealing with. You just listen to me. Make sure this Bernard character is working Friday evening. I want to see him. I'll take care of this entire matter. Everyone."

"Sure I can, Randall. Let's see, *hmmm*, I can have him stay a little later and clean the floors in the front hall between seven and seven thirty."

"Good. I'll take care of the rest," Zilbar said with a confident smile.

"I knew you would, Randall. I just knew it."

Randall Zilbar and Clarence Wolfe tipped their glasses. Clarence Wolfe ordered a second whiskey, sat back, and pulled out a pack of Lucky Strikes. He hit the pack against his left hand and reached out to Randall. "Have one."

"Don't mind if I do. Why thank you, Clarence." Zilbar leaned over and accepted the light from Wolfe. With a slight smile on his face, he took a soothing sip of his martini and then a long drag of the cigarette and thought, *All three of these witnesses will be handled. Handled my way.*

PART VII

PLANS AND RESCUE

MEETING THE WITNESSES

Randall Zilbar—October 31, 1958

RANDALL Zilbar turned into the long drive of the reform school. The night was clear and cool. Stars filled the sky. The moon was full. The parking spaces in front were empty with the exception of one gray-and-white two-tone 1955 Oldsmobile and an older model green pickup truck that was parked at its side. Zilbar pulled up and parked next to the truck. He thought of how out of place his brand new Cadillac looked.

After getting out of the car, he straightened his long coat, adjusted the collar once, and secured the wide brim of his hat. Advancing up the steps with complete confidence, he entered the building. The wide main hall pulled his gaze to the back of the building and the cross hallway. He remembered the room to the left. Zilbar paid no attention to the lone figure at the end of the hall, sliding the mop back and forth across the terrazzo floor. The figure looked up and stared and then continued to push the mop back and forth. Zilbar didn't notice the glare.

The door of Wolfe's office was open, and the lights were on. Two men stood, waiting for his appearance.

"Good evening, Mr. Zilbar."

"Clarence." Zilbar, having removed his hat, glanced at the younger man in the flannel shirt. "You must be Atkins?"

Homer didn't reply to the much taller, well-dressed Zilbar.

"This is Homer Atkins. He's here to meet you," Clarence said nervously.

No handshakes. Homer nodded. He purposely gave a cold shoulder.

Zilbar wasn't accustomed to being stiffed. *Goddamn, it could be him. No mistake,* Homer thought.

"Mr. Zilbar, yes, you haven't changed much in twenty-four years."

"Don't know what you're talking about. Now what's this all about Wolfe? Let's get on."

Clarence took Randall's tweed topcoat and carefully set it across Miss Gardner's desk, the nearest location without leaving the two. "Let's go into my office. We'll talk."

Atkins's first words were, "No need. We'll talk in the room."

Immediately Wolfe's face grew red. "I'm sure Mr. Zilbar would prefer the comfort of my office."

"I'm not here to make Mr. Zilbar comfortable."

"Exactly why are you here, Mr. Atkins?" Randall Zilbar calmly asked the younger man.

"One reason, make no mistake. To identify Gordon's murderer."

"Sure, I can understand your conviction. At the same time, I will assure you this is the first time I've ever stepped foot in this school," Zilbar insisted.

"Are you sure about that, Mr. Zilbar? You sound a little defensive. Take us to the room," Atkins ordered Wolfe.

Zilbar nodded once to Wolfe. "Go ahead."

"If you say so. Gentlemen." Clarence Wolfe opened his hand to the door. "Follow me." He led the way down the hall.

There he is. Wolfe looked down the hall and saw Bernard Bednar as planned. Back and forth with the mop. Bernard looked up, not expecting the three men approaching at this time of the evening. Wolfe passed Bernard. Homer stopped, looked, and smiled a guarded smile but didn't say a word. *That's him.* Having seen Bernard, Wolfe's mind flashed back. Over Bernard's shoulder, Homer saw the staircase to which he had run that night twenty-four years ago. *That's him. I remember his face as I rushed out the door,* Homer remembered looking back at Bernard.

Zilbar approached the solitary figure gripping the mop handle last. Bernard's chin rested on his two hands at the end of the mop, anticipating Zilbar's approach. Tightly, Bernard gripped the handle as if it was Zilbar himself. Zilbar passed without even a glance at Bernard. Twenty-four years hadn't erased Zilbar's thin face, brown hair, and cold eyes. The desire to attack Zilbar was instant. Having paid no heed to the man with the mop, Zilbar turned left, following Atkins. Bernard continued, back and forth over the terrazzo floor. Wolfe unlocked the door. Atkins walked in. Zilbar followed.

First to speak, Zilbar said with complete ease, "Comfortable-looking room. Are we going to talk here? This will be fine, but I have little to say."

"Just a question or two," Atkins replied.

Zilbar's back was still to the open door. Casually, he stood with his hands in his pockets, trying to act relaxed. His heart raced. Not knowing exactly what to say, he said, "Mr. Atkins, what is it you have to say? Have a question?"

"That's a handsome suit, Mr. Zilbar. Gray, isn't it?"

Zilbar lifted his lapel. "Yes, gray. A hint of charcoal."

"Do you wanna take it off, along with your tie and white shirt?" Atkins asked, catching Zilbar off guard with the alarming request.

Zilbar's shoulders tightened. His gaze clashed with Homer's. He looked to Wolfe for an answer. "What the hell you mean by that?"

"I meant no offense. Just asking if you would be more relaxed if you took off your clothes and stood naked in front of the couch. That could better remind you of when you stood right there. Maybe like old times' sake. Remember July 1934?" Atkins asked, jarring Zilbar with a slap of sarcasm. "Think back twenty-four years to that dreadful night you stood over Gordon. I can still hear you breathing, Mr. Zilbar. I mean panting, as you hovered over defenseless Gordon."

"Stop right there! I don't know what you are talking about."

Atkins continued. "Gordon was crying for help. He begged you to get off. I remember his 'No', so you smothered him. Smothered him to save your ass! From the corner of my eye, I saw you cup your left hand over his face, extinguishing every sound from his body. Then suddenly you yelled, 'He bit me! Goddamn little bastard!' Blood gushed. 'He took a chunk!' Maybe this time Gordon won't bite a chunk from your finger. Remember?"

Zilbar slammed the heels of his hands together. "I have had enough of your insults. I'm leaving now!"

He turned around. Before he could exit, Zilbar stiffened at the figure of the man, this time without the mop, blocking the doorway, both arms spread. Bernard's hands gripped the door frame. Zilbar turned into his clutches.

"Grab his left hand!" Atkins shouted. "Palm up!" Like a vise, Bernard's right hand clamped Zilbar's left wrist. "Turn his hand over, Bernard! Open it up! Look at his middle finger!"

"Let me go!" Zilbar pleaded.

"Open it!" Immediately detectable was the large diamond ring on Zilbar's middle finger.

"Diamond ring on it. *Uumpgh.*"

"Pull it off, Bernard!"

Zilbar jerked back. "No!"

Bernard paid no heed. With one pull, the giant ring came off, revealing a noticeable missing chunk of finger from an injury sustained twenty-four years before.

Homer Atkins walked over. "Open your hand." He looked up at Zilbar. "Gordon took a part of you to his grave. That's why the diamond on the middle finger."

Zilbar was mute.

Wolfe blinked, speechless. "Get out of Mr. Zilbar's way."

"No. Not yet. *Uumpgh.*" He stared directly at Zilbar. "I never forgot your face. You killed Gordon. I was there. *Uumpgh.*"

"Holy shit, Bednar, what the hell you saying?" Wolfe asked, stepping one pace forward.

Homer watched as Bernard took control.

As the words unfolded, Zilbar, having had enough, stepped forward. "Outta my way, you retarded son of a bitch!"

Hand open, Bernard slammed Zilbar's chest with the thud of a Floyd Patterson punch. "Halt! I'll mess your pretty face. *Uumpgh.*"

Zilbar stopped, feet planted.

"You touch me, you killer, and I won't give you your tie clasp back," Bernard said to Zilbar. "*Uumpgh.*"

Zilbar stood in shock.

"RZ initials. I have it," Bernard said.

"Don't know what you're talking about. Tie clasp? Initials?"

Bernard's face broke into a small smile. "You do, killer man. *Uumpgh.*

You left it. Right there." Bernard pointed toward the end of the couch. "*Uumpgh*. RZ."

Zilbar knew he was had. Reaching up, he grabbed Bernard's wrist as if to take it away. *Stiff like steel.*

Wolfe's mind flashed back to Krueger's contorted, bloody face. "No. No. Don't hit him, Bernard. Let's be calm about this. Let's talk." Wolfe stepped forward.

"Get back, Wolfe," Bernard said, stepping away from Zilbar. "*Uumpgh.* I saw you there that night with this gray suit. You were there too," Bernard said, looking directly at Wolfe and his full mustache. "I saw you both run out of the room. You, Wolfe, and this Zilbar. You both there. Been watching you for years, Mr. Wolfe. *Uumpgh.*" Bernard looked directly into Zilbar's piercing eyes.

"No, no, that wasn't me," Wolfe said fearfully. "It was him. He did it." He instinctively pointed to Zilbar.

Bernard lowered his hand, stepped forward in front of Wolfe, and looked up. "Know you were there. Now I know both you. Little Gordon's dead because of you two bad guys."

He's right. Now I see. Yes. Square jaw, mustache. Those eyes. We're all here, Homer thought, looking at Wolfe. He stood there, not saying a word as he watched Wolfe and Zilbar incriminate one another. *Good job, Bernard.*

Zilbar turned and walked through the doorway. He had found exactly what he wanted—the witness, Bernard Bednar. Bernard turned around and followed Zilbar into the hallway. He quickly came up behind Zilbar before he turned into the main hall. Bernard reached out and slammed his powerful hand on Zilbar's shoulder. With the iron clasp of his left hand squeezing like a vice, he turned the taller man around.

Looking up at Zilbar and squinting his eyes, he said, "I want to kill you just like you killed Gordon. You are a bad man. *Uumpgh.* I will get you soon!" he threatened.

Randall tried to push Bernard's hand away. Bravely, he looked down into his eyes as Bernard let go of Zilbar's shoulder and closed both his hands into a single fist.

"Fuck you, you ugly bastard," Zilbar warned. Then he turned and walked toward the front door.

Bernard followed into the main hall and watched Zilbar walk away. He waited until Zilbar was out of sight. Then Bernard walked over, retrieved his bucket and mop, turned, and walked back toward the lower level stairs. *Back and forth. Back and forth.*

Back in the room, Atkins stared at Wolfe. "This is not what I planned, but now I know. It was you with Zilbar that night. That guy remembered. Now I can see you, you decrepit, deceitful bastard. My eyes are open this time."

"Bednar didn't know what he was talking about. I wasn't here, I mean there, that night," Wolfe said to Atkins. "To be honest, I don't even think Zilbar was here. You've made this all up. You just want money. Now I know. Go ahead and go to the police. They'll never believe you against Randall Zilbar."

Homer Atkins smiled. "Don't worry, Mr. Wolfe. Now I know it was you. Now I know who Zilbar is. It was you who said: 'Randall, stop over there. Back off. You'll smother the kid.' You were right. He should have stopped. He killed Gordon Yoder. He didn't even hear you. He was in heat, raging, an uncontrollable craze for his own. He's an animal just like you. You bastard, I remember you heaving, panting, and moaning all over me. I gagged. You made me vomit. I could take a knife to you right here." Homer lifted his knee in the direction of Wolfe's belt. "You haven't seen the last of me, you filthy hypocritical bastard." Homer slammed his hands together, turned, and left the room.

Clarence Wolfe stood alone. All he could hear was, "I'll get you, you son of a bitch!" The words echoed as Homer Atkins charged down the hall and out of the building. Clarence Wolfe realized a perfect storm had come together after twenty-four long years. The course had changed in a manner he had not expected.

Homer left the building, walked to his truck, and sat alone. He was out of breath, and his mind raced. *Now I know. Now I can do something.* Homer Atkins laid his head back on the seat and thought about what had just transpired. There was a knock on the front fender. *Bernard.* Homer reached over and rolled down the passenger window.

Bernard filled the frame. "I'm Bernard. You were the little boy. *Uumpgh.*"

"Yes, I was. Now I remember you. Sit down inside? It's cold."

"Cold don't bother me. Zilbar bothers me. Wolfe bothers me."

"Thank you for what you did tonight," Homer said, looking kindly at Bernard.

"I'm not done. *Uumpgh*. Gonna get him. Wolfe too. They killed little Gordon."

"Did you understand how Gordon died?" Atkins asked Bernard. "Zilbar smothered him."

"Why?" Bernard asked.

"Gordon yelled for help. He pleaded 'no', so Zilbar smothered him. That's when Gordon bit the chunk of his finger. Proof! That and the tie clasp RZ."

"*Uumpgh*. He wears that diamond to cover it."

"You are totally right, Bernard. I know. I was there. Zilbar killed Gordon. Wolfe had me. I escaped. I saw you then. Now here we are twenty-four years later. The two of us. We meet a second time."

"Gordon was little. He left a little mark. Bernard will have to do a better mark. *Uumpgh*. Yep." Bernard looked at Homer. "I'll get 'em both. Give me some time. *Uumpgh*."

"Maybe I can help?" Homer asked.

"Nope. Let me. Got a phone?"

Homer reached for a pencil in the glove compartment, took a book of matches from it, and wrote down his number. "Here, call me at this number."

"Need some time. Call you in December. I'll take care of those two bad men. They killed little Gordon. Gotta go." Bernard turned and walked back toward the side of the school.

Someday, he thought, *I'll leave my mark on that bad man who killed little Gordon Yoder*.

Homer Atkins stepped on the clutch and turned the ignition as he watched Bernard walk away around the building and disappear into the darkness.

CHAPTER 96

PLANNING FOR JUSTICE

Bernard Bednar—October 31, 1958

THE ground was already beginning to freeze in late October. Winter was around the corner, a whole month early in 1958. There were a few scattered traces of snow as Bernard walked back home on that dark cold night. The full moon lit his way. He walked beyond the school in the direction of home.

The frozen grass crunched beneath his boots as he took the shortcut along the Wabash River toward Friends Cemetery. Soon he saw the hill ahead and the peaks and shadows of the ancient headstones. Instinctively, Bernard walked over to the crest and then down the hill to the simple stone on the far side. The shadow was small: *Gordon Yoder. April 2, 1922–July 22, 1934.*

Bernard stood in front of the gravestone. *Promised you, Gordon. I found him. It'll all end soon.*

He thought of Zilbar as he walked home along Pike Street. All was quiet in Monkey Town. Bernard first noticed the lit pumpkins on the Stouffer porch. 1-2-3-4-5-6-7-8 he counted. Every year he looked for the pumpkin with the frown on its face. *Sad pumpkin. Billy's pumpkin.* Most people were home, settled in after their Friday shopping trips to downtown Wabash. Bernard could see the flickering lights through the windows of a few who had televisions. He looked in the direction of his house at the end of Chestnut Street. Only a dim light from the kerosene lantern gave a small glow through the kitchen window. He kept walking in the direction of the faint light. He accidently stepped on a smashed pumpkin in front of his drive. *Mean kids.* Bernard reached the screen door and went inside to the warmth of the black stove, which was still giving off radiant heat. The only sound was the purr of the cat comfortably curled on the rocker in the front room.

Bernard knew his parents had retired for the evening, early, as they always did, sheltered in the darkness of their individual rooms. He threw a couple hickory logs into the stove. The immediate crackle of the split wood was soothing after the long, traumatic evening. Bernard put a pot of coffee on the stove. Soon hot, he filled the porcelain cup and headed up the enclosed stairs. He could hear the sounds of his parents sleeping as he walked by their separate rooms. Snores, blubbers, and old folk noises.

Once in his own room, Bernard took off his shirt, pants, and ankle-top leather work shoes. He unstrapped the sheath from his right calf. Asked to work late, he had decided to strap the blade on that early morning. Bernard was glad he hadn't needed his knife when he was in the room with Zilbar and Wolfe.

His room was chilly but not cold, as some warmth was filtering upward through the register beside the potbelly stove downstairs. Bernard walked over to the dresser, opened the drawer, and pulled out an old mustard-colored wooden box. He reached inside, lifted the gun, and spun the empty chamber. He leafed through his missal, flipping through the pages. Looking at the liturgy of the Mass, Bernard glanced at the picture of the priest and two altar boys. He remembered how badly he had wanted to be an altar boy—a dream like so many others unfulfilled. Putting the box away, Bernard walked over and sat on the side of his bed. He rocked back and forth, contemplating his plan.

Bernard figured exactly how he would find Zilbar. Wolfe would come later. He would check the phone book at work for Zilbar's home address. He heard it was a big stately house somewhere around Thorne Street. Bernard was familiar with the street name but not the neighborhood.

Bernard's Tuesday and Thursday work shifts always ended at 2:00 a.m. On Mondays, Wednesdays, and Fridays he was usually off work after the 5:30 dinner hour. There was plenty of time to walk home east on Pike, down the hill, and across the river at the Carroll Street Bridge. From there it was an easy walk through town to the north side and the Thorne Street neighborhood.

Randall Zilbar—October 31, 1958

Randall Zilbar lived in the old Cowgill Estate built back in the early twenties. Flanked by century-old oaks, the house stood on a crest above Thorne Street. A long drive meandered up to the portico on the south side. Just beyond, the carriage house provided space for four cars.

Zilbar enjoyed driving up to his house. *My wealth. Showcase. Only the finest.* His weekday evenings were usually busy either at work, at out-of-office business meetings, or at social events often held at the Indiana Hotel. Most often he arrived home around 7:00 p.m. at the earliest or as late as 10:30–11:00 p.m. or even around midnight. Every so often he would drive late at night west on Pike and Mill Creek Road to a house in the country.

The Indiana Hotel and the country club were his favorite establishments. Randall Zilbar was well-known in the Wabash area. One day soon, he would have other thoughts as he drove up his drive.

Bernard Bednar—November 3, 1958

Having scouted Zilbar's home during daylight hours on Saturday, Bernard made his first evening trip to Thorne Street and began his lookout for the man in the black Cadillac the following Monday. Bernard swept aside the cold evening air, bundled in his oversized brown wool coat. He pulled down the earflaps of his brimmed hat. His cold breath in the air was his only companion.

Large elms lined Thorne Street, one of which provided a comfortable lean for Bernard while he waited across the street from Zilbar's house. The driveway was on the far side of the house on the dead-end street. From there, one could look over the city of Wabash and the river valley below. The view was spectacular.

Bernard remained by the south side of the tree, hidden from the headlights of oncoming cars finding their way home after a long day. Two boys, hooting and hollering, rode by on their Schwinn bikes. One turned around and looked as he passed Bernard but paid no heed, panting as he pumped. A cocker spaniel was trying to keep up. *The boy's just turning around for the dog, not me,* Bernard thought.

The dog stopped and flashed his teeth at Bernard. Brow lowered,

Bernard pointed his finger at the toothy canine. The dog whimpered and darted back toward the boy, who was racing away. Sometime before 7:00 p.m., Bernard was joined by an owl that perched itself in an elm farther up the street. Bernard enjoyed the hoots. As the temperature dropped, so did his expectations of confronting Zilbar this first evening. *Waited twenty-four years. Few more days don't matter none.*

Bernard returned on Wednesday evening to find the same results. No Zilbar. He was equally disappointed that the old hoot owl, along with the boy on the bike and the snarling dog, didn't join him. Three weeks into November, each and every Wednesday, provided the same no-show of the big black car. However, Bernard did see Zilbar leave on Thanksgiving Day after dark, joined by his wife and three kids. Bernard walked home, knowing his time would soon come.

CHAPTER 97

ALL'S SAFE

Sheriff Thurow—November 26, 1958

SHUFFLING through a stack of papers on his desk, Sheriff Thurow came across some letters. One envelope was addressed to Ed Small in Muncie, Indiana. He immediately thought of the little man he had visited several months before.

That afternoon, the sheriff found himself driving alone. Just ahead, a sign read *Muncie City Limits, Population 41,602.* A man of conviction, Sheriff Thurow remembered his promise that he would return to visit Ed Small. When he called the reform school last week, he had been told that Eddie Small had not been involved in any incidents lately. *How can they really know what takes place behind closed doors? But a promise is a promise.*

Walking up the side stairs to apartment 2, Sheriff Thurow heard the same squeaks as his last trip. He knocked, waited a moment, and knocked again. Two fingers, cracked and grimy, pulled the shade aside behind the broken glass. Two eyes appeared, looking from the top row of glass panes. Cardboard now replaced two of the panes.

"What do ya want?" the edgy voice easily traveled through the unprotected window.

"Mr. Small, it's me, Sheriff Thurow."

"Oh yeah, yeah. Just a minute. Gotta put my shirt on." Soon the door opened. "Come in, Sheriff. Sure. Sorry. Come on in. Sorry not to recognize you. Some strange characters in this neighborhood," the disheveled little man said, still buttoning his shirt. "Yes, yes, so good to see ya. Come over here. Have a seat," he said, picking up a stack of newspapers from the one upholstered chair in the room. "Coffee? I'll make us some."

"No, no thank you. Just wanted to say hello. Then I'm gonna stop and see my sister. She lives here in town."

"How's my Eddie? How's my Eddie, Sheriff? I haven't heard a word. No letters since before the last time you were here."

"That's why I came to see you. I've checked with the school, and there's been no incidents involving Eddie," Sheriff Thurow informed him. "Of equal importance, Mr. Krueger is now gone. He's gone. No one knows where to find him. So Eddie's safe."

"That's good to hear. Safe from that grimy bastard? Good, good," Ed Small said as he anxiously leaned forward on a distressed kitchen chair. "What's most important is that Phillip Krueger is no longer at the school. Remember, his name in Eddie's letter?"

Sheriff Thurow looked at the unshaven man, who wore a smile across his face. He heard a squeak and then saw a mouse scurrying across the dirty torn rug directly behind the man's chair. *How does anyone live in a place like this?* "Strange thing happened after he was arrested."

"What do you mean, Sheriff? You gotta be kiddin'! How'd he get arrested in the first place?"

"He was abusing some boys. Caught cold turkey. And yes, Mr. Small, he had abused Eddie at the school. Then Krueger disappeared, skipped bail. Gone. We don't know where."

"Eddie was one of the boys?"

The sheriff hesitated. "Yes, Mr. Small. I'm afraid he was. I apologize. I should have informed you sooner—"

Ed small cut him off. "No, no. That's okay. You're here today. This means a lot to me."

"We don't know where Krueger is. He's just gone. Months now."

"That's no care of mine, sir, 'cause now I know the pervert can't get at my Eddie," Mr. Small said with a big smile on his face. "Hope he's rotting in hell," the little man said with conviction.

With that, the sheriff stood and said, "Well, I just wanted you to know Eddie's safe now. Promised you I'd come back."

"That you did, Sheriff. That you did. I'll be forever grateful."

"Just my job, Mr. Small. Gotta care for the victims. Those preyed upon. Glad I could help." Sheriff stood. "Now don't you worry anymore. Maybe you will be able to get your life back together," Sheriff said looking around the unkempt apartment.

"Yes, sir. Yes, sir, Sheriff. Maybe now I can get rid of these wine bottles, clean the place up a little. Even could go out and find a job now knowing my Eddie's okay."

"I hope you do, Mr. Small. Hope you do." As the sheriff opened the door, he turned and said, "You take care now, Mr. Small."

"Sheriff, you can count on that. This is the best news I've had in years. You know, Sheriff, things gonna start workin' out for me. Just gotta hunch." His wide smile revealed a number of missing teeth.

As the sheriff drove to his sister's, he thought of how strange and different parents' love could be for their children. Although Ed Small had not seen his son in a couple years, Eddie was the most important person in his life. Even more important than all those empty wine bottles.

Peter Goodnar—October 7, 1958

The long nightmare continued. Peter Goodnar's friends had noticed a changed, aloof, sullen, and very negative Peter. He now deterred any friendships he once enjoyed. Slender and of medium height and build, Peter's parents noticed he was losing weight. His brown hair was more matted and straight.

Anthony Gordon noticed Peter's continuing change of character. Anthony would walk to the park during recess and console Peter whenever necessary. They talked. Anthony had remained his friend. During Peter's downturn, in almost every aspect in his daily life, it was Anthony in whom he confided. Peter did not, however, reveal the monster in the dark hidden closet of his mind. To Anthony, Peter was just a shy boy with few friends and little confidence. Anthony found Peter nice, and they simply enjoyed one another's company.

Walking home with Anthony after school on that blustery October day, Peter heard, "Homo man, homo man, better run if you can."

Anthony stopped dead in his tracks. Placing his hand on Peter's shoulder, he said, "Wait. Here, hold my books."

With glare in his eyes and calm in his stride, Anthony turned and approached Herbie Ratski, who was just ten yards away. While not invading Herbie's space, Anthony pointed his finger directly at the bully's chest. Herbie's two chums stood behind him.

"You leave Peter alone, you hear? Or else your eyes will blacken, your nose will bend, and you will be missing some teeth. You understand?" he warned the intimidating bully. "If I ever hear you call Peter a name, if I ever see you pass him one of your nasty notes, then you will contend with me."

Herbie said nothing as he stood with his hands on his hips, just above his wide black belt. "Ah, piss on you. You don't scare me one bit, you nearsighted son of a bitch."

"Go ahead, talk tough, Herbie. You mess with Peter, or even Gene for that matter, you'll find out that your tough talk will quiver in the wake of my fist."

Anthony calmly turned his back on Herbie. No more words were exchanged. Herbie knew well enough to not cross Anthony.

Peter was happy to have Anthony as his friend. When home alone and absent from Anthony, Peter would gag and vomit. Daily, Peter's parents became more concerned. Talking with Sister Mary Michael did not help. When the sister tried to talk with Peter, it made matters even worse, as he felt more humiliated and embarrassed. Fortunately for Peter, Anthony was alwayss there for him. As Peter grew further apart from his parents and few friends, the bond with Anthony helped him through each agonizing week.

The visual image of Father Jaeger hovering over him overpowered Peter most every day. The image of the abusing priest was always in Peter's mind. The sight of the rectory was a reminder of the den upstairs, a place of entrapment he could not escape. Once the idea crossed his mind, Peter tried to evoke the courage and confidence to share his overwhelming secret with Anthony. He had yet to gain the courage.

CHAPTER 98

TRUSTED FRIEND

Father Girouard—October 7, 1958

THE overcast skies moved with a reckless abandon. Fathers Girouard and Holtz walked to the car, which was parked just outside the Steak 'n Shake.

"Best burgers in town," Father Girouard said, opening the car door. "Better put our windows up. Look at that sky."

Closing the door and cranking up the window, Father Holtz said, "Thanks for lunch, Ronald. That really hit the spot. Next time, White Castles are pretty good. They're only a nickel."

"Let's not keep our distance. We have to do this more often. I won't be here forever."

Father Girouard shifted into first gear, let out the clutch, pulled onto the street, and headed back to the rectory. About a block away, they could hear raindrops on the tinny uninsulated roof. Glancing over the plain metal dashboard, Father Holtz said, "I can tell you're an unimposing priest. You don't have a radio."

"Thanks, Ben. Give credit to Cardinal Cullings. This is his car."

"A black, what is this, a '55 or '56 black Plymouth?" Father Holtz asked.

"I think a '55. The cardinal is no-frills and no-pomp, just a regular good priest who happens to be a blessed cardinal."

I'm even more impressed. "Ronald, I've been wondering. I'd like to intrude upon you and ask for your help."

"Of course. Anything," Father Girouard responded.

"If you have just a little more time, I'd like to talk with you about something very important"

After Father Girouard drove into the side cathedral lot, he threw the gear shift into reverse and turned off the ignition.

"Yes, of course. What's it about?" He turned in his car seat as if to talk there.

"If you would, Ronald, could we sit inside the cathedral? It's more tranquil, and I want to feel our faith, our church, around us. Nothing against the cardinal's car, of course."

"Sure."

They both smiled.

"This time of the afternoon, everything is quiet. Okay, let's go. Rain is falling harder. Let's just dash," Father Girouard said.

The two priests ran lickety-split from the car and up the steps of the magnificent cathedral. Father Girouard opened the tall original oak doors. Their cassocks flew behind in their wake.

"That wasn't bad. Your hair is a little matted," Father Holtz told him.

"It'll dry. Let's go in. Come on," Father Girouard said, opening the tall paneled vestibule door that led into the cathedral.

Father Holtz was first hit by the vastness and beauty of the seventy-year-old church. The dome was far oversized in proportion to the sanctuary, giving a feeling of a more European, even baroque, design. Gold leafing outlined corners, crowns, pillars, and the altar. The confessionals were located on the sides. Wooden doors protruded into the aisles. The ornately carved doors with pointed Gothic panels across the top presented a majestic yet a welcoming look, making one want to see what was inside. Everyone knew ... just solitude and darkness. "This cathedral reminds me of a local parish church I attended in Milwaukee, St. Josephats. Absolutely stunning, just like here. Both make me feel like I'm in Europe," Father Holtz commented.

The pews were a dark blackish-brown stain. The ends of each pew were much higher than normal, duplicating the Gothic painted panels of the confessionals. Father Holtz stood in sheer amazement as he scanned the stunning grandeur. All the pews were original to the church.

"This place is unbelievable. I almost expect to see the pope suddenly appear in the sanctuary," he said, still looking around.

The clouds and dark skies of the day prohibited the entrance of sunlight. Few lights had been turned on. They could see an elderly man with his head bowed kneeling in front of a statue of St. Peter far over on the right side of the sanctuary. A lady wearing what looked to be a long, dark woolen scarf low over her shoulders knelt alone in the middle of the church. Father Holtz could hear the sounds of the rattling beads of her rosary as she loudly whispered her prayers. A few candles glittered in front of the Holy Mother Mary statue on the left side of the church.

Slowly, Father Girouard walked up the center aisle, five or six pews from the back. His visitor followed. Their shoes echoed on the wooden floors, which were also original to the cathedral.

Turning his back to the altar, Father Girouard extended his hand, motioning to Father Holtz. "How's this?"

"Just fine, Ronald. Can I sit here for a moment and take it all in?" he asked, taking a deep breath. Sitting and placing his hands on his knees, Father Holtz now stared ahead, directly toward the altar, which was almost hidden in the depth of the sanctuary.

A door from someplace beyond the pillars toward the front left side closed. Echoes. Footsteps. A man walked along the front communion rail, past the statue of the Blessed Mother, and then by the large canopied pulpit elevated six steps above the broad spectrum of front pews. Father Holtz imagined Cardinal Cullings speaking his righteous sermon to the vast congregation filling all the pews before him. *Oh, the magnificence of it all*, he thought. He absorbed all the emotions of why he had taken his sacred vows and became a priest. *This is what it's all about. Why can't it always be like this? Peace, solitude with one's Lord and Savior*, he thought, so transfixed in this holy space.

The sound of a door opening and then gliding closed was heard from the front corner of the church. Both priests watched Cardinal Cullings. He walked toward the center, genuflected, and then bowed his head. Their eyes followed him as he walked directly toward the center of the altar. He went up the marble steps, placed both hands on the altar, and slowly genuflected again. He stood there. From the rear of the church, they could not detect his purpose, as his back was to them. He stood in front of the gold tabernacle. A minute passed. A click echoed in the hollow chamber.

Stopping for just a moment, the cardinal looked into the side chapel, right of the altar, and then further looked around. He seemed to be looking at the old man in black. Stopping, he beheld the man kneeling before St. Peter. Fathers Holtz and Girouard watched as Cardinal Cullings walked over to the communion rail. At the same time, the elderly man stood and walked in the direction of the cardinal. The old man knelt and bowed his head. Cardinal Cullings reached out, and the man looked up as Cardinal Cullings gave his blessing. The cardinal then turned and walked back to the altar, slowly genuflected, and walked into the side of the sacristy.

Father Girouard pointed to the corner by the statue. Father Holtz looked just in time to see the man in the black coat leave through the side door. With a most puzzled look, Father Holtz looked at Father Girouard.

"I don't know. I have seen that man before Cardinal Cullings approached him. I don't know, Ben. I don't know. The cardinal does have a mystique about him."

The Catholic Church is not without mystery, Father Holtz thought. Turning toward Father Girouard, he said with efficient directness, "The reason I asked to talk is that our church right here in Indiana has a tremendous problem."

Father Girouard lowered his brow, waiting for his friend's next words.

"Ronald, I'm going to get right to it. Over the past several years, and ever since I've been in South Wayne, we've had … " Father Holtz took a deep breath. "We've had numbers of—and I don't know exactly how many since the beginning before my arrival two years ago—well, you see, priests … " He stopped, pressing his lips closed, shaking his head, and then looking down. "Priests abusing boys," he shamefully told Father Girouard. "Ten, eleven, twelve, thirteen years old. Not really teenagers. There have been at least six priests accused of abuse within this diocese. Once the bishop confirms the truth, he transfers them to other parishes. No real investigation. No reporting to the police. Ronald, he just covers it up. Sweeps it under the rug and sends them off to other parishes, where they can do it all over again. I have this—"

"Excuse me, Ben. Sorry to interrupt." Sitting on the end of the pew, turned sideways, and listening to his friend, Father Girouard rested his right arm along the top the pew. "Listen, Ben. I must first tell you that your situation is not unique. We have abusing priests in numbers of parishes in the diocese. Some of the abused, now even in their twenties and thirties, have come forward after so many years of hiding … tormented years. Now, after all this time, they are speaking up. As young boys, they couldn't. They were scared. Their parents wouldn't believe them. 'All priests are good.' You know, Ben."

Father Holtz responded, "What? What are you telling me? Is Cardinal Cullings aware?"

"Yes, Ben, he is. As cardinal in the Catholic Church, he is disgusted and abhorred by the actions of just a few bad men. He knows it's not the collar, the priesthood. In each terrible, pathetic case, it's the man who degrades the collar, not the order, not our holy church."

"Then what's he doing?" Father Holtz asked in amazement. He was totally shocked. "Where have I been? Ronald, I'm so unaware of all this."

"Ben, I can assure you that Cardinal Cullings is aware, but has no knowledge about South Wayne. I guarantee you. He will be upset, but he won't be surprised. Across the country in other dioceses in other states the same thing is happening. Right now the media is not really aware. If they are, it's all being hidden. You know, who wants to go up against the Catholic Church? Many are hurt, but few know."

"Why not?" Father Holtz asked, bewildered.

"Two reasons. First, numbers of the bishops have done exactly as you described. Covered it up, we believe. It is hard to know. Secondly, Cardinal Cullings and another cardinal out in the east, who he is in constant contact with, are doing something. Ever since he first became aware, the cardinal has been working with local authorities, specifically with prosecution right here in Indianapolis. He has written to the Vatican with some, but he has gotten minimal results. Pope John Benedict keeps everything *confidential*. There is something else, but I'm not at liberty to say. Everything is so slow. Most don't respond. Yet daily the abuse goes on."

Father Holtz was not only surprised, but he was also encouraged to hear that someone higher up was doing something. An authoritative person, a cardinal, was addressing the cancer within the church. "Are you telling me that they can possibly bring these priests at least to legal justice, even if not moral justice?"

"Yes, Ben, he can, and he will, but justice is slow."

Father Holtz spent the next hour describing in detail the cover-up in South Wayne to the best of his knowledge. He named the priests involved, the transfers, and the excuses. He stressed the absence of concern for the victims. Father Holtz talked only about situations of which he knew for sure, omitting at this time, the bishop's and Father Schmidt's abuse.

"Yes, I understand. We must be fair and factual," Father Girouard clarified.

Then with deep conviction, Father Holtz said, "Unfortunately, the bad far overshadows good in our minds, almost eliminating the good. Ronald, all they think about are the priests, the diocese, but never the victims."

Both priests had a sixth sense that, with heaviness of the subject, their discussion should end for the day, as time had flown by and Father Holtz had to get back to South Wayne.

"One last thing. A good priest, an assistant at St. Thomas Moore in Wabash, has stepped forward to bring justice for some victims. His name is Father Michael Sullivan. It's his fellow assistant, Father Jerome Jaeger, who has terrorized victims in the parish. What did the bishop do? Well, he brought the troubled priest back to South Wayne. The priest spent two sessions a week for a month with a psychologist. Just one month!"

"Then what?" Father Girouard asked.

"Ready for this? They transferred him to a parish in Eastville, Indiana, just west of Terre Haute. St. Vincent is the name of the parish. Unbelievable! I'm sure he is back to his old deeds. This has to stop. Here's my question. Would you please ask Cardinal Cullings if he'll meet with Father Sullivan? He will organize and present everything he knows fairly and factually to the cardinal."

Father Girouard replied, "Of course. You know, since I've been here for three months now, one of my assignments is to be aware of and involved with the cardinal on all these abuse cases. There may be as many as twelve to fifteen. The good cardinal is hands-on with every case. He told me the church must address this now. Otherwise, in ten or twenty years, the cancer could be out of control."

Father Holtz stood up. "That's my concern. It's real, and I'm so surprised and pleased that you are aware and involved." Father Holtz knew they had gone on longer than planned. "This can tear at the very heart of the church. I know you have to leave, Ronald. I can't thank you enough."

Together they walked back to the vestibule. Father Girouard opened the big oak door for Father Holtz. They both stepped outside. The rain had stopped. The skies were opening up.

"So glad we got together today. It's been too long," Father Girouard said, extending his hand to Father Holtz.

"Same here, Ronald. I'll never forget this day."

"Now listen, Ben, I'll talk to the cardinal about the entire situation in South Wayne and Wabash. I know he'll meet with Father Sullivan. Like I said, once I share your story, I will ask him if I can confide in you about some confidential information that may give you hope. This will also give hope to Father Sullivan. I'll call you the day after tomorrow at 7:00 p.m. sharp. Then you'll be able to go to Father Sullivan." Father Girouard extended his hand again. Clasping Father Holtz's hand with both of his in a more hardy handshake, he bid Father Holtz good-bye. "Take care," he said.

Father Holtz bounded down the steps. Turning toward the parking lot, he glanced back at his friend, who was still standing in front of the cathedral doors. *Maybe after these months of trials, suspicion, and disappointment, we finally have someone who can help stop this madness.*

Driving back to South Wayne that late afternoon, Father Holtz could not wait to share the good news with Father Sullivan.

CHAPTER 99

THE GOOD CARDINAL

Cardinal Cullings—October 7, 1958

AFTER Father Holtz's request for Father Sullivan to meet Cardinal Cullings, Father Girouard stopped by the cardinal's study late that afternoon. Father Girouard knew the cardinal would be open to meeting Father Sullivan; the issue was just finding the time.

The tall ceilings, full wall of bookshelves, and leaded glass windows gave the cardinal's study an old European feel.

"Good afternoon, Your Eminence," Father Girouard said as he walked through the open door.

"Come in, Father. Have a seat here at the table. Easier to talk. You look pretty serious. Is anything the matter?"

"It is kind of urgent. You know, Your Eminence, you asked me to work with you on these abuse issues regarding a number of priests in the diocese."

"Yes, go on," the cardinal responded.

"Father Holtz had another reason to visit with me in addition to friends getting together. You see, Cardinal, I'm sorry to report that there are more problems involving abuse beyond what you and I are currently aware of," Father Girouard said reluctantly.

"Oh, Father, don't tell me. I was hoping it would remain isolated with the cases we already are addressing. I am naïve, I guess," Cardinal Cullings said, propping his elbow on the table and resting his forehead on his hand. His body language said it all. *Not another child.*

"Father Holtz has a friend, Father Sullivan, an assistant at St. Thomas

Moore in Wabash. Father Sullivan became involved because his fellow assistant, a Father Jaeger, was abusing boys."

"What a shame. Beautiful church that St. Thomas Moore. I said Mass there a couple of years ago. I remember, good parish, good people. I believe they have a very fine pastor. A Father, let me see ... Oh yes, Father Warren. My dear Lord, how can this happen there?"

"Father Sullivan would like to explain the situation directly to you."

"That's fine, but why doesn't he first go to his bishop in South Wayne? Bishop Powers?"

"He already has. Father Holtz says the bishop is handling the situation with a month or two of psychological evaluation, and then he transfers the priests to another parish where they can start over again. In other words, he's passing the problem on through reassignments."

"Same thing that's happening down here. These bishops just pass the problem to another parish. How awful this all is," Cardinal Cullings said, shaking his head.

"Well, you're not covering up, Your Eminence."

"No, we aren't, Father. By the way, did you say anything to Father Holtz about my paper, the presentation I'm giving in January at the Vatican?"

"I'd like to, but not without your permission."

"Do you trust Father Holtz?"

"Yes. Absolutely. Ben is one of the finest people I've ever known. He's a good priest and a good person."

"If you share my involvement with the Universal Bishop and Cardinal's Conference in January, that will be okay. If he's so dedicated, he will be even more confident that we are taking this to the Vatican. I keep saying address it now before the problem grows over the next decade. The harm could be overwhelming to our church. I know I've told this to you so many times, Father. Eventually, this will all come down to the courts, lawsuits, money settlements. The victims will want restitution. We must address this now. Most importantly, just look at the needless pain and suffering ... and the victim's families, to say the least."

Cardinal Cullings sat back in his chair. He clasped his hands and raised them to the back of his head. Father Girouard could tell he was thinking.

"You know, Father, hopefully Pope John Benedict will meet this issue head-on," Cardinal Cullings went on to say. "*Hmmm*, Father, what do you think of this idea? Nothing replaces the truth. What if we invite Father Sullivan and we include the other assistant, the so-called perpetrator, Father Jaeger, to visit together? Get them all here in the same room?"

"Why not? This is not a trial. You are inquiring. Sure," Father Girouard said as he saw the cardinal nod in agreement.

"Listen, we don't stop there. We feel that Bishop Powers and Father Schmidt may be hiding their own sins."

"I'm all for this. We'll simply have an informal inquiry. Truth never lies."

"Good idea," Cardinal Cullings said to Father Girouard. "Then I'd say only one thing is missing."

"What's that?" Father Girouard asked.

"The boys, the victims, should be here. It could be risky. Eventually some may need lawyers. Maybe not. They could speak separately without the priests in the room."

"I'm for it, Your Eminence. Let's get everything out in the open. If no one has anything to hide, they shouldn't care. Truth will back them up."

"It's settled then. Father Girouard, you are to organize the agenda. On Monday, bring the list of those who should attend. We will find the truth. I will make this work. For the good of the church and the victims, this must end."

"I'll have it completed for you," Father Girouard said.

"One last thing. I want to call and invite Bishop Powers myself. Let's set the meeting for…let's say, how about the week after Thanksgiving. How about Wednesday. That would be December 3. I know I'm free that day. How about one o'clock?"

"Works for me. I'll get started immediately. You'll meet Father Sullivan for the first time that day," Father Girouard said to the cardinal.

"Father, if everyone is open and honest and puts it all on the table, we'll be okay. I am going to get to the bottom of this." *Now before it's all too late*, Cardinal Cullings thought.

Father Holtz—October 9, 1958

On Thursday evening, Father Holtz was sitting in the comfort of his own room. Father Girouard called exactly at 7:00 p.m. Getting right to the point, he told Father Holtz all about the cardinal's idea.

Father Holtz was astonished by the magnitude and scope of the cardinal's response and asked who would attend the meeting. Father Holtz agreed that having the priests and victims together would be the best way to shake things out.

After Father Holtz agreed to the meeting on December 3, Father Girouard said, "Remember when I told you there was something confidential?"

"Sure, I remember. How could I forget? Why, can you tell me now?" Father Holtz asked.

"In January, Cardinal Cullings is going to Rome. There he will present a paper to the Conference of Bishops and Cardinals. Pope John Benedict will attend. When Cardinal Cullings was first made aware of the scale of child abuse within the church in 1952, six years ago mind you—the bureaucracy of the church takes so long—he gave it his immediate attention. Like I said, he's working with local authorities, but the politics make it very slow. He is also talking with someone in the Vatican. Along with another cardinal from the United States—can't mention his name—they have been addressing this issue for three years. Three long years! He is really concerned that if child abuse in the church is not addressed now, it will get out of hand. See why I respect him so much?" Father Girouard asked.

"I surely do. How fortunate we are to have a man of his character and position addressing this problem," Father Holtz added.

"Ben, you need to contact Fathers Schmidt, Sullivan, and Jaeger. Keeping it quiet, we need to have Ned Thornbauer in attendance but not for the whole meeting. I think you said there are several other victims of Father Jaeger. I recommend two of them."

"Ronald, I never thought the meeting could happen so quickly."

"Cardinal Cullings is focused and decisive. I told you, Ben, he is a good and devoted cardinal. I believe he is a holy man. I will leave it to you and Father Sullivan to contact the boys and their parents. We want to hear from the parents. Once we have everyone here, Cardinal Cullings will conduct the meeting and the agenda," Father Girouard said, believing he had covered everything with Father Holtz. "Are you all right with this, Ben?"

"All right. You bet. I'm a bit apprehensive, but I know it needs to be done," Father Holtz replied.

"Okay then, let's call each other two weeks from today to see if everything is on schedule. December 3 is a good time because Thanksgiving will be over and it will be weeks before Christmas."

"Sounds good. God bless, Ronald."

"To you also, my friend," Father Girouard said. *Yes, let's pray for everyone. We are all going to need it*, he thought.

Clarence Wolfe—November 28, 1958

"Operator, I'd a like to place a call. Wabash, Indiana, person-to-person. Clarence Wolfe."

"Where did you say, sir?" Mario Molinaro was asked by the operator.

"The Wabash Reform School."

"Wait one minute, please."

"Don't take long. Gotta talk with 'im." After about two minutes, Mario's patience grew short, and he began breathing heavily.

"I have Mr. Wolfe. Go ahead please."

"Clarence Wolfe? This is Mario Molinaro calling from Cicero."

Just the name sent a chill down Wolfe's spine.

"Please, with what you're doing for Randall and me, I wanna thank you and ah … and ah maybe talk about stepping up our operation. So I wantcha to come visit with me here in Cicero."

"Cicero? Up by Chicago?"

"Hell yes. It's not by Indianapolis. Cicero's by Chicago. Not goin' down there to Wabash. Don't like cows."

"But, ah, but Mr. Molinaro, I can't."

"Listen, pal, no one says *no can't* to Mario. When I wanna thank someone, they better cooperate. Know what I mean?"

Startled by the response, Wolfe thought about Krueger and his disappearance. Thinking fast, he cleared his throat. "Sure, it's not that far.

Up and back in a day. When should I come?" he answered with a total change of heart.

"Wednesday at two o'clock. Let's see a, December 3. Just a little meeting 'bout our plans. You call Randall. He'll tell you how to get here. See you Wednesday, two o'clock sharp."

Wolfe heard the phone slam. *Must be Mario's usual way.* "Damn! Goddamn it!" he said out loud to himself.

"Yes, Mr. Wolfe? What did you say? Need something?" He identified Miss Gardner's voice from out front. *Should've had the door closed.*

"Nothing, nothing at all, Miss Gardner. Just my brother calling," he said so she wouldn't come into the room. "Close the door, will you?"

Reaching down, Wolfe pulled his bottom desk drawer open. The bottle of Jack Daniels was half full. Slamming the bottle on the desk, he poured himself a stiff one. *This is all I need. Damn Mafioso calling me. Thanks, Zilbar. Thanks a lot, Randall, you arrogant, untrustworthy prick!*

CHAPTER 100

CRUELTY AND HUMILIATION

Gene Kowolski—November 13, 1958

SISTER Mary Michael kept a close eye on Gene Kowolski. Sister Joaugusta informed her earlier about Gene's progress, or lack thereof. Each week she became more concerned about the declining change in his attitude and performance in class. Gene seemed to have few, if any, friends. Unaware of his physical problem and the ever-increasing taunts and minor bullying from the tough kids, Mary Michael asked Gene to stop by after class. She wanted to talk even though he was no longer in her sixth grade class.

At the end of the day, the school bell rang. The class cleaned their desks, put away their books, and began their orderly routine to leave school. Sister Mary Michael knew Gene would soon arrive from his seventh grade class. The children began to file out of the classroom. Sister Mary Michael was standing across the hall and happened to hear some boys leaving Sister Joaugusta's class, following Gene.

"See ya tomorrow, homo man." Herbie Ratski sneered at Gene and then said, "Oops. Sorry, Sister." He hurriedly scurried down the hallway before she could stop and reprimand him.

The cruel comment was humiliating to Gene as he noticed the sister's reaction. Her concern for Gene elevated to a new level.

"Gene, come into my classroom. Let's visit," she said once the room had cleared. He felt closer to Sister Mary Michael than his seventh grade teacher.

Gene slowly approached the front desk. "Thank you, Sister," was all he said. Looking around, he felt comfortable in his old classroom. He liked old things. The classroom was surrounded by vertical wainscoting and blackboards with wooden chalk trays. Four oblong light fixtures hung from the high plaster ceiling. He did remember some good times in the beginning of last year, before Father Jaeger.

Sister Mary Michael tried to relax Gene and understand what he must be going through. "Gene, you're not in any trouble. I just wanted to ask you if there's something really bothering you. I think maybe there might be."

"Not really. No, nothing much, Sister," Gene replied as he looked away, gazing out the large paned glass windows on the far side of the room.

"I heard what Herbie said to you out in the hallway. I'll address that tomorrow. Are the kids in your class causing you problems?"

"Not really," Gene said, not wanting to tattle on anyone. He felt he could handle himself.

"Gene, could I do anything to help? What about having your parents come in and we could all talk together? I'm sure they might be concerned also."

"No, no, Sister. Not my parents." Her comment alarmed Gene. "I gotta go now." He paused and then said, "Please, Sister."

Sister Mary Michael knew she wasn't getting through. "Yes, Gene, you can leave."

Gene stood up, books in hand.

"Gene, I'm here for you, just across the hall. Please remember that. I know Father Sullivan is also."

Gene couldn't reply. He felt the need to cry. He knew the sister cared. Feeling embarrassed, his eyes filling with tears, Gene stood. "Excuse me, Sister." He hurriedly left the room. He was at his lowest point since his last encounter with Father Jaeger. Walking home, the haunting and scary feeling of loneliness overwhelmed him to the point of gagging, almost choking. He bent over, more from emotional pain than physical.

I'll take the long way home. Detouring left on Market, he walked downtown. Noticing a bench by the curb in front of the Wabash State Bank, he sat with plans of going nowhere. Alone. Pedestrian traffic was increasing in the late afternoon. A group of eighth graders jumped and hollered as they walked on the other side of the street.

Looking right, Gene was startled by the appearance of a black Studebaker turning the corner. Couldn't miss it. *It's him*, he immediately thought, *Father Jaeger*. As the car approached, Gene slumped on the green wooden bench. Straining to see if it was the haunting man in black, he lifted his school bag to cover his face and peered at the car from the side. The setting sun gleamed off the car's windshield. He knew the lone driver would be Father Jaeger. *What's he doing here?* Just as the car was about to cross in front of him, a large moving truck coming from his left totally blocked the view of the passing black car.

Gene only saw *Red Top Movers* in large letters painted across the truck's side. He saw the tail end of the car passing his bench, so Gene immediately stood up. Back lights, bumper, and a single driver of the priest's car were all he could see. The back of the driver looked exactly as he remembered—the man in black.

Immediately Gene raced down the sidewalk. He had to make sure. The brake lights went red. He gained ground on the stopped car. He neared the corner … Then he stumbled on a raised crack in the concrete sidewalk. Gene lost a step but kept going. Parked cars on his right blocked his view. Hitting the corner at full stride, Gene stopped with a jump. Dropping his schoolbag, he threw his hands on his hips as the black car moved out of sight. *It was him. I know it was him.* Gene was convinced Father Jaeger was back in town. He walked directly home. Somehow he had to figure how to tell his dad that he had seen Father Jaeger.

Gene was nervous and anxious about talking to his dad that evening. He picked at his supper. Pops was in his usual good humor, keeping the conversation around the supper table lively, though the pain of his cancer was increasing daily. Pops was determined to be around for Christmas, one last time with his wonderful family. Still mobile with the help of his trusty wooden cane, his concern was to keep driving his old '47 Plymouth for as long as possible, hopefully through the Christmas season.

"Hey, Dad," Gene said to his father after the rest of the family had left the supper table. It was Susie's turn to clear the dishes and help Mom clean up the kitchen. The other kids hurried to their rooms for home-work. "Could we talk? Something I gotta tell you. It's about *him*," Gene said in a concerned, serious voice.

"Oh sure. It's quiet in the living room. Maybe Pops should hear," Gene's dad said, knowing what Gene meant to Pops.

"Pops, gotta a minute?" Gene's dad asked as his father was just leaving the table.

Gene sat in the middle of the sofa. His dad sat next to him on the end. Pops sat in the lone armchair across from the sofa and in front of the porch window; the seat always reserved for him. With his head down and voice soft, Gene told his dad of the meeting with Sister Mary Michael and how she wanted to help.

"She's so kind and caring, but she can't do anything. My problem is I … Dad, I just hate school. Now the kids are giving me … oh, they're calling me names like … names like *homo man*. I don't even know what it means. Well, kind of, but not sure. It's all because of Jaeger. I hate school. I hate him. I hate him."

Pops took a breath and shifted in his chair. He could feel his blood pressure rising. Gene's dad kept listening.

"Worst of all, Dad, I saw him. Saw him driving downtown today in his black Studebaker. I'll never forget that car. He's back. Back! Father Jaeger came back!"

"Now, Gene, he's not coming back. I promise you. It's almost Thanks-giving. He can't be transferred now."

"Then why was he here? I hate him. I hate him. Dad, I don't want to go back to school."

"I know, son, but you can't quit school."

"Okay then, I'll run away. Jaeger ruined my life. I'm not going to school. I hate him! I quit!" Starting to cry, Gene jumped up and headed for the stairs. "I quit!"

Herb Kowolski didn't try to stop him.

Pops glanced across the room. "Something's got to be done about that man. Look at our Gene. He's not the same kid. This guy should be strung up by his … you know what I mean."

"I know, Pops. I agree, but what? What can we do? This has gone on so long. Maybe I'll go back and talk with Father Sullivan. At least I'll find out if Jaeger's coming back."

"That bastard deserves ... deserves—" Pops stopped himself again. "You go see this ... this father and let me know. I'm old. I'm sick." He stood up, coughing, and bent over. "I only care about my family and justice for Gene..."

"What's wrong, Dad?"

"Oh, it's the damn pain. Would you get my pills, Herb? Please?"

Herb went to the kitchen and returned with the two pain pills and water.

Pops swallowed them both. "One more. One more!"

Herb ran back to the kitchen.

After taking the third pill, Pops plopped back in his chair. Hand pressed against his side, he said, "Better. Thanks, son." He leaned his head back on the chair, breathing heavily, and said in a raspy voice, "You know, son ... " He looked at Herb, who was kneeling on one knee.

"What is it, Pops?"

"The pills help. Temporary but ... " Another breath. "Temporary but I feel better." Catching his breath, he said, "The real pain, the real pain's right here." He placed his palm on his heart, with his head still resting against the back of the chair. "It's here. My heart breaks for our Gene." He paused. "We've gotta ... we've gotta take care of that devil." Still clutching his side, he said, "Let me rest here for a while." His breathing was easier.

Herb stood, walked over to the lamps, and turned the lights out in the room. *He's right. Something's got to be done.*

CHAPTER 101

LAST TIME

Father Sullivan—November 29, 1958

ONLY a single light on his desk slightly illuminated the room. Books were hidden in shadows of darkness in the case on the far wall. The moon loomed behind a late November cloud cover. His late-night glass of merlot was half full and waiting. *Doctor Zhivago* lay to the right of his desk, as he had just finished reading the best-selling novel. Wondering how he ever found time to read, he derived comfort and escape from the good novel and a glass of wine.

As he sat quiet and alone, the late-night atmosphere provided time for wandering thoughts and dreams. He thought about Holtz's friend Father Girouard and Cardinal Cullings and all they were trying to do to eliminate the cancer of abuse in the church. Wondering to himself, Father Sullivan could not comprehend why the Vatican was not addressing the problem. Pope John Benedict had been elected by the conclave of cardinals more than a year ago, yet nothing had been publically addressed regarding abuse. He asked himself, *Why hasn't the pope decreed that any abuse will not be tolerated? Zero tolerance. Laicization. Never to wear the collar again.*

With his head tipped forward and his eyes closed, Father Sullivan's mind drifted away. The boys, the pope, and the awfulness of it all. Temptation loomed when he thought of that which could not be. He thought of Linda. For how long, he did not know. Dreams of her were his only images, his only thoughts. He woke to the sound of wind through the window beyond his chair. Startled, he sat up. The image of Linda was still permanent in his mind. Putting his hands on his knees, he slowly stood up and sauntered over to his desk.

Reaching into the top drawer, Father Sullivan picked up the unopened letter he had set aside yesterday. Not sure of its contents, he had waited. The merlot suggested he read the letter. Picking up his carved wooden letter opener, a gift from his mom several birthdays ago, Father Sullivan slowly tucked it under the flap. He wanted to make a perfect incision. A memory of his mother flashed by. He opened the envelope.

Delicately, he removed the one-page letter. Intuition had earlier warned him that he might not like its contents.

November 24, 1958

Dear Michael:

The difficulty I find in writing this letter is overshadowed by my need to share these words with you. For so many years, you have been an all-consuming part of my secret private life. My love for you has no limits. That love includes my respect for you and the collar you wear. You are a good person and a wonderful priest. Michael, you are truly blessed. Good-byes are too difficult. I will forever remember our last visit.

On Tuesday, December 2, my brothers and I will be packing all my belongings and furnishings, and I will leave this house that night for the last time. Although the timing is during the middle of his first semester, Joey has agreed with my decision.

I do and will always cherish my last time there with you. Your words, your kindness ... your touch will always remain in my heart. Forever, I will remember you and all the times we shared together.

Take care, my dear friend.

Love,
Linda

Father Sullivan laid the letter on his desk. He stared at it for a minute.

Then he took a long slow sip of merlot, thought of what could have been, and drifted back into the darkness.

CHAPTER 102

EXTREME JUSTICE

December 1, 1958, late morning

THE plans were complete. Pulling open the top drawer of his simple cherry dresser, he reached far back under the stack of old seldom-worn shirts. As his fingers touched the cold steel of his revolver, he gently lifted it from its twenty-year hiding place. As he patted the gun in his left hand, the handsome weapon brought back sad, dark memories from a time long ago.

Walking across the worn wool area rug to the closet, he stretched and reached high overhead for an old worn cigar box. Lifting it down, he heard the roll from inside like marbles. Still standing in the closet, he opened the lid. One by one, he picked up the cartridges, twelve in all. He placed them gently in his right jacket pocket, grabbed his worn newsboy hat, turned off the light, and walked out the door.

Now everything had been taken care of. The long-distance call had been made. The family all knew he would be gone for a couple days visiting an old friend. Only he knew his true destination. Leaving in the early afternoon, he drove south for a couple hours until a little before darkness and the supper hour. He enjoyed the time alone. He knew it would be the last time he ever drove his trusty 'ol Plymouth. His car was once a friend. Ahead, a neon sign flashed—*Motel*. Seeing the vacancy sign, he pulled in.

An elderly gentleman with stubble on his stacked chins sat behind the front desk. His expanded gut spread his shirt, putting heavy stress on the middle buttons. Suspenders hung tightly to the sides of his nonexistent waist. The smoke curling above the counter trailed back to the cigar clutched between his teeth. The color of a dirty white undershirt was visible under his green mechanic's shirt. Long black and gray hairs curled over his unbuttoned collar. The name *Clyde* was circled above the right breast pocket of his shirt. A small warehouse of several different pens adorned the blue-and-black ink-lined pocket holder in his left pocket.

"Howdy. Four dollars a night, cash. Clean sheets and one bar of soap. Two rooms left. One's got a broken spring, but has clean sheets. You can have it for three dollars," he said as he greeted the traveler. "Anything else ya wanna know?"

"Thanks. You're quite a salesman. Got that spiel down pat. What would you say if there were no vacancies?"

"Ah, I'd say no room. Got a stable in back. You can sleep with the sheep for a buck," the man said, chomping his cigar. "Merry Christmas, stranger. Get it? Manger in the back?"

He handed the innkeeper a five dollar bill. "I'll take the one with the good spring."

"Sorry, got no change. I'll have it in the morning. Will leave a buck on the counter if you're pullin' out early. If you leave before 10:00 a.m., just throw the key on the desk. I'll get it when I start cleanin' rooms. Lots to do around here. Do it all. Chief cook and bottle washer. Plugged toilets too. Almost a full house except for that room with the broken spring. These days travelers want nothing but the best."

"Give the buck to the maid," the traveler said, trying to be polite to the disheveled innkeeper.

"Got no maid. I do that. You saying the dollar tip's for me?"

"Yeah, as long as the sheets are clean."

"Sure are. Changed 'em last week. Your room, the guy stayed only one night. Looked clean to me when I pulled up the bedspread. Pay no heed. I knew the guy had showered. Saw some hair in the tub." he said proudly, not leaving the comfort of his displaced upholstered chair. "Sign there on the desk. Just your name." Reaching over the worn arm of his chair, he picked up a Maxwell House coffee can. He leaned forward. "*Spppt.*" The brown stream from his chew shot from his mouth. "Bull's eye! Bingo!"

He tossed the traveler a key from the rack on the other side of his chair. "Number eight ... last on the end. Sleep well." As the traveler turned to leave for his car, the old man behind the desk said, "Don't forget your soap." He pointed to the basket at the end of the counter. "Just one, remember. Say, what brings you here to Crawfordsville?" the old clerk asked before the traveler could get out the door.

Replying in a raspy voice, the traveler said, "Just passin' through. On my way south to visit an ol' friend. Name's Lang. He's a barn builder when he's not off in his boat fishing."

"Old friend? Guess guys like you and me can't have too many old friends."

"What do you mean too many?" the traveler asked as if to challenge the oversized jerk behind the counter.

"Old friends. Guess that's all you and me got. Just old friends."

The traveler looked back in disgust. "Speak for yourself ol' man. I've got both old and young friends. I'll let you know how clean the sheets are."

As the traveler opened room 8, a newfound smell exited through the door. He flipped on the one-bulb light in the ceiling, and the whiff of dank and dullness permeated the room. Throwing the worn gray bedspread aside, he checked the sheets. *Damn, just one.* He pulled the bedspread back up on the bed. *Hope it's clean.*

It wasn't the room that made the night sleepless. Anticipation of tomorrow crowded his mind long into the wee hours of the morning. Dawn could not come too soon. Then he'd be on the road again, just seventy more miles. All was on schedule as planned.

The Old Man—December 2, 1958

After the long night, the old man woke early as usual. He left the hotel before the innkeeper arrived at the front desk. *Just a few hours to drive this morning. All I need is hot coffee.* Nausea was part of his morning regimen. *Maybe a donut too.* After pulling into the Texaco station, the old man stopped in front of the second pump.

"Fill her up, sir?" a young man of thirty eagerly asked as he bent down and peered into the driver's window. His billed hat, bowtie, and light brown uniform looked as if he just arrived for work.

"No, just two dollars' worth. You're two cents higher than the guy back in Crawfordsville. Shoulda filled up there."

"Out here in the country, guess you can charge more."

"Oh, go ahead. Fill 'er up, son. Just got a lot on my mind."

"No problem, sir. I've heard plenty worse 'round these parts."

"I'll pay twenty-four cents a gallon. Not a problem. Any coffee and doughnuts?"

"Yes, sir. Both inside. Coffee's ten cents. Donut's a dime. Cheaper though if ya buy both. Just leave two dimes on the counter. Second cup on the house."

Clever young man, the traveler thought.

After walking into the station, he looked the doughnuts over. *Hmmm.* He poured his coffee and dropped a quarter on the counter. The attendant walked back inside. "That's two dollars and seventy-five cents, sir. I checked your oil and cleaned the windshield. You're all set to hit the road."

"Thanks, thanks," the old man said, handing him a five dollar bill. "Quarter's right here. Good coffee. Say, how far to Eastville?"

"Eastville, Indiana? Small place. Let me see," he said as he pointed his finger to the map. "I'd say … 'bout … I'd say 'bout two hours driving time. Take 41 down toward Terre Haute, continue south and you'll come to Sullivan, Indiana. Turn west 'bout four miles and you'll be in Eastville. Been there once. Nice little burg. Gotta real good coffee shop. Let's see… Dick and Jackie's. That's it. Now, there's a place for the best donuts."

"Thanks, I'll remember that, though don't plan on being there long. Got just one stop."

The old man walked out to the car, and the attendant said, "Say that car of yours sounds like a sewing machine. Running real sweet. Those Plymouths have a perfect purr."

"Yeah, a '47 Plymouth. You're right. Purrs like a kitten. Almost brand new," the elder man said. "Thanks again, my friend. Good doughnut." The old man got in his car and pulled away from the station.

"Hey, mister, I owe you a nickel!" The attendant only heard the tires spin in the gravel as the old man drove onto the highway.

Traffic was light with the exception of a few tractor trailers and a random school bus. Though he kept both hands firmly on the wheel, his eyes would drift to the austere December countryside. He noticed a lone farmer on an orange Case tractor, still harvesting corn late into the season following the unusually wet and cold fall. The old man loved the Indiana countryside.

Within two hours, the picked cornfields gave way to a grain elevator along the tracks that headed north to Chicago. A sign ahead read, *City Limits, Eastville, Indiana, Population 1,850.* The main street through town was a visage of late Victorians with gabled clapboards. The corner grocer in the midst of the tranquil neighborhood on the way to the downtown was a hub of activity on this blustery Tuesday in December.

The old man carefully applied the brake as a flatbed truck stocked with lumber pulled out of the yard. A bronze statue of an obscure local Civil War hero marked the town square. Ahead, he saw a single church spire. Assuming it was St. Vincent's, he turned right on Maple, drove one block, stopped, and then parked in front of the church. Looking around the four-way stop, he noticed a mailbox next to the phone across the street. *Fate has its ways.*

Sitting behind the wheel, he inhaled a drag of his cigar. *Might be my last.* He dropped his spent ashes on the rubber mat below his feet. Flipping the cigar out the door, the old man reached inside his jacket and checked the small slip of paper located inside his shirt pocket. He felt his left jacket pocket for the letter, which was far offset by the weight in his right pocket.

Time to move. Reaching for his trusty wooden cane where it lay against the right front seat, he opened the car door, stood, and looked over the top of his car at the simple brick church. He walked around the front of the car and directly to the mailbox. Pulling the letter from his left pocket, he glanced at the name—*Herb Kowolski and family*—and dropped the envelope into the box.

As the old man walked across the street to the church, he noticed the aged cornerstone, sacredly original: *St. Vincent's. Dedicated to those who gave of themselves to erect this holy church. March 1884.* Only two stone steps and he opened the black paneled front door. Immediately the old stood inside the sanctuary. The wooden pews with their hand-carved crosses represented one of the few ornamentals within the old church. Simple wood trusses spanned the dark ceiling. Blessing himself, he half-genuflected and took a seat in the back pew, opposite the side that housed the confessional in the other corner. Setting his cane on the pew, he attempted to kneel but then half sat back against the wooden seat. *Please allow me to know that what I am about to do is right for my family. Please assure me now that I am justified.*

The silence was broken by the movement beyond the front corner door, which was hidden by an archway that leads to the sanctuary. A door closed behind the arch. Remaining still, the old man watched from the opposite back corner of the church. Like a shadow emerging from darkness, the priest appeared. Genuflecting in the direction of the small plain altar, the priest turned—he thought unnoticed—and walked down the side aisle just below the stations of the cross. *The devil himself*, the old man thought.

Walking below Christ agonizing in the Garden of Gethsemane, the priest stopped at the confessional door and slid his name into the brass nameplate. Standing in the confessional doorway, he noticed an elderly man in the last pew on the far side of the church. *Must be him*, Father Jaeger assumed. Not expecting such an older man, the priest opened the confessional door and stepped inside. Turning around, he sat in the wooden armchair facing the door through which he had just entered. *Didn't recognize him. In the name of the Father and of the Son and of the Holy Ghost.* The priest prayed and waited.

Leaning forward on the pew, the old man stood. *Bless me, Father, for what I am about to do.* Slowly he walked across the back of the church toward the confessional. The elder dipped his fingers again in the holy water as if reaching for strength. He genuflected, bowed his head, and proceeded to the confessional where the unsuspecting priest waited. The tapping of his cane echoed through the church as if someone was calling from a deep valley. As he approached the confessional door, the man glanced over his right shoulder at the altar and the oversized crucifix. He thought, *Died for our sins.*

The old man confirmed the name of the priest on the middle confessional door. Opening the first door, he stepped inside and gingerly knelt before the sliding black veil. As he took one last deep breath, he felt the presence of calmness, a sanctity he had not experienced in more than thirty years. The door slid open, releasing a smell with which he was not familiar. "Ah, ah, bless me, Father. I'm here to confess my sins."

"This is good," he heard the priest whisper in response. "You called for this special time. I'm always available for my flock. Now we are here."

"I, ah, want to thank you for accepting my call last Saturday evening and then I want to thank you for agreein' for this here special, or should I say personal, confession?"

"That's quite all right. Forgiving sins is an important mission in my life," the priest reassured the old man. "We all make mistakes, but our Lord is forgiving."

I'm sure not, the traveler thought. "I'm a sick old man, Father, about to die soon. I have no more in life to experience. All I care about is peace for my family." The old man paused and then cleared his throat. "And in one case, all I care about before I leave … is *justice*. No more to lose. My time is near, maybe as little as a month. I do want to make Christmas though."

The priest detected the man's personal acceptance of his fate. "If you feel you are soon to meet your Lord, God, and Savior, then this should be a satisfying, personal, and blessed experience."

"Yes, I'm sure. It will be an experience all right. Blessed, I don't know. Satisfying; that it will be, Father. Long overdue justification."

From the darkness, a frown creased the priest's brow. He did not know what to make of the old man's comment. "Go on."

"Father, know that any day could be my last. I want to go in peace. Before I leave though, I want to even a few scores. You know, bring justice. Sort of level the playing field with a no-good coward in my family's life. I want to bring justice for someone who has been terribly abused."

"Well, now's the time to come forth. We all want justice, so go ahead, my friend," the priest said, listening intently while first reflecting on the old man's choice of the word *abused*.

"Okay then. I haven't been … Well, let's say I haven't been to confession in about thirty years or so."

"How long has it been?" Father Jaeger questioned.

"*Hmmm*, thirty, maybe thirty-five years, Father."

"Yes, it has been a long time. However, our Lord would feel that this day is even more special considering your fate in life. It's never too late."

"Well stated, Father. That's what I say. It's never too late. Matter of fact, Father, late for me would be never."

Odd choice of words, the priest thought.

"I've been thinking about and kind a preparing for this day for a while. Actually for a short while since I discovered this ah…this perverted injustice I mentioned to you. Father, I have sinned by my absence from any of the sacraments for many years. I was a good family man, but I feel grave sin in my absence from my religion. I've done some or may be about to. I've had these thoughts, Father. I'd say it is my intent, as I haven't committed the sin yet."

"Yes?" the priest confirmed as a question. "You mentioned injustice and then absence from the sacraments together. First tell me about the injustice, yet you haven't committed the sin. Strange I ask. Please explain," Father Jaeger encouraged with trepidation in his voice.

"Well, I could be violent, brutal to a man."

"Why?" the priest asked for more detail. A sense of uneasiness began to gather in his dark place.

"Well, this certain man, a very perverted evil man, was unjust. He harmed my family. He harmed my grandson. It's been over the last year or so. Took advantage of him and affected our lives forever, all because of the lustful pursuit of his own carnal gratification. He, this man, sodomized my grandson."

Immediately, faces flashed across the priest's mind. He disguised his almost uncontrollable need to gag or hyperventilate. "Then in this case I'd say … " Father Jaeger groped for words. "I'd be sure. I mean, in your frame of mind, seeking justice would be wrong. You're talking about revenge, not sorrow, not forgiveness."

"Ah, well no, no, Father. I believe justice and fairness should always be served. Weren't the Romans punished for killing Jesus?"

"Yes, I understand your thinking."

Beginning to focus on his true intention, the old man asked, "Is it wrong, Father, to kill a man in the name of justice?"

Startled, Father Jaeger asked in an effort to make a point, "Was this self-defense or an act in a just war?"

"No, Father, it wasn't either. I mean, it wouldn't be because it ain't happened … yet."

Father Jaeger replied, "Then I would tell you killing a man is morally unlawful and unjust, no matter the reason. It is a grave mortal sin for which you would be condemned to the fires of hell."

"I'm glad you said that, Father. Thank you. I agree. Killing is wrong."

"A justifiable act against someone who harmed you would have to be of less consequence ... let's say a verbal response and communication with the person who harmed your family. Do you agree?"

Silence. The old man waited to respond. Father Jaeger listened. Not a word. He readjusted his position in his chair.

Bless me, Dear Lord, to say the right words, the elder man thought. "Father, I cannot escape the nightmare of the harm brought by this cowardly cruel culprit. I live with it daily. I can't forget or forgive this man for how he affected my family. He shows no remorse, feels no guilt, and discards any plea."

"Understandable, but you must think forgiveness of this man."

"Maybe I could, but he shows no remorse for what he did."

"But you can't kill him," the priest reiterated.

"I don't plan on killing him, Father. That would let him off too easy. He needs to suffer for his sins like the way my family is suffering. You say forgiveness, Father, for one who has harmed your family? To one who took advantage of *my grandson* and selfishly affected this boy for the rest of his life?"

Father Jaeger was now most concerned for his safety. He could feel his pulse rise. Beads of perspiration everywhere.

My grandson ... abuse ... justice. Now Father Jaeger had a strange feeling about the old man's response. His own dark closet of hidden sins was now surfacing during another man's confession. Straightening his back, Father Jaeger became emotionally uncomfortable. He felt tightness in his back. "Sir, I believe you may be too emotional for repenting for your sins. I suggest you leave."

Pops leaned closer, his lips nearly touching the black veil. "Father Jaeger ... " He paused. "Do you know a twelve-year-old boy by the name of Gene? Gene Kowolski?"

Like reacting to a sudden piercing sword in his side, the priest's adrenaline spiked. He felt heat on his face. The confessional became an oven. Trying to stay calm, the confronted priest said, "Gene, Gene, I know several Genes. What did you say the last name was?"

"Kowolski. Gene Kowolski. Same last name as mine."

Father Jaeger's immediate reaction was self-defense. "I don't know any Gene Kow ... " The priest regretted knowing the name.

Silence was deafening from within the confessional. Father Jaeger did not hear breathing, not a sound from the other side of the black veil. The priest felt as if the confession was turning into an inquisition. *Stay calm. This man may be ...* Father Jaeger suddenly felt a stream of light as he saw his confessional door pulled open. The priest squinted at the sudden light and then looked straight into the face of the old man looking down at him.

"Gene Kowolski. The boy you abused, molested, and raped over and over again!" Pops lowered his head. "Gene Kowolski! He's my grandson, you sick bastard! I'm here to bring justice for Gene and his family. Now, Father Jaeger, do exactly as I say. I am about, about to..." Herman Kowolski turned his head and coughed. "I am about to cause great..." he coughed again.

"Holy shit! I mean ... " the priest made the sign of the cross. Dropping his priestly face, Father Jaeger's mode instinctively changed to defense in this most surreal situation. Survival. "What the hell are you talking about? I did no such thing. Your grandson's a liar—a sick, disturbed little boy."

"Thought you said you didn't know him. You're right, a sick and disturbed little boy. All because of you, you filthy bastard!" Now with stark hate in his voice, Pops said, "I'll ask you just one last time. Did you—" Sensing the priest was about to move, Pops stepped back one pace and simultaneously pulled the steel revolver from his right jacket pocket.

Father Jaeger started to lunge, his heart pulsating in his chest.

"Sit down, I say!" Pops pointed the gun straight at the priest's head. *Stay calm. This old man's serious.*

"Last time. Did you abuse my boy?"

"Now, Mr. Kowolski, I was always good to Gene. Always loving to him."

"Don't bullshit me, you son of a bitch. You are a phony two-faced bastard hiding behind that collar."

Father Jaeger's eyes bulged as he looked directly into the single barrel.

"One more time!" Pops pointed the gun straight between the priest's eyes.

"Dah, I know!" Jaeger stuttered incoherently. He watched as the gun tipped back and forth directly between his eyes. He squinted. His eyes closed in anticipation. *Bang!* The repercussion vibrated within the smoking barrel. Father Jaeger slumped in terror as the bullet whizzed just six inches above his head. Brown soundproof board flew like grenade fire.

"I'm hit! I'm hit," the priest whimpered.

"Sit up, you snake. The next time, I shoot to hit!"

Father Jaeger braced himself back in his chair, his two hands pushing against the seat. Herman Kowolski bent closer to the priest and steadied the smoking barrel directly between his eyes. In a low voice, he said, "I may be old, I may be dying, only weeks to live, but you should know I was a sharpshooter in World War I, France. I may be on my deathbed, but I still have one final aim, especially if I have one bullet left for a monster like you."

"Now, listen. Calm down. We need to talk this out. The Lord can be forgiving!"

"Quiet. I don't give a crap about forgiving. I'm here for justice. Did you molest Gene? Last time I'll ask!"

The priest said, trying to calm his aggressor as he faced the smoking barrel, "Yes, yes! I did!"

"How many times?"

"Don't know. Didn't count. Often," he said in rapid succession. "Several, many. I can't remember!" The priest covered his face with his hands and began to sob. "I'm sorry. I'm sorry. Forgive me. Please, please don't kill me!"

"I assure you, Father, I won't kill you. Not unless my aim is off," Kowolski said. "Forgive you?"

"Please, never again."

"What about what you've done to Gene? Were there others?"

"Yes, yes, there were others."

"How many?" the old man asked, now feeling his own pain in his side. Pops coughed as he forced himself to steady the gun. He used his left hand to brace himself on the door frame.

"Many. Lots. I didn't count."

"How long did you do this?"

"Years."

"How many?"

"Ever since the seminary. There! There, you old man. You have it all, but ... but I didn't mean to ... to ah ... Don't kill me!"

"You're a disgrace to the priesthood, to the church, and to manhood. You're just a sick, sick disgusting ... you son of a bitch! You've soiled and tarnished the collar you wear! It's not the Catholic Church. It's you—a bad, bad man." The pain in Pops' side intensified. He pressed his left hand against his side much harder. "Take it off! Take that collar off!"

"Why?"

"Take it off, you coward. It's tarnished. Your collar's tarnished forever!"

Father Jaeger reached up, pulled the collar from his neck, and flung it to the floor.

Pops was now in excruciating pain, but he held the gun steady. "Make the sign of the cross!"

Father Jaeger shook in terror.

"I said make the sign of the cross! Sit up! Put your filthy decrepit hands on your knees!" Pops quickly turned his head and looked around. *Nobody. Church is still empty.* He felt the rush of time.

Both men were in emotional and physical pain beyond what they had ever expected in their lives.

Steadying the barrel directly between the eyes of the priest, Pops said, "On your knees! Your hands on your knees!" Father Jaeger obeyed. "Now pull them apart!"

"A-a-apart? What apart?" Perspiration poured from the priest's forehead.

"Pull your knees apart. They are not to kneel on anymore. Make them touch the walls. Push, push with your hands. Spread your knees, you filthy bastard!" Pops steadied himself. The moment of his intended plan arrived, along with a sudden commitment to get it done. The priest's knees bounced against the walls of the confessional. He felt exposed, unprotected beneath his cassock. Vulnerable.

"Here's for all the acts you committed upon Gene and how many more … God only knows. You'll never rape again! Spread your knees! I said spread your knees!" Pops Kowolski lowered his head and kept the gun steady. "Now one last time, I want you to think of all those boys. Unzip your pants."

"What! Holy Jesus. No!"

"Unbutton your cassock. Now! Unzip!"

The priest, shaking and quivering, immediately obeyed. *Zipper? He's gonna.* "No, please, no!"

"I said keep your knees to the walls!"

The priest's hands shook. "No, please no!"

"Hold tight. Now think of Gene. I'm going to count to five while you say five of the boys' names. One, two … their names!"

Father Jaeger first stuttered, "G-G-Gene, Ed, D-Danny … "

The old man continued, "Two more!"

"J-Joey, Pete-Peter, I mean!"

In one motion, the frantic priest watched as Herman Kowolski slowly lowered the gun to the priest's shoulders … then two more feet to his belt.

"No! Please don't! You can't!" the priest screamed in horror as the old man gently squeezed the trigger.

Before the priest could instinctively close his knees … *Bang!* One shot fired. One direct hit. *Bang!* A second shot and a scream of unimaginable pain and horror resonated throughout the vacuum of the church. Pulling his hands together, the priest instinctively clasped the entrance wound and keeled over into an agonized fetal position.

Herman Kowolski stepped backward staggering. He watched as the man screech in agony. The priest, drenched in blood, lay rocking on the floor, curled up like a cat yearning for warmth. The old man felt a shock of horror at his action, almost as if he had imagined the act.

The cries and screams assured Pops Kowolski that the deed was real. Stunned, neither Father Jerome Jaeger nor Herman Kowolski heard the far front door open and close. Herman turned and staggered to the closest pew. He emptied four unfired cartridges from the revolver. They fell to the floor. Carefully, he laid the gun on the pew seat. Images of Gene in all his agony flashed through his mind. *Over. I'd do it again. For you, Gene, and all the rest of those abused souls.*

Kneeling, he quietly whispered, "Bless me, Father, for I have sinned. I have sought justice. I had to do what I did. I'm sorry, but the man has to suffer. I'm more sorry for Gene and my family." Herman Kowolski knew his days were short-lived. *Just Christmas, Dear Lord.*

The janitor appeared in the archway. Father Jaeger's bloodcurdling screams were unending. Seeing the fallen priest reeling on his side, Gorman Kelly streaked down the aisle toward him.

"Help me. Oh God, help me! I'm bleeding, bleeding. The pain, oh my God, the pain! That old bastard shot me. He was going to kill me. *Ahhh!*"

Gorman saw blood on the priest's hands, and his cassock was ripped open. The soaked blood turned black on the cassock. Kelly didn't hear the footsteps, but Father Jaeger saw Father Arnold peering over Gorman's shoulder.

"Help me, Father. Oh, oh, God, help me!"

"Judas Priest! What happened, Father?"

"That old bastard shot me!" Father Jaeger pulled his hands tighter in a futile attempt to stop the pain in a pool of blood.

"Gorman, go call the hospital," Father Arnold said.

All Father Arnold could see was blood and the priest wreathing in pain. Father made the sign of the cross and prayed. *Help this poor man.*

"No, no!" Jaeger pleaded between his horrifying *ahs* and deep moans. "Take me now. Now, or I'll, oh God, I'll bleed to death! Goddamn this pain. Help me!" his cries echoed through the vacuum of the church.

Gorman Kelly and Father Arnold did not see the old man in the pew just a few feet away.

"Better call the police," Herman Kowolski said, still staring ahead in a peaceful trance. *All for you, Gene. May you now rest without suffering.*

Father Jaeger looked up from his crouched position. He saw the back of Herman Kowolski's head. "You, you!" he yelled. Goddamn you!"

"Don't worry, Father. I'm not leaving. Justice has been served," the old man said to the priest reeling in pain.

Immediately assuming what had happened, Father Arnold said, "Later, later," dismissing any urgency to call the police, as he was totally focused on aiding Father Jaeger.

The side door, opposite the archway where Father Arnold and

Gorman had entered, suddenly opened. Sister Gregory heard the commotion. The sounds of her rosary jumping up and down at her side echoed as she hurried down the center aisle. Seeing the huddle in the far corner, sister sidestepped through the pews in the direction of Father Arnold, who was hovering over the fallen priest.

"What happened? Oh my dear God in heaven!" she exclaimed, making a quick sign of the cross when she saw Father Jaeger reeling in agony on the floor.

"He's been shot, Sister. We've got to get him to the hospital fast," Father Arnold said in a low voice, trying to maintain control of the situation.

"I'll get a couple of the big eighth-grade boys." She turned and without hesitation ran up the side aisle.

"Gorman, keep him comfortable as best you can."

Gorman looked up at Father Arnold with a puzzled expression. "I'll get some towels and blankets," he said, thinking of comforting the wounded priest.

"No, never mind. You just go get the car, Gorman. My car." Looking down at the terrified, anguished priest, he said, "Father, we'll get you to the hospital. Just you hold on while Gorman gets my car. It's parked In front. Drive across the lawn to the front door." Gorman turned in a rush.

"Oh God, hurry. The pain is killing me." Father Jaeger said. His screams had subsided and were now reduced to continuous groans, as if he could not stand the intolerable pain. Shock was his partner.

As Father Arnold turned, Herman Kowolski said, "Father, I'll wait here till you return. Please call the police. I'm not going anyplace. I did what I came to do."

Herman Kowolski remained in the side pew close to Father Jaeger, his deed done. Father Jaeger lay in shock, helpless to relieve the excruciating pain. Father Jaeger looked up to see Herman Kowolski staring down at him.

"Here, take this," Kowolski said as he took off his woolen gray coat and laid it atop the suffering priest. Moaning in his own pain each time he moved, the old man bent over and then fell, catching himself on the pew in front of him. With all his effort, the anguished priest moved his bloodied, trembling hands, as he reached to grip the old man's arm trying to pull him closer. Then he said, "May you ... you ... may you burn in hell, you goddamned ol' bastard." Father Jaeger had the look of Lucifer across his face.

Not responding, Herman Kowolski reached for the top of the pew and, struggling in his painful, weakened state, slowly walked to the front of the church row by row. Each pew served as an anchor, leaving small remnants of blood he had inadvertently acquired from the wounded priest. The tap of the cane in his left hand was muffled by the moans of the fallen priest. For the Kowolski family, justice had been served.

Once he reached the front row, Herman Kowolski dropped himself into the first pew seat. Hunched over at first, he slowly sat up. Looking at the statue of St. Joseph behind the communion rail, Herman Kowolski prayed for Father Jaeger.

Although it seemed to Father Jaeger like hours passed, Herman slowly turned toward the commotion in the back of the church minutes later. By then, more help had arrived. He could not tell from his vantage point who was removing the priest from the church. Herman Kowolski could only hear the intermittent moans and yells of the priest enduring the intolerable pain. For a moment he heard nothing. Then, "May you rot in hell, hell, hell!" The echoes ruptured through the empty church. "You, goddamn old bas, bas, bastard!" Then silence filled the church as Herman Kowolski sat alone, prayed, and waited.

Father Sullivan—December 2, 1958

It was late afternoon. Darkness was soon to arrive. His mind had remained confused since reading Linda's letter three nights before. It was a chilly day. Slipping on his long black overcoat, Father Sullivan decided to take a drive. After reaching for his black fedora, he turned out the light, walked to the end of the hall, and went down the steps to his car. Not in any kind of a hurry, Father Sullivan felt like his body was almost moving in slow motion. He was thinking more than he was walking. He imagined music, violins.

Pulling the collar up on his black woolen coat, Father Sullivan felt the chill of the cool winter air. He tugged the front of his hat brim down closer to his eyes. He backed his car up and shifted into first gear then drove south out of the rectory. He knew his destination. He did not yet understand his intentions or purpose.

Main Street was busy. School had let out, but now businesses were closing. It was sometime after 5:00 p.m., and darkness was falling on the early December evening. Tomorrow's meeting with Cardinal Cullings was absent from his mind. He was thinking about someone else.

Families were gathering in their homes for the supper hour, random cars were pulling into driveways, and kids were scurrying home on their bikes. Turning onto Harrison Street, Father Sullivan noticed   the side streets were quiet except for a few returning cars pulling into their driveways. In front of him, a paperboy slowly rode his bike, accurately tossing the papers on to the waiting porches.

Slowly, very slowly, Father Sullivan drove down the tree-lined streets. There were only traces of snow on the ground. A few leaves still clung to the trees. He passed a man burning leaves at the edge of the street. *Late for the season.* As he cranked down the driver's window, the aroma of the burning leaves took him back to his childhood days—he and his dad raking leaves on a late fall afternoon. *Oh, the memories.*

Ahead, Father Sullivan could see a long panel truck backed up to a house on the other side of the street. Slower and slower, he drove. He stopped on the opposite side of the street, a few hundred feet short of the moving truck in front. Father parked in the darkness provided by a large solitary oak. Turning the motor off, Father Sullivan remained in the car, outside the beam of the closest street lamp. He pulled his collar closer around his neck. He sat, thought, and waited.

The priest watched intently as the movers continued their trips in and out of the house, always coming back from the truck empty-handed. Most of the time, he could see her silhouette through the front window. He assumed she was giving directions and of what to take next. Time stood still.

Hearing the slam of metal, Father Sullivan assumed the back doors of the mover's truck were closing. He watched as the two movers got into the truck. He noticed a boy jumping into the middle front seat. *Joey.* The headlights beamed forward about thirty yards in front of his car. Slowly the truck moved forward, stopped, and then carefully pulled over to the curb. The truck turned left, and Father Sullivan watched the taillights disappear into the dimming evening light.

Looking back toward her house, he watched Linda carrying a box down the steps and then placing it in the trunk of her gray two-door Chevy. Reaching for his door handle, he hesitantly extended his fingers, feeling the cool metal. He waited. She returned to the house. He saw her through the front window, standing as if she was making one last check. *Now's the time*, he thought. Squeezing the handle, he quietly opened his car door. After placing his feet on the ground, Father Sullivan stood up behind the open door and braced his arms horizontally across the top. He watched. He waited.

The closing of the front door of her house sent an echo down the street and a chill down Father Sullivan's spine. He watched as the house went dark. *Now's the time*. Stepping around the car door, he slowly closed it, keeping his right hand in the jamb. Rubbing his eyes with his left hand as if he could push for the decision, Father Sullivan let the door close without a sound. Linda walked around her car. He took two steps forward. *Now's the moment. I will*. Barely, he could see her silhouette inside the car.

The lights of her Chevy beamed ahead. Still in the shadows, he walked up the street toward Linda, stepping faster. Then he stopped, hidden in the darkness of another towering oak. Linda's car pulled into the street. Father Sullivan noticed the right red brake light. The car stopped. He froze. Then he thought he saw her hesitate, turn around, and look directly at him. Standing still in the middle of the street, he hesitated one last time, stepped forward in her direction then hurried faster, closer to her car. His efforts were futile, as the brake lights went dark. Father took a deep breath. His heart stopped, as he watched the Chevy pull away and then disappear into the darkness.

Father Warren—December 2, 1958

Father Warren prayed about Father Sullivan's meeting tomorrow with Cardinal Cullings. It was late afternoon. With his day complete, he walked outside and then toward the front of the church. Lifting his cassock as he walked up to the church, he could feel the worn pattern in each step. The priest was in a private state of reflection.

Inside the church, Father Warren's eyes scanned the surroundings. Solitude and sanctuary gave him comfort. He reflected on memories still contained in this holy place. Walking down the center aisle, he stopped and took refuge in his usual twelfth row pew on the St. Joseph's side. Kneeling, Father Warren lowered his head in prayer. Thoughts of his friend Father Sullivan and the boys he was fighting for remained constant in his mind and prayers. His mind wandered to the future, wondering how this sickness could continue, where it would lead, and how it would end. The good priest begged God and his Savior Jesus Christ to let these good men—Fathers Sullivan, Holtz, and Girouard and Cardinal Cullings—bring an end to the crisis, achieve justice for the abused, and bring sanity back to his beloved Catholic Church.

An hour or so passed. Deep in thought and meditation, Father Warren prayed that tomorrow would be the beginning of the end to this unbelievable nightmare. The good priest sat back in his pew. He prayed about his own appointment tomorrow. His prayers subsided, he closed his eyes and felt the Spirit in his presence. *Dear God, let there be peace. May these good men come together, and with your divine spirit may the fallen seek forgiveness and come back into the good graces of God.*

CHAPTER 103

FINAL JUDGMENT

Father Sullivan—December 3, 1958

FATHER Warren and Father Sullivan breakfasted together before the younger priest left for his meeting with Cardinal Cullings in Indianapolis.

"Anxious, Michael?" Father Warren asked, glancing at the morning paper. Setting the sports page down, he picked up the front section before Father Sullivan could respond. "Are you ready?" Father Warren asked his friend.

"I am, Father. Our Lord and justice are—" Father Sullivan started to assure him.

"Oh my Dear Lord," Father Warren said, immediately startled by what he read. "Michael, look at this … *Priest shot in confessional. Father Jerome Jaeger, formerly assistant pastor at St. Thomas Moore, was shot while hearing confession at St. Vincent Parish Church in Eastville, Indiana, where he presently resides as assistant pastor. Late Tuesday afternoon, Father Jaeger was found by the church janitor, Gorman Kelly, lying on the floor, apparently shot by a man going to confession. The priest was rushed to Union Hospital in Terre Haute. The hospital reported that Father Jaeger is in serious but stable condition. After the incident in the church, the accused waited for the police to arrive. The suspect was taken into custody without incident. The name of the assailant was not released.*"

Father Warren thrust the paper down. "Michael, I can't believe this! This is horrible. Just horrible!"

"I agree, Father. Why haven't the police called here? Although I want Father Jaeger to be brought to justice, I must say not in this way."

"Who would do such an awful thing? This is so terribly wrong," Father Warren said in a raised voice.

Father Sullivan hesitated with his answer. He thought. Looking at Father Warren, he said, "God only knows. It could be a number of people. Who knows what people will do when their children, their defenseless children, are so horrifically abused? Who are we to judge the reason? We can only forgive."

"What about your meeting this afternoon?"

"Oh yes, of course. Excuse me. I'm going to call Father Holtz." Father Sullivan thought he might still be able to contact Father Holtz before he left South Wayne.

He called, but there was no answer. Then Father Sullivan remembered Father Holtz had said the bishop and Father Schmidt had planned to drive to Indianapolis the day before the meeting. Father Sullivan knew he would not be able to contact him. Although he had not met Father Girouard, Father Sullivan felt comfortable calling.

"Person-to-person to Father Girouard, 555-3662 at St. Peter and Paul rectory in Indianapolis." He waited for the operator to connect.

"I have him on the line, sir."

"Hello, Father Girouard speaking."

"Father Girouard, this is Father Sullivan from St. Thomas Moore in Wabash."

"Oh yes, I'm glad you called. Father Holtz hasn't called yet. Did you hear about Father Jaeger?"

"Yes. Just read it in the paper this morning," Father Sullivan replied. "That's why I called. What about the meeting?"

"Cardinal Cullings and I already discussed that as soon as we read the paper only a few minutes ago. The cardinal decided we are meeting as planned. This is all the more reason. Now the news will travel. *The Star* already called this morning."

"I'm ready to leave now," Father Sullivan said. "Just a couple hours' drive. Look forward to meeting you. Trying times, Father."

"Yes they are," Father Girouard said as he hung up the phone.

CHAPTER 104

JUSTICE AT A CROSSROAD

Clarence Wolfe—December 3, 1958

THE rain had turned to sleeting snow, and the clouds still hovered low in the morning sky. To the north in the direction Clarence Wolfe was driving, darker clouds rolled and tossed in the sky. He had allowed plenty of time to get to his final destination. He didn't even tell Miss Gardner where he would be this day.

Driving through the windy city was never to Wolfe's liking. The cars were bumper-to-bumper, and the tension in driving seemed to elevate his anxiety and stress. However, the anticipation of the meeting far exceeded the stress of driving in city traffic. *What does he want from me? How are they going to step up the operation? Why did Randall Zilbar insist I make the meeting?*

Hours passed. The drive was tense. The hovering clouds, the slick highway, and the meeting with Mario all weighed heavily on Clarence Wolfe's mind. Ahead he could see the tallest building in Chicago. The mighty Prudential. Forty-one stories, new and gleaming, it seemed to stretch to the clouds as far as the eye could see. *A half hour. I should be there by noon. Plenty of time.*

Driving north on Route 50, Clarence Wolfe could see the planes flying in and out of Midway Airport to his left. *Watch for Ogden.* Stretching his neck under the top of the windshield, he looked at the street signs … 55th Street, 47th. He kept driving. There it was. He turned left on Ogden, traveled three blocks, and then turned right onto Polermo, number 666.

Slowing down, Wolfe was at first confused. The address was both a trucking and cement company. Surrounded by cyclone fence and barbed wire, the space looked more like a minimum security prison than a trucking company. The area took up an entire block across from a working-class residential neighborhood. Wolfe pulled up to steel bar gates. Showing his authority, the security officer held up his hand, indicating Wolfe needed to stop, as if he thought the '55 Oldsmobile might proceed through the double-fenced gate without stopping.

"Whatcha need?" the burly uniformed guard asked.

"I'm here to see Mario Molinaro."

"Let me see your driver's license."

Carefully, the guard scrutinized the card, front and back. After running his hairy finger down the page on the clipboard anchored above his belt, he said, "Name's here. You're okay. Drive right over there and park behind that black Cadillac."

"Which one? There's a dozen black Cadillacs," Wolfe asked.

"The black one with the large fins. Don't hit the bumper. Then walk up to that front entrance," he said, pointing to the sign over the front door. "The one that says Molinaro Bros." Pointing above the sign, he said, "That's the office."

Wolfe could tell the guard had not appreciated the "all black" comment, as he was still leaning over, looking into the car, scrutinizing the driver, and not saying a word.

The steel gate slid open. *They're all black*, he thought, pulling away. *Small-time dego.* In the rearview mirror, he could see the guard still watching him. Rolling up the window, he felt the car should be locked. From inside the car, he watched another security guard walking a dog around the corner of the office, a German shepherd. Clarence wondered, *Where's his Tommy gun?* The guard wore a gun. Clarence Wolfe's gray-and-white two-toned Oldsmobile seemed lost in the sea of black cars. All big. The Cadillacs were parked closer to the building. A huge array of trucks, semis, concrete trucks, and large flatbeds were arranged toward the back of the lot.

Clarence parked his car as directed. *No time to dick around.* Looking left and right as he walked to the front steps, he stopped ... *Molinaro Bros. Construction and Cement Company. Cement?* After straightening his tie and adjusting the lapels of his jacket, he deliberately walked up the concrete steps and opened the half-glass *Molinaro Bros. Co.* front door. *They sure like their name. Meatballs Cement Company*, he snickered to himself.

A wide hall with chairs on one side led to a closed solid wood-paneled door. *Wonder what's behind that.* He opened the door to another half-glass *Molinaro Bros.* door. A middle-aged receptionist sat at her desk with her back to the wall. She had a perfect view of those who entered. Wearing a solid black dress, she looked more daunting than attractive. He imagined her being Mario's younger sister, though he had yet to meet Mario. There were three other desks, and two other ladies were busy tapping on their typewriters. *Smarter than I thought. They can even type.* The last desk, closest to the far closed door, was unoccupied.

"Good afternoon, sir," the receptionist said.

"To you too, ma'am. I'm here to see Mario."

"You mean, Mr. Molinaro?" she asked with a corrective inflection in her voice.

"Oh yes, of course. Sorry."

"Yes, he's expecting you. Rosie is with him now. When she returns to her desk, I'll tell her you're here. Meanwhile, have a seat in the hall … Mr. Wolfe," she said with an emphasis on *mister*.

"Do I need to go back through both doors or just the first?"

"Both," she said, with some disdain.

Clarence nervously waited in the hall for about twenty minutes. He spent the time imagining Mario Molinaro and the purpose of the meeting. The door opened. He sat up and looked at the attractive thirty-five-year-old dressed in a plain black dress with a red scarf draped over her shoulders. As she approached, he stood up.

"Good morning, sir. I'm Rosie Riccardi. Please follow me. Mr. Molinaro is ready to see you."

I'll bet he is. Clarence just nodded and then said, "Thank you, ma'am. I'm anxious to meet him. Heard many good things."

Returning through the same door, they passed a formative looking guard just inside. Rosie never looked up. Following Rosie, Wolfe couldn't help but notice her long wavy black hair that hung almost to her waist. He remained behind the click of her tall black heels. *Nice dego ass.* Past her desk, right down a long hall, and toward the back of the building, Clarence followed the lady in black. His sense of direction told him this would be a corner office. Few windows. Almost hidden. *Wonder why.*

"Mr. Molinaro, this is Clarence Wolfe," Rosie announced as they walked into his remote, dark office.

Mario Molinaro was standing behind his desk, back to the door. As Rosie announced the visitor, he turned, reached across his large oak desk, and extended his hand. Wolfe shook it in return. A lamp, pen tray, and a small stack of files were overwhelmed by the exposed wood desktop. Clarence Wolfe was totally surprised by Mario's stature. All of five feet nine with dark curly hair, Mario, dressed all in black, commanded an imposing presence. "Have a seat," he directed.

As Wolfe sat down in the straight back wooden chair, he noticed a worn black leather book to Mario's right. He wondered. Accepting the power and authority commanded by Mario, Wolfe listened tentatively.

"How was your trip, Mr. Wolfe? See you found us okay."

"Easy drive. Just a little busier around Chicago than I'm used to."

Mario nodded.

"Quite a place you have here. Much larger than I expected."

"Yeah, we're into a number of things. Like to keep the family busy, and the family's family, if you know what I mean," Mario said very convincingly. "Getting down to business, you know we have this little project, ya know, with Zilbar. Good ol' Randall Zilbar."

"Sure, sure, glad to do my part," Wolfe responded without using Mario's name.

Leaning forward in his chair, hands folded, elbows on the desk, Mario asked, "That's one of the reasons you are here. You know, we're expanding, and I want to discuss your role."

Feeling a little more relaxed, Wolfe said, "If it can ... if it can help Randall--and you, of course, I want to continue."

"Good. That's good to hear. Think you know the ropes there, Mr. Wolfe?" Mario paused, leaned back in his chair, and clasped his hands behind his head. "There is one little thing, however, that you and I need to talk about." He leaned forward and spoke in a lower voice. "Ya know, make sure we both understand. You owe Randall some dough, right? Maybe twenty-five thousand?"

"Yes, yes, I do. I'm gonna pay though. Right now it's a lot of money, but Randall can trust me. He knows that. I'll pay him," Clarence replied in advance of the question.

"Sure, sure, I'm sure he knows. Like a ... like Randall trusts you. He can, can't he?"

"Sure, always. You too. You too, Mr. Molinaro. You both can trust me."

"That leads me to my question. Can I trust you?" Mario asked, his eyes narrowing and his brow furrowing. "Can Mario really trust you?"

"Trust me? Of course ... course. Just as I said. Just as Randall can," Wolfe said, feeling his pulse elevate with Mario's inquiry.

Mario's voice dropped even lower, just above a whisper. He leaned another inch closer. "You see, when I received the last delivery, you know, in August when the boys came down?"

"Yes, sure, I remember. Packed the briefcases myself," Wolfe assured him, accepting the baited question, hook, line, and sinker.

"Yeah, but one little problem there, Mr. Wolfe. One case just wasn't fully complete. Don't think you packed it all. So a ... so that makes Mario wonder. Wonder what you could have done. You look like a bright man. Of course, you can count 1-2-3-4. Know what I mean? This disappoints Mario. Everybody knows, ya know, I don't like disappointments, surprises, or failures. So tell me straight. What happened?"

"What the hell? You tellin' me you think I kept some?" Wolfe asked, his voice and body both elevating.

"Settle down, settle down. You raisin' your voice to Mario, Mr. Wolfe? Not accusing. Just asking. All I want is da truth. You tella me the truth, then, then, then Mario's happy." Mario nodded and pressed his lips together. "All done. Completo. No problemo."

"The truth is I don't know why you asked me. I took nothing. Nothing from you. Nothing from Randall. I know the danger of that. I wouldn't think of it. Goddamn no! No way! I'm not crazy," he said and then leaned back in his chair. He wiped the perspiration from his brow. "I come up here to be accused of something I didn't do? No way. Not to you, not to Randall," Wolfe said, his voice stammering and head shaking.

"No way! Not me! Wouldn't do that, especially not to important powerful people like you, Mr. Molinaro, or to Randall. I mean Mr. Zilbar. No, never."

Lifting his shoulders and opening his palms, Mario Molinaro calmly said, "Relax. That's fine. If that's the truth, then that's the truth." Judging by Wolfe's response, Mario knew Wolfe was not telling the truth. Sitting back in his chair, he looked directly at Clarence. "Now I understand. Thanks for the truth there, Mr. Wolfe."

Wolfe breathed easier. Mario knew, however, that there was no room in business for doubt. Doubt would fester and turn easy decisions to harmful hard choices. Mario knew the importance of Randall Zilbar. Life has choices.

There was a knock on the door. "Come in, come in," Mario said.

Slowly, it opened. Any light from the dim hall was blocked by the large man standing in the doorway. "Come on in, I said. Want you to meet a friend of mine. This here is Clarence Wolfe from the reform school in Wabash, a friend of Randall Zilbar."

The big man, now standing a few feet inside the closed door, said, "Yeah, Wabash. Think I might have passed through there once."

"Clarence, I'd like you to meet my friend, Lucco. Lucco Gagliardi."

The name meant nothing to Wolfe. He said, "Glad to meet you, Lucco. I mean, Mr. Gagliardi."

Hands clasped, feet spread, Lucco waited.

"As I was saying, I wanted you to come here, as we are going to be stepping up our operation with Randall. If you're going to remain a part of our little operation, you need to know a little more about us. Lucco's goin' ta show you around. You do want to remain a part, don't you, Mr. Wolfe. You know me and Randall, and, well of course, my friend here, Lucco?" Lucco looked straight ahead.

With relief and a semblance of returning confidence, Wolfe replied, "Of course. Why of course. You can count on me, Mr. Molinaro. Just like Randall can."

"I'm sure we can. Yes, I'm sure of that, Mr. Wolfe." Mario stood up. "Lucco, you drive Mr. Wolfe over to the other office down the block. I have to meet with Louie for about ten. Then I'll be right over."

Clarence turned toward Lucco. Lucco opened the door.

"Mr. Wolfe, one more thing. Thanks for the truth. I knew I could count on you," Mario said with a big smile stretched across his face.

"You bet. You can count on me, Mr. Molinaro. Good to meet you," Wolfe said and then turned to follow Lucco down the hall.

Lucco said nothing as he walked to the front door. Clarence Wolfe followed. Mario stood and watched them leave.

In the parking lot, Lucco opened the door of his black Buick and said, "Get in."

I'm not comfortable with this tour guide, Wolfe thought, but he got in the front as directed. Pulling ahead, Lucco turned right away from the front gate. Adrenaline shot through Wolfe's body. His heart immediately raced. "Aren't we going to another office?"

Lucco said, "Yeah."

"This doesn't look like the way."

"Gonna show ya somethin' else first." Driving back around a large brick building, Lucco stopped the car next to a set of double doors. He straightened his tie, got out of the car, walked around the front, and opened the passenger's side door. "Come with me."

Now Wolfe knew for sure that this was not looking like a fun poker game. "No," he said emphatically. "I'm leaving. Don't like this. Going back to Mario's office." All he could think of was how to reach his own car and get the hell out of this construction boneyard. Turning away from Lucco, Wolfe walked toward the corner.

"Stop!" Wolfe heard Lucco's deep, dark voice from behind.

Turning around, Wolfe looked at the big man, whose huge hand was wrapped around a barrel of cold gray steel. Looks said everything. Lucco did not say another word. He motioned toward the double doors with the barrel of the gun. Another man in a black suit stood solitary by the open door, leaning against the brick wall, his right foot braced back solidly against the bricks. His only movement was his thumb and finger inserting a cigarette in his mouth.

Clarence Wolfe knew he had no choice. Walking ahead of Lucco through the double doors, he nodded at Wise Guy, who was still leaning against the wall with a Chesterfield dangling from his lips, his dark suit with gray stripes shielding him from the cool dampness of the brick. Wolfe could not help but notice his pug-like nose and the large curved scar over his right eye. Wise Guy just stood there with the expression of a rock.

Entering the building, Wolfe could hear the steps of the silent one following. The creak of the hinges informed Wolfe that this was a seldom-used building. Nobody was around. Wise Guy closed the doors. Clarence watched the cracked concrete floor as the dim light narrowed to a slim triangle and then disappeared. The building was empty with the exception of a flatbed truck and a front-end loader close to the door. The bucket was flat on the ground and pointed at the closed double doors.

Lucco stopped next to a tall gray beam. Most of the paint was chipped away. He looked directly at Wolfe as he slid his gun back into the holster beneath his left arm. He didn't say a word. For a flash, Wolfe relaxed his shoulders. Then Lucco reached his right hand into his jacket pocket. *Left it there.* He stepped forward closer to Wolfe. "Turn around. Face da wall." *Silence.* Wolfe looked over at Wise Guy. *I could use that cigarette*, he thought as he felt his body beginning to tremble.

Lucco removed his hand from his right pocket, secured the wrapped leather end of the wire in his hand, reached with his left hand for the other leather end, and stretched the wire taut. In one motion, he wrapped and secured the wire around Wolfe's neck. Wolfe's eyes bulged. "Ah, ga, ga!" Wolfe instinctively reached for his throat. He flung his shoulders from side to side. Gagging, he felt the tight clutch of the thin wire around his throat. Although a big man at 240 pounds and as tall as Lucco, Wolfe was no match.

Thrusting his feet forward and then high was useless as Lucco's big arms tightened. Lucco then moved the wire from side to side like a saw. Wolfe struggled with all his might. His life flashed before his eyes. He saw family, children, boys. Only his constant gagging for air interrupted the silence.

Zilbar's deranged face appeared in a cracked mirror. Number 1934, leather couch, Zilbar's naked body hovering over Gordon Yoder, Homer Atkins gagging, Bednar. Images raced across the screen in his head. The fight for air was more painful than the wire itself. Screams and noise did not exist. There was no exit. The flinging of arms and thrashing of feet soon gave way to the total absence of air. Wolfe reached inside for every bit of strength. He flung his body to his right as if to free himself from the hulk behind him.

Lucco suddenly lurched forward and sideways as he got caught off balance. The wire remained secure as both men fell to the ground. On his side, his hands grasping for his neck, Wolfe thrust and kicked, his heels digging into Lucco's shins. With one last burst of energy, Wolfe thrust his elbow into Lucco's ribs, delivering one last powerful blow but to no avail. As if in slow motion, Clarence Wolfe felt the last movements of his worldly body. His hands slowed, and then currents of fire raced to his feet until his legs went limp. Lucco put his hands together. The wire fell to his side. Clarence Wolfe lay sprawled on the cracked concrete floor. Still. Dead.

Lucco fell backward, his left hand still clutching the wire, his right hand bracing his fall. He half sat, leaning against the steel column next to Wolfe on the dirty, damp concrete floor. His heavy breathing continued. His mind swirled. Gasping for breath, Lucco leaned back, hands at his side.

Wise Guy lit another Chesterfield. *Let them be.* He looked at Lucco leaning against the column, his stomach heaving, his chest pounding for air. Wolfe's dark blue suit had split down the back seam from the violent struggle. Looking over at Lucco, Wise Guy walked over, bent down, straightened the lapels on Lucco's suit, and loosened Lucco's tie. He then placed his cigarette between Lucco's lips. Lucco closed his eyes in thanks.

Walking back to the wall, Wise Guy propped his foot against the brick once more and tipped his hat backward, exposing his thin black hair. He lit another Chesterfield. Some time passed until Lucco and Wise Guy regained lost momentum.

Then Lucco said, "Let's clean this up. Take him to the loader." Having caught his breath, Lucco pulled himself up, bent over, and turned the body with one flip of his powerful right hand. Wolfe's face was contorted in frozen agony. Wise Guy lifted Wolfe's feet as Lucco manhandled his shoulders. The two pulled the body to the front of the loader and then heaved the lifeless body into the bucket.

Dusting off his hands, Lucco looked at Wise Guy. "I'll report to Mario. You take care of the rest."

Wise Guy knew exactly what to do. He was experienced. Clarence Wolfe never returned to Wabash. Randall Zilbar never inquired. He had already received a report from Mario.

Miss Gardner--December 4, 1958

Sitting quietly at her desk, Miss Gardner wondered why Clarence Wolfe did not come to work yesterday. *He didn't even call*. Her Corona was silent as she could not keep her mind on her work. She assumed he was most likely sick.

Today she became more concerned. Her repeated phone calls went unanswered. Noon time came and went. Finally, she made up her mind. After asking Jim Duncan to watch the office, she left the building.

Clarence Wolfe's house was only a few miles away, a fairly quick trip. Pulling into his driveway, she noticed right away that his car was gone. *Odd. Sick?* She went up to the house and rang the bell repeatedly. No answer. She peered into the windows. Nothing seemed amiss.

As Miss Gardner drove back to the school, she began to feel fearful of what could have happened.

Decision made. When she was once again seated at her desk, she put in a call to Sheriff Thurow. After telling him of her concerns, he questioned her about how he seemed when she last saw Wolfe. Sheriff Thurow paused in deliberation, then more to himself rather than to Miss Gardner. He mused, *Something mysterious is going on up at the school. First Phillip Krueger disappears and now Clarence Wolfe.*

CHAPTER 105

FINAL MEETING

The Clergy—December 3, 1958

FATHER Holtz stood in the doorway of the side waiting room of the archdiocese rectory, waiting for Father Sullivan. Around the front corner, he could see Father Sullivan moving at a brisk pace.

"Good morning, Michael."

"Hello, Ben. Have you heard the news this morning?"

Father Holtz replied, "Yes, just a while ago. I read about Father Jaeger this morning when I picked up a paper at the hotel. Unbelievable!"

Father Sullivan responded, "You know, Ben, I am shocked. I do feel for the man, but I'm ... " He paused. "Between you and me, Ben, I am not surprised. All his dirty deeds and God only knows how many victims. Something like this was almost bound to happen. This was drastic to say the least. Imagine if you had a son and a priest took advantage of your defenseless eleven- or twelve-year-old. Ben, what would you do? Honestly? Hear his confession and say the rosary every day? Forgiveness? Yes, but some things ... " Father Sullivan shook his head. "Some people would address it in ways, well, ways like what happened to Father Jaeger. We are not to know how far one can be pushed. Whoever did this, and of course I don't approve, must have felt helpless, and this was the only way to find justice."

"And yes, Michael, just my usual reminder, but remember, we have never talked. I barely know you. Only through the meetings in South Wayne with the bishop did we meet," he reminded his friend. "Only

Father Girouard and the cardinal know of our friendship, but they brought us all together today. They can be trusted ... totally."

"Yes, I can't wait to meet him," Father Sullivan said, assuring Father Holtz of his appreciation for making this meeting come together. "I keep telling myself it's for the boys, for the victims. My belief is that today will be the beginning of justice being served."

"Speaking of the boys, are they coming?" Father Holtz asked.

"Peter Goodnar and his parents will be here at two thirty. Didn't want them to have to sit and wait too long. Unfortunately, Gene Kowolski's dad called me two days ago. He said Gene could not handle any confrontation. The poor lad is having a terrible time—a terrible time with school, friends, and his family, not to mention his health issue. Mr. Kowolski said it's a very dark time for Gene. He said the continuous nightmares about Jaeger never stop. They are concerned and oh, it's awful. Mr. Kowolski said Gene has a lingering infection from the ordeal. You know, Ben, I've talked with Gene's dad several times. Met once in my study. That didn't end well."

Father Holtz responded, "Michael, I got ahold of Ned Thornbauer. He'll be there. He said the two of you had a clear understanding after your meeting. You know, Ned is twenty-two. He's mature, strong, and really committed. Ned really opened up after nine years once he heard about his brother. Hard to believe Danny is going through the same thing with Bishop Powers as Ned experienced so long ago."

Father Holtz looked down the hall then continued, "Shows how Bishop Powers has kept everything under cover. By the way, I didn't tell you why I drove separately from the bishop and Father Schmidt. I'm sure that Bishop Powers won't bring his driver. He'll be hush-hush. I told the bishop I'm driving on to Terre Haute after the meeting. Can't imagine riding with him and Schmidt back to South Wayne. Told him that I'm going to see my Aunt Mame and Uncle Bill. They live on a farm west of town."

"Yeah, that ride home should be quite the conversation after today," Father Sullivan said with a half-smile.

As they waited together in the library, Father Girouard walked in and said in a robust, welcoming manner, "Hello, Ben."

Father Holtz proudly introduced his two friends to one another.

"It's all my honor, Father. A friend of Father Holtz is a friend of mine. I've heard so much about you, although I'm sorry to meet under these circumstances," Father Girouard said, extending his hand to Father Sullivan.

The three priests discussed the meeting, who would be there, and their hopes for the outcome.

Father Girouard said, "Cardinal Cullings is meeting with the bishop right now. Just informing him about the agenda without going into great detail."

"I kind of feel badly for the bishop, especially since Ned Thornbauer will be here. Is the cardinal going to tell the bishop that Ned will be speaking with us?" Father Holtz asked.

"No, he's not," Father Girouard said. "I disagree with the tactic, but the cardinal was adamant. I suggested that Bishop Powers should be informed before. However, I never second-guess Cardinal Cullings. He has incredible judgment. Regarding the shooting of Father Jaeger, I find this to be a tragedy, a very concerning state of affairs. Any idea who could have done this?" Father Girouard asked Father Sullivan.

Father Sullivan pressed his lips together, thought for a moment, and then said, "I have an idea, but it's too early to say. I want to hear officially." Father Holtz looked at Father Sullivan and furrowed his brow, but he didn't inquire.

"Totally understand. I respect that. We don't want any leaks or rumors, especially about such a sensitive and traumatic situation," Father Girouard replied. "Sister Catherine will greet Ned and Danny when they arrive. Same with Peter. I suggested she let them wait in different rooms. They'll all be nervous, so separate rooms will be less awkward."

"Good idea, Ronald. You're always on top of things," Father Holtz commented.

"Thanks. I received good instructions on manners, courtesy, and protocol in the Vatican. They are sticklers for details." Father Girouard patted Ben on the shoulder. "Why don't we go on down? We will be meeting in the cardinal's conference room. The center table seats fourteen. There'll be plenty of space, so we all won't be shoulder to shoulder. A little less intimidating."

"Especially for the bishop," Father Sullivan said with a slight smirk on his face. "He'll need some extra space between himself, the other priests, and the victims."

Fathers Holtz and Sullivan smiled at each other.

Fathers Holtz and Sullivan wore black suits. Father Girouard looked official in his black cassock. He knew Cardinal Cullings would be in all red.

Both Fathers Holtz and Sullivan looked up and around as they entered the conference room from the side double doors. Just off the main hall, beyond the front foyer, the conference room was impressive, featuring floor-to-ceiling walnut paneling, original paintings on the walls, and a high ceiling of crossbeams with antiqued plaster between. The windows opposite the side doors were framed with Italian tapestries.

"I've never seen such a table. Looks like mahogany," Father Sullivan said to Father Holtz. The beautiful table with long, heavy carved legs and the fourteen matching wood and black leather chairs surrounding it were as impressive as the room itself.

"Maybe, Father Sullivan, you and I will sit on the window side," Father Girouard said, opening his hand to the other side of the table. "I'll sit closest to the cardinal, who will be at this end to the right of the side doors. That door behind him opens to the back hall. You can sit on this door side, Father Holtz, and that will place Bishop Powers and Father Schmidt here with their backs to the door. Ben, just scoot down two more chairs to give additional space between you and Father Schmidt."

Two pitchers of ice water and several glasses had been placed a third of the way from each end of the table. Father Girouard could hear the cardinal and the bishop coming down the hall.

"Here they come," he said to Fathers Holtz and Sullivan.

Cardinal Cullings entered the room. Wearing his cassock and scarlet sash, he was the epitome of religious stature. Bishop Powers was at his side, totally expressionless. Bishop's suit jacket was open at the waist, a rather wide expanse from side to side. His thinning hair slicked back over revealing a somewhat disheveled appearance, only intensified by the strain in his eyes.

"Good morning, Your Eminence," Father Girouard was the first to greet the cardinal.

"Father Girouard, you met Bishop Powers earlier. Bishop, I believe you know everyone else."

The bishop barely nodded. Saying nothing, Bishop Powers pushed his rimless glasses upward on the bridge of his nose, which looked redder than usual.

"Why don't we all have a seat?"

Bishop Powers instinctively walked to the chair next to Father Schmidt sitting in the middle of the table, back to the double doors. Father Holtz sat closer to the end of the table with two chairs between himself and Father Schmidt.

Cardinal Cullings was the first to speak. "Gentlemen, as you all know by now, a tragic event happened yesterday. Father Jerome Jaeger, who was invited to be with us today, was shot while hearing confession. This is under any condition a wrong, sinful, and sad immoral act. May Father Jaeger recover. May the culprit be brought to justice. That said, it was my decision that this meeting still take place. If the accusations stated here today about Father Jaeger are factual, fair, and true, then the shooting yesterday will not exonerate him."

Father Sullivan internally agreed. Bishop Powers had not heard a word Cardinal Cullings said; he was concerned only for himself and what the meeting would bring.

"We all know why we are here today," Cardinal Cullings said. "I especially want to listen to what you, Father Sullivan, have to say. I understand that your words are very accusatory of our good Bishop Powers." Cardinal Cullings looked to his left, acknowledging the bishop's presence. "Of equal importance, Bishop Powers, I want to know exactly what your response is to Father Sullivan. Both of your words are of extreme importance regarding these most unfortunate circumstances. After your words and the following discussion, we will hear from the boys who say they have been involved. I understand we also have some parents."

Bishop Powers leaned to his left, cupped his hand to his mouth, and whispered something to Father Schmidt. Father Schmidt seemed to sink a little lower in his chair.

"We should feel good about this meeting if the truth comes forward. We cannot escape or fear the truth," Cardinal Cullings said with steadfast conviction. "I'm in hopes that what we have here is a *failure to communicate.* When it comes to misunderstandings, coming together and placing everything on the table is the best way to address any difficult and challenging situation. We will find answers regarding this plague that is affecting our beloved Catholic Church. So I suggest we begin with the truth, gentlemen." Cardinal Cullings paused. "Yes, the truth. Now, Father Sullivan, could you tell us why you asked for this meeting?"

"Thank you, Cardinal Cullings." Father Sullivan took a deep breath, while looking directly at Bishop Powers. "My main purpose is to bring justice for the abused victims. My goal is for the church to provide for the safety of all children within our church. We should organize a structure that solidifies a common pledge of zero tolerance for any priest who is an abuser of children. Cardinal Cullings, it is my belief and conviction that elimination of sexual abuse by any of the Catholic clergy must begin in Rome. However, we must do our part to stop any and all abuse here at home. Then we must make sure that all cases are reported to the Vatican," Father Sullivan said as he continued to look across the table at the stoic bishop.

A couple of eyebrows raised. Father Holtz sat silently. Father Schmidt leaned over, covering his mouth, and whispered something in the bishop's ear. Father Girouard displayed a confident look of agreement. Cardinal Cullings, for reasons he would later disclose after Bishop Powers and Father Schmidt left, quietly agreed. Father Holtz felt the bishop was now getting the point.

"Before we invite the young boys waiting to join us, I want to express my factual feelings of how I see this situation," Father Sullivan said.

Everyone noticed as Sister Catherine stepped into the room and handed a note to Father Girouard. She left as quietly as she had entered.

Sensing the need to clarify his previous comments, Father Sullivan said, "It is my observation and conclusion ... " He paused and then said, "With all due respect, Bishop Powers ... " Father Sullivan reached for a glass of water. "With all due respect Bishop Powers ... " He looked directly at the bishop and continued, "I believe you have been hiding the abuse within our diocese and covering it up by transferring the priests to different and new parishes.

"I assume but do not know for sure that you probably don't even inform the pastors about the priests' histories of abuse. You are covering up for these wicked men, priest after priest. You hide them away. Bishop Powers, do you hear me? You hide them away. The cover-up is almost as sinful as the deed. You are guilty, just as the abusers. They preyed on other young boys. That may not have been your intention, but that is the result. Scores and scores of abused lives ... and you ... you—"

Bishop Powers' face beamed pink. Tiny blue vessels appeared on his cheeks. "Now that's just enough!" As lost in the moment as Father Sullivan, Bishop Powers stood up. He bent over the table, braced himself with his left hand, and pointed his finger directly at Father Sullivan. "For God's sake, you ... you are a liar! There is no truth in what you say. I'll have no more of this! You are out of order referring to your superior. I'm your bishop. Show respect! I remind you, Sullivan, even suggesting an ill-founded cover-up ... it's a damn lie! A lie! You hear me?"

The bishop was out of breath. His face was flushed red, and spittle oozed from the corners of his mouth. The vein in his neck enlarged above his collar. Stammering, he stopped, knowing he had lost control in front of Cardinal Cullings. Huffing noticeably, Bishop Powers tried to regain his composure. Still standing, now with both hands resting on the table, his glare and look to kill was printed across his face. *I went too far. I lost it.*

Bishop Powers stood erect and shook his finger at Father Sullivan. He straightened the lapels on his coat, stiffened his posture, and then sat back down. Although he tried, he could not formulate any coherent words to follow. He sat back and slumped in his chair. The room was as quiet as snowfall on a windless day. Cardinal Cullings thought, *The unexpected truth can bring out the worst in a person.*

Within a few moments, the bishop tried to hasten composure. "Excuse me, Cardinal, gentlemen."

The cardinal did not say a word, empathetically allowing the bishop to compose himself. His attempt to cover up his outburst was unsuccessful, but it was very telling. The emotional eruption was not retractable. Bishop Powers knew he had just become his own worst enemy.

The silence in the room was uncomfortably overwhelming. Even Father Sullivan felt a brief moment of compassion for the now overexposed bishop. Showing his calm, controlled resilience to confrontation and sincere empathy for the bishop, Cardinal Cullings placed both hands on the table as if to prepare to push himself away from a satisfying meal. He said, "Gentlemen, let's all have a glass of water and reflect for a moment."

Like a balloon releasing stagnant air, everyone accepted the appropriately timed invitation. Rather than confronting the embarrassed bishop, the good cardinal said, "Those are strong words and accusations, Father Sullivan," hoping to balance the awkward moment as the bishop still sat in silence.

After waiting for the perfect time, Father Girouard discreetly slid a piece of paper to Father Sullivan. All eyes focused on Father Sullivan, who was visibly alarmed. "*Hmmm*, gentlemen, may I change for a moment to another subject?" he asked calmly. "Father Girouard has passed word that Father Warren, my pastor and mentor, called and left a message that the man who shot … "

Blinking, he carefully read the note again. "The man who shot Father Jaeger was Gene Kowolski's grandfather. Just a moment please." Father Sullivan was noticeably shaken. Gathering his thoughts, he said, "Gene's grandfather? Actually, Gene informed me that his grandfather was very ill with cancer. I know Gene, the ah, the grandson, very well. I invited Gene and his parents to be here today. Gene is one who has been, might I say, severely affected by the abuse of Father Jaeger." Father Sullivan was trying to decipher the news. "I know the Kowolski family very well. I met with Gene's dad, Herb, a few months ago. Excuse me." He reached for his water glass. It was empty. As he picked up the pitcher, everyone could hear the rattle of ice cubes.

Father Sullivan took a breath. As he tried to steady his hand, Cardinal Cullings said, "Let's all take a short recess."

"Oh no, please. I'll be okay," Father Sullivan said. He continued, "Herb Kowolski was most concerned, upset as any parent would be. During our visit this past summer, I could tell he was an intense man—emotional, very fiery. I listened carefully and just let him talk. After a few minutes, I tried to calm him down. Mr. Kowolski became even more agitated. All of a sudden, he stood up and said something like, 'You priests are all the same. Holier than thou.' Then he walked to the door. Looking back, that's when … that's when he threatened Father Jaeger and said, 'I'm gonna kill him. That's what he deserves.' Bursting down the hall before I could even reach the door, he cursed and threatened again. Before I made it to the foyer, I heard the front door slam closed. I felt terrible. I was concerned, but I just, ah … I accepted his agitated state of mind."

Throwing his head into his palm, supported by his elbow, Father Sullivan rubbed his forehead and took a deep breath. He took a long drink of water and then a short sip. He tried to gather himself.

"Gene had told me about his grandfather's illness. They were very close. Gene said they called him Pops. Mr. Kowolski was, I'd guess, in his late seventies. He had terminal cancer. Pancreatic, I was later told. Gene said all his Pops wanted to do was make it … live through Christmas. Now what?" he asked, looking at everyone in the room. "It looks like he wanted far more than just Christmas. I feel so badly for him. For Gene and his family. I feel badly for my fellow priest, Father Jaeger. If somehow I could have reached out to help. I was concerned about Gene's dad. But his grandfather? Who could have known?" Father Sullivan leaned back in his chair without saying another word.

Cardinal Cullings could tell that Father Sullivan had said his piece … at least for now. "Gentlemen, now we will take a recess," he said, standing to signal to everyone that it was time.

After about fifteen minutes, the concerned cardinal returned with the entrapped bishop, and the conflicted priests sat back down at the conference table. Conversations had been on task during the break. The disclosure about Gene's grandfather remained an undercurrent to the gathering with the exception of Bishop Powers and Father Schmidt both focused on their ensuing demise.

Cardinal Cullings approached the bishop as they all geared up to return to the meeting. "Bishop, I know how difficult this must be."

"Thank you. It is," the bishop replied in a low, stoic, monotone voice. "This is most difficult."

Cardinal Cullings expected a comment in return from the bishop but received no defense from the beaten man.

Cardinal Cullings began, "I see Sister has kindly refilled the water pitchers. Thank you, Sister, wherever you are," he said, trying to lighten the moment. "Would you like to continue, Father Sullivan?"

"Yes, I would very much. Thank you for the recess. I need to say that my heart goes out to Gene Kowolski, his grandfather, and family."

Father Sullivan looked around the table. "My heart does reach out to Father Jaeger. I'd say the primary reason we are brought together in this room. Yes, he is a sinner. A very vile sinner, but in so many ways I feel for this man. I, I want," Father Sullivan stopped. He shook his head. "I can say no more." Clearing his voice, "Well, let's begin again. I knew we needed that break, as it gave Sister a chance to refill the water pitchers," Father Sullivan kidded. This time there were a couple of feeble chuckles. Looking as if he had regained his earlier momentum before the news about Herman Kowolski, Father Sullivan decided to begin with startling directness.

He continued, "As I said earlier, I want everyone in this room to see your actions, Bishop Powers, as a simple cover-up to hide the truth." Then he looked directly at the bishop. "If I am wrong, correct me right here. I wish I didn't have to make these accusations about you with such directness. The truth has to be told. We both know my words are real and factual. I would not intend to deliver any ill words at your expense, Bishop Powers. But for the sake of all these boys, I must."

Father Holtz looked down the length of the table at his friend Father Girouard. He raised his eyebrows and received a nod back from Father Girouard. Each knew the other could not help but feel the oncoming tide of the bishop's self-inflicted demise. Father Schmidt had sat noticeably mute, waiting only for Bishop Powers to speak.

"Father Sullivan," Cardinal Cullings interjected. "Since we have decided to listen to the accusations directly from two—or is it three of the boys—maybe it's time to invite them in to speak with all of us. One at a time, of course," Cardinal Cullings suggested. "We must remain conscious of how traumatic this could be for each of them. At the same time, their words might be disturbing to you, Bishop Powers and Father Schmidt."

Father Sullivan said, "Since I am confident that there is a cover-up, I ask your Eminence, Father Girouard, and Father Holtz to watch carefully the quiet expressions of Bishop Powers. He will be there listening to these abused boys, and he knows what they are saying is true, even though he might deny it later. Watch for his face to turn red. He will perspire at the brow. Why? Because he knows."

"Thank you, Father. Let's move on. Hear from the boys, Father Girouard." The cardinal nodded.

"Excuse me, Cardinal Cullings, might I add three are here," Father Girouard whispered to the cardinal as a reminder. "Would all agree that we should listen to what the boys have to say?" he asked everyone.

Cardinal Cullings replied, "Yes, the only fair way."

Father Holtz and Father Sullivan concurred. Bishop Powers knew the words and accusations could be his downfall. However, he convinced himself that the accusation of cover-up was only opinion and conjecture. A twelve-year-old boy would also lack credibility. But he did not know which of the three would speak first, let alone their names.

"Would you like to begin with Peter Goodnar? Being the youngest, I'm sure he is the most apprehensive," Father Girouard asked.

"Yes, good idea," Cardinal Cullings agreed. "Let's begin with the youngest first."

Father Sullivan left the room. Bishop Powers closed his eyes and breathed temporary relief. The cardinal mentioned again the sensitivity of the matter, imagining how difficult it would be for the boys to speak in front of six priests. Bishop Powers, now wringing his hands hidden under the table, thought, *How can I endure any more of these lies and fabrications?*

CHAPTER 106

LAST STRAW

Gene Kowolski—December 2, 1958

THE days had grown shorter. More hours were hidden in the darkness. Nightmares accompanied by hideous looming images of the priest would not abandon Gene's mind.

On Tuesday afternoon, the bell rang. Another awful school day ended. As he was leaving the classroom alone, Gene noticed Herbie Ratski and his two buddies just ahead. Walking toward the stairs, Gene saw Herbie turn and walk straight toward him. *Pow!* Herbie let his right elbow fly into Gene, hitting his arm. In the same motion, Herbie kicked Gene's schoolbag down the stairs. The flap opened. Books flew, and papers fluttered in the stairway like seagulls in the sky.

"Hey, you dropped your books, homo man. Gene, Gene the homo machine," Herbie rhymed out as he headed toward the stairs.

The clasp of Sister Annaclario's hand around Herbie's arm could have lifted a skid of cinder blocks. Sister was the school principal and eighth grade teacher. Nobody ever wanted to be at the mercy of her wrath. With her other hand, she reached over and took the top of his ear and guided him straight back into the classroom. His head tilted sideways as she pulled his left ear toward the sky, making him tiptoe like a ballerina.

Herbie's two buddies stepped back and hovered against the wall by the top of the stairs. With a final tug, sister flung Herbie into the room. Looking back outside, she saw the other two still standing by the stairs. "You two heathens get in here now! Right now!"

Both boys marched to her command. Sister Annaclario walked to the top of the stairs. "You okay, Gene?" she asked as he scrambled to pick up his books and gather his papers. Susanne and Margaret were both helping Gene.

"Thank you, thank you," he said.

As Gene tried to make his way down the stairs, having assembled his books and with his papers askew in hand, three of his classmates—Sally O'Newell, Carol Strider, and Shirley Macey yelled, "You three creeps are scum!"

"You should be kicked out of school," Sally said, disgust written across her face.

Gene felt his last straw break. He headed directly home, walking with committed purpose, one hard step at a time. *Why, oh why, dear God? Why me? Please understand, I can't take this anymore.*

"Damn that Herbie. To hell with them all! I hope they all burn in hell! Pricks! Pricks! Pricks, all of them!" Gene muttered out loud to himself as he stomped down the sidewalk. Three fat *pricks* were tough words for Gene to muster. "Goddamn Herbie! He's a no good son of a bitch!" he yelled louder to the world, not caring who heard him with language that he had never uttered in his life.

After turning into the yard, Gene opened the screen door to the house and stomped up the stairs to his room. He threw his bag on the bed and slumped in his chair. Within a minute, he was up and in the bathroom. Once he was back in his room, he checked the Boy Scout calendar to the side of his desk. Gene sat at the desk and flipped through the pages of *Huckleberry Finn*. Gene couldn't concentrate. Picking up a piece of paper, he began to write.

Meticulously, he carefully chose each word and signed his name. *Love you, guys. Gene.* After folding the paper, he placed it in an envelope. On the front, he simply wrote, *To My Family.* When he laid the pen down, some ink bled onto the envelope.

Gene leaned the envelope against the front of his desk. Then he reached into the drawer on the left side of his desk and pulled out a deck of cards. Shuffling through, he pulled two aces, two jacks, and two jokers. Setting the remaining forty-eight cards aside, Gene fanned the six cards across his desk. He then set the letter on top.

I can't stand all this. Jesus help me. He thought of his mom and dad,

Pops, and the kids. How he loved them. Suddenly, Gene was blinded by the face of Father Jaeger. Calmly, he stood up and grabbed his yellow baseball cap and plaid button-up coat. Gene calmly walked down the stairs, not wanting to draw attention. *The last straw. I know what I must do.*

"Oh hi, Mom," he said as if nothing was wrong. He saw that she was preparing chicken and noodles for supper.

"Hi, honey. How was school?"

"Just an ordinary day," he said, lying through his teeth. "Going for a ride on my bike. It'll be dark in an hour."

"Be back before dark," his mother ordered. "Chicken and noodles. Yours and Pops favorite. Your grandfather should be back from his trip soon."

"Oh, I will." Looking up at his mom, he gave her a big hug and said, "Oh, Mom, I love you and Dad. I love you so very much. Pops and the kids ... all of you."

Gene bounded for the door. He stopped and looked back at his mom. Then he jumped down the stairs, leaped on his bike, and pedaled down the street. Only a light dusting of snow was left from the weekend. The sun was setting in the west. Gene was glad for a little light on the now gray, overcast December day.

His mom followed Gene to the front door. Standing on the porch, she watched. *What a good boy, our Gene. That seemed like an odd time to express all that love.* She continued to watch as he rounded the corner and pedaled out of sight. Just like the wind. *Yes, a good, good boy.*

Gene's heart beat faster and faster as he pedaled with all his might around the corner. He stood up, pumping his bicycle as hard as he could heading straight for the gravel road adjacent to the Big Four Trestle. He coasted downhill and then off the road and onto the service drive next to the looming trestle. At the base of the giant wood bridge, Gene jumped off his bike, dropping it to the ground all in one motion. Bending over with his hands on his knees, he tried to catch his breath. He felt a semblance of peace, escape, and confidence about what he was about to do.

Walking toward the river's edge, Gene bent over and selected some flat stones from the road. He found three. Just a few feet from the water, Gene sidearmed the flat rock across the top of the water. Five times it skipped with a perfect throw. Six for the second stone. Shooting for the magic ten, he flipped the third rock, only to watch it land with a thud and drop directly into the current. *Not ten.* Gene remained committed to his plan.

Looking across the river, he saw a misshapen tree configured like a man, grotesque in its shape. *It's him. It's him.* Gene's mind played games with reality. "Jaeger! Jaeger!" he yelled, turning his head away. His pulse raced.

Looking left of the trestle, Gene scrambled up the embankment on all fours, heading directly toward the tracks. Near the top, he slipped and scraped his hand on the crusty cinders. Skidding back, he caught a foothold and then willed himself back to the top. Thin lines of red streaked on his left hand. Feeling no pain while standing by the track, Gene looked ahead at his escape toward the middle of the trestle. For a minute, he thought, *no, go back home. I can't.* He glanced over at his favorite resting place, the rock aside the giant oak. Remembering the past, Gene saw the image of himself passing time during better days. His thoughts revolved helter-skelter within his head. *The pain, monster, bastard!* He thought of the words *homo man. No friends. Mom, Dad, and Pops know all about me. The confessional, the bed … the hurt. I have nothing. Nobody.*

Gene felt his legs walk in the direction toward his final destination. Stepping onto the tracks, he walked forward thirty paces and then stopped as usual. He looked straight ahead down the long distance of iron rail, which spanned atop the trestle to the other side of the giant Wabash River Valley, then disappeared around the curve. *Far enough? No!* Feeling no fear, Gene walked forward, railroad tie by railroad tie, step-by-step.

Looking down, he could see the ground between the wood ties moving farther away. Without thought, Gene kept walking fearlessly, selecting the center of the wooden ties. He looked over the sides. Height lost its meaning. Seconds passed. Purposely and with abandoned fear, Gene kept walking. He stopped. Placing his left black tennis shoe securely on the sparkling rail, fearlessly Gene lifted his right foot in front and then his left foot and the right again, easily balancing like a tightrope walker as he spread his arms like a bird's wings and walked the rail. *If only I could fly.*

I hate the man! A gross image entrapped his mind. Arms spread like an vulture, Gene took three and then four steps forward, one step in front of the other on the single narrow rail. He swayed and shifted his hips for balance. Two more steps.

"Goddamn it all!" he yelled. "To hell with everyone! Damn the bastard to the fires of hell, hell, hell … "

Gene heard his own voice echoing through the valley below. With a deep breath, he leaned over, stood back up, and jumped, as if in slow motion, landing between the two rails. *Fear doesn't exist. I can handle fear. I fear not.* With a quickened pace, Gene continued toward the middle of the trestle. Slight traces of snow had found a home in the cracks of the blackened railroad ties. A few patches of ice gathered and lay hidden under snow and depressions in the wood.

The silence of the valley below was interrupted by a call far ahead, beyond the curve on the other side of the giant trestle. The whistle resounded—a familiar noise. Looking forward, Gene saw the puffing smoke spewing from the stack. Again and again, the whistle blew. It became louder and louder with each passing warning. No train in sight, Gene stood motionless, facing the direction of the oncoming invader. *I feel no fear. I feel no pain. Soon it will be over. Do not be afraid.* The smoke rose higher. The train was still out of sight, but the huffing grew louder. Smoke bellowed into the gray sky. Sporadically, clouds gave way to the setting December sun falling in the west. *There she is!* The circular front of the steel horse rounding the curve was in direct line with the trestle.

The vast area of the Wabash River Valley exploded in full view as the train was about to traverse the long, high wooden trestle. From inside the giant engine, the engineer, his left elbow hanging out the window, looked ahead at the oncoming track. His red bandana flapped in the cold breeze of early December. His blue-and-white striped engineer's hat was pulled tightly to his ears. His leathery face rebuked the wind. The engineer watched the oncoming skeleton of wooden beams and trusses supporting the steel rails spanning the Wabash Valley. The tracks took a turn and disappeared into the horizon beyond the trestle. Squinting his eyes once, twice, he detected a figure. *No, can't be!* The coal man was pitching the black rocks to the open door, burning bright red within.

"Joe, Joe!" The engineer tugged at the whistle. "Look ahead! Judas Priest! Is that ... is that someone on the tracks?"

Hooking both hands on the pullman's bar, the coal man leaned outside the train beyond the top step. The cold wind blew darts into his lined face. "Can't tell. Slow 'er down! Stop!" the coal man yelled over the loud thunder of the mighty engine.

"Can't stop! Too late! A stop will take us beyond the end of the trestle. Holy God Almighty, it's a boy! He's just standing there!"

The sound of screeching wheels, steel on steel, resounded throughout the valley below. Gus Dorais, standing outside his Chevy garage on Canal Street, heard the screeching a mile away. Ruth Stouffer, shooting pictures of the Christmas tree in front of the courthouse, looked toward the mighty trestle ... *a daunting wooden skeleton. A visual masterpiece*, she immediately thought to herself. Then the shrieking sound she heard with alarm.

Gene froze. His plan was being executed. Never again would he have to face life, its problems, nightmares, and the sight of that looming monster.

Gene heard the frantic warning of the whistle, and the shrill sound of grating steel pierced his ears. His life flashed before his eyes. *Oh my God, I am heartily sorry for all my sins. Say it, Gene. Say it! With all my heart, dear Lord, I'm sorry! I don't want to go to hell! I do forgive him! I do forgive!*

Ahead twenty yards toward the side from which he had come, Gene saw a four-foot safety platform to the side of the service walk and right of the shimmering steel tracks. *Should I? Can I? Oh my God, I'm sorry!*

"No, Gene, no!" he yelled over the roar of the train. One step and then two, Gene frantically looked down to the river far below. His heart exploded. His knees crumbled at the roar and vibration of the oncoming monster. A few more steps. *I can't! I can't! God, I'm sorry!* The oil bucket on the engine ramp was in sight. *Too late! God, I'm sorry! I'm going to hell forever!* With all his might, Gene leaped. His last feeling was the steel of the bucket grazing his left tennis shoe. He slipped as he thrust himself headfirst in the direction of the platform and the mighty Wabash River one hundred feet below.

The roar of the slowing train was deafening. Now it didn't matter. His life flashed. He felt the wind. The haunt of the deadly priest was finally gone. His mind raced a thousand frames in just two agonizing seconds. Slow motion. Gene was free.

The train squealed and scratched the tracks like nails on a chalk-board, raw to the ear. The clatter of the tracks subsided. Far ahead, past the trestle, the roaring locomotive finally came to a halt. The engineer and coal man leaped from the train. Along the rocky sides of the track, they scurried, running directly toward the back of the train. Huffing and puffing, the engineer and coal man bent over in stride, looking all along the way for any signs of the missing boy.

"Do you see any blood, any unusual sign? Clothing?" The caboose was far behind the engine of what seemed like a thousand black coal cars.

The flagman in the caboose had jumped from the train and was running alongside the tracks then onto the service walk along the side of the train. He yelled to the engineer and coal man fast approaching the middle of the trestle. "Why'd you stop? What are you looking for?" The flagman looked puzzled as he yelled to the engineer far to the other end of the tracks.

"A boy! I saw a boy in the middle of the tracks," the engineer responded.

"Yeah, I looked back. I saw him leap," the coal man said.

"Holy shit! Jump? For Christ's sake, look down there!" the flagman yelled ahead to the engineer, still fifty yards between them, as he pointed to the valley below. He continued walking at the edge of the rails, along-side the coal cars, into the direction of the engineer and coal man.

The roar of the river echoing through the valley seemed even louder as the three men scanned the vast open space below. *Nothing.*

The coal man, having caught his breath, said in a defeated voice, "I think I saw him leap. Not sure, but that was it! We were still goin' too fast."

The engineer and coal man were covered in soot and grime.

"Goin' too fast my ass. That was our normal speed for this giant trestle," the engineer snapped back.

The three trainmen walked along the train of cars toward one another. The flagman getting closer to the engineer and coal man. "Can't see a thing!" The engineer and coal man focused, still shading their eyes. The flagman walking toward the engine side, held on to each car as he transversed the trestle. They strained to see any glimpse of life. The coal man, followed the engineer. The flagman advanced closer toward them, now only a mild yell away. "See anything?" the flagman called out.

"Hell no. All I can see is the space below these tracks and that muddy river below."

"I feel nauseated," the coal man said, bent over. "He's probably floating face down in the current of that river halfway to Attica by now. Why would a boy do such a thing? He didn't even run. Just leaped to his death. Why? Why? God, why?"

"God only knows, Joe. Wait! What's that?" George, the engineer, asked, pointing down the track alongside the continuing line of coal cars.

"Where, where?" the coal man asked.

"Look straight down the rail, thirty yards in front of Mike!" Who now stopped as he too saw movement in front of the engineer. "Something's moving!" the engineer said, still pointing. "There! Moved again!" The engineer yelled as he quickly walked along the side of the train. "Don't move! Stay there! We're coming!"

The coal man stood stationery, not believing his eyes. Focusing, both hands cupped over his forehead, he saw a boy rising to his knees. Clutching the handrail around the safety platform, the boy stood up and struggled back onto the service walk and hugged the wheel of a giant coal car. Miraculously, Gene started walking cautiously down the walk toward the trainmen as if each step was his first. Slowly, he got his bearings and made his way to the waiting men.

"Oh my God," said the coal man. "Impossible! Can't believe what I just saw," he said in total amazement.

"Praise the Lord. You are one lucky little guy," the flagman added having caught up to Gene. He reached out and put his hand firmly on Gene's shoulder. The flagman looked to the heavens, made the sign of the cross, and said, "Judas Priest! Praise the Lord!"

The engineer looked over Gene's shoulder at the long span of train and track disappearing around the curve. "After that brush with death, I hope you live to watch the sunset as an old, old man."

Gene couldn't find words. He was breathing heavily as the three trainmen guided Gene alongside the train to the safe side of the trestle from where Gene's journey began.

After making sure the boy was okay and unhurt, the three trainmen bid Gene farewell. Gene thanked them and was happy they would never know his original intention.

Gene turned and walked over to the rock by the giant oak. He sat on the rock, and watched as the train pulled away. The endless train of coal and lumber cars passed. Gene waved to the flagman, as the flagman ran alongside the train then leaped to the steps of the red caboose. He hung on to the railing and continued to wave to the boy, resting in the safety beneath the giant oak. The train now only a departing sound in the distance had come and gone. Gene thought, *maybe the demon has left.*

Gene stood, walked over to the tracks. All was quiet. He looked across the abandoned trestle. *It's almost dark, I better get home.*

Gene turned and walked back to the embankment. Down he skidded, hopped on his bike, and headed home for supper. For the rest of his life, Gene knew he would never forget that almost fateful day in December 1958.

CHAPTER 107

TOTAL TRUTH

Peter Goodnar—December 3, 1958

WITHIN a few minutes, the door on the side wall behind the bishop and Father Schmidt opened. Peter and his parents followed Father Sullivan into the conference room. The presence of six priests was overwhelming for the boy. They all stood as Father Sullivan led Peter Goodnar and his parents around to the side of the table opposite Bishop Powers.

Father Girouard, to the right of the cardinal, watched as Father Sullivan pulled a chair out for Mrs. Goodnar. Mr. Goodnar sat to her right toward the end of the table opposite Father Holtz. Peter, wearing a white shirt, a poorly knotted tie, and black trousers, sat between his mother and Father Sullivan in the middle of the table. Peter looked so intense, scared, Father Girouard wondered if he would even be able to talk. Dismissing formal introductions, Father Sullivan simply mentioned the individual priests around the table. Anything to reduce the obvious nervousness and tension within the room.

Father Sullivan thanked the Goodnars for attending. He explained how everyone at the table is here to help, even though he knew all too well his concern about Bishop Powers and Father Schmidt. Father Sullivan began by asking, "Peter, could you tell us about Father Jaeger and your relationship with him?"

Peter looked to his mother. "Yes, I think I can," he said with guarded hesitation. "Last November, I was in Father Jaeger's study. He came and sat at the end of the couch. Then he scooted next to me. He touched my leg," Peter explained matter-of-factly. "I was very uncomfortable with him. Didn't feel right. He ... he," Peter looked over to Father Sullivan. "Father Jaeger was too close. His leg touched mine." Sounding relieved, Peter said, "Then Father Sullivan came in. Isn't that right, Father?" he asked as he looked over at the good priest sitting next to him.

"Yes, I saw you with Father Jaeger together on the couch," Father Sullivan calmly confirmed.

"When you left, Father Sullivan, Father Jaeger moved away. Nothing happened. He did give me his missal and asked me to bring it back in a week. Maybe it was two. Sorry, can't remember exactly." Peter looked over at father. "Am I doing okay, Dad?"

"Yes, Peter. You're fine. Go ahead."

"I did bring it back. I think it was a Tuesday. I mean that was the day I came back. Father Jaeger wasn't ready." Peter's delivery to the priests who were listening intently was almost rote, as if he had memorized every word.

"He told me to come upstairs. I wondered why. When I went up to give him the missal, he took it and set it on the table. Then he went into his bedroom. He called me in. Father Jaeger showed me the crucifix." Peter was still talking as if he was on automatic. Everyone could tell this was difficult for him. Cardinal Cullings gave his full attention to Peter while intermittingly looking at the expressionless face of Bishop Powers. The bishop's only concern was for himself.

"As he led me into his bedroom, he was taking off his shirt. I was scared. He told me to take my shirt off and be comfortable like him. Then he reached over and pulled off my sweater and my shirt at the same time. I didn't know what to do. I was scared. Really scared." Peter stopped. He looked down at his clenching hands.

"It's okay, Peter. Just tell as you remember. We are all listening," Father Sullivan added, trying his best to assure Peter.

"Ah, yes. Thank you, Father, I will. Just as it happened. Father Jaeger wanted to show me his scar. He said he had a scar just like Jesus and pointed to the crucifix. He said it wasn't from a sword. It was a scar from his appendix. We knelt by the side of the bed and prayed. Then it was awful.

"Father Jaeger stood up, his pants came off. He was naked then he

713

pulled me up. 'Take your pants off like me.' I didn't know what to … he said it again, 'take 'em off' like he was hurrying me. So I … I wanted to run, but I, I took off my pants. I was cold then he pushed me on my back. I was embarrassed. All I could do was look at the crucifix overhead. Then I distinctly remembered him on my backside." Peter stopped. Now he was speaking with emotion, and everyone in the room saw that he was crying.

Father Holtz noticed Peter's dad, who was red with anger, a look of rage.

Horror crossed Peter's face. "I was so scared. All I could remember was closing my eyes, praying, and feeling this awful, awful pain as he moaned and groaned in my ear. It was the worst experience in my life." Peter stopped and tried to catch his breath, hands covering his face. "Help me. I can't get him out of my mind."

Father Sullivan reached over in front of Peter's mother and slid a glass of water to Peter.

"Excuse me, Mrs. Goodnar."

"Thank you, Father." Peter took a drink. Tears rolled down the boy's cheeks. His face was crimson, and he stared down at the table. Peter's mother continually wiped tears from her face. Peter's dad's hands twisted and wrenched as he looked ready to explode.

"That's fine, Peter, no more. We understand," Father Sullivan said, giving Peter relief. There was silence in the room.

Father Girouard spoke up, "Peter, could we ask another question? Again, is this the only time you were in a bed with Father Jaeger?"

Peter put his head down, ashamed. He covered his eyes, trying to stop the tears. "No, Father, there were more times. That was just the first." Looking over to Father Sullivan, Peter added, "Two more times. It was terrible. Two more times, he did it to me." Then he was quiet.

The silence in the room crept in like emerging fog. Words were not spoken in the moment. Cardinal Cullings took a deep breath and sat back, his hands folded on the table. Mr. Goodnar experienced fire in his blood. Bishop Powers was stoic and contemplated how to leave the meeting.

"Peter, just one more question. May I ask?"

"Yes, Father Sullivan." Peter rested his elbow on the table, put his hand in front of his mouth, and waited. Shame, embarrassment, *just one more question, I hope.*

"Would you be able to tell the story, exactly as you say it happened to the authorities specifically to the police, a detective?"

"Yes, Father. Yes, Father, I could, exactly the same."

Again, silence fell over the room. Cardinal Cullings nodded as if to say, *Give him time.* Within moments, Peter looked up, wanting to finish telling his nightmare.

Peter's father leaned forward, looking in front of Peter's mother toward his son. Instinctively, Mr. Goodnar lightly pounded his fist on the table. "That man's a monster!"

Mrs. Goodnar reached over and gently patted his hand. "George, George, let's not get angry here in front of all these priests. We know, we know. We all feel the anger."

"You need say no more," Father Sullivan looked at Peter. He then asked if Peter's parents would like to say a few words.

"Yes, I would," Mrs. Goodnar said. She sat up straight, folded her hands, and cleared her throat as if trying to speak properly and stay in control. "Fathers, I'm very nervous, so please bear with me. I truly can't describe the trauma Peter has endured. He has done that far better than George and I could have—" she said, referring to her exasperated husband.

"We can't … " Mr. Goodnar said, interrupting his wife. He wiped the back of his hand across his forehead. "We can't understand how and why a priest would do this. You guys are supposed to be good men for our kids. Good men."

Cardinal Cullings sensed that all six of the priests, including himself, were being included in some guilt by association. He hoped Father Schmidt and Bishop Powers were feeling some form of guilt.

"What Peter described is unbearable for a parent to hear. His younger brother and sister know, but they don't know the details. Thank God for that," Peter's mom continued.

Bishop Powers listened with excruciating intensity. *The boy's telling the truth. Did I really cover this up? I must deny, deny.* The bishop wanted no more. His denial would be overshadowed by Peter's most believable and horrifying story.

Mrs. Goodnar continued, "Peter's brother is now fearful of any priest. He asks if the same thing will happen to him. Can any of you imagine yourself in their shoes? We are sorry that Father Jaeger is not here. I'd give the world to have him look us in the eyes. We do, however, hope he recovers."

"Excuse me. I'd like to add one more thing," Mr. Goodnar said, gently placing his hand on his wife's forearm. "In my darkest hours, I too have imagined bringing justice by some act of physical pain to that awful, despicable man. Something … " He stopped, bowing his head and regaining composure. "Something inside makes me want to harm him. What he's done to Peter and the other boys is beyond … beyond words. There is nothing worse than seeing your child hurt and in pain, and for someone to intentionally harm … " He shook his head. "No matter. Prayer and forgiveness won't do it. At least not for me. I want to bring justice. I, as a parent, can understand why someone shot that man. I could, I could … "

"Now, George, *shhh*! Stop. Not in front of these priests. *Shhh*."

"I wish I would have been there. After listening to Peter again just now, I think I could … " He looked at his wife, paused, and then said, "I think I too could have pulled the trigger." The priests and Cardinal Cullings listened intently and with compassion, trying to understand.

As his emotions continued to rule, Mr. Goodnar stood up. Placing both palms on the table, his arms rigid, his face intent, George Goodnar leaned forward. Mrs. Goodnar took hold of his wrist.

Looking directly at each of the six priests, "Anyone who does harmful, unjust, despicable actions or deeds that hurt your children and affect their lives must be brought to justice. That person must pay a price for his actions." Pausing, he finished by saying, "Today, Father Jaeger was brought to justice. He deserved what he got, being shot to suffer, but not to die." Mr. Goodnar looked around the room at each of the priests. "Fathers, Bishop, and ah … and Cardinal Cullings, I know you are all good men. For me, I will not judge myself, good or bad. I do, however, approve the man that shot that priest." Not caring of their reaction, George Goodnar added, "I applaud the shooter. That priest deserved justice." Feeling he may have said too much, "Fathers, forgive me. It's ah … ah too hard to explain right and wrong. I just think he got what he deserved." Mr. Goodnar stopped, took a breath, and sat down. Mrs. Goodnar gently patted his hand and then held it tightly.

The silence within the room overwhelmed the six priests. Inwardly, they felt speechless. *How convincing*, Father Girouard thought. *What do I do now?* Bishop Powers asked himself. Cardinal Cullings clenched his lips together. He raised a finger to his eye. Such conviction and passion he had never heard before. Father Sullivan was moved beyond words, listening to Mr. Goodnar. He also thought about Gene, Joey, and all the others. Passion, conviction, outrage clung to each word of George Goodnar. Not one of the priests or Cardinal Cullings could agree with George Goodnar's support of the violence perpetrated on Father Jaeger. Each in his own way, however, understood Mr. Goodnar's willingness to pursue justice for his son.

Father Schmidt was numb. Father Holtz felt more determined to press forward. If he had heard the words of Mr. Goodnar, Father Jaeger would have turned around in his own filthy bile that day. Father Holtz thought, *If that was my son, I would have felt the same*. Immediately, he made a fast sign of the cross. *Forgive me.*

Tears welled in Peter's eyes. He clutched his mother's hand, leaned forward, looked past his mom, and gave a most grateful smile to his dad.

"Now, honey, be calm. I know. These men understand," Peter's mother said as she squeezed her husband hand. "All we are asking now, as parents, is to stop this from ever happening again to anyone," she then said, looking directly into Bishop Powers' eyes. "What we don't understand is when you knew what he did to Peter, how could you send this man to another parish? How can this be? How can children be safe?"

Bishop Powers sat, expression absent from his face. Father Schmidt looked directly at his folded hands.

"Yes, she's right," Peter's dad interrupted. "He should be in jail and rot in hell! We deserve an answer."

Bishop Powers looked to the ceiling for escape. No reply.

"Now, George, these men know what to do. I guess after what happened yesterday, this Father Jaeger will no longer be a threat. That's all we have to say." Taking a tissue from her purse, Mrs. Goodnar dabbed her eyes. Then she reached over and once again took hold of Peter's hand.

Cardinal Cullings responded, "Thank you, Peter, Mr. and Mrs.

Goodnar. We all know how difficult this is for you. Be assured that by coming forward you are helping us to better understand so that we can do the right thing. I will do all that I can so this does not happen again."

Cardinal Cullings paused and noted the expressions of hope and trust on the Goodnars' faces. Peter looked at the cardinal. *Dear Jesus, this man is going to fix things.*

Father Sullivan stood. Bending over, he patted Peter on the shoulder. "You did well, Peter. You did very well." Still standing, Father Sullivan turned and placed both hands, palms down, on the table. He leaned forward looking Bishop Powers directly in the eye. "Deny that. Tell me this boy's lying. Can you?" The bishop was stone cold, silent. "And you transferred Father Jaeger to...to a..."

"That will be enough, Father. We all understand," Cardinal Cullings said in a calm voice.

"Yes, excuse me, your Eminence."

The relieved look on Peter's face reflected a heartfelt thank-you to Father Sullivan. Father Sullivan pulled back the chair for Mrs. Goodnar. He walked with them to the door, which was directly behind Bishop Powers. Opening the door, Father Sullivan motioned for Mr. and Mrs. Goodnar to step through into the hallway. He quietly closed the door and followed them down the hall.

Mrs. Goodnar stopped, looked at Father Sullivan, then at his collar and said, "Father, we will always be grateful."

"Yes, we will, Father. I hope that ... well, I hope that I didn't say too much, the wrong thing," Mr. Goodnar said sheepishly.

"I was so taken by your heartfelt words. Nobody could have said it better. Your love and concern for Peter, and for all the victims, was expressed so passionately, with such conviction. Although I cannot condone violence, I totally understand your love for your son. Your willingness to right a wrong."

Mrs. Goodnar smiled slightly. *He's such a good man.*

"Far better than what any of us priests could say." Father Sullivan clasped Mr. and Mrs. Goodnar's hands in his.

"Father, was that a real cardinal?" Peter asked. "He's almost like a pope."

"Yes, Peter. Cardinal Cullings is a very fine and holy man. He will do good for you, good for everyone."

As Peter and his dad turned to leave, Mrs. Goodnar looked at Father Sullivan. She reached out her hand. "You, too, are a good man, Father. We will always be gratified." Father squeezed her hand. He smiled. Mrs. Goodnar turned and followed Peter and his dad.

Father Sullivan smiled as he watched them walk down the hall.

When he returned to the conference room, everyone was waiting for Cardinal Cullings to speak. Visibly touched by Peter's concise description of the traumatic events, the cardinal spoke with directness and simplicity. "How can we not believe that boy? He did not make those terrible deeds up. I believe every word."

Father Girouard said, "I totally agree. Peter's words were compelling."

Father Sullivan and Father Holtz both nodded in agreement.

Cardinal Cullings looked to Bishop Powers. He did not ask for comment. Bishop Powers stared out the window on the other side of the table. His expressionless face said it all.

After Peter Goodnar's convincing words, the heaviness of the hour loomed for Cardinal Cullings and Father Girouard. Tension mounted, as they knew Ned Thornbauer was waiting just down the hall. Bishop Powers was still unaware of Ned's presence, although his intuition was becoming suspicious. *Could there be anybody else?*

Father Girouard silently prayed that Cardinal Cullings had made the correct decision by not telling Bishop Powers the name of the second boy. "Rather than discuss Peter's case, let's not make the next person wait any longer," Father Girouard suggested, looking directly at Bishop Powers.

"Before he comes in, I would like to comment," Cardinal Cullings added, to Father Girouard's surprise. Addressing Bishop Powers, he said, "Bishop, when I called you last week, I asked you to come here to discuss some concerns regarding your diocese. I considered two possibilities regarding the next person. If there is no truth in what he might disclose, then you need not address or be concerned about the matter. If, however—and I emphasize *if*—we all conclude that he does speak truthfully, then I must give my complete attention to the situation and decide what action should be taken. We cannot disguise the truth. We will put the issue on the table. That we will do today." Watching for a reaction from Bishop Powers, Cardinal Cullings looked directly at him. Seeing no response, he said, "If any accusation comes forth and it is false, then I depend on you, Bishop Powers, to deny and explain. We just want the truth. We do want to hear from you today. And I might add, you too, Father Schmidt." Father Schmidt immediately felt his mouth go dry and his heart race. *Oh please Lord, not me. No.*

Father Girouard raised his eyebrows as he eyed Father Holtz at the other end of the table.

The bishop knew Cardinal Cullings's statement put him into a potential entrapment. He knew it was best to wait and then respond. Over the past hour, Bishop Powers had tried to contemplate a response to his alleged cover-up. His efforts had been to no avail. *No matter what,* he thought, *deny, deny, deny is my only option.*

Cardinal Cullings decided it was time to inform the bishop that Ned Thornbauer was the second boy to speak today. "Bishop Powers, you might know a Ned Thornbauer." Hearing just the word Ned shocked Bishop Powers and sent a chill down his spine. *Oh my god!* He immediately remembered the cabin on the lake, an image of a naked boy. *Oh dear Lord, no, not him.* He thought Ned's little brother, Danny, might have told Ned of the trips to the cabin this past summer. Now he faced his own exposure. He assumed what would be said and concluded. The accusations could be his downfall totally. For this, he was not prepared.

Father Holtz walked down to a small waiting room. "Hello, Ned. Sorry to keep you waiting." Ned was not alone.

"Not a problem, Father. I've been waiting a long time. This wait was very enjoyable. Hope it's okay, but I convinced Danny to come with me. I assured him he would be safe."

Raising one eyebrow in wonderment, Father Holtz asked, "Danny?"

"Yes, Father. Danny's my brother. You know, he's the reason I came forward. He confided that he has made several trips to the bishop's cabin. As I told you before, he's taken some time, but he has concluded that he will speak up."

Father Holtz looked dumbfounded. "Oh yes. Yes, of course. I just didn't expect him today," he said, caught off guard. *This surprise visit brings a new twist to our discussion. I'm not sure how the bishop will handle being face to face with both Ned and now Danny.*

"Yes, Father. Danny's an altar boy, just as I was. Same thing happened to him."

How can I deny Danny an opportunity to speak up? Father Holtz said, "I knew you said Danny had been approached by the bishop. It's just that I … I thought it would be just you, Ned."

"Father, please, let Danny come along and tell his story," Ned said convincingly.

"Okay, let the cards fall as they may," Father Holtz said.

As he was about to take Ned and Danny back into the room, he suddenly heard loud shouts coming from the conference room. "Excuse me one minute, Ned," he said. Then he walked back toward the conference room.

Immediately, his pulse raced and his heart pumped as guilt reared its ugly head. *If only I would have gone into the cabin and protected Danny from the bishop. Dear Lord, I too have sinned.* Father Holtz was ashamed of his own weakness. Opening the door, Father Holtz immediately heard the outburst.

The bishop pounded his fist on the table. "This is not a meeting! I've been set up! This is an inquisition!" he exclaimed, pointing his finger at Father Girouard. The bishop made sure he made no eye contact with Cardinal Cullings.

"I beg your pardon, Bishop. You are the one who is out of order," Father Girouard's sixth sense was coaching him that Cardinal Cullings was quietly authorizing his comments.

"Listen to me," Bishop Powers said, raising his voice. "I was invited here to discuss my handling of priests in our diocese. I made decisions based on professional psychological reports. I relied on the analysis of honest, well-intentioned psychologists. I've listened as you've accused me of a cover-up."

He pointed directly at Father Sullivan. "Now, without warning, you are bringing forth some kid I befriended years ago. A kid from a poor family. No, Father. I took an interest to help him, to influence him, and to give him what was lacking in his life. Yes, I took him for trips to my cabin. That was an award, not abuse. What does Ned do but turn on me, making up these wild stories. For what reason, I do not know. I tell you he's up to no good. He just wants … " Bishop Powers thought for the right word. "Money. That's it. He just wants money. Once poor, always poor. That is called blackmail. Then I'm accused by this priest in front of you and Cardinal Cullings," he said, again pointing his finger directly at Father Sullivan.

Father Holtz stood and listened. He knew it was not the time to bring Ned into the room.

Father Girouard stood up and pointed his finger back at Bishop Powers. Cardinal Cullings listened. *This situation is not out of control, though it is headed in that direction*, he thought.

"You've had your say. Bishop Powers, please why all the denial? Defense? Nobody has said anything about your relationship with Ned Thornbauer. Now let's just all compose ourselves and listen to what Ned has to say," Father Girouard said to the bishop.

"Yes. Let's listen to this Ned. But I know he lies. All I want is the truth!" Bishop Powers knew there was no recovery. "This boy holds a grudge. He's going to come in here and lie, lie, lie! Just you listen and see," Bishop Powers said, taking a breath. "All I want is the truth!"

Cardinal Cullings spoke up, "I agree, Bishop Powers. We all want the truth. May I suggest you sit down and let's listen to what Ned has to say."

Father Girouard immediately responded. His voice now raised, he again pointed his finger at the bishop. Clenching his teeth, his eyes on fire, Father Girouard said, "Bishop Powers, by what we've observed today … *you can't handle the truth!*" Knowing he had said exactly what he intended, Father Girouard took a breath. His eyes were now steel and focused directly on the bishop. He said not another word, sat down in his chair, and waited in silence.

"I do not have to take any more of these accusations and insults. Cardinal Cullings, I'm sorry you had to listen to all of this … this military tribunal orchestrated by these two priests." Looking down at Father Schmidt, who remained in shock, the bishop added, "Gather your things. We are leaving now!"

Father Schmidt, who had not said a word all afternoon, stood, raised his eyebrows as if to say, *Gladly. Let's leave before they fry me. Father Schmidt* closed his file, and followed Bishop Powers to the door. Father

Holtz looked down the table at Father Sullivan and Father Girouard, who was trying to regain his composure. Bishop Powers stopped at the door and looked directly to his right at Father Holtz, who had sat down at the end of the table.

With a furrowed brow and sternness spreading across his face, Bishop Powers said, "Father Holtz, upon your return to South Wayne in three days, you are to come directly to my office," he said in what was obvious to all a very threatening manner. Bishop Powers then turned and left the room.

Cardinal Cullings didn't say a word. He calmly stood up and followed the backs of Bishop Powers and Father Schmidt as they left the conference room, heading directly for the front foyer. Neither the bishop nor Father Schmidt noticed Ned and Danny standing at the far end of the hall.

As they approached the front door, hats and coats in hand, Cardinal Cullings called out, "Bishop Powers, may I have a minute?"

Bishop Powers turned around.

"Alone," the cardinal said, looking directly at Father Schmidt.

Father Schmidt took the cue and walked out the front door and into the sleeting snow. *God, yes. Thank you. I'll take this cold rather than face the cardinal.* Standing in the foyer, out of the sight of Ned and Danny, Cardinal Cullings said, "I'm totally taken aback by your words and your conduct. I assume now your deeds are somewhat in line. Remember what I told you when we met together before this meeting? Don't forget those words. You will be hearing from me. Hearing from me soon."

Bishop Powers sent an unexpected look of disdain toward the cardinal. "Good evening, Cardinal. Yes, do have a safe trip to Rome. I'm sure you now think you have all the answers," he said with disrespectful sarcasm.

"Yes, Bishop Powers. After all, what I've heard today and observing your reactions, I believe I do. We'll talk about that when the two of us meet. It will be soon."

Bishop Powers then put on his black wool coat and brimmed hat. After briefly looking back at Cardinal Cullings, he turned, and stepped out into the driving sleet, not knowing what Cardinal Cullings meant.

Ned and Danny were still standing around the corner at the far end of the hall. They did not hear the exact words, but they did hear an exchange between the cardinal and the bishop. Ned and Danny waited for Father Holtz to return. Ned was disappointed to see the bishop leave, as he had anticipated directing his accusations at the bishop face-to-face.

Father Holtz walked down the hall to where they were still waiting. "Well, I guess you saw the bishop leave."

Ned replied with a scowl across his face, "Sure, he left. He doesn't want to face me. He didn't even know Danny was here. Danny was with the bishop just last month. Isn't that right, Danny?" Ned said, looking at his younger brother.

"Yep. In the sacristy, he touched … well, you know. I told you," he said, looking up at his older brother.

"That man has no shame. He has no soul," Ned said of the bishop.

Father Holtz shook his head without a verbal reply.

"So now what, Father?" Ned asked.

"Cardinal Cullings and Fathers Sullivan and Girouard are still inside. We'll go in as planned."

"Works for me, Father. I want them to hear all that has happened at the hands of Bishop Powers. Everything," Ned said.

"You too, Danny?" Father Holtz asked.

"I can as long as Ned's with me."

"Don't worry, brother. I'm here for you."

Ned and Danny Thornbauer followed Father Holtz into the conference room. Ned's confidence was equally matched by Danny's reluctance. Once in the room, Father Holtz made introductions to all those still present and explained the reason for Danny's presence. Ned and Danny sat in the chairs Bishop Powers and Father Schmidt had vacated, immediately across from Father Sullivan. Cardinal Cullings remained at the head of the table to their right. Father Holtz moved up a couple of chairs, just one away from Danny.

Father Holtz began, "Although we planned for the bishop to be here, plans have obviously changed. I'm sorry. Cardinal Cullings, would you like for Ned to tell you what happened at the hands of Bishop Powers?"

"By all means," the cardinal replied.

"Ned, would you like to begin?" Father Holtz asked.

"Thank you, Father Holtz. I will be direct and brief."

"Take what time you need to tell us the truth," the cardinal said, reassuring Ned.

"The reason I came forward this summer and informed Father Holtz about all that happened years ago between me and the bishop is Danny. He too has been abused. I was shock this past summer when Danny confided in me. He was at a low point because he had been traumatized by Bishop Powers. Danny had been to the cabin just like me. Danny was stripped of all his defenses and raped by the bishop, the man who just left this room."

Everyone in the room could tell that Ned would not mince words.

"Excuse me, Ned. Do I understand that for what has it been, nine years and you said nothing?"

"That is right, Father. It was this summer when Danny told me about his trips to the cabin with Bishop Powers that I decided to come forward. It was for Danny. He's my little brother. I must protect him."

Are you saying Danny was experiencing sexual abuse at the hands of Bishop Powers?" Father Sullivan asked.

"Yes, that is exactly what happened. First, it was me when I was thirteen, nine years ago. I've tried to forget. Now he's come after Danny, who is only eleven. I guess he assumed he had his way with me, so he could do the same with my brother."

Father Sullivan did not reply, but threw himself back in his chair, shaking his head in exaggerated animation. *Just like he told me before.* Father Sullivan remained outwardly calm as he raged inside, filled with disgust.

Ned explained his experiences with Bishop Powers in the same exact detail as he had months earlier with Father Holtz. He described the summer trips to the cabin. Danny was hearing this for the first time from Ned, though his experience with the bishop had pretty much been the same. Father Sullivan, having heard the story previously, listened to Ned intently, verifying his credibility. Cardinal Cullings and Father Girouard were amazed at the bold daring of Bishop Powers and what he allegedly did to these two brothers.

"The swimming in the nude was very awkward as the bishop tossed, splashed, and fondled while I was underwater. That was the first time we were together. I didn't know what to do. When the bishop exited the lake, I noticed he was already very aroused. I was embarrassed. I immediately wanted to head back to the cabin. He stood at the end of the pier, looking out at the lake. I couldn't believe it, but he just turned nonchalantly—you know, he was nude—and then walked toward me. He said to follow him to the cabin. I had already put my trunks back on.

"We walked the fifty yards from the lake to the cabin. He was breathing heavily. Although that could also have been the hill. You know, he's not in good shape, and he wasn't nine years ago either. So far nothing happened other than his foreplay in the lake. I knew that might change, though I didn't know what exactly to expect. I could tell only one thing was on his mind, and that included me."

Ned looked directly at Father Girouard and described clearly and vividly, "Bishop Powers had one thing on his mind, which he acted out physically, sexually, and so perversely on me. I was at his total mercy. Mercy, he showed none."

Cardinal Cullings listened calmly without showing any outward expression. He was focused on every word Ned said. Father Girouard's forehead was propped in his hand. Father Sullivan periodically shook his head from side to side.

"Once we were in the cabin, Bishop Powers directed me upstairs to show me my room. On command, I followed him. As I looked around my room, he walked out on the deck in his. I thought, *Oh good, he's gone.* It wasn't too long … Well, it was long enough for me to think I might be safe. Then he called me to come onto the deck. There were double doors that opened from his bedroom onto a deck that looked out over the hill and the lake. He was standing on the porch, leaning with both hands on the rail, looking at the view. I slowly walked toward his back. I immediately noticed a reddish patch above his waist on the right side. To me it looked like a birthmark.

"He said for me to come over by him. Once I was by his side, I felt him place his right hand around my shoulder. He, of course, was still naked. Now when I look back nine years, I can still see him aroused to full sexual excitement. It's such a horrid image that I fight to rid from my mind. His breathing was heavier. His physical changes provided no barrier as he walked me back to the room next to the bed. Everything was like a blur, happening so fast.

"Somehow, he removed my trunks and pulled me close. We were there, together on his bed. The last thing I remember was his sweaty clutch, heavy breath, and the invasive pain that followed. For the first time in my life, I experienced pain with which I was not familiar. Unfortunately, it wouldn't be the last time." Ned sat back in his chair, looking at the priests around the table. The room was quiet. Ned knew he had told the true facts convincingly. Minutes passed. Danny reached under the table and squeezed his brother's hand.

Father Girouard spoke first. "Hearing your story, Ned, is very, very … I can't even think of the right words." He thought and then said, "Sickening, alarming, and very disappointing to hear that about Bishop Powers. I wish he would have stayed to confirm, explain, or deny."

Ned immediately responded, "Father, you don't forget things like that. Truth is easy to remember." Father Girouard nodded twice.

Looking at the younger brother shyly sitting next to Ned, Cardinal Cullings then asked, "Danny, did the same thing happen to you?"

"Yes, sir, just like Ned except the first time we didn't go swimming. It was raining. He, ah, he took me to bed that afternoon. Then after supper he made me go back and do it all again." Danny paused for a minute. "I hate rainy days."

"Could I add a few more words?" Ned asked.

"Sure, sure, go ahead," Cardinal Cullings replied. "Say whatever's on your mind, but I can't imagine anything else you could add to your heart-wrenching words."

"Danny and I have both been terribly wronged by this very bad, bad man. He doesn't deserve to be a bishop. He doesn't deserve to wear the same collar all of you wear with such dignity. All I want to say is that I will bring justice for my brother, Danny. Bishop Powers will never be free from *my* pursuit of justice. I am committed to a quest to avenge the wrong done to Danny and myself."

"After hearing your story, we can understand your feelings of hostility toward the bishop. Remember though, you must be rational and not do anything that would cause you more trouble," Father Girouard said, trying to tone down Ned's rhetoric. "You can be assured, we, all of us in this room, seek the same justice."

"Excuse me, Father Girouard, maybe you don't understand. Justice has to be served. If the church doesn't act, if the police don't act, if the legal system does not bring justice ... " Ned paused and then continued in an almost threatening manner, "then I will bring justice. I will do whatever it takes. There is nothing I would not do to get back at him for the harm he has caused my family."

Father Girouard did not respond. Cardinal Cullings didn't say a word. They both knew there was passion in the moment. Quietly sitting across the table from Ned, Father Sullivan had a different take. He felt the threat in Ned's tone. That day, Father Sullivan knew Ned Thornbauer would do anything to get back at the bishop. Anything. He thought, *The person who is wronged knows what happened, knows the absolute effects, and has the passion for justice. This passion could become an obsession.* He believed every word Ned said.

"Ned, Danny, we thank you for all you have shared today," Father Girouard said. "I have one more question. Would you ever swear under oath in a court of law to all that you have said today?"

Ned did not hesitate. "Give me the chance. I intend on making that happen. Every word I have spoken today, I'd say directly to Bishop Powers. Obviously, he does not want to hear the truth. His weak character and lack of principles and integrity can't handle the truth. One thing I do know," Ned said as he looked around at the priests. "Every day he looks in the mirror, every day he is alone, he has to face himself. He knows what he has done to our family—Danny, my grandmother, and me. His months and years are numbered. He will face justice. Of that I am sure." Ned then added, "Bishop Powers has affected my family, and that can never be taken away. Never undone. Bishop Powers is narcissistic. He will drown in his own arrogance. However, before that he will be on the receiving end of my wrath. Justice will be served."

Father Sullivan looked across the table at Ned. "Ned, you need to be careful. You can't threaten harm. You are very articulate. You stated your feelings. I saw your passion for how you were wronged." He paused and then continued, "I believe you are obsessed with seeking justice. I, for one, believe you will be successful, and there's nothing we can do to stop you. However, it is your responsibility to work with us in the church and the legal system to bring Bishop Powers and the others to justice. Please give us some time to accomplish this. We all want to bring the justice you so eloquently seek. Please, as I say, give us that chance."

"Thank you, Father Sullivan. Thank you all for listening to our plight. Danny and I are both appreciative."

Cardinal Cullings spoke and simply said, "I am so sorry this has happened to both of you. Rest assured, I am giving this matter my full attention. Thank you both for coming."

Father Holtz stood and escorted Ned and Danny to the front door. "Thank you both. Indeed, this was a worthwhile day. You explained very well. I could tell that they found you credible. We were all moved."

Ned and Danny thanked Father Holtz.

"I can assure you both that Bishop Powers hasn't heard the last of Cardinal Cullings. He is pursuing justice for the many victims. I know Cardinal Cullings is committed to ending this tragedy," Father Holtz assured them.

"Thank you, Father. I believe you. Just remember though, Bishop Powers will still answer to me. Maybe he doesn't believe that, but time *will* prove him wrong. Let's go, Danny." The two brothers walked out the door and disappeared into the darkness of the gray December afternoon.

The snow continued to fall that day. After leaving the meeting, Father Schmidt drove carefully back to South Wayne, but the trip was stressful. Most of his anguish was created by the passenger in the backseat. Bishop Powers sat alone, just staring out the window at the bleak, cold countryside. Ned and Danny were on the same route back to South Wayne, about an hour behind the bishop's black Imperial.

In the conference room, Cardinal Cullings reached for the pitcher of water. "About empty. Maybe we are all running on empty. I want to say a few words before you all leave. Let's retire to my study. I may have a good bottle of wine or something even stronger if any of you would like to indulge."

Father Sullivan looked at Father Holtz. "I know I'd be game for that," he said, the Irish in him awakening as he raised his eyebrows a couple times to Father Holtz.

As they entered Cardinal Cullings's wood- and book-filled study, the cardinal observed three smiles for the first time that day. He turned to his guests and said, "Father Sullivan, I now know what you've been up against. Did Father Girouard inform you I am going to Rome next month? Bishop Powers, along with several other cases, will be on my agenda. I will of course be meeting with Bishop Powers first. I told him so today. However, the appearance of this cover-up and moving the abusive priests from one parish to another must be addressed. We need support from the Vatican. I believe the hierarchy of our church must be involved with the discipline and hopeful rehabilitation of these priests. The ultimate punishment to defrock a priest is in the hands of the pope. I do know from a friend on the inside of the Vatican that our Holy Father relies heavily on Cardinal Paul Ratican."

"Who is he?" Father Sullivan inquired.

"Well, this dates back to the Inquisition. You know, a time in our church's history that we aren't so proud of. That's when the Grand Inquisitor, really the church's enforcer of dogma, ruled with an iron hand. Today, we are more civilized. We are structured under the Supreme Sacred Congregation. In other words, Pope John Benedict depends on Cardinal Ratican to discipline priests who are abusers. I'm afraid this curse is not being addressed by those in authority. That is what I will be addressing next month in the Vatican."

Setting aside the serious discussion, Cardinal Cullings said, "I thank you all very much."

Walking over to a small counter between the elegant bookshelves filled with fine leather-bound volumes and other assortments of quality-looking books, the cardinal gestured toward standing bottles of cognac and scotch. Father Sullivan noted one bottle of Bushmills Irish whiskey. To the left was a rack of fine wine.

In that meeting room in the archdiocese rectory in Indianapolis, Indiana, a most memorable meeting had taken place that day. The lives of six men of the Catholic Church were irrevocably affected. That day would forever be etched in their minds.

After the meeting with Cardinal Cullings and the priests, Danny Thornbauer's main concern was being confronted by Bishop Powers again. He was scared about what the bishop might do to him because he and his brother had come forward.

Ned's whole state of mind had changed as a result of the meeting. Feeling confident that the cardinal and the priests believed the truth in his story, Ned was formulating his plan for exposing the truth and bringing justice.

"Danny, you must believe me. The bishop will never take advantage of you again. Just trust me. I will handle all of this for you. I will handle the bishop for good."

CHAPTER 108

TRIP BACK TO SOUTH WAYNE

Bishop Powers—December 3, 1958

THE windshield wipers were close to useless. The heavy snow became frozen slush across the windshield of the bishop's black Imperial. With both hands secured to the wheel, Father Schmidt was bent forward, trying to see through the slush-covered glass. Only his head moved up and then down as he tried to peer between the streaks of ice.

Accumulating some courage, Father Schmidt spoke. "I've got just a quarter tank of gas." He looked in the rearview mirror, which he had turned onto the bishop's face instead of the dark, gloomy road behind them. "I suggest we stop in Kokomo and fill 'er up. Maybe catch a bite to eat."

"Stop for gas. No time to eat. Have to get back before this weather gets worse," was all Father Schmidt could coax from the passenger in the backseat.

Within a few minutes, Father Schmidt could see a small, dimly lit Phillips 66 gas station ahead, standing solitary on the crossroad of Route 31. He carefully turned into the station. Fortunately, there was a cover that hung over the two single pumps. An old attendant stepped out. The ear flaps of his black-and-gray plaid hat were pulled tight under his chin. *Strange-looking character*, Father Schmidt thought.

"Fill 'er up?" the man asked as the priest walked past him into the station.

"Yes, please."

Father Schmidt stepped inside and warmed his hands by the black potbelly stove. He grabbed a half dozen stale doughnuts and two cups of coffee. Soon the attendant walked back into the station, clapping his gloved hands together. "Colder than a witch's tit. Ha-ha. Oh sorry der Father." The attendant noticed the priest's collar.

Father Schmidt did not respond. He asked for two bags. Using his greasy, dirt-stained hands, the old man grabbed a dull pencil and wrote up six doughnuts at twenty-five cents, two coffees at ten cents each, and twelve gallons of gas for three dollars and sixty cents. Carefully, he counted.

Impatiently, Father Schmidt said, "That's three dollars and ninety-five cents," and handed the attendant a five dollar bill.

"Wait, wait. Can't forget those doughnuts are half price after six o'clock."

"That's okay. Just give me a dollar. Thanks." Father Schmidt turned to leave.

"Say there, Father, that's a pretty fancy car. You got the pope there in the backseat?"

Father Schmidt looked and said, "Yeah, I do. He's visiting here from Rome."

Back in the car, leaning over into the backseat, Father Schmidt handed the coffee and doughnuts to the bishop. He listened for a thank-you but did not receive one. As they drove north, the weather continued to deteriorate

About an hour south of South Wayne, Father Schmidt heard the voice from the backseat. "Those relentless young priests are influencing the cardinal with lies, twisted stories, and false accusations. You know, those kids are all set up. Thank goodness I've planned well. To think of this, after all I've done for the church, especially this diocese, during the last eighteen years. I'm seventy-two and simply don't need this stress in my life."

Startled by the sudden outburst, Father Schmidt added, "You had every right to speak up as you did today." He knew he had good reason to stay on the bishop's good side, knowing the bishop could connect him with Billy Donovan. The bishop had not said a word about it, but Father Schmidt knew Bishop Powers would do anything if it was self-serving. The bishop needed Father Schmidt's cooperation for a few more days.

As if the bishop had been devising a plan during the first most of the trip, he now spoke up and said, "From you, Father Schmidt, I expect your unyielding support. First thing tomorrow, I want you to review every single file on any of our transfers—psychological analysis results and all written comments, letters, or correspondence that could be damaging. You know what to do with them. Of most importance, I want all files, records, billing files, patient records, and everything of Catholic Services Testing Co. to be destroyed or burned. Leave not a trace. You handle that all personally. In two days, you should have all this completed. Place only the checkbook and the credit of deposit accounts on my desk in the study before noon tomorrow. Through next Tuesday, I will take no phone calls. Make no appointments. That includes His Honor Cardinal Cullings."

Father Schmidt was first startled by the bishop's commands. "I will handle everything just as you say," Father Schmidt assured the bishop, still hovering over the steering wheel, focused on the increasingly dangerous road ahead.

The conversation ended as quickly as it began. The weather did not relent. Father Schmidt kept his eyes glued to the road as best he could. Off and on, the driving snow made visibility only a few yards in front of the car. Fortunately, the roads were almost barren except for the occasional monster semi-truck that drove past, temporarily engulfing their car with a deluge of snow and sleet.

The bishop sat quietly, glaring out the steamed and frosty windows in the backseat. Just south of South Wayne, he felt confident about the next several days. By this time next week, he knew it would all be over. *Safe and secure in Rome.*

Father Schmidt could barely make out the name on the snow-covered city limits sign to South Wayne. *One more mile,* he thought. Soon he pulled up to the garage at the rectory. Father Schmidt shifted the car into park, got out, and opened the double garage door. He drove inside and turned the engine off.

"One minute before we go in. I want to say something in absolute confidence," Bishop Powers said to Father Schmidt as he leaned closer to the front seat. "A very little secret will remain hidden between you and me," the bishop said, alarming Father Schmidt.

I hope this is not the Billy Donovan issue, he thought.

"I expect your total support in all that I have directed. I will leave here with a clean, exemplary record. All evidence of anything relating to today and any past indiscretion will be eradicated. Everything we talked about earlier this evening will be executed. Am I clear?"

"That will not be a problem for you, Bishop. You have my seal of confession," Father Schmidt responded, now looking at the bishop through the rearview mirror.

"Make no mistake about what I just told you. Understand?"

"Absolutely clear," Father Schmidt assured him. "I totally get it. I know how you want everything to work out. I'll make sure it does."

Bishop Powers thought Father Schmidt sounded overly accommodating. Leaning his arms on the back of the front passenger seat, his chin resting on his forearm, the bishop said, "Oh yes, one more thing."

Father Schmidt did not turn around.

"I have totally wiped clean from my mind, absolutely forgotten that night in September when I knocked, opened the door to your room, and saw you naked in a … what we'll call a compromising position with Billy Donovan. I assume I'm the only one who knows. I believe you and I were in a meeting that evening. If for some reason this Donovan kid decides to step forward, you were in my study. I will vouch for you, provided—"

Father Schmidt interrupted, "Study. Yes, sir. That's where we were. Your study."

"Does that give you some relief, Father Schmidt? Now you carry out everything as I directed. I don't want my legacy to be jaded. You know what I'm getting at?"

Father Schmidt responded, "Yes, sir. Thank you for understanding, Bishop. Just forget it all. Everything will be handled just as you expect. I'm here for you. I promise you won't ever have to remember that night."

While Father Schmidt cleaned the car, Bishop Powers went inside, not to be seen again that evening.

Ida Thornbauer—December 3, 1958

As the snow continued to fall, Ida Thornbauer became more concerned about Ned and Danny. Then she heard a sound, stomping on the porch. She rushed to the front door. "I'm so glad you're home. I've been so worried about you, these terrible roads and all."

"The meeting lasted longer than we planned, then the weather. Will tell you all about it after supper," Ned said, hoping she had prepared one of her fine meals.

"Good Land of Goshen … it's almost eleven o'clock. The stew is simmering on the stove. Your favorite, Ned. Beef stew."

"Okay, Grandma," Danny answered.

"But we want to talk with you after," Ned added as he took off his coat. "Going upstairs now."

"I just don't like you both being out so late," Ida reminded them.

"That sure smells good. We'll be back down soon." Ned took off toward the stairs, anticipating how she would take the horrible news.

"Oh, Ned, before I forget, I'm going down to Wabash on Friday to see Helen. She's having some problems." Ida was close to her younger sister, Helen. "We need to be together for a couple days. I need you to check on Danny."

"Of course, I'll be around for Danny. Maybe he should come stay at my place."

"That would be great, Ned. Just great."

The boys both rushed upstairs.

Ida Thornbauer was a kind, caring, and resilient woman. Never married and having raised one son alone and now two grandsons, she always had a way to deal with the challenges of life. Over the past three days, Ida had gathered all her strength anticipating something was happening with her boys. Why did they go to Indianapolis to meet with those priests? The cardinal? Why was Ned acting so suspiciously and more concerned than usual about Danny? Attending daily Mass the past three days as she did every morning, Ida said extra prayers for her boys. She said a rosary for each. Ida lit more candles than she ever had in her life.

"*Yoo-hoo!* Supper's ready now," Ida called upstairs to Ned and Danny.

The boys came down and followed the aroma into the kitchen. The three of them sat together at the kitchen table. Ida said evening grace and then closed with, "Okay, boys, tell me about your day."

Ned was not that hungry, so he talked first. "As you know, we went to Indianapolis for our meeting with Cardinal Cullings. Bishop Powers was there but unfortunately left prior to Danny and I meeting with the cardinal. I might have mentioned that Bishop Powers was to be there."

"Yes, you said, but why?" Ida said with a proud look. "I don't understand."

"Grandma, I don't know how to tell you this. It's difficult. Embarrassing. I'm so ashamed." Ned's face turned red.

Ida leaned forward. "You can tell me anything."

Ned hesitated but knew he had to tell her. "Grandma, about nine years ago, remember when I went on those trips to Bishop Powers' cabin?"

"Yes, that was so nice of him."

Danny looked to Ned in wonderment. *How will he answer?*

"Grandma, Bishop Powers is a bad man. There's no other way to tell it. While there, he took advantage of me. He … he … " Ned stammered. "Grandma, he touched me like … like my privates. It was awful."

"He what? Oh, my good Jesus."

"He touched me and more. Grandma, now that I look back, Bishop Powers abused me physically. He made me … made me … Grandma, please understand, there is no need to tell you more."

Danny saw tears in his grandma's eyes.

"Tell me it was just that one time. Only once."

Ned did not respond. He shook his head.

Bursting into tears, Danny left the room and rushed upstairs.

Ida started to stand up. "No, no. Stay here, Grandma." Ned reached for her arm. "Stay with me. I want to tell you all. Danny doesn't need to hear this again."

"Oh, Ned, please. There can't be more."

"Yes, there is, Grandma."

Without a word, Ida looked at him with horror in her eyes.

"Grandma, I found out that … that, well, the bishop has been doing the same to Danny."

"What? To Danny? Pray God, tell me that's not true." Ida put her face in her open hands in shock.

Ned waited. He heard her whimpers. Ida stood up and slowly walked over to the window. She looked into the darkness with her back to Ned. "Here I encouraged Danny to go with the bishop this summer. I think they made three trips to the cabin. Oh, Ned, I can't imagine this. Our Danny with that beast, that horrible man. How can he be a priest? Now a bishop? They are supposed to do good for us." Quietly, Ida remained transfixed on the darkness outside the window.

Ned stood up and walked over to stand behind his grandma. "It's over. We told everything to Cardinal Cullings today. Three other priests were there. We told them how, when, and what he did for all these years. They will take care of this, and Bishop Powers will be brought to justice."

Ida turned around. "Promise?"

"Yes, I promise. Danny is safe. Bishop Powers will have to pay for his sins. Not only to the church and God, but I'm sure he will have to answer to the police. He'll never touch a boy again."

Ida looked up to Ned. She reached around to give him a hug and then felt Ned's arms around her. Just his words that Danny was safe lifted the immediate burden of anger and fear from her shoulders. Inwardly, she felt her own strength surface as it had all her life.

Now that Ida knew the plight of her boys, memories from her past returned. But she asked herself, *Is there any relevance?* The secret in her life she had tried to remove for so many decades was resurfacing.

With the late hour and bad weather, Ida encouraged Ned to stay the night. Before they retired, she reminded Ned that she was going to visit her sister, Aunt Helen. "I'm leaving Friday after Mass. I'll be safe, as I'm riding with Charlie Schroeder. He's going down to visit his brother and sister, who live on a farm south of Wabash. Out there beyond the reform school. You've never been there. I'll be safe with Charlie. He's a good driver." With all this horrid news, Ida knew there was now another reason to go to Wabash. There was something she knew she had to do.

Ned thought nothing of her trip. He knew it would be good for her to get away from all this. Although Ned knew little about Wabash, he was aware of how much she loved her family, especially Helen.

CHAPTER 109

JUSTICE IS SERVED

Randall Zilbar—December 3, 1958

BY late afternoon, Randall Zilbar knew Mario would have executed the plan. The faulty underpinning of Zilbar's grand scheme would have been removed, zeroing out the chance of any future misgivings or mistakes by Clarence Wolfe. The trust Wolfe so flagrantly violated would not raise its ugly head in Zilbar's business ever again.

Disclosing important details, even if only partially, to Phillip Krueger had been the beginning of the questionable principles through which Clarence Wolfe had betrayed Zilbar. Wolfe's demise was of his own making. Zilbar had not completely disclosed to Mario Molinaro the plot he had planned. Zilbar's corrupt scheme was supported by arrogance and his exaggerated self-worth. He alone would control the plan.

Clarence Wolfe had foreseen the impending calamity. However, the leverage of Randall Zilbar, so carefully schemed, had been a barrier Wolfe could not challenge, let alone defeat. The deceptive means by which Zilbar had eliminated the long-held secret between them was never compromised. Zilbar's self-indulgent maneuvers, always at the expense of others—including friends—were always justified, but only to himself. The man simply had no soul. He was totally controlled by his own narcissistic personality.

Late that Wednesday evening in December 1958, Zilbar, dressed in a smoking jacket and smooth leather slippers, discreetly walked down his baroque carved staircase. Knowing his family had retired into their own private slumber, he pivoted at the last step, his hand rotating on the oversized hand-carved newel post. Feeling triumph in the success of today's event—the elimination of Clarence Wolfe—Zilbar walked directly to his private study in the back center of his grandiose late nineteenth-century manor house on the north edge of Wabash. As he walked the few paces between the staircase and the study, the quiet steps of his slippered feet were further muffled by the elegant Persian runner in the center hallway.

Two eight-panel mahogany doors protected his study from uninvited friends and family members. The back wall was bookended by two individual sets of double lead-panel windows separated by a twelve-foot expanse of a one-foot thick masonry wall. The space provided the perfect backdrop for his handsomely paneled dark teak desk. Wall bookcases adorned both ends of the room. Just to the right of the center double doors, off the main hall, Randall Zilbar stood in front of a small three-drawer marble-top chest. An ornate mirror of beveled glass surrounded by a frame of hand-carved serpentine entwined botanicals overshadowed the less predominant chest of drawers.

He opened a humidor centered on the marble top. Selecting one of his finest hand-rolled Cubans, Zilbar smoothed the cigar across the bottom of his nose. *Only the finest.* Six bottles of single malt Scotch stood to both sides of the humidor. Three right, three left, as if soldiers guarding the precious Cubans. The Scotch, the least of which was twenty-one years old, waited his selection. He picked up a thirty-year-old Glenlivet. Pouring it straight into a glass tumbler from his private collection of vintage glassware, Randall Zilbar realized the ecstasy of triumph. He stared straight into the nineteenth-century mirror. A satisfied smirk of complete confidence crossed his face. He had no limits for his own self-aggrandizement.

Cigar and scotch in one hand, the man slowly walked over, picked up his briefcase from the side of the desk, and strategically placed it on his leather-bound desktop. He reached over and unbuckled the alligator band on his gold studded Hamilton watch and laid it open below the desk lamp. Looking past his wedding band, he admired the oversized diamond on the middle finger of his left hand. *Size of a marble when I was a kid.* He spread all his fingers, twisting his hand and approving of the prominence of the ring. Reaching over with his right hand, he rubbed the middle finger encircled by the gold band with the brazen diamond. Damp weather still affected the scarred finger. Temporarily, he set the scotch down beside a silver-plated ashtray. Cigar smoke curled under the beams above his head.

Noticing the large embossed leather initials *RUZ* centered on the front flap of his briefcase, Randall Zilbar methodically unlocked the one-strap combination. *There they are.* He removed the meticulously wrapped package and held it in both hands. The secret of the missing package that only he knew was forever hidden from Mario and Clarence Wolfe.

Bernard Bednar—December 4, 1958

The gray metal alarm clock ticked back and forth, louder and louder with never-ending annoyance. It was nearly 2:00 a.m. Sleeping restlessly, Bernard threw the multi-patched wool blanket to the side. His shoulder-to-ankle long underwear provided minimal protection from the cold in his unheated room. Bernard sat up, reached for his woolen dark brown coat, and slipped into his ankle-top leather work boots. Walking over to his dresser, he pulled out his worn, faded mustard-colored wooden box. Holding it in both hands, Bernard walked down the hall, past the separate rooms of his mother and father. He proceeded to the kitchen.

After setting the box on the kitchen table, he reached down, picked up three splits of hickory wood, and tossed them into the black potbelly stove. The crackle of dry hickory broke the silence in the room. He set a cold pot of coffee on the flat top of the cast-iron stove. Then, sitting at the table, Bernard absorbed the increasing radiant heat. During the last few months, he had dwelled on the past. He thought about Little Eddie and Billy. Phillip Krueger's deeds were etched in his mind. Deep into the early hours of the morning, when he could sometimes see his own breath in his room, Bernard thought back to his cold, stark childhood and his early years.

Poking his wide index finger between the lid and the side of the box, he gently raised the lid. After carefully reaching in, Bernard removed the worn *Saint Joseph's Daily Missal* he had once used as a student at St. Thomas Moore. Inside the cover, Bernard noted his printed name in pencil—*Bernard Bednar, 1922*. Setting the missal down, Bernard reached beneath it and pulled out his eighth grade report card. Sister Augustine and Father Gilner's signatures were most familiar. On the back side, Bernard read the printed X above his father's signature line.

As he reviewed his spelling, arithmetic, and reading grades, Bernard proudly pointed to each grade with his finger. His worn gray nail pointed at the letters one by one—C, D, D+, C-, D, C, D. The D+ in geography still bothered him, as he had studied so hard the locations of countries around the world he knew he would never see. Bernard thought about being most proud of all the *excellents* in conduct, obedience, and hard work. Around his ankle, Bernard felt the gnarly house cat rubbing itself on his wool sock.

The aroma of coffee broke Bernard's focus. He stood up and reached for the hot coffee pot. After pouring a cup, he sat back down, warming his hands with the hot porcelain cup before taking a drink. Pulling the box back toward himself, Bernard poked around, pushing aside some marbles, a wooden slingshot, and three silver dollars. Below his report card, which was now pushed into the back corner, Bernard picked up a gold tie clasp. He stared at the raised gold initials, tracing them with his finger.

The horror of that terrifying night in 1934 when he was only twenty-two still haunted him. Bernard rubbed his finger along the cold smooth black barrel at the bottom of the box. Placing his finger on the trigger, his mind imagined. He knew he could. After so many years, Bernard now knew their identities. *This time gonna get that man. Gonna hurt 'em. That man killed little Gordon Yoder.* The tie clasp remained a constant reminder to seek justice for Gordon. Bernard could still see the monster's face in his mind. Now he knew who the murderer was. He would avenge the death of Gordon. The time for justice had come. Bernard took one last drink of coffee. *Today is now.*

Closing his treasured box, Bernard carefully carried it back to his room. The cat followed. Bernard set the box on the dresser. He looked in the aged mirror above the dresser and stared at himself. Tears welled in his eyes. His conviction looked back. Bernard imagined the little boy lying on the couch. Then the image disappeared. His own face was blurred in the mirror. Zilbar appeared. Bernard could see the cold in Zilbar's eyes. *Chilling.* A blank stare, a reflection of Zilbar's soulless being, the man who had taken the life of little Gordon Yoder so long ago.

Bernard looked down and then back up to see himself. He knew the time had come. *Time for justice.* He gently pulled his only sweater over the box, in some manner protecting his precious possession. Leaving his wool coat on, he lay back in bed and pulled the heavy woolen blanket over his head. Peeking out, he noticed the time—2:48 a.m. He listened to the cold night air whistling through the cracked window sash. When he closed his eyes, thoughts about the regrettable night in 1934 continued to race through his mind. Gordon Yoder, a victim of a deranged monster and a boy he never knew. *Today.*

Bernard spent several hours late the next afternoon chopping wood. He figured he made enough to last a couple of weeks. Before he finished, he filled the box with small chopped kindling. Bernard delighted in the sound of the dry hickory splitting and separating along the grain of the wood. His precision with the hand ax and the big knife was true and accurate. Filling the wood box, Bernard carried the kindling back into the kitchen and set the box by the black stove. He rubbed his cold hands by the stove as he watched his mother stand at the sink, pumping water into a kettle. She began to slice potatoes. Bernard said, "Cold outside. *Uumpgh.*"

She kept peeling, never looking up.

"Supper soon," Bernard's dad spoke in his low gruff voice from the front room. The cat rested in the rocker. With darkness approaching, the kerosene lamp flickered on the table next to the old man's chair. The glow from the lamp was faint as he rested in his aged upholstered chair.

Bernard threw a couple of hickory logs into the potbellied stove.

"Bernard, come here, boy," the old man commanded.

Bernard clanged the black, heavily sooted metal door closed on the crackling embers. He walked into the front room. Pushing the cat aside, he sat forward in the rocker.

The old man leaned forward, elbows on his knees. In a hushed tone, he said, "'Member what I tolds ya. When bad men hurt little boys, you do what ya gotta. Know what ya mean?"

Bernard nodded. "*Uumpgh.*"

"'Member, show 'em so they'll never forget. Remind 'em forever."

That said, the old man sat back in his chair knowing Bernard knew what to do.

Bernard walked back to the kitchen and stood in front of the stove. "*Uumpgh.*"

His dad got up and limped to the kitchen. Right hand on his ailing hip, he sat. "Let's eat."

"Not hungry. Goin' out. Just takin' a walk. Fresh air, exercise. *Uumpgh,*" Bernard announced to both his parents.

"You been choppin' wood all afternoon. That's exercise. Ain't it?"

"Yep. Love to chop wood."

"Then take your walk on this cold night. Do what you gotta."

"Love to walk. *Uumpgh.*"

Bernard ambled over to the stairs, opened the door, and trudged up, step by step, his heavy leather ankle-top boots sliding on the worn wooden steps. Inside his room, he walked over to the dresser, opened the drawer, and reached toward the back. Pulling out his treasured mustard-colored box, Bernard looked at the missal, ivory knife, and revolver. He stared at the revolver again, paused a moment, and then made the decision.

After closing the box, Bernard carefully set it back inside the drawer. The wind whistled through the wide crack on the window sash on the other side of his bed. Bernard reached into the top drawer and pulled out a blue bandana handkerchief. "*Uumpgh.*"

Feeling the draft, he pulled the ten inch knife from a sheath hanging on the bedpost. Using the back side of the blade, Bernard meticulously stuffed the bandana into the wide crack, sheltering the room from the blast of air.

"*Uumpgh.*" Satisfied, he settled on the side of the bed.

As Bernard pulled his right pant leg up to his knee, he turned and saw the dark leather sheath hanging on the bedpost. He lifted the leather and then strapped it to his right calf. He slid the knife in and then reached over to the table at the side of the bed, where he picked up an empty cigar box and slid it into one of the large saddle pockets on the side of his heavy wool coat. *Just fits.*

Bernard walked downstairs. He knew his destiny. Ma and Pa were sitting down at the kitchen table. Ma served potatoes. Pa bent over his plate with his elbows on the table.

"Dark. Real cold out there. Don't be gone too long. May need some more wood tonight," Pa said not raising his eyes from his plate. He cut into the chicken as Ma plopped another heaping mound of potatoes on his plate. Pa spooned his own gravy.

Bernard turned around and shuffled down the back hall. Pa heard the back door slam. Instinctively, he knew the purpose of his son's intention. Remembering back long ago in his life, the haunting memory crept forward. *My son's following me.* Before he could finish his potatoes, he heard the back door slam again. Boots shuffled down the hall. Bernard's arms were full with seven splits of hickory.

Setting them in the wood box, he said, "Feed your face. Now feed the stove. There's your wood. *Uumpgh.*" Bernard didn't say another word.

Ma never raised her eyes from her plate. The clock above the mantel in the front room broke the stillness. The cat rested in the rocker. Without a word, Bernard walked to the side screen porch and disappeared down the driveway.

Unbeknownst to Randall Zilbar, Bernard Bednar walked toward Pike Street. Just ahead on the north side of Pike, Bernard saw the Stouffer farm.

"Hey, Bernard," he heard a little boy say. The boy was reaching into the mailbox for the newspaper. "Come on over and help us milk. You can pull the teats," little Billy Stouffer teased. "You like them teats! You can sit on my milking stool. Come on, Bernard!" Billy started running backward toward the house. "Come on, Bernard, it's teat time! It's dark. Watch out for the boogey man!" he yelled.

Uumpgh. Nice little boy, that Billy Stouffer. Teats, uumpgh.

Bernard continued east on Pike. *Five more minutes.* He could hear the water below singing from the current of the mighty Wabash as he crossed the Carroll Street Bridge. *I'll get him, little Gordon.* Bernard pictured the black couch, the startled face, and Gordon's solitary tombstone. *I'm coming, Randall Zilbar.* "*Uumpgh.*"

In the meantime, Randall Zilbar was driving over to the Indiana Hotel. This night was much colder. The wind had settled. He anticipated his favorite time of the day. He knew Armond would be waiting.

Within a few minutes, Bernard looked into the office of Yarnell Lumber. The lights were still on. From the back of the yard, he heard the high shrill whine of the buzz saw tearing through a long board as someone was still ripping and cutting through the tight grain of wood like a cleaver through meat. The front office had closed for the day. Just ahead, a group of teenage boys ran from the Honeywell Center, jumping and hollering as if they were still playing basketball.

"Hey! *Uum-uum* man!" one hollered as he ran by Bernard.

Bernard paid no attention as he stared ahead toward Thorne Street. His hand clutched inside his right coat pocket. He could feel the treasured metal. Cold and smooth.

In the distance high on Hill Street, Bernard gazed at the beautifully lit Christmas tree atop the courthouse. The spirit of the season was not present in his mind on this night. Reaching Hill Street, he turned left and headed a few blocks to Thorne. A dog barked in the distance. Bernard stopped, reached down, and rubbed his right calf. Left on Thorne and down a few houses, he stopped at his private solitary elm.

He looked out over the river valley beyond and thought of the spectacular view Zilbar had of the valley far below. Bernard leaned against the tree and waited. Calmly, in the cold stillness of the early evening, Bernard Bednar could hear his heart thumping. He thought of the altar boy he had wanted to be, his secret mustard-colored box, the boys at school, and then as always, he thought of little Gordon Yoder.

Randall Zilbar—December 4, 1958

The Christmas lights illuminated the skyline as Randall Zilbar drove up Carroll Street. *'Tis the season.* Any joy of the season was heightened by Zilbar's time spent at Armond's bar. Slowly, he turned left onto Thorne. He loved the view of the valley beyond. More importantly, he fixed his eyes on the grandeur of his home just a few doors up the street.

To his right, leaning on the far side of the giant elm, Bernard froze as he caught sight of an approaching car. Never conscious of his surroundings other than what focused on himself, Randall Zilbar passed the shadow standing against the elm, his mind transfixed on the grandeur of his house. The black Cadillac turned left and eased across the sidewalk and up the drive on the near side of his house. Bernard's gaze followed. He pulled down the brim of his wool hat and felt the cold steel barrel in his pocket and the power strapped to the calf of his right leg. He secured his top button. His cold breath in the night air preceded him as he crossed the street. His boots were silent on the concrete walk. A hoot sounded, and Bernard knew an owl was watching. A lone dog barked in the distant valley below. Bernard heard the curse of an angry man. One word.

"Damn!" Zilbar cursed his son. Clifford had left his car under the portico. Randall parked in the drive behind it. He took one long drag of his cigarette and then flicked it out the window. As he looked up, he caught the dark shadow of a figure in his rearview mirror. Instinctively, Zilbar reached his long arm under the seat, not daring to move. He felt cold steel at the ends of his fingers. *Yes, slow now.* Always paranoid of strangers, he slid the revolver carefully into his jacket pocket, concealed from the intruder. Lifting his briefcase from the front seat with his right hand, Zilbar got out of the car.

Looking back down the drive toward the valley, he cried, "Holy shit!" He jumped back. "What the hell are you doing? Who are you?"

Bernard stood directly behind the trunk of Zilbar's car, his eyes piercing from below the bill of his dark wool hat, which was pulled low over his forehead. He didn't say a word.

"Who the hell are you?" Zilbar called out.

Bernard's right hand was buried deep in his coat pocket. His left hand hung next to the hidden cigar box.

"Get the hell out of here!" Zilbar turned toward the house

"Want your tie clip?" Bernard asked in his low guttural voice.

Zilbar froze in his tracks. "It's you. Bednar. You ugly son of a bitch. You goddamn liar." Zilbar slowly turned around, gun in hand but still hidden within his coat pocket. *Don't alarm him. Slowly.*

"I'm here for Gordon Yoder. *Uumpgh.* You killed him. Long time ago."

Zilbar turned and looked straight at the stranger while his hand clutched the metal in his pocket.

"Let me see the clip. You want money?" Zilbar felt the protection in his pocket. "That's it. You ugly freak, you want money?" Zilbar could barely see the shorter man's eyes.

"Don't want no money. You gonna suffer just like you made Gordon Yoder suffer." His gaze was hard and cold with conviction. "One thing different. Little Gordon died. You killed him. You ain't gonna die." Bernard leaned forward, his words slower. "You gonna suffer a long, long time … 'cause"—his voice was now a harsh whisper—"I'm gonna hurt you. Hurt you bad."

Zilbar looked at Bernard from head to toe. His mind raced. Bernard stood without moving, still behind the trunk. *Safe. He can't do anything*, thought Zilbar, his hand tightly gripping the gun within his right pocket. Then slowly Bernard took a pace back. Randall noticed the hand moving inside Bernard's right pocket.

"That's it. You gotta gun. Think you're gonna kill me? Shoot me?"

"Killing's wrong. Not gonna kill you like you killed Gordon. Don't need no gun." Bernard secured the handle in his right hand, hidden within his coat pocket.

Feeling confident that he had the upper hand, Zilbar edged to the back of the giant fin-shaped fender of his Cadillac, his hand still clutching the gun in his pocket. Tighter, he squeezed. His eyes focused on Bernard's hand hidden in his own jacket pocket.

"That was Wolfe. He killed Yoder. Not me," Zilbar said with authority.

"Take care of Wolfe later. *Uumpgh*," Bernard replied as he stared at Zilbar's face, long nose, and extended ears.

Get the clasp and then shoot him; the thought raced through Zilbar's mind. "I've got an envelope full of hundred dollar bills in my glove compartment. Twenty of them. More money than you've ever seen, you freak." Zilbar stepped forward toward Bernard. "Let me by. I'll get the cash in the glove compartment. Step back."

Immediately, Bernard pulled his right hand out of his pocket. Opening his hand, palm up, Bernard exposed the metal clip. Zilbar saw the initials RZ.

"That's it!" Randall exclaimed.

"You left it on the floor by Gordon. You're a bad man. *Uumpgh*."

Bernard leaned forward and set the clasp squarely in the middle of the trunk lid. Zilbar stood still at the corner of the trunk. He could feel the sharp point of the tail fin of the fender against his side. Zilbar and Bernard were squared off with the clasp between them.

"Want it? Take it," Bernard challenged Zilbar.

Slowly, Zilbar reached forward with his left hand across the top of the trunk toward the metal clip. He looked down at Bernard. Bernard stood his ground, knees almost touching the bumper. His gaze was frozen on Zilbar. Zilbar looked at the clasp. He knew with one swift movement he could pick it up and then throw his shoulder into Bednar, knocking him to the ground while he pulled the gun and ended it all.

Bernard's eyes, still tucked below the bill, focused only on Zilbar's left hand. Just before Zilbar clutched the clasp, Bernard lowered his right hand to his pant leg. In one continuous motion, Zilbar closed his left hand around the clasp as Bernard raised his left arm and slammed his giant hand around Zilbar's forearm, pinning it to the trunk. Feeling the force of Bernard's lock on his arm, Zilbar reached for his gun, only to see Bernard's right hand rise from behind the trunk and reach high above his head, holding a silver blade that reflected the light of the starlit sky.

Zilbar gasped. His gaze froze on the shining metal. Instinctively, he pulled his right hand from his pocket without the gun and reached for Bernard's hand, still high overhead. Zilbar was defenseless in trying to stop the downward thrust of Bernard's right hand; his left forearm secured to the trunk against the cold metal. Zilbar strained to free his left arm.

"No, you bast—Noooo!"

With the force of a mighty piston and the ten-inch blade in hand, Bernard used all his brute strength to bring the blade down like a bolt of lightning in perfect alignment with Zilbar's wrist. The knife sliced through skin, nerves, and tendons, splintering bones and spewing blood. They both heard the sound of the blade making contact with the black steel of the trunk. The jarring sound rang through the silence of the cold December night. Blood gushed in all directions, splattering against the rear glass window of the car and across Bernard's face, spotting Zilbar's white shirt, and blotting his stylish woolen coat.

"*Ahhh!* My God!" Blood now ran onto the trunk. "You cut off— *Ahhh!*" Zilbar grasped for his left arm. He saw a red stump. His hand lay on the trunk.

Zilbar tried to reach for his gun, but instinctively he clutched his fragmented wrist. A neighbor next door turned on the porch light at the sound of horror. Dressed only in his white shirt, trousers, and slippers, he rushed across his yard. The cries grew louder. He looked toward the sound coming from the direction of Zilbar's car, and rushed forward. "Randy, that you? Randall, that you?" Zilbar bent over in excruciating, mind-numbing pain as his screams of horror sounded through the neighborhood. He squeezed his forearm like a vise pulling the carnage to his chest.

Meanwhile, Bernard watched the devil screaming in agony. He looked at Zilbar's contorted face. "Look at me!" he commanded Zilbar. "You pay for murdering little Gordon Yoder!"

Zilbar did not hear.

"Justice has been served!"

Bernard stepped back as he watched Zilbar stagger toward his house. Bernard bent down and wiped the blade of his knife across the dead grass. Traces of blood smeared the dark leather when Bernard slid the knife into the sheath. Pulling the cigar box from his pocket, Bernard stepped back toward the trunk and picked up Zilbar's hand. While holding the tie clasp in his left hand, he wrapped his right hand around Zilbar's fingers, securing the diamond ring. Then Bernard whipped the wrist end of the severed hand toward the ground, draining as much blood as possible. Carefully, he placed Zilbar's hand into the box, turned, walked down the drive, and disappeared into the darkness.

Lights across dark front porches lit up the neighborhood one by one. A man down the way stepped out onto his porch as he heard the reverberating screams. One man shouted, "There he goes!" as he pointed to Bernard walking away.

Clutching his left forearm, Zilbar tried to stop the bleeding.

"Holy God, Randall!" His neighbor saw Zilbar running while holding his handless arm. The neighbor rushed to Zilbar's aid.

"Get my hand! On the trunk! Bastard! Goddamn that freaky bas—!" Shock was setting in. Blood dripped across the porch. Zilbar's wife heard the screams, opened the front door, and shrieked at the sight of the red arm. "Pull my belt! Fast! Oh God, my hand! *Ahhh!*" he screamed as pain and terror overtook his entire being.

Blood dripped on the white shag carpet. "*Ahhh*, there above the wrist. Pull! Goddamn that freaky bastard!"

His wife frantically pulled the belt as she tried to steady his left arm. "Oh God! No! I can't!"

Blood splattered as she fumbled with the belt.

His neighbor, Reuben, charged in. "It's gone! Your hand is nowhere! I looked all around the car. There's a giant blood smear on the trunk, like it was dragged away. Can't find it anywhere!"

"What's gone, Reuben?" his wife shrieked not realizing what she was seeing.

"His hand! His hand is gone!" Reuben yelled in dismay. "Look, look! All that blood, no hand!" Reuben shouted, pointing directly at the stub on the end of Randall's left arm.

"Oh my God, the pain! My hand? It's gone?" Zilbar became glassy-eyed. He swayed. His legs turned limp as he struggled to the kitchen. He plopped into a chair, frantically holding his left forearm. Zilbar's wife braced her left hand on the arm, still tugging the belt.

"Tape, black tape? Any tape?" Reuben pleaded. He yanked the belt as she went to the kitchen drawer. Reuben pulled the belt with all his strength and then wrapped the tape around and around, pulling with all his might. "Towels! Bring a lot! Then I'll get my car."

"No! No, take mine. Keys are in it," Randall remembered. Zilbar's head fell against his right arm. "Where's Clifford? Left his damn car in the drive. Goddamn, this wouldn't of happened!"

"Dad, he went over to Mickey's!" Zilbar's daughter, Ruthie, shouted from upstairs above the cries of pain.

"He's going into shock. He's white. Get cold water!" Reuben demanded, now taking charge.

Elenore could hardly move. Her hands were shaking out of control. She couldn't talk. Chaos reigned. Ruthie ran downstairs at the sound of the screams. As she ran into the front room, she shrieked at the sight of blood on the white carpet.

"Let's go, Randall. Fast!"

Holding his arm bundled in towels, his wife and Reuben stood him up and guided him back across the blood-stained carpet and through the front door.

Reuben alarmed the neighborhood as he screeched out of the drive and around the corner at Thorne and Hill. He broke all limits racing across town. The lights from the courthouse exclaiming the joyful season, unaffected by the horror happening below, still glistened over the quiet city as Reuben sped by. Randall lay in a fetal position on the backseat. He was in unimaginable pain, shock, and horror. He clutched his left arm to his chest. He felt the protruding bones. The towels were saturated with blood.

The eleven long blocks to the Wabash County Hospital lasted an eternity. His knees were pulled up as he tried to mitigate the pain. Speed was Randall's only friend. As Reuben ignored stop signs and speed limits, he took the corner at Hill and East Streets nearing fifty miles per hour. The moans and cries from the backseat spurred him to drive even faster. *Hurry. Hurry.*

God, I didn't find his hand, Reuben thought. Elenore Zilbar sat at Randall's side, half on the floor of the big car. Her blouse and hands were covered in blood. She imagined the nightmare ahead. *A man with no hand.* "Hold on, Randall. Almost there." *God, he's got no hand.* His condition worsened. She gently patted his left forearm. "Almost there."

Delirious, Randall Zilbar fainted into a dark place.

"Two more blocks. I'm hurrying, Randall." Reuben's hands squeezed the wheel.

The night was long and torturous. Dr. Inden, the emergency room doctor, tended to Randall, along with a horrified attending nurse. Inden remained calm and focused, ice in his veins. They were all at Randall Zilbar's side long into the morning hours.

His wife and daughter stayed close, both heavily sedated in the aftermath. Having lost a lot of blood, Randall Zilbar received the best of care. The next day, an infectious disease specialist arrived from Indianapolis. After three days, Randall Zilbar was out of intensive care, his life saved. He now had to face the reality of the future. His life had been changed forever.

Bernard Bednar—December 4, 1958

Bernard could still hear the screams as he approached Hill Street. He looked ahead and could see the Christmas lights of the courthouse. The lights illuminated the spirit of the season, and light flakes of snow began to fall.

All was quiet around the Honeywell Center. Only a faint light of the electric wall clock could be seen in Yarnell Lumber. As Bernard walked toward the Carroll Street Bridge, his leather shoes were now tracking in the snow. The cigar box was wrapped in a gunny sack he had brought along and left by the elm tree while he confronted Randall Zilbar. Blood dampened the interior of the cigar box. Bernard walked on. Ahead, the Carroll Street Bridge. *Home, contentment, and peace.*

The light flakes continued as Bernard left his tracks west on Pike Street. All lights were out at the Stouffers'. He continued beyond the city along Mill Creek Road. Walking west toward Friends Cemetery, Bernard could see the lights of the reform school farther west. The snow continued with soft white flakes.

The stone pillars at the gate of the cemetery were within sight. The moon was full. Bernard ambled toward the base of the hill. He could see the small shadow of the headstone. After walking over slowly, he stopped, dropped to his knees, and laid the sack at his side. Reaching out, Bernard gently rubbed his fingers across the engraved letters—*Gordon Yoder.*

Justice served, little fellow. You didn't deserve to die. To die all alone. Bernard turned, picked up the sack, and pulled out the cigar box. He laid the folded sack on the ground in front of the stone and opened the lid of the box, exposing the contents to the face of Gordon Yoder's headstone.

"Twenty-four years ago, little Gordon. See the ring? *Uumpgh.* The bad man used that to cover the scar from your bite. Looked like it went all the way to the bone. *Uumpgh.*" Bernard stretched the finger open as if Gordon could see. "You took a little part. Now, I took the rest. Here for you. Justice has been served. You can rest in peace, little fellow. Justice for you. Bad man suffers forever." Closing the lid, Bernard set the box against the headstone and folded the sack over, protecting the box from snow, wind, and varmints.

The tranquility of the cemetery permeated the night air. Bernard stood, backed up, and walked away from the tiny headstone. A short distance beyond, he stopped and looked back at Gordon Yoder. Bernard Bednar thought about what he had done and what else he had to do. In his own way, Bernard had brought justice to Gordon Yoder while branding Randall Zilbar forever.

Knowing it was wrong to kill, Bernard knew he had left Zilbar with an unexplainable scar for the rest of his life. *Justice has been served.* Bernard pulled his hat low over his eyes as the snow turned to heavier flakes and the wind began to whirl. Pulling his coat tighter against his body, he hunched his shoulders, turned, headed home, and disappeared into the darkness.

CHAPTER 110

ALL SO SUDDEN

Bishop Powers—December 4, 1958

SOUTH Wayne woke up under the attack of six-wheel dump trucks pushing large plows as they forged down the snow-covered streets. After Mass, Father Schmidt was about the bishop's business. Most files would eventually be stripped of at least half their content. As directed, he returned the check and certificate of deposit books of the Catholic Services Testing Co. to the bishop's desk an hour before his deadline. He found the bishop at his desk, looking through files.

Father Schmidt wondered what all this was about. Stripping the files of the accused priests was understandable. Checking and deposit accounts and no appointments through Tuesday seemed so secretive, clandestine. *Why all so sudden? Why so definitive?*

Father Schmidt knew not to question. He wanted to keep himself safe from Bishop Powers' wrath. While the bishop was sitting at his desk, Father Schmidt informed him that the file work was all on schedule and that everything would be complete by tomorrow evening, as directed.

"Thank you, Father. Keep me informed of the balance of your work, results, and completion of all that I asked. I'll be taking a walk after lunch today, in case anyone asks."

"Sure, Bishop, I'll be here." Father Schmidt left, closing the door behind him.

Bishop Powers reached down to the lower left drawer of his desk and pulled out a previously opened letter.

November 22, 1958

Dear Bishop Powers:

I am in receipt of your letter of September 10, 1958, per your request for a permanent reassignment to the Vatican. I have presented your letter and resume to Cardinal Angelo Tomarelli. He, in turn, has met with Bishop Rinaldi. Both have the last word in a Vatican transfer before the recommendation is presented to Pope John Benedict.

On November 20, 1958, His Holy Father approved your request. Your new position, yet to be determined, will commence on February 1, 1959. Hopefully this will allow you time to progress on your end.

You may commence your transition, as your acceptance is effective immediately upon receiving a copy of your letter of resignation.

We look forward to working together with you. Your teaching, organization, and language skills will offer you an advantage in obtaining the right position here at the Vatican.

I look forward to hearing from you soon.

Very respectfully in Christ's name,
Cardinal Alberto Martini

Early that afternoon, Bishop Powers walked two blocks to the Second National Bank of South Wayne. There he withdrew $166,000 from the Catholic Services Testing Co. business account. In addition, he withdrew $142,000 from his own personal account. Within half an hour, he was presented with two individual money orders. He thought it proper to leave $1,000 in each account.

After asking for the keys to his lockbox, Bishop Powers signed the card and followed the safe deposit attendant to the vaulted lockbox safe. Once inside the private cubicle area, he removed his file of personal legal documents, including his last will and testament. Using the second key, along with the attendant, he opened a larger box and set it next to a small black suitcase. The paper on top totaled his last calculation of $96,000 in various cash denominations.

Gleefully, he looked at the stacks and stacks of cash and piled them neatly within the suitcase. Having squeezed all the cash in, he securely closed the case. He left the vault, handed the keys to the attendant, signed the withdrawal card, tipped his hat, and left the bank. Holding the briefcase carefully in his right hand, Bishop Powers felt relief, as he was bringing more and more to closure.

Later that afternoon, Bishop Powers drove to the telegraph office and sent a telegram to Rome.

To: Cardinal Alberto Martini, Vatican City, Rome.

Accept new position. Will send letter of resignation to Cardinal Cullings effective December 31, 1958. Arrive in Rome January 6, 1959. Will be staying in the Florentine Sebastian Hotel. Will call upon arrival for further instructions. Ready for assignment February 1, 1959, as directed. Thank you. See you soon.

Very respectfully in Christ's Name, Bishop Lawrence M. Powers.

Feeling empowered by the results of the day, Bishop Powers looked forward to quiet time in his office, a nostalgic visit and prayer in the cathedral, all followed by a meal and bottle of red wine in the main dining room. The reality of an earlier departure to Rome was now set in motion.

Ned Thornbauer—December 4, 1958

Ned Thornbauer spent the day working at Miller O'Connell Printing Company. As an apprentice pressman's helper, Ned looked forward to making something of himself in the printing business. He was a smart apprentice. He worked hard, listened, learned, and was accepted by the printing shop staff.

By the end of the first shift at 3:30 p.m., Ned's plan was formulated. He raced home to his apartment, cleaned up, and quietly made the phone call he had been anticipating all day. The streets were plowed well, but the temperature had dropped. The evening was clear, cold, and windless. The snow was now dry and crunched when he walked to his car. Ned drove down to the corner gas station and asked Bernie to fill his car up and check the oil. Ned's Chevy was eight years old. He walked to the phone booth in front of the station. Dropping in a nickel, he made a local call.

"Good evening, St. Leonard's Rectory. This is Sister Joelda."

"Good evening, Sister. May I please speak to Father Holtz?"

Ned waited about a minute before he heard, "Good evening, Father Ben Holtz."

"Oh good, you're home. Father, this is Ned Thornbauer. That was quite a day yesterday."

"I have to agree, Ned, quite a day. I just got home an hour ago. I was going to Terre Haute, but I decided not to," Father Holtz informed him.

"Father, this won't take long. I need your help. I'd like to meet with Bishop Powers."

"Really? Meet with the bishop? That's a surprise, but knowing you, maybe not. First thing, Ned, he's not here. He left about twenty minutes ago to go over to the cathedral. It's not unusual in the evenings. He finds quiet, solitude, and prayer time."

Not wanting Father Holtz to know that it was the perfect situation, Ned said, "How about tomorrow?"

"That would be better. Why don't you call in the morning? Talk with Father Schmidt to see if we can set some time. Remember, Ned, there could be a chance he won't see you."

Ned didn't respond. His plan was already set. "Thanks, Father. We'll talk tomorrow."

Ned drove a few blocks over to the cathedral. *Please, God, let him be there*. His timing was perfect. The cathedral was just next door to the rectory. He walked up the snow-packed steps, pulled the giant cathedral doors open, and stepped into the vestibule. His cold breath followed him inside.

Looking through the windows in the door to the sanctuary, Ned saw a lone figure just beyond the darkness toward the front pews. Lost in his own solitude, Bishop Powers was thankful for an end to the events of the past few days. He was still a man of religion and was praying for his future. The silence in the sanctuary was broken by the opening and closing of the main door into the cathedral. Bishop Powers heard the entry but paid no attention. He was in church. No reason for concern.

Ned blessed himself with holy water, genuflected, and walked to the right aisle along the darkness of the outer wall. He could not completely muffle the sound of his footsteps on the tile floor. Large marble columns running parallel with the sanctuary flanked the left side of the side aisle. The silence was broken by the clicking of his leather shoes on the wooden floor. Bishop Powers halted in his prayer and listened.

The intruder walked halfway up the aisle and stopped. Bishop Powers took notice and turned his head in the direction of the steps. Silence. He continued to pray but saw and heard nothing. The bishop knelt, resting back against the wooden pew. His bowed head and rounded shoulders showed a man deep in prayer. The steps continued.

Ned approached the pews about halfway up the sanctuary of the voluminous cathedral. He was within ten rows of Bishop Powers. The small amount of available light hung directly over the communion rail. Bishop Powers was about two rows beyond the dim rays of the lights high overhead. Ned stopped. The echoes subsided.

The bishop looked around. "Somebody there?" he asked. Silence. "Speak up!"

He turned and saw no one. Silence. Then he heard what he thought to be the sounds of shoes sliding from side to side between the pews. Coming from the darkness, the sound grew closer. Bishop Powers turned and saw only a silhouette in the darkness several pews behind him. The man still wore his hat, the brim pulled low over his eyes. The dark collar of his coat was erect.

"Who's there? Who are you?" the bishop asked with instinctive alarm in his voice.

The cathedral was a safe haven. Break-ins or intruders had never been a problem. However, Bishop Powers felt threatened by the presence of the stranger.

The bishop heard a low, unfamiliar voice say, "Turn around, face the altar, and stay where you are. Do not move. For now, you are safe."

"I'm leaving," the bishop said as he stood.

"Yes, I suppose. That's your style. Run rather than face the truth. Now sit down!" the voice rang out with commanding authority.

The bishop continued to stand.

"Sit down now or I will pull from my pocket … " the stranger said in a threatening tone as he stood in the pew behind the bishop.

This time the bishop stopped.

"Sit right where you are or I will endanger you with one slam of my hand to the back of your head. Your face will meet the top of the pew in front of you with full force. Your nose will break, and several teeth will fall to the floor in advance of the stream of blood close behind. Lots of blood! I'll make sure. Remember, the steel is still in my pocket."

"Show respect to an old bishop, whoever you are."

"I would if you had not shown total disrespect, terror, and pain to me nine years ago. These past years have been a total nightmare because of you. You're not going to control my life or my family's life. I can still see your panting, overweight, aroused body pulling me into submission. I was all of 120 pounds. Am I coming back to you now?"

Immediately, the bishop thought it could only be one of two possible people, yet he could not recognize the voice. He slowly started to stand.

"Sit down! You move, I shoot," the voice ordered in a tone the bishop did not want to confront. He rested back on the pew seat. "Remember the swim, your walk of nature back to the cabin? You were breathing heavily, and it wasn't because of the walk. You pointed in the direction of the cabin and followed your lead."

No reply. Ned knew he was now in control. "You were as excited as a stud horse. It was sickening. You took me upstairs, showed me my room, and then called me into yours. Looking over the balcony, you turned around, naked, and walked toward me. Your aroused body still sickens me. Your excited breathing muffled your words as you whispered vulgarities in my ear."

Now the bishop knew. He remained motionless. There was silence. Words came from neither man. The quiet was broken by the sliding of shoes across the tiled floor as the intruder slowly shifted to the center aisle.

"I said don't turn around! I'm the one who will overpower you this time."

The shuffling stopped. The bishop's mouth went dry. He could hardly swallow. His breathing was irregular and heavy. He could hear nothing.

Silence. He waited in fear. *A gun? A hit? A rope? An arm?* Nothing. Moments felt like an eternity. Bishop Powers knew not what lurked in the darkness behind him. Suddenly, without warning he could hear calm, steady breathing. Then a hand cupped his right shoulder. The bishop sat frozen, shuddering in anticipation of what was next.

"I'm here, remember? The table has now turned. For nine long, horrifying years, I've seen the patch … the slimy reddish-brown mark on your back waist. You had all the power. Now I have the power. You are no longer safe. You can't get rid of me now. I want justice. Justice for my family and all the other lives you have ruined.

Startled, the bishop said, "But I—"

The right hand of the man in the darkness rose, cupped, and then moved horizontally from right to left. *Smack.* It struck the bishop's ear, jarring his head into his left shoulder. "Quiet, I said!" The sound resonated through the bishop's head like a shot.

The calm steady voice continued just above a whisper, "I didn't hit a bishop. I didn't smack a priest. I gave a reminder that you are just a man. Your arrogance, power, and self-serving assuredness will not protect you anymore. You are narcissistic, thinking only of your personal gratification, always at the expense of ones weaker than you. Then you took advantage of me when you could. I've waited seven then eight, nine years. Now it's my turn. Justice is on the horizon. Wait and watch."

"You're lying. There is not a bit of truth in what you say."

Without warning, the cupped hand rammed into the bishop's right ear much harder, causing his whole body to bound left, almost knocking his head to the seat of the pew.

"Don't lie and make me do that again."

By the sheer force of the blow, the bishop knew he was indeed overwhelmed. He did not feel safe. "I know who you are. What do you want from me, Thornbauer?"

"I want justice for my family and myself. Most of all, for my family and all they have gone through dealing with me and my trauma … all because of you. Tonight, I want only one thing. You are to believe every word I have said. Tomorrow, you are not safe."

"Don't turn around," he said, delivering a much lighter reminder to the right side of the bishop's head. "You will be hearing from me, Bishop

Powers. You're not safe. I am bringing justice in a manner you have never experienced, never imagined. You will pay for what you started nine years ago. Justice will be unexpected, like from nowhere. Pain is in your future. Pain just like what has been in my past."

Trying to regain his composure, the bishop sat. Reaching for a handkerchief, he wiped the perspiration from his brow. He did not hear another word from the stranger behind. His right ear still rang with pain. He heard the sound again, the sound of shoes walking into the distance. Bishop Powers was now alone but no longer did he feel safe. He knew someone was committed to doing him harm. Silence from the back of the church was interrupted by the sound of the door closing. Bishop Powers remained in place. The door close and Ned Thornbauer was alone as he left the church then disappeared into the darkness.

Thornbauer, Wolgameyer – December 5, 1958

Warmer temperatures initiated an early melt the next morning. Walking up the steps of the South Wayne County courthouse, Ned Thornbauer noticed the letters chiseled in granite above the two-panel glass front doors. *Justice for All* was most fitting for what he was about to do.

Entering the courthouse, Ned was greeted by an elderly janitor who was trying to keep up with the slush and snow being tracked in from the mess on Hill Street. The man said hello to Ned and then replied to his request for directions by pointing down the hall to the district prosecutor's office. *This is the right thing to do*, Ned thought as he read the black lettering painted on the top glass of each door. Having passed *Probate Judge* and *Register of Deeds*, he read the name *Thomas Patrick Wolgameyer, Chief Prosecutor* on the next door. Although confident, Ned was a little nervous as he opened the door to face the toughest-looking receptionist he had ever seen.

"Good morning," Ned said. "I'd like to see Mr. Wolgameyer."

"You and the other dozen a day reporters."

"I didn't say I was a reporter." She brushed Ned off.

"Name's Mrs. Horner. He's not in. What's this for?" she quickly asked. Her wide neck and broad shoulders gave her an authoritative look, matched by her snappy, quick, short questions and answers.

"I'd like to report a crime," Ned replied.

"What kind?"

"Child abuse. Sexual child abuse."

"What's your name?"

"Ned. Ned Thornbauer."

"Is this regarding a family member?"

"Yes, Ma'am."

"Have a seat," she said with a glare in her eye.

Ned immediately followed her directive and took a chair against the back wall. After about five minutes, Mrs. Horner showed Ned into the prosecutor's office. Tall, thin, and bald with a complementary beaklike nose, Mr. Wolgameyer stood behind his desk, peering over the top of his spectacles. His tie was perfectly matched to his impeccable gray wide-lapelled pinstripe suit.

"Sit down," he said to Ned. "Tell me why you're here. Be brief and to the point."

Boy, this is a friendly place, Ned thought. "I was sexually abused by Bishop Powers in 1949. He raped me seven times. I didn't tell anyone for nine years. I was scared and didn't want to hurt my grandmother. However, I found out this summer that Bishop Powers was doing the same thing to my brother. How's that for brevity?"

"That's brief and to the point." He sat down and leaned back. "You mean to tell me you expect me to believe that Bishop Powers, our respected bishop, the leader of the diocese who says Mass at the cathedral, raped you?" the prosecutor said, bowing his head even more as he peered over his glasses at Ned.

"Absolutely," Ned responded. "I have no reason to lie."

"So are you telling me one brother is verifying for the other brother? How much money you boys looking for?" Mr. Wolgameyer asked. "That's what you're after."

"Money? Never even thought of it. We want him to stop before he hurts someone else. We want him exposed, brought to justice for what he did to us."

"You telling me the truth, Mr. Thornbauer? Pretty big accusation. You say this is true?"

"I'd swear on a Bible in court."

Wolgameyer gave Ned a stern look. "You better be tellin' the truth, son. Mrs. Horner, fill out a criminal complaint with this young Mr. Ned Thornbauer. We'll take a look at it under the proper procedures," the prosecutor stated, continuing his dry delivery.

After completing his ten minute tell-all to the prosecutor and completing the complaint, Ned stepped out into the chill and dampness of the cool gray December day. He put on his brown wool gloves and clapped his hands together, trying to beat off the cold. Now Ned was even more determined to take things into his own hands. *Legal authorities. Bull shit!*

The office of *The South Wayne Journal* was only three blocks away. Ned briskly walked through the slush and damp air as a sign to himself that he was committed to his pursuit of justice. Ahead, he could see the four-story brick building. Ned was confident that the paper would be interested in what he had to tell them. *The Journal* was the premier morning newspaper for the entire tri-county area. They had readers as far south as Indianapolis.

Ned walked up the five steps of melting slush and walked through the front door. A second set of doors led to the main reception area.

"Good morning, sir. Welcome to *The South Wayne Journal*. Mary Beth Robeck is my name, and yours?" she asked featuring a most pleasant smile.

"Ned, Ned Thornbauer," he replied. "Miss Robeck, ma'am, I'd like to talk with a crime reporter."

"A crime reporter? You committed a crime?" she asked, unabashed, and half chuckled.

"No, no, ma'am."

"Just kidding," she said.

Ned smiled while maintaining his serious look. "Ma'am, you're the first contact. I can go to another newspaper if you are not interested," Ned said with a stern look, baiting her for an answer.

"How many papers are you going to talk to?" she asked inquisitively.

"That's confidential, ma'am. I keep my sources nameless. Can I please see a reporter?" Ned asked, becoming a little more impatient.

Her curiosity aroused, she replied, "Have a seat. I'll be right back." Her blue flowered velvet dress hung just below her knees and swayed from side to side as she walked into the newsroom.

Within two minutes, Miss Robeck returned to her desk. "Mr. Gary D'Amato, our assistant editor, will be with you. He's just finishing a meeting with a gentleman from out of town. He said he would see you." She immediately sat down at her desk and pointed her nose at her type-writer. Miss Robeck began to peck away, periodically glimpsing up at Ned.

Inside his office, Gary D'Amato and his visitor, George Griffin, were meeting and talking over old times. More social than business. Both had studied journalism at Indiana State back in the

'20s. Although George was a teacher, he was a part-time reporter for the *Wabash Plain Dealer*. Over the years, he and Gary had made a point to get together at least once a year. George was always interested in the larger stories that took place in South Wayne. Gary did concede that Wabash had its share of mystery, murders, and an occasional robbery every ten years or so. Most of George Griffin's reporting was about car wrecks, deaths, and domestic violence when it became public.

Gary was intrigued by the case of child abuse in Wabash that had surfaced in 1947. In addition, he had heard rumors about the strange death of a young boy back in 1934. George had learned of the abuse from parents of a boy in the reform school who was allegedly abused by an administrator. His investigation had led to a suggested accusation by the same parents of one of the prominent businessmen in town. Within two days of Griffin's first report, the parents had suddenly reversed their accusations, telling Griffin off the record that their son had stretched the truth and they had overreacted. In their retraction, they had been adamant about the misunderstanding and denied any mention of the businessman in the first story.

As they sat in D'Amato's office, Gary said, "George, I asked you to visit for a specific reason. Remember that abuse case back in '47 in Wabash?"

"Don't forget those. And?" George was a man of few words, but they were always well thought out. His demeanor was reserved, his emotions kept under seal.

"Remember back in '53 when we spoke off the record about Bishop Powers? There were rumors and innuendos about possible child abuse. I mean, by the bishop himself. We were also pretty certain that some priests within the diocese, especially over the last several years, were a … well, let's say mysteriously being transferred."

George Griffin nodded. D'Amato knew he understood every word.

"Then everything was suddenly dropped. Nobody would step forward and verify the accusations or comment about the transfers. Bishop Powers is very connected in this town. I also know from a reliable source that he has strong connections in Rome. So where's this going?" D'Amato asked himself the question for Griffin. "I've been told, confidentially and off the record—can't release my source—that Bishop Powers has been covering up for Father Jaeger, the assistant in your town. Transferred him several times. My source said he or she knows for sure that Jaeger has been accused of molesting young boys in the last four parishes he has served. Now you know where I'm going," Gary informed Griffin.

"Yeah, St. Thomas Moore. I have friends there," George Griffin responded.

"Bingo! I read about Jaeger in Wednesday's paper in Wabash. Glad it was your article there, Clark Kent. This guy, this priest from Wabash, gets shot."

"Hard to believe," George commented.

"Shot in the confessional? Are you kidding me? What a story, and part of the factual reporting was where he was shot. You know, right here." D'Amato gestured, pointing his finger under his desk. "Holy shit, George, this story could be a bell ringer. And the shooter was in his eighties, dying. George, my friend, there's probably as much as a book hidden under the cover of this kind of story. This one could have legs."

"Yeah, working on it. Right, Gary. Lots more than meets the eye." Griffin responded in his slow, sullen way.

"Okay, we're on the same track. Here's the deal." D'Amato leaned forward. "There's a connection between Wabash and South Wayne. We know the bishop, and you know the priest. My gut is usually right."

"You always were good at tying knots together, Gary, or I'd call it a keen sense for the obvious."

"Thanks, Clark. You're always so encouraging."

"My turn," George said in his low raspy whisper. "When you called, I came immediately. I can't link Jaeger. I mean it's all hush-hush in Wabash." His words were slow and deliberate. "Nobody—parents, parishioners, the pastor—nobody's stepping forward at St. Thomas Moore. I wanna know why. Now you tell me today about the bishop."

"Yes, George, that's why I called you. Now you make it clear. It's gotta be the bishop. He's covering up, or should I say shutting up, the parish. Then you ask, who's he directing? It has to be the pastor. What's his name?"

"Father Warren. You figured it out again, Gary. I've known Father Warren for fifteen years. Absolutely the finest priest I've ever met and a wonderful man," George Griffin confirmed.

"Finest? Wonderful? George, then why hasn't he addressed this Jaeger character? Why, George? Why, I ask you."

George leaned back in his chair and rubbed his forehead. Shaking his head, he said, "It's like this, Gary." He then leaned forward. "Maybe the good priest is handling it, or maybe he's not. Now with this possible connection with Bishop Powers, what you say about the bishop, I'm going to find out. Maybe it is a cover. Maybe Father Warren is hiding something, but then it can't be. Father Warren is just too good of man. That's it, Gary." George Griffin put his hands on his knees. "You got somebody waiting for you out there. Stay in touch."

George slowly stood and walked to the door but stopped, turned, and looked at Gary with his piercing gray eyes. Pointing his finger, he said, "I'll be back to you. I have a few things to check out. You've made my day."

Within minutes, Ned heard the newsman walk out of his office in conversation with his out-of-town visitor. Not noticing Ned sitting against the wall, D'Amato said, "That's not to say there couldn't be a connection. Let's stay in touch, George."

Ned kept his head in that morning's *Journal*.

"Thank you, ma'am, for the coffee," George Griffin said as he left the office, paying no attention to the man leaning against the wall behind the paper. "You too have helped make my day."

"Is that the gentleman who wants to see me?" D'Amato asked, looking at the paper hiding a face.

"Mr. Thornbauer, please come in. Mr. D'Amato is ready to see you."

Ned folded the paper and walked to the desk, where Miss Robeck introduced him to Gary D'Amato. Ned was immediately impressed with the editor's office, which displayed an eclectic array of a newspaperman's interests. Ned especially enjoyed seeing the large John Deere tractor calendar and array of metal models of tractors, including Case, Farmall, and Massey Ferguson.

"See you're a baseball fan," Ned said as he perused black-and-white photos of Ernie Banks, Willie Mays, and Duke Snyder.

"Sure am. As you can tell, I'm partial to the National League," D'Amato said. "However, golf is my favorite pastime. Ben Hogan, Sam Snead, Byron Nelson—now those guys are the real athletes," D'Amato said with a slight smirk on his face.

Ned was concerned that D'Amato might not listen to his story.

"So what's this about a crime? I'm all ears there, young man."

Sitting in a straight chair in front of D'Amato's desk, Ned was about to begin when he was interrupted.

"You just relax, take your time, and tell me what this is all about. I just need to hear the truth," Gary instructed him. "Go ahead. Sorry for the interruption."

"It all started when I was thirteen. I was a server for the bishop in South Wayne. This would have been back in '49." Ned went on to tell how at first the bishop had made some groping and touching advances toward him.

"Hold it right there. Are you telling me this is about Bishop Powers? He's involved? What kind of groping?" the newspaperman asked.

"Sexual, my genitals. What else?" Ned said.

D'Amato just listened as he took notice and began to write in his spiral notebook. The reporter's heart began to race as he could not believe the possibility of the coincidence being presented. *Did I just talk with George about this?* His mind momentarily distracted from Ned's words. Ned just kept talking. He explained in detail the first trip to the bishop's cabin, the swim in the nude, the trip to his bedroom, the porch, and the hours in bed. Ned even made sure he directed the reporter's attention to the bishop's red birthmark.

"Didn't you tell your parents?" D'Amato asked still not believing what he just heard.

"No, there's just my grandma, Ida Thornbauer. Mom left a few years after Danny was born. She couldn't handle life with Dad. I kept Bishop Powers inside, not telling anyone, for nine years until it got to be too much. I was plagued every day for all these agonizing years. Still am."

"What makes you come here then if you were keeping it all inside?" D'Amato asked now wishing George Griffin was still here in the room to hear Ned's story.

"I found out this summer that Bishop Powers was doing the same thing to my brother, who is now eleven. He started taking Danny to the same cabin. Grandma was all for Danny going with the bishop. She works at the library but only two days a week. Loves books. We don't have much. To her, the bishop was a respected, important person in our church and community. She wanted Danny to be around better, more important people, so she encouraged him to go with the bishop. She had no idea anything could be wrong. Everyone trusts priests, she'd always say. Ever since I can remember, my grandma would go out of her way for a priest. To her, they truly were holy men."

D'Amato sat up in his chair, still taking notes. Ned could tell he had the editor's attention.

"Who all knows of this?" D'Amato asked for information to see if this could possibly be an exclusive story.

"All those in the meeting."

"What meeting?" the reporter asked.

"On Wednesday, I met with Cardinal Cullings; Father Girouard, the cardinal's assistant; Father Sullivan, the assistant pastor at St. Thomas Moore in Wabash; and Father Holtz from the bishop's office. Bishop Powers was also in the meeting, along with his secretary, Father Schmidt, but they left abruptly before I came into the room. I'm sure he did not want to hear me tell the truth about his abuse of Danny and me."

D'Amato loosened his bowtie, giving relief to his neck as his temperature rose at the same level as the possibilities of the scope of this story. "When did you first tell anyone?"

"Oh, a several months ago, early summer, I believe," Ned said to the reporter.

"Wait one minute there, Ned. Why did you wait nine years?"

"That's easy to explain. I have a younger brother, Danny. As I said, Mom left after Danny was about two. Very hard on the family. That's when Grandma moved in."

"What about your grandfather?"

Ned paused for a minute. He bowed his head. "The truth is we never knew him. Grandma never married. Lived alone all her life. So you see, this all would break her heart. She's the one who really raised us. Dad was always travelin'. He has a drinking problem. Grandma does her best to keep us on the up-and-up."

"Back to why you came out with this now." D'Amato could tell something heavy was on Ned's mind.

"I had noticed this summer that Danny—you know, my younger brother—wasn't quite himself. Quiet, forlorn, he just kept to himself. Then one day I asked if anything was bothering him. That's when he just gushed open. I was shocked and then infuriated when Danny told me that the bishop was doing the same thing with him as he had done to me nine years prior. Danny had already made three trips to the cabin," Ned explained in anger. "I informed another priest, but I can't use his name. Eventually I was asked to the meeting with Cardinal Cullings. There, I told everything."

"You mean you've told all this to Cardinal Cullings?" D'Amato asked.

"Yes, everything," Ned replied.

D'Amato walked over to the window, thought a moment, and then said, "Okay, Ned, you've given me enough. You stand by your story? If not, you are liable, and I'm in trouble."

"That's right. Everything happened exactly as I told you. Nothing to hide anymore."

"Let me take it from here. You gave me enough to begin asking questions. For now, you and I have not talked. Wait to hear from me, Ned. Keep this confidential between you and me."

"By the way, I must tell you that I've already been to the district prosecutor. He's looking into the situation," Ned informed D'Amato.

"Looks like I'm the last to know," D'Amato said. Ned didn't respond. "*Hmmm.* When did you see the prosecutor?"

"This morning," Ned replied.

"I'm sure he'll be looking into this if you are accusing the bishop. This is a very serious accusation. You better be telling the truth, or you are going to be up to your eyeballs in hot water from all sides."

"I accept the seriousness of the accusation." Ned stood, turned, and walked to the door. "I assure you, Mr. D'Amato, I'm telling the truth."

CHAPTER 111

BIZARRE CRIME

George Griffin—December 6, 1958

GEORGE Griffin walked into the *Plain Dealer* to catch up on the latest news about domestic violence, traffic reports, and the obituaries. Saturday morning, the newsroom, containing three metal desks, typewriters, and a bulletin board, was quiet. He made a phone call to verify a lead on a story he was pursuing. Every so often a story of real interest would hit the streets of Wabash. Griffin noticed a story pinned to the board. *Businessman Loses Hand in Violent Attack. Randall Zilbar brutalized in his own yard. Culprit on the loose.*

George Griffin immediately approached Jerry Durnbaugh, who had written the feature story.

"Don't know a thing, George. Not a clue. No weapon, no witnesses. The hand is even gone," he said, sharing the scoop with his fellow reporter.

"Gruesome! Can you imagine Randall Zilbar, a real big shot, with no hand?" George looked at Jerry. "His golf and tennis days sure will be over."

"Nice shot, George. Crime scene, right in his front yard, is all clean. Zilbar won't talk with anyone. He's still in the hospital."

"Nowhere to go." George Griffin turned and left the newsroom.

Driving straight uptown, Griffin pulled to the curb and parked his car. He walked into the Rock City Bar and Grill and took a stool at the bar. Gilbert, the bartender, asked, "Same?"

"Yep, straight up. Make it a double. Two cubes."

"What's up with you, Griffin?"

"Just heard about Zilbar. Hand hacked off."

"Yes, happened Thursday." Gilbert knew all happenings around Wabash. "Nighttime in his own yard. I heard nobody's talking. Well, nobody except—" Gilbert was cut off by a customer.

"Hey, Gil! Two more Falstaffs down here."

"No, make mine a Wiedemann's," the guy's buddy shot back.

"Right back, George. Got something for you." Gilbert served the two beers and then returned to George a few moments later. "There was a guy in here earlier. Never seen him before. Says he heard some guy talking about the hack on Zilbar. They were in Dye's Tavern. You know they got some strange customers out there. Not decent ones like you, George."

"Me decent? Any more exaggerations from you, Gil, and I'll take my business to Dyes. I'll check it out tonight."

The temperature outside dropped to freezing. Griffin hung around the Rock City and had another with no cubes. Around 5:35 p.m., he threw two bucks on the counter. "Next time." He buttoned his coat, turned, and left.

Slushy snow was turning heavier now that it was below freezing. George Griffin made his way in his car to the far side of town. The neon lights of Dye's Tavern were his only beacon. The wiper blades gained little traction against the heavy wet flakes.

The ring of the bells above the door of Dye's were drowned by the sound of cue balls smacking the break across worn green felt. Flying chalk dust from the tips of the cues was dampened by circling smoke from a selection of Luckies, Old Golds, and Chesterfields. Three old-timers hung low at the front end of the bar. The eldest, in a red flannel shirt, bent over his gin and tonic. A lone patron sat at the end of the bar with his head down. His green uniform blended into the aged cracked walls. Dye's was known for regular customers. Some more than others.

George pulled up a stool in the middle and pushed aside an ashtray still smoldering from a dying butt.

"What you say there, George? Been a while." Reg slammed an empty scotch glass in front of George Griffin.

"Johnny Walker Black. One rock. Just one tonight."

Reg went about his business, restocking the beer chest and tending to his too few customers. George Griffin laid two one-dollar bills next to the glass.

"See you changed your mind, George," Reg said as he reached around and set a bottle of scotch in front of him.

"Anything new this end of town?" George asked, baiting Reg.

"Come on, George. Everyone knows 'bout Zilbar. Lost his hand and all. He deserves it though. Rich prick. Never comes in here, except, well one time. Came in with this lady. You could tell she wasn't his wife. Knew the lady. Gretchen. Waitress around town. Think she's the one murdered last spring." George Griffin looked down. "Yeah, one time. Can't forget a rich prick. I mean a one-handed rich prick. Ha!" Reg wiped the counter and walked to the old guys at the front of the bar.

Griffin thought to himself, the memory of her still filled his soul.

Reg walked back. "Yeah, George, the guy must of used a meat cleaver."

"Yeah, I hear nobody knows who did it," George responded.

Neither Reg nor George noticed the startled look from the loner at the end of the bar when he heard *meat cleaver*. Reg looked to the front of the bar where the trio of elders were lost in their gin. The loner at the end just looked straight ahead but listened to every word Reg and George were saying.

Reg put his elbows on the bar, leaned forward, and said, "Okay, Griffin, here's the scoop. There was a guy in here earlier today before noon from over in Huntington. Out of nowhere. Never seen the feller before. Had a few beers, actually a few too many. Told me that"—Reg lowered his voice—"some guy out at the reform school knows. Then after he had another beer, he said, 'Had something to do with that boy murdered back in '34.' Don't get the connection. That boy in '34? What was he talkin' about, George? Soon the guy was three sheets to the wind, so I had to cut him off. His beer, not his hand. Get it, George? Ha! Just a slip of the tongue."

"Yeah, Reg. You're a real Milton Berle."

"He threw down a buck and left. All there was. Said no more. Here, I'll pour your second. Just don't get it. Stranger from Huntington, murder in '34, now Zilbar, the reform school. I'm no Sherlock Holmes. Means nothing to me, George."

George shook his head. "Reg, did you get his name?"

"Son of a bitch! Should have asked."

"Nice going, Dick Tracy."

From the other side of the bar came a call. "Hey, Reg, 'nother gin!"

Reg reached up for the half-filled bottle. "This is the last one, you guys. You had your limit. This stuff can be mean." As Reg put the lid back on the bottle, he said, "Bingo! Yes, that's it. Romer." Reg turned to George. "When the guy walked in, I can recall Larry. See the guy there in the middle of the three musketeers? I remember him greeting that guy from Huntington, 'Hey, Romer. Been a long time.' Easy to remember. Romer begins with an R, just like my name. Yeah, guy's from Huntington. Romer. That's it."

"Clever association. You're a genius there, Reg."

"Thanks, George. Inherited it from my Ma. Pa was a drunk."

George poured another scotch. Without him saying anything, Reg dropped in a new cube.

George Griffin hunkered over his Johnny Walker for another hour that evening. *Huntington, meat cleaver, well-known victim, reform school— they don't tie together!* And then it wasn't his story anyway. George knew Jerry Durnbaugh was a good reporter, and George didn't want to cross the line with Jerry. The relaxing warmth of Johnny Walker settled in. George's mind drifted. *Swimming in the Wabash River with Sandy.* He thought of *Gretchen. Oh, the days. Gretchen.* George relaxed as Johnny did all the thinking. Reg looked over at George Griffin. Reaching up on the back bar shelf, Reg pulled down another Johnny Walker and set it in front of Griffin. The loner at the end of the bar turned to the clang of the discarded bottle below the bar.

"One more, Reg."

The war, mustard gas, trenches, cold, wet, wire with thorns. Griffin's mind paused as Reg added two cubes. *The old guilt, darkness, Gretchen. If only. If ... was not to be.* George had a capacity for knowing his own limits. "Cup of coffee before I leave, Reg."

Elbows on the bar, chin on his folded hands, George heard the scrape of the bar stool to his right but paid no attention to the loner at the end. Reg set the thick gray mug on the bar.

George took a sip. "Goddamn, Reg. Coffee's black as hell and just as bitter."

"You need it to camouflage the Johnny Walker. Otherwise, I'd have to drive you home, George."

"That's the last thing I'd want, in a car alone with you."

"You mean black coffee?"

"No, you driving me home. Wouldn't trust you, ol' pervert." George half laughed at himself.

George took a second sip of coffee. "This is like mud, Reg," George sensed someone moving to his right. He saw the loner stand while taking one last swig from his longneck beer and then slam the bottle on the bar. He tugged his hat low over his eyes. The longer walked over and stopped behind George Griffin's stool.

"Ya wondering who did it? Check over at the butcher shop on Wabash. City Market. Used the meat cleaver. Ask Ollie, the owner, 'bout the gypsy who lives upstairs. Maybe he did it."

George put his hand on the back of the stool and slowly twisted right to catch a glimpse of the strange whisper from behind. Turning back around to his left, he saw only the back of the loner heading for the front door. "Reg, get 'em!" Griffin said with a half slur.

"You mean another scotch?"

"No, meathead. *Him*. That guy leavin'. Stop him."

"Oh, you mean stop Bednar?" Reg dashed to the door and opened it. A flash of wet snow blew in. Halfway down the walk, he shouted, "Bednar! Stop! Wait there!"

With indifferent nonchalance, Bernard Bednar stopped as directed but did not turn around. He knew. Bednar stood at the curb in the wet falling snow.

Griffin managed his coat and pulled on his hat. "Thanks, Reg. Next time," he said as he walked outside, only to see the back of Bernard Bednar standing and waiting.

Griffin walked over and looked down at the stout man standing still, his hands pushed deep into his coat pockets. Bernard's eyes were hidden under the brim of his hat, now accumulating heavy flakes of snow.

"Can you help me?" Griffin asked.

"What kind of help?"

"Who was the hacker?" George asked in blunt terms.

"Find the meat cleaver. All 'bout little Gordon Yoder. *Uumpgh*."

"Who's Yoder?"

"Little boy in cemetery. Rich man killed him in 1934."

George responded, "How you know?"

"I was there."

"You were there in '34?"

"That's what I said. Do you know … *uumpgh* … rich man naked all over little Gordon Yoder."

"Naked?" George flinched. "You say naked?"

"Yeah, no clothes. Big and hard. Then he suffocated little Gordon. *Uumpgh.*"

"You know for sure?"

"Yeah, Gordon got justice. Find the hand. Check the finger. You'll find little Gordon's killer. Gordon bit chunk from his finger."

Griffin couldn't believe what he was hearing.

"That's all. Cold. No more. Find the hand. The finger will tell you. *Uumpgh.*"

As the snow turned to heavy wet rain, a puddle gathered around the loner's work shoes. Griffin looked down. No socks.

The loner repeated, "That's all. Find the hand. Check for Gordon's bite." Pulling his hat even lower, Bernard Bednar walked away from Griffin. The rain grew heavier. Through the sounds of the beating rain, George heard the muffled words: "Find the hand." *Find the hand*, he thought, as he watched the loner walk around the corner and disappear in the darkness.

CHAPTER 112

THE LAST DARK NIGHT

Ned Thornbauer—December 6, 1958

FATHER Schmidt was walking down the hall of the rectory. The phone rang. He picked up after two rings and sat at the small table, just off the foyer. "Hello. St. Leonard's rectory. Father Schmidt speaking."

"Good evening, Father. This is Jake Summers, a friend of Father Holtz," Ned said, muffling his voice with a handkerchief over the phone. "May I speak with him about the Christmas pageant?"

"Sure. Let me get him for you," Father Schmidt set the phone on the table, stood, and called for Father Holtz. As he walked down the hall, he saw him. "Ben, there's a call for you."

"Thanks, Father. I've got it! I'll take it in my room!" Father Holtz yelled down the hall to Father Schmidt so he could hang up the line. Father Holtz double-timed it up the stairs to his room and then yelled back down, "I've got it, Father!"

Father Schmidt went back to the table to hang up the phone. Leaving the phone at rest atop the maple table, he leaned his ear close to the arm of the chair, just three inches from the phone. Through the line, he could hear Father Holtz's conversation.

"My plan is to protest in front of the cathedral on Sunday," Father Schmidt heard Ned say.

"Protest how? Protest what?" Father Holtz asked.

"I'm making signs and will display them in front of the church. I'll be carrying one, of course, and so will Danny. We both agree."

"What will they say?"

"The truth … Bishop Powers sexually abused me in 1949."

"Are you sure you want to do that, Ned? You might be stirring things up too soon. Bishop Powers is liked and respected. Many or most may be hostile to you."

"It's not a problem. Just telling the truth. I'm going to bring justice for me and my brother. This is a start. I also called Gary D'Amato at *The Journal*. If people hear about my protest … hundreds will want to know."

"You know, Ned, you better have perfect timing 'cause he has tickets to fly from Chicago to Rome on Tuesday. Remember, you're not going to be accepted as a hero in front of the bishop's cathedral. Few will believe you."

"I know, Father Holtz, but truth is on my side."

"I sure give you credit, Ned. You are committed. Be careful."

"Father, I promise you, nothing will stop me. No matter how long it takes, I'll never stop my quest to bring justice for Danny and Grandma Ida. She has been hurt deeply."

"I know, Ned. I believe you."

"Bye, Father. Please say some prayers."

Ring, ring. "Hello, this is the *South Wayne Journal*."

"Yes, may I speak to Mr. D'Amato?"

"Just a minute. I'll check. I think he's in."

Ned felt anxious waiting for the reporter.

"D'Amato here," the reporter said as if he was talking with someone in the next county.

"Mr. D'Amato, this is Ned Thornbauer. Remember me? Bishop Powers abused me."

"How could I forget that story, Ned? If true, that's a front pager." D'Amato listened to Ned's news. He was not prepared to hear that Ned was going to protest. "What is your plan?"

"My plan is to go to the rectory tomorrow afternoon at 4:00 p.m. when I'm sure Bishop Powers will be there. I'll carry a sign about his abuse of me in 1949. I hope to have someone from the newspaper there to take my statement. It will be a small protest. That is when I will expose him publically."

"We promise to be there, but I can assure you that you won't be looked upon favorably by the parishioners, many of the Catholic and city leaders, and most of the people in this downtown. You are accusing their bishop of a heinous crime. That's what it is."

"I assure you there is going to be an ongoing story. So you might as well start in the beginning with me," Ned told the reporter.

"You can count on me to be there for a while. Low-key. Shouldn't be many people."

"Up to you. See you then," Ned said.

Ida Thornbauer—December 5, 1958

Charlie Schroeder drove his gray 1947 Pontiac up to the curb of Ida Thornbauer's home. After tooting his horn, he got out and walked up the shoveled walk to the steps of her porch. Charlie was a nice man. Single with no family, he worked as a janitor at Robertson's Department Store. With a round face and average height, Charlie always had a smile for everyone he met. He spent his evenings and Saturdays helping friends with odd jobs, for which he never accepted pay. He was never short of cookies, Cokes, homemade meals, and presents at Christmastime, which usually included an array of new plaid flannel shirts.

"Good morning, Miss Ida."

"Same to you, Charlie."

He held out his hand and helped her down the shoveled steps.

"Snow sure is crunchy this morning," Ida said.

"Yes. Twenty-eight degrees out. Real chilly today. At least there's no wind," Charlie said as if he was giving a full weather report.

"I packed a lunch for us in case it takes a while." She handed Charlie her brown suitcase, which was locked at the top. The two brown bands wrapped around the suitcase gave away its 1920s style.

The roads were still packed with patches of snow. "Charlie, you sure are a good driver," Ida said as she comfortably sat in the back right seat, knitting a sweater for Danny. "I can relax and enjoy the ride with you. My grandson, Danny, is spending a few days with his brother, Ned Thornbauer."

"You just tend to your knittin', Miss Ida. Ol' Charlie will have you there in no time," he said. He heard her chuckle from the backseat. "I'm the best driver in the county."

"You're a cheerful and thoughtful guy, Charlie. I love how you take interest in everything you do. You're so nice and helpful to everybody."

"That's the way my daddy taught me, Miss Ida. Chip off his old block."

After twenty minutes, "Charlie, you better keep your mind on the road. I'll tend to the knittin'," Ida said hoping to just enjoy the ride and tend to her knitting.

Time lapsed. "That's the way. Hold on, Miss Ida!" Charlie yelled as if they had never stopped talking. Ida leaned into the right side with the sharp turn as Charlie turned east toward Wabash. "Have you there in twenty minutes. Any chance you've got one more of those ham salad sandwiches … and maybe a pickle?"

"Charlie, you've had two."

"But they're good, Miss Ida. How about just a half one?"

"Okay. I'll give you Helen's. That's fair, you being so nice to let me ride with you."

Charlie was proud of his 1947 four-door Pontiac Chief. He loved to follow the chief—the best hood ornament on any car in the country. The mighty Chief purred along the road as if she was brand new. Ida hummed the rest of the way to Wabash. She always got a nostalgic feeling every time she rode into town. Ahead, she could see the courthouse high on the hill, Abraham Lincoln proudly standing in front. Her heart always warmed when she saw the twin spires of St. Thomas Moore, her beloved parish. What memories. *What could have been*, she thought.

"Miss Ida, I'm pretty low on gasoline. Is there any chance I could stop here at this Sinclair Station to fill up?"

"Of course, Charlie. We've made real good time."

Having the tank filled, Charlie pulled back onto Wabash Street and drove through town in the direction of the Wabash Bridge. After crossing the bridge, he turned right on Columbus, up the hill to Orchard.

"There it is, Charlie. Turn there on Orchard. Third house on the right."

Charlie drove up to Aunt Helen's small white clapboard house. Snow was sparse. The air was dry. Ida saw her sister waiting in the front window. Helen, with a shawl wrapped around her shoulders, hurried down the steps to her beloved sister Ida.

"Go on in," Charlie said. "I'll bring your bag."

Ida and Helen wrapped their arms around each other.

"Oh, so good to see you, Helen," Ida said as she gave her sister an extra squeeze. With her hands on her sister's shoulders, Ida pushed Helen back, looked her in the eye, and said, "Just look at you, little sister. It's so good to see you. Been what? Almost ten months?"

"Yes, it has. Back in February. Uncle Oscar's funeral."

Arms around each other, Helen and Ida walked up the porch stairs together.

"Better reunion I've never seen," Charlie said, holding his brimmed hat with both hands.

"Have some time for coffee, Charlie?" Helen asked.

"Thanks, ma'am, but Arthur's waiting. Another time. You two just catch up, and I'll be back Sunday. How's two o'clock sound, Ida? That gives everyone time for Mass and lunch."

"That would be fine, Charlie. We can get home before dark." She reached in her pocket and handed Charlie a dollar. "My share for gas."

He pushed it away.

"Now, Charlie, I insist."

"Okay, okay, but this will more than cover our ride home Sunday. Thank you, ladies. Have a great weekend together. Don't stay up too late, though. Bye."

"Bye, Charlie. Thanks again!" Ida waved as Charlie stepped down the walk toward the Chief.

Chief Pontiac, what a car, Charlie thought proudly.

Ida heard the mantel clock strike three times. "Three o'clock. I'm going to stoke the fireplace, and we'll have time to visit and catch up before I take you out this evening," Helen said.

Ida looked at Helen. "We're going out this evening?"

"Yes. Remember Dorothy Tate? We were all such good friends. As fate would have it, there's a potluck dinner down at church. Dorothy's going to pick us up, and we're all going together. She's still good for driving at night. She is such a hoot, smart remarks and all, that Dorothy. You know she's always got her little girl-boy jokes."

"Ah now, Helen, remember we're all good Catholic girls." Ida pursed her lips. "But sounds real good to me, Helen. I don't get out too much. Would love to go down to the old church. Might see someone else we know."

Helen stoked the fireplace well. The room was filled with warmth and the smell of hickory crackling in the fireplace.

"Yes, Helen. This will be good time to catch up. Lots to talk about, I know."

Father Schmidt—December 6, 1958

A few days had passed since the traumatic meeting in Indianapolis. Bishop Powers was a little more content, especially considering his upcoming trip to Rome.

"Hello, Bishop," Father Schmidt said as he saw the bishop walking down the first floor hall. "Have a few minutes? Think you better know something."

"Sure. Let's go into my study. It's more private in here. You never quite know where Sister is lurking," Bishop Powers said as he sat in his favorite overstuffed chair.

"You wanted me to keep you up-to-date," Father Schmidt said. "Well, this is unexpected. I have word that Ned Thornbauer is going to carry a sign in front of church on Sunday. A sign that reads, *I was sexually abused by Bishop Powers.*'"

"What? A sign? Abuse? In front of my cathedral? No way! Call the police and have him taken away!" Bishop Powers said harshly.

"I already did that, Your Excellency. He has a permit. We can't stop him. Free speech."

"Then make sure that doesn't happen. That's all I need before I leave for Rome," he said. "It was that damned Thornbauer in church the other evening," he then muttered to himself. The bishop turned red. "To hell with him anyway! I should have taken care of him that night."

A puzzled look swept across Father Schmidt's face. "The other night? What do you mean, sir?" *Never heard such language from the bishop before.*

"Oh, nothing. Damn it! Just talking to myself. I'll have that … that … I'll have him busted if he does. I know people at city hall," Bishop Powers threatened. "He won't get away with this, that little bastard!" Before Father Schmidt could respond, Bishop Powers stood up, headed back down the hall, and said in a disgusted voice, "Do you have my tickets? Did you pick them up?"

"Yes, sir. They're on your desk."

"What time's the flight?"

"It's at 4:45, Tuesday. Indianapolis to New York to London and then on to Rome. You'll soon be away from all of this."

"Good. Not a word. Remember, or else. Understand? I'm not available."

"Yes, sir. Not a word," Father Schmidt said. "But there is one other thing, Bishop Powers. I hesitate to ask you at this time, but Father Holtz insisted. He wants to see you."

"See me? Didn't he go to Terre Haute after our meeting with Cardinal Cullings?"

"Don't know. Was supposed to, sir, but he's here and wants to see you. Remember, you said you would see him when he got back."

"I know, I know, but that was Wednesday. I'm busy today."

"Sir, he insists."

"Okay, okay then. Find him and send him up here."

"Thank you, Bishop."

Bishop Powers turned and disappeared up the stairs. Father Schmidt only heard the bishop's bedroom door slam.

Behind the closed door, Bishop Powers went over to his desk, picked up the tickets, checked the times, and then flipped them on the bed. Walking over to his closet, he pulled out three leather suitcases and set them on the sofa in the small sitting area by the fireplace. He pulled the chains on the floor-mounted lamps at both ends of the sofa. *Hate overhead lights.* He confidently stared at the suitcases, knowing their contents. He dressed for the evening in casual clothes and a robe. *Three days. Time to start planning. Tuesday, 4:45, peace. Thursday, safe.*

About fifteen minutes later, Bishop Powers heard a knock at his door. *Holtz, I imagine.* "Hold on. Be there in a minute." Bishop Powers reluctantly walked to the door. "Who is it?"

From the other side of the door, he heard, "It's Father Holtz, Your Excellency. I just need a minute."

Bishop Powers opened the door. "Yes?"

Not being invited in, Father Holtz said, "Sir, you mentioned you wanted to see me when I returned."

"Well, I guess I did, but I'm busy now. I'm busy."

"Sir, it's not what you think. I hesitate to ask, but it is very important to me."

"Yes, yes, what is it?"

"Well, sir, I would like for you to please hear my confession."

"Hear your confession! Now? I thought you always go to confession at St. Justin's at the other side of town."

"I do, sir, but I feel a special need now, and I do not want to wait."

"Okay, okay. I … I cannot deny you. This is a very inopportune time. How about tomorrow afternoon?"

"Whatever is best for you, sir."

"Three o'clock tomorrow afternoon. I'll be in church in the confessional. As I said, this is a very inopportune time."

"I appreciate it very much, sir. I have a lot on my mind, and I must say that though I am a priest, I am not without sin. Thank you."

Bishop Powers closed the door. Father Holtz closed his eyes. *Thank you. Thank you, Dear Lord.* He turned and walked away.

Gary D'Amato—December 5, 1958

Good reporter that he was, Gary D'Amato decided to make a few calls to cover as many bases as he could. Picking up the telephone, he dialed Lance Christian over at CBS.

"Lance, Gary here. Gotta little scoop for you. Seems our good Bishop Powers might have dipped his toe in the wrong pond this time. Remember that situation he had about twelve years ago with a … let me see … What was that kid's name?"

"Ah, give me a minute … Richards, Orville Richards. Bishop went off and got in all kinds of problems. As I remember, not much happened. Everything kinda blew over. Someone from city hall helped the bishop on that one."

"Well, this one might have legs. I can smell it. This could be big. As I said before, Bishop Powers may have done it this time. Know what I mean? I'll give you the location. Front of the rectory at St. Leonard's, four o'clock, Sunday. Tomorrow. That's all I'm givin' you. On your own. Bye, Lance."

Damn that snoop. Just gives me droppings to serve his own good. Sunday, 4:00 p.m., cathedral, Lance said to himself. *Bet he was dipping more than his big toe. Dirty ol' guy.*

D'Amato hung up the phone and then immediately picked it again to make another call.

"I'd like to place a long-distance call, operator."

"Yes, sir. Where to?"

"Mr. George Griffin, 563-5333, in Wabash, Indiana."

D'Amato patiently waited for the operator to place the call.

"Yes, I have George Griffin."

"Hello, George here," George said in his deep, slow monotone voice.

"George? Gary D'Amato up here at *The Journal* in South Wayne."

"Oh yeah, Gary. Good to meet with you the other day."

"George, I didn't make this call. Between you and me, forget we even talked. Totally off the record. Just a tip from me to you. Let's say I owe you one from years back."

"What's up?" George asked.

"Remember our conversation? May be a connection between the bishop, South Wayne, and Wabash. Think I was right. The bishop's in town. Think he's going to have a visitor Sunday around four o'clock outside the cathedral. That's all I know. If we were right, you might want to be here."

"Yeah, maybe. Maybe I would," Griffin responded.

"Now, there's a little three-story hotel—the Wolford—to the side street across from the rectory. It's in the middle of the block. From there, you can see the entire side of the rectory and the front corner to the sidewalk. Closest you can get to the cathedral itself. As you told me, you don't want to be seen or involved. You said you just want to know for yourself."

"Yeah, that's the way I want it. Just want to put a few pieces together from over the past thirty years. Actually, Gary, I'm going to come on my own time, not as a reporter."

"Works for me. Gotta go. Remember, George, we never talked. Don't know your intentions. Don't want to either. You're on your own. See ya."
Click.

George Griffin had never met the Thornbauer kid, but he'd had a few run-ins with Ned's dysfunctional small-time failure of a dad when he was working in Wabash. Some connection between South Wayne and Wabash. George never did piece it together.

Griffin sat back in his chair. Reaching around to the side table, he poured another scotch. Both arms resting on the oversized chair arms, scotch hanging from his right hand, he thought, *Yes, maybe there's a connection.*

Ida Thornbauer—December 6, 1958

Mid-afternoon on Saturday, after an excellent time at the social the previous evening and a morning of visiting with Helen, Ida decided to take the chance. She had been planning this all along. Her intention weighed heavily on her mind. The afternoon was cold and crisp.

"Helen, I'm going to take a walk," Ida said. "Just want to spend some time looking around the neighborhood."

"That's good, Ida. I've got a few things I want to do around here. Making your favorite meal this evening. Remember?"

"Oh yes, chicken casserole and potatoes. Don't forget the onions."

"When you're back, the smell will fill the house. I'll have a fire in the fireplace for you. Enjoy your time."

The weather was perfect for a brisk walk. A few remaining oak leaves still hung on the trees. Few traces of snow still clung to the low stone cliffs along the road to the bridge. At the foot of the hill Ida could see the steel trellis of the old Carroll Street Bridge. Not sharing her predetermined destination with Helen, Ida headed straight downtown, across the old bridge. Ida concluded that this was the right thing to do. Keeping her hands warm in the pockets of her long plain wool coat, she moved her fingers from bead to bead on the rosary deep inside her right front pocket. Spry for her age of seventy-one, Ida enjoyed the pace. She walked by the elegant old Indiana Hotel, where guests were arriving. Saturday afternoon a few weeks before Christmas, Wabash was abuzz.

Having walked up the hill past the courthouse, Ida turned right toward St. Thomas Moore. It was 4:30 p.m., beginning to get dark. Sentiments and memories rushed through her mind as Ida ascended the steps of the twin-spired church. She felt nervous in her anticipation. Her black wide-heeled shoes settled into each worn footprint in the granite steps.

Once inside the church, Ida felt melancholy by the mystic memories of a time long past. She could still see herself in her white lace confirmation dress and veil, with her family and friends, the men in black worn wool suits and the ladies in shoe-length dresses and black hats. The church was cool then, even in early May. Heads were all bowed reverently for the Virgin Mary and Her Son and Savior. Confirmation day 1899, almost sixty years ago, and Ida felt like it was yesterday. She could feel the hand of her sponsor on her right shoulder—her Aunt Margaret. Ida thought about those pleasant memories as she escaped into the past.

Blinking, Ida noted the short lines for confession. As planned, she looked to the confessional on the right. The center door light was on. Ida genuflected, blessed herself with holy water, and slowly walked with her hands folded, rosary entwined beneath her fingers, eyes focused on the name on the center door. Two more steps: *Father Warren.* Walking past the center confessional door, Ida stepped into line. As she tightened her black-and-brown wool scarf, she didn't notice the frayed edges.

"Hail Mary full of grace, the Lord is with thee," she whispered. Pulling both sides of her black knee-length coat around her, Ida protected herself from a slight damp draft within the church. Her black purse hung from her left forearm. She felt vulnerable and sought the protection of the enclosed confessional. Confession, Ida prayed, would exonerate her past.

The confessional door opened. A bright, smiling young lady holding an infant stepped out and held the door for Ida.

"Thank you, miss."

Kneeling down, Ida felt the familiar pad on the kneeler. The black sliding door was the same. Ida thought about what she was about to do, unlocking a secret of half a century. A secret she had never once disclosed. A secret lodged in her mind, forever kept in the darkness of her own private thoughts. *Little did I know that my prayers would come to this moment.*

Ida was slightly startled as she heard the confessional door slide open. Her heart raced. She whispered, "Bless me, Father, for I have sinned. My last confession was two weeks ago. My last confession in this church was forty-nine years ago."

Hidden on the other side of the screen, Father Warren took the acknowledgement in stride. He heard confessions of most of the elderly.

"Father, I'm an elderly lady. I'm getting old. Seventy-two now. At this time in my life, my sins are few, small, and infrequent."

"That's very normal," Father Warren said. "We learn in life that there is a time for all seasons. As we enjoy our later years, we learn daily the importance of life, and what truly matters. We can, however, still harbor on the past," he said, feeling an unexpected inspiration. "Our past sins, if we have repented and have been forgiven, are no longer a part of the present. They are fleeting, hopefully forgiven, and just forgotten memories."

"Oh, Father, thank you. That's the way I feel. Your words are so welcoming, so wise and comforting." Ida felt a closeness to the man whispering on the other side of the dark curtain. "However, Father, I have one sin in my life for which I have never asked forgiveness. I've never told a living soul. For so many years, I have prayed and now I," Ida paused. "Father, I conclude, I have decided for sure, I must confess someday. Someday, Father, is now." Ida paused and then went on, "I feel a moral obligation to disclose, to be mindful of another person who deserves as much and has a right to know. It's not for me. It's not for the one I sinned with. Father, I must do this to help bring justice to my children," Ida said and then paused.

"I understand, my spiritual friend. Please go on. Repent as you feel you must," Father Warren said, blind and unknowing of the person on the other side of the curtain.

"Father, this happened fifty years ago this past summer. Fifty years. So much has taken place since. Father ... " Pulling together, reaching into her soul for the courage, she said, "I was with a man. A man I desperately loved. However, we both knew a life together was not meant to be. Unselfishly, we both knew it couldn't be. I believe our love was mutual, but we could never be one." Ida stopped for a moment. She thought again of what she was about to disclose. "We, my dear, dear friend and I, spent a night together. Was it planned? I'll never know. Deep in my heart, as I look back ... " Ida paused again. "Father, what I am about to say is most difficult." Ida pulled a handkerchief from her purse. "Oh, excuse me, Father. We both knew the man I loved was going to be leaving. We both knew he loved another more than me. It had to be that way. I accepted it, as did he."

Father Warren said, giving her some relief, "It sounds like your love was true, but you each knew and accepted that it couldn't be. I understand." He spoke slowly, barely above a whisper, his word filled with compassion. "However, sometimes in life, love can't be separated even though two people are apart. That separation, however, sometimes can't extinguish emotions, feelings, and passion for true love."

"Father, you're so correct." Ida felt tears welling in her eyes.

"So what is your sin?" Father Warren asked.

Ida Thornbauer paused and felt as if her mouth was sealed tight. *After fifty years, can I?* She felt almost unable to say the words. There was a long pause.

"Take your time. I am still listening," Father Warren said in the kindest way. "I am here to assist you in acknowledging your love, free yourself from this secret you say, this secret of fifty years."

He understands. Taking a breath and arousing her courage, Ida said, "My love and my sin of omission is for, oh Thomas, my dear Thomas, my love, a lifetime of love is still for you. Father Warren, please forgive me. I am so sorry. This is Ida … Ida Thornbauer." Her hands were shaking so much that Father Warren could hear the jingle of her rosary.

"Ida, Ida? This is you? I never. No, I never thought about sin. I can remember. No, not sin." He paused as he groped for words.

"Father, that's not all. Oh, Father, it was love. God told me it was okay because our love … " Ida was trying to muffle her sobs.

"Go on, Ida. It's okay. Say what you must. I'm here. I may not know what to say to you, but please go ahead. Say it all. We are in the privacy and confidentiality of the confessional."

Ida placed her handkerchief to her nose. "Oh, Thomas, I loved you so. I still carry that love just as—oh, Father, forgive me—I carry that love just as I carried our son, Thomas." Ida did not know what to expect. She couldn't see Father Warren as he fell back against the chair, hand to his brow. "Thomas, are you okay?"

"Yes, Ida. Yes, I am. I just never knew. No idea. That's why. That's why you stayed away? That's why we never spoke again?"

"Yes, that was when Thomas was born. I had to move. I couldn't tell you. I couldn't keep you from becoming a priest. You had years until ordination. I couldn't be in the way. I accept the blame. All of it, but I knew then, deep in my heart, that your first love was to become a priest."

The seventy-two-year-old priest tried to gather his thoughts. The calm, wise man, always in control, was there for others. Father Warren was at a temporary loss for what to say to a woman he loved, but left behind. So unexpected were the words from this lady that his mind was immediately engulfed with guilt of his own. *How strong Ida was to hold this secret for fifty years. How unselfish of her.* Father Warren could feel the silence on the other side of the black curtain. Images of the back porch, the staircase, the coverlet, the feel of her skin, then her lips, the touch to her breasts all shot in the speed of light as if it was yesterday. For a fleeting moment, Father Warren thought not about the confessional. Forgiveness. Ida. All he could see was together that night fifty years ago, then the darkness. Gathering himself, "Ida, was there anyone in line after you when you came into the confessional?"

"No, Father. I saw no one."

Father Warren leaned forward and opened his confessional door a couple inches. Nobody was in line. He turned off his light as he reached around and pulled his name card from the door.

"Excuse me, Ida. Go ahead."

"Father, I'm so sorry to tell you now. Believe me, I didn't want to. However, there is reason. Good reason."

"Ida, I must ask, how do you know of the paternity, that I'm the father?"

"Thomas, it is very simple. I had never before been with a man. You were the first, Father. I loved you so much." Ida paused. "Then after that weekend, knowing we would never be together again, I just knew. I kept the feeling of being with you. I didn't want to lose that. Then within a couple months, I discovered I was ... " Ida paused. "I knew I was ... knew I was going to have a baby. I could not tell you. I could not destroy your dreams, your family's dreams of you becoming a priest. I know, Thomas, that I made the right decision. The only connection I maintained were the memories of being with you and his name, Thomas. I was not with another. The right one to marry never happened. Nobody could live up to you. I was never with another man. Only one man, one time in all my years. If this was a sin, Father, then it was a sin with a man I loved deeply. My love was not with a priest."

Father Thomas Warren was most touched, more than any other time in his life. He felt love, real sincere love for this lady, this good, unselfish person ... the mother of his child. "Ida, I have to ask why. Why now after all these decades of our lives? Why do you come forth now? And, dear

Ida, please understand, I am most grateful to know, to know your secret. Ida, you are not alone, the secret we now share together."

"Oh yes, of course. Father, I planned on carrying this secret to my grave, but something happened, something awful. I needed help. I decided I had to tell you," Ida said with some hesitation. "When Thomas was born, I moved away within the first year. My older brother, Stanley, lived in South Wayne. He helped me find a small second-floor flat. I was able to get a good job as a receptionist in a law firm—Wolgamot, Kirk, and Meyer. Worked there for forty-five years. They were good to me. Thomas had a difficult life. He did marry, but Elizabeth left after their second son, Danny, was born. Thomas was always away, traveling. Never there much for the boys. I really raised them by myself."

"Ida, I must ask about … " Father Warren could hardly say the words. "What about Thomas?" He paused and then asked, "What about our son?"

"That's so kind of you to ask, Father. I obviously named him after you. That's what makes it even more difficult. You see, Thomas always had a troubled life. I did my very best. He was in and out of trouble. Small scrapes with the law. Two years in jail. Two failed marriages and then … and then the alcohol. He tried to be a good father for Ned and Danny, but he was never there. He traveled. He was a salesman, hardware supplies. A salesman on the road, but he drifted from one job to another. Thomas, he was never you. Then … then … " Ida simply could not form the words. Trying to hold back the tears, she somehow said, "They found him."

Father Warren thought, *troubled life. Sure, he had no parents. No father in his life. I wasn't there for him. All my fault.*

Trying to hold back the sobs, she said, "The police found him in a broken-down motel by himself, alone, with a gun still in his hand. He's been gone since 1952. I hadn't seen him for years. My son, Thomas … our son … alone. He died alone." Ida paused and wiped her eyes.

Father Warren's mind swelled with grief.

Ida continued, "The boys, however, are the exact opposite of their father. They are good boys. Both did well in school. They never caused one problem for me."

"You said there are two boys? I have two grandsons?"

"Yes, Father, both good boys. Ned, the oldest, is twenty-two. Danny is eleven. Father, I must tell you now, I have to get this out. The only reason I'm here … This is hard to say. I need your help."

"What is it, Ida? You can tell me."

"Father Warren, both boys have been … Thomas, Thomas, please help me. This is so hard to understand. So hard to say … sexually abused. Taken advantage of."

"Oh, Ida, sexually abused? This cannot be. Our grandsons? Do you know who?" Father Warren asked. "Who could do this?"

"Father, I'm a good Catholic. I actually don't have sins to confess. I would not lie. A priest abused them … many times. I do not know the details about things like that, but I believe my boys. They wouldn't lie to me."

Knowing she had to say the name, with trepidation, Ida said, "It's Bishop Powers."

The shock struck Father Warren. He could feel his blood rush. "No, Ida. No. I don't want to hear that name. Are you sure?"

"Yes. He took advantage of both my boys. He's so powerful, and he just used them. My only choice was to come to you."

"I understand, Ida. You have every right," Father Warren said. "You did the right thing, Ida. But Bishop Powers? Our very own bishop?"

"I'm so sorry, Thomas. I just had to tell you. I hope you are okay, Father. I thought all my life I'd never have to tell you. These past fifty years, I would have kept this secret forever … forever for your good."

Father Warren gathered his composure. "I can always handle the truth. Now I know. It's up to me."

"Father, I have one more favor. Fifty years is too long to wait to see one another. It is my decision that we are bound by our words in this confessional. I must stay this way. Separate in the future as in the past. The black veil must forever be between us in the confessional, and also in our lives. I do not want you to tell our secret to anyone. Can we vow to take this to our graves, never to tell a living soul? I had to tell you because maybe you could do something so this bishop is brought to justice. I felt an obligation to tell you. I simply need for you to be aware. Now, Thomas, this is most difficult. The secret that I told you is for you and me only. What you do for Ned and Danny is up to you."

"Of course, Ida. Our secret … and … our secret as it should be but I will be the judge of Bishop Powers." He leaned forward very closely to the black curtain. Ida could feel his breath. "Ida, I will address Bishop Powers. Justice will be served."

"Oh, Thomas, I knew you'd be there. Now there is one more thing. Please, please, my dear, dear friend, we cannot see each other. Ever!"

There was a moment of silence. "You did the right thing, Ida. I will honor your wish," the good priest told her. "For whatever it is worth, Ida, I did have love for you during those years, but I chose the priesthood. I still do think about you. This moment in our lives we are together. If it's meant to be, then never again will we meet. We will never share what we once had. Memories, Ida. Memories I will cherish more than ever."

"Those are welcomed words from you, Thomas. I will cherish them always." Ida thought for a moment. "I will continue to have my love for you every day of my life." There was silence. Ida was still holding her tears, along with a lifetime of feelings inside. Ida took a breath, pulled her scarf tight under her chin, and said, "I must go now. Please do not leave the confessional until I'm long gone. Please, Thomas. For me. For us. This is the way it must be." She paused. "I love you, Thomas. Good-bye. I'll … I'll never forget you."

Ida took one last look at the black curtain, hoping she could get just a glimpse of the good priest. Making the sign of the cross, she stood, pressed her fingers to her lips then touched the black curtain with her hand, not expecting to feel his hand from the other side. But, for several moments, their hands met together, separated only by the black cloth.

Ida stood frozen in time. The feel of his hand would be a memory that would last forever. Slowly, she stood, opened the confessional door, and left. Walking to the center aisle, Ida blessed herself, bowed her head, and genuflected. With one last glance toward the confessional door, which was still closed, Ida solemnly closed her eyes for just a moment, tucked her hand inside her black coat, turned, and left the church forever.

Father Warren sat alone in the dark confines of the confessional. The most unexpected moment of his life had begun to take hold. He sat alone with just one thought. He felt as if his heart would break. He remained there, for how long he never did know. He prayed as Ida left the church, and disappeared into the darkness.

Father Warren—December 6, 1958

Father Thomas Warren walked back to the rectory that late Saturday afternoon. He remembered back fifty years to the summer of 1908. He recalled the week at home with his folks and his brother, Jack, and the time he spent with Ida. Not once in the past five decades had he even thought about the physical consequences of their time alone. He thought of Ida from time to time, so fleeting until today. He knew Sister Agatha would have supper ready at 5:30. He thought he might pass and go back to his room until he saw Father Sullivan walking toward the dining room.

"Oh hello, Father. Good evening," Father Sullivan said as he saw Father Warren walking in his direction. "Dinner together? It's Saturday night."

"Sure, why not, Michael. That would be nice," Father Warren responded, trying to lighten the burden of his thoughts of the previous hour in addition to the nagging pain in his stomach. Walking into the comfortable dining room, both priests immediately felt the warmth and comfort of the fire Sister Agatha had prepared. The front tapestry drapes were drawn closed. The side window curtains were still open, allowing the light of the moon to offer an extra glow of warmth.

"Little red wine this evening, Father?" Father Sullivan asked, sensing Father Warren could use a relaxing moment. "Did you hear the choir practicing for Christmas Mass?"

"Oh yes, I did, Michael. So solemn. So beautiful. Seems every year they get better. I cherish the time alone in church, just listening to our choir."

"Yes, I agree, Father. Just like this bottle of 1952 merlot. Better with age," Father Sullivan said, tipping his glass to Father Warren.

"Yes, Michael, better with age. Wish I could say that about myself," the elder priest took a sip.

"If anybody gets better with age, it's you, Father. Wiser, experienced, more knowing … on and on," Father Sullivan assured his friend, as he sensed the mood within the room. Excuse me, Father, but is something bothering you? Something on your mind?" Father Sullivan asked. "I know you, Father. I can tell."

"You are astute, my son. You know me well. Yes, there is something on my mind. Something I learned. Sad, but beautiful. I will need time to reflect. Something is so new to me. New in this solemn stage of my life." Father Warren sat back in his chair. "But this is good. I need to be with you now, Michael. I will reflect another time. I have the rest of my life to do so. Meanwhile, I have a new issue to address. A most important and serious Issue."

"Can I do anything to help?" Father Sullivan asked.

"No, Michael, this only I can address. It will be done."

"Well, I hope your new issue is going to the doctor."

"Michael, I did. Must have forgotten to tell you. Had a check-up before Thanksgiving."

"Everything fine? Okay?" Father Sullivan asked his friend.

Father Warren hesitated. "Everything fine you ask?" Pressing his lips, "Michael, let's say everything will work out by next week's end."

For several moments, the two priests sat in silence, only broken by the crackling fire. Father Sullivan sipped his merlot…and waited.

"Michael. I just want to enjoy these later days of my priesthood. I thought they would be longer, but these years have the same challenges and rewards as those years since ordination."

"Father, you have many good years ahead of you."

"Well, Michael, kind of you to say, but I would not say that be the case."

"What's that supposed to mean?"

"Oh nothing. I…" Father Warren scooted himself up in his chair. Father Sullivan noticed a grimace across the elder priest's face.

Father Sullivan continued. "I'm feeling the same in my middle years." Father Warren did not comment. "I want to tell you that I received a call from Father Holtz a few hours ago, just before confessions."

"What's that, Michael?" Father Warren asked trying to hide his mood.

"Let's just say he overheard something. You know, he's rather close with Father Schmidt, more on a parish basis than a close friendship."

"Yes, I know what you mean, Michael."

"Anyway, he said that Bishop Powers is resigning his position as head of the diocese effective immediately. Father Holtz heard just this morning. He informed the cardinal by special letter. He would have received it today. Now listen to this," Father Sullivan said, leaning over his plate. He continued in a low whisper, "He has received a position in Rome. He is leaving Tuesday. That fast. Tuesday."

Father Warren was shocked. "Why so quickly? Well, that speaks volumes for all we learned from the meeting this week. That's only three days," Father Warren said, an expression of concerned surprise crossing his face. *The immediacy. Ida, my grandsons.*

"Father Holtz told me that one of the boys who is accusing the bishop of abuse is picketing tomorrow in front of the cathedral. Guess he's carrying a sign, *I was abused by Bishop Powers.*"

"Did Father Holtz say who the accuser was?" Father Warren asked.

"Yes, he did. His name is Ned Thornbauer. I don't think I told you about him. He's the one the bishop abused for a couple summers about nine years ago. Now the bishop is doing the same to his younger brother."

Hearing Ned's name jolted Father Warren. He felt reality tremble within his body. He asked, "How could he do this to two brothers? How close in age?"

"Let's see, Ned is twenty-two. Danny must be about eleven," Father Sullivan replied. "Father, your face Is red. Did I say something wrong? Did this shake you?"

"Nothing shakes me anymore, Michael. Just two brothers?" Father Warren asked, trying to disguise his knowledge. "Just the two? *Hmmm!* Do the parents know?"

"As Father Holtz told me, their mother left them just after the younger brother was born. The father, I think, may have also died. Don't know for sure."

"What's his name?" Father Warren immediately asked, just wanting to hear the name.

"I think, but I'm not sure, it is Thomas. Yes, Thomas Thornbauer."

Father Warren felt a piercing sensation in his heart. Trying to look unaffected, he sat back in his chair. "Well, who cares for the boys? Who raised them?" he asked, already knowing the answer. His mind was so unsettled. He was trying to find words to hide his emotions.

"Father Holtz said the grandmother does. Says she is a very nice, caring lady. Gave her life to the boys. Strange thing though."

"What's that?" Father Warren asked Michael.

"She had only one child. She never married. No husband and now no grandfather. Just strange."

Father Warren didn't respond. He sat expressionless.

"I met both the boys. They spoke to us at the meeting with Cardinal Cullings on Wednesday. Very nice, both of them. Ned, of course, I think is ten or eleven years older than Danny. Ned is very protective of his brother. Seem like just good kids. The older one, Ned—well, he's not a kid—seems very confident, strong, and driven to expose the bishop. If he's going to carry a sign Sunday, he better be strong. The parishioners won't take kindly to accusations about their Bishop Powers."

Father Thomas Warren could not believe what he had just learned what he was hearing. Everything whirled. It all seemed so surreal. *Am I dreaming? Is this happening?* "You know, you're right, Michael. Sounds like Ned and Danny are good boys. I'd assume reflective of their grandmother, who raised them. She must be quite a strong and good woman," Father Warren said and then paused while rubbing his cheek and chin. "But what about the son? What'd you say his name was? Thomas? Strange, very strange."

"Just so you know, Father, I'm going to drive up to meet Father Holtz after Mass tomorrow," Father Sullivan told the elder priest. "Father Holtz mentioned that the newspaper and maybe a television station might be there around four o'clock. I'm interested to see what the bishop does under those circumstances."

"I've known the bishop a long time. I didn't say much to you, but he and I go back to our seminary days. I was ordained two years ahead of him. Those days are a whole 'nother story."

"Say then, you want to ride along with me? We could leave after the 11:30 Mass tomorrow."

"Thanks, Michael. I'll pass on this one. I have another matter to attend to. Besides, I must tell you I am not feeling my best. I'm sure you'll handle everything just fine."

"What is it, that cough again? Father, I've noticed lately, it sounds worse. You haven't been quite yourself lately. I'm worried about you."

"You go on, Michael. Tell all about what happens when you return. How about tomorrow?"

"Will do, Father. Just as you ask, but it's Saturday. Please get some well-needed rest."

"I'm sure you'll handle everything just fine."

Father Warren and Father Sullivan sat together for a time, finished their dinner. Few more words were spoken. They were both in their own thoughts. Time passed. Father Sullivan stood, "Father, thank you. This was the right time for our discussion. You and me."

"Thank you, Michael, yes it was. The right time." Father Sullivan turned and walked to the hall. "Michael?" He stopped and turned around.

"Yes, Father?"

"Michael, I might like to meet this Ned. Ned and Danny. I'm sure they are fine boys, knowing what you said about their grandmother. Ida was her name, you said?"

"No, Father. I don't know her first name. You said Ida?"

Father Warren paused. "No, I don't think I said her name. No. How would I know?"

"Sure, Father. Maybe you were thinking of another grandmother."

"That's it, Michael. You know I am the oldest in here."

"Good night, Father."

"Good night, Michael." He paused, "Remember, I'd like to meet those boys someday.

Father Sullivan turned and walked back to his room. *I'm sure he said Ida. How would he know her name?*

Father Sullivan—December 6, 1958

The fire crackled in the fireplace. A third glass of merlot sounded like a good way to escape the tense moments of the week. Sitting in a chair by the fireplace in the front parlor, Father Sullivan felt a sense of melancholy. Merlot in hand, book on his lap, he stared into the fire. The wine was talking to him. The half-empty bottle rested to the side of his novel on the small table next to the chair.

He kept thinking of the bravery of Ned Thornbauer in speaking out against the abusive Bishop Powers. He reflected on the young man's courage, passion, and commitment. Ned was seeking justice for his brother, himself, and all of the unknown victims who had fallen prey to the gluttony and perverseness of sick and evil men who also happened to be men of the cloth. His mind traveled to thoughts about Linda, Father Warren's comment about his few years ahead. He thought of Gene, Peter, and Joey.

Surrendering to the impending slumber from the wine, Father Sullivan looked at his watch and thought he would have one more glass. Reaching over, he gently poured the red wine into his stemmed goblet. After taking a sip, he leaned his head back on the doily atop the firm upholstered chair. Then another sip ... and Father Sullivan thought of her. *How can I ever forget?*

The flames of the fire were subsiding, along with Father Sullivan's mood. The embers flickered in deep shades of glowing red, orange, and yellow. Random crackles broke the surrounding silence. Father Sullivan's relaxed feelings brought on the sensation of evolving melancholy and loneliness. He liked who he was, but then he thought of who he could have been. Who he would have been with her.

As the evening waned and the wine continued to talk, Father Sullivan watched the dying embers and drifted to a place his mind would often wander. Suddenly he was startled by the ring of the telephone. Assuming it was a parishioner calling about her dying mother or a concerned parent whose son was just in a car wreck, Father Sullivan was surprised when he picked up the phone and heard the voice of Father Holtz.

"Good, Michael, you answered," Father Holtz said in an alarmed voice.

"Hello, Ben, what's up at this hour? Just lonely? Need me to talk to?" Father Sullivan said, gathering his senses.

"Well, I'm always up at this time of the evening," Father Holtz cracked right back. "Seriously, Michael, I told you that Ned's going to be in front of the cathedral tomorrow. I think there could be some trouble. Meaning some parishioners aren't going to like this. Some have pull and friends downtown. They might call and the cops will show up. Also, I just learned that Bishop Powers decided not to say any Masses tomorrow. Father Schmidt and I are going to cover all five."

"That speaks a lot for the bishop. Hiding. Covering up," Father Sullivan said. "I plan on driving up tomorrow afternoon. I want to be there when Ned makes his statement. I want to be there for him. I would defend him and I would speak out for him. However, out of respect for Father Warren, I am concerned. I don't think he approves of Ned being so open, so in the face, accusing Bishop Powers. If Ned goes through with this, he's going to draw attention. Just one reporter and it will explode."

"I know, I know, Michael. Listen, the main reason I called. I need your advice. You hear? I gotta talk to someone."

"Is there a problem besides all this, Ben?"

Father Holtz did not respond immediately. Then he said, "Michael, I have a decision. A big decision that I have to make. Could you meet me tomorrow? I really would like to talk with you."

"Let's see. I have the 7:00 and 10:15 Masses tomorrow. I could leave by eleven thirty. Let's say about two o'clock, and I'll do my best for one thirty. What's it all about?" Father Sullivan asked.

"I can't talk over the phone. Trust me. When you arrive, call me from the edge of town. There's a pay phone next to the Shell station. I'll be in the rectory. There's a little diner a couple blocks down the street. We'll meet there."

"Count on me. I'll call at one o'clock. Might have to stop at our favorite truck stop for chicken though," Father Sullivan said to Father Holtz, laughing at himself.

"Good-night, Michael."

The embers had faded to a low warm glow. *Just one more glass. All will be better.*

George Griffin—December 7, 1958

George Griffin thought long and hard after receiving the tip about Ned Thornbauer's protest. On Sunday, he rose at his usual 6:30 wake-up time. A brisk walk, a cup of coffee, and the *Indianapolis Star* were his constant morning companions. Having made his reservation at the Wolford Hotel in South Wayne, George thought he would leave around 11:00 a.m.

He wondered if Gary D'Amato was leading him on a wild chase. Although he had a hunch about the connection between Father Jaeger in Wabash and Bishop Powers in South Wayne, George Griffin concluded the trip would be worth his while. He usually trusted his intuition.

George sat in his chair, reading the paper. Within fifteen minutes, he stood up and meandered to the kitchen for his second cup of coffee. He noticed the bottle of Balvenie scotch sitting on the counter, just waiting for company. *Not now, old friend.* He still had an hour and half before leaving for the city up north. George Griffin was glad it was a clear day, despite the temperature being in the low twenties. He looked forward to his trip into the unknown.

CHAPTER 113

ON TO SOUTH WAYNE

Bishop Powers—December 7, 1958

SATURDAY night had been a sleepless night for Bishop Powers. The bottle of Beefeaters advised him that a quick departure to Rome would relieve him of this self-inflicted situation. For the past day, Father Schmidt had been his only connection to the outside world. A temporary wall of protection was needed until he departed for Rome.

Father Schmidt's quarters were two doors down the hall from Bishop Powers' room. Bishop Powers, Father Schmidt, and Father Holtz were the only ones who lived in the rectory. Having opted out of saying Sunday Mass, Bishop Powers got out of bed and reached for his black silk robe. Tying the tasseled belt, he cautiously opened the door. He walked toward Father Schmidt's room, bracing himself against the wall with his right hand. He knocked twice.

"Yes?" he heard from behind the locked door.

"Open up. It's me," he ordered Father Schmidt.

The door immediately opened three inches. "Morning, sir. I'm getting ready for my 6:30 Mass."

"That's good. All Masses covered?"

"Yes, sir. Father Dirsch from St. Paul's will cover the 8:30. Father Holtz and I have the rest."

"Don't forget the special second collection for the roof repair fund. After the ushers make the count, bring it all to my room. Just anxious to see how well we did. I'll prepare the deposit for you. I can still manage that job before I leave. You understand?" Bishop Powers instructed. "Last thing. Before your 6:30 Mass, have Sister make a pot of coffee and any-thing for breakfast. Tell her to set it outside my door. Remember, tell her it's the flu. I need rest today." As he braced himself with his hand on the door frame overhead, Bishop Powers looked directly at Father Schmidt. "I need not remind you. Everything is confidential. Confidential forever. You wouldn't want me to raise your direct ties with that boy in your room. Remember that night?"

"Yes, Bishop, I understand everything. Forever."

Bishop Powers turned and made his way back to the safety and comfort of his own room. After walking directly to the windows, he opened the blinds, letting in the thin shred of light escaping from the gray clouds. As he noticed the empty gin bottle, a sudden feeling of recurring nausea jolted his system. Throwing the bottle into the wastebasket, his immedi-ate thought was the comfort of black coffee and toast. *God, glad no Mass today!* Not ready to dress for the day, he lay back in the protection and comfort of his oversized ornamentally carved bed. Waiting for the first sound of the arrival of coffee, Bishop Powers looked directly at the white ceiling and calculated his mission over the next few days.

The fifteen-minute relief was gladly interrupted by two soft knocks at the door. He knew the sister would set the tray on the floor, turn, and leave. She knew the bishop's ways. For a few moments he gathered energy, and then with all his collective strength he pushed himself up and sat at the side of the bed. Gathering equilibrium, he put his feet into his black leather slippers. His right hand grabbed for the post at the foot of the bed. Steadily, he left in pursuit of the equalizer just beyond the door in the hallway.

After setting the tray on the table between the chairs in front of the neglected fireplace, Bishop Powers poured his first cup. *Relief at least.* After two cups of black coffee, along with an equal number of pieces of crisp, dark toast, his mind was on track to some semblance of clarity. He walked toward his desk. Passing the dark mahogany dresser, abound with photos of his clerical history, he stopped and looked in the horizon-tal mirror. His look was disheveled. Salt-and-pepper stubble highlighted his jowly face. His uncombed thinning white hair crisscrossed in uncon-trolled directions. The puffiness below his eyes motivated him to think, *Everything will soon be better. A forgotten, dark memory.*

Sitting down, he picked up the phone. "Operator, will you please connect me with Bassett? Meryl and Sue Bassett." Head in hand but feeling better, he waited. A first smile crossed his face as he stared at the envelope containing his plane tickets to Rome on Tuesday.

"Okay, sir, go ahead," the operator said in her shrill voice.

"Hello, Sue? This is Bishop Powers."

Startled, Sue said in surprise, "Your Excellency, what brings this ... this call? Can I help you?"

"Yes, Sue. I've received a call and have been summoned to Rome for a conference. Can't say what it's about. Father Schmidt bought my tickets, you know."

"Yes, I noticed they were just one-way," Sue said, wondering why.

Her comment caught the bishop off guard. Flustered, he said, "Just one-way will be fine, as I don't know the exact date I'll return."

"Okay, I understand. You can telegraph to me, and I can book your return flight."

"Oh, yes, that will be fine. Thank you, Sue," he said agreeably, knowing he would not need the return ticket. "Anyway, Father Schmidt is saying Mass, so I called to ask you to confirm my flight for Tuesday."

"Oh, sure. First thing this morning, sir. I'll call back with your confirmation."

"Do your best. And, Sue, this is very confidential."

"Oh, of course, Bishop Powers. Not a word."

"Thank you, Sue. Knew I could depend on you. Call my personal number anytime today or tomorrow. Have to have it, and don't forget, make sure it is confirmed for first class."

"Do you need transportation to Indianapolis?"

"Not necessary, Sue," he replied. "Father Schmidt will be driving me. I'll wait to hear from you."

Knowing that his plans were all set, Bishop Powers decided it was time to pull a few more things together. The next few days would be fleeting.

Ida Thornbauer—December 7, 1958

Standing by the door, peering from behind the curtain, Helen watched as Charlie drove up to the curb. "Your chauffeur is here, big sister," Helen kidded. She looked over at Ida, who was fixing her bun with a wooden comb and pins.

"Yes, my chauffeur, Charlie. Oh, I hate to go. What a wonderful time we've had, sister. Stayin' up and talking things out with you was so good for me," Ida said appreciatively

"It was just like ol' times and all our wonderful visits. Our weekend was topped this morning with Mass and breakfast after. I'm so glad Father Warren said Mass," Helen said. "He's such a good, caring pastor."

"I'm sure he is," Ida responded, thinking back to yesterday's confession. She felt her emotions stir.

Helen saw the perplexed look. "What's wrong, Ida?"

"Oh, nothing. Just don't want to leave." Slipping on her long wool coat, Ida adjusted her hat and picked up her purse. "I can hear Charlie honking. Have to go now. You take care, dear sister. I love you so much, Helen," Ida said as she kissed Helen's forehead. Ida wrapped her coat tightly around herself and pulled the belt snug.

Helen opened the door. There stood Charlie, hat in both hands.

"Good morning, Miss Ida, Miss Helen. Here, let me take your suitcase." Charlie tipped his head. "Ladies." He turned and walked to the car.

Helen reached out and wrapped her arms around Ida. "Bye, dear sister. Hope all works out for you and the boys."

"Thank you, Helen. We'll both keep praying. God will provide the answers."

Helen stood in the open door, pulling her gray sweater together. Folding her arms, she watched as Ida walked to the car. Charlie stood holding the back door open. Ida waved and stepped inside the vehicle.

As Charlie drove away, "Charlie, would you mind driving by St. Thomas Moore? It's up on Hill and Wabash."

"Sure, I'll find it."

"I'd like to see, I'd like to see the church one more time."

Helen noticed her sister's footsteps in the morning's light powdering of snow. She knew her sister's journey with her grandsons had a long way to go.

Father Sullivan—December 7, 1958

Looking up from the Sunday paper as he sat with a cup of coffee at the kitchen table, Father Warren heard some muffled footsteps in the hall.

"Father," he heard Father Sullivan's voice. "Leaving now. Just wanted to say good-bye. I will be back tomorrow afternoon. I have my Mass covered tomorrow. Father Melanowsky will be here."

"Good. He is a good man. I look forward to seeing him. I know I can coax him to stay for one of Sister Agatha's big breakfasts and maybe even a game of chess on a cold Monday morning. Jolly man, that Father Melanowsky. Loves his football. Great Steelers fan." Father Warren gave his last instruction, "Now be careful, Michael. I hope that all works out. I'm sure you and Father Holtz will be stabilizers for those boys." Father Warren looked at Father Sullivan. "None of us can predict the behavior of the bishop. What did you say the young man's name was?"

"Ned Thornbauer. He's a good kid. I think he'll be respectful while getting his message across. He does have the best of intentions for his family, although a couple times he comes off a little aggressive, maybe threatening toward Bishop Powers."

"Maybe, Michael, he has reason to," Father Warren said. "Keep an eye on that young man. Will you? Didn't you say there's a younger brother?"

"Yes, Danny. Of course I will," Father Sullivan said, making a mental note of the concerned look on the elder priest's face when the boys were mentioned. He passed it off as Father Warren's usual concern for anyone under duress.

"Take care, Michael. Drive safely. I'll pray for all of you, especially those boys … and of course for our own bishop. I'm afraid he's going to need lots of prayers."

Maybe Father Warren has a reason for not coming along. That sounded strange from him, Father Sullivan thought to himself.

Father Warren walked with Father Sullivan to the door. Placing his hand on the younger priest's shoulder, he bid him a farewell. *How on God's Earth could I have ever known?*

Father Sullivan was anxious during his ride north to South Wayne. He could not figure out the mystery behind Father Holtz's requested visit. The snowplows were keeping the highway clear. Approaching the South Wayne city limits, Father Sullivan saw the Shell station just ahead. He stopped and called Father Holtz promptly around 12:15 p.m.

Traffic was light in the city. Mass and church services were over. All businesses were closed on Sundays, as usual. Fortunately, the Blue Plate Diner was open seven days a week. Father Sullivan drove past the huge cathedral and rectory. Turning on the side street, he drove by the Wolford Hotel to Market Street. He could see the diner. Pulling up to the curb close to the front door, he noticed the neon red *open* sign hanging in the window.

As he walked in, Father Sullivan observed just a few tables were occupied. Two elderly men hovered over their coffee at the far end of the counter. Father Sullivan immediately noticed Father Holtz in a corner booth. Father Holtz waved.

"Hello, Ben. It's always good to see you, although I sure don't know what to expect today."

"Oh, I just like clandestine meetings with you in diners and truck stops, Michael," Father Holtz smiled as if he had just cracked a wild joke. "Just kidding. Good to see you, too, Michael. Ma'am, another coffee please. Well, you made good time this morning," Father Holtz said, looking down at his watch while lifting his cup to the waitress behind the counter.

"Yes, took me a couple hours. What time is it? Ten till one? Smells good in here. Ah, a good cigar," Father Sullivan said, as one of the elderly gentlemen at the bar had just lit up his stogie. The diner was quiet.

"Your trip okay? Roads safe?"

"Easy ride. Actually relaxing as long as I didn't think about what lies ahead for us today. I do feel a little stress. Our meeting here, Ned, Danny, and of course the bishop."

Father Holtz looked at his friend. His face was stern. "I can't relax. Getting right to the point and why I asked you to come early today, I have to tell you something. Then I need your advice. You see, I haven't told you everything during these past months. Now I see I should have come forward earlier." Father Holtz looked down into his coffee. He looked concerned.

"What is it, Ben?"

"I feel awful, ashamed, and quite guilty. I should have spoken sooner to be fair to you and everyone involved in this tragic mess."

"Good morning, Fathers. Here's your coffee. Would you like to order? Can I tell you about our Sunday special? We over—"

"Please, ma'am, thank you, but we need some more time. Later. Coffee's fine."

"Fine. I'll be behind the counter. Just give me a holler."

"Michael, when Ned came to me last summer, he wanted to talk. He wanted to come forward because he found out about Danny and what the bishop was now doing to his brother."

"Yes, of course, I remember," Father Sullivan said. "I was deeply affected. Still am."

"Well, last August on a hot Friday afternoon, Father Schmidt had asked me to cover the bishop's Saturday Mass. 'Of course,' I told him. Then he added, 'Guess the bishop's going up to his cabin in Michigan.' Immediately red flags went up. I had my suspicions about the bishop. The next morning, I said the 6:30 Mass, and then I was free for the day. I was not scheduled for confessions that afternoon, as we had a visiting priest for the weekend.

"After Mass, I checked the garage. The bishop hadn't left, so I parked my car on the street about a block and a half from the garage. I walked into the kitchen after Mass. I was drinking coffee when Bishop Powers came downstairs. I heard the back door close, so I went out the front door and watched from around the corner of the rectory as he drove out of the garage. He headed toward Market. I hurried down the street, got into my car, and followed him. Being a Saturday, the streets weren't so busy, but I was able to keep hidden from his view. I'm sure he had other things on his mind."

"Yes, but didn't you think he'd eventually notice you if you followed too close?"

"Fortunately, Michael, he gave the cabin keys to Father Schmidt and me. We spent a Wednesday evening there last June, so I know how to get there. Mostly, I wanted to see if he was taking anyone with him."

"What happened then?" Father Sullivan asked anxiously.

"Sure enough, Bishop Powers pulled up to a little house over on

Oxford Street. I stopped a block away. Didn't turn on Oxford. Within a minute, Danny Thornbauer came bustling down the steps. An elderly lady stood on the porch and waved. I knew it was Danny, as Ned had previously mentioned the street where they lived. I'm sure a few in that neighborhood noticed the big black Imperial and then thought a rich uncle or the like."

"Ben, why didn't you mention this before?"

"There's a reason, Michael. In hindsight, I should have. I was wrong. My omission has torn me apart ever since. I feel so guilty."

Father Sullivan agreed and then said, "Go on. What happened?"

"Danny jumped in the bishop's car, and off they drove. Once I saw they were heading north, I knew they would be going to the cabin, so I didn't bother to follow closely. Actually, I knew of a shortcut and took it, knowing he'd take the main highway route. I knew where the bishop was taking Danny."

"Don't you think Ned knew?"

"No, Ned has his own apartment. Remember, Danny said he was scared to say no to the bishop. His Grandma Ida encouraged him. Nice lady. Ned speaks so lovingly of her. Ida Thornbauer. Anyway, it took me until about three o'clock to drive to the lake. Genesee Lake, I think it's called. I drove north, crossed the Indiana-Michigan state line to Three Rivers. As I said, I took some back roads. Was faster. Wanted to get there before him. I knew I was close. Then a few more miles on 131 to Howardsville. Took an old gravel road a couple miles, and I was there."

"The place was easy to find. Remember, I said I'd been there with Father Schmidt. I just watched for the Burma Shave signs on the farmer's fence. It was the next drive after. No mailbox, no address sign, just a little dirt and pea gravel lane. The cabin was set back, hidden from the road by a heavy growth of underbrush and trees. I continued past the drive, following the bend in the road where it was wide. I pulled to the side of the road and parked my car right by a walking path that led to the lake."

"Good grief, Ben, what if he had seen you?"

"Since I was past his drive, I knew he would never by chance see me. But if he did, I would have had a lot of explaining to do, like 'Bishop … you forgot your fishing pole, so I brought it to you.'"

"Funny guy," Father Sullivan responded.

"No, I just had to be careful. I quickly walked back to his drive and followed the gravel lane into the woods. Glad he doesn't like dogs. Halfway up the drive, I saw the cabin from an angle. I could see the back, the west side, and the corner of that porch. The lake was beyond, down the hill. The day was beautiful. Perfect weather. I noticed there was no Imperial in the drive. I first thought maybe this was a wild goose chase. I carefully looked around for five minutes, and then suddenly I heard the sounds of a car on a gravel road beyond the first bend near the entrance. I dashed deeper into the woods toward the west side. My heart was pounding.

"The sounds of tires on the gravel grew closer. As God is good, I saw some dust through the trees. Then I could hear the purr of an engine. Immediately, I dove behind a fallen elm tree. There, I lay on the ground, parallel with the trunk. From that tree, I was hidden from the drive. I was completely out of sight but had full view of the cabin and half of the front porch. I had one and only one option: wait behind the fallen tree, listen, and watch. My stakeout was almost perfect. I had thought to bring binoculars. Fortunately, mosquitoes don't bother me. I prayed to God, please no snakes. Lying there hugging the ground, I thought, *Now what do I do?*"

"What did you do?" Father Sullivan asked.

"Waited and watched. Actually, I was quite comfortable. There was a padding of some grass on the ground. Hey, I was alone in nature. The location was so comfortable. I almost wished I brought my sleeping bag. Coulda spent the night. Glad I wore dark clothes. Feeling like a secret agent, I kept checking the front of the cabin, as much as I could see, and watched the hill to the lake. Hey, the lake looked inviting. I thought I might ask the bishop if I could go for a swim. Actually, I make fun, but, Michael, I was scared. How could I confront the bishop? What would I do? God, he's my supervisor! Allow me to kid a little. I feel stressed like I'm going to hyper-ventilate just telling you."

Father Sullivan asked, "What did you plan on doing?"

"After they went into the cabin, I didn't hear anything. Within about fifteen minutes, the screen door slammed. I saw them as if they had stepped out onto the porch, gone down the stairs, and started walking down the hill. I darted for the edge of the woods for a better look. From that angle, I could see the bishop and Danny walking together toward the lake, both wearing trunks and carrying towels. The bishop is no picture of well-hewn manhood. While they were going to the lake, I moved quietly along the edge of the woods. Now I was within thirty yards of the cabin. I could see most of the deck and some view of the water.

"The bishop was the first to go in. I was a bit taken aback when he dropped his trunks and jumped feet first into the water. Danny followed, but he left his trunks on. For about ten minutes or so, they frolicked and rousted in the water. I watched as they walked out about thirty yards close to a patch of lily pads. A couple times, the bishop lifted Danny up, and he jumped from the bishop's shoulders. Danny seemed to be going along with the whole deal. Then a strange thing happened. I watched as the bishop came back close to the dock. He was about waist high in the water. He flipped something up on the dock, what looked to be Danny's red trunks. Then he turned and swam back to Danny. They both went underwater. When they came up for air, the bishop was tussling Danny up for the third time to his shoulders. Danny looked like a little Roman statue without the red trunks, as naked as the bishop."

"You're kidding me, Ben."

"Saw it through my binoculars."

"You know, as kids we sometimes went swimming nude in the creek," Father Sullivan reminded Ben.

"But this older man and naked boy frolicking close … and I'm sure grabbing. Well, it's sick. Actually, I felt sick myself just watching. You know, like a peeping Tom. Soon they both were walking up to the cabin. Still no trunks, towels over their shoulders. Danny looked a little timid. I could see his face through my binoculars. I watched as they went inside the cabin. That's when it happened. Within about five minutes, the bishop walked out on the porch from his room, which was on the second floor. I saw him stand by the railing. I felt sick. I could tell he was anxious. I hated looking at him. Within a minute, Danny came out wearing a towel and stood by the bishop while the bishop gazed out over the railings toward the lake.

"Michael, I'm about to end this saga, but I felt you should know what happened. This is exactly how it happened. I watched as long as I could. The bishop pulled Danny's towel off and put his arms around him. Then I saw them disappear. I did see a lounge chair between the slots of the porch where two could … where two could lie down. I heard some no's. I heard quiet … and then lots of moans. It was quiet outside. I was only yards from the cabin."

Father Ben sat back and looked at the ceiling as if to shake his head in shame. "Oh, Michael, I should have charged to Danny's defense. I didn't. I was a coward. I just couldn't confront my bishop. I am … I'm so ashamed."

Knowing he would have charged the cabin to save Danny, Father Sullivan said, "Ben, I can imagine looking back how you would have done differently, but in the moment, you didn't. I will not pass judgment."

"I know, Michael. I live with this every day. I'm so sorry, but that didn't help Danny. I should have rushed the porch, called the police. I didn't. I went back to my car, drove back home, and have lived with this ever since. It's my own private nightmare. If I had to do this over, I would have confronted him inside the cabin. But then I knew I would have blown my cover. He, of course, did not know I was giving you all this information. The consequences and retaliation from the bishop could have been extensive. Unfortunately, at the time I was thinking more of myself than I was of Danny. I still regret my decision."

Father Sullivan looked his friend in the face. "Who am I to judge?" he said in a consoling tone.

"No, Michael. When I saw Danny in the meeting, I felt a ton of guilt. No, I must make up for the lost time. What do you think I should do?"

"My friend, I will not comment about what you should have done. I will help you now. With Ned and Danny's story, with the cardinal behind us, it is time for you to go straight to the prosecutor. You are an eye witness. We'll go together on Monday."

"I agree. That's what I've been thinking. You know, this man in his powerful seat is just as bad as Father Jaeger."

"No, Ben. The bishop is far worse. He is not only an abuser himself, but he is covering up for all the other abusing priests in the diocese," Father Sullivan said quite emphatically. "Ben, look at me. Bishop Powers personifies all that is bad. All that is evil in the Catholic Church. You and I are going to bring justice. Monday, you and me. I will also ask Ned and Danny. The time has come."

"Will you go with me tomorrow to see Prosecutor Wolgameyer? I found out his name yesterday."

"Ben, I will be there for you tomorrow. We'll both go."

"Michael, I know that was a long story. I should have come forward long before. Now we have what lies before us these next few days. You and I together must bring justice. I made a mistake. Now I will do what is right for Ned, Danny, and all the others." Father Holtz took a last sip of coffee. "I need to go back to the rectory. You better not come until four o'clock, just in case. The bishop might see you."

Father Sullivan nodded in agreement. "I think he's so bad, with the abuse, rape, cover-up, and now fleeing to Rome. I have a hard time thinking of forgiveness for this pathetic man."

"You're right, Michael," Father Holtz said as he laid a quarter and a nickel on the table. They both stood up. "Michael, there is one thing I am doing." He looked at Father Sullivan and started to say something but then stopped. "Michael, I will fix this. Fix this for Danny."

"Hey, Fathers, what about our Sunday specials?" the waitress asked as she saw only the backs of the priests' black suits.

Ned Thornbauer—December 7, 1958

Ned was overwhelmed with conviction. His sign was made. It was 2:00 p.m. He heard a knock at the door.

"Come in!"

In walked Danny. "Hi, brother. Told you I'd show up."

"What do you think of this?" Ned asked, holding up the sign that read, *I was abused by Bishop Powers in 1949.* "Do you have warm clothes on?"

"Sure do, Ned. How do you like my new muff hat?"

"Great ear flaps, kid," Ned replied.

"Now here's your sign. Same sign, different year, 1958."

"Real good, brother," Danny said, taking his own sign.

"I have a charcoal bucket with holes and some kindling. A little fire to draw attention. There won't be many people. Need only one. Mr. D'Amato from *The Journal*. He promised. We'll leave here at three thirty, Danny. I plan on knocking on the bishop's door at exactly four o'clock."

Time passed slowly. "Ned, let's make some sandwiches," Danny suggested.

"Yeah. We'll listen to the Bears playing those lousy Cardinals."

"Aren't they a baseball team?"

"No, the Chicago Cardinals, a windy city team, just like the Bears."

"Is Stan, what's his name? Musal playing?"

"Mus-i-al's baseball, Danny."

"My favorite quarterback's playing. Had a rough game at Pittsburgh last week."

"You mean Musial?"

"No, Danny, Zeke Bratkowski. He can throw a ball seventy yards. When we were in the meeting Wednesday, I talked a little football with Father Girouard. I mentioned the Bears. He told me Cardinal Cullings mentioned that Zeke was later from the same town where the cardinal was a pastor. Danville, over in Illinois. Said Zeke played at a Catholic high school. He and the Bears gonna win today."

"Gotta pull for a Catholic football player. Right, Ned?"

"Okay. 'nuff football. Let's make the sandwiches."

Together, they put some bologna on bread and poured some milk. They ate. Ned turned on the radio, and they listened to the Chicago Bears. Danny dozed off.

"It's 3:20, big fella. Let's get ready. Almost time to leave," Ned said, shaking Danny as he lay on Ned's old, worn green couch. After the brothers put on their coats and left, they jumped into Ned's Chevy and headed across town directly to the bishop's rectory. Their time had come.

Father Schmidt—December 7, 1958

Father Holtz rapped on Father Schmidt's door a little after two o'clock that afternoon.

"Hello, who is it?" he heard from inside.

"Father Holtz. Got just a minute?"

"Yes, come on in," Father Schmidt responded in a low, hushed voice. Father Holtz walked in to find Father Schmidt sitting on the end of his sofa, looking despondent. His eyes were almost half closed.

"You've been very quiet today. Just stopped to see how you are doing. This whole situation has to be so much," Father Holtz said to the sullen priest. "Now you have the stress of the bishop leaving for Rome. Are you handling everything?"

No response.

"Anything I can do?"

"Who knows? Who knows?" Father Schmidt responded, still looking straight ahead. "I'm sick to death of the whole thing. You've seen me have to work with these priests. Transfer here. Psychiatric care. We both know that doesn't do much good. Then they come back, and the bishop says to transfer again. He just wants no problems from the higher-ups. Now he can go and be one of them in Rome."

"Yes, Leonard, but what about the bishop? Do you think he's guilty as his accusers say he is?"

"Ben, let's be honest. You know, I know, and our Lord knows. Bishop Powers is aware of everything he's done. Why do you think he's leaving? I feel so terrible, so guilty for being a part. Besides that, I've also—" Father Schmidt stopped midsentence. He just could not say it out loud while privately thinking of his own indiscretions. "As I see it, it's like putting a fox to guard another fox from raiding the chicken coop," Father Schmidt admitted.

"Let me ask you this," Father Holtz questioned. "What if someone sees a priest in the act with a minor?"

"Well, if he's telling the truth, I guess the priest would be guilty."

"I would agree with that," Father Holtz confirmed. "Now, Father Schmidt, what if—"

"Wait a minute. Where you going with these kinds of questions? What are you trying to say?" Father Schmidt asked as his own guilt caused him to feel an oncoming question of implication. He started to give himself away before Father Holtz asked the next question. "Listen, Ben. I only do what the bishop tells me. You know that better than anyone."

"Yes, I do, Leonard. Yes, I do. But you're ahead of yourself. Relax. I'm talking about the bishop. Not you, of course," Father Holtz said, deflecting Father Schmidt's defensiveness.

"Come on, Ben. Get to it. What are you saying?"

"Did you ever see the bishop sexually abusing a child?"

"For God's sake, no! No! Of course not!" Father Schmidt's voice rose with his blood pressure.

Father Holtz leaned forward. Using his index finger, he motioned for Father Schmidt to come closer. Inside Father Schmidt's room, their faces were only two feet apart. In a low whisper, Father Holtz said, "Guess what, Father Schmidt?"

A blank, startled look raced across Father Schmidt's face as if he was waiting for a gun to go off.

"I did. I saw our holy bishop stark naked, hugging a little boy. I heard the cries of no! I heard the moans of passion. Yes, I did, Father. I swear I did!" Father Holtz calmly sat back in his chair as if he had just lifted the burden of the world from his shoulders. Resting his elbows on the chair's wooden arms, he folded his hands and simply gazed at Father Schmidt.

Father Schmidt's face was white, as white as the curtain behind the sofa. Then he flushed. "No, that can't be. I don't believe you. You couldn't have seen him. Where?"

"Let me ask you, Father, are you familiar with his one-night trips to his cabin in Michigan?"

"Yes, yes, of course. I probably knew every time he went, at least most."

"Has he ever invited you to go? Has he ever invited other priests?"

"Well, I guess not that I am aware of, except for the time you and me went to his cabin," Father Schmidt replied.

"Then who does he go with?" Father Holtz asked. Now Father Schmidt was showing discomfort in his seat. "I asked, who does he take with him?" he asked again. "Could they be altar boys? Eleven-, twelve-, thirteen-year-old altar boys? Does that seem a little strange, Father? Did that ever make you suspicious?"

"You are right, Ben. Yes, boys, young boys. I said before, I knew about what he was doing. Yes, I was suspicious."

"Were these boys from St. Leonard's? And you say you knew?"

"Yes. Yes, I did say that. I was suspicious. I mean, I don't know what I mean. It's all just sick. Well, maybe, sometimes. Can this be over? This is enough, Ben. You're acting like you're still at that meeting with Cardinal Cullings. Actually, I don't like this. Enough, Ben. Enough! I'm so confused. What do I do?" Father Schmidt stopped and raised his outstretched hands above his head. "I can't take this anymore. I don't care if he hears me. I'm done!"

"Just one more question and I will leave. Could you have been covering up for Bishop Powers?"

"No, absolutely not. Just doing what I'm told. You're going too far with all this, Ben, and I don't like it," Father Schmidt said, now standing up from the sofa. "You can leave now."

"Okay, okay, I will. But first, I'll leave you with one … let's call it a sobering thought, a question," Father Holtz said, looking squarely at Father Schmidt.

Then he made a statement of fact he already knew for certain: "Maybe you are covering for Bishop Powers because he is covering for you. You're both holding a trump card on each other. Blackmail?" Before Father Schmidt could respond, he went on, "If the truth is difficult for you, then I'll do just that. I will leave. Don't want to upset you. By the way, are you aware that Ned Thornbauer is coming to see the bishop this afternoon at four o'clock?"

"Yes, I am."

"Does the bishop know?"

"Yes, I told him. But too bad. He's up in his room, sick."

"Well, we all know where his room is. Maybe the bishop will see Ned up there."

"I wouldn't count on that. You can leave now, Father Holtz."

Father Holtz turned and walked to the door. He stopped, snapped his fingers, and walked a couple paces back toward Father Schmidt. "Can you believe I almost forgot the main reason I came to pay you a visit?"

With mounting concern on his face, Father Schmidt asked, "What's that?"

"Do you by any chance remember where you were on September 15, 1958?"

"Now how can I recall without looking at my appointment book?"

"Let me help. Look at the couch you're standing in front of."

"Yes, of course, it's a couch. What does that mean?" Father Schmidt asked in wonderment.

"Do you ever pray there?"

"Pray there? Of course not. What you getting at?"

"Let me reword my question. Have you ever been with a certain Billy Donovan on the couch?"

"What? What are you talking about? No, of course not! Now it's time for you to leave!"

"*No!* I will have the last word. Have you ever sat there naked with

Billy Donovan kneeling in front of the couch just for your hideous satisfaction? After that, did you throw him facedown on the sofa with you to follow? Did Bishop Powers open the door and see you in an awful sexual act? You—yes, you, Father Schmidt—are an abusive sexual pervert ... just like ... You are an abuser just like Father Jaeger. I'm accusing you to your face right here and now."

Father Schmidt turned and walked toward the back of the room.

"Truth hurts, Leonard. That's why you are dancing at every whim of the bishop as he prepares to leave for Rome, leaving his own abuse and corruption behind him. You are a criminal, a sodomizing rapist, and you should go to jail for a long, long time. And while I'm at it, you are not safe. It's all coming down and sweeping you along. Sweeping you right along with Bishop Powers. Today, I am bringing finality to both of you." Father Holtz turned and walked toward the door. Turning around, he calmly said, "Finality, Father Schmidt. For you and Bishop Powers. You must answer for your sins. Good afternoon, Father. See you again at four o'clock."

Father Schmidt did not hear the door slam. He walked back to the couch, threw himself prone onto its cushions, and buried his head in anguish and shame. The truthful words had ruptured his soul.

Father Holtz—December 7, 1958

After leaving Father Schmidt, Father Holtz walked downstairs, removed his coat from the foyer closet, and left the rectory. *Finally, finally, I did it. Had to tell him like that. Monday will be his undoing.*

Snow was in the air as Father Holtz looked at his watch—2:49. *One more.* Walking to the front doors of the church, Father Holtz entered the foreboding darkness of the holy place. The day was dark and gray. *Echoes.* Sunday afternoon, not a soul. He genuflected. A light from a hanging fixture barely reached the sanctuary. Father Holtz listened to his own footsteps as he walked up the side aisle. He knew the side where Bishop Powers would enter the confessional.

Father Holtz walked a dozen rows up. After draping his coat over the pew, he knelt in prayer, knowing Bishop Powers would be able to see him before the bishop entered the confessional. *Our Father, who art in Heaven, hallowed* ... He heard footsteps. Father Holtz watched as a dark shadow entered from the sanctuary, genuflected, and walked down the side aisle toward the confessional in the back corner of the church. Kneeling on the opposite side, Father Holtz peered at the advancing shadow. *It's him. On time, as usual.* He knew Bishop Powers would look for him. The confessional door closed. Father Holtz looked at his watch—2:56. *Two minutes.*

Bishop Powers heard the confessional door open. Reaching over, he slid the small black screened partition. He heard Father Holtz take a deep breath. *It's him.*

"Bless me, Father, for I have sinned."

"How long has it been since your last confession?" Bishop Powers asked.

"One month to be exact. Friday. Four weeks ago, Friday. My sins are few. Two to be exact."

"Yes, go on."

Somewhat hesitantly, Father Holtz continued. "I am sometimes tempted by the devil. I lust. Making sure to provide clarity, definition, the devil sometimes sends images. Female images. In desire, the temptation can be ever so wrong. It is difficult to determine when thought becomes sin. It comes and goes. Weekly to be sure."

"And more?" Bishop Powers asked, pursuing the penitent's sins.

"Yes, there is." Father Holtz paused a moment. "Yes, yes. I have committed a sin of grave omission. Every day for months, I am plagued about not what I did but what I didn't do."

"Yes. Can you be more specific?"

"It was a Saturday afternoon this past summer. I witnessed a terrible, horrific sin, and I … My sin was that I did nothing."

"Explain specifically," Bishop Powers demanded as his curiosity heightened.

"Well, Father, I saw a man molest a young boy."

Immediately, Bishop Powers' adrenaline raced. His system shocked like the prick of electricity. There was a long pause. The bishop waited for the voice from behind the black screen to continue.

"They were together at a lake. I watched as they frolicked in the water together, both naked." The flash of a boy being tossed from the water sent a sensation through Bishop Powers. "Then I watched as they walked together back to the man's cabin, still naked."

Feeling a rush of excitement more than the penitent's words, Bishop Powers asked, "Then what happened?"

"I waited in the woods close enough to hear the sounds, the sounds of passion, moaning, then 'no'."

Maintaining the masquerade, the bishop asked, "Did you become a part of this so-called sin?"

"Oh no. No," Father Holtz responded.

"Then you have not sinned," Bishop Powers responded, placing the onus on the penitent.

"I confess that I did sin by omission. I did not step forward to defend the boy. I did not go to the authorities. I did not go to my superiors." Trapped, Bishop Powers was speechless to reply. "While I confess this grave sin, the sin of watching a sinner, I must ask what to do."

"As I see it, you did not sin," Bishop Powers said, protecting the charade. "You have confessed. That's all. You are forgiven."

Knowing Bishop Powers was feeling entrapment, Father Holtz continued. "But, Bishop, I can't live with myself until I sweep this away. Become clean. I must tell beyond the confessional. If our Lord forgives me, then the abuser must also confess. I must go to my superiors and inform them."

A long moment of silence overwhelmed the confessional. *Silence.* Playing his hand, the bishop said, "I do forgive you. Our Lord forgives you, Father. Now for your penance, I want you to be sure you say the rosary each and every day for a year to remind you of the gravity of your sin. With that, this episode in your life should be over. You are forgiven. Go in peace."

As Bishop Powers raised his hand in blessing, he slid the confessional door closed, ending the ordeal.

"Please, Father, or should I say Bishop Powers, I do accept our Lord's forgiveness, but I will go to the authorities."

Not wanting to expose himself by threatening Father Holtz, Bishop Powers nodded. Concerned, he said, "Go in peace."

"Thank you, Bishop Powers. I will do what I must." Father Holtz remained kneeling. "Now you know, Bishop Powers, you are the abuser, molester, the sinner. You are the one that should be repentant." Bishop Powers did not respond. Father Holtz stood, then bent over and leaned close to the black screen. "Bishop Powers, your time has come. It's over. No more abuse. No more cover-up. Your days of reckoning are here. Bless you, Bishop." Father Holtz returned to his pew, knelt, and prayed. *Forgive me, Dear Lord.*

Within a minute, the sound of the confessional door opening and then closing echoed throughout the cathedral. Footsteps slowly followed the side aisle. Father Holtz watched as Bishop Powers walked down the side aisle, genuflected then disappeared into the darkness.

Father Sullivan—December 7, 1958

Father Sullivan knocked on the rectory door at 3:40 p.m.

Father Holtz promptly answered. "Hello, Michael. Welcome to Happyville."

"What's that mean?" he asked as he took off his hat and followed Father Holtz into the parlor.

"Sit down. Rest for a few minutes. Could I offer you a bottle of wine? How about a full bottle of scotch or gin? Just name it. We both could use it, I'm sure," Father Holtz said with a whimsical look on his face.

"What's with you? Have you popped some pills?"

"No, but I'd like to. Maybe a bottle later. Quickly, one more thing before the boys arrive. Surprise! Are you ready for this?"

"Probably not," Father Sullivan said.

"Bishop Powers saw Father Schmidt raping Billy Donovan last summer. I know. I was there in this rectory when it happened. That's how the bishop has such a tight leash around Father Schmidt's neck. All makes sense. I have to be right," Father Holtz said, trying to justify his assumption.

Father Sullivan interrupted, "Ben, yes I know. You told ... "

Father Holtz cut him off. "Michael, listen to me."

"Okay, okay. Tell me again," Father Sullivan went along. "How could you know all this, Ben?"

"Well, Michael, I must tell you, I did see Bishop Powers peeking into Father Schmidt's room that night. I heard sounds when I first walked by.

I know it was a boy with Father Schmidt. Then a week later, let's just say Billy Donovan confided in me."

"What? Are you kidding me? You sure know how to hit people over the head. You pull surprises like rabbits out of a hat."

"Yes, I held that back too. I knew about Father Schmidt," Father Holtz admitted. "Billy Donovan told me everything."

So you are telling me you saw Bishop Powers at the cabin with Danny then you found out about Father Schmidt from Billy Donovan. Ben, I can't believe this. Any more confessions you'd like to make? I might have to stay a week," Father Sullivan said. "Of course, now are you going to tell me Bishop Powers asked you to tag along to Rome with him. Like a traveling companion?"

"Stop it, Michael. I'm serious. This is not the time to joke around."

"I know. Sorry. Just trying to lighten the moment," Father Sullivan said with a slight smile.

"Michael, it's all true. This is like a perfect storm. Everything all at once. What else could possibly happen today?"

"Oh let me see, Ben. Maybe one of the sisters has some dark hidden secret."

"Your humor is going too far."

"Are you finished? Relax." Father Sullivan put both his hands squarely on Father Holtz's shoulders. "You are under so much stress, and I must remind you, your own guilt, Father. We both know Bishop Powers, Ned, Danny, Father Schmidt, Billy, Father Jaeger, Gene, Peter … more and more, and god only knows who else."

"Yes, I knew all along. I was so wrong. You're right, Michael." Father Holtz took a deep breath then relief. "I forgot to ask earlier about Father Warren. How is he? How is he handling all this? I thought he might come with you."

"You know, Ben, he's such a good man and wonderful priest. He's so concerned about our church and all these … these misfits. He just goes about his business, uninvolved, and simply depends on me. I love him like a father. We talked last night, then this morning. I could just tell something was on his mind. Maybe something new. Don't know. Concerns me though."

"Yes, I understand what you mean. Wish I had a priest in my life like that. Now just look at what I have. Two pedophiles living with me in this big house. Some days even I don't feel safe, but of course I'm not thirteen," Father Holtz said, looking up at the ceiling. "I see where Father Schmidt learned all his bad habits."

There was a knock at the door. Both priests looked at their watches. The clock on the wall struck 4:00. Daylight was losing hours.

"Is sister here?" Father Sullivan asked.

"No. She'll be back early in the morning. Good thing she's not around all these shameless perverts," Father Holtz said as he walked to answer the door. "Just you and me, Father Schmidt, and our invalid bishop, who is upstairs supposedly resting from his illness."

"You leave my name out of the discussion with Schmidt and the bishop," Father Sullivan instructed.

"I'll answer the door," Father Holtz said as he entered the foyer. Opening the door, he expected to see Ned and Danny.

"Good evening, Father, I'm Gary D'Amato from *The Journal*. I have an appointment with Ned Thornbauer."

"He's not here yet. I do expect him."

"I met Ned the other day. He's not out front yet. I thought I might see him carrying a sign. Said he would be here. Something about Bishop Powers, abuse?" D'Amato said vaguely. "I found his story to be almost unbelievable."

"You might as well come in out of the cold and join our party. Did you bring some wine? Just kidding."

D'Amato was very Italian-looking. Courteous, unassuming for a reporter. He wore a brimmed hat with a wide bill; it was set back on his head. The hatband was distorted and streaked with lead, a landing area for hundreds of pencils from a truth-seeking, tenacious, and honest reporter.

"Thank you, Father. You're very kind. Ah, while we wait, could I ask you a few questions? Your name? What do you do here?"

"Not right now. Ned and the bishop are the ones you need to talk with."

There was a knock on the door. *Saved by the bell*, Father Holtz thought as he opened the door. Surprisingly, he saw Fred Newman standing in the doorway. "Oh, good evening, Mr. Newman. Can I help you?"

"I just saw two young men walking down the street, heading this way. One had this sign over his shoulder. Couldn't believe what I read. I even stopped to make sure I was reading it correctly."

"This really isn't a good time."

"Maybe not for you, but it is important to me. I must see the Bishop Powers," Mr. Newman said, stepping across the threshold.

"Mr. Newman, our hands are kinda full. Ah, Father Sullivan, Mr. D'Amato, this is Harold Newman, a member of our parish council."

"What's going on, Father? What's a reporter doing here?" Mr. Newman asked, looking directly at Father Holtz. "I happened to be checking some things in the basement at the cathedral. Walking up from the side stairs, I saw these two kids. What a disgrace to our good bishop. As a member of the council, I demand to know what's going on." Fred Newman said with self-appointed authority.

Gary D'Amato stood back against the wall, trying to be unnoticed, just taking it all in.

"Please gentlemen, let's all keep calm and wait in the parlor. The Thornbauers will be here soon."

As they all proceeded to the parlor, there was a third knock at the door. Father Sullivan answered this time. *Trick or treat,* he thought.

"Good afternoon, Father," Ned said politely. Danny stood behind him, hat in hand.

"Come on in, boys. The party is just beginning. Our guest of honor isn't here yet," Father Sullivan said, trying to lighten the moment as he perfectly described the situation. Ned and Danny followed him into the parlor.

In the meantime, Gary D'Amato had walked over to the fireplace and was looking around. *Maybe there is more to this story than I thought.*

A tall man of about seventy, gentlemanly dressed in a suit and tie, Mr. Newman said, "This looks like diocesan business. The parishioners have rights. I'll stay out of the way, but I'm staying." He sat down. His long legs kneed the high tea table in front of the couch. "I need to see Bishop Powers. He'll straighten this all out."

"Gentlemen, make yourself comfortable. I will call on Father

Schmidt, and he will bring the bishop to talk to you all," Father Holtz said to everyone.

In what he knew would be a futile cause, Father Holtz walked up the back stairs. Father Sullivan remained in the parlor and sat rather tensely in a comfortable armchair at the end of the sofa. Everyone waited.

George Griffin—December 7, 1958

Meanwhile, across the street in the Wolford Hotel, George Griffin—the reporter from Wabash—sat by the window on the fourth floor, positioned along a street side, with a full side view of the rectory. He could not distinguish the faces of the guests who had been entering the front door, but he was able to see them as they approached. He did, however, decipher a young man and a boy, both with signs he could not read. He wondered if his friend D'Amato was somewhere close by.

I should have gone with him. He waited closely to see if anything would happen. He thought about D'Amato's suggestion that he be here. His gut asked about a connection between Wabash, St. Thomas Moore, and the bishop in South Wayne. George Griffin waited and observed. His trusty scotch was his only companion.

Father Holtz—December 7, 1958

Knocking on Father Schmidt's door, Father Holtz hoped he would find him in a composed state of mind. *I really did hit him with a heavy message this morning,* he thought. Considering the circumstances, Father Holtz assumed Father Schmidt would be in his room. There was no answer. Holtz then went down the hall to Bishop Powers' room, looking for Father Schmidt.

He felt a little awkward as he approached the bishop's door, thinking back an hour earlier when he was so close to Bishop Powers in the confessional. He now wished he had those pills he and Father Sullivan had joked about.

The bishop's apartment was in the front corner on the Wolford Hotel side of the rectory. For a minute, Father Holtz stood in front of the door. Taking two deep breaths, he knocked. The response was immediate.

"Who is it?" a growl sounded from the other side of the panel door.

"It's Father Holtz, Your Eminence."

"Eminence, Eminence, I'm a sick bishop. Got any coffee? I was expecting Schmidt. Where is he?" The booming voice sounded closer. Father Holtz could tell the gruff man was just on the other side, close to the door.

"Sir, you have guests." Father Holtz gritted his teeth at that one.

"Guests?" Suddenly the door opened, a slight crack. "Hello, Holtz. What do you want? Do you offer room service?" the bishop asked with a huge catlike smile.

Father Holtz noticed some gold on both sides of his teeth. He was in a robe, peering through the three-inch opening in the doorway.

"Excuse me, sir, but Ned and Danny Thornbauer would like a few words."

"Oh they would, would they? Have some fresh new lies? You can tell those two lying little bastards to turn around and head home to Grandma's house or maybe to their drunken ol' man."

"He passed away, sir. They don't have a dad."

"Sorry."

"Also, Harold Newman from the parish council would like to see you."

"Did he bring a check?" the bishop asked with another big cheesy smile. "You can tell him to go home to that snobby bitch of a wife he has."

Through the crack in the doorway, Father Holtz caught a quick glimpse of an empty Beefeaters bottle. That explained it.

"Well, Father Holtz, you little turncoat, I watched you at the meeting last week, sitting there by yourself with a smirk on your face," he said, pointing his fat index finger through the door. He made no reference, however, to the confession he had heard just a few hours before. "Naughty, naughty there, Father."

Father Holtz was caught off guard.

"Now, you do this, Father Benny," the bishop said in a sarcastic, derogatory tone. Then he said quite calmly, "Now you tell all my guests I'd love to visit, sip some wine, and sit by the fire except for ... *I'm sick. Sick of all of you!* Invite them to all come back this Wednesday, same time, and we'll spend some quality time together. Understand, Father

Redcoat? And one last thing. Tell good ol' Father Schmidt, my trusty companion … *to get up here immediately!*" He slammed the door in one quick motion.

What was that? Father Holtz asked himself as he headed back down the hall. He stopped at Father Schmidt's door and knocked, waited, and then knocked again. He turned the handle. No answer. Still locked.

Father Holtz proceeded back down the stairs and into the parlor. He noticed that they were all still in their stations, just as he had left them. Folding his hands together, he said, "Gentlemen, the bishop asked me to say—"

Instantly a huge noise like shelves and cans falling over was heard by all.

"Sounded like it came from the basement. Excuse me again, gentlemen," Father Holtz said.

A remnant sound like a can rolling on a concrete floor came to a slow stop. Father Sullivan stood up. He looking at Father Holtz and furrowed his brow in question. Father Holtz gave him a nod.

They walked into the foyer. "Michael, the bishop was totally drunk. Maybe he fell."

"No, Ben, that sound was from below. Where's the basement door?" Father Sullivan asked.

Father Holtz pointed to the end of the hall.

Father Sullivan asked, "Burglars?"

"Nah, not here."

The basement door was unlocked. Father Holtz saw that the light was already on. *Unusual.* He slowly walked sideways down the steep steps. The old, dark, rough wooden stairs creaked. One bulb hanging from the ceiling, just beyond the bottom of the stairs, gave faint illumination toward the center of the room. Rows of shelves lined the walls of the dark, damp basement. Three rows of shelves ran parallel in the back half of the basement. The boilers and a half-full coal bin, two shovels leaning against the wood walls. Suddenly, the house cat streaked across the floor and shot up the stairs.

"Ah, just darn ol' Jefferson, our friendly housecat. She probably pounced on a mouse and knocked the cans over. Let's head back to our guests and break the tension."

"Ben," Father Sullivan said with a gulp. Thrusting the back of his hand against Father Holtz's chest, he exclaimed, "Stop! It wasn't Jefferson. Look over there in the corner, above the ladder. Oh my God. It can't be."

Father Holtz choked. Shivers quivered through his body. Father Sullivan took a couple steps forward. He looked up at the black lead waste pipes attached to the dark floor joists that traveled the ceiling of the high stone basement walls. In the far corner, above the ladder, a hemp rope was securely tied to the sturdy pipes. Three feet below, a rope encircled the neck of Father Leonard Schmidt. His tarnished collar was a good six inches below the taut rope. He was clad in his black cassock, black shoes, black socks, and a black Good Friday chasuble hung over his shoulders. He was motionless. His eyes bulged in stark horror.

Father Holtz made the sign of the cross. "Oh my God."

Both priests rushed over to the ladder.

"Let's think clearly, Ben." Father Sullivan saw a stack of dark towels on a shelf at the far wall. He grabbed out two. "Ben, let's stand the ladder up. We should not move him. We'll have to call the police, the coroner."

Slowly and carefully, they straightened the ladder. First, Father Sullivan felt Father Schmidt's wrist for a pulse. He shook his head. "Nothing there." Then he opened the towels.

Father Sullivan stepped up the ladder. Carefully and gently, he covered the priest's face with the two towels and then draped them over his shoulders.

"Father, look at the left side of his chasuble. Is that a paper?" Father Holtz asked.

"No, it's an envelope, pinned."

"Can you reach it?"

"Yes, need two hands to unpin. Hold the ladder."

Father Sullivan reached over and unpinned the envelope. He looked at the name. "It's addressed to you."

Father Sullivan leaned over, handed it to Father Holtz, and then stepped down from the ladder. Holtz turned the sealed envelope in his hand, checking it over.

"Should I open it?"

"Yes, of course. Open it."

The Tarnished Collar

Father Holtz slid his thumb neatly through the back of the envelope. Stepping away from Father Sullivan, he turned his back.

December 7, 1958

Dear Father Holtz,

All you said this afternoon is true. I deserved your wrath. I want to leave no secrets. I'm sorry. I have failed. I have not honored my sacred vows. I'm not a good priest. May God someday forgive me.

I was a puppet for Bishop Powers. I executed his immoral plans. I arranged the transfers of abusive priests. I altered files. I aided his money scheme and implemented the cover-up of all his lies.

All along, I knew of his trips to Michigan and the altar boys who went along. Other times, I made the arrangements for them to meet in the guest apartment. Bishop Powers thought he was being sly and didn't really understand that I knew the purpose of his trips and meetings. I am ashamed to say, I was his pimp. He trusted me, but I knew what was really going on.

Bishop Powers has tickets to fly to his safe haven in Rome. He has friends there. He leaves for Indianapolis on Tuesday. I made all the arrangements. He will be in Rome on Thursday if you do not stop him. Check his room. You will find two satchels of cash. Both are filled with cash that he siphoned from the collection baskets and his own personal money in a form of a cashier's check. He stole the money for years and years. He disclosed this to me when he told me to destroy all the books.

You must understand that your words today did not drive my decision. I have contemplated this rope for weeks. You just reminded me of my sins. I was immoral. I defied my church, my God, my collar, and all that I know and love. Worst of all, I hurt and abused boys. There were more than Billy Donovan.

In the top drawer of my desk are six letters written over the past several weeks. One is to my mother, who lives in Ashford, Wisconsin. Three are addressed to the victims of my sinful abuse, one of which is for Billy Donovan. The fifth is a letter to you. The last is to Bishop Powers. Would you please make sure they receive them?

Father, thank you. I hope this is not a burden. Do with this letter as you see fit. Bishop Powers must be brought to justice.

May God someday in His almighty wisdom be able to forgive me. I am truly sorry.

Peace be with you,

Father Leonard Schmidt

P.S. I swear to our God above that every word in this final letter is the truth, the whole truth, and nothing but the truth.

Father Holtz put his hand to his forehead, knelt down, and prayed for Father Schmidt. The disclosures he had just learned made total sense considering his and Father Sullivan's discovery in the basement. The power of Father Schmidt's words left him speechless. The overwhelmed priest handed the letter to Father Sullivan.

Father Sullivan read the letter and then calmly said, "Why don't you go to his room now? Get the letters he asked you to deliver. Do it now before we call the police."

"Good idea, Michael. You should have been a detective. I'll meet you downstairs."

"Wait a minute. Oh my…we should…we're priests, we need to give the last rites for Father Schmidt. Where was my head? More important than the letters, bring the oils also. Hurry, Father," Father Sullivan commanded.

Father Holtz rushed, with letter in hand, to Father Schmidt's room. Using the rectory master key, he opened the locked door, and went directly to the desk. There sat the six letters. He picked them up, then immediately went to his own room where he grabbed his stole and the holy oils. Tucking the stole inside his cassock, Father Holtz rushed downstairs, walked calmly through the hall to the basement door.

Hurriedly, he descended the stairs, "Michael, I have the stole and oil. You be the one." Pulling the stole from his cassock, he handed it to Father Sullivan.

Father kissed the stole and placed it around his neck. "We can't take him down yet. The ladder."

Ben reached over and set the ladder back up.

Holding the oil in his left hand, Father Sullivan, stepped up the ladder until he reached the dead priest. Father Holtz knelt at the base of the ladder. Dropping the towels from around Father Schmidt's head, Father Sullivan touched the oil to his right thumb then anointed the forehead of Father Schmidt. "Through this holy oil, may our Lord in his love and mercy assist you with the grace of the Holy Ghost. May our Lord free you from your sins and raise you up to life everlasting."

Both priests bowed their heads. "Amen."

Father Holtz handed the note to Father Sullivan.

Ben, I wrote out a copy of all letters in my hand. Keep them safe and please get them into the right hands. Every word is painstakingly written, word for word, all the same, all the truth. Hope you find these before anyone else.

Both priests were taken aback by Father Schmidt's written words. They could feel the remorse, shame and the anguish Father Schmidt left behind.

Father Sullivan looked at Father Holtz. "Father, this troubled priest, this troubled man…" Father Sullivan shook his head. "For him, this was the only way out."

"God rest his soul."

"For sure," Father Sullivan replied, putting his hand on Father Holtz's shoulder. "Time to go upstairs, we have much to do." Father Holtz ascended the stairs.

Father Sullivan followed, but stopped on the second step, turned, and raised his right hand to Father Schmidt, giving one last blessing. "*di te incolumen custodiat.*" Yes, *please God, guard him safely.* Bowing his head, Father Sullivan turned and followed Father Holtz and their challenge ahead.

George Griffin—December 7, 1958

George Griffin continued to watch from the hotel window. Light flakes of snow began to fall peacefully. As he watched them flutter softly from the windless sky, he noticed a figure round the corner of St. Leonard's School, directly behind the rectory. The man's hat was black with a wide brim pulled low to the erect black collar of his dark overcoat. His hands were hidden deep within the safety of his pockets. He walked slowly. As he approached the rectory, the dark figure turned to the right in the direction of the back door.

George Griffin stood up and walked a few paces to his right so he wouldn't lose sight of the man dressed like the darkness he disappeared into. Griffin rubbed his chin and watched. Then he observed a back second floor light turn on. Seemed like a light in a staircase. He watched. Suddenly the dark figure walked in through the light. Then he was gone. George Griffin was tempted to go outside to get a closer look, but the man in black was only in view for a moment. Then he disappeared inside.

Griffin waited and continued to watch, also keeping his eye on the front of the rectory. He did not want to risk losing the view of the front or back entrances. Although George Griffin did not know what or who he was watching for, he did not want to chance missing the connection.

Fathers Sullivan and Holtz—December 7, 1958

Father Sullivan stood alone, overwhelmed at the ghastly sight above him. He heard cautious steps on the stairs behind.

"I have the letters," Ben said, patting the side of his cassock.

The body of Father Schmidt hung motionless in front of the two priests.

"In the name of the Father, the Son, and the Holy Ghost. Amen."

Both priests looked at the surreal situation. It demanded immediate attention. They knew they had to calculate their options.

"The newspaper reporter is already here. We can't tell him to go, as he soon might be suspicious. Though I'm sure he already is in our absence." Maintaining a clear head, Father Sullivan suggested, "I say we go upstairs. I'll first call the police. We'll ask D'Amato to leave. You should immediately tell the bishop. Take control. I'll tell those in the parlor. By then the police will be here."

Both priests took one last look upward.

Turning to walk back upstairs, Father Holtz said, "I simply can't believe this. Now all I can remember are the words, what I said to him."

"You were only telling him the truth. He made his decision before. The letter shows us that."

"Yes, but just a few hours ago he—"

"Stop, right now. I won't hear of it, Ben. It's not your fault. He's been bringing it all upon himself for God knows how long. He decided his own fate. Not you," Father Sullivan assured his friend.

Father Holtz looked up at Father Sullivan as they began to ascend the stairs. "Maybe God decided for him."

"No, Ben. That's wrong. God would not take this way out."

"Of course. What was I thinking?"

Opening the basement door, they were immediately confronted by Harold Newman.

"What is going on around here? What were you doing in the basement for so long? Canning beans? Tell us what's going on. The members of the church deserve to know. We've all been hanging around here waiting for you two. Conversation is awkward. We're running out of things to say, although the Bears did win."

"You're not the only one, sir," Father Holtz shot back, not thinking what he said. Father Sullivan glared at Father Holtz.

"Sorry, Michael. That was uncalled for."

"Relax, Mr. Newman. You'll know soon enough."

Gary D'Amato stayed calm. The story was coming to him. His reporting instincts told him that something had either happened or was going to happen. *Maybe both*, he thought. He had gotten all he needed from Ned and Danny. His questions and Ned's and Danny's replies had connected the dots regarding their accusations of Bishop Powers.

"Mr. D'Amato, we suggest it's time for you to leave." Father Sullivan placed his hand on D'Amato's arm.

"Please, Father, I have a right to be here. People deserve to know. This is their parish. Things are really getting exciting."

"That, I'll agree with." Father Sullivan shrugged and then walked over to the hallway phone and called the police. He expected them within ten minutes. Father Holtz slowly ascended the stairs to the second floor. Approaching the bishop's room, he thought he heard voices within. He did, though they were low. He couldn't recognize who the bishop was talking to.

. *Here goes.* He knocked. "Bishop Powers? It's me, Father Holtz."

"Thought I told you to send Schmidt up here."

"You did, sir, but I can't."

"Can't what?" Bishop Powers shot back.

"Can't get him up here. May I please talk to you? It's extremely important. Is someone with you?" Father Holtz boldly asked the bishop.

"No one's with me. Give me five minutes. Let me put my cassock and collar on. Go back downstairs," he demanded.

"Okay, sir. I will, but we should talk now. Back in ten minutes. It's important about Father Schmidt."

Father Holtz kept his ear to the door for a few more seconds. "We've got ten minutes to finish," he heard the bishop say in a low monotone. "Continue." Father Holtz turned and walked down the hall. *Ten minutes, that's all,* Father Holtz thought to himself.

"Okay, he's gone," the bishop said to his visitor. "I don't like doing this, but you are forcing my hand. Time is fleeting. After all these years, I will admit I have little choice. I know you well enough that you wouldn't lie," Bishop Powers said to his visitor. He walked over to his desk, raised the satchel, and checked the contents inside. The visitor waited as the bishop counted and then handed one of the satchels over to him. "After forty-eight years, this makes us even."

"I agree, Bishop. You have my word. We are even." The visitor put on his coat. "Is that all?"

"Yes, that's everything. More than I'd like to give you." Bishop Powers added, "Forever. The table is level again."

They shook hands. Bishop Powers said, "We'll never see each other again."

The man in black looked the bishop directly in the eye. He nodded, put on his hat, and then turned toward the door. Opening it to the empty hall, he first checked both ways and then immediately headed for the back stairs. He turned and looked back at Bishop Powers, nodded and descended the stairs. The bishop watched then closed the door for good. His back to the door, Bishop Powers took a deep, satisfying breath. *It's over.*

Opening the back door, the visitor pulled his black hat low, the satchel secure in his right hand. He heard sirens. Feeling the intensity of the blowing snow, he bent his head down lower and left.

"Father Schmidt! Where are you? Father Schmidt!" the bishop yelled down the hall, having heard the sirens.

Meanwhile, across the street, George Griffin had also heard the sirens and now watched two police cars pull up in front of the rectory. An ambulance soon followed.

With an instant glance through the light fluffs of falling snow, George Griffin spotted the man in the long black coat heading back down the sidewalk toward the corner of the school. This time he noticed the man carrying something in his right hand. The man's hat was pulled low on his head. His left hand was tucked into the safety of his long coat, and his right gloved hand was carrying something like a briefcase, a satchel. Griffin kept his gaze glued to the man in black, watching him walk down the street, around the corner and disappeared into the darkness.

George Griffin sat back in his chair and poured another scotch. The light atop a police car turned in his left peripheral. He was more concerned about the man who had just disappeared. He thought, *Of course, two plus two is four. Why didn't I figure that before?* He thought about the priest back home in Wabash. George Griffin now knew ... or at least he thought he did.

Back at the rectory, Father Sullivan heard a knock at the door. He opened it. "Thank you for coming so quickly. I'm Father Sullivan."

"Good evening, Father," the police captain said. "I'm Captain Campbell Hamilton, South Wayne police. There's a problem?"

"Yes, there is. Please come in. There's quite a problem," Father Sullivan replied. "Please follow me." He led Captain Hamilton into the parlor. "Gentlemen, this is Captain Hamilton of the South Wayne Police Department. Father Holtz and I decided it would be best, considering the odd circumstances of this evening, to tell you all at the same time."

"What is going on here?" Mr. Newman asked. "Level with us. Where is the bishop?"

Father Sullivan said to the reporter, boys, and Mr. Newman, "We waited until the police arrived. About thirty minutes ago—"

"It's been at least forty-five minutes," Mr. Newman interrupted.

"Thank you, Mr. Newman. I knew there was a purpose for you being here."

"Please, sir, let Father Sullivan continue. He needs to inform you of what's happened," Captain Hamilton said, already aware of the evening's event.

Father Sullivan went on, "You remember, we all heard a commotion in the basement, like something heavy falling and then small follow-up racket. Father Holtz and I both went to the basement. The light was on. There in the corner, we found Father Schmidt, the bishop's secretary, hanging by a rope from the pipes above."

"What!" exclaimed Mr. Newman. "Oh my good God!"

D'Amato said nothing. He frantically started writing. Ned put his arm around Danny. They both showed little reaction.

"I've already called the coroner," Captain Hamilton said. "Who has the key to—what's the priest's room?"

"I do," Father Holtz responded.

"Father Sullivan, you come with me downstairs. You gentlemen wait here. When the coroner arrives, direct him to the basement." Captain Hamilton told Father Holtz to go and make sure Father Schmidt's room was locked and then to come back downstairs. "As soon as he arrives, Detective Riley should first inspect the priest's room."

Father Holtz headed back upstairs. Having already checked Father Schmidt's room, he walked directly to bishop's room. As he approached the door, he listened carefully for a second voice. Before knocking, he waited outside. Not a sound. He knocked twice.

"Schmidt, is that you?" the bishop called.

"No, it's me, Father Holtz. I must talk to you right now."

"Later. Can't talk now. Send Schmidt in here. I need him now!"

"Bishop Powers, I can't send Father Schmidt," Father Holtz said. Knowing the immediacy and his inability to get through to Bishop

Powers, Father Holtz simply said, "I can't, Bishop. I'm sorry to inform you that Father Schmidt is dead."

Silence was immediate. This time, the door opened slowly. Father Holtz could see the bishop walking away toward his chair. He fell back into it. Dressed in his cassock, he looked with a blank expression at Father Holtz. Father Holtz followed him into the room.

"Dead?" the bishop asked, both as a question and a statement of fact.

"Yes, Your Excellency. It is true, and I'm sorry to inform you. Father Sullivan and I found him in the basement about forty-five minutes ago. He was … he was hanging from rope tied to the pipes above. The police are here now. The coroner is on his way over. It all happened after four o'clock when Ned and Danny Thornbauer arrived."

"Damn boys," the bishop muttered to himself. "I know some things about those two guys," he said, disgusted. *Little bastards.*

"*The Journal* is here. They want a statement."

"Hell, the body's not cold, and they want a statement already? We'll have an official one tomorrow," Bishop Powers confirmed. "I want to understand more of what happened."

"Sir, they want you to come down now."

"No, not yet! Send those boys home. I've had enough of their lies. Tell *The Journal* no comment. Just let the police and coroner do what they have to do. Maybe we should go check Schmidt's room."

"Can't sir. They locked it. Off-limits. Orders of the police." Father Sullivan turned and looked out the window for a moment. "Okay, sir, I can't force you to come down. I'll be back to check periodically if you need anything."

"We'll address this all tomorrow. All heads will be clear," was the only response Father Holtz received from the bishop. *Now what does he mean?*

Father Holtz gathered his thoughts as he slowly walked back down the hall to the stairs. A gaggle of curious onlookers awaited in the front hall for a reply from Bishop Powers. Folding his hands in front of him as if he were about to deliver a parable, Father Holtz cleared his voice and looked around at the men standing in the parlor. The coroner had just walked in and was heading straight to the basement along with Detective Riley, who had arrived five minutes before.

"Gentlemen, I have spoken to Bishop Powers. He will have a statement tomorrow," Father Holtz informed them.

Two orderlies walked through the front door.

"The coroner's in the basement," Father Sullivan said, pointing to the open door off the hall. "Ned, Danny, you've waited a long time," he continued. "We understand about your signs and giving a statement. By the looks of things, a far bigger statement than anticipated has been made. Maybe you should leave for the evening. Ned, are you available tomorrow?"

"Well, I have work, but of course, I will be here for you, Father. What time do you have in mind?" Ned asked.

"Oh, let's say ten o'clock. I'll explain then. We are going with Father Holtz to file a criminal complaint. Danny, you should come along." Both boys were agreeable. "I think your protests are going to be made in a much more visible venue," Father Sullivan explained.

"I'll take tomorrow off," Ned assured Father Sullivan. "I look forward to being there, Father."

"Danny, if you can come with Ned, I'll give you a letter to take to school. Long night, boys. Now you say not a word to anyone. This is all highly confidential."

D'Amato started to ask Father Sullivan, "Father could—"

"Mr. D'Amato, not now, please," he said, turning toward the basement door.

"Absolutely, Father. Got enough for tomorrow's edition anyway," D'Amato said as he headed toward the door.

"Guess this includes me," a mellowed Mr. Newman said. "I simply can't understand why the bishop won't see me," he sort of muttered to himself.

Father Sullivan walked down to the basement.

"I'm sure Detective Riley and the coroner will be here for a while," Father Holtz said, following him down the stairs. Looking toward Detective Riley, Father Holtz asked, "Sir, any chance you'd have a few minutes? I'd like to show you something that you might find helpful. I can take you upstairs."

Father Holtz nodded for Father Sullivan to follow. The three men ascended the stairs and walked into the parlor.

"Have a seat." Father Holtz opened his hand to the sofa.

The detective sat at the end of the sofa. Father Holtz eased into the nearest chair. Reaching inside his cassock, he pulled out a letter and then handed it to Detective Riley. "Please note my name on the front." Father Holtz pointed to the signature. "Take your time. It's long, but it says it all now."

Detective Riley leaned to his right, closer to the table lamp. Looking over the top of his spectacles, he began. Father Holtz sat back in his chair, folded his hands, and waited.

Father Ben Holtz:

By the time you read this letter, it will all be over. I have come to the end. I can no longer face the person I have become.

As our Good Lord is my witness, I have no choice but to disclose the truth before I end it all. I accept the seriousness of my written statement. On the Bible, on my sacred vows, and to my Dear Lord, Jesus Christ, for whom I attest my sins, the words that follow are totally true.

I am a dreadful sinner. I have abused young boys. Billy Donovan will confirm the sins I committed. There were others. Three more to be exact. First was Johnny Smith, and I also betrayed Larry Dilland in the early '50s, Jimmy Foster in 1955, and most recently, Billy Donovan. To all four, I am truly sorry.

Bishop Powers is truly ruthless. Not only did he cover for so many priests, not only did he transfer these bad men to other parishes, but he too was an abuser. I am sure there are many victims, and I assume, like most, his weak ways go back decades. For sure, he took total advantage over the past ten years of two good boys, Ned and Danny Thornbauer. I know this for sure because I covered for him, especially his trips to his private cabin in Michigan. I believe there was no end to the lengths he would go for his own gratification.

Lastly, during the past weeks, I assisted Bishop Powers in preparing for his departure to Rome. He commanded me to destroy files of abusing priests. He instructed me to bring collection baskets for him to count and then confiscated cash for his own use. He did this for years. I have tried to find some good in this man, but as of today, I can definitely say my search has been fruitless.

Father Holtz, my friend, please accept my words of appreciation for being there for me these past few years. You are a good priest and a good person. You are the kind of priest I wish I could have been.

May our Lord be with you always,
Father Leonard Schmidt

Detective Riley shook his head like he could not believe what he had just read. "You knew him well?" the detective asked, handing the letter back to Father Holtz. Father Holtz then passed it to Father Sullivan.

"Very well. We have been working together for two years. We both handled the child abuse cases within the diocese, coordinating the priests' psychological evaluations, testing, and reassignments for the bishop. We almost always reassigned them to other parishes."

"Yes, I am aware of some of that happening but in an unofficial way. This letter sure implicates the bishop in no uncertain terms," Detective Riley said.

"Father Schmidt knew every case. He kept Bishop Powers totally informed. Bishop Powers made all the final decisions."

"If the statement from Father Schmidt is true, then the reassignment of known abusers is one issue. Probably endangering minors." Detective Riley hesitated and then stood up. "But if the abuse was included, now where's the proof? If there was actual rape and these were minors, then you are talking felony. If convicted, decades in jail. But where's the proof? Where are the witnesses?" he asked in a very procedural manner.

Father Sullivan looked at Father Holtz to see how he would respond. Like a lawyer knowing the answer before he asked the question, Father Holtz said, "Do you think the district attorney would be interested in being made aware of this?"

"District attorney? Ha, you're talking federal in this case if he was crossing state lines. Did the letter say Indiana to Michigan?"

Father Holtz looked for Father Sullivan's reaction.

"State lines. If the man above … " The detective looked up to the ceiling and pointed, referring to Bishop Powers. "If he took these boys into Michigan, you're talking the big boys, federal prosecutors, FBI.

When he hears that, he'll rock in his boots, or do I say sandals?" he said sarcastically.

Father Holtz could tell this guy wasn't Catholic.

"Regarding the witnesses. Are there any?" the detective asked. "Any who will attest to being abused?"

"I'll have two in your office tomorrow."

"You'll what?" he asked.

"Yes, absolutely. Two of the boys will file charges tomorrow," Father Holtz replied with confidence.

"Reliable witnesses?"

"Yes, reliable. They were all there with the bishop and ... " Father Holtz nodded. "And I'm one of them. I saw Bishop Powers with a boy."

The detective jerked his head back in surprise, raised his eyebrows, and made a note in his small pocket notebook. "See you tomorrow at ten o'clock. Good evening, Fathers. It's been quite a night." Detective Riley tipped his hat and then was out the door.

No sooner did the detective leave than the basement door at the end of the hall opened, made apparent by the groans of the orderlies bringing the body upstairs.

"Damn, that's a narrow stairway. Hold on, Charlie," one orderly said as he backed into the door while holding the gurney at a drastic tilt.

The coroner followed. Once through the door, they set the gurney legs down in the hall. Fathers Holtz and Sullivan stood in the hall off the foyer, watching the whole thing. The white sheet tied across the body and tightly tucked through the bar of the gurney looked eerie in the dark hallway. Charlie rested against the wall, more concerned about his aching back than getting the body to the ambulance.

"That's everything, Father. Would you please sign this release? He couldn't have been there for more than an hour. Seen many a suicide but never a priest before. Thought you guys were all happy and did no wrong. That's what I thought, but I'm no Catholic."

"Guess sometimes anyone can fall astray," Father Sullivan said, looking over at Father Holtz.

"Okay, boys, let's go. Few more steps. Careful. There will be ice."

Father Holtz and Father Sullivan stood side by side on the front step. Their breath signaled the cold December evening. Not a word. The sound of silence was broken by the slam of the back door of the ambulance behind the feet of Father Schmidt. Both priests watched as if in a surreal did-this-really-happen trance. The ambulance tires crunched through the fallen snow, pulling on to Church Street and then disappearing into the darkness beyond.

"Everybody has departed," Father Holtz said to Father Sullivan after the coroner left.

"Yes, Father. All gone. Just you and me," Father Sullivan responded with a deep breath.

"Why don't you stay the night here? We have three beautiful extra rooms. You can have your pick. Don't worry. They are at the opposite end of the hall from Bishop Powers. I'll take you up, and you can have your choice."

"Maybe I will. Been a long, long day. Don't look forward to driving back to Wabash. Besides I'm going with you tomorrow to the prosecutor's office."

"Good. Then I'll check on the bishop. How about a glass of your favorite merlot? Knock off the edge of this day?"

Father Sullivan nodded. "Thanks, Ben, that sounds good. I'll take merlot over a dark drive back to Wabash."

"Can we call it a tumultuous day?" Father Holtz asked. "Let's meet in the parlor in a few minutes. There should be enough embers to stoke up the fire," he said as he headed upstairs with Father Sullivan following.

"Sounds perfect, Ben. I could use a glass—or maybe two."

"Good. I have just what the doctor ordered," Father Holtz assured his friend.

Father Sullivan found the accommodations more than satisfactory. The room looked like a time warp with its dark empire furniture, tall ceilings, and gray plaster walls. The room gave an appearance of being older than its sixty-five years. Father Holtz walked in the other direction, toward the bishop's room. He knocked and then knocked again. Not a sound.

"Bishop Powers?" he called. No response.

He tested the knob. It turned. He pushed the door open an inch or two. Tapping the door again, not wanting to startle the bishop, he stepped inside. There was no sign of him. The light on the desk in the parlor room let off dim illumination. In the far corner of the room, Father Holtz noticed the bedroom door ajar. Light glowed through the half opening. "Bishop Powers? It's me, Father Holtz. Do you need anything? Everyone's gone now."

Garbled yet understandable, he heard, "That you, Father Schmidt? Give me a minute. Just reading."

"No, Bishop. This is Father Holtz. Remember, I was here an hour ago? I told ... Remember, I told you about Father Schmidt? Remember what happened?"

The door suddenly opened. The haggard bishop appeared, dressed in his robe.

"Sorry Bishop, your door wasn't locked, and I was"—Father Holtz touched his forehead—"a little concerned."

"Must have dozed off in my chair. Father Schmidt. Oh yes, I remember. He never was of strong character. Still a little groggy. Is everything taken care of?"

Father Holtz, feeling no reason to explain, replied, "Yes, everyone has left. We do have a guest in the house this evening. Just wanted you to know Father Sullivan is staying overnight rather than driving back to Wabash in these hazardous conditions. He's in the far spare room at the other end of the hall."

"Sullivan? What's he doing here?"

"He drove. Drove up from Wabash today—"

Bishop Powers cut him off. "Don't bother. I don't need or want to know anything more about that, that bastard, renegade priest. Never really liked Schmidt anyway. Same for Sullivan. Two of a kind as far as I'm concerned. Be around tomorrow. I may need some help before I leave town."

Father Holtz didn't respond. *Useless.*

"That's fine. I do have a ten o'clock appointment downtown. Private matter."

"Young priests don't have private matters," the bishop said. "You answer to me now," he furrowed his brow. "Now that Schmidt's gone, just be here in the afternoon. By the way, I'm feeling a little better. You got my Mass covered for tomorrow?"

"Yes, sir, I do. Bishop, there is just one other thing. I called Father Schmidt's parents in Wisconsin. The operator couldn't connect. Maybe it would be best for you to tell them? Father Schmidt looked up to you and all. I bet the police will notify them tonight … but, but I'm sure they would like to hear some words from you."

"Sure, sure, I will a little later. Bet the police have already notified them."

"I don't know that. For whatever reason, they haven't contacted me."

"Write their phone number on a piece of paper and leave it outside my door. I'll call in the morning. Father Holtz, that'll be it. I'll see you in the morning. If I need anything else, I can do things for myself. Raised on a farm, you know."

"Goodnight, Bishop Powers." *Hope he gets a good night's sleep. He's going to have a big day tomorrow.*

The fresh hickory logs popped and crackled in the fire. Father Sullivan stood with his hand on the mantel, staring at the glowing flames as if he was waiting for some answers to reach out to him from the burning embers.

"I'm back, Michael. Bishop's tucked in. His manner was strange, at times jovial. So different from this afternoon. He wasn't his usual grumpy self. Wait. I'll be right back. Left something in the kitchen." Father Holtz soon returned with a bottle of wine, two glasses, and a corkscrew in hand.

"We earned this today," he commented to his friend. Then Father Holtz continued, "The bishop acted, he acted almost unfazed. Very removed. Said nothing about Father Schmidt. Then I asked him to call Father Schmidt's parents, and he said he would in the morning."

The glow from the brick fireplace cast minimal light in the room. Shadows danced on the ceiling. The sound of the red spirit bubbled as Father Holtz poured two glasses a little over half full. Crystal clinked. Their toast was mutually silent, only revealed by the looks of exhaustion and mixed emotions on their faces.

"Do you think tomorrow is the end of this saga?" Father Holtz asked his friend.

"I would hope so. By the end, do you mean the end for the bishop?"

"No, Michael, I mean for all of us involved. Can we ever go back to normal?"

"In reality, I believe if this problem exists here, all over Indiana, it's everywhere else. Let me add, tomorrow could be a turning point. Look at it logically, Ben. In many ways, this could be the beginning of something very big."

"What do you mean?" Father Holtz asked as he savored another sip of the soothing red liquid.

"Ask yourself, how can the bishop escape his deeds?" Father Sullivan asked. "How can any abuser?"

"You're right. Probably can't. I'm definitely going to tell the prosecutor that the bishop has resigned and is leaving town Tuesday. In a way, I feel badly, as Father Schmidt confided to me about the bishop leaving for Rome. He shared a lot. Then that letter. I unleashed my wrath on him today. I do feel badly about that. Maybe, he wouldn't have—"

"We don't know, Ben, but he brought that on himself," Father Sullivan said, trying to lighten any of Father Holtz's guilt. "Ben, what you said is all true. You could not have known," he said, trying to console him with the truth. Father Sullivan took a slow sip of Merlot.

"You know, Ben, staring into the fire reminds me of being a kid again. Back in the twenties, Scout camping trips, we sat around the fire just like this with friends. We had so little, yet we had so much. I long for those simple days. No televisions, supermarkets, and fancy cars … " Father Sullivan remarked, his wine beginning to talk.

"Ben, look at all the good that can come of this if Bishop Powers is arrested, tried, and convicted like any other rapist. He will go to prison for what he did. Other abusing priests will have to change their ways. Bishops Powers will no longer be shuffling priests from parish to parish."

"I hope you are right, Michael. We do have Cardinal Cullings as our leader. Now if all this could come to the pulpit of Pope John Benedict. Michael, that's the key."

"You're right, Ben. The Vatican has to take the initiative. Defrock a known abuser. Set an example. Make priests chose between abuse, sin, and keeping their sacred vows. You know what's that called, Ben? Zero tolerance."

"Yes, Michael, also called jail."

Father Sullivan continued, "Pope John Benedict must face this crisis. Let the world know our church will not accept, not condone, not cover-up for these pedophiles. These sinful abusive priests."

"Ho, Michael! Calm down. But I agree with every word. Someone has to get to the pope."

"You're right, Ben. Pope John Benedict has to lead our church in a crusade." He paused.

"What do you mean, Michael? Crusade?"

"Battle against abusing priests." Father Sullivan took a breath, looked deep into the fire. Calmly, he looked up at Father Holtz, "We both know, Ben, that someone is Cardinal Cullings. If the pope leads our Catholic Church, it is he who can eliminate this hideous scourge … this cancer. Ten years from now, abusing priests will only be bad memories. This one case with Bishop Powers can be the turning point. Justice can be brought to the victims." Father Holtz's words started to fade along with the dying embers. "God is on our side, Michael. He is leading the way."

The two priests seized the moment. Pouring the last two glasses of wine in the bottle, they both felt a soothing calmness. A bond of friendship had been forged over this past eventful year, all for a common cause. All for the good of the church and the victims.

The next morning, Father Michael Sullivan, Father Ben Holtz, Ned and Danny Thornbauer met at Detective Riley's office. They discussed the events of the night before. After signing the complaints, Detective Riley escorted them to the federal district attorney's office. The truths about Bishop Powers, Father Schmidt, and the cover-ups were disclosed.

"Gentlemen, I must first warn you that what you say here today, you will eventually be questioned about under oath," Federal Prosecutor Daniel J. Brink warned.

"I agree," Father Sullivan said.

Father Holtz, Ned, and Danny confirmed the same. The complete litany of misdeeds of Bishop Powers was addressed. Father Sullivan related the horrors experienced by boys of St. Thomas Moore at the hands of Father Jerome Jaeger. He described how he and his pastor, Father Warren, met with Bishop Powers and pleaded for Father Jaeger to be removed. He informed them about Father Jaeger's one month of psychiatric evaluation and transfer to another parish to teach and work with children.

In descriptive detail, Ned told about the salacious sexual acts Bishop Powers committed. Danny and Ned both told of the trips to the cabin in Michigan. They told how they were coerced to perform sexual deeds in the name of "love." Father Holtz related his suspicions of the bishop's excursions to the cabin and then Ned's informing him that he had not only been molested nine years ago but that the bishop was now preying on Danny.

When asked by the prosecutor to describe what he witnessed, Father Holtz explained to the district attorney his daily regret for not interfering between the bishop and Danny that day.

"You should have regret. That does not speak well of you. However, you are a material witness, which would be most helpful if this were to go to trial."

Federal Prosecutor Daniel Brink asked if all would stand by their statements in a court of law.

"It's easy, sir, to tell the truth," Ned replied.

"Your statements are all very strong and convincing."

"Don't forget the birthmark above his waist. Danny and I both saw it," Ned added.

"We have all of your statements, I can assure you."

"Mr. Brink, there is one issue. Bishop Powers is leaving for Rome tomorrow. He has been appointed to receive a position in the Vatican. He does have friends higher up."

"Tomorrow?" Brink asked, looking concerned. "That gives us no time. I'll have to act today. Thank you, Father Holtz. I think that will be all, gentlemen. We will expedite from here. The quick arm of the law may be put into full use. If you will just sign the final statements for Mrs. Petersen. Thank you and good day, gentlemen. I have much to do."

Fathers Sullivan and Holtz walked out of the prosecutor's office along with Ned and Danny. "Well, gentlemen, the prosecutor was convincing. He took our words seriously."

"Yes, he did, Michael. And, did you hear him? He's going to act today."

"I commend you both for your convictions and willingness to do what is right," Father Sullivan said to Ned and Danny.

"Thank you, Fathers. You are good priests. Danny and I are proud to know you both."

"Remember, boys, when he is arrested, this isn't over. You will probably need to testify."

"Let's go, Danny. Got to get you to school," Ned said.

As Ned and Danny walked away, Father Sullivan and Father Holtz stood alone on the front steps of the courthouse. "Guess I better get back to the rectory. I'll be the only priest there. Oh, of course, along with Bishop Powers. At least for today."

"After tonight, you may be the only one. I better drive south. Father Warren's going to want to hear all about this. He's been in Wabash all weekend. He'll worry about me."

Father Holtz said, "Well, ol' friend, we've done our best. I think the victims will now see the beginning of justice."

"Let's hope this curse is eliminated and there won't be any other victims," Father Sullivan said.

They gave each other a two-handed handshake and exchanged pats on the back. Father Holtz stood for a moment and watched Father Sullivan pull his car in front of the courthouse, give a hearty wave, turn south, and disappear around the corner on his way back to Wabash. Father Holtz was warmed by Father Sullivan's waving hand outside the driver's side window. *We did something special together, all for the good of our church and the victims.*

Father Holtz—December 8, 1958

The morning was long. Noon passed. Just after 1:00, having concluded the extensive details of the case, the accusations, and the reliable witnesses, Prosecutor Brink walked across the hall to request a warrant for Bishop Powers' arrest. The warrant was given to the US Marshal, who was ordered to deliver it that very afternoon.

Meanwhile, Father Holtz returned to the rectory. He was anxious in anticipation of a visitor that afternoon. He was not hungry and had a feeling of relief except for a real concern for Bishop Powers. Father

Holtz sat alone in his most comfortable chair. He tried to read. His mind wandered. His immediate attention was the bishop, who was spending his last hours in the rectory, preparing to leave Tuesday for his safe haven in Rome.

At 1:05 p.m., Father Holtz walked up the wide center staircase. His pace was slow as he approached Bishop Powers' room. He knocked. "Good afternoon. It's Father Holtz."

The door immediately opened. "Good afternoon, Father Holtz. Quite a sick spell we've had these past few days. Come on in. Could you have Sister prepare a nice lunch in the main dining room? It's late, and I haven't had anything to eat today. Just working on a few last-minute things before I leave tomorrow."

"Sure, whatever you like."

"Maybe you can join me."

Caught totally off guard by the invitation, Father Holtz could only accept.

"Then we'll talk about a couple other last-minute details I'd like you to handle before I leave tomorrow. I may take the train to Indianapolis. We'll see. You let me finish up here, and I'll see you in the dining room, let's say 1:30. Now tell Sister. Could be our last supper, Father," Bishop Powers said, half in jest.

"Yes, Your Excellency, last supper. Never know who might be coming to see us. Will see you in, let's say, thirty, forty minutes. Give sister some time to prepare your ... " Father Holtz paused. "Prepare your last lunch." Bishop Powers smiled. *He seems to be preparing for the wrong trip*, Father Holtz thought. *Closure has yet to arrive.*

"Good afternoon, Sister," Father Holtz said, walking into the kitchen. "Bishop Powers would like a good lunch at 1:30. He invited me to join him."

"What would he like?"

"He likes everything you prepare. Make it special. It could be his last here."

"Last here?" she asked.

"Oh, you know. His conference in Rome."

"Oh, of course, I see what you mean. I'll make one of his favorites. I just got back from the store."

"And maybe plenty of coffee. He'll need to stay awake."

"Glad to see he invited you. That's unusual. It must be a special occasion."

"Oh yes, Sister. Surely is special. A day he'll never forget."

Marshal Gerald Cooper picked up the signed federal warrant for Bishop Powers' arrest that had been dropped off at the prosecutor's office. A note was attached that directed him to deliver it at exactly 2:00.

Sister Joelda set the table for lunch. Father Holtz was waiting in the dining room when the now-jovial bishop entered.

"No need to wait. Begin," the bishop said.

"Would you say grace?" Father Holtz asked him.

"Of course, My honor, Father. Bless us, O Lord … "

Father Holtz was pleased to hear the bishop pray.

"It's been a good tenure here at St. Leonard's. I'm appreciative of all your assistance, along with Father Schmidt, God bless his soul. I have not received an acceptance of my resignation from Cardinal Cullings. I assume it will be this week. All will work out fine. I'm looking forward to going to Rome," Bishop Powers said almost gleefully. "Someday, I hope you can visit, Father Holtz."

"Thank you. I assure you that if you arrive, you can count on me."

"I was thinking later, Father Holtz."

"Oh yes, sure.

Father Holtz just listened as Bishop Powers shared his kind words. *It's almost as if he has completely blocked yesterday's confession from his mind. Amazing.* Father Holtz felt a moment of relief. In his mind, he knew he had not only confessed his sin yesterday, but he had also warned Bishop Powers that indeed the long years of abuse were over and justice would soon follow. *Didn't he listen?*

Meanwhile, an unmarked car pulled up in front of the rectory. A tall man in a long gray coat stepped out from the passenger's side. "Let's get this done," he said to his partner. "I've been looking forward to this for years." Marshal Gerald Cooper pulled his topcoat tight around the collar. They walked side by side up to the front door. The tall man knocked twice.

Moments later, Sister Joelda stepped into the dining room. "Excuse me, Bishop, there's someone here to see you."

"Who is it?"

"Says his name is Cooper, Marshal Cooper, sir. He has another man with him. I think he said Karsavich. Anyway, they want to see you, your Excellency."

"Probably wants a donation. Tell him to wait. I'm having lunch," the bishop responded nonchalantly.

"He says he needs to see you now."

"Okay, show him in. Excuse me, Father," the bishop said, standing up, wiping his mouth with a napkin. "Always someone looking for money."

Father Holtz could not move. He knew what was about to happen. He folded his hands and waited at the table.

The marshal walked to the entrance of the dining room. Looking at the bishop, he said, "Bishop Powers, I presume?" The marshal took a few steps forward and handed him the warrant. Karsavich watched, clearly seeing the look of concern on the bishop's face. Father Holtz remained seated with his arms now folded across his chest.

Bishop Powers read the warrant. "What? There must be a mistake! Are you saying now? Not now. I'm not going anyplace. I haven't done anything wrong. I want to see my lawyer."

The marshal replied, "Bishop, you will be able to call your lawyer. Right now I have orders to serve this warrant and bring you down to the courthouse."

The bishop balked. "Young man, sir, I am not leaving."

The marshal replied, "You are coming with me now, sir. You have no choice."

"Father Holtz, tell him I can't go now. I'm leaving for Rome tomorrow."

"The only place you are leaving for, your Highness, is jail. If I may be so abrupt."

"Did you know about this, Holtz?"

Looking very sheepish, Father Holtz replied, "Bishop Powers, I expected something like this would happen. Everyone has warned you."

The marshal spoke up, "Bishop, read the warrant. Bishop Powers, you are initially being charged with seven counts of sexual abuse of minors."

"Here I'm trying to be good to those boys, helping this diocese, and this is what I receive?" Bishop Powers slowly walked over to Father Holtz. Pointing his finger, he shook it in the young priest's face and glared at him with despicable distain. He leaned close and whispered with hot breath into Father Holtz's ear. Father Holtz did not back away. "It was you! I knew it all the time!" His face got red. "You were the mole who brought all this down. May you rot forever in hell, you deceitful bastard. I should have gotten rid of you when I could." Bishop Powers walked over to the marshal. "I need some time. Going upstairs. I need some time to get some things together."

"That will be fine. Take all the time you need. You have ten minutes."

Bishop Powers proceeded upstairs. Marshal Cooper nodded at Karsavich. Karsavich followed the bishop.

Father Holtz stood up and walked to the window in the dining room. The sky was as gray as the mood within the rectory.

Soon Bishop Powers returned. He walked to the closet. Buttoning his black overcoat, he walked over to the marshal. He looked into the dining room. Father Holtz turned and walked toward the foyer to bid farewell to Bishop Powers.

With one last glare, Bishop Powers sent hate into Father Holtz's eyes. Then he looked at the marshal with equal disdain. "Marshal, let's get this over with." As he stepped to the door, the bishop said, "You haven't heard the last of me, Holtz. I will get you for this." The bishop looked back and walked away with the marshal.

Father Holtz stepped to the window in a state of shock. His heart pounding, he watched the marshal's car pull away. Father Holtz could see the bishop through the back window of the car. *I think Bishop Powers is going to be gone for a long, long time.*

Herman Stahl—December 9, 1958

Herman Stahl lit the pile of wood before he began digging another grave. The ground was frozen and needed to thaw. While waiting that early afternoon for the fire to burn down, he gazed across the span of tombstones—a lifetime of work. He clenched his pipe tightly in his half-toothless mouth.

Dead brown grass peaked through patches of snow. The gravedigger leaned against the giant oak tree, smaller now without the huge limb that fell in the storm this past week. Bent with a stoop, slight limp, and slow gate after fifty-two years of digging graves and caretaking Friends Cemetery, Herman Stahl caught a glimpse of a peculiar looking object in front of a small headstone. He pulled long and hard on his pipe and then stood and meandered toward the grave, followed by the smoke from his pipe.

Herman Stahl drew closer, he saw what he thought to be a brown blanket. Having cared for the site for the past twenty-four years, Herman knew it could not have been left by any next of kin of Gordon Yoder. *That boy, we'll never know how he died. He was just left behind. Has no one.* A few paces away, he could clearly identify a burlap feedbag. His brow furrowed as he stood before the tombstone. Dirt, weather, and dead moss had found its way into some sides and turns of the chiseled and now faint letters.

Hands on his knee, Herman eased himself down, kneeling before Gordon Yoder's headstone. Slowly, he reached out and lifted back the bag with his gnarled and cracked fingers. *What the hell? Cigar box.* Carefully, he picked up the box and turned it around while slowly lifting the lid with his thumbs. Herman instantly was startled by the grotesque severed hand he saw inside the box. "Judas Priest! Oh my God!" He thrust himself back, sending an excruciating jolt of pain through his knees. "Oh, my God! Holy shit!"

The sight startled his senses. He dropped the box, and it rested on the sack, the lid open against the stone. Raising his hand to his chest, he gasped for air while staring at the pale shrunken skin. Palm down, the fingers were jammed against the back of the box. *My God! Son of a bitch!*

"What can … what can this … " he spoke aloud in frantic alarm, with nobody around to hear.

Frozen dark blood covered most of the bottom of the box. Smears were on the side. His hand shaking, he extended his finger, first touching the blood-covered diamond on the middle finger. Carefully, he slid his finger above the thumb exposing the fingers of the severed hand. Twisting his head to the right, he saw what looked like letters. Blood-covered … BZ. He scratched the blood away with his nail. RZ was visible like the day. *What the hell. A tie clasp?*

Herman braced his left hand on the ground, relieving some strain on his aching knees. The old man closed the lid, pushed the box back against the stone, and lifted the sack over the top. Bracing himself with both hands on the headstone, Herman lifted a knee and then agonizingly pushed himself upward and stood before the headstone. A few moments passed. Then he quickly walked back to the maintenance shed. *Gotta call the sheriff.*

Herman Stahl jumped into his truck as if being chased by a wild dog. Shifting into first gear, Herman drove his green pickup hurriedly back to his house, a half mile west of the cemetery in the direction of the reform school. Figuring this would be a county matter, he frantically flipped through the phonebook and made a call. Having alerted the sheriff, within ten minutes, he was back at the cemetery.

Herman waited by his truck, which he parked in the drive by the big oak, about thirty yards from the grave. He paced back and forth for a long five minutes like an expectant father. *Holy shit! In all my days, can't believe.* He saw two sheriff cars drive into the cemetery. The second car flashing the red bulb on top of the car. The siren screaming. He walked over and stood by the grave. As the officers approached, they noticed the strange sight in front of the grave.

Herman said, "Just like I found it a short time ago."

Accustomed to the harsh realities of accidents and trauma, both officers were startled at the grotesque finding inside the box. Using his writing pen, sergeant moved the hand, which held the tie clasp. "Belongs to the hand," the young officer said.

"How'd you figure that out, Sherlock?" the sergeant shot back, looking over his shoulder at his junior officer.

"I'll get my Brownie camera. It's brand new." The younger officer ran back to his car.

"That's a pregnant idea. Don't forget the film!"

Snap, focus, *snap.* Randall Zilbar's left hand was recorded forever.

Within less than fifteen minutes, the two officers were back at the sheriff's department. The senior officer commanded, "Call the hospital. Check to see if they have any patients with a missing hand."

"I'll tell 'em it's the left."

"Brilliant detective work there, Joe Friday," the senior snapped back. "Be sure and ask if he still has the right hand."

The sheriff's office connected the finding with Randall Zilbar, who was recovering in the hospital.

The young officer put his hand over the phone's receiver. "Sergeant, they have a patient with no hand. I told 'em we've got a left hand. He still has his right hand though."

Sergeant shook his head. "Great detective work there, Mr. Holmes. I'm gonna recommend you for the FBI."

Herman Stahl later read the police department's official statement, which appeared in the *Plain Dealer*. *Randall Zilbar assaulted outside his home late Thursday, December 4, 1958. Robbery was the apparent motive. The attacker remains at large.* Somewhere between the sheriff's report and the identification by the Wabash City police, the presence of the diamond ring, the clasp, and the hand were not mentioned. It was most surprising to Herman when he read the newspaper account. He didn't understand why the police didn't disclose the location of the cigar box along with the contents. Not wanting to be involved with the police or the victim, Herman Stahl would take the secret to his grave.

CHAPTER 114

THE COVER-UP

Randall Zilbar—December 8, 1958

FOR the first time since his assault, Randall Zilbar agreed to talk with the police. His feelings of coherency awoke that Monday morning. Continuous IVs helped control the dreadful pain. He thought he could feel his hand until he realized the large white wrappings at the end of his arm revealed the undeniable truth. Knowing the police were only hours away, Randall Zilbar strategized his plan.

Absent of shame or remorse for the death of Gordon Yoder, Randall Zilbar planned his explanation for the life-changing event. Identifying Bernard Bednar as the assailant was the least of his problems. Explaining the reason the cigar box, containing his severed hand, his ring, and possibly, the tie clasp, had been left at the gravesite of Gordon Yoder, was the most difficult challenge. However, in the end he knew it would be his word against the strange, unknown attendant at the reform school, Bernard Bednar.

"Did I say who did it?" he asked his wife when she came into the hospital room.

"Well, kinda, but not really. You mumbled, 'the ugly one, ugly one,' quite a few times yesterday when you first started to talk, but you were on so many drugs." She leaned over. "Who did this to you, Randall? Tell me who did this."

He tried to look back four nights ago, but it was too terrifying to recall the moment that blade flew down with uninhibited fury. "It was dark.

Couldn't see," he mumbled. The pain intensifying, he dozed off. Randall Zilbar knew he was at the crossroads of yet another lie. He closed his eyes in the pursuit of unconsciousness.

Hours later, the detective arrived. Zilbar instructed Elenore to leave the room. Then Randall exposed the awful truth. Torn between identifying Bernard and the link to the Gordon Yoder murder or lying, he vowed to himself to quiet Bednar in his own way later.

He told the officer, "I couldn't get a look at his face. It was dark. He wore a hat pulled low over his eyes. I've never seen him before. Couldn't catch his face. It all took only seconds when he rushed me. All I can see is the large knife high overhead. I do remember one thing. The guy said, 'Give me your cash and watch.' His coat was long and dark. He had a dark beard. Never saw his eyes. Everything went blank. The next thing I remember was waking up here. This bed, and oh, oh the goddamn pain. You have to catch this guy. I want the bastard to pay for … for … Look. I'm ruined!" He looked down at the huge white wrap at the end of his wrist. "Oh God! What am I going to do?"

"Calm down, Mr. Zilbar. Calm down." The officer patted Zilbar's leg.

"You tell me, how do I do anything? Baseball? How do I play tennis, golf, anything? Can't lift … lift a … a goddamn chair! Everything with one hand? Hell no. Get the bastard!"

The police found it hard to believe he couldn't describe a face. Outside the room, the detective said, "But there was a full moon."

Although his mind swirled in and out of semi-consciousness, Randall Zilbar knew he was right. *If they find the clasp and connect it to Bednar, they might go back to Yoder. All will unravel.* He continually reminded himself, *He's got the tie clasp!* Not identifying Bednar would only leave the police with the conclusion that the motive was a failed robbery attempt. *Wolfe's gone. Krueger's dead. Time. Time. I'll make sure Bednar and Atkins never talk. Nobody will deny my credibility.* He knew Bednar had trapped him. His adrenaline flowing, Zilbar scooted himself up in bed with his dirty secret about Gordon Yoder.

Bednar will never step forward. There's always Lucco.

CHAPTER 115

MAKING THE CONNECTION

GEORGE GRIFFIN—DECEMBER 9, 1958

GEORGE Griffin pondered the possible connection between Father Warren and Bishop Powers. *If what Gary says about Bishop Powers is true and Powers covered up and transferred Jaeger, then Father Warren could be aware. Gotta make the call.*

George Griffin stopped at the Rock City Bar and Grill for lunch. He had already called and informed the school secretary that he wouldn't be in today. George liked the atmosphere of Rock City. He knew he'd never meet a teacher there. George sat alone in his usual spot at the end of the bar.

Gilbert was working the day shift. "Scotch up or on the rocks, George?"

"Too early there, Gil. Just a turkey club and coffee."

"Lots on your mind, George? Too early in the day?"

"Yeah, Gil, lots on my mind, but too early for scotch. Later."

Three cups of coffee and an hour and half at the bar was plenty of time for George to construct his plan. Taking his last sip of coffee, he stood and walked back down the hall to the phone booth. Behind the glass-and-wood doors, privacy was complete. He flipped through the yellow pages for Catholic churches. "St. Anthony's, St. Barnard's." *Here it is.* "St. Thomas Moore." He dropped a nickel in the slot.

"Good afternoon. St. Thomas Moore."

"Hello, ma'am. Father Warren please. Tell him George Griffin's calling."

Within just a minute, Father Warren picked up the phone.

"This you, George? Been a while."

"Yes, Father, except when you heard my confession last month, but I didn't give you my name."

"Now, George, I always recognize your voice."

Oh no. George cleared his throat but didn't respond. "Father, I would like to know if I could stop by this afternoon, maybe talk privately and confidentially."

"Why of course, George. Let's see, it's 1:35. I've got ... Wait, that'll work. How about four thirty."

"I'll be there, Father."

"Good. Say, George, if it is really important, personal, we could meet in church. Nobody will be there at that hour. I like the solemnity. I spend a lot of time there by myself. Actually, George," Father Warren rubbed his chin. "I would like to share something with you."

"Sounds good, Father. Four thirty. Thanks."

"God bless, George."

Father Warren hung up the phone. He thought a moment. *I'll be in church. Perfect timing. I cannot put this off any longer.*

Father Warren walked upstairs and knocked on Father Sullivan's door. "Father, you have a moment?"

Father Sullivan opened the door. "Yes, Father, of course."

"Michael, would you be available this evening to hear my confession? It's been a while."

Not expecting a request, "Sure, Father. I would be honored."

"How about 6:00pm in the church?"

"Expect me there, Father."

"Thank you, Michael. This is very important to me."

Father Sullivan thought, *Important, why so sudden?*

Having confirmed his visit with Father Warren, George slid open the folding doors of the phone booth, walked back to the bar, and checked his watch. Father Warren walked upstairs and

"Let's have just one, George?"

"Straight up. A slow sipper."

After a half hour, George thanked Gil, placed two dollars and two quarters on the bar, and headed for the front door.

"See ya next time, George."

George Griffin tipped his hat. He left his car parked in front of Rock City. *Little walk will do me good.* Standing at the corner of Market and Wabash Streets, he looked up the hill toward the courthouse. From there, he could see the Great Emancipator stoically protecting the hill overlooking the city. He thought, *Lincoln's looking out the corner of his eye at St. Thomas Moore. His brow must be furrowed.*

Griffin meandered up the street and then stopped and stood in front of the majestic statue of Lincoln. He looked up at the twin spires on the brick church kitty-corner from the courthouse. Further to the east, the school was in clear view, towering over the rectory. Knowing there were a couple hours until he would meet Father Warren, Griffin turned west on Hill Street toward the Carnegie Library. He walked a block and entered.

"Good afternoon, Mrs. Bush," George Griffin said to the friendly and helpful librarian. He then sauntered over to the history section and pulled out volume three of *Lincoln* by Nicolay and Hay. Griffin then walked over to a single table by the window and lost himself within the pages of the book about the man from Indiana.

Time lapsed. George Griffin enjoyed the solitude of the library—a perfect place to be alone and read. Soon, he checked his watch giving himself five more minutes before heading to St. Thomas Moore. *4:20.*

"Enjoy the rest of your day, Mr. Griffin."

"Will do. Tell your husband, George, I said hello." *Great first name.*

George Griffin left the library and walked down the street, tipped his hat to Mr. Lincoln, crossed the street, and entered the church. The front doors looked welcoming. Inside, he blessed himself, genuflected, and then knelt down in the back pew. Just two lights overhead dimly illuminated the sanctuary. Darkness was falling outdoors. *Almost four thirty. Bless me. May I say the right words to this good priest.*

The sound of a door opening echoed from the far corner of the church. Griffin watched as the white-haired figure in a long black cassock walked between the communion rail and front pews toward the center aisle. After genuflecting and then pausing, Father Warren stood. Griffin noticed the reverent bow of his head and sign of the cross. Griffin gave the priest time and watched him take the left pew about twelve rows from the communion rail.

George walked up the center aisle. "Good afternoon, Father," he whispered in a low, slow voice.

"Same to you, George."

"No, no. Stay seated, Father."

"Here, George, sit here." Father Warren patted the pew seat. "You see why I suggested this solemn place. I find peace here."

"Yes, I can see, Father. Very peaceful. I'll have to also come here alone someday."

"Good for the soul, George."

Father Warren spoke in his clear, gentle voice, "You're looking good, George. What's on your mind? Tell me."

"Father, please allow me to be direct."

"Why, of course. Between you and me. You know I have lots of practice in the confessional."

They both smiled.

George paused and then took a breath. "Father, I have heard over, oh, let's say the last several months about your assistant, Father Jaeger. Rumors, innuendos, and then accusations he was molesting boys, maybe one or more in your parish. It's all been very hush-hush and secretive. Of course, we both know what happened last Tuesday."

"Yes, George. Father Jaeger is in very serious condition at Union Hospital in Terre Haute." Father Warren thought and then said, "For some reason, I expected this from you, George. Surprised not sooner, but"—he raised his finger—"yes, it's true. However, Father Jaeger was transferred last spring. Well, better yet, he first left here last spring. His reassignment was official this summer. Bishop Powers transferred him to another parish west of Terre Haute." He looked up at the crucifix over the altar. "Most unfortunate. Poor man."

George felt more at ease now that Father Warren was accepting his forthrightness about Father Jaeger.

"Can we be, as you would say, George, totally off the record? By that

I mean this is between you and me," Father Warren asked. "Totally confidential. Just like confession, a seal between you and me."

"Of course, Father. No doubt. Totally off the record. Confidential. Just between friends."

Both heard the front door of the church open and then slowly close. Father Warren turned toward the back. He noticed an elderly man genuflect and kneel in the back of the church.

The priest tapped Griffin's arm. "No bother. Roy Porter. He stops every day about this time. Good man. Where do I begin? Let's see. I mentioned Bishop Powers."

Griffin nodded.

"Bishop Powers governs this diocese. He made the decision to reassign Father Jaeger. I had no say. George, we have a hierarchy in the Catholic Church. Pope John Benedict is here." Father raised his hand. "Cardinal Cullings—I'm sure you know of our Eminence in Indianapolis—is here. Then there's Bishop Powers. And, well, at the bottom of the ladder, there's me. That's the way structure works in the Catholic Church."

"One covers the other?"

"Is that a question, George?"

Griffin nodded.

"Yes, if you want to put it that way. Yes, one covers the other. There is an exception, or should I say intention? I do not want to cover for Father Jaeger, but"—Father Warren tilted his head—"I must, I was told."

"Let me be open with you, Father. I was in South Wayne on Friday."

Father Warren raised his eyebrows as if to ask a question. A concerned look came across the priest's face.

Griffin didn't detect the nuance. "I have an old friend. A reporter, Gary D'Amato in South Wayne. He informed me about a priest from Wabash, and what he alleges is a possible cover-up by Bishop Powers."

"I see," Father Warren cautiously replied.

"My friend implied, and that's all, that he has heard accusations over several years that Bishop Powers may also be guilty. I mean not just of a cover-up."

George looked toward the altar. Dim light left the crucifix unprotected from the darkness.

"He suggested that Bishop Powers may also be covering up his own transgressions."

Father Warren looked straight ahead and made the sign of the cross. "God bless us all," he murmured.

For some time, George Griffin and Father Warren were silent. Father Warren prayed and thought to himself. He struggled in silence as George Griffin sat by his side.

"Decisions are sometimes less painful when made in the presence of ... in this holy place." Father Warren looked over at Griffin. "I need to talk openly." He paused and rubbed his chin. "I've known Bishop Powers since we were in the seminary together back in 1909-1911. He's not a principled person. I'm sorry to say, Bishop Powers is not a good man. I knew that then, and after Sunday, I now know for sure that this will all come out, as I believe this latest incident will be Bishop Powers' demise." Father Warren looked straight ahead at the altar. "Yes, George, I confirm there is a connection between Wabash and South Wayne. Father Jaeger indeed abused boys. Several we know for sure. How many beyond? We may never know. There was a definite cover-up in South Wayne. Yes, we are connected just as you concluded."

"Father, do you wish you would have come forward sooner?"

"George, I can make the case that I should have defied Bishop Powers and spoken more openly about Father Jaeger, but I didn't. You see, George, one of my vows is obedience. I kept that vow well until Sunday evening."

"What do you mean, Father?"

Father Warren looked at George Griffin, wondered, paused then said, "I was with Bishop Powers Sunday evening. I needed to address him not only Father Jaeger, but also discuss our past between Bishop Powers and myself. As I said, I have known him since the seminary. Excuse me..." Father Warren turned to his side and coughed several times.

"You okay, Father?"

"Oh yes." Father Warren went on. "I needed to straighten an issue with Bishop Powers, so I went to see him. I did give him a call. He expected me that evening. That's when we met."

"Met where? His rectory?"

"Yes, George. We ironed out an issue."

George gave the priest a discerning look, trying to better understand the connection. He could see the difficulty Father Warren was having divulging a secret about his superior. About what he had seen, about what he hadn't done.

"George, let me answer your question. The purpose of our meeting here tonight, I do know much about Bishop Powers, most of which I will take to my grave. I believe from what I know happened these past months and actually over the past several years, Bishop Powers will live with his sins for the rest of his life. However, there is good in all of us, George. Let me explain."

"Father, you say Sunday night? Would that have been around five thirty to six o'clock? It was snowing. You wore a long black coat. You walked up the back stairs of the rectory?"

"Yes, George, it was about that time. How do you know?"

"I was there, Father. Gary D'Amato suggested I be in South Wayne. Be there to observe. Of course, I didn't know it was you. I was in the hotel across the street. I saw someone walk up the street, stop at the back of the rectory, and then go into the darkness of the back stairs. You must have been inside with the bishop maybe forty-five, fifty minutes. You left with a briefcase. Now I understand the long relationship with Bishop Powers, but why the briefcase, Father? You didn't take it in when you walked up the stairs."

Father Warren didn't answer. "What prompted D'Amato to call you?" he asked.

"He knew one of the accusers was going to come to confront Bishop Powers that late afternoon. He told me a Ned and his brother. I think his last name was Thornbauer."

"What was the name?" Father Warren asked.

"Ned Thornbauer. Don't know his younger brother's name."

Father Warren rubbed his forehead with his fingers. He looked directly at George and then back to the altar. There was silence between the two men. Patiently, George Griffin waited for Father Warren to see if he'd speak first.

"Are you saying these two boys were in the rectory? The same building I was in? Same time?"

"Yes, Father, I am. I know for sure they were both there."

George saw tears on the priest's cheeks and placed his hand on Father Warren's shoulder. Father Warren looked at George, who was now kneeling beside him. He placed his hand on George's arm. "This remains between you and me, George." Father Warren thought of Ida and his two grandsons. Father thought of his son, his namesake. Looking directly at the altar, *I cannot tell, cannot disclose Ida's name. No, Thomas,* he said to himself. *Do not break Ida's trust.*

George Griffin noticed the look on Father Warren's face as if he wanted to say more. "Yes, Father, forever between you and me. But, Father, just one unanswered question. The black briefcase?"

Father thought a moment, "George, please understand, there is a connection between Father Jaeger, Bishop Powers, and myself, as I just told you. Your friend, Mr. D'Amato was right." Father Warren stopped, turned his head away from Griffin, and coughed several times.

"Are you all right, Father?"

"Oh yes, just a cold coming on." Father wiped his nose with his white handkerchief. "As I was saying, you now understand the connection. The black briefcase you ask?" Father Warren looked directly at George Griffin. "Please understand, George, I must keep this connection of the briefcase to myself."

"Yes, Father. Sure, as you wish."

Father Warren added, "Bishop Powers and I continued to talk, revisiting our relationship and connection to the past. I did say that he and I were in the seminary together. I have known him a long time. It was not until this incident with Father Jaeger that our connection resumed, bringing us to where we are today." Wanting to say more, while holding back his secret about Ida Thornbauer, he continued, "George, there are many bad people in this world. However, we must give credit where credit is due. I truly believe there is some good in everyone. In spite of the abuse, the cover-up, and Bishop Powers' indiscretions, he, too, has good in him. He has governed our diocese, contributed many positive reforms, and has shown generosity for others on occasion. That I know for sure."

Father Warren slowly stood. "I hope I have answered your questions, George." Father Warren placed his hand on George's arm. "God bless you." That said Father Warren walked to the end of the pew. Raising his right hand and bracing himself, he genuflected and then proceeded toward the side entrance.

George Griffin made the sign of the cross. "Dear Lord, give me the strength to hold the secrets of this good man." He remained in the pew and thought of the abused boys, the wickedness of Bishop Powers, and the wounded priest, Father Jaeger, in the hospital. He reflected on Father Warren's comment about 'good in all of us'. Raising his hand, he placed his elbows on the pew and bowed his head in prayer. *That good man was tortured for many years regarding his knowledge of Bishop Powers.*

Most of the church was now hidden in darkness. George's mind wandered, as he thought of his love for Gretchen, his own loneliness, and despair. He heard a noise in back of the church, shuffling of feet. Turning, he saw, from the corner of his eye, a man in a long coat standing in the center aisle. George watched. Slowly, Roy Porter genuflected, turned, and walked away.

After making the sign of the cross, George Griffin stood, walked to the center aisle, genuflected, and went to the back of the church. There he stopped and looked back toward the altar. He noticed Father Warren kneeling in the second pew. George Griffin turned and walked out the front door of the church.

"Oh good evening, Father," George Griffin said to Father Sullivan, who was walking up the steps.

"And good evening to you, George. Fancy meeting you here." Father tipped his hat.

"Making a visit, Father?"

"Oh yes. Prayer helps us all, especially in this solemn church."

"Same here, Father, just a visit. Must admit, it's been quite a week, especially this weekend."

"You can say that again. It sure has."

"Have a nice visit, Father."

"Thank you. Let's hope it's a good visit." Father Sullivan stepped to the door and looked back at George Griffin. *Didn't think George Griffin makes special visits to church. He must have had something important on his mind.*

Father Sullivan stepped into the church. A slight chill permeated the dark interior. Two ceiling fixtures cast a dim light across the center of the church. Father blessed himself, genuflected, and walked over to the far side confessional. Taking off his long black coat and brimmed hat, he laid the coat over the last pew, tightened his stole across his chest then stepped into the confessional. Switching on a dim light hidden above his chair, Father Sullivan sat back and prayed for the confession he was about to hear. For several minutes, he thought about so much that was on his mind. He thought most about Father Warren.

Several minutes passed. Quiet, darkness encased the confessional. Father Sullivan heard the side confessional door open. He waited a moment, then slid open the small confessional door. Only the black curtain separated Father Sullivan and the penitent on the other side.

"In the name of the Father, Son, and the Holy Ghost. Bless me, Father for I am a sinner. It has been some time since my last confession."

Father Sullivan did not ask the length of time to Father Warren on the other side of the black curtain. There was a pause. "Go ahead, Father. I'm here to listen."

"My sin is that of omission. Something I have held inside for over fifty years. We all have secrets in our lives. I am no different. When I'm in this holy place, I feel closer to God. The confessional inspires me to admit my weaknesses, my sins. I need to confess after so many years of denial, my omission regarding Bishop Powers. I have also committed a second sin. A grave sin. I have lived with guilt. I have lived with it the better part of my life." Father Warren paused. "You need to know, Father. I met with Bishop Powers Sunday evening in his rectory. Yes, two days ago around six o'clock."

"Same time I was there with Father Holtz," Father Sullivan responded.

"I was with the bishop for maybe an hour." Father Warren rubbed his chin. "I've known Bishop Powers since we were in the seminary together back in 1909-1911. He's not a principled person, I'm sorry to say. Although Sunday, I did see some kindness."

Father Warren continued, "It was so long ago, but I can see it like yesterday. A cold January. Bishop Powers and I were both seminarians. 1911, as I recall. I was walking up the side aisle in the chapel and heard some words. They weren't clear. Then I heard very clearly--'No, please, not again!' I continued to the sacristy. Over in the corner, down a short hall, I saw Lawrence Powers--that's the bishop's first name--with an altar boy. There was resistance, and then..." Father Warren struggled with the words. "I'll just say, they were in…it was horrible. I don't even want to tell you what I saw. They didn't see me. I watched for just a moment, trying to be sure what I was seeing. I didn't move. Then I had to do something. That poor boy. 'Lawrence,' I said. 'Stop! What are you doing? Stop now!' I could see the startled look on Lawrence's face. He stopped immediately. I didn't say another word. I turned and left. My heart was racing. If I could go back forty-five years, I would, I'm sure I would have handled it differently. You know, I should have confronted Lawrence directly, and taken the altar boy away from him, but I didn't. I saw them and I failed to pull the boy away. That's my omission. That is my sin."

Father Sullivan could tell the difficulty Father Warren was having divulging a long held secret about his superior. About what he had seen. About what he hadn't done.

Father Warren continued, "Two years later, Lawrence Powers attended my ordination, not because of me though. Until that day, I never told a soul about that horrid January day. About one hour after the service, I saw him standing outside alone. He was smoking a cigarette. I walked over and said, 'Lawrence, I've never forgotten that day. The day I saw you in the sacristy. You were so wrong. Why, Lawrence? Why?' He did not reply. Not one word. I've never understood. He stared at me, then simply turned and walked away. I decided to avoid any confrontation, but I still wanted him to know I hadn't forgotten. I knew. I should have forced an answer then. An apology, but, no I didn't."

Father Sullivan knew Father Warren was a man of conviction. *Yes, he should have.*

Father Warren continued, "I saw him again in…I believe 1938 or 1939. Can't remember the year exactly. We were at a conference together. The subject never came up between us. Again, I wish I would have confronted him."

Father Sullivan responded, "Father, I do realize, I acknowledge the sin of omission. Are you asking for forgiveness?"

"Yes, Father, I am."

"Forty years? I must say carrying that burden is a punishment in itself.

So may I ask, do you think you should have confronted Bishop Powers over these past few months?"

Father Warren thought a moment knowing his confessor was totally involved with Bishop Powers. "Father, I know I have vows which include obedience and chastity, both of which I must confess." Father Sullivan was taken back. *Chastity.* "I am obedient in the hierarchy of our church. I am at one level, then Bishop Powers, then Cardinal Cullings, and of course, our Holy Father. That said, I will not cover for Bishop Powers any longer. If the church and or civil authorities come forth, I will cooperate fully. Let the full truth be told, no longer hidden. Of course, now I am aware of Bishop's abuse in addition to the cover-up. Forgive me, Father, I am sorry for this sin." Father Warren paused. "I need to confess an even longer held grave sin, which I have never confessed in all these years of my priesthood." Father Sullivan listened, but could not imagine what the penitent could possibly confess. "The truth must be told. This is difficult, but I must."

Father Sullivan sensed the gravity of what he was trying to say, but knew not the sin.

Father Warren continued, "Before I was ordained, I had a very dear friend, a most wonderful lady. She will always be a special person who affected my life in an extraordinary way. We were close, but we both knew we could never be together. Let me say it this way, as my commitment was first to our Lord." Father Warren rubbed his forehead and thought a moment. "We both knew and accepted that. It was difficult for both of us." Father Warren hesitated again, rubbing his forehead. "Several years before my ordination, I was home for about a week here in Wabash. As life would have it, we spent time together. Two days and…" Father paused. "And two nights. That's when it happened."

"Did you love her, Father, might I ask?"

"Love? Oh Father, how do we define that cherished word? Looking back, I'd say yes. Yes, I did love her, but I chose the priesthood. After fifty years, I'd still do the same. I made the right decision. Yes, fifty years since I had seen her. Then from out of nowhere--you may find this difficult to believe--I spoke with her for the first time. It was on Saturday. Three days ago."

Father Sullivan sat back and tried to comprehend what he was hearing. He immediately thought of Linda, stopped, and focused on Father Warren.

"We had not been in touch all these years. And can you believe she lives in South Wayne? Still has a sister in Wabash."

"Father, two people, who once were in love, can be apart for many years, yet that love can still exist," Father Sullivan said to his penitent.

Father Warren knew his moment of truth was at hand. *I'm doing the right thing. I must tell it all.* "Yes, Father, fifty years is a long time. Never heard from her. Then…" He searched for the courage and clarity to say, "Michael, like I said, Saturday is when she contacted me," Father Warren said, but did not disclose the confessional.

"Please, Father, take your time. Tell your sins as you feel best. I'm here for you."

"Thank you, Michael. After all these years, she told me…" Father Warren's eyes began to tear in the darkness behind the black curtain. With his fingers, he wiped away a tear, then continued, "Her name is… well, we'll leave it at that. She told me I was a father. I mean a natural biological father. She told me I was the father of our son, Thomas. He would have been Thomas Warren. Same as me, except this beautiful, caring woman never disclosed my name as the natural father. She knew my vocation and that my lifelong desire to be a priest was what I truly wanted."

Father Sullivan sensed the tears on the other side of the black curtain. He felt his own eyes water.

"Now I know. Thomas had a difficult life. He died some years ago, alone. It haunts me, Father. My son died alone." Father Sullivan could hardly believe the enormity of what Father Warren had just told him. Father Warren lowered his voice to a whisper. He fought for each word. The priest blessed himself, then said, "Thomas had two sons. They are… Father, I have two grandsons. They live in South Wayne." Father Warren closed his eyes, took a deep breath. "Father, there is more. Please understand I am still having a difficult time comprehending the sheer magnitude and heartbreak of what my grandsons have endured. You need to know, Father." Father Warren stopped for a moment. The secret is about to be divulged. He closed his eyes, made the sign of the cross. "Their names…my grandsons' names are Thornbauer. Yes, Ned and Danny Thornbauer."

A shock wave charged through Father Sullivan. His heart raced like a bolt of lightning. He leaned forward, his lips close to the curtain, "You're telling me your grandsons are Ned and Danny both abused by Bishop Powers? No, Father, this can't be. The same man you saw abusing the altar boy back in the seminary? Please say 'no'!"

"Yes, Father, it is regrettably true. I was with Bishop Powers Sunday evening." Father Warren paused, and then said, "Father, listen, you'll understand. I confronted him about coming forward and disclosing his cover-up and abuse. So much crossed my mind; revenge, justice, forgiveness. I broached the subject with Bishop Powers. He absolutely denied everything. I explained that I was aware of the outcome of last Wednesday's meeting with Cardinal Cullings. I accused him that leaving the meeting, not facing the accusers, was truth unto itself. More importantly, I reminded him about the horrid day in seminary when I happened on him with the altar boy. His immediately response was his word against mine…and that he is the bishop. With those statements, he confirmed the cover-up and abuse. All of it. I knew, he knew. When I responded with, 'cover-up, abuse, and you, Lawrence, are all one in the same.' The bishop didn't respond. He backed up and collapsed in his chair. I watched him. Poor man caught in the web of his own denial and lies."

Father Sullivan interrupted. "Excuse me, Father, but please tell me he realized his sins, his many sins."

"Yes, Father. That was his breaking point, his moment of coming to grips with his sins. He knew that I was aware of his abuse in 1911, and now his abuse with Ned and Danny. In the end, I believe it was because of his guilt, the guilt I knew. I watched him sitting there, struggling with the truth. Despondent, to say the least, head in hand, lost in his hypocritical life of sin, he began to cry, sobbing almost uncontrollably, as if all his sins broke the dam, the monsters were unleashed. I cannot repeat what he said. I turned and stepped out into the hall so the poor man could be alone in his misery. Ten minutes or so passed, then he called my name, 'Father, please come back in,' he said in a low despondent monotone. I did, but he wasn't in the chair. 'Just one minute', I heard from the other room. You see, Father, once I mentioned Ned and Danny, Bishop

Powers knew he was trapped, like a clever fox or a hungry wolf. The monster was out. I felt for him. I could not imagine the horror inside or maybe he felt relief, as a great balloon of bad deeds had been punctured. I'll never know. He had to do something. He realized the truth. He faced his own demons. I believe he wished, he just wanted to atone, maybe give a sign of his remorse."

"Do what?" Father Sullivan asked.

"Soon Bishop Powers came out of the room. His face was flushed, his eyes still red, and he was carrying a briefcase. I was confused. I thought, *what's he doing?* He set the briefcase on the table. I watched his eyes. He opened the case exposing stacks of twenties, fifties, and some one-hundred dollar bills that I could see. 'Thomas,' he said, 'I know I have definitely caused irreparable harm to these boys. God only knows what happened to the boy back, you know, back in 1911 at the seminary. And, yes, Father, there were others. I am so sorry. I can never take back my dastardly deeds with, with…' I couldn't believe his statement of contrition, remorse. Then he said, 'Go ahead, this is a significant part of my personal savings. I have it in cash. Why? I'm planning a trip. Sin is sin. Remorse is remorse, but I know I can't buy back the sins I committed. Please, this is the least I can do--education, living expenses, whatever they want. Please, Thomas, it's simply a personal gift. Give this to the Thornbauer boys, but under one condition. The boys can never know this came from me.' I was so taken aback. I told him I would accept and honor his request. Then the bishop said, 'This is not because you know what I have done, Thomas. I know you will come forth about me as you must. This is not to silence you. All I ask is for you to give this to Ned and Danny. You're not to say where it's from. Just tell them to use the money for education, live a good life, and never, never hurt anyone.'

"The bishop reached forward, shook my hand, and looked in my eyes. He wrapped his right hand around me and patted my back. Not once but two, three times. He said, 'I'm sorry for all the hurt I caused you and others, Thomas. Good-bye.' He turned and walked into the bedroom from which he had come. I just stood there. I saw a broken and defeated man. What does it mean?"

"I will always remember the kindness I saw for the very first time. I must ask if his generosity was for Ned and Danny. I do hope so, while at the same time, maybe for me, because of all that I knew about him for so many years. Maybe just guilt. I never really know. I thought of Ned and Danny. I saw sorrow, remorse in the bishop's face. I decided to believe the good and fulfill his wish. He asked me for nothing. I closed the case and held it to my side. I left Bishop Powers forever. Donned my hat and coat, tightly clutched the briefcase and left the rectory. My sin of omission is not confronting Lawrence Powers that horrid day with the altar boy. I confess and I am sorry."

"There are some things in life, Father, for which we may never know the answers," Father Sullivan said trying to ease any doubt in the penitent's mind.

"Lastly, Dear Lord, I ask for forgiveness for a sin of fifty years. I am sorry for my sin of being with a woman outside of marriage and waiting these many years to confess. I hurt her. I hurt the son I never knew I had. And now even my grandsons. My Dear Lord, I am truly sorry and I ask for your forgiveness."

Father Sullivan thought about the enormity of the two sins. He knew Father Warren to be a good man and a good priest. "Our Lord and God, absolves you from your sins. He knows of all your goodness, and he recognizes the sincerity of your contrition. Heed the words of our Lord to go and sin no more. You are forgiven."

Father Warren felt the lifting of the weight, the weight of fifty years of denial.

"Father, before I go in peace, there is one other thing, not a sin, mind you, but something I want to say to you. Now the timing is perfect. Michael, over these past years, you and I have shared much. I have observed your goodness, your caring for others, and your love of God and our church. Beyond that I have felt--and so much during this past year--that you, Michael, are like…like the son I never had. And with what I have learned, about my birth son and grandsons, I have not changed my feelings about you. Always, Michael, I will love you."

Father Sullivan felt his eyes water. "Father, I am truly touched. You have been my mentor. I always look up to you. Inside this confessional, I am a priest. When you leave, I will carry your words always as I treasure you in my heart. As your confessor, all that you hold true and repented for this day will always be sealed within this confessional."

"Thank you, Father. Thank you, Michael. Now before I leave, you need to know two things. Under the second pew in front of the confessional is a briefcase. Yes, the one given to me by Bishop Powers. I ask you to give it in the best way you see fit to Ned and Danny. Never disclose the gift is from Bishop Powers or that I passed it on to you. They are never to know about their grandfather. It is simply too late."

"Too late, Father? They would handle this quite well. You would fill such a vacuum in their life."

"No, Michael. Cannot be. First of all, I cannot disclose this secret that their grandmother has sheltered all these years. Secondly, this has nothing to do with my confession, my secrets of the past fifty years. Please listen, Michael."

"Sure, Father. If not a sin, what is it?"

"You recall the coughs as of lately? You actually asked me to go see the doctor. I knew I had put it off far too long. I knew it was more than a cold. Maybe I was not ready to face reality until this time to repent, clear my conscience."

Father Sullivan immediately thought of his mother. *Oh no. Please, God, no.*

"I did go to the doctor just before Thanksgiving. I was examined and tested. While you attended your meeting last Wednesday with Cardinal Cullings, I went back to the doctor and learned of the results. Let's just say they were far less than what I prayed for." Father Warren took a deep breath.

Father Sullivan closed his eyes, shook his head. *Dear Lord.* "What is it, Father? Please tell me."

"Yes, Michael, I will. The good doctor informed me that I have a form of lung cancer called *small cell lung cancer*. Unfortunately, it is aggressive and has already spread outside of the lung. He told me my cancer is terminal. There is no cure. Too far gone, Michael."

Father Sullivan listened. Then quiet. "I dread asking. How long, Father? Pray tell."

"Couple of months. Sometime this winter."

Father Sullivan did not respond. He felt the true meaning of shock and sadness what he had just heard.

"Michael, this past hour I'm sure has been exhausting. Exhausting for both of us. I suggest we talk tomorrow. I will explain how we will handle this week and my departure. You see, you will be the only one to know. No good-byes, no announcements from the pulpit, and no farewell dinners."

"Yes, Father, but where will you go? I know you have no family here."

"Right, Michael. I called my old friend, Father Gilner. We went to the seminary together. Father Robert Gilner, a good man and a devoted priest. Father has a place for me in the rectory at Holy Hill, up in Wisconsin. We have kept in touch over the years. I'm sure he will have some good stories and a few Irish golf jokes to make me laugh during my time there. Of most importance, I will have a friend by my side during what I assume might be challenging days. I know he will be there for me. I will be leaving for Holy Hill sometime next week. He is making the necessary arrangements for me, especially during the final days."

"Father, I am having difficulty accepting this. I can't let you go. I need for you to stay here, right here in this confessional. You are...you mean so much to me. Father Warren, please, if you could only deny. Bless you, my dear, dear friend."

"Michael, we all have to face death. It's a part of life. We'll talk tomorrow." Father Warren stood, opened the door, then stopped and looked back at the curtain. "Please remember the briefcase."

Father Sullivan remained in the quiet and darkness of the confessional. So much had just been revealed. His mind swirled. His heart ached. He felt overwhelming empathy for Father Warren. Father Sullivan thought of himself and his love twenty-five years from now.

Linda is forever on my mind. How, my dear God, will this be for me? For Linda? Will I be like Father Warren? Have I done the right thing? Dear Lord, please help me. Will I someday regret giving up another life I could have had? What I lost? I pray I made the right decision. My true vocation is to be a priest. Never in my life have I felt such emotion, such sadness. Dear God, I cannot lose this man. The moment seemed surreal. Tomorrow Father Sullivan would face the finality of losing Father Warren.

Father Warren felt relieved, his soul cleansed. He put on his long black coat he had left in the vestibule. Stepping outside, he stood in front of the tall oak doors, looked around, buttoned his coat, and pulled the brim of his hat low over his eyes. Step-by-step, he felt the worn limestone. Breathing deep, Father Warren took in the cool fresh air. To his right, he looked toward the lights of the courthouse and the statue of Lincoln standing guard over the city.

A slight wind blew through the barren branches of leafless oaks. A new moon was obscured by dark gray clouds drifting across a fore barren sky. The street was blanketed in a gloomy malaise. Only a solitary street lamppost cast a little relief from the darkness at the corner of Wabash and Hill. The elderly priest looked to his left. *Dear Lord, I am sorry. I am free. I accept my decisions and will live with them the rest of my days.* The drab lights to the side of the front doors faded. Father Warren's shadow diminished as he walked up the street and disappeared into the darkness.

Bernard Bednar--December 10, 1958

Bernard Bednar made his way to work that Wednesday morning. The temperature was unseasonably cold. The sky was covered with clouds. Walking on Mill Creek Road toward the reform school, Bernard approached Friends Cemetery. Knowing he had time before his shift started, he walked down the drive in the direction of Gordon Yoder's grave. Just at the bend, he stopped and looked across the cemetery until he identified the small headstone, thirty feet away. Bernard walked toward the grave. Just a few steps away, he suddenly stopped, squinted staring at the headstone. *The box is gone.* Bernard nodded. An ever so slight smile crossed his face. He stood in place for a minute and then turned and left the cemetery, his deed having been completed. *Gordon's safe. Randall Zilbar's life is forever scarred.* As always, Bernard Bednar was on time for work that day. That first week in December 1958, Wabash Indiana, had indeed been a long, long week.

CHAPTER 116

ADDRESSING THE CONCLAVE

Cardinal Cullings—January 20, 1959

CARDINAL Gustav Anthony Cullings stood before an assembly of bishops and cardinals in Trinity Hall, deep within the confines of the Vatican. Ten marble columns etched in gold supported the massive arched ceiling, which was painted in a beautiful array of gloriously divine hues of blue, white, and crimson.

Before him, a sea of men in red and black respectfully awaited his address. One, however, dressed in white, sat to the front left of the first row with his secretary, a cardinal, and two other priests.

Cardinal Cullings began by welcoming His Holiness and fellow cardinals and bishops. He eloquently and tactfully outlined the growing problem of clerical abuse of children within the Catholic Church. Speaking with compassion, he defined the problem and brought attention to the evolving exposure from the media. He explained that the time was now for the hierarchy of the church to lead by publically acknowledging the problem and developing a judicial structure within the church to address each and every case. He stated, "We, the bishops and cardinals of the church, must come together. We must agree to create a policy, a *zero tolerance policy* that will reach out to all priests around the world. Abuse, molestation, and pedophilia will no longer be tolerated. Let our words be written as policy. Policy that will be executed. That will be adhered to by all our clergy from Rome to South America, Asia, Africa, across North America, and our European brethren and clergy all around the world.

Cardinal Cullings stopped, looked across the room observing his fellow bishops and cardinals. Turning his head left, he glanced at the Holy Father then continued, "Priests will no longer say Mass, administer sacraments, teach the young. They must be relieved of all privileges, all duties and responsibilities of the priesthood. May the echoes of our words fall on every priest, every seminarian, every deacon in the Catholic Church. From the leadership here in Rome, from we, the hierarchy of our beloved Catholic Church, set the example, set the tone. Law must be made to eradicate this cancer within our church. From this day forward, we here gathered today must not accept any form of abuse within our Catholic Church!"

Moving his head from side to side, scanning the assembly as he spoke, Cardinal Gustav Anthony Cullings screened the attentiveness and visual responses of all gathered before him. With distinct inflection and clarity, his words were meant to pull in and command the attention of all those assembled. Cardinal Cullings noticed Pope John Benedict turn, cover his mouth, as if to speak discreetly into the ear of his secretary.

With vigor, Cardinal Cullings called for action. "The church, beginning with all of us assembled here today must immediately come together and exchange our knowledge, experiences, and procedures so that we can set a policy that we can execute in unison, as one for the good of our Holy Mother Church. We must set standards of conduct and expectations with emphasis on our sacred vows."

Everyone's eyes were focused on Cardinal Cullings, though some of the cardinals and bishops discreetly whispered to one another. As he spoke, Cardinal Cullings assumed some dissension by the gestures and movements of those assembled before him.

"We must acknowledge and recognize those who have already been victimized. A policy and program must be set for expected demands for restitution. The highest of all standards must be adopted, adhered to, and enforced by all of us in authority. As long as our church continues to demand a mandatory vow of celibacy as part of our vows of ordination, then those vows must be honored, obeyed, and protected in all forms of sexual conduct and sexual gratification by each and every priest who has been ordained."

Then without malice, Cardinal Cullings looked directly at all those gathered and said, "We, the hierarchy of the Catholic Church, must come together and act in unison today, this week, so that we can return home and speak as one church all around the world. If we fail to address this growing plague, we will be passing on to the next generation of Catholic clergy and laity a problem that may consume, scandalize, and deface the church. In years to come, moral and financial bankruptcy could engulf our most blessed church if we do not act together now. So let us join together this very day and do what is right for our Holy Mother Church. Let no one, priests, bishops, cardinals, and the abused … let no one stand alone!"

As Cardinal Cullings looked out over his fellow cardinals and bishops, he could tell by the positive expressions on some of their faces that many supported his cause and agreed with his proposed solutions. Equally so, he observed cardinals and bishops who harbored denial, oblivious to his passion and commitment. During his presentation, from time to time he could see heads turning right to look directly at Pope John Benedict, searching for his expressions of approval. Nothing.

Having spoken his last words, Cardinal Cullings stood silent, his arms straight, the fingers of both hands spread as he gripped the side of the lectern. Numbers of the cardinals and bishops in the audience stood in applause, others remained seated, and some just stood and watched their fellow bishops and cardinals, looking for support, reactions, and denials. Those still seated whispered, sharing private comments among themselves with no visible displays of approval. Still others sat almost in a state of disbelief or boredom. Immediately, Cardinal Cullings could foresee that much of what he said this day in Rome before the total assembly of the hierarchy of the Catholic Church had fallen on deaf ears.

The future of our church will depend on the collective decisions and policies of these learned, powerful, and hopefully responsible men. Our Holy Father must lead, Cardinal Cullings thought as he looked out over the assembly. He glanced to his left. The movement of the man in white was obvious to all in attendance. Cardinal Cullings looked over at His Holiness. Pope John Benedict leaned over and whispered something quietly to the cardinal sitting by his side. For a moment, the pope looked up and locked eyes with Cardinal Cullings. Stone-faced, Pope John Benedict stood, turned, and walked away.

THE END